National Baker Pub. Co.

The national baker

National Baker Pub. Co.

The national baker

ISBN/EAN: 9783744640435

Printed in Europe, USA, Canada, Australia, Japan

Cover: Foto ©Andreas Hilbeck / pixelio.de

More available books at **www.hansebooks.com**

VOL. XXVII. ENTERED AT THE PHILADELPHIA POST OFFICE AS SECOND CLASS MATTER No. 312

THE NATIONAL Baker

DEVOTED SOLELY TO THE BAKING INTERESTS

PUBLISHED MONTHLY BY
THE NATIONAL BAKER PUBLISHING CO.
411 WALNUT STREET
B. F. WHITECAR, Pres. and Editor

PHILADELPHIA, PA., JANUARY 16, 1922

Price per year, U. S.
and Canada $1.00
Foreign Countries $1.50

HUBBARD OVEN COMPANY
CHICAGO
1140 BELDEN AVE.

HUBBARD OVEN & MFG. CO.
303 Wool Exchange
NEW YORK CITY

KANSAS CITY
303 SCARRITT ARCADE

Introducing John:
Pan - Room Boss

John is a six-foot husky; pan-room boss of a bakery. When the emptied sets pile up, he hasn't time to be gentle. He nests them with a *slam!*

But John knows that no matter how rough he is Ekco Everstay Strapped Bake-Pans stand up. They are built especially for this hard work. And John knows too, that the patented rounded corners of Ekco Sanitary Bake-Pans, are easy to keep spotlessly clean. That's two more reasons why "you'll equip with Everstay Some Day".

Your supply house carries Everstay for prompt shipment.

Complete General Catalogue No. 20 sent on request

EDWARD KATZINGER CO.

131 N. SANGAMON STREET - CHICAGO, ILL
Dept. K DREXEL BLDG. - PHILADELPHIA, PA.

Largest Manufacturers of Bake Pans in the World

STOCK SIZES

Single and Double Loaf

Pan No.	Top Inside	Bottom Outside	Depth	Capacity Ounces
06	8 x4	7⅝x3⅜	2⅜	12-13
06A	8 x4	7⅝x3⅝	2⅛	12-14
07	8⅝x4⅜	7⅜x3⅝	2⅜	16-18
07A	8⅝x4⅜	7⅝x3⅝	2½	15-17
08	8⅝x4⅜	7⅜x3⅜	2⅜	16-18
017	9⅝x4⅜	8⅛x3⅜	2⅝	16-20
017A	9⅜x4⅜	8⅝x3⅝	2⅜	16-20
044	9 x4⅝	8⅜x3⅜	2⅜	16-18
045	9⅜x5⅜	8⅛x4⅜	2⅜	20-24
046	10⅜x4⅜	9⅛x4⅜	2⅛	24-26
047	9⅜x5⅜	8⅜x4⅜	2⅜	24-26
047A	9 x5	8⅜x4⅜	2⅜	24-26
048	9⅜x5⅜	8⅛x4⅜	3	24-28
055	9½x5	8⅝x4⅜	3	24-28
056	10 x5	9⅜x4⅜	3	24-30
027	9⅜x4⅜	8⅜x3½	3⅛	18-22
027A	9½x4⅜	8⅛x3⅜	3	20-24
084	7⅜x7⅜	7⅜x7⅜	2	24-28
085	8 x8	7⅜x7⅜	2⅜	24-32
088	8½x7⅜	8 x7	2⅜	32-36
088A	8 x7	7⅜x6⅜	2⅜	24-32
086	8½x8½	7⅜x7⅜	2⅜	32-36
086A	8⅜x8⅜	7⅜x7⅜	2⅜	32-36
087	8½x8⅜	8 x8	2⅜	36-44
089	9 x8	8⅜x7⅜	2⅜	32-36

There's an Ekco Guaranteed Product for every baking need.

Flat Baking Sheets for Drop-Cake Machines. Stock size 17x35 special sizes to order. Specify Ekco for satisfaction.

Republic Rapid Transit, with Panel Body and Fore-Door Open Cab, Cord Tires, Electric Starter and Lights. Price on application.

Cuts the Cost of Delivery & Increases Bakers' Profits

Other body types include

Carry-All
Canopy Top
Stock Rack
Screen Enclosed
Tank Body
Open Express
Double Deck
Platform Stake
Bus Body
Police Patrol
Grain Body
Bottlers' Body
Dump Body

Republic Rapid Transit enables bakers to make quicker and more deliveries over a wider area at much less than the usual expense.

The low first cost of the Republic Rapid Transit plus the saving it effects in operation and upkeep have earned its recognition as the most economical delivery equipment.

Customers' good will and bakers' profits are increased through the use of the Republic Rapid Transit.

The Republic Line: ¾, 1, 1½-2, 2½-3, 3½-4 tons capacity.

REPUBLIC TRUCK SALES CORPORATION,
ALMA, MICH.

REPUBLIC
RAPID TRANSIT©

Republic has more trucks in use than any other exclusive truck manufacturer

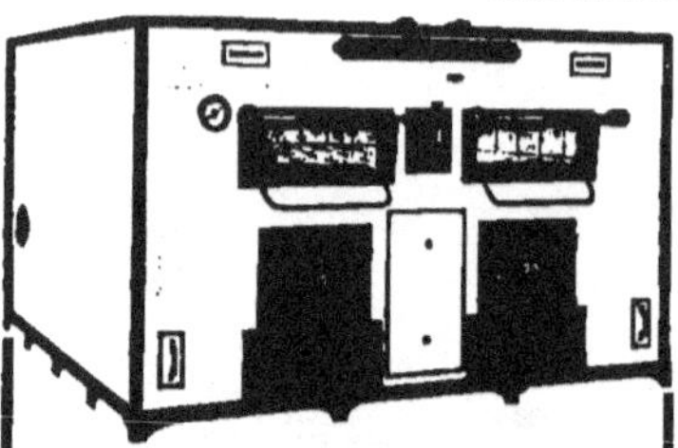

Bennett Ovens Make Busy Bakers

Are you worrying along with an old style oven? Are you turning down new business because you cannot turn out the goods?

Install a modern, efficient Bennett Oven and you will be able to handle an increased demand on a profitable basis. Others are doing it. So can you.

BENNETT OVENS ARE BETTER OVENS

BENNETT OVEN CO.,
Ave C & 22nd Street,   Battle Creek, Mich.

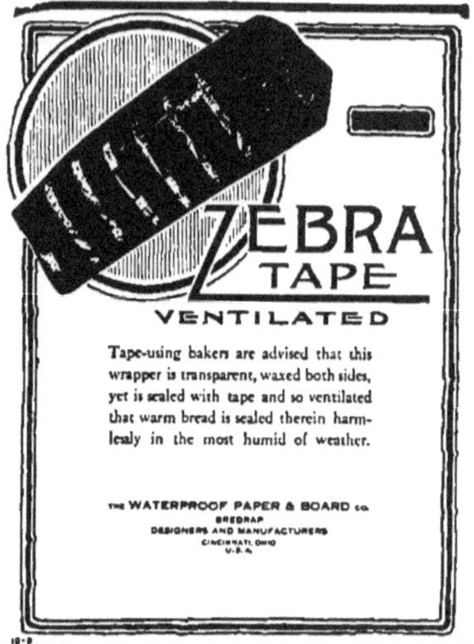

ZEBRA TAPE
VENTILATED

Tape-using bakers are advised that this wrapper is transparent, waxed both sides, yet is sealed with tape and so ventilated that warm bread is sealed therein harmlessly in the most humid of weather.

THE WATERPROOF PAPER & BOARD CO.
BREDRAP
DESIGNERS AND MANUFACTURERS
CINCINNATI, OHIO
U.S.A.

BIG DIAMOND FLOUR

BIG DIAMOND MILLS CO. MINNEAPOLIS, MINN.

LIKE a treasure ship of olden times, full fraught with precious things, so may 1922 come to you laden with all that will make for you Happiness and Contentment.

LAMBOOY LABEL & WRAPPER CO.
KALAMAZOO, MICHIGAN

THERMOMETERS
STANDARD OVEN THERMOMETERS
MADE TO FIT ANY OVEN

Dough Testing Thermometers
Vacuum Pan Thermometers

Long experience has gained for us an invaluable fund of knowledge on the subject of Thermometers. Write for information and Prices.

THE PHILADELPHIA THERMOMETER CO.
54 No. 9th St.   Philadelphia, Pa.

There is no place where dependable high-speed production is so essential as it is in the modern bakeshop.

Where the baker is called upon to supply a greater demand for his product than he usually produces, he must be in a position to furnish the goods or lose the business.

And losing extra business is a step down instead of up.

With a Thomson equipped shop, and every unit of equipment ready to work in perfect unison with the other, the baker need not worry about quantity production.

Quantity production, as said before, is essential.

"Take it up with Thomson"

THOMSON MACHINE CO.
BELLEVILLE, N. J.

Be a Bakery Superintendent

No matter what your present job may be, there is always room for better men at higher wages—**AT THE TOP.**

Experts are scarce. Cheap Help is plentiful enough. Employers want **CAPABLE** people in their employ—men who know their business thoroughly. To such they will pay big wages.

You cannot know too much about the Baking Industry.

The **SIEBEL INSTITUTE OF TECHNOLOGY** has a plan whereby you can earn while learning great proficiency in baking.

Their Home Study Course in Scientific Baking enables you to train yourself for a better paid position in the Bakery business. *You owe it to yourself to make more money.*

It is easy to learn these simple lessons which have been written for your benefit by **TWENTY LEADING AUTHORITIES** in the Baking Industry.

Your Home Study is rendered still more interesting by practical laboratory work which you do at home in your spare time with the **FREE LABORATORY OUTFIT,** included with the Home Study Course.

If your pay ranges from $30.00 to $50.00 a week—or even higher—the Siebel Home Study Course will show you how to command *much more.* It will help you to attain greater efficiency—greater earning capacity—and *more money.*

Therefore send **TODAY**—without obligating yourself—for full particulars by filling out and mailing the accompanying coupon to the

SIEBEL INSTITUTE OF TECHNOLOGY
Specialists in Flour Analysis

(ESTABLISHED 1872)
935 Montana Street, Chicago, Ill, U. S. A.

- -

SIEBEL INSTITUTE OF TECHNOLOGY, Dept. "NB"
935 Montana Street, Chicago, Illinois.
Please send me full particulars of the Siebel Home Study Course in Scientific Baking FREE.

Name ....

Address ....

Town ....

State ....

Position I Now Hold..

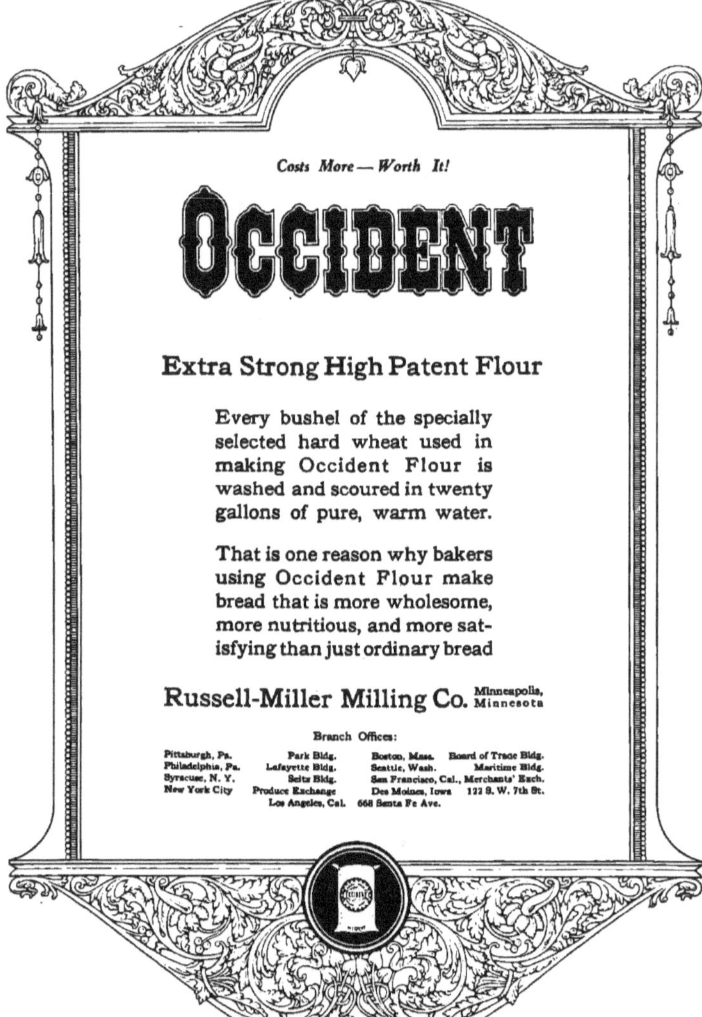
Costs More — Worth It!

OCCIDENT

Extra Strong High Patent Flour

Every bushel of the specially
selected hard wheat used in
making Occident Flour is
washed and scoured in twenty
gallons of pure, warm water.

That is one reason why bakers
using Occident Flour make
bread that is more wholesome,
more nutritious, and more satisfying than just ordinary bread

Russell-Miller Milling Co. Minneapolis, Minnesota

Branch Offices:

Pittsburgh, Pa.
Philadelphia, Pa.
Syracuse, N. Y.
New York City

Park Bldg.
Lafayette Bldg.
Seitz Bldg.
Produce Exchange
Los Angeles, Cal.

Boston, Mass.
Seattle, Wash.
San Francisco, Cal., Merchants' Exch.
Des Moines, Iowa
668 Santa Fe Ave.

Board of Trade Bldg.
Maritime Bldg.
122 S. W. 7th St.

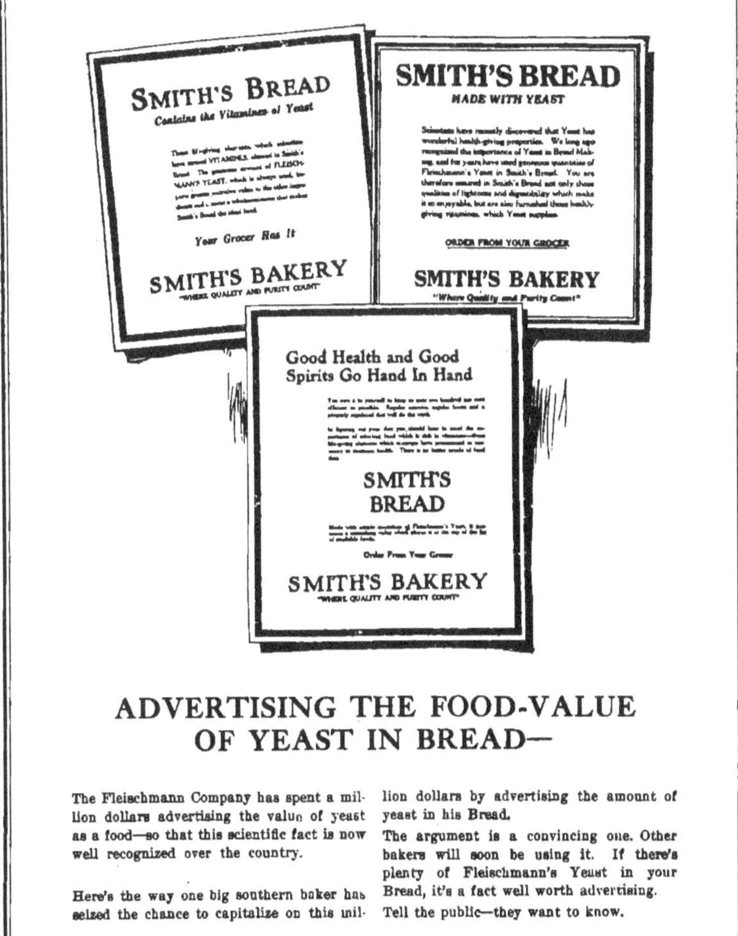

ADVERTISING THE FOOD-VALUE
OF YEAST IN BREAD—

The Fleischmann Company has spent a million dollars advertising the value of yeast as a food—so that this scientific fact is now well recognized over the country.

Here's the way one big southern baker has seized the chance to capitalize on this million dollars by advertising the amount of yeast in his Bread.

The argument is a convincing one. Other bakers will soon be using it. If there's plenty of Fleischmann's Yeast in your Bread, it's a fact well worth advertising.

Tell the public—they want to know.

THE FLEISCHMANN COMPANY

Fleischmann's Yeast   *Fleischmann's Service*

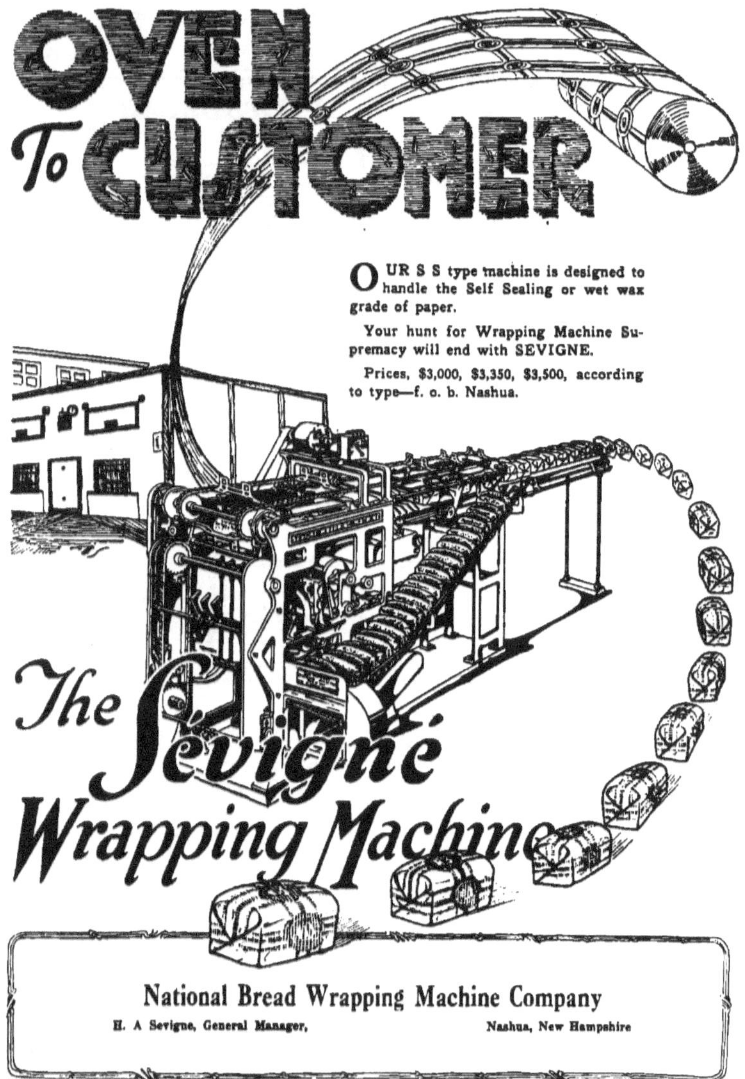

O UR S S type machine is designed to handle the Self Sealing or wet wax grade of paper.

Your hunt for Wrapping Machine Supremacy will end with SEVIGNE.

Prices, $3,000, $3,350, $3,500, according to type—f. o. b. Nashua.

National Bread Wrapping Machine Company

H. A Sevigne, General Manager,   Nashua, New Hampshire

(When addressing advertisers kindly refer to THE NATIONAL BAKER)

Other ovens may resemble the "Universal"
on the OUTSIDE, but not on the INSIDE

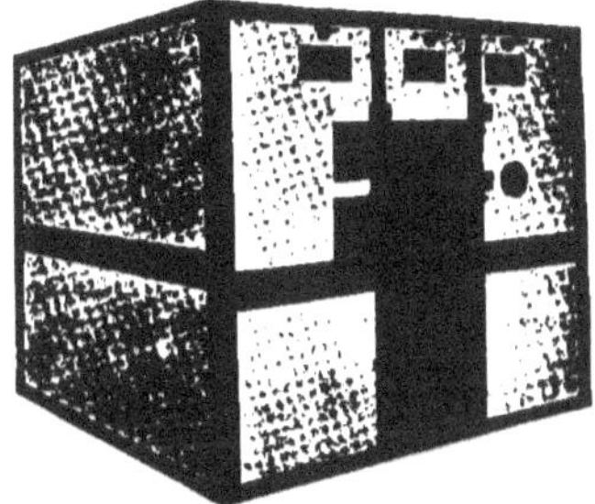
"UNIVERSAL" DOUBLE CONTINUOUS OVEN

This is the only oven of this type with fire-brick construction **all through.**

It must be good
Every user satisfied

Write today for catalog and list of users near you

MADE, INSTALLED, AND GUARANTEED BY

MIDDLEBY OVEN COMPANY 41-45 PARK ROW NEW YORK

The Test of Time

is the surest test

OP Malt Extract

has stood this test and has not been found wanting.

Prudent bakers do not experiment—they place full reliance in

OP MALT EXTRACT

Malt-Diastase Company

79 Wall Street, NEW YORK

Warehouses: CHICAGO, PHILADELPHIA   *Laboratories,* BROOKLYN, N. Y.

PUBLISHED ON THE FIFTEENTH OF EACH MONTH

AT

411 WALNUT ST., PHILADELPHIA

BY

THE NATIONAL BAKER PUBLISHING CO.

B. F. WHITECAR, PRESIDENT AND EDITOR
W. W. GALE, SECRETARY AND TREASURER

MEMBER OF THE AUDIT BUREAU OF CIRCULATIONS

SUBSCRIPTION RATES
UNITED STATES, ITS POSSESSIONS AND CANADA ..$2.00 per year
FOREIGN COUNTRIES .... 3.00 per year

PAYABLE IN ADVANCE

ADVERTISING RATES ON APPLICATION

Make all remittances payable to the order of
The National Baker Publishing Company

*Changes for displayed advertisements must reach this office
by the 5th of the month*

VOL. XXVII   JANUARY, 1922   No. 312

CONTENTS

Allied Trades 47	Flour and the Baker's Loaf 42
Bakers' Prices and the Tariff 34	Indiana Convention 37
	Information Department:
Bread Prices Fully Reflect Drop in Flour 31	Icing and Filling 55
	Cream Puffs 55
Bread Is Your Best Food 36	Cocoanut Macaroons ... 55
Cake Recipes:	Cocoanut Balls 55
Birthday Cake 62	Drying Out of Cake 55
Fruit Genoa Cake 62	Spice Cake 55
Madeira Cake 62	Butter Cakes 59
Fruit Cakes 62	Black Ants 59
Venetian Lunch Cake .. 63	Royal Icing 60
Almond Cakes 63	Cheese Cake 60
Cherry Cakes 63	Preserved Pineapple Cake 60
Drop Buns 63	Legal: A Business Man's
Rock Cakes 64	Will 33
Hoop Cakes 64	Moisture in Bread 38
Fermented Buns 64	New England Bakers Re-
Short Paste 64	Organize 39
Almond Tarts, Swiss ... 64	Pennsylvania Convention . 37
Layer Cake 64	Repeat Orders 35
Court of Industrial Rela-	Secretary-Manager H. E.
tions 48	Barnard 37
	Survey of the Sugar Situa-
	tion 35

The Customer's Angle—A Good Thing To Get

A RETAIL baker ought to be an all-around man, but in far too many cases he has not proved to be as good a salesman as he is a workman. He can bake, but he finds it hard to sell. This is not to be wondered at, either, for a large proportion of the retail bakers are men who have graduated from the ranks of the journeymen and have gone into business on their own account after gaining their experience in some other man's shop.

They have the technical part of the business down pat, but they have neglected the selling side; they have not developed as merchants while they were making progress and improving themselves as bakers. To the average baker this may sound like a wrong statement of the case. He has never noticed it. But he does not go into his shop or into any other man's shop as a customer. He comes into his own as proprietor of it —he has the proprietor's angle. He goes into another shop in the same town as a competitor—he has the competitor's angle. He goes into another town as a professional brother of that other baker—he has the professional angle. But he does not do business with himself, with his competitor or his trade brother. He serves the customer, and he should get the customer's angle on his business.

Coming into his own shop he will note how the rolls are going and how many are likely to go stale, then begin to figure how far short he is of breaking even on the batch for the day, or getting out ahead. He will consider where he has plunged too deeply here or misjudged the demand there. In his competitor's shop he will be comparing notes on his own and his competitor's shop and stocks, but from the professional and not from the customers' point of view. In another town he will have the same professional interest unmixed with any personal feelings. There is mighty little to keep him on the alert, and trying to see things out of his customers' eyes.

Right here, however, is one of the big secrets of success in any retail business. The merchant who sells at retail comes into contact with all kinds of people. He must please all kinds. The more he considers his business through the eyes of his customers, the better he will be able to meet their wants and the better he meets their wants, the more business he should do with them. There are many ways to get the customers' angle, which, after all, is the normal, wholesome, average person's point of view on storekeeping and the way he or she is treated in that store. It is a personal matter with every customer, and the sooner the retail baker realizes this principle, the better for verybody.

In order to get good bread, rolls or pies, many people will more or less cheerfully submit to little inconveniences, little slights or occasional inconsiderate

is the best in town, and who dismisses complaints of incensed customers by the statement that it is easier to get customers than it is to get salespeople. He may "take it out" on the girl behind the counter later on, but he certainly neglects his opportunity to make a friend of the customer with a grievance. That customer may continue to come to the shop, but he comes without feeling that he is welcome. Good wares may do this, but think of the opportunity this baker is missing to build up his trade among the chance customers whose memory of the slight they had to submit to is stronger than their memory of the excellence of their purchases. It is the new customer whose angle is the important one to the retail baker.

There is no magic in regulating a business so as to please the customers. A merchant does not have to be a professor of psychology to figure out the kind of treatment that the patrons of his store are going to like and the treatment they will object to. The baker who feels that the personal relations between his store and his customers are not as pleasant as they ought to be, who must realize that there is friction, can mend his selling ways if he will take up the proposition from a common sense angle. It can be done without much difficulty; the baker can develop a "customer's eye," and by so doing will be putting his shop in a position to gain increased business.

Two principal points can be made in this connection, and if they are appreciated and put into effect the result is bound to be good. First, the store and the disposition of the baker's wares has got to be attractive to his trade; and, second, his trade ought to leave with its purchases or ought to receive its purchases from the delivery man with a sense of having been treated in a courteous and a complimentary way, with that warm feeling that comes when a person feels he has been appreciated. The baker spends most of his time in his shop and gets so familiar with things as he has been handling them that he comes to accept them as they are, and to follow methods of display already in use just as a matter of course. His delivery service is pretty sure to become routine and mechanical, and he and his employes are liable to become so absorbed in their regular work that they will fail to appreciate the impression the customer gets and carries away with him.

The "looks" of a tray of pastry will often do more toward selling it than the price or the nature of the goods. The same thing is true of bread, cake, or anything the baker handles. Good, honest wares, whatever they are, can be displayed to advantage, can be made to show their good points; can be made to attract. Here is where the baker can combine the competitor's, the professional and the customer's angle, if he will look through the customer's eyes at the arrangement of these goods in his and other retail departments. On almost everybody's customers' list, too, there is sure to be one or more customers who are above the average

of the others, whose ideas as to taste and orderliness and effective display are definite and practicable.

The baker who is seeking to improve his relations with his trade can single these out and make use of them. They will gladly respond if he asks them to tell frankly just what they think of the way he conducts his shop. Some of them may even volunteer, if he gives them half a chance. In any case, he ought to receive the suggestions in the spirit in which they are given, if he wants to keep that customer as an appreciative one. A case came under the writer's attention some time ago which illustrates this point, though it applies to the treatment of customers more closely. It involved one of the leading bakers and confectioners in a certain city, who one day received a note to this effect:

"Dear Mr. Blank.—Last evening my husband and I stopped in to buy some cakes, but we did not seem to be able to get waited on. We stood for five minutes or more in front of the cake counter, and waited for some one to come up. No other customers were in the store and there were several salesgirls deep in conversation. We did not know but what they were assigned to their own special counters and so did not call for service, and, becoming considerably indignant, we went out without making a purchase.

"Now, we have always liked to trade with you, because among other reasons we get just what we like and big values for the money, and it is very convenient for me to telephone my husband to step in as he comes home from the office to get some cakes for dinner. He had been refusing to go lately, saying that he always got insulted by some 'fresh' clerk, and I had to use some persuasion to get him to stop with me last evening. You can understand how difficult it will be to overcome his aversion to your shop hereafter.

"Please don't misunderstand the spirit of this note. I am writing it because I believe you will be glad to know how a customer feels or has been treated, so that you will be able to prevent similar treatment of others. Very truly yours."

The woman signed her name—and it was one the baker had known for years. She expected to get a response in due time, or to get the baker's thanks the next time she passed him on the street. He made no acknowledgment of the note, and carefully avoided seeing her the next time they met. The consequence is that he has lost a good customer, and a customer who will retail the experience every time the baker's name is mentioned. He did the riot act to the salesforce, but he neglected to do the most obvious thing to restore good relations between himself and his customer.

Things to eat must look appetizing to people who eat them, not merely to the baker who makes them. It is from customers who will resent slights like the one referred to who will be the most particular about the "looks" of a tray of lemon wafers, or of coffee cakes. Instead of repelling interest of people like these, the baker can learn from them and he can be sure that if he will arrange his wares and order his store so as to please the customers who demand particular treatment of what they eat and of themselves, he is going to please those who are less exacting in these respects.

Courtesy is preached in season and out of season by everybody who believes he has a message for the retailer. Yet this first requirement in handling customers is so often neglected that all this haranguing appears to have had little influence. A good way to get the customer's angle here is for the baker to go as a customer into some other retail store, not a bakeshop. The sales-force will not recognize him as a tradesman and will treat him the way they do anybody else. Half a day devoted to a series of calls in other retail establish-ments in his own town will give the baker a lot of pointers on what not to do in his own shop and likewise what to do. He will get both a lot of positive and a lot of negative ideas, if he goes looking for them.

It is the easiest thing in the world for a baker to get up from his desk, where he has been comparing his sugar bills for the month just past with those of the year before, to find that his sweets have cost him a third more and that his profits were cut in half on them last month, and wait on a customer with a scowl on his face. He is not thinking of the customer; he is thinking of his factory. The customer goes away with the impression that the baker is a grouch. This is bad for everybody. The customer is the important thing, every bit as important as good bread. The less good the bread is, the more important the manner in which customers are handled becomes. The baker, the sales-girl, the delivery wagon boy should consider the customer first, last and all the time. Some of them will get a little overbearing now and then, but their money is what the baker is after, and it will pay him to please them as well as all the others to whom he sells.

Every baker has his own particular problems; his customers have their own particular preferences. His problems in a large part are to find out and to satisfy these particular preferences of the particular custom-ers. The way for him to do is to get his customer's angle.

—†—†—†—

Repeat Orders

HOW many bakers are there that have not been tempted, at some time in their career, to sac-rifice quality for cheapness in their goods, thinking to make more profit? Those who have tried it have found to their sorrow (and loss of trade that it does not, nor ever will, pay.

The trade that can be relied on to create a steady demand, month after month, for the baker's goods, does not want, nor will it have, poor goods. The great middle class, formed of persons of aver-age ability in the things of the world, want and are willing to pay for goods of a standard, good quality. This holds good, no matter whether it be wearing apparel, housefurnishings, or baker's goods. They may take in a bargain sale now and then, to be sure, but when it comes to something for which there is a regular, every day demand (and of what can this be said more surely than of the baker's goods?), they want something that they can depend upon being good, not only to-day and to-morrow, but all the time.

It may not be hard for the baker to convince himself that it will do no harm to use butter that costs him quite a bit less than he has been paying. He may assure himself that his trade will not notice it, and be right, as far as the first or second batch is concerned. They won't know that the in-ingredients of that particular piece of goods have been cheapened, at first. But they will notice that the quality (the things that have so far brought them back to that baker's store when they wanted anything in his line) has deteriorated. Possibly they may give the baker the benefit of the doubt at first, though, as a general rule, they do not do so. They may tell themselves that it is an accident and will not happen again for a long time. But let the baker continue to use that cheaper butter, his trade will buy less and less of that article, until the demand has become *nil*.

The baker, then, not only has *not* made money on that particular piece of goods, but he has lost money and *good-will*, that intangible asset for which business men are willing to pay a good price, and that spells success, if fostered.

This principle of keeping up the quality of all his goods is the life of the baker's business. Let him use the standard, good-quality supplies of all kinds, spices, flavors, etc., remembering that not only are they much cheaper, in the end, but they go a great deal farther than the cheaper, just-as-good grades.

The baker must depend on the regular, qual-ity-demanding trade for his livelihood. The trade that is satisfied with cheap goods is inclined to flit about, dodging landlord's and other bills. They cannot be depended upon to consume even the cheap goods made for them.

Let the baker who wishes to succeed, then, strive to keep his goods of the best at all times, nor think anything is as good as might be. Let him strive to please, making a good variety of goods, each of the best, attractive in appearance, reliable in quality. Then let him put a price on them that gives a reasonable profit, all things considered, and he will have no trouble in disposing of the proceeds of his labor.

Let him patronize the supply houses that give him just what he wants, being sure to want the best; taking no just-as-good materials, remember-ing that only the best gives the best results, both in flavor and appearance.

The baker who does these things is bound to

Bread Is Your Best Food—Eat More of It

IT is bad practice to engage in controversies and bakers are wise in paying little attention to the outbursts of dietetic cranks who from time to time rush into print with their maledictions against all kinds of food except those to which for the moment they are addicted. But while it may be wise to keep silent it is a good policy always to know the exact facts, and so bakers will be interested in reading a recent book by McCollum and Simmonds, which the authors have called "The American Home Diet, or What Shall We Have for Dinner," and in which they have much to say of adequate and satisfactory diets. The authors discuss at length the cereal grains and the different parts of the wheat berry and as well the relative nutritive values of the several types of flour. Some of the paragraphs which are of special interest to bakers are as follows:

"*The cereal grains.* The most important food grain in Europe and America is wheat. Its most important use is as a bread grain, because when mixed with water, wheat flour forms a better dough than can be obtained with flour from rye, barley or buckwheat. *The custom of eating as a part of every meal the spongy white bread made from bolted flour has a very strong hold upon us.*

"White flour represents the part of the kernel which is very rich in starch and gluten (protein) and which crushes so readily under the blows of the rollers as to make its particles fine enough to pass through bolting cloth, hence the name bolted flour.

"There are great differences in the nutritive value of the proteins of the different parts of the wheat kernel. The proteins of the germ are of better quality than those of other parts, but *the germ is not suitable for human food because* the oil seems to have slightly detrimental properties. *Bran is not a good human food* because it is so coarse and irritating to the digestive tract. The proteins of bolted flour are among the poorer proteins which enter into the diet of man. This does not constitute a sufficient reason for regarding flour as an inferior food because *when used in proper combinations with other foods* the proteins of the flour are supplemented so as to greatly enhance their value.

"Bran is now widely employed as a remedy for the correction of constipation. *Its action depends on its irritating nature* and on the greatly increased bulk which it confers on the residues of food which escape absorption in the intestine. It cannot be denied that much relief is experienced by many persons taking bran, but the same object can be attained by an extension of the use of such vegetables as spinach, cabbage, and other related plants, also turnips, beets, radishes, onions, carrots, etc., and the *latter are to be recommended rather than bran,* because they are less irritating and possess valuable food properties in addition.

"Not only is bolted flour a source of proteins of poor quality, but it is very poor in those mineral elements which are essential constituents of the normal diet. The most important deficiency in this respect, because of its limited content in other foods, is calcium, the principle constituent of lime. Bread falls short, therefore, of furnishing sufficient mineral salts for the nutrition of the body.

"Bread is, therefore, a very incomplete food. It is, notwithstanding its shortcomings, a *good food provided it is combined with the proper foodstuffs to make it complete,* and the statements made to its discredit are not to be construed as a justification for seeking some substitute for it. Wheat is one of our best agricultural crops and we should continue to use it freely, but with a full understanding of what should be eaten with it.

"Whole wheat flour is superior as a food to bolted flour provided that the bread made from it is to be used as the sole food for a considerable period, as has happened and may happen again under conditions approaching a famine. *This fact is, however, of little importance in ordinary times,* when a variety of foods are available, for either kind of flour is incomplete from a dietary standpoint and will not long support health when used alone.

"The reason for the manufacture of bolted flour is purely a commercial one. The unbroken wheat kernel can be kept for a long period without undergoing changes which affect its food value, but when it is milled, either by the old grinding process or by the more complex roller mill process, it soon undergoes changes which make it less palatable. The fats in the germ decompose and spoil the flavor, and the presence of the germ in the flour encourages the development of worms and weevils, which render it unfit for human food. This can be strikingly demonstrated by anyone by a simple experiment. If some bolted flour is placed in a container, and some fresh wheat germ in another, and the two are loosely covered and kept in a warm room for a few weeks, the germ will be found to be alive with insects, while the flour will be almost free from them. The insects which infest cereals place their eggs almost entirely in the germ, and this part most closely approximates a complete food for the larvæ.

"*It is not probable that whole wheat flour will ever become widely used* for the reasons just stated. *There seems to be no good reason why the use of white flour should be discouraged.* The present practice in milling returns over a quarter of the grain to the farm as cattle feed, and avoids danger of loss in the distribution of that part which is used for human consumption. The important fact to be appreciated is not the difference in the food value of whole wheat and ordinary flour, a difference which is decidedly in favor of the former, but that *the entire wheat kernel is itself not a complete food. Many of our natural foods are incomplete,* even when not manipulated or changed in any way. *The watchword of modern scientific nutrition is proper selection of foods* and their consumption in the most desirable combinations."

In the preceding paragraphs the authors have told the story of wheat flour. They have pointed out that whole wheat flour is superior to bolted flour in cases "where nothing but bread is used as the sole diet for a considerable period." Of course, such a condition has never yet arisen in this country and there is no good reason to expect that our families will ever have to adjust their diet to famine conditions.

The objections to the use of bran are pointed out and substitutes for bran, such as vegetables, are shown to be more wholesome, just as efficacious and decidedly rich in nutritive value. The authors are evidently not in sympathy with the desire of the public for white flour or with the practice of bleaching by which it is obtained. In this connection they say "there are several competing interests in the milling industry, and their most effective appeal to the housewife is the whiteness of the flour. We naturally associate whiteness with purity in flour, as with garments, walls and furniture; hence arose the practice of bleaching flour which is not naturally as white as was desired. There is no justification for the demand for white flour by the public. It has been created artificially for commercial reasons."

Siebel Tech Commencement Exercises

ON THE evening of December 20th, at the Chicago Lincoln Club, the Commencement Exercises of the Fall Term Baking Class of Siebel Tech were held, under the auspices of the Siebel Alumni Association. Genuine enthusiasm, utmost friendship, and a warm undercurrent of fellowship congeniality characterized the occasion, and to those who had the privilege of attending the exercises will remain a cherished recollection.

Promptly at 7 o'clock Alumni President Maegerlein called the gathering to order, and, with a few well-chosen words, introduced, as toastmaster for the evening, Dr. F. P. Siebel, the President of Siebel Tech. The speaking was confined exclusively to the faculty and class members nad some very interesting and instructive talks were given by Dr. Siebel, Professor Stuhlmann, Mr. Fox and Mr. Boecker. The Class President, Joe Martin, of White City, Kansas, has prepared a splendid valedictory, which will be reprinted in the Siebel Alumni Bulletin.

—‡—‡—‡—

More than twenty-five salesmen of the Taggart Baking Company, Indianapolis, Ind., attended a banquet at the Claypool Hotel and a theatre party. The banquet, which was the eighth annual affair of its kind, came as the conclusion of the 1921 fiscal year. The banquets are held to stimulate interest in the business and to cause a better feeling of fellowship among the salesmen and the executives of the company, according to E. B. Taggart, secretary of the company.

The New Secretary-Manager of the American Bakers' Association

THE prompt activities of the recently appointed Board of Governors of the American Bakers' Association brings into the limelight the important appointment of Dr. Harry Everett Barnard, the man selected for the management of all the activities of the Association which will include directorship of the American Institute of Baking.

This is a selection truly fortunate, for Dr. Barnard has had a career of experience in the varied phases of chemistry, not alone in their scientific relation, but in their contact with practical, political and community life; he is not only a scientific analyist, but an administrator with many civic accomplishments to his credit.

From almost his boyhood days Dr. Barnard has had a busy life in the creation of scientific standards for the safeguarding of the public. Born in Dunbarton, New Hampshire, he grew up on a farm, atending country school, graduating from the Nashua high school and gnishing with a course in New Hampshire College as Bachelor of Science at the age of 25. Now, at the age of 48, he is a fine specime nof physical and mental agility, with none of the traditional storybook appearance of "the typical Yankee.'

His first venture into practical chemistry was right after his exit from college, as assistant chemist of the New Hampshire Experiment Station. Later he became research assistant to Dr. Wolcott Gibbs, then assistant chemist of the United States Smokeless Powder Factory, at Indian Head, Md. He dropped the manufacture of powder to become State Chemist of New Hampshire. This was in 1901. His constructive abilities manifested themselves in the organization of the food and water departments and the establishment of State laboratories. Four years later he resigned to become chemist to the State Board of Health of Indiana.

Dr. Barnard was now entering the broader field to which his ambition aspired. Here he began a record that won his ronown. He established food, drug and water control; created laboratories in Indianapolis; secured the passage of a model pure food and drug law; and became State Food and Drug Commissioner. In 1901 he wrote and secured the passage of a model sanitary law which, within the next few years became the law in most of the States and the sanitary code of many large cities. Two years later he secured passage of a model cold storage law, and two years after that a law on weights and measures, becoming administrator as commissioner of this branch of public service.

Wartime brought special responsibilities to Dr. Barnard, placing him in close contact with conspicuous national figures, such as Food Controller Hoover and Dr. Wiley. In the early days of Federal control he was in charge of the Indianapolis laboratory and of inspection work under Dr. Wiley. In 1917 he became Federal Food Administrator for Indiana and chairman of Federal food control activities in Illinois, Indiana, Michigan, Wisconsin, Ohio and Kentucky. Under Hoover he organized Indiana for war administration affecting bakeries, sugar distribution and other conservation measures.

The close of the war did not end Dr. Barnard's zeal for social service. In 1919 he secured the passage of an oil inspection bill, abolishing political control and organizing the new department of State Oil Commissioner. It was in this year that he resigned his several State offices and became director of the American Institute of Baking at Minneapolis.

This record of science and the public does not tell the whole story of an active career. Dr. Barnard organized the Indiana section of the American Chemical Society, being its first chairman, later its counsellor, and then director for ten years. For ten years he was associate editor of the society's journals. Here is a bit more of his history:

Fellow of Indiana Academy of Science and editor for three years.

Member Food Standard Committee in 1907, 1911, 1914 and 1919.

Chairman Food Adulteration Committee, Association of Official Agricultural Chemists, 1914, 1915.

Organized and was first president, Indiana Sanitary and Water Supply Association.

Editor American Food Journal), 1918.

Editor pure food page New York Evening Mail, 1916, 1917.

Editor food column Leslie's Weekly, 1912.

Writer on food subjects in Ladies' Home Journal, Good Housekeeping, Pictorial Review, Munsey's National Magazine, McCall's Magazine and other publications.

Received Doctor of Philosophy degree from Hanover College in 1913.

Member Board of Trustees New Hampshire College, 1903-5.

Member Executive Committee National Conservation Congress, 1913.

Secretary Indiana Conservation Association, 1912.

President Lake Michigan Sanitary Commission, 1916.

Member Society Chemical Engineers, American Public Health Association and American Home Economics Association.

With this background of achievement in view, the caliber of Dr. Barnard becomes evident. What he has to say of the baking industry of the past and its hpes of the future becomes of consequence. Asked to review the in:dustry, he said

"I have always felt, since I began the study of the baking industry intimately in 1909, when we began its inspection, that it is potentially the greatest food industry of the nation, with the exception of beef. No, I will not except beef, for the consumption of cereals is potentially greater than that of beef. A great opportunity is at hand for the baking industry. At the time I mention the industry was unorganized and in the hands of small men. They had a small outlook on their business and the small ambition to keep their families supported.

"I have watched the development of the sanitary bakery from its beginning," continued Dr. Barnard. "I have seen it change from production by a craftsman to the output of a big manufacturing plant—transform from a mere trade to a technical and scientific calling.

"I think the home industry of baking has passed out of the kitchen with the advent of scientific methods. While the art of breadmaking is not wholly lost, it will no longer be practical. The housewife has finally had to admit she can buy better bread from her baker or grocer than she can make at home—that she can get a finer loaf, day in and day out, than from her own oven. The old notion that bread is best because it is home-made is not advanced in these days by the home manager.

"When I turn to the future of the baking industry, and base my prophecy on a knowledge of what the industry stands for today, I can say that the forward-looking men who hold its destiny in their hands must believe in the future of their own business, or they would never have adopted the constitution presented at their recent convention. They believe in science, or they wouldn't have founded the Institute on Baking. They believe the business must be carried forward by trained men, or they wouldn't have made possible a school for the training of bakers."

Dr. Barnard concluded the interview with this frequent statement:

"I believe the baker is going to step out in his community and take his stand with the banker, the railroad magnate, and other business men. It is a noble profession, an essential of civilization and something above the mere labor of baking bread and cutting prices. The baker today is a merchant and manufacturer, a scientist and captain of industry; and the sooner he realizes this and lives his part the sooner will the industry arrive at destined prestige and prosperity."

New England Bakers Re-Organize

AT a meeting held at the Boston City Club on December 28th, 1921, a complete reorganization of the New England Bakers' Association was effected and a full list of officers chosen.

There had been several preliminary mettings held, as per resolution adopted at the New England Bakers' Convention, held in Springfield, Mass., August 23, 24 and 25, 1921, which was as follows:

Be It Known, That it is the opinion of your Committee that the Baking Industry can be better served by a duly and properly organized New England Association, and we recommend to this Convention assembled that they instruct the several Baking Organizations represented to forthwith elect delegates to be called together by the President of the Western Massachusetts Bakers' Association for such a purpose, together with a Committee made up of all the Presidents of the now organized Bakers' Association in New England.

New England Bakers' Association.
A. J. Arnold, Chairman,
Joseph Dube
C. H. Swanson

The following officers were elected and standing committees appointed:

OFFICERS AND MEMBERS OF COMMITTEES NEW ENGLAND BAKERS' ASSOCIATION

President—Hugh V. Keiser, of Dexter's Bakery, Springfield, Mass.

General Vice-President—Frank Eighme, of Grocers' Baking Corporation, Providence, R. I.

Secretary—Walter Dietz, of Massachusetts Baking Co., Hartford, Conn.

Treasurer—Arthur G. Swanson, of Worcester Baking Co., Worcester, Mass.

Vice-President of Wholesale Bread Department—Frank R. Shepard, of General Baking Co., Boston, Mass.

Vice-President of Retail Bread Department—George Ochsner, Springfield, Mass.

Legislative Committee—Chairman, Frank R. Shepard, General Baking Co., Boston, Mass.; Henry Blair, New England Baking Co., Pawtucket, R. I.; Charles O. Swanson, Massachusetts Baking Co., Hartford, Conn.; W. L. McKee, C. H. Cross Co., Montpelier, Vt.; O'Neil Cote, Cote Brothers, Manchester, N. H.; John J. Nissen, John J. Nissen Baking Co., Portland, Me.

Membership Committee—Board of Governors and all State Standing Committee.

Finance Committee—B. S. Ferguson, General Baking Co., Boston, Mass.; Ernest J. Arnold, Saylesville, R. I.; William Davis, George H. Cross Co., St. Johnsbury, Vt.; Melvin Calderwood, Jr., Portland, Me.; Charles Cram, Meredith, N. H.; W. L. Gilbert, New England Baking Co., New Haven, Conn.

Industrial Relations—Chairman, Charles O. Swanson, Massachusetts Baking Co., Hartford, Conn.; George West, Vermont Baking Co., White River Junction, Vt.; Andrew Webber, Laconia, N. H.; E. B. Harris, Waterville, Me.; A. J. Arnold, General Baking Co., Providence, R. I.; Alton Hathaway, C. F. Hathaway & Sons, Boston, Mass.

MEMBERS OF STATE STANDING COMMITTEE OF EACH STATE AND STATE GOVERNORS

Connecticut—O. F. Parker (Governor), Chairman, Parker-Buckey Co., New Britain; C. H. Swanson, Massachusetts Baking Co., Hartford; L. L. Gilbert, New England Baking Co., New Haven; E. Malpass, Sonderheim Baking Co., Bridgeport; George B. Beroth, Beroth Food Shop, Hartford; Mr. Gilman (Governor), Blanchett & Gilman, Willimantic; Joseph Byers, Byers Brothers, New London.

Maine—John J. Nissen, Chairman, John J. Nissen Baking Co., Portland; Joseph Brazier (Governor), Cushman Baking Co., Portland; Edward De Lorge, Biddeford; E. B. Harris (Governor), Waterville; Harry E. Dahlberg, Bangor; I. Simard, Lewiston; Melvin Calderwood, Portland.

Massachusetts—Frank R. Shepard, Chairman, General Baking Co., Boston; Richard Dietz, Sr., Dietz Baking Co., Holyoke:; A. G. Swanson, Worcester Baking Co., Worcester; A. L. Martin, New Bedford; George Oschesher, Springfield; Alton Hathaway (Governor), C. F. Hathaway & Son, Cambridge; Feitz Wachanleim (Governor), Boston, Mass.

New Hampshire—Andrew Webber (Governor), Chairman, Laconia; Mr. Tousiant, Berlin; O'Neal Cote (Governor), Manchester; R. R. LeForme, Nashma; P. J. McManus, Dover; L. B. Pahl, Portsmouth; Seth Rich, Claremont.

Rhode Island—H. J. Blair, Chairman, New England Baking Co., Pawtucket; George S. Ward, Ward Baking Co., Providence; A. J. Arnold, General Baking Co., Providence; Frank Eighms (Governor), Grocers' Baking Corporation, Providence; Mt. Bastastini, Providence; Ernest J. Arnold, Sayesville; Daniel F. Joy (Governor), Providence.

Vermont—George West (Governor), Chairman, Vermont Baking Co., White River Junction; William Davis, George H. Cross Co., St. Johnsbury; William L. McKee (Governor), G. H. Cross Co., Montpelier; Ralph Hamblett, Newport; Fred Moquin, Burlington; Homer Ladd, Barra; Mr. Davenport, Bennington.

The Constitution adopted follows the same general lines as the new Constitution of the American Bakers' Association. In fact, many of the men prominent in the reorganized New England Association are also members in the American Association. The number of ovens being the basis of dues.

The next regular meeting of the New England Association will be held in Hartford, Conn., March 1, 1922, at 12.30, under the auspices of the Connecticut State Governors.

Application for membership is hereby printed and all desiring to fill out such application may do so and forward it to Walter Dietz, Secretary, New England Bakers' Association, care Massachusetts Baking Co., Springfield, Mass. All applications received prior to the meeting of March 1st will be considered as charter members.

      192

I, ...representing ....do hereby signify my desire to join and become a member of the New England Bakers' Association, and agree to abide by its Constitution.

    (Signed)....................

    Address....................

......Number of ovens

—:—:—:—

The United States, 1822-1922

COMPARISON of the conditions under which the United States entered the year 1922 with those of the corresponding year of the preceding century gives us renewed confidence, says the Trade Record of The National City Bank of New York, in the industrial and commercial future of our country. The population, which in 1822 was less than 10,000,000, is now 107,000,000, or more than ten times that of a century ago, while the population of the world as a whole has increased but about 150% meantime. Our international commerce even in the present moment of depression is 60 times as much as that of a century ago, having grown from $109,000,-000 in 1821 to nearly or quite $7,000,000,000 in 1921, while international commerce of the world in 1921 may possibly total forty times that of a century ago, when it stood at $1,659,000,000.

This growth with us has been largely due to increased facilities of transportation. In 1821 our great Mississippi Valley, with its wonderful producing possibilities, had but about 2,000,000 people, and their only method of sending their products to tidewater was by the rivers and the Great Lakes, for even the Erie Canal was not yet finished at that date and steam railways for commercial service were then a thing unknown in any part of the world. Of the 750,000 miles of railway built in all the world since 1821, over one-third was constructed in the United States, chiefly to connect the great interior with the ocean frontages, and the "Middle West," which had then 2,000,000 population, has now 50,-000,000, and is not only the world's biggest producer of grain and meats, but is turning out over one-third of the manufactures of the country. The manufactures of the whole world in 1820 are estimated by Mulhall at $4,250,000,000, while our census of 1920 puts the value of those of the United States alone

at $62,000,000,000, or nearly fifteen times that of the whole world a century earlier. With this tremendous growth in our manufacturing industries our exports of domestic manufactures exclusive of foodstuffs have grown from less than $8,000,000 in 1821 to over $2,000,000,000 in 1921, or 250 times as much in the "lean" year just ended as in the corresponding year of the preceding century. With this increase in industrial, commercial and business activity has come a corresponding advance in the financial requirements of supplies, and the total "money in circulation," which was officially reported at $67,-100,000 in 1820, is officially stated at $5,676,711,000 on December 1, 1921. Meantime the centers of industry and business have grown amazingly, the population of New York having increased from 130,-000 in 1822 to over 6,000,000 in 1922; Philadelphia from 108,000 to nearly 2,000,000, and Chicago from "a hamlet of log houses, inhabited by less than 100 people" in 1830 to approximately 3,000,000,000 in 1922.

Not all of this growth in the industrial and prosperity of the country has come from a mere increase in population, for our area has doubled meantime, the total area of the United States having grown from 1,792,000 square miles in 1821 to 3,620,-000 square miles, including Alaska, at the present time. Our additions of territory since 1822 consist of Texas, Arizona, New Mexico, and the entire Pacific frontage, and thus includes enormous additions to the agricultural and mineral wealth of the country.

Thus the year 1922 finds the United States the world's chief agricultural, manufacturing, commercial and financial nation. The possibilities of a further expansion in all these lines are found in the fact that with our population, exclusive of Alaska, is still only 36 per square mile, or less than one-tenth that of certain of the most prosperous of our European neighbors.

—:—:—:—

Celebration of the fact that business has more than doubled during the past seven years was a feature of the seventh annual banquet of the Reynolds Baking Company to its employes at the plant, Buckingham Street and Cleveland Avenue, Columbus, Ohio, last week. More than 150 employes and members of their families attended. Dancing followed the fine dinner. The employes presented the officers with flowers. J. W. Cartzdafner is manager; S. L. Seelig, assistant manager; W. H. Palmer, sales manager, and Robert Cartzdafner, traveling representative.

—:—:—:—

Dr. Pillem—Are you going to call a consultation?

Dr. Bolus—I think not. I don't believe the patient has that much money.

Bread Prices Fully Reflect Drop In Flour

THE first concrete proof that cheaper bread is a reality and that recent reductions in the price of flour and other materials have been fully passed on to the consumer, has been furnished by the W. E. Long Company, Chicago to the clients of its accounting department.

This proof, in the form of a Composite Profit and Loss Statement, shows by comprehensive analysis of the costs of July, 1920, and September, 1921, that not only has the industry absorbed and reflected in selling prices all lowered costs, but that a still further reduction has been made in their effort to meet the public demand for cheaper bread.

Through the courtesy of the W. E. Long Company the following statement, containing the essential facts disclosed, is made available. The detailed figures are, of course, of a confidential nature, and as such are available only to their clients.

"The price of flour is down, while, according to a number of so-called authorities, the price of bread is still up. Is this true, and if it is true, what is the reason? Has the baker passed on to the consumer the full reduction in his costs, or is he profiteering by retaining an abnormal profit? We are going to reply to those questions by quoting actual facts supported by figures taken from the Comparative Cost Report, which, in turn, reflects the unit costs and operating results of wholesale bakers representative of every section of the United States.

"Are these costs representative of the baking industry as a whole? We have no hesitancy in answering in the negative. Unfortunately, the status of the average baker is such that he has no adequate cost records to show whether he is making or losing money, hence the undetermined losses due to ignorance of costs and the factors responsible for these costs.

"Because of the very fact, however, that our figures are taken from the larger, more efficient plants, the costs are going to be considered at their lowest possible level, for it goes without saying that the greater the efficiency the lower the costs. It, therefore, follows that if bakers are making an abnormal profit, as a whole, then the more efficient ones are making an even larger profit, because the selling prices being fixed more or less by competition are approximately the same.

"We have before us the Comparative Cost Report for September of this year, comprising unit Profit and Loss Statements of wholesale baking plants located in all sections of the country, also figures of these plants, from month to month, for a considerable period prior thereto. The highest average cost of wheat flour per barrel was $12.90, during July 1920, which again proves that these plants are efficiently managed, as the peak of flour prices was somewhere between fifteen and sixteen dollars. However, what we are interested in is not the market quotations, but the actual cost of flour to the baker, and as above stated, the highest average cost was $12.90 per barrel, effective for the month of July, 1920. The average cost for September, 1921, was $7.45 per barrel.

COMPARISON OF COSTS

"The following schedule is based on 100 pounds of baked bread, and shows the Increase and Decrease in the average unit figures for September, 1921, as compared with July, 1920 (when the flour cost was highest).

	Increase.	Decrease.
Total Sales Value of Production..		$2.6175
Less: Loss on Damaged, Stale, etc...............$.0423		
Net Selling Return..............		$2.6598
Cost of Sales:		
Flour		$1.9941
All Other Material............		.3147
Direct Shop Labor		.0236
Indirect Shop Labor..........		.0097
All Other Shop Expense.......		.1252
Total Manufacturing Cost.....		$2.4667
Gross Profit		$ .1931
Overhead:		
Selling and Delivery Expenses.$.0290		
Administrative Expense		.0461
Total Overhead		$ .0171
Net Profit		$ .1760

"It will be noted that the cost of flour decreased $1.9941 per hundred pounds of baked bread. The yield was 288 pounds per barrel of flour used. The decrease in the cost of flour per barrel was $5.45. This means that the decrease in the cost of flour per barrel was responsible for a decrease of $1.8923 in the cost of one hundred pounds of bread. ($5.45: 288—$1.8923). This leaves a further decrease in unit cost of flour of .1018, due to causes other than the decrease in cost per barrel. The figures show an increased Absorption, and a decrease in "Invisible Loss" and Evaporation. These constitute the controllable factors which are either high or low, depending upon the degree of efficiency. The increased efficiency shown was, therefore, responsible for .1018 of the total decrease in unit cost of flour.

"A comparison of the average wholesale Selling Prices and Scaling Weights in effect for July, 1920, as compared with September, 1921, shows the following:

	Small Loaf.	Large Loaf.
Selling Prices decreased...	1 4-5c	2 3-4c
Scaling Weights increased..	1 1-2 oz.	2 oz.

"It will be noted that not only do Selling Prices show a considerable decrease, but Scaling Weights were increased—in other words—the small loaf selling at a decrease of 1 4-5c, contained an additional 1½ oz. of dough. The foregoing schedule, which is based on actual pounds baked, regardless of the number of loaves or the Scaling Weights thereof, shows a total decrease in Production Value or Selling Prices of $2.6175 per hundred pounds. This, of course, includes both the decrease in price per loaf, and the increase in the size of the loaf, consequently $2.6175 constitutes the total decrease in the average Selling Price of 100 lbs. of baked bread. The total decrease in the cost of flour was $1.9941. From this it is apparent that the baker has not only passed on the total decrease in the cost of flour, but has made a further reduction in the price of bread amounting to .6234 per hundred pounds, over and above the entire saving in flour cost. So much for flour. What about the other costs? Have these other costs decreased, and if so, has this decrease been fully reflected in the decreased Selling Prices? As shown in the foregoing statement, material, other than flour, shows a decrease of .3147 per unit of one hundred pounds of baked bread, making a total decrease of $2.3088 in unit cost of material, as compared with a decrease of $2.6175 per unit in Selling Prices.

"Direct Shop Labor decreased from .5507 per unit for July 1920, to .5277 for September, 1921. Wages show an average decrease of $2.02 per week, which accounts, for the most part, for the decrease in unit cost of Direct Shop Labor. Indirect Shop Labor decreased .0097, while other Shop Expenses decreased .1252 per unit. These added to the decrease in material cost make a total decrease in manufacturing cost of $2.4667 per hundred pounds. Still the decrease in Selling Prices ($2.6175) is larger than the decrease in costs.

"Losses from Damaged Bread and Bread Unaccounted For shows a satisfactory decrease, but Stale Bread increased from .0331 per unit for July to .0915 for September, making a net increase of .0423 per unit in total losses of the finished product. Selling and Delivery Expense increased .0290 per unit. This, together with the increased loss on Stale tells the story of the increased selling effort on the part of the baker. Production shows a decrease of 6.76% for September, as compared with July, 1920. It is evident, however, that a part of this decrease is due to seasonal causes, as a comparison of the average production for September, 1921, with September, 1920, shows a decrease of but .33%.

"Administrative Expenses shows a decrease of .0461 per unit in spite of the decrease in volume, which means that this is due entirely to greater economy.

"To sum up, the foregoing comparison shows a total decrease in costs of $2.4415 per hundred pounds of baked bread, against which the baker has decreased Selling Prices to the extent of $2.6175 per hundred pounds. This means that the baker has not alone passed on to the consumer all of his decrease in costs, but has granted a further decrease of .1760 per hundred pounds, thereby causing a decrease in profit to this extent. In this connection it is noted that the average Net Profit for September was less than ½c per pound, which effectually disposes of any charge of profiteering on the part of the baker. This means, in fact, that a further reduction in Selling Prices of but ½c per pound would, as shown by September figures, result in an operating loss in place of any profit. Please remember also that these figures are taken from the larger, more efficient plants. The condition of the small baker with no adequate knowledge of costs and cost factors, and a consequent lack of control thereof, may well be imagined. Why not give the Baker a 'Square Deal'?"

—‡—‡—‡—

The members of the Sales and Production Forces of the National Biscuit Company Bread Bakery, Pittsburgh, Pa., held a dinner in the company's cafeteria, on Wednesday, December 21st, in honor of Manager James J. McVeigh, to celebrate the sales and production records gained under his leadership during the past two years.

Mr. McVeigh was presented with a gold pen and pencil by a stirring presentation speech by Superintendent Charton C. Frants, which was followed with a very interesting talk by Mr. McVeigh. The cafeteria was decorated with Christmas trimmings and National Bread colors.

As guests at the dinner were F. F. Barkow, manager of the Cracker Bakery at East Liberty, Pa.; George B. Curley, cashier, and Mr. Mick, of Cincinnati, Ohio. Among the members present at the dinner were: H. T. Freley, J. G. Spain, J. Turner, W. C. Watkins, J. Bradley, W. Craig, J. Laner, S. Guenther, F. DeForest, C. Koerner, C. Hoerger. C. Grombach, A. Schwartz, C. Fess, F. Gimble, P. Schaidt, R. Kirstein and Charton C. Frants.

—‡—‡—‡—

Be sure of your aim in life before moving into a glass house.

Some people never seem to tire of making other people tired.

If you can't do anything else to benefit your town move away.

LEGAL

No. 116—What Sometimes Happens When Business Men Make No Wills

Cleveland, Ohio.

I AM the sole owner of the above business, which I established about twelve years ago and which has been prosperous since the first year. I am getting along in years and my health is not what it should be, yet I do not intend retiring from business until I die, as I believe that is bad policy for any man, if he is able to keep at it. I have never made a will, and would ask your advice about it. I have a wife and two sons, one of which is with me in the business. I have been told that when a man is on good terms with his family there is no reason to make a will, as the law makes a good enough will for any man, disposing as it does of a man's property who has left no will with the utmost fairness. Please let me have your views on the subject, which may be of general interest to business men throughout the land. I cannot expect a personal reply, but if this letter is answered publicly, please do not attach my name to it. ⸱ ⸰ L. R. A.

Once in a great while there may be a case in which a business man, dying without a will, can look back from where he is and see the law disposing of his estate exactly as he would have done it, but my experience and observation lead me to believe that probably there is not one such case out of fifty thousand.

A man who has nothing but ordinary personal property to leave, such as stocks and bonds, or even real estate, and who is as this correspondent expresses it, on good terms with his family and wishes to favor them equally, can sometimes afford to make no will, because usually the law will make an equal distribution of his property among his heirs. But leaving a business is vastly different. You can't *distribute* a business very well, especially when some of the heirs want to continue it and some want to sell it out.

Every business man who is the sole or part owner of an unincorporated business should make a will. If the business is large enough he would save a lot of trouble if he incorporated it before he died, for after he dies it can be handled much more easily in that form.

Not long ago a business man whom I knew died without a will. He was the sole owner of a thriving business which he had founded, and through many years had carefully built up. When he died it was his chief asset and a very good asset.

He died leaving a second wife, and a son by the first wife, who did not get along well with his stepmother. The latter was keenly interested in the business, in fact, the father had married her out of the office. The son had no interest in the business whatever.

The owner of this business should of course have made a will leaving the business to the wife, who was both able and willing to run it. Instead of that he died intestate, that is, without a will, and under the law the business descended to the wife and son in equal shares. The result was dissension from the first, and finally the sale of the business at a great sacrifice.

The making of a four-line will would have saved this.

In another case a business man with a fair-sized estate had also been married twice, first unhappily, the second time very happily. There were children by both marriages, but he had no relations with the first crop at all. It would have been a very simple matter to leave a will giving his entire estate to the second wife and her children, but instead of that he died without a will, and now the children by the first marriage also share in the estate, and really get the greater part of it, as there are more of them.

In a third case the owner of a good wholesale business had a son who was most devoted to the business and highly efficient in it. He also had another son who had made his life a burden, and who was a liar and a thief. He should have made a will leaving the business to the good son, and leaving the other, if he wished to leave him anything, a bequest of a different sort. Instead he left no will, and the two sons inherited the business equally. Of course they at once began to fuss, and as the good son was not able to buy out the other's share, the business was finally sold, being bought in by a competitor, with whom the good son got a job.

All these business men doubtless turned in their graves if they knew what their carelessness had allowed to happen.

A man who builds up a business usually likes to feel that it will be held together, as a sort of monument to him, after he dies. There is only one way to be sure that it will be, and that is to make a will which will get it into the right hands. Only in exceptional cases will the intestate law get a business into the right hands.

(Copyright by Elton J. Buckley.)

—‡—‡—‡—

The man who is liberal with his sympathy seldom hands out anything else.

But the beauty that is only skin deep is better than the kind that rubs off.

The man who makes good doesn't sit down and wait for his ship to come in.

Unless a man is personally interested in a thing his enthusiasm soon drops to zero.

There may be plenty of happiness in sight, but distance doesn't lend enchantment to the view.

There are two things calculated to make a man's head swim—a merry-go-round and a merry widow.

Empty heads are the easiest turned.

When might makes right it is often wrong.

It takes a good judge of whisky to let it alone.

Bakers' Prices and the Tariff

By Dr. H. E. Barnard, at the Indiana Convention.

WITH the cry in the air for a return of the 5-cent loaf of bread, and certain bakers having a very specialized place in the industry, satisfying it by announcing such loaves, every baker knows that with railroad rates where they are, coal prices where they are, rents where they are, and delivery service costs where they are, the 5-cent loaf represents a dream impossible of general fulfillmnt.

At least until deflation progresses along more general lines than it has so far followed, and reaches into the general field of bakers' costs, this is so because wheat alone is but a small part of the expense of preparing and delivering bakers' bread to consumers' homes.

For that reason we have visited to-day the newspaper offices of Indianapolis and have explained to their editors that thd dream of the 5-cent loaf, which they have played up on their front pages as returning, has been fulfilled only by department stores and chain stores. The department store, we explained both in letters to the editors and in interviews, did not have to care about either costs or profits on bread, as it got the bread customer when she had much else to buy, and it did not intend to let her get away merely with her bread.

It looked to her visit, as a whole, for general profits and used the 5-cent loaf as a lure.

We shall make it a constant practice to notify the press in this manner of cases in which it is perfectly possible for it to go all wrong, and raise false expectations which bring down on the baker a burden of proof that is grossly unfair to him.

We shall continue to educate the public to the bill of costs in the baking industry and how generally this bill is affected by high transportation, high rents, high overhead and high delivery costs.

As the baker faces an editorial demand that his prices "get back to normalcy," he finds himself surrounded by news of the new agricultural bloc in Congress and its cry for great and unusual tariff raises on everything that grows in California.

This agricultural bloc plan turns out to be a plan to make the baker foot a pretty bill for many of his most valuable materials, while the Republican leaders in Washington pat Senator "Hy" Johnson, of California, on the back and tell him they have done everything he asked for, so why should he not be a good fellow and let harmony prevail within the party.

I do not bring this up as a partisan political matter. The agricultural bloc's fight for a walnut tariff, a cocoanut tariff, an almond tariff, an egg tariff and a filbert tariff is not a political fight. It is a sectional fight. It arouses in America a new sectionalism.

The would-be tyrants are the California overlords of orange, lemon, walnut, egg, almond—and I was going to say, filbert and cocoanut industries.

But I would be in error if I said that. The bloc is so dog-in-the-mangerish that it wants a huge tariff on filberts and cocoanut products just to drive American good consumers off those foods, hoping they will take to California walnuts and almonds instead.

They want to raise the almond tariff from a cent a pound to fifteen cetns a pound. That gives you an idea of what the California coersiveness has come to.

Now, if they only had the almonds to give us, their move to break up industries depending on the millions of pounds of shelled almonds imported yearly, would appear a little different from what it does. But California has almond-growing lands for sale, not almond nuts, for the most part. California can meet only 9 per cent. of the almond demand, and all of its crop goes into table use. Bakers have found a sweet almond in Spain and have built up almond-cake sales built on this meaty, deliciously flavored almond.

California, which is famous for flavorless fruits and odorless flowers, now seeks a reputation for conscienceless tariff demands, by offering us a fibrous and untast:y almond, with a 9 per cent crop, compared to the demand. And asks her to help out a land-shark and real estate selling program based on her proposed new tariff.

This is news that the bakers must get across to the public of the Eastern cities, instead of merely sitting back until bakers' cakes become a luxury and then taking the blame because the agricultural :bloc has forced the hoisting pf prices on eggs, almonds, walnuts, cocoanuts and other ingredients of the cakes that now have 20,000,0000 satisfied users.

In China American capitalists, headed by Mr. Keith, of Boston, invested their money in egg refrigerating plants. They did it to serve the American baking industry. They found eggs there good enough (for England to import and sell in the shell to London users as first-quality eggs.

They found a great surplus of fine fresh eggs that could not be profitably imported in the shell to America because of breakage. So they refrigerated them, taking only eggs very fresh from the nest. Thus the finest of eggs reach the American baking industry. And thd price is only 20 cents per pound, a pound being the shelled contents of one dozen eggs.

Imagine our Petalums friends forcing us on the American shell egg market. We have to work a year ahead in the industry, and to order ahead. Egg prices here are the most volcanic of any prices, ranging from 25 cents a dozen to one dollar a dozen. And if bakers had to compete with the American housewives, the housewives would surely have to pay more than they do.

California seeks a monopoly market to exploit. Her plan is a raiding foray against the American residents of Eastern cities. Shall we let her get away with it? Not, at least, without our letting the public know what conditions intrude themselves upon its notice.

The matter of bread standards calls for attention. It is being taken up in Washington. We hope within a few weeks to bring the matter to final adjustment.

At our new home for the baking industry we are finding most interesting work in analyzing costs of bakers' materials and final costs in delivering bread to consumers. We find now, through averaging costs in many cities, that it costs the baker 3 cents a pound for material and more than 3 cents a pound for shop labor and delivery costs, so that material is only 41.68% of the total costs of a loaf of bread. That is something the public must learn and we are teaching them the lesson by establishing all possible contact with those who feel that cheaper wheat alone can give us cheaper bread.

—:—:—:—

Words of Cheer

DAYTON, OHIO.—The National Cash Register Company made satisfactory progress during 1921. It gave steady employment to more than 5000 men and women in Dayton, and as many more in the selling and making fields throughout the world.

Compared with 1920, its working force was slightly reduced. This was done in the interest of efficiency, however, and not to reduce the output of the factory. In fact, more cash registers were built during the year than were constructed in 1920, which was the biggest year in the history of the Company.

Three things contributed to the success of its business in 1921. They were the redoubling of efforts for efficiency in the factory and selling force, the demand of business men everywhere for a machine that would enable them to control their business, and a campaign of national advertising.

Business conditions will gradually improve throughout 1922. There is every reason for conservative optimism. Unquestionably the low mark in the industrial depression is past, and from now on there will be decided improvement.

The United States is at peace with every nation. It is the wealthiest country in the world. It has stemmed the tide of depression in 1921, and I am certain will make greater strides during the coming year.

　　　(Signed) FREDERICK B. PATTERSON,
President, The National Cash Register Company.

—:—:—:—

Albert Salzmann, 101 Abeel Street, Kingston, N. Y., has built a new annex which practically doubles the size of his bakery, and is adding new ovens.

A Survey of the Sugar Situation
By EARL D. BABST
President, American Sugar Refining Co.

BROADLY speaking, the United States controls about one-half of the sugar of the world outside the former battle lines of Europe. Since the armistice little progress has been made in reviving the sugar industry within the war area, so there still is little exportable surplus. The world's supplies and demands remain in about the same proportion as during the war.

The United States sugar industry as a great world factor is an incident and accident of the Spanish War. We went to war to save Cuba and by accident got the Philippines. Porto Rico was an incident. Cuba was not so fortunate as either of these.

The signing of the Treaty of Paris in 1898, at the close of the Spanish War marks the beginning of a noteworthy period in the sugar development of the United States and of Cuba. The Reciprocity Treaty with Cuba, as well as other organic law, distinctly recognizes a trade alliance. One billion of American capital was invested in Cuba, bringing about an increase in her sugar production. The Hawaiian Islands were annexed early in that year. while Porto Rico and the Philippines were ceded by the Treaty of Paris. Recently the United States has acquired the Virgin Islands and has established closer relations with Santo Domingo and Hayti.

The so-called United States field may be described. therefore, as comprising the beet and cane sugar of the United States, the cane sugar of Hawaii, Porto Rico, the Philippines, Santo Domingo, Hayti, the Virgin Islands, and, by reason of the Reciprocity Treaty and of our investments, the cane sugar of Cuba. The total production of the United States field in the year 1898 is set forth in the following table:

	Tons
United States Beet	41,000
Louisiana and Texas Cane	310,000
Hawaii	225,000
Porto Rico	54,000
Philippines	150,000
Santo Domingo and Hayti	48,000
Virgin Islands	13,000
Cuba	315,000
Total	1.156.000

At the outbreak of the European War, in 1914, there had been the large development shown by the following table of production for 1913:

	Tons
United States Beet	624,000
Louisiana and Texas Cane	153,000
Hawaii	488,000
Porto Rico	350,000
Philippines	155,000
Santo Domingo and Hayti	84,000
Virgin Islands	6,000
Cuba	2,428,000
Total	4,288,000

EUROPE WAS BIG PRODUCER

Before 1914 almost half of the world's sugar was produced in Europe. The Great War came and one-half of Europe's production was enclosed within the battle lines. What with devastation, neglect, and the substitution of other crops, the sugar output of the war area is now 2,000,000 tons less than in pre-war days. The Old World's loss has been the New World's gain, however, for these 2,000,000 tons have been added to the productions of the United States and Cuba. At the present time, therefore, half of the world's production is in the Western Hemisphere, Europe and the Far East together constituting the other half.

The United States and Cuban fields were the only ones available to the allied countries when war was declared. Consequently, at the outbreak of hostilities Great Britain, France, Italy and other European countries immediately entered the United States and Cuban markets. Prices naturally rose under this forced draft, giving greater impetus to the already increased production of the United States field. In contrast with the foregoing tables, the one below gives the production for that field in the year 1921, which shows an increase since the outbreak of the War of over 2,000,000 long tons, most of which has been in Cuba.

	Tons
United States Beet	969,000
Louisiana and Texas Cane	157,000
Hawaii	508,000
Porto Rico	437,000
Philippines	252,000
Santo Domingo and Hayti	191,000
Virgin Islands	4,000
Cuba	3,936,000
Total	6,454,000

The United States and Cuban fields are sufficient to meet for some years all the needs of the United States and of Europe. It would have been a wise provision if some commitments, aside from informal assurances, had been secured by Washington before it inaugurated its war programme of stimulation of sugar production in the United States field. If, however, the industry of the United States and of Cuba has the continued support of the respective governments, there are many reasons to expect that it will be able to hold a large part of the business which came so unexpectedly during the war. This can be made of special advantage to the consumers of the United States, and that, too, without scrimping on domestic requirements.

HIGH PRICES DETRIMENTAL

The recent inflation period has demonstrated once more that high prices are detrimental. A lower range of prices is beneficial, not only to the public, but to the industry. Less capital is involved and hazardous risks are eliminated from the business. A smaller manufacturing margin becomes possible and the consumer and industry benefit equally: the consumer by low prices, industry by increased sales.

During the war the producers and refiners of the United States and Cuba fitted their operations into a world programme, making possible a period of moderate world prices and an international division of supplies of boundless benefit to consumers, both domestic and foreign. The initiative of producers and refiners and the investment of hundreds of millions of American capital have made possible in Cuba and the United States a vast increase in the production of a food staple of pre-eminent world importance. The world needs this sugar. The United States has the excess capacity to refine a million tons for export. Not another brick need be laid.

There is bound to be a race for foreign markets. Will the ultimate prize go to Cuba and the United States, or will it go elsewhere? Washington can help by giving permission, as proposed, to refine in bond in the manner already accorded by law to other manufacturers, smelters and refiners. The ultimate answer, however, must be made by the industry itself. It had the pioneer courage to invest hundreds of millions in production. Without doubt it will have the courage and the vision to find and to hold foreign markets rather than cut production unnecessarily and so lead to a period of high prices.—*New York American, Jan. 9, 1922.*

—‡—‡—‡—

Pennsylvania Bakers Advisory Committee

C B. CONNELLEY, Commissioner of Labor and Industry of Pennsylvania, has appointed the following advisory board on bakeries to assist the Industrial Board in all matters relating to the enforcement of the safety standards in bakeries: L. J. Schumaker, president Pennsylvania Bakers' Association, and Louis Orthwein, president Retail Bakers' Association, both of Philadelphia; R. K. Stritzinger, Norristown; George W. Fisher, Huntingdon; William Freihofer, Philadelphia; R. M. Allen, Ward Baking Company, New York; Horace W. Crider, president, Western Pennsylvania Bakers' Association, Homestead; C. J. Layfield, Scranton; J. Fred Schofer, Reading, and Fred C. Huller and C. C. Latus, secretary of the Pennsylvania Bakers' Association, both of Pittsburgh.

Preparing for the Pennsylvania Convention

WHILE the annual convention of the Pennsylvania Bakers' Association to be held at Bedford Springs, Pa., June 12 to 14 is still six months distant, time flies, and ere the bakers of the Keystone State realise it the time will be at hand when preparations for the journey to the convention place must be made. The 1922 convention of the Pennsylvania bakers will, according to well informed bakers, be the largest and best gathering of bakers ever held in the State.

It is the plan of the committee to have but one business session each day. This will be an innovation in Pennsylvania. The business session will be called to order in the spacious auditorium of the Bedford Springs Hotel at 9.30 A. M. and continue in session until 1.30 P. M., when adjournment will be taken for luncheon. This will be followed by the amusement and sporting events. Raymond K. Stritzinger, Vice-President of the Association has been designated as general chairman of the committee on amusements and entertainment and he is arranging a live wire program.

The event of Monday evening, June 12, will be a costumed masquerade ball in the hotel ballroom, which will be under the direction of George P. Reuter, of the Malt-Diastate Company, of New York. Those who took part in the masked ball at Scranton, in June last, well understood how successful Mr. Reuter can be in making an evening of merriment and good fellowship. Valuable prizes will be awarded for costuming at the ball that night.

There will be all sorts of games during the periods after the business session and the evening's entertainment. The golf players will have their innings as well as the baseball enthusiasts. Ralph D. Ward, of the Ward Baking Company, has been appointed captain of the Bakers' golf team, while Horace W. Crider, of the Homestead Baking Company, Homestead, Pa., and president of the Western Pennsylvania Bakers' Association, will captain the Bakers' baseball team.

Marshall Holt, of A. D. Acheson & Co., will be captain of the supply men's ball team. Appointment will be announced later by Mr. Stritzinger of the captain of the supply men's golf team. Candidates for these teams are to apply as early as possible to their captains, stating experience and golf handicaps at home

The Fleischmann Company will donate a mate to the above cup, to be given to the baker shooting the next best medal score.

The Duhrkop Oven Company has donated 16 medals to be given to winners of individual golf matches.

Other prizes donated thus far are as follows: Hamersley Mgr. Co., silver cigarette case; American Diamalt Company, either a cigarette case or a piece of the famous Rockwood pottery ware; Falk American Potato Flour Corporation, large bag of potato flour.

One enterprising supply firm, it is understood, will donate a wrist watch to be awarded to the best costumed lady at the masquerade ball on the opening night.

The following firms have notified Mr. Stritzinger that they will donate suitable prizes and give the particulars later: Jaburg-Miller Company, Menasha Printing and Carbon Co., Trueheart & Russell, Triumph Machinery Co., Marshall Milling Co., Samuel Knighton and Son and the Larabee Flour Mills Corporation. These prizes will be utilized for miscellaneous events that will be held during the three days of the convention at Bedford Springs. All bakers who register at the convention will have ample opportunity to win a prize.

It is possible that special train fare can be arranged to Bedford Springs from all sections of Pennsylvania for the convention, as negotiations are now on to that end, through C. C. Latus of Pittsburgh, the secretary of the Association.

An interesting list of speakers who have some vital and compelling messages for bakers will be heard at Bedford Springs, June 12-14.

—‡—‡—‡—

Indiana Convention

THE Indiana Bakers' Association at its annual convention at Indianapolis on January 4th and 5th, adopted a number of important resolutions, among which were the following:

"RESOLVED that the Indiana Association of the Baking Industry hereby approves the recent re-organization of the American Bakers' Association in its endeavor to further promote the activities of the baking industry of this country, and

BE IT FURTHER RESOLVED that our members co-operate individually with the American Bakers' Association and join with them to further the great

we believe it advisable at this time that those sections not in accord with the principles of Standard Weights try out the other theory of fractional units, assuring them of our friendly interest, and still reserving for their use our help and experience in event that their experiment fails to answer the purposes they seek.

RESOLVED that the name of "Indiana Association of the Baking Industry" be changed to read hereafter, "Indiana Bakers' Association."

RESOLVED that in furthering the work of our Association we add the name and title of "Business Manager" to the office of secretary.

Resolutions were also adopted favoring an equitable tariff on frozen and dried eggs, and on shelled almonds and walnuts, and protesting against the increased rates as designed by bills now before Congress.

The following officers were elected: President, E. K. Quigg, Richmond; Vice-President, A. W. Wilkinson, Rushville; Treasurer, J. A. Dietzen, Franklin. Other details in our next issue.

The ordinance adopted at St. Louis, Mo., in June last, and which was to become effective on August 14, 1921, prohibiting bakeries selling their products after 9 A. M. on Sundays, has been upheld by Circuit Judge Hamilton, who refused a permanent injunction against the enforcement of the law. It is reported that an appeal will be taken to the Supreme Court.   •

—‡—‡—‡—

Ohio Association

THE Ohio Association of the Baking Industry will hold its annual convention at the Hotel Chittenden, Columbus, Ohio, on January 17th and 18th, and the following program has been prepared:

Tuesday, Jan. 17th

10.00 A. M.—Registration.

2.00 P. M.—Meeting called to order by President A. G. Reck, Columbus.

Reports of Secretary H. B. Apple and Treas. H. M. Miller.

"The Service Ideal in Business," Address by Galen Starr Ross, Columbus.

"Why Bakers Should Advertise," Address by J. Adam Payne, of The Fleischmann Co.

"Humps," and Address by John M. Hartley, Chicago.

Report on past year's work, by H. N. Dixon, Field Manager.

Nomination of officers for ensuing year.

7.00 P. M.—Banquet and entertainment.

Wednesday, January 18th

10.00 A. M.—Meeting called to order.

Address by L. J. Taber, Chief of the Ohio Department of Agriculture.

Address by R. M. Black, State Dairy and Food Commissioner.

"Allied Trades and What They Are Doing for the Baking Industry," Address by Williams, Evans, Chicago.

Election and Installation of Officers.

Moisture in Bread

Address by C. B. Morison, of the American Institute of Baking, at the Chicago Convention.

THE subject of moisture in bread is of particular importance to the baking industry at this time when so much is heard about present and impending legislation affecting the sale of bread by weight, the standardization of composition, and of food value.

The problem of the relation of moisture in bread to high absorption flours, different amounts of dough ingredients, such as sugar, malt, yeast, lard and other constituents, fermentation conditions, oven temperature and storage, for example, has not been exhaustively studied as far as we have determined from a survey of the literature on the subject.

The Institute has been conducting a systematic series of observations on some of these points and considerable data has already been collected bearing on the moisture content of different kinds of bread, and the amount of loss in weight which these breads undergo when subjected to various conditions of temperature and humidity for twenty-four hours or longer. At present we are continuing these experiments and the investigation will not be concluded until we have obtained a fairly representative collection of data bearing on all the important aspects of the problem. It will then be possible to present to the baking industry figures which will show the moisture content of bread made from various formulas, conditions of fermentation, baking and storage. Therefore, for this reason, we do not intend to dwell specifically upon the data so far observed in these studies, although we now have information on the moisture content of bread and losses in weight during various conditions of storage that will be of importance to the industry in relation to present and future legislation concerning bread.

Various articles on the moisture content of bread have been published in the trade papers and other journals, but no extensive data has been published sufficient to establish the contention of the baker, that the losses in weight shown by various types of bread exposed to a wide variation in atmospheric and storage conditions is of greater magnitude than is supposed by those who have not investigated this subject. The lack of such data is deplorable, when arbitrary systems of tolerances are incorporated in legislative enactments which are unfair to the baker.

The problem of the losses shown by bread during storage is also extremely complicated, and a recent published work by Whymper has pointed out the interesting observation that bread may lose weight, and at the same time determinations of moisture made on the crumb and crust may show increases in this constituent. The whys and wherefores of this phenomenon are conjectural, but this example is offered to emphasize the difficulty of drawing up arbitrary tables of moisture losses in bread.

The fact remains, however, that if the sale of bread is to be regulated in relation to weight, the legislative bodies responsible for such laws should be fully informed of the difficulties inherent in formulating just statutes for this purpose. This information can only be obtained by an intensive study of moisture in bread and the resulting losses of weight in storage under a wide variety of conditions; embracing obviously regional and local influences, as well as manufacturing conditions and variations in the breadmaking process. No arbitrary assumption regarding tolerance can be made effective without attention to observed facts and these should be comprehensive enough to include all probable conditions.

A bread containing about 38% moisture and weighing 16.5 ozs. after baking may lose enough moisture (when subjected to certain conditions of storage, such as high temperature and low humidity) to cause the baker selling it to be liable to prosecution by certain existing laws; while the same loaf of bread under a different set of conditions may conform to the legal tolerance. The final weight of the two loaves with an original moisture content of 38% and a weight of 16.5 ozs. may vary considerably at the end of a given period under different conditions of storage, but nevertheless if the amount of total dry solids is calculated on both loaves, the results may be identical. The laws regulating the sale of bread by weight should be based on the actual amount of dry solid matter present in the bread after baking, and no just system of tolerance can be formulated which fails to recognise this fact.

ACTUAL NUTRITION A MAIN FACTOR

The consumer of bread is more concerned with the amount of actual nutrition which can be obtained from a loaf of bread than with its weight. A loaf of bread may weigh one pound when purchased and contain an excessive amount of moisture which would reduce the total nutritive value of the loaf, while another bread with a lower moisture content would also weigh one pound and at the same time be more nutritious. This point has not been exploited by popular proponents for weight laws, who appear to consider bread as a food product of an exceedingly uniform character, the moisture content of which can be easily controlled or subjected to variable conditions of storage from oven to consumer without much change. It would be a very difficult matter for the state to regulate the sale of bread on the basis of nutritive value and such a step is not regarded with favor except by a few theorists; but if the idea could be driven home to the public that the baker does not stand behind bread of excessive moisture content because such a condition does not produce good bread, much of the criticism directed against the baker would be ended.

In a previous article by the writer, it was stated that "unfounded statements that influence the public in the belief that bakers' bread is lacking in nutritive value through the addition of excessive and abnormal amounts of moisture are detrimental to the industry." We are fairly convinced of the truth of this statement, and believe that the work of the Institute in gathering information on the moisture content of bread from all sections

sold today does not carry an abnormal amount of moisture, but on the average conforms closely to the demands of an economic popular nutrition. The idea of "high absorption" has led to incredible assumptions as to the amount of water to be found in a loaf of bread, and we advise those who are addicted to such statements to indulge in a few simple calculations and moisture determinations. The Institute is not only engaged in a study of storage losses, but also has considerable data of oven losses which are important in their relation to the moisture content of bread as influenced by baking. In this connection we might suggest that slack doughs are apt to lose some of their characteristics before they reach the oven, and the bread baked from them is not as uniform in high moisture content as some suppose.

EXPERIMENTS WITH WRAPPED BREAD

During the last year the Institute has conducted a series of experiments on the efficiency of the protection afforded by wrapping bread with commercial papers of different types and weights. We have not included in our study of the effects of breadwrapping, quantitative observations on the protection against contamination from micro-organisms and other sources. This has been well worked out by Jacobs, LeClerc and Mason, and others, who have found that the surface of wrapped bread purchased on the retail market is more nearly free from organisms than unwrapped bread obtained at the same time and from the same source.

Our work has been concerned particularly with the losses shown in twenty-four hours by bread wrapped in commercial papers and the effect of such wrapping on bread quality. We have found that the loss in weight of one-pound loaves at the end of twenty-four hours, when wrapped in so-called self-sealing paraffine papers, weighing from 25-35 pounds per ream, varied from 0.15-1.01%, or .02-0.16 ounce. The lowest loss was obtained from the heaviest paper, which weighed 35 pounds to the ream.

Papers waxed on one side gave slightly higher losses, ranging from 1-3% or 0.16-0.48 ounce, while dry waxed papers showed greater variations of from 0.32-3.4% or .051-0.54 ounce. The so-called ventilating stripe paper (familiar to many as the type of which "Zebra" is an example) gave losses of from 0.86-3.70% or 0.14-0.59 ounce. Ordinary wrapping paper, unparaffined, gave an average loss of 4.54% or 0.73 ounce.

The much lower loss in weight shown by wrapped bread in comparison with unwrapped bread under the same conditions is striking, and the effect of wrapping on the retardation of staleness is generally favorable.

In our experiments the bread was wrapped one hour after baking, which is not a sufficient length of time for the bread to cool to room temperature, which varied from 68-77°F., with a relative humidity of 40-45%. Thorough cooling of the loaf to room temperature may take as long as five hours when the initial temperature of the loaf is about 210°F., and that of the room is about 70°F. This is easily determined by thrusting a thermometer into the

until that of the room is reached. The time will vary with the size of the loaf and with the temperature of the room. Nevertheless we did not find at the end of twenty-four hours evidence of mold growth, though the spores of molds were present on the surface of the bread. Mold growth is an index of too high a humidity and bread wrapped warm and then subjected to rapid cooling, favorable to condensation of moisture, is liable to develop mold with comparative rapidity, this, of course, varying with the species of mold, degree of the infection, and other conditions. If the bread is consumed within twenty-four hours after baking, even under unfavorable conditions of temperature and humidity, there does not seem to be much reason for worry as far as the development of mold is concerned. Unless there are present abnormal conditions of contamination, of temperature and humidity, we should not expect mold to develop within twenty-four hours. In recent experiments it is interesting to note that when we reduced the relative humidity to 35%, with the temperature as high as 86°F. in the storage room, we were unable to find external or internal growth of mold after observations extending over six days, though the surfaces of the loaves were contaminated with mold spores. When the same loaves were placed in a tight bread box containing several pounds of moist bread, mold growth developed in from 48-72 hours. Bakers should appreciate the fact that moldy bread is often due to conditions favorable to high humidity. There are other factors in the mold problem which are not so easy of explanation, but we have drawn attention to the influence of humidity because many bakers do not seem to understand the importance of this factor in practical measures to prevent mold.

It is hoped that the few points developed in this discussion may be helpful in our consideration of the problems surrounding the subject of moisture in bread, and that the data which has been collected by the Institute on this subject will be of benefit to the baking industry in its relation to the legal and other aspects of the problem.

—⁂—⁂—⁂—

A Course in Cake Baking Now Offered To Women Bakers

During the past year the Siebel Institute of Technology has received many requests from women all over the country for admission to its Special Two

Special Kinds of Pies and Pie Fillings.

Tartlets; Frosted and Fancy Cakes.

Wine and Ice Cream Cakes—various kinds of Torten.

Finishing of Torten, Petits Fours and French Pastry.

Also Sponge and Box Cakes, Pound Cakes, Commercial Cakes.

Cookies, Snaps, Jumbles, etc.

SECOND WEEK

Almond and Cocoanut Macaroons; Fancy Macaroons.

Ice Cream Confect—Tea and Coffee Desserts.

Meringues; Plain and Fancy Kisses.

Sweet Doughs, Coffee Cakes, Sweet Rolls.

Danish Pastry.

Different Fillings for these cakes.

Ornamenting and Decorating.

Marzipan Work.

Students' Decorating Contest.

It has also been decided to limit the class to a small number to permit personal instruction whenever possible, and also to afford students every opportunity to do some of the practical work herself. There is no question that this Course should appeal to the many women bakers who are desirous of introducing into their shops a superior attractvie line of cake and pastry goods.

Requests for information regarding this Course should be addressed to the Registrar, Siebel Institute of Technology, 964 Montana Street, Chicago.

—⁂—⁂—⁂—

CUP CAKES

Two and a half pounds of powdered sugar, one and a half pounds of butter and lard, twenty eggs, one quart of milk, two ounces of ammonia, four and a half pounds of cake flour, mace. Cream sugar and butter in the usual manner, add eggs, then milk and ammonia, which has been previously powdered and dissolved; then add flavor and flour, fill in richly greased cup-cake molds and bake in moderate heat.

ORIENTAL CAKES

One pound sugar, fourteen ounces flour, ten eggs, essence lemon. Beat up the sugar and eggs in a bowl or machine, the same as for sponge cakes, then mix in

Flour and the Baker's Loaf

By F. G. Atkinson

Vice-President of Washburn-Crosby Co., at the N. Y. Wholesale Bakers' Convention

YOUR Program Committee has assigned me the subject of "Flour." I imagine the discussion of this subject has been worn almost threadbare at your previous conventions and in your places of business. So if you will permi tme, I will not only speak as regards flour, but will also give you some of my impressions resulting from my study extending over a good many years of the baking business in general.

The reasons why a baker should use the best flour obtainable I brought out in a talk at the New England Bakers' Convention, held in Springfield in August. Therefore, to avoid repetition, would refer you to the report on this talk, which appeared in the August 27th issue of the Bakers' Weekly.

Being a miller, I am not going into details and try to tell my friends, the bakers, how to make bread, for you all know more about it technically and practically in five minutes than I know in a day.

In starting an organization to produce high-grade flour or A-No. 1 bread, the miller and baker must first make a thorough investigation of his subject. He then proceeds to form an organization and plan his business. He starts operations, and if he is a careful business man, keeps a sufficient quantity of records to tell him accurately what he is accomplishing. Then he proceeds to standardize his business and provide incentives for his employees, each and every one in his own department, to make the business a success.

If he does all this and used good judgment, he is going to have a wonderful business, and he is going to produce something that the American consumer wants. That American consumer is not happy unless he gets it, and the better it is, the more he wants it. As millers and bakers we want the people to eat more bread and less of other food products. I have a distinct conviction that if we all work together, that is, the millers, the bakers, the yeast man, and the bakers' supply man. we can

Wheat has a God-given power in it not possessed by any other cereal. This factor is known as gluten, and I often marvel that such a high percentage can be found in a grain of wheat. Quoting from a pamphlet by one of our large yeast companies:

It is on account of the gluten that bread can be raised with yeast. The gluten is that elastic, resilient, tenacious substance that holds the gas when it is formed by the action of the yeast on the sugar. It forms the sustaining walls of the whole cellular structure of the loaf. Gluten supplies the characteristics that make wheat and wheat products superior to all cereals. Therefore, let us mark well—bread is the most easily digested of all cereal products.

PREPARATION OF THE WHEAT

It is not generally known to what extent the miller goes to produce a clean, pure and high-grade product. Let me tell you what takes place up to the point of actual grinding.

The wheat from the cars immediately goes to a machine that removes all straws, coarse grain and other large-sized foreign matter. From there the brushing machines take it and remove all of the so-called beard and dust and dirt that may be adhered to the outside of the berry. From these scouring machines the wheat then goes to the washers and is thoroughly washed. Thence to the driers. Then, after a period of tempering, which is necessary in order to properly remove the bran coats, the wheat goes to the first break-rolls, where it is cracked open. At this stage of the process there begins the work of the famous middlings purifier, which removes any impurities that may have adhered to the kernel, especially to that portion which we call the "crease."

The mill then proceeds to make flour. However, I won't attempt to describe or enumerate the details of manufacturing flour, as the process is a long one.

HIGH QUALITY FLOUR

Extreme care is necessary in the manufacture of such a product.

The use of BUDWEISER Barley Malt means a better loaf of bread at a lower cost, for *pure* malt gives a healthier fermentation by energizing the yeasts, and its maltose content reduces the quantities of sugar necessary. Full development of gluten means greater nutrition value.

BUDWEISER Barley Malt—100% pure—develops a bigger volume with a finer texture and a better flavor—and the richer appearance and golden bloom of the loaf will mean a steadily growing volume of business.

Fresh supplies are constantly available from Anheuser-Busch distributors without the need of a contract.

ANHEUSER-BUSCH SALES CORPORATION
ST. LOUIS, U. S. A.

Incidentally, at this point I might say that any baker who is putting extra money into his quality, should see to it that his salesmen and representatives are talking that quality continuously. Sometimes moral influence has a great deal to do in the maintenance of a man's business. For instance, if a manufacturer and his men are sure of their quality, proud of it, and talk it, there is much more likelihood of that brand of bread being kept up to high standard of quality than if the enthusiasm in the manufacturing and selling department were lacking.

Another feature should be considered in this matter of maintaining high quality. It has been proven that it is not good business to try and manufacture too many varieties of the same article. To illustrate, a cotton goods manufacturer in Pennsylvania some years ago did a large business in various varieties of cotton goods. Said manufacturer turned out something over fifty varieties. Year after year, however, his profit and loss account did not show satisfactory results and, of course, he began to wonder why.

From some source he got the inspiration of determining to confine himself to a few standard high grade qualities and make his fatcory conform to the standardized product. The change resulted in a pronounced success financially, and his troubles were reduced in many other ways accordingly.

In the bakery business there are many temptations to add a new department here and there, and also to increase the number of brands. The standardized program, I believe, would appeal to me if I were in the baking business.

If a baker uses some certain brand of flour as a backbone for his mixture, why is it not good business for said baker to use such a flour exclusively? Everything except water that goes into the making of a loaf of bread these days is of a costly character. Therefore, flour should be of the best quality obtainable

Bread is the most perfect all-around food known to man. What an opportunity, therefore, exists for the bakers This commodity is used at least three times daily by every man, woman and child. Work on this enormous, potential trade assidously, endeavoring to give the people the natural flavor. You are bound to win. Look to the high quality loaf as something lively and beautiful to look at as well as something delightful to eat. Don't worry too much about big absorption and much volume.

What wonderful opportunities there are for the baker. His business is bound to succeed if he adheres to the simple proposition of handling the commercial side of his business carefully and giving the public a high quality loaf.

A COMMERCIAL LOAF OF BREAD

loaf of bread may get into it various ingredients so costly in price as to make the net result of his business show unprofitable.

Bakers using ingredients other than flour, water, yeast and salt, must to a great degree be scientific in their methods, for it takes a good level head, with lots of experience, to know just what the mixture should be from day to day. Here is where a high-grade flour becomes so important. A flour properly milled from a carefully blended mixture of wheat can carry a tremendous load, but, of course, cannot be expected to perform miracles.

Where a baker endeavors to produce a loaf of bread with a flavor different from the natural flavor of bread made from wheat flour, he thereby attempts to educate the palate of a certain section of the public to a new flavor in bread. Sometimes, unwittingly, he gives himself an insurmountable task, as we all know that the public is mighty particular and does not like to have its customs and tastes interfered with. You will find this particularly true in the case of children.

If these statements are nearly correct, should we not say, therefore, that the nearer we can keep our loaf of bread in flavor to the natural flavor of bread produced from flour, water, yeast and salt, the more successful we will be in presenting the public for its consumption the much-desired commercial loaf of bread?

From the above do not infer that we are not in favor of the use of such ingredients as milk, malt, mineral salts, sugar and shortening, for we are emphatically of the opinion that these most necessary articles of food for the human body have their place in the commercial loaf of bread. What should be avoided is the overloading of the flour with richness, because in the commercial loaf of bread the public is expecting bread, and not something that approaches cake in taste and constituents.

ABSORPTION

After the war, when restrictions were taken off and bakers were permitted to make bread just as they pleased, there was naturally a strong tendency to improve the quality of the loaf. The public encouraged this, as the people were anxious for the old-time quality and flavor. Naturally, this effort on the part of the bakers continues, but, in addition, we have noticed, during the last six months, that much more attention was being given to the adding of moisture to the doughs. Ingredients are being used that help to increase the absorbing power of the flour and, in addition, we have the high-speed mixer, with helpmates, that help to run the moisture content higher. Instead of 58 or 60 pounds to the hundred of flour, we now have reports running from 65 up to 70, all of which is commendable, but certainly there must be some

add to the moisture content; that is, if the loaf is going to prove satisfactory to the consumer. The only reason for this remark is that we all want to make bread so attractive to the palate of the individual that there will be no question but what the percentage of bread in the diet of American people will gradually increase. There is much room for such a development.

CHANGING BREAD BRANDS

If you have been observing the matter, you will have noticed that it has been common practice in the past for some bakers to change their bread brand once in a while, or possibly add another brand to the list.

Such a :plan has some advantages, but it looks to me as though a baker should decide on one or two brands, and stick to them through thick and thin.

The only good reason for changing a brand is where there has been a laxity on quality, resulting in the old brand getting into disrepute.

One can readily see that this is another reason for a baker always using good flour and avoiding a mixture of poor grades with the better.

Advertising is very costly; hence it is imperative that the article advertised should be of unquestioned quality.

I am departing from my theme in the mentioning of these matters of advertising bread. Really, however, it is a kindred subject, especially in my ·case, as my company manufactures a very high grade of flour and, naturally, is anxious that its customers have as wide a distribution as possible. Therefore, my remarks on advertising are apropos.

Speaking from long experience in the advertising game, I should say that much care should be exercised in the arrangement of an advertising program. If a baker is to erect a new bake shop, he studies his plans day and night for some time. In fact, he does his best to produce a perfect shop. So it should be with the bread advertising program. The whole thing should be discussed pro and con with those who know the game, and a plan laid out that will show the details from start to finish.

CUTTING PRICES

There is another feature in the bakery business

and a nicely arranged advertising plan that will tell the people of the community what a very palatable and fine loaf of bread we are offering the public.

STANDARDIZATION

A standardized, dependable and unform flour is what 99% of the bakers should have. Many have already learned the lesson, and others will come along gradually. A well-arranged shop has its storage room for flour, where there is a free circulation of air, and the temperature somewhere about 68 or 70. The baker running a standardized shop wants his flour to reach the mixing machinery at about the same temperature all the time, and he wants to feel that the quality of the flour that he is using today is the same as that which he consumed yesterday, and which he expects to consume in the succeeding days. I do not need to leave to your imagination the other hundred and one things necessary in a shop that is to produce regularly a high-grade bread, as you know all about them.

There will always be individuality in breads, as we very seldom see absolutely the same kind of bread made out of the same flour when the product comes from more than one shop. There are exceptions to this, as we know of at least one brand of bread that has been standardized, and which is making distinct advances in its popularity with the public, and the location of the shops are quite widespread.

If a flour in a bake shop could always be the same, what a great opportunity it gives the proprietor and his foremen to attune the whole institution to the successful manufacture of high-grade bread. Barring changes in temperature and atmospheric conditions, and granting that a shop is kept cleanly in every respect, this much-desired good quality bread would come out just like clockwork.

GREATER USE FOR BREAD

Now that we have made our plea for the use of high-grade flours, and have told you something about their manufacture and use, let me urge all bakers and others interested in the increased consumption of bread to study ways and means of inducing the public to more completely get on the

and bakers as to the uses of bread. We all know that a white bread can be turned into toast, French toast, toast for puddings, dressings, toast for soups, breakfast foods and other purposes that any good cook could easily suggest.

France has the reputation for being able to save money rapidly. The great bulk of the French nation is tremendously thrifty and provident. Is there not some explanation for this in the fact that France consumes double the quantity per capita of wheat breadstuffs than is used here in the United States?

That people or race that is a large consumer of wheat breadstuffs inevitably saves tremendous sums of money, and who knows but what they become in many ways the leader or leaders of the nations of the earth?

—:—:—:—

Greeting From the Allied Trades

CHRISTMAS comes to us from the Festival of Ceres—the Feast of the Harvest. It is the time of great rejoicing. This year we are thankful for life, love and abundant harvests. This gratitude finds form in greetings to our friends. No blessing of the Creator exceeds the Divine gift of friendship.

At this season we are reminded that, after all, life is more than a mere chase for profits—important as these are. To you and to us life (and business) means the the satisfaction of *serving*. It means, too, the formation of valued personal relationships, such as we are glad exist, and we trust will long continue to exist.

We want our Baker Friends to fully understand and appreciate the activities and influence of the Allied Trades of the Baking Industry—this vast army of energetic, progressive emissaries of trade, and commerce. "Optimism" is our middle name, and it is the principal ingredient in stimulating business, and particularly now during this period of reconstruction.

The financial reports of the great commercial agencies tell us we are near the "turning point" and that this country is on the eve of great prosperity. They add that all we need is *confidence*.

It is the purpose and ambition of the Allied Trades to co-operate in assisting our Baker friends to attain this prosperity—with the contentment and happiness it brings. We are at your service, and hereby promise by thought, word and *act* to do our *level best* to bring about the prosperity you should enjoy. May the NEW YEAR bring you all, and more than you anticipate.

And to each individual member of the Allied Trades may the coming year be the most prosperous you have ever experienced.

Sincerely,

(Signed) WILLIAM EVANS,
Pres. of the Allied Trades of the Baking Industry.

The Court of Industrial Relations

An address by Governor Henry J. Allen, of Kansas, at the Chicago Convention.

IT IS said by those who have taken the pains to place themselves in possession of statistics on the subject that practically six million laboring men are out of employment in the United States at this hour. All who have made any study of the situation realize that this is an unnatural condition. During the latter part of 1918 we were all hopefully pointing to the prospect of the discharge from service of three million men who had been giving themselves to the war activities. It was pointed out with optimistic spirit that the country would experience no difficulty in finding employment for all. We were four years behind in our building program. All of our constructive energies had been devoted for many months to the creation of facilities for carrying on war. Public work, commercial building, general manufacturing —all were to a certain extent sidetracked and we had a right to believe that the task of getting caught up would provide a high pressure of work as soon as the manufac- turing and commercial energies of the country could again be turned back into their natural expression. Apparently there was not a single obstacle in the way of the high tide of prosperity which would bring the energies of every element of the country into full plan.

In the very midst of these high and reasonable ex- pectations, there came a slump which seems to have jarred the entire machinery of our commercial and industrial life. Men do not agree upon the causes for the unexpect- ed condition which has brought so many activities to a standstill. Possessing all the symptoms of robust health, the commercial and industrial life of the country suddenly became paralytic

I am asked today to discuss particularly the relation- ship of labor to the problem which the depression has brought us. I realize that this great organization has given too thorough a survey to all the factors in the problem to harbor the thought that the labor has been more than *one* of the elements in the situation. There has been a tendency on the part of all to hesitate before entering upon the descent which leads to pre-war condi- tions. Every man who was enjoying a war profit natural- ly held on as long as he could. The man who made brick and the man who laid brick were both grasping at the desirable opportunity to continue the high prices of ma- terial and of labor. The trust which manufactured cement, the trust which sold it and the trust which worked it into buildings—all in their several ways decided that they would not reduce the war profit until compelled by circumstances so to do.

Organized labor formed early the determination to keep up war prices. On the day we signed the armistice, Samuel Gompers, president of the American Federation of Labor, addressing at Laredo, Texas, an internationa l labor council, said, "The fight of labor in the United States is to keep what it won during the war." For the purpose of carrying out a program which was intended to strengthen labor's condition, the doctrine of doing less work for larger pay was promulgated. It had been preached before by a radical leader here and there, but it had not been made the general program of organized la- bor. It had not been adopted until this time as labor's remedy for keeping wages at a high level. Now we know that the plan was an artificial one and it broke down of its own ponderous weight.

Slacking is not an American doctrine. It does not fit a land of achievement where we are behind with our con- structive activities. It is ruinous equally to the man who labors and the man who employs. Out in the Middle West this multiplication of personnel upon the task has had a wrecking influence, not only upon the industry it has touched directly, but upon all which are affected indirect- ly.

Probably in the Middle West no graver deterrent to the general activity exists than the present status of the transportation problem. If a farmer ships four carloads of stock to the market it takes one carload to pay the freight upon the other three cars. It costs him one-third of the selling price of his wheat to land it in his ultimate market. Railroad freight rates are incredibly high. The wildest dream of the early railway financier never con- templated the present earning schedule, yet when you bring to his attention the disastrous results of these ex- tortionate rates he has no difficulty in proving that the government still owes him money to make up the deficit between these rates and the operating cost.

The factor of labor in this problem has been very conclusive and here again the multiplication of personnel has had more to do in causing the wreck than the wages paid per man. It is not that they are paying too much for the men—they are paying too many men to do one man's work. Recently I examined the new regulation of crafts in the railway business. One sample is sufficient to show the extraordinary effect that has followed the illogi- cal expansion of the personnel. This typical case relates to the removing of a nozzle tip from the front end of a locomotive. Mechanically it is as simple an operation as the unhitching of a team of mules, yet here is the elaborate provision of the crafts regulation for perform- ing this task:

It is necessary to send for a boilermaker and his helper to open the door of the boiler, because that's a boilermaker's job. Then you must send for a pipe man and his helper to remove the blower pipe, because that is a pipe man's job. Then you must send for a machinist and his helper to remove the nozzle tip, because that is a machinist's job. Thus they have used three master me- chanics and three helpers to perform a simple task which

in the pre-war days was performed by a handy man around the place who was called a helper. Has it brought prosperity to the railroad man?

More railroad men are out of employment in the United States today than at any other time since the administration of Grover Cleveland. The doctrine of doing as little as you can for as much as you can get has killed the goose that lays the industrial egg. Labor is not the basis of all wealth. It is only the basis of wealth when combined with it there is a program which carries forward the energies of labor in a just and co-operating spirit which recognizes the mutuality of the problems between labor and labor's employers.

Germany is the only country in the world that has given sufficient recognition to the influence of labor as a governing factor in the economic situation. Germany is the only country that has gone back to work in the right spirit. She is probably no farther behind in her various activities than is England, but while England still listens to the voice of labor and her government trembles under the threat of its solidarity, German labor has just voted for its own good to do away with the eight-hour day and substitute the ten-hour day, because Germany needs the labor and labor needs the added hire.

I am not urging that it is necessary in America to do away with the eight-hour day, but it is necessary to do away with the pernicious idea that labor prospers most when it works least.

THE COURT OF INDUSTRIAL RELATIONS

I have been asked to discuss the relation of the Kansas experiment to the problem. I am naturally prejudiced in favor of the Court of Industrial Relations, which Kansas created for the purpose of giving the state jurisdiction over the industrial quarrel. The state reasoned that government had put a stop to every other quarrel which threatens the welfare and good order of society. The industrial quarrel is the only one which government anywhere allows to proceed at its own destructive will. And so, reasoning that the state by the broad exercise of its police powers has the right to protect the public against the danger and the waste of the industrial controversy, it adopted a law which declares that neither labor nor capital shall conspire to close down an institution which is engaged in the production of an essential commodity such as food, fuel, clothing or transportation.

It prohibits any employer of labor from establishing a lockout or a blacklist. It tells him that he shall bring his labor cause into a court of impartial justice and in the meantime he shall keep his institution running while the court determines upon the rights of the employer.

It denies to employees the right to enter into a conspiracy to close the factory.

It says to both the same thing—the public has come to depend upon this great institution for that which is necessary to sustain its life and its health and its welfare. The state cannot permit the dangerous thing called "economic pressure" to be used upon the helpless public. Therefore, it has provided for the adjudication of your quarrels by a court of justice and has pledged you in the name of righteous and responsible government that your cause shall have prompt and just determination.

Surely, if moral principles do not exist in American institutions for the extension of the powers of government to meet this emergency, then American institutions are doomed to failure. If government cannot settle this quarrel, who can?

God help us in this country if at any time any considerable number of men may rise to seriously question the capacity of government to provide justice. When a man or a group of men may seriously question the ability of government to render justice through its courts, then for them government no longer exists.

Labor leaders sometimes tell you that the Kansas Court of Industrial Relations does not function. This Court has been upon our statute books a year and a half. Something over thirty cases have been brought, mostly by the leaders of union labor, and of these twenty-eight have been decided. Of the twenty-eight decisions, which affect wages, working conditions and contracts, twenty-seven have been accepted as entirely just and satisfactory both by the laborers and the employers. Show me a court with a better record of accomplishment than that.

This court has met its test from every angle. When it had been upon the statute books a year, it was necessary for the members of the legislature and the chief executive, who had created the court, to come before the people for approval. In every industrial district these men were opposed by union labor leaders. Practically an unlimited campaign fund was created by contributions from the American Federation of Labor and the United Mine Workers. Imported orators were sent into every industrial neighborhood, and yet those who believed in the industrial court and were responsible for its existence without a single exception were re-elected.

Why? Because labor itself, when given the opportunity to vote the sentiment of its individual members without coming into direct conflict with its radical leaders, voted to give the Court of Industrial Relations a chance. It voted its discontent with its own secretaries of war. A few months later the constitutionality of the court was unanimously confirmed by the Supreme Court of the state.

PRODUCTION STABILIZED—INDUSTRIAL CONTROVERSY DECREASED

A few weeks later a survey of the industrial conditions of the state proved beyond question that the result of the court had been to stabilize production and decrease industrial controversy. Probably nothing more significant has come to light than the official report of the state mining engineer who investigated the coal production. When the Court of Industrial Relations was created, fol-

How to make it: Use a rich layer cake mixture. For filling, chop uncooked pitted Sunsweet Prunes fine enough to make a paste. Moisten with currant jelly and spread between layers, then ice with flavored water icing. Sprinkle shredded cocoanut on top and sides.

Yes—it's the filling! That's the in-between secret of *any* layer cake. That's the flavor-secret that explains why some layer cakes go big and others fall flat.

A filling made of Sunsweet Prunes gives your trade a new taste-sensation. It puts novelty into an everyday bakeshop specialty. Easy to make, too—especially when you use Sunsweet *Pitted* Prunes.

Prepared by a recently perfected process, they are superior to any pitted prunes on the market. They fall apart without extra handling. They do not break apart in the dough. They do not discolor the dough. They are right easy to handle. And—they save labor. No fuss; no bother; no time lost!

Other profitable variations you can make with Sunsweet Pitted Prunes are pies, tarts, coffee cake, fruit slices, etc. Ask your jobber or supply house for Sunsweet Pitted Prunes—and see that you get them.

Also, write for our new formula folder, "I never knew what prunes could do!" Every formula has been proved in the baking and it's free! And, if you ask for it, we'll send along window pasters and other sales-helps that are bringing in new trade to live bakers all over the country.

Simply address Bakery Department, California Prune & ApricotGrowers Inc., 192 Market Street, San Jose, California. An association of 11,000 growers.

SUNSWEET *Pitted* PRUNES

lowing the general coal strike, Alexander Howat, the president of the Kansas mining district, announced that if this court were created all the miners would leave the state of Kansas. Five hundred of them left, but in 1920 those who remained produced 900,000 tons of coal more than the larger number had produced in 1919. Why? Because in 1919 there was an average of 13½ strikes a month in the coal mining district. In 1920 there were no strikes. In 1919 the average number of working days of the miners was 141. In 1920 it reached above 200. The smaller number of miners received in wages $4,000,000 more than they received in 1919. Therefore, when an opportunity came to cast a secret ballot upon the subject of the Industrial Court, a majority of them voted to sustain it.

Last month at Columbus, Kans., the law met its final test. Howat, the miners' leader, had been prophesying for a year that if opportunity were ever presented to try out this law before a jury in an industrial neighborhood it would not be possible to secure a conviction—that the prejudices of the labor men against it would prevent an effective trial. It became necessary to try Howat in the heart of the mining district before a jury of his peers upon a criminal charge. He sent out to the other labor unions of the state a Macedonian cry. He invited every union to send a delegate or delegates to Columbus to attend the trial, in order that there might be indicated to the jury the solidarity of labor's resentment against this law. He informed them that the crowd of union labor people would be so great that the houses of Columbus wouldn't be sufficient to give them shelter, and to meet this emergency he had rented tents and provided for a tented colony of union labor sympathizers. He evidently believed that labor would send its delegates, Columbus believed it, the newspapers believed it, but when the morning of the trial arrived the only outsiders were the band, which had been hired, and the newspaper correspondents. The delegates didn't come.

The trial was held, as all other trials are, and when the case was given to the jury it returned a verdict, holding Howat to be guilty of an offense under which he was sentenced to jail for six months and to pay a fine of $500.

Every cause the court has touched has been benefited. Permanent adjudication has come. A new spirit of justice prevails; a new state of expectation on the part of labor and labor's families. The leaders of labor still fight it, because they realize that if the government may find justice for the laboring man in his quarrel with his employer then there will no longer be any reason why the laboring man should pay out of his pocket every month a percentage of his salary to keep in idleness a lot of agitators who live off labor. Today 150,000 paid labor leaders in the American Federation are drawing out of the slender purse of labor more than $60,000,000 a year. This is an industry which is interfered with, of course, if the state makes it unnecessary in the future for labor unions to hire secretaries of war.

The idea of substituting adjudication for arbitration is growing in this country. The packers and their employees have for many months now been submitting their controversies upon wages and working conditions to Judge Alschuler, of Chicago. He has been their court of industrial relations and under his impartial adjudication conditions have very much improved.

A few months ago, when the mining difficulties in Alabama had reached a point where they threatened to paralyze all activities and when the strike was generally recognized to be no longer endurable, the miners and the operators were persuaded to submit their controversy to the governor of the state. They chose him as their industrial court and, accepting his decision as final, went back to work.

These instances, where by common agreement employees and employers have pledged themselves to submit their controversies to impartial adjudication, merely follow out the idea of the Kansas industrial court. The Kansas industrial court does not do away with efforts at conciliation and arbitration. It merely says that when these efforts have failed to bring about a composition of the quarrel and the strike or the lockout threatens, then the state shall have the power to step in and adjust the situation.

Recently there have come into the controversy in Kansas a few of the worst type of employers fighting the law. When labor was scarcer these men were glad to have the protection of the court against the termination of their operations. Now that depression has brought a surplus of labor, they are afraid that the court will deny to them the liberty of taking advantage of the surplus for the purpose of driving wage levels to an indefensible minimum. But in spite of the opposition of the radical leaders of labor and the radical representative of organized capital, the law has made steady progress and its success in the state today is regarded as a most hopeful indication that the government may through the exercise of its judicial powers bring a guarantee of peace and justice to all who labor in the essential industries and to all who are affected by their production. Isn't this better than warfare?

It wouldn't be possible for that to happen in Kansas what has just occurred in West Virginia and in Illinois. The government steps in at the inception of the quarrel and puts a stop to the war before the war has organized itself into the explosive qualities which characterized it in West Virginia and Illinois.

—:—:—:—

Roscoe Conkling said: "When a man climbs the ladder of fame, the fellows behind him catch hold and try to drag him down. The higher he gets, the more there are hanging on his skirts." The same is true of the man who wins success in business. The greater his success the greater the number of the dogs of envy who snarl at him. But he can afford not to care.

Trade Items

A permit was recently issued to Essig & Busenlehner, Birmingham, Ala., for the erection of a $16,000 bakery at Fourth Avenue and North 14th Street.

Jasper & Rosetter, Charleston, Ark., will soon open a bakery there.

The Mutual Creamery Company, Oakland, Calif., has opened a large bread, cake and pastry shop adjoining their main office at E. 14th Street and 37th Avenue. The company has sixteen retail stores.

Work on Diehl's new bake shop, Brewster, Conn., is progressing rapidly, and is expected to be completed within a short time.

The Boston Baking Company, Hartford, Conn., recently opened an up-to-date bakery and delicatessen shop at 401 Albany Avenue, carrying a complete line of baked goods. It is a branch of the Boston Baking Company, 148 Bellevue Avenue.

O. J. Vanasse, Meridan, Conn., recently opened a bakery at 334 Pratt Street, and will carry on both wholesale and retail business.

J. Firlik & J. Dzialo have purchased the half interest of Morris Fields in the Fields Brothers' Bakery, 47 Union Street, Middletown, Conn.

O. O. Anderson, of Stony Creek, Conn., has opened a bakery on Concord Street, Morris Cove, Conn.

Wehrle Bros., Centralia, Ill., will erect a large new and modern bakery, and will install new outfit, fixtures and furniture.

The Fishbein Bakery has recently been opened at East St. Louis, Ill., under the management of Harry Fishbein.

Evans Bros., of Edwardsville, Ill., are moving their plant to 1107-9 North Main Street, that city, and are adding a retail department.

P. W. Brown, of Stewardson, Ill., has just completed his moving from the west end of town into his new and much larger quarters and will do both a wholesale and retail business from now on.

Homer Achleman recently became proprietor of the Decatur Bake-Rite Store, Decatur, Ill., purchasing same from Raymond Harting and Joe Lose.

The Brudi National Bakery, Ft. Wayne, Ind., was incorporated at Indianapolis, Ind., for $50,000, by H. E. Brudi, M. C. Brudi and H. M. Wonker. The firm recently moved into its new plant at Rudisill and Lafayette Streets, Ft. Wayne, Ind.

A. A. Sheet, Madison, Ind., will open a bakery in the building at West and 5th Streets, Madison.

T. B. Carlock has purchased the bakery located on the southeast side of the public square, Shelbyville, Ind., from George Harding.

Jacob Cox plans to build a bakery at 65 Franklin Street, Portland, Me., to cost $4,000.

Elmer E. Skedd has purchased the Irving Home Bakery, in the Commercial Block, Beverly, Mass., taking possession at once. Mr. Skedd formerly owned the same business.

The Toussaint Baking Co., Berlin, N. H., are making extensive repairs on their modern baking plant on School Street. The wrapping and shipping rooms are to be enlarged to twice their present capacity and a new private office will be added.

Alterations and improvements are being made to the bakery of Frank A. Rogers, Franklin, N. H.

The Dainty Baking Company has been incorporated at Irvington, N. J., with capital of $100,000, by George E. Christine, Henry Noll and Alfred H. Peoples.

A new concern, with $200,000 capital, known as the Travis Baking Company, will open a bakery at 133-35 North Hamilton Street, Poughkeepsie, N. Y., if the present plans materialize. Walter J. Travis, formerly president of the Bridgeport Baking Company, and a director of the Massachusetts Baking Company, and several of his associates from Bridgeport, have purchased the property and expect to build a bakery 78 by 100 feet.

The Acme Bakery, of which J. G. Dodd is proprietor, is soon to open at Belhaven, N. C.

A large, new bakery, handling both wholesale and retail trade, has been established at 543 Clarendon Avenue, N. W., Canton, Ohio, and will be known as the R. & Y. Baking Company. O. C. Yant and C. B. Robinson are heads of the concern.

The Haggard & Schubert Company has opened its new bake shop at 513 Walnut Street, Cincinnati, Ohio. The establishment is one of the most modern and the second they have opened in the heart of the city, the other being located at Sixth and Main Streets. Edward Schubert will be in charge of the new store.

The S. E. F. Baking Company has been incorporated at Cleveland, Ohio, with capital of $10,000, by Herman Steinfeld, Harry Epstein, Saul S. Danaceau, A. Barbian and Lee Gerwin.

Sterling Donaldson has purchased the interests of George W. Bollinger in the Top-N-Och Baking Company, Columbus, Ohio. These two gentlemen recently bought this business from Harry Meyer, now connected with the Columbus branch of the Holland Bread Co.

It is reported that the Ward Baking Company will build a $100,000 bakery at Warren, Ohio.

The Blackwell Baking Company has been incorporated at Greenville, Ohio, by F. Auketman, J. S. Blackwell, F. Kerwood, J. Mathews and W. A. Zimmerman.

Employes of the Seyfang Bakery Company, which plant was sold recently to the F. Bissell Company, have organized the Seyfang Biscuit and Macaroni Co., with capital of $25,000, at 1165 Grand Avenue, Toledo, Ohio, and will take over the cracker, biscuit and macaroni business of the former company.

The International Baking Company, Green Street, Brownsville, Pa., have purchased property on Middle and Cherry Streets, where they will erect a new, modern sanitary bakery.

The Easton Baking Co., Easton, Pa., have about completed their new plant at 34-36 North Seventh Street, containing two ovens, for the making of bread, pie and cake.

Schaible's Bakery, Easton, Pa., have moved to their new plant at 24th and Northampton Streets, which is a very handsome structure, in white brick, 150 by 150 feet, including a battery of eight ovens and full equipment of machinery.

W. E. Knisely has purchased the C. H. Pangle Bakery and Grocery Store at Red Lion, Pa., at a cost of $10,500.

The Hazleton Baking Company and the Hazleton Cake Company, of West Hazleton, Pa., following the distribution of an annual bonus to their employes, gave a complimentary dinner and dance to all their officers and employes. G. Stuart Engle is president and J. B. Gould vice-president and general manager.

Goronwy Williams, West Hazleton, Pa., will build a new steam bakery at Seventh and Alter Streets, 32 by 80 feet. A new oven and machinery will be installed.

Jacob Fischer, of Cheltenham, Pa., has bought the bakery of John L. Simon, on West Market Street, West Chester, Pa., and will take charge January 23rd. Mr. Fischer is an experienced baker, and Mr. Simon has for many years conducted this business and is well known throughout Chester County.

C. J. Layfield, of Kolb's Bakery, Scranton, Pa., on January 2nd gave a dinner in the Hotel Casey to 650 guests, including his sales force and the grocers in that territory. Mr. Layfield has been proprietor of the Kolb's Bakery for three years, during which time he has built up a large trade.

FLAWS IN CAKES

REGARDED from a figurative point of view, a cake is anything made up with butter, sugar, and flour with or without added eggs or fruit; described in homely parlance it is a compound of flour, fat, sugar, with some currants and baking powder in it, and these being subjected to the ordeal of an oven becomes caked, and is therefore a cake. The sugar-bedecked, flower-draped, artistic production, the piece for the bridal breakfast table is a cake, and so is that delight of children, that sharpener of teeth, the all-too-rock-like cake. The delicious, rich gateaux is a cake. The lordly, richly, clothed Savoy mould is a cake, and so is that abomination, that compound of dried molasses and flour, called parkin, a cake.

I have been asked to say something about the cause and cure of "flaws in cakes," and have thought and thought about it until I am forced to confess, sitting in judgment upon my own knowledge, that it is well-nigh impossible, by means of printed words, to make the matter plain to the reader. For instance, there are cakes which cut coarse and crumble, cakes which are heavy, solid, and sodden, which have holes, which sink in the middle, which burst open across the top with a rugged, harsh, hard fissure, and cakes which, though looking nice, are not nice to the palate. Many of these imperfections are different in degree, there are different kinds of cracks and sinkings, slight or acute, arising from quite a different cause, each type being peculiar in itself, which may be caused by excessive richness or poverty in the ingredients. Too much or too little moisture, too high or too low a temperature in the oven, or wrong manipulation.

Experience and reason lend their aid, imagination calls up, embodies, and locates the individual flaw, and outlines the cause and the cure in the mind. But how to describe each of them upon paper with a reasonable chance of the amateur cakemaker understanding and profiting by the explanation seems to me to be well-nigh impossible, but with the actual cake or article before us, in our hands, and with physical ears listening to spoken words, doubtless the speaker would be able to make his hearers understand what he thought to be the cause of the particular kind of sickness then under observation. Perhaps if I begin by writing a few lines about mixtures and the mixing of them, inspiration may proceed and guide my pen, and that which to me is now dark and obscure may become clear and luminous; for the readers' sake may it be so.

THE THREE DIVISIONS OF THE CAKE FAMILY

Recipes and formulas for cakes are very numerous, but, whether for a quarter-pound or a quarter hun-

dred-weight cake, there are but three bases upon which they can be built up, i. e., very rich, very plain, and intermediate between the two. Oscillating between these three, up and down, the interchange, the preponderance of certain ingredients, the free play of the desire of a kind to enable him to excel, does not interfere with these divisions or bases; no, not even if by thought and experiment he has found and incorporated a new ingredient; the cake is still rich, poor, or intermediate.

As there are three divisions in the character of the cake family, so there are three divisions in the mode of preparation and manipulation, and only three; the scone tribe, wherein eggs are a minus quantity and everything, from rocks and rice and brioche to the currant and seed cake, is prepared by rubbing all the ingredients—fat, flour, sugar, aerating powder—together, and then adding the liquid and mixing the whole; the tribe of intermediates, compounded with a moiety of eggs and made up with liquid to moisten and powder for aeration and shortening, make up medium quality, Genoese, Madeira, sponge, pound, Genoa, slab. The modicum of eggs have to be beaten to their maximum of expansion, and the balance of saturation and lifting and aeration has to be supplied by baking powder and liquid, milk or water, according to the retail price charged. The third, the tribe of goods made up regardless of cost, with as many eggs, as much of best butter and best other ingredients that can be mixed in, the eggs beaten and butter incorporated with them, and the other ingredients mixed in so as not to destroy the perfect emulsion of the whole, is the law governing this third basis in the division of "cakes" making. Each of these divisions and their sub-divisions are controlled in their perfect making by these known laws, and each of them depends, in its simple perfectness, on what is called in the trade "Experience," but what I prefer to call the cultivation of the sixth sense, the sense of touch. A preponderance in the cause of the flaws comes not from having a wrong recipe, but from a wrong manipulation of the prior stages, or from being wrong in the final finish and amalgamation of the whole.

IMPERFECTIONS AND FLAWS

I will give a few typical mixtures and their manipulation to try—for that is all that can be done, because their name is legion—and show wherein is the imperfection and how it is caused. (1) An eggless cake of the scone tribe: Four pounds flour, one pound fat, two pounds sugar, three pounds currants, two and one-half ounces aerating powder, one quart of milk or water. Beat the fat and sugar together until quite smooth and shiny (the fat and sugar should be prepared in this way for this class of goods, it mixes more evenly with the other ingredients and makes the baked surface clearer and brighter); then rub into it the flour and the powder, then pour in the liquid, the egg yellow, and flavoring (a few drops of essence of spice

is best), slightly mix the whole and add the fruit, and finish the mixing. (2). These cakes are mostly made in loaves, or blocks of four pounds, seven pounds, or fourteen pounds each. Fifty-two pounds flour, fourteen pounds sugar, fourteen pounds fat, one pound aerating powder, and essence spice, and about three gallons water or milk and twenty-five pounds fruit (currants, peel and sultanas mixed), prepare and mix same as the foregoing formula.

The probable imperfections in this class of goods arise from insufficient beating, or rubbing together, or in the final mixing, and are shown on the face of the cut cake by lighter or darker small patches, the lighter eating dry, rough and not nice, being merely flour with but a poor share of the other good things. Another class of flaw arises from the mixture being too dry and firm, it does not rise much, and cuts too solid and hard, or by being too wet and not toughened enough, it frets in the oven and cuts coarse and crumbly.

All goods which depend upon aerating powders for their lightness should be as moist as they can bear, and when the liquid is added in the final mixing, thoroughly toughened to prevent the gas escaping or playing about too riotously inside. The finished cake, after it is in the frame, should be allowed to stand fifteen minutes, or more, before being put into the oven.

The sense of touch, of feel, must be cultivated by the cake maker himself. It cannot be imparted from one person to another, its only teacher is named Experience. This greatest of all teachers is mostly misused by the worker. What he calls his experience is a perfunctory, a rotary kind of usage, thoughtlessly performed and automatic. One lot of finished goods is good, the next, from the same mixture, is bad. Why? The worker thinks it does not feel right, it does not look right; and as quickly, or more quickly, than the lightning's flash Experience, ever in attendance and quick to the voice of inquiry, as need to instinct, touches the eyes and the fingers, they see, they feel, Experience touches the spot, and the why and the wherefore is in the workman's possession. He is a student at the footstool of experience, he is safe.

MACHINE-MADE LOAF CAKE

Seventy pounds flour (containing high percentage of soft and unstable gluten), twenty-seven pounds butter, forty pounds white sugar, thirty pounds currants, ten pounds drained and chopped peel, ten pounds sultanas, two pounds glycerine, twenty pounds eggs, seven ounces cream tartar, five ounces bicarbonate soda (or twelve ounces of any other aerating powder), and essence spice, and ten quarts milk (if stale or sour the better). Procedure: Put butter and sugar in machine and beat, on the slow motion, until creamy and shiny, then add the eggs, a few at a time, until two-thirds are in and the mixture is running smooth and clear, then put on the fast speed, give it one minute, and then add, by a continuous dribble, the rest of the eggs, the flavoring, the glycerine, and a dribble of the flour and liquid concurrently; watch the mixture and as soon as experience tells it is light, smooth, and clear, put on the slow speed, and dribble in the rest of the flour (which, of course, has the aerating powder thoroughly mixed into it) and the rest of liquid and the fruit, all as near concurrently as possible, and then when all is in, watch for a minute until the whole is smooth and homogeneous, then stop machine, weigh off into frames, let stand ten, twenty, or more minutes, and then put into oven at a temperature of about 300 to 310 degrees F. Steady cooking and solid. (Experience of individual behavior of individual ovens must come in here.)

If a cheaper mixture is required substitute a butter substitute for the butter and proceed the same. If a still cheaper mixture is required use nut or vegetable oil or fat; there are several on the market, but in this case start the beating of sugar and fat, or oil on the fast motion, 500 to 700 revolutions to the minute, and add at the same time seven to ten pounds of the flour so as to give the beaters something to work upon and make into a foam. It is of very little use adding the eggs to oil or a fat that oils, because the oil either prevents the expansion of the eggs or

Do You Know What Your Goods Cost?

ONE of the hardest things in bake-shop practice is to keep an accurate account of the cost of each piece of goods, so that the baker will know just how much profit each piece or each dozen pieces will yield, with raw materials at certain prices.

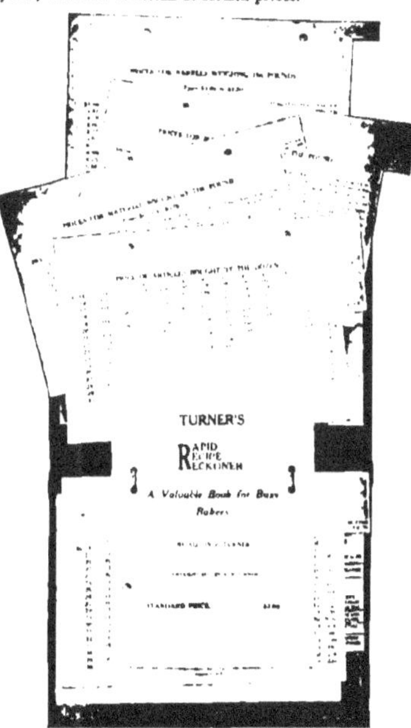

Turner's Rapid Recipe Reckoner

saves a baker all trouble in reckoning up the cost; it is already done for him, and all he has to do is to pick out the desired item at the given price per pound or dozen.

Tables are given of the cost for each ounce of flour at a price per barrel from **$4.00 upward**; and of lard, butter, sugar, eggs and of all other supplies by the ounce or measure at what price you pay in quantities.

Turner's Rapid Recipe Reckoner

simplifies cost accounting so that it is a matter of only a few minutes to get the cost of a batch of any size, and of any class of goods.

The tables are printed on heavy serviceable cardboard, placed in a substantial loose-leaf cover, bound in cloth. It will last a life-time and you can add new sheets or tables, if desired.

In these days of close competition one is needed in every bake-shop, and the cost is but **$2.00**, postpaid. Address

411 Walnut Street
Philadelphia, Pa.

Information Department

The object of this department is to help our readers, as far as possible, to solve the various difficulties that come up from day to day. We will also answer questions about all kinds of machinery and give every possible assistance in securing detailed information. No names or addresses of manufacturers will be given in these columns. When wanted they will be sent by mail. Address,

INFORMATION DEPARTMENT **THE NATIONAL BAKER**

A FINE ICING AND FILLING

F. W. T., Ohio: The trouble with your icing is that you do not whip it light enough. We give herewith a very fine icing which can also be used as a filling:

No. 1—Boil 2 1-2 lbs. of glucose, 5 lbs. sugar, granulated, 1 pint water. Boil to 240 degrees.

No. 2—Dissolve 9 ounces whip powder in 1 quart of water, add 2 lbs. of XXXX sugar; beat it to a meringue.

Pour No. 1 into No. 2 while hot. Beat all for 10 minutes. Add any flavor. You will find the above very satisfactory.

CREAM PUFFS

J. R. M., Pittsburg, Pa.: Answering your favor of recent date we advise as follows:

Put on a brick fire 1 qt. water, and 1 lb. lard. Crush lard in pieces to melt fast, and when it boils up good, add 22 oz. Spring wheat flour. Now stir as fast as you are able, stirring till it is all one lump—a full minute after the flour is added. To make it light, get 1 quart of the best eggs you can secure, and drop them into the cooked mass in a mixing bowl on cake machine, adding two eggs at a time until all is smooth and shiny before you add more eggs. If it is too stiff add a little milk. Drop on pans and bake in an even oven. If bottom is too hot double-pan them. After baking pies the oven is just right for cream puffs. If they crack too much to suit you, use more milk and less eggs.

The darker color is caused by what you use. May be the flour or the frozen eggs. I always add a grain of ammonia, but you do not want them to crack. Fresh eggs make a light cake. Try our way, and let us hear from you again.

S. A. M., Mass.: Answering your favor of the 10th instant, we give you herewith two formulas for Cocoanut Macaroons:

COCOANUT MACAROONS

No. 1.—3 pounds macaroon cocoanut, 4 1-2 pounds of sugar—half granulated, half powdered, about 2 1-4 pounds egg white or more, according to dryness of cocoanut. Mix this together in kettle on the fire and stir so it becomes clear and hot without boiling. Take off and let cool a little, then drop out with bag and plain tube. The mixture should not be too soft. Flatten tops with damp cloth and bake the same as al-

No. 2.—2 pounds macaroon cocoanut, 2 pounds granulated sugar, 1 1-2 pounds powdered sugar, 8 ounces corn flour, 1 to 1 1-4 pints egg whites. Mix on fire like No. 1. Let cool and drop on greased and flour-dusted pans.

COCOANUT BALLS

5 lbs. cocoanut, 5 lbs. sugar, 1 1-4 qts. whites of eggs.

The whites of the eggs are beaten with the sugar and stirred together with the cocoanut. Form round balls and place on dusted pans. Bake in a cold oven.

We trust these will be of service to you. Glad you find business good. In our judgment, you are wise if you would make certain specialties for certain days and push on those.

DRYING OUT OF CAKE

L. E. S., Illinois: It is caused by:

1. Baking too dry in a slow oven.

2. Too stiff a mixture.

3. A short dry flour. You should use only winter wheat.

4. Not enough oil in the mixture. Use pure lard.

5. Beating eggs too light makes dry cake.

6. Too much baking powder.

Do not use sweet milk, but cream up condensed milk with sugar and lard. 3 lbs. condensed milk to 10 lbs. sugar. Do not beat up eggs, but cream them with the sugar and lard until smooth only. Add some flour with eggs, one pound eggs to half pound flour.

Add hot water after eggs are creamed in, 9 pints water to 10 pounds sugar, and after stirring 2 minutes add pastry flour, 9 lbs. 5 oz., together with 1 lb. sugar and 1 lb. cornstarch, and 4 oz. baking powder, which is 1-9th of the amount of pastry flour. Mix 5 minutes on high or "fast." Bake in wooden frames lined with wax paper in a pound cake temperature of oven, 270 degrees.

C. E. W., Ohio: Either or all of the following formulas should answer your purpose. They have been good sellers in several other places.

SPICE CAKE NO. 1

1 1-2 lbs. crumbs, 4 ozs. lard, 1 teaspoon soda, 4 ozs. citron and orange peel, 1 1-2 lbs. flour, 1 pt. molasses, 4 ozs. currants, 1 oz. mixed spice, 3-4 lb. sugar, 8

SPICE CAKE NO. 2

3 lbs. crumbs, 1 qt. molasses, 8 ozs. citron and orange peel, 1 lb. flour, 1-2 teaspoon soda, 4 oz. currants, 2 oz. lard, 6 eggs. Mix with a little water.

SPICE CAKE NO. 3

1 qt. molasses, 1 lb. lard, 5 eggs, 4 ozs. currants, 1 qt. water, 2 oz. soda, 3 lbs. crumbs, 4 ozs. chopped peel, 1 lb. sugar, 1 oz. mixed spice, 3 lbs. flour.

Rub the crumbs through a coarse sieve. Dissolve the soda in water. Cream sugar and lard; add molasses, spices, water and soda, and mix in the crumbs and flour. Add more water if required to make a soft mixture. Bake in well greased muffin cups. When done ice either chocolate, white or pink.

BUTTER CAKES

T. J. W., Mass.: The cakes made in lunch rooms, known as butter cakes, are in fact English crumpets, for which we give the following recipe:

Take two quarts of water, or use half milk, one ounce of yeast, half an ounce of salt, and a good bread flour.

Make a soft dough, work it well, but make it slack like a sponge: set it about lukewarm, let raise to the drop, beat it down again, and let come up half.

Bake it in about two ounce pieces; dust over a little flour, cover and let prove until nearly double in size. Handle carefully.

These can be cooked on a griddle either with or without muffin rings. When done on one side turn over carefully with a cake or palette knife, and finish baking.

The quality of these can be improved by using all milk.

BLACK ANTS

C. E. W., Kentucky: We have your favor of the 26th, in relation to getting rid of black ants. One remedy is to soak a sponge in a thin syrup of sugar, place it where the ants can reach it, and they will swarm through it; then take the sponge and immerse in scalding water, then soak the sponge again in syrup and repeat the operation.

Try and find the nest of the ants. When found, fill repeatedly with scalding hot water. If you can thus kill the "queen ant," the others will leave.

Or if you can place a broad band of lard around the next, or at some other convenient point, the ants cannot cross the lard.

We do not give you any poisonous remedies, as they are hardly safe to use in a bakery.

R. Y. H., Missouri: We have your favor of recent date, and give you herewith a recipe for Royal Icing, which is used for decorative purposes.

ROYAL ICING

This is an icing used especially for ornamenting

and piping purposes, but also for frosting cakes, such as wedding, birthday, angel cakes, etc., in which case it is kept in more of a creamy substance and not quite as stiff as for ornamenting. It is made as follows.

Take 1 pt. of egg whites in a very clean basin and beat into it some sifted pulverized sugar, with the aid of two wooden spatulas until it becomes a medium stiff batter; then add a few drops of acetic acid or the juice of half a lemon, or a little cream of tartar, if none of the others are convenient. Beat again until the frosting has become quite stiff, and stands up when drawn to a point with the spatula. To improve the white pure color add a few drops of bluing.

This frosting must be kept covered with a clean, wet towel all the time, as it dries quickly if exposed to the air, and thus makes it unfit for use. If kept this way in a cool place it will be good for quite a long time.

Care must be taken that the bowl, the towels and the material used are free from all grease and flour. The egg whites must be absolutely free from yolks and should be fresh, as otherwise the frosting will get soapy.

A cheaper piping icing is made from gelatine.

CHEESE CAKE

J. A. M., Illinois: Referring to your inquiry for cheese cake, there is a number of varieties of this, which vary considerably. We give, herewith, a good one:

Rub eight ounces of dry curd through a sieve, add four yolks, four beaten whites, six ounces of sugar, a little cream, two ounces of melted butter, the grated rind of one lemon, a little grated nutmeg. Fill the mixture in puff paste lined molds, dust some cinnamon over and bake. When done sift over some powdered sugar and serve.

This may be altered or added to, to suit your trade. We can give you several finer varieties if you will advise.

PRESERVED PINEAPPLE CAKE

Three pounds flour, two pounds pulverized sugar, two pounds preserved pineapple pieces, one and one-half pounds butter, one pound chopped blanched almonds, two ounces baking powder, twenty eggs, one-half pint pineapple flavoring.

Cream the butter and sugar together, and stir with them one pound of flour. Whip the eggs to a froth, and work them into the cream. Add the flavoring and milk, after which sift the baking powder with the remaining flour, and incorporate them with the mixture. Rub the chopped almonds with the pineapple pieces and blend them with the previously mixed ingredients. Spread the batch on a papered baking tin and bake in a moderate oven.

Flaws in Cakes
(Concluded from page 57)

falls upon the air globules as fast as they are formed and breaks up and dispels them, therefore use some flour at the beginning, and then dribble in a little more with the dribbled-in eggs, all the time running on the fast speed, and do not give the eggs more than a minute or two's beating, just a quick thrashing, and then the slow speed, and mix in the other ingredients as before directed. In this formula mix slightly at the finish, and when filling the frames draw the mixture well up at the sides and ends from middle, so as to prevent pinched sides and bulging middle, and when filled in the frames and nicely flattened and smooth on top, let stand for thirty minutes for the powder and the mixture to recover, and free itself before putting into oven. In baking cakes where the top is required to be quite level and flat, leave the oven door open for half of the time of baking at the beginning, that is unless the worker knows that the oven is cold or does not carry much top heat; here again experience comes in, as the judge in this court of final appeal is the oven.

Pinched thin sides and bulging, possibly burst top, are the most common flaws in large cakes, and I have outlined a preventive or a cure above, but there is another and very serious flaw frequently seen in this kind of cake, i. e., a long thin gap just under the top crust, which causes the crust to fall off when it is cut. This is usually caused by a firm mixture being flattened on top when going into the oven, and the mixture not having time to recover, and in the oven a free top heat which quickly sets the top service and draws it up: the mass, being too slow and solid to follow, parts with the top crust and leaves this gap between.

—‡—‡—‡—

ESTABLISHED 1864
THOS. MILLS & BRO., Inc.
MANUFACTURERS OF
BAKERS', CONFECTIONERS' AND ICE CREAM
MACHINERY AND TOOLS
1301-1311 NORTH EIGHTH STREET :-: :-: PHILADELPHIA, PA.
ALL SIZES OF TUBS AND CANS IN STOCK
EGG WHIPS
COMBINED ICE CREAM FREEZER
AND BREAKER
LARGE ASSORTMENT OF INDIVIDUAL
ICE CREAM MOULDS
PEELS AND SWAB POLES
ALL SIZES OF TIN, STEEL
AND RUSSIA IRON PANS
ALL STYLES
OF BRUSHES
ALL SIZES OF
PIE PLATES
ICE CREAM REFRIGERATORS, HARD
WOOD OR MARBLE FRONTS
PATENT BEATING MACHINE
WE ISSUE THREE DISTINCT CATALOGS—CONFECTIONERS'
BAKERS' AND ICE CREAM

Recipe Department

In this department we will publish new and valuable recipes and want our readers to forward to us any recipe from which they have had good results, or that is not generally known. We wish to make this department as interesting as possible and ask our readers to help us to this end. Address.

RECIPE DEPARTMENT   THE NATIONAL BAKER

BIRTHDAY CAKES

One pound of butter, one pound of brown sugar, one and one-half pounds eggs, one and one-half pounds soft flour, one-quarter ounce of burnt sugar, the zest of two lemons, two pounds of currants, one pound of sultanas, twelve ounces cut peel, grated nutmeg, a pinch of baking powder. Cream up as usual. Bake in an oven at 320 degrees F. Almond ice and ice with royal icing, decorate with colors. A chocolate medallion is very pretty for a centre.

* FRUIT GENOA CAKE

Two pounds butter, two and one-quarter pounds pulverized sugar, three pounds of eggs, three pounds soft flour, three and one-half pounds sultanas, one pound cherries, one pound citron peel (cut in squares), one pound candied lemon peel, grated nutmeg, one teaspoonful essence of vanilla, pinch of baking powder. Cream as usual. The above will make a cake twelve and one-half inches by sixteen and one-half inches. Bake in an oven at 310 degrees F. It will bake in three hours. Sprinkle almonds on the top. In case currants are used only take three pounds.

PLAIN OR SEED GENOA

Two pounds butter, two and one-quarter pounds sugar, three pounds eggs, three pounds flour, one-quarter ounce baking powder, one-half ounce seeds, one-half grated nutmeg, teaspoonful essence of vanilla. Cream as before. Put in a frame eleven and one-half by fifteen and one-half inches. Bake in an oven at 320 degrees F. Should be baked in two and one-quarter hours.

GOOD MADEIRA CAKE

Three pounds butter, three and one-quarter pounds pulverized sugar, six pounds of eggs, two and one-half pounds strong flour, two and one-half pounds soft flour, one ounce baking powder, one-half grated nutmeg. The butter and sugar should be thoroughly well creamed, add the eggs gently (six at a time). As soon as the mixture curdles, begin adding a little flour, and continue doing so until the whole six pounds of eggs are in. This mixture will rise and break open with a cauliflower head and will keep moist for a long time. Some consider a little corn-flour an improvement, and should anyone care to try it, he should substitute eight ounces of corn-flour for eight ounces of flour. These cakes should not be dusted with sugar. Bake at 350 degrees F.

MADEIRA CAKE (NO. 2)

Two and one-quarter pounds of butter, two and one-quarter pounds sugar, three pounds eggs, three and one-half pounds of flour, a little milk, essence of nutmeg, three-quarter ounces baking powder. Cream as usual. Dust with sugar. Place on thin strips of citron. Bake at 350 degrees F.

FRUIT CAKE (NO. 1)

Six pounds butter, six and one-half pounds sugar, six pounds eggs, twelve pounds flour, four ounces ground almonds, five ounces baking powder, eight pounds sultanas, two pounds peel (orange and lemon), one-half pound citron peel, six drops essence of lemon, one-half grated nutmeg, four pints new milk, egg color. Cream as usual. Put almonds on top or a strip of citron. Bake in an oven at 350 degrees F.

FRUIT CAKE (NO. 2)

Four pounds butter, two pounds lard, five pounds eggs, fourteen pounds flour, nine pounds currants, one and one-half pounds peel, sugar, six ounces baking powder, six drops essence of almonds, six drops essence of lemon, five and one-half pints new milk, egg color. Cream as usual, but give more mixing when flour is in. Bake in an oven at 350 degrees F. A strip of citron should be placed on top of cakes.

FRUIT CAKE (NO. 3)

Five pounds of lard or compound, five and three-quarter pounds sugar, sixteen eggs, fourteen pounds flour, six and one-half ounces baking powder, nine pounds currants, two pounds peel, essence of lemon, egg color, six pints skim milk. Rub sugar and fat together on board, add eggs then mix well, scaling off in four-pound or two-pound tins. Some like sugar dredged over, others wash over with milk. Bake in oven at 350 degrees F.

In all these cakes, if you can afford it, it is preferable to add a little almond paste, about eight ounces to every fourteen pounds of flour. Ground almonds are not so good, but they give the cakes a delicate flavor and serve to keep moistness in the goods. On no account add to much milk, as it is one of the worst things for a powder cake, causing that shrinkage and dark streaks from which so many have suffered.

VENETIAN LUNCH CAKES

Twelve eggs, one pound, twelve ounces sugar, one pound, ten ounces soft flour, one-quarter pint hot water, essence of vanilla. Put the eggs and sugar in the sponge machine and when well beaten up, add gradually the gill of hot water, keep beating until the mixture is thoroughly well up and then add about two tablespoonfuls of essence of vanilla. Give a turn round to thoroughly blend. The mixture should then be turned out into a round bottomed bowl and the flour mixed in. Fill into oval pans with hands, and bake in an oven at 400 degrees F. This mixture should make nine cakes.

Orange flavor, lemon, almond or cherry essence can be used with good results. If you use raspberry, or strawberry, it will be necessary to make a separate mixture and tint it a delicate pink. These cakes if made properly should break open with a cauliflower head. The heat of the oven is an important factor in keeping the cakes moist and giving a good break.

ALMOND CAKES

Six pounds flour, two and one-quarter ounces baking powder, three and one-quarter pounds butter, three and one-quarter pounds sugar, one quart eggs, twelve ounces chopped almonds, two ounces ground almonds, few drops essence almonds, one and one-half pints milk. Beat up sugar and butter and eggs in the usual manner, add the essence, chopped and ground almonds, and mix lightly. Weigh at thirteen ounces each and cover with chopped almonds. Almond paste instead of ground almonds is an improvement.

A splendid cocoanut cake can be made from this mixture by adding one pound of desiccated cocoanut with the milk of a fresh one, in which the desiccated nut has been soaked. Cherry cake should be made from a different recipe, as the cherries are likely to disappear. Bake at 400 degrees F.

CHERRY CAKES

Seven pounds flour, two ounces baking powder, one pound cherries (cut in quarters), three pounds butter, three and one-half pounds sugar, one quart eggs, eight ounces citron peel (cut small), essence of cherry, one quart new milk. Beat up as usual. Place four or five halves of cherries on top, and bake at 400 degrees F. Weigh at fourteen ounces.

DROP BUNS

LEMON, ALMOND, COCOANUT, ETC.

Five pounds flour, four ounces baking powder, eight eggs, one and one-half pounds lard, one and one-half pounds sugar, one quart milk, essence, egg color. Rub

---

lard into flour, then make bay, place sugar and eggs in centre, adding milk gradually, giving a good mix at the same time. Lay out on tins and then egg wash, putting currants, almonds, or cocoanut on top. Bake at 460 degrees F.

ROCK CAKES

Ten pounds flour, seven ounces baking powder, two and one-half pounds lard or compound, three pounds of sugar, six eggs, three pounds of currants, one-quarter pound chopped peel essence, egg color, three pints of milk. Mix on board as previous mixture, only this should be a stiff instead of a soft one. Lay out with a fork on sheets, and bake at 430 degrees F.

CAKES FOR HOOPS

Six pounds of flour, four ounces of baking powder, two and one-half pounds of lard or compound, four pounds of sugar, twenty eggs, essence, egg color, about one quart of milk. Cream up, mix lightly, and allow to stand for quarter of an hour, when you should lightly mix again. Lay out in small hoops or any sorts of pans. Bake at 450 degrees F. for small cakes, and 430 degrees F. for large size.

ORDINARY FERMENTED BUNS

Ferment one quart of milk, one quart of water, at 95 degrees F., five ounces of yeast, three-quarters of a pound of sugar, one pound of flour. When dropped, add: eight pounds flour (strong patent), one and one-quarter pounds lard, one pound of sugar, one and one-half pounds of currants, one-half pound of peel, one-half ounce of salt. Give the dough an hour and a half proof, and then mould up, prove in steam. Egg wash and bake at 460 degrees F.

SHORT PASTE

Four pounds of flour, two pounds of lard, eight ounces of sugar, one pint of water, one-quarter ounce of salt. The above paste is an excellent one for custards, jam, tarts, etc., taking a golden-brown color when baked.

SWEET PASTE FOR STRIPS, ETC.

Four pounds of flour, two pounds of butter, one and one-quarter pounds of sugar, nine eggs. Mix without handling too much. This paste will make almond strips, etc.

FILLING FOR STRIPS

Put on stove twelve ounces of chopped almonds, four ounces desiccated cocoanut, eight whites of eggs, essence of almonds. Bring this up to 140 degrees F., when it should be turned on to the strips (which have previously been in the oven for ten minutes). Sprinkle with chopped almonds.

GENOESE CAKE

This cake is well adapted for cutting up and will keep moist for a considerable time if kept enclosed in a tin with a lid. Three pounds of flour, one quart of eggs, two pounds of butter, two pounds of sugar,

one ounce of baking powder, essence of vanilla. Cream up well and lightly mix. This mixture will fill an ordinary sized tin. Ice with various colored fondants, and decorate to fancy.

SWISS ALMOND TARTS

Cream one pound of butter, one-half pound of pulverized sugar, four whites of eggs, then add eight ounces of ground almonds, twelve ounces of flour. Have a number of small pans slightly greased and floured, place the mixture in a bag containing a large star pipe. Pipe a round ring round the inside of the tin, and in the centre put a little raspberry jam. Bake in a slack oven, just hot enough to tinge the tops a golden brown, slightly dust with icing sugar when done. These tarts are favorites wherever introduced, as they are delicious to the palate and agreeable to the sight.

LIGHTNING CAKE

One pound of powdered sugar, one pound of butter, twelve yolks of eggs, twelve whites of eggs, one pound of pastry flour, the grated rind of one lemon. Cream up sugar and butter, gradually adding the yolks; then beat up the whites, adding same together with flour and lemon and mix thoroughly. Put the mixture into papered square moulds and bake in medium heat. When cold ice top with a punch icing.

LEMON SNAPS

Five pounds of sugar, two pounds of butter, five pounds of flour, fifteen eggs, one ounce of ammonia, lemon flavor. Mix sugar and butter, add gradually the eggs, flavor and the ammonia, finely powdered; roll out and cut out with a small cutter, lay on greased pans, and bake at good heat.

A GOOD CHEAP LAYER CAKE MIX

Twelve ounces of powdered sugar, five eggs, one pound, two ounces of flour, half a pint of milk, one-half ounce of soda, one ounce of cream of tartar, flavor either lemon or vanilla. Mix sugar and eggs together, adding soda flavor and milk and give it a few more turns. Lastly, add the flour. Spread this mixture upon greased layer cake pans and bake in good heat.

SPONGE SANDWICHES

These sandwiches are very popular, but they need to be much lighter, so as to present a greater bulk than sponge cake. Volatile is often used in the cheap kinds, but it has a tendency to dry them. A little ordinary powder tends to give both lightness and moistness.

Five pounds eggs, four and one-half pounds sugar, four and one-half pounds flour, one ounce baking powder. Beat as usual. Lightly mix, and bake at 420 degrees F. if thin sandwiches; if thick, bake at 400 degrees F. They can be dusted with sugar or brushed with apricot pulp and then cocoanut dusted on. A little apricot jam brushed on the top will keep the sugar from falling off.

Business Chances

"WANT" and "FOR SALE" advertisements inserted in THE NATIONAL BAKER for three cents a word, payable in advance. Stamps accepted in payment.

BAKERIES FOR SALE

FOR SALE—MODERN EQUIPPED wholesale bakery with good established business, owns corner lot, 200 x 125, upon which bakery is situated; also 15 automobile trucks, 5 ovens, and two 7-room dwelling houses. Located in Jacksonville, Florida, a city of 100,000 population. An exceptional opportunity for any one interested in a wholesale bakery. For further information communicate with Morgan F. Jones, Receiver, 104 Law Exchange, Jacksonville, Florida.

FOR SALE—BAKERY AND ICE Cream Parlor. Good business. Established 40 years. Death of owner selling reason. Town 16,000. For price and particulars address Mary K. Storck, 226 Gilman Ave., Marietta, Ohio.

FOR SALE—ONLY BAKERY IN thriving tobacco and college town. Hubbard three deck oven. Hobart cake machine. Baking outfit complete. Cheap for quick cash sale. Ill health reason for selling. Address Blackstone Bakery, Blackstone, Va.

INFORMATION WANTED

OWEN F. ALVEY, A FIRST Class Baker, formerly of Texas, worked several years in shops of Oklahoma, then in about 1916 disappeared from his friends. He is about 39 years old, small, height 5 ft. 9 in., weight 125 lbs., black hair, brown eyes, red lips and cheeks, artificial eye on left side, wore No. 5 shoe, usually a derby hat, several front teeth crowned with gold, a quiet man, saving and well liked, musical voice, sang in choirs and theaters, played the guitar, religiously inclined, a northern man by birth. (A prominent nose and large hands.)

His son age 12 is very anxious to locate his father and any information leading to his whereabouts will be greatly appreciated. Address Special Efforts Department, Salvation Army, Dallas, Texas.

MACHINERY FOR SALE

1—20-inch Thomson Moulder Extension, new. .
1—Thomson Zerah Baller.
2—Bake Right Gas Ovens, Reel.
1—2½-bbl. Day Dough Mixer.
1—2-bbl. Read Dough Mixer.
1—1½-bbl. Read Dough Mixer.
1—1-bbl. Read Dough Mixer.
1—Sugar Pulverizer, never used.
2—Union Bun Rounders.
2—Day Dough Brakes.
1—Day Automatic Dough Brake, Cincinnati.
1—No. 3 Day Clipper Beater.
3—Day Wood Flour Sifters.
2—Triumph All-Steel Flour Sifters.
1—2-bbl. Triumph Dough Mixer.
2—Wood-Proof Closets, for public view bakery.
2—Steel-Proof Closets, for public view bakery.
1—1½-bbl. Peerless Dough Mixer.
1—Giant Cake Mixer and Motor. Like new.

Cake Machines, Bread Racks, Troughs and Equipment of every description ready for immediate shipment, new or rebuilt. Rebuilt machines guaranteed same as new ones.

J. H. BAST & CO.
649 W. Pratt St.　　　Baltimore, Md.

BUSINESS CHANCES

FOR SALE—1 MIDDLEBY MARshall Oven No. 103. Double Deck 270 loaf capacity. A bargain for cash if taken at once. C. H. Alderman, Ashtabula, Ohio.

Help Wanted—Male

SALESMAN WANTED—A HIGH class representative, capable of closing large advertising contracts with wholesale bakers, and willing to travel, will find a splendid opportunity and big earnings by writing to Fink and Paine, Inc., 299 Madison Avenue, New York City.

MACHINERY FOR SALE

FOR SALE—FOR A VERY LOW price you can secure the following slightly used equipment:
Two Yankee Reel Ovens, $100 each.

DOUGH MIXERS

1 Dutchess, 4 bbl. J. H. Day, 3 bbl.
1 Rockwell, 4 bbl. 2 Rockwell, 3 bbl.
J. H. Day, 2 bbl. Double Jacketed.
1 Century, 3 bbl.

CAKE MACHINES

Read
1 Little Giant　　　　1 Champion
1 Hobart with D. C. Motor attached
Dutchess Two-Pocket Divider
Dutchess Roll Dividers
Bread and Pan Racks
Proofing Closets　　　　Troughs
Work Tables　　　　Bread Pans
1 Day Egg Clipper　　Shipping Boxes
Sheet iron pans for the following ovens: Yankee, Barker and Federal.
Dough brake, A-1 condition
2 Doughnut Fryers with trays

I. KALFUS COMPANY
175 Stanton St.　　　New York City

MISCELLANEOUS

TURNER'S RAPID RECIPE RECKoner simplifies cost accounting so that it is a matter of only a few minutes to get the cost of a batch of any size, and of any class of goods. The baker is saved all the trouble in counting up the cost; it is already done for him. Tables are given of the cost of each ounce of flour at a price per barrel from $4.00 upward, of other materials from $0.01 to $0.60 by the pound, and the cost of each ounce. One is needed in every bake-shop, and the cost is but $2.00 postpaid. For sale by THE NATIONAL BAKER, 411 Walnut Street, Philadelphia, Pa.

A Classified List of Goods Needed by Bakers

Automobile Trucks—
Republic Truck Sales Corp., Alma, Mich.

Almond Paste—
Henry Heide, Inc., New York.

Bakery Advertising—
I. B. Nordham Co., N. Y.
Schulze Advert. Service, Chicago.

Bakers' Institute—
Siebel Institute, Chicago.

Bakers' Machinery—
Champion Machine Co., Joliet, Ill.
J. H. Day Co., Cincinnati, O.
Dutchess Tool Co., Beacon, N. Y.
Freymark Steam Generator Co., St. Louis.
Jaburg-Miller Co., New York.
Peerless Bread Mch. Co., Sidney, O.
Read Machinery Co., York, Pa.
Reeves Pulley Co., Columbus, Ind.
Syracuse Steam Generator Co., Syracuse, N. Y.
Thomson Mch. Co., Bellevue, N. J.
Thomas Mills & Bro., Philadelphia.
Union Machinery Co., Joliet, Ill.

Bakers' Pans—
J. W. Allen & Co., Chicago.
Jaburg Bros., New York.
Jaburg-Miller Co., New York.
Edward Katzinger Co., Chicago.
The Aug. Maag Co., Baltimore.
Thomas Mills & Bro., Philadelphia.

Bakers' Tools—
J. W. Allen & Co., Chicago.
Jaburg Bros., New York.
Jaburg-Miller Co., New York.
Edward Katzinger Co., Chicago.
The Aug. Maag Co., Baltimore.
Thomas Mills & Bro., Philadelphia.
Union Steel Products Co., Albion.

Books for Bakers—
Malsbender's Recipe Book.
Turner's Rapid Recipe Reckoner.

Bread Labels—
Mirror Printing Co., Kalamazoo.
National Binding Mch. Co., N. Y.

Bread Wrapping and Sealing Machines—
National Bread Wrapping Machine Co., Nashua, N. H.
Lambooy Label & Wrapper Co., Kalamazoo, Mich.
Union Machinery Co., Joliet, Ill.

Cash Registers—
National Cash Register Company.

Chocolate—
Walter Baker & Co., Ltd., Dorchester.

Cooking Oil
Corn Products Ref. Co., New York.
Patent Cereals Co., Geneva, N. Y.

Dough Mixers and Kneaders—
Champion Machinery Co., Joliet, Ill.
J. H. Day Co., Cincinnati, O.
Read Machinery Co., York, Pa.

Eggs-Desiccated—Egg Products—
Joe Lowe Co., N. Y.

Flour—
Atkinson Milling Co., Minn.
Big Diamond Mills Co., Minn.
Commander Mills, Minneapolis.
Empire Milling Co., Minneapolis.
W. J. Jennison & Co., Minneapolis.
Russell-Miller Milling Co., Minn.
Updike Milling Co., Omaha.
Washburn-Crosby Co., Minneapolis.

Food Colors—
National Aniline & Chem. Co., N. Y.

Fruit Growers—
California Associated Raisin Co.
California Prune & Apricot Growers.

Honey—
Arthur A. Beals, Oto, Iowa.

Ice Cream Tools and Supplies—
J. W. Allen & Co., Chicago.
Atlas Mfg. Co., New Haven.
Chr. Hansen's Lab., Little Falls, N. Y.
The Aug. Maag Co., Baltimore.
Thomas Mills & Bro., Philadelphia.

Malt, Extract and Dry—
American Diamalt Co.
Anheuser-Busch, Inc., St. Louis.
P. Ballantine & Sons, Newark.
Freihofer Baking Co., Philadelphia.
Malt Diastase Co., N. Y.
Stein-Hall Mfg. Co., Chicago.

Milk, Powdered and Condensed—
Consolidated Prod. Co., Lincoln, Neb.
I. H. Nestor & Co., Philadelphia.

Ovens—
Bennett Oven Co., Battle Creek.
Duhrkop Oven Co., New York.
Hubbard Oven Co., Chicago.
Meek Oven Mfg. Co., Westport, Conn.
Middleby Oven Co., New York.
Middleby-Marshall Co., Chicago.
Standard Oven Co., Pittsburgh.
Superior Oven Co., Chicago, Ill.

Oven Lights and Doors—
Dutchess Tool Co., Beacon, N. Y.
Chas. Robson & Co., Philadelphia.

Papers (Parchment and Waxed)—
Lambooy Label & Wrapper Co., Kalamazoo, Mich.
Menasha Ptg. & Carton Co., Menasha, Wis.
Waterproof Paper & Board Co., Cincinnati.

Pie Machinery—
J. H. Day Co., Cincinnati, O.
Union Machinery Co., Joliet, Ill.

Potato Flour—
Falk American Potato Flour Co., Pittsburgh, Pa.

Pyrometers—
Hubbard Oven Co., Chicago.
Philadelphia Thermometer Co.
Chas. Robson & Co., Philadelphia.

Shipping Boxes (Wood and Paper)—
A. Backus, Jr., & Son, Detroit.
Rob't Gaylord, Inc., St. Louis.

Shortening—
Corn Products Refining Co., N. Y.
Procter & Gamble Co., Cincinnati.

Stoves for Bakers and Confectioners—
Edward Katzinger Co., Chicago.
Thomas Mills & Bro., Philadelphia.

Sugar and Sugar Syrups—
American Sugar Ref. Co., N. Y.
Corn Products Ref. Co., New York.
Franklin Sugar Ref. Co., Philadelphia.

Supplies—
J. W. Allen & Co., Chicago.
Jaburg Bros., New York.
Joe Lowe Co., N. Y.
Stein-Hall Mfg. Co., Chicago and N. Y.
Ward Baking Co., New York.

Thermometers—
Phila. Thermometer Co., Phila.

Vermin Exterminator—
Berg & Beard Mfg. Co., Brooklyn.

Washing and Cleaning Material—
J. B. Ford Co.

Yeast—
The Fleischmann Co., New York.

INDEX TO ADVERTISEMENTS

	Page
American Diamalt Co.	14
Anheuser-Busch Sales Corp.	43
Baker & Co., Ltd., Walter	57
Ballantine & Sons, P.	15
Bennett Oven Co.	4
Berg & Beard Mfg. Co.	62
Big Diamond Mills Co.	4
Business Chances	65
California Associated Raisin Co.	17
California Prune & Apricot Growers	51
Carter, Rice & Co., Corporation	12
Commander Mills	55
Corn Products Ref. Co.	9
Day Co., The J. H.	6
Duhrkop Oven Co.	13
Dutchess Tool Co.	8, 14
Empire Milling Co.	16
Fleischmann Co., The	11
Ford Co., J. B.	68
Freihofer Baking Co.	59
Heide, Inc., Henry	63
Hubbard Portable Oven Co.	Cover
Jennison Co., W. J.	16
Katzinger Co., Edward	Cover
Lambooy Label & Wrapper Co.	4
Maag Co., The Aug.	Cover
Malt Diastase Co.	16
Malsbender, M.	13
Meek Oven Co.	46
Menasha Printing & Carton Co.	55
Middleby-Marshall Oven Co.	49
Middleby Oven Co., N. Y.	15
Mills & Bro., Inc., Thomas	61
National Bread Wrapping Mach. Co.	12
Philadelphia Thermometer Co.	4
Procter & Gamble Co.	6
Read Machinery Co.	47
Reeves Pulley Co.	8
Republic Truck Sales Corp.	3
Robson & Co., Charles	13
Russell-Miller Milling Co.	10
Siebel Institute	7
Standard Oven Co.	5
Superior Oven Co.	41
Thomson Machine Co.	7
Turner, A. R.	57
Union Steel Products Co.	
Union Machinery Co.	8
Ward Baking Co.	22
Washburn-Crosby Co.	Cover
Water-proof Paper & Board Co.	4

Entirely Different from Any Other Pan on the Market

Their construction, the most rigid and sanitary ever devised, entirely eliminates strapping, therefore neither dirt nor grease can collect.

The outer face of the end pans is protected by a sheet of steel which acts as a piece of armor-plate. This steers the peel underneath the pans, eliminating all danger of battering the end pan.

Kleen-Krust Rivetless "Steel-Shod" Bread Pans are manufactured under letters patent granted by the U. S. Government. We are sole manufacturers.

The advantages of Kleen-Krust Rivetless "Steel-Shod" Bread Pans go a long way toward creating a demand for your bread by improving the appearance of the loaf. In order that you may find out these advantages for yourself, we will forward a sample set of open Pans for immediate practical use in your oven room.

Specially Adapted for Traveling Ovens

We have issued a New Catalog illustrating and describing our Kleen-Krust Rivetless "Steel Shod" Bread Pans and Kleen-Krust Rivetless Pullman or Sandwich Bread Pans. Catalog mailed on request.

THE AUGUST MAAG CO.

509-11 W. Lombard St.

VOL. XXVII. Fe 21 '22 — ENTERED AT THE PHILADELPHIA POST OFFICE AS SECOND CLASS MATTER — No. 313

THE NATIONAL Baker

PUBLISHED MONTHLY BY THE NATIONAL BAKER PUBLISHING CO. 411 WALNUT STREET B. F. WHITECAR, Pres. and Editor — PHILADELPHIA, PA., FEBRUARY 15, 1922 — Price per year, U. S. and Canada $3.00 Foreign Countries $4.00

Bake Better Bread and Build Bigger Business

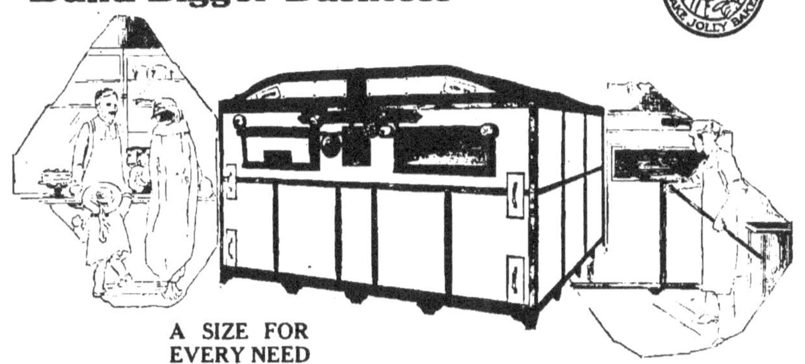

A SIZE FOR
EVERY NEED

HUBBARD OVENS

HUBBARD OVEN COMPANY
1140 BELDEN AVENUE, CHICAGO

STOCK SIZES

Single and Double Loaf

Pan No.	Top Inside	Bottom Outside	Depth	Capacity Ounces
06	8 x4	7½x3¾	2½	12-13
06A	8 x4	7½x3½	2¾	12-14
07	8½x4½	7½x3½	2½	16-18
07A	8½x4½	7½x3½	2½	15-17
08	8½x4½	7½x3¾	2½	16-18
017	9½x4½	8½x3½	2½	16-20
017A	9½x4½	8½x3½	2½	16-20
044	9 x4½	8½x3½	2½	16-18
045	9½x5½	8½x4½	2½	20-24
046	10½x4½	9½x4½	2½	24-26
047	9½x5½	8½x4½	2½	24-26
047A	9 x5	8½x4½	2½	24-26
048	9½x5½	8½x4½	3	24-28
055	9½x5	8½x4½	3	24-28
056	10 x5	9½x4½	3	24-30
027	9½x4½	8½x3½	3½	18-22
027A	9½x4½	8½x3½	3	20-24
084	7½x7½	7½x7½	2	24-28
085	8 x8	7½x7½	2½	24-32
088	8½x7½	8 x7	2½	32-36
088A	8 x7	7½x6½	2½	24-32
086	8½x8½	7½x7½	2½	32-36
086A	8½x8½	7½x7½	2½	32-36
087	8½x8½	8 x8	2½	36-44
089	9 x8	8½x7½	2½	32-36

There's an Ekco Guaranteed Product for Every Baking Need

Velvediron Bun Pans

Velvediron is the perfect metal for Bun and Cookie Baking. Will not buckle. Lies flat on the oven. Look for the Diamond Mark when you buy. See the catalog for sizes.

Perfection in the Parts
means
Perfection in the Whole

E KCO Everstay's better qualities are built into its parts. Each does its share to add durability, economy and good baking.

Examine a set. For durability there are the sturdy spreaders and band-iron. For economy in use see the flat band-iron, the rounded pan edges, the protection plates. And Ekco Sanitary Bake Pans, combined with the patented riveless construction makes clean, well-baked bread.

Ekco Everstay Sets are the first choice of bakers who ask for good baking and economy in use. Leading supply houses carry stock sizes for prompt shipment.

EDWARD KATZINGER CO.

131 N. SANGAMON STREET - CHICAGO, ILL
Dept. K DREXEL BLDG. - PHILADELPHIA, PA.

Largest Manufacturers of Bake Pans in the World

Republic Rapid Transit, with Panel Body and Fore-Door Open Cab, Cord Tires, Electric Starter and Lights. Price on application

You *Can* Cut Delivery Costs!

Other body types include

Carry-All
Canopy Top
Stock Rack
Screen Enclosed
Tank Body
Open Express
Double Deck
Platform Stake
Bus Body
Police Patrol
Grain Body
Bottlers' Body
Dump Body

Lowest first cost of any truck of similar capacity, lowest operation cost plus Unequalled Service make the Republic Rapid Transit with Panel Body the most Economical Delivery Equipment bakers can use.

This truck has proved its ability to make more and quicker deliveries in town and country at a cost considerably below the average. It enables bakers to cover a much wider territory. It will place your delivery system on a permanently profitable basis.

Write for Vocational Catalog showing how Republic Trucks save time and money for bakers.

The Republic Line: ¾, 1, 1½-2, 2½-3, 3½-4 tons capacity.

REPUBLIC TRUCK SALES CORPORATION
ALMA, MICH.

REPUBLIC
RAPID TRANSIT©

Republic has more trucks in use than any other exclusive truck manufacturer

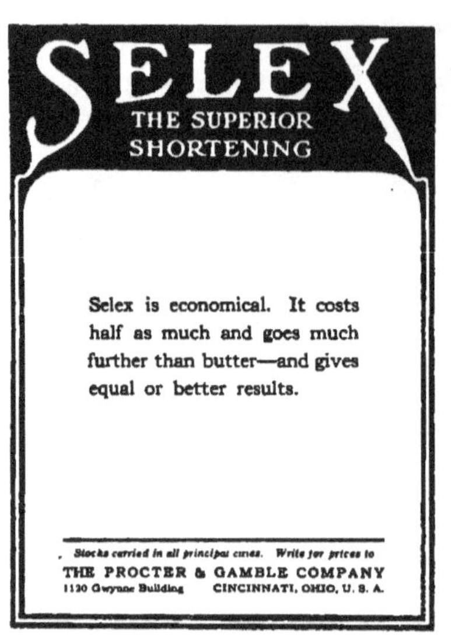
SELEX
THE SUPERIOR
SHORTENING

Selex is economical. It costs half as much and goes much further than butter—and gives equal or better results.

Stocks carried in all principal cities. Write for prices to
THE PROCTER & GAMBLE COMPANY
1130 Gwynne Building   CINCINNATI, OHIO, U. S. A.

THE BIBLE OF SPEED CONTROL

"The Reeves"   Variable Speed Transmission

CATALOG T-29

JUST OFF THE PRESS

All structural details, dimension diagrams and installation data. Complete and authoritative. 52 pages of facts covering every conceivable speed control problem, the result of 25 years of experience.

SEND FOR YOUR COPY TODAY

Reeves Pulley Co., Columbus, Indiana
Chicago Branch: Cor. Clinton & Monroe Streets

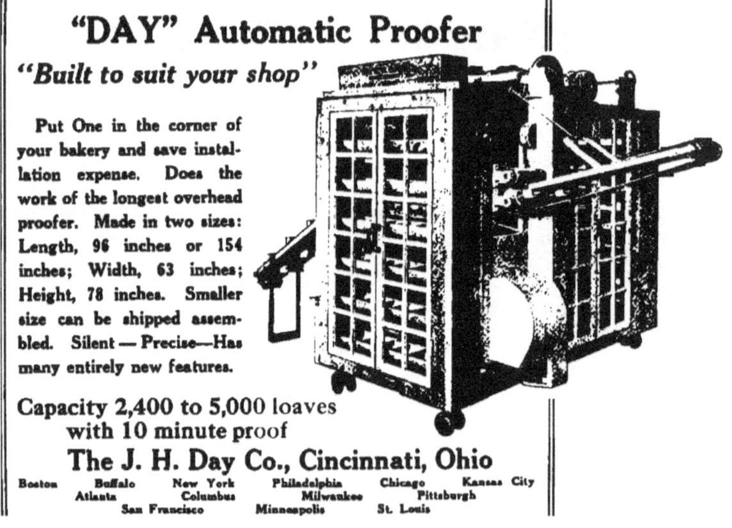
"DAY" Automatic Proofer

"Built to suit your shop"

Put One in the corner of your bakery and save installation expense. Does the work of the longest overhead proofer. Made in two sizes: Length, 96 inches or 154 inches; Width, 63 inches; Height, 78 inches. Smaller size can be shipped assembled. Silent — Precise—Has many entirely new features.

Capacity 2,400 to 5,000 loaves with 10 minute proof

The J. H. Day Co., Cincinnati, Ohio

Boston   Buffalo   New York   Philadelphia   Chicago   Kansas City
Atlanta   Columbus   Milwaukee   Pittsburgh
San Francisco   Minneapolis   St. Louis

BAKE BETTER BREAD

Increase Your Profits

Model C—Double Oven—This is but one of the types we make. Our catalog describes many others. Our line comprises a size and style to meet your particular requirements.

Every baker knows that the better bread he bakes, the more sales he will make and the greater will be his profits.

Regardless of how good the quality of the materials used in the mixture and how careful you are in the various steps of preparations, unless you have a reliable oven you cannot assure yourself of a quality loaf that will satisfy your customers, and hold your trade.

But why take such a chance?

With a Middleby-Marshall Oven you will be absolutely sure of your product being properly baked regardless of whether it be bread or cake.

For all 'round work, Model C, Double oven, pictured above, cannot be equalled. The purchase of this oven is not an expense, it is an investment. Repeat orders are constantly being received from bakers everywhere who are using this oven with the greatest satisfaction.

Let us tell you more about this All 'Round Continuous Baking Oven. Upon request we shall be glad to send you our catalog free. Write for it today. You will be glad you did later.

MIDDLEBY-MARSHALL OVEN CO.

Largest Builders of Ovens in the World

760 W. Adams St.

Branch office and factory at
St. Louis, Mo.

Chicago, Ill.

Address all correspondence to
main office at Chicago

The New Refined Cerelose Ready NOW

AN improved quality Cerelose Corn Sugar of 99% purity with approximately 95% Dextrose or gas-producing substance. Pure white. Low in moisture, making an ideal bread sugar. Costs less than Cane sugar. If unable to obtain this sugar through your jobber, write us direct.

CORN PRODUCTS REFINING CO.

17 BATTERY PLACE

NEW YORK

OCCIDENT

Extra Strong High Patent

Occident has grown in favor each
year because the attempt has never
been made to see how cheaply,
but how *uniformly good* it can be
milled.

Costs More --- Worth It!

Russell-Miller Milling Co.
Minneapolis.   Minnesota

Branch Offices:

Pittsburgh, Pa.   Park Bldg.   Boston, Mass.,   Board of Trade Bldg.
Philadelphia, Pa.   Lafayette Bldg.   Seattle, Wash.   Maritime Bldg.
Syracuse, N. Y.   Seitz Bldg.   San Francisco, Cal. Merchants' Exch.
New York City   Produce Exchange   Des Moines, Iowa   122 S. W. 7th St.
                     Los Angeles, Cal. 668 Santa Fe Ave.

OCCIDENT

Raisins 40% Cheaper

means a new opportunity in—

—millions want it daily

Start it Now

Don't wait too long with your raisin bread!

Raisins are now 40% cheaper than formerly. That means a new opportunity for you—a good reason why you should lose no time in again featuring raisin bread.

Another good reason—here are even *finer* raisins that will make a *better bread*. Use the delicious Bakers' *Seeded* Sun-Maids—the raisins with that real raisin flavor.

We are constantly advertising raisin bread. Most all women see this advertising. They will come to *you* for it, because we tell them that the neighborhood bakers have it, and that they make it *best*.

Raisin bread enjoys a permanent popularity. It has been the favorite bread for ages and ages, just as it is the favorite loaf of today. The demand for it is constant—and always large.

So with better raisins today, 40% cheaper, you can now realize larger profits with seeded Raisin Bread. Start baking it regularly—now!

SUN-MAID RAISINS
Delicious *Raisin-Bread* Raisins

Bakers' Seeded Sun-Maid Raisins are especially for bakers' use in bread, cakes, cookies, snails, "race tracks," pie, etc., are selected, washed and sterilized, to make them perfect raisins for your use.

Now cheaper by 40% than formerly. Rely safely on prices and other information given you by our own direct representatives who will call on you.

Bakers know that Seeded Raisins absorb 10% more water.

California Associated Raisin Co.
Membership 13,000 Growers
Dept. E-6-1 Fresno, Calif.

Free

The coupon below is for your use, no matter what position you hold in any bakery, large or small.

If your raisins, no matter from whom purchased, have deteriorated or lost quality for any reason, if you have an unused stock of raisins, ask us for suggestions to help remove the difficulty—no matter what it is. We maintain a Bakers' Service Department which will supply free formulas for mixes on request. Use coupon below.

Free Service to Busy Bakers

Write us about your difficulties, if any, with any variety of raisins—see our offer below. We will gladly place at your disposal, without charge, the resources of our Bakers' Service Department, composed of practical bakers familiar with *your* problems and methods that have solved the same problems for others.

We came in contact with one baker not long ago who found that placing the raisins on a sheet pan in the oven for a while caused the white sugar-spots, when there were any, to disappear quickly, the sugar going back into the raisin, and thus restoring it to the same condition in which it left our California packing plant.

That is but an instance of the various helpful little hints we pick up all along the line, and incorporate in the service we offer you.

California Associated Raisin Co.,
Dept B-6-1, Fresno, California.

Please send me free formulas for mixes for raisin products that you have found to be practical sellers through large and small bakeries.

Name......................................

Street......................................

City................State................

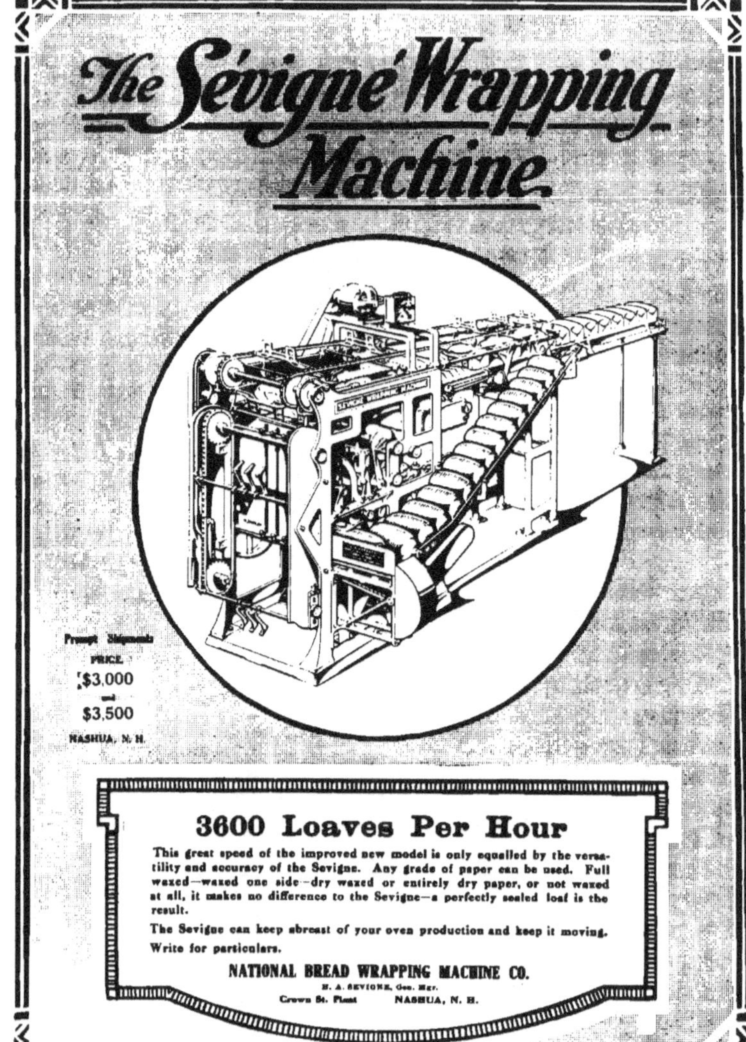
The Sévigné Wrapping Machine

Prompt Shipments
PRICE
$3,000
and
$3,500
NASHUA, N. H.

3600 Loaves Per Hour

This great speed of the improved new model is only equalled by the versatility and accuracy of the Sevigne. Any grade of paper can be used. Full waxed—waxed one side—dry waxed or entirely dry paper, or not waxed at all, it makes no difference to the Sevigne—a perfectly sealed loaf is the result.

The Sevigne can keep abreast of your oven production and keep it moving.

Write for particulars.

NATIONAL BREAD WRAPPING MACHINE CO.
H. A. SEVIGNE, Gen. Mgr.
Crown St. Plant   NASHUA, N. H.

DUTCHESS

Roll Dough Dividers, Oven Lights, Oven Doors, Fire Doors, Etc.

Make your work easy, accurate and profitable with a DUTCHESS Roll Dough Divider. These great labor and material savers are built in two sizes—a heavy floor machine, and a lighter machine for bench use. They can't be equalled for making rolls. Each machine cuts 36 pieces of equal weight at one operation. Don't waste your time breaking off rolls in the old fashioned, slow, wasteful one-at-a-time method. Save your time and material. Use a DUTCHESS.

New Prices Effective May 2nd, 1921

Stand Machine $180.00

Bench Machine $80.00

For That New Oven

Insist on DUTCHESS Fixtures and you may be sure that they will give you lasting dependable service. They are made only of the best grade of grey iron castings, carefully fitted, no leaky joints, and resist the effect of heat and hold their shape.

Ask Your Supply House

Your Competitor—

You bet he's on the lookout for something better!

How about you? Have you tried Diamalt?

Beat the other fellow to it. Use Diamalt. It will improve the quality of the loaf you bake. Makes bread whiter, better flavored and finer in texture. Saves sugar and makes more dough from less material, and bigger loaves of solid bread.

The American Diamalt Company
424 Bankers Investment Bldg...San Francisco, Cal.
1182 Broadway.......................New York City
327 So. La Salle Street...............Chicago, Ill.

Home Office: 419 Plum Street, Cincinnati, Ohio

The Test of Time

is the surest test

OP Malt Extract

has stood this test and has not been found wanting.

Prudent bakers do not experiment—they place full reliance in

OP MALT EXTRACT

Malt-Diastase Company

79 Wall Street, NEW YORK

Warehouses: CHICAGO, PHILADELPHIA   *Laboratories:* BROOKLYN, N. Y.

IT isn't often possible to increase the quality of an article and at the same time lower the production cost. But it can be done in the baking industry through the use of

In these days of price-cutting and bitter competition every baker is struggling to keep loaf quality UP and manufacturing costs DOWN.

Small wonder then that bakers who are already using Arkady are patting themselves on the back.

For they have found that with the addition of a trace of this wonderful yeast nutrient they are able to produce better bread than ever before and at the same time make undreamed of savings in raw materials, yeast, sugar, and flour.

The story of Arkady is one of the most interesting romances of American scientific achievement and of the utmost importance to every American baker. Let us tell you about it.

Write for the Arkady booklet or, better, order a trial shipment of Arkady today.

Arkady is sold in 50-lb. drums and 180-lb. sacks. Price 13c. per pound. In lots of 900 lbs. or over, 11c. per pound. All prices f.o.b. New York and subject to change without notice.

Research Products Department

WARD BAKING COMPANY, NEW YORK, N. Y.

PUBLISHED ON THE FIFTEENTH OF EACH MONTH

AT

411 WALNUT ST., PHILADELPHIA

BY

THE NATIONAL BAKER PUBLISHING CO.

B. F. WHITEOAR, PRESIDENT AND EDITOR
W. W. GALE, SECRETARY AND TREASURER

MEMBER OF THE AUDIT BUREAU OF CIRCULATIONS

SUBSCRIPTION RATES
UNITED STATES, ITS POSSESSIONS AND CANADA .. $2.00 per year
FOREIGN COUNTRIES .... 3.00 per year

PAYABLE IN ADVANCE

ADVERTISING RATES ON APPLICATION

Make all remittances payable to the order of
The National Baker Publishing Company

*Changes for displayed advertisements must reach this office
by the 5th of the month*

VOL. XXVII   FEBRUARY, 1922   No. 313

CONTENTS

Activity of Allied Trades........ 31
Bakery Standards in Pennsylvania 28
Bakery Accounting 33
Bakers' Score Card 42
Baking Technology 34
Bread Weight Bill, Massachusetts 26
Calculating Dough Temperatures 46
Calorie, What Is It?.............. 50
Cake Recipes:
  Cocoanut Cream Patties 62
  Cocoanut Sponge Balls 62
  Almond Honey Cakes 62
  Almond Biscuit 62
  Pistachio and Almond Cake... 62
  Moonbeams 63
  Domino Squares 63
  Primrose 63
  Ice Cream Tartlets 64
  Engagement Doublets 64
  Fruit and Rice Eclairs...... 64
Increased Operating Costs 23
Information Department:
  Chocolate Fried Cake 55

Spices and Flavors............. 55
Bread Troubles 55
French Pastry 56
Danish Pastry 56
Fried Cakes 56
Lunch Cake 56
Nut Cake 56
Prune Cake 57
Kansas Bakers Meet 42
Magic Four 25
Modern Methods in Shop Control 50
National Prune Week 42
New England Association........ 32
Ohio Convention 40
Pennsylvania State Convention.. 24
Pennsylvania Bread and Milk Week 27
Recipe Building 58
Small Fancy Cakes.............. 56
Trade Items 44
Western Pennsylvania Association 32
1922 Loaf and What It Should Contain 29

Increased Operating Costs

*Greater Efficiency of Organization and Increased
Volume of Business Required to Meet Them.*

WHEREVER a group of business men gather together these days, one of the topics of conversation is the increasing cost of doing business, and all sorts of suggestions are made on how to keep down the "Overhead."

The nervous business man meets his difficulties by lopping off expenses in every possible way. He looks about him with an eye not to increasing sales, but to reducing operating costs. He forgets that there is great danger of reducing the efficiency of his whole organization by this plan, with the result of cutting down the volume of business and getting in worse condition than ever before. Cutting expenses without considering results is, therefore, a policy in keeping with cyclone cellar methods, and not in line with hustling, courageous, up-to-date Americanism.

The business man who is aggressive in his methods, and who pushes for business, seldom needs to worry about what will happen if he doesn't get the relatively big volume which is needed to take care of his expenses. He gets the business because his methods are calculated to develop it, whereas if he shrank back and eliminated promotion work, with the necessary expense connected with it, he would have trouble getting the volume which even the smaller expense would necessitate having in order to get by. The business which is strong enough to maintain a "big drive" seldom has to worry about results.

Of course, this does not mean that one is justified in extravagance. The baker is not going to spend a great deal of money without seeing some return in sight, but the point is that where that return is logically to be expected, it is a mistake not to go after it, on the ground that it costs too much to do the necessary promotion work. Right now the opportunities of the bakery business are probably the greatest in the history of the trade—considering permanent good-will, contribution to the welfare of the community and other things involved in the operation of a first-class bakery at present—and consequently this should be an era of development for every member of it. Don't get the idea that because it costs more to do business you must cut down expenses in proportion.

As one baker said the other day, "I don't care how much my expenses are if I am making enough money to take care of them." The man who is making $100 now where he made $50 a year ago is able to absorb an increase in expenses of similar amount. The merchant who is so scared by the increase that he loses his nerve and fails to go after the larger profits that await the right kind of effort is caught both ways. Nothing succeeds like success, and nothing brings success like a determination to get in line for it. Nothing venture, nothing have, applies in a business way as to other things and that means being willing to keep up with the faster pace set by business today.

There is no getting away from increased operating expenses. No matter in what branch of the business the baker may be, he will realize how much more it costs him to carry on his enterprise than it did before the war. In the first place, it takes more capital to handle the same quantity of product. The bakery which is not increasing its output must put more money into everything involved in production, from the flour to the labor and machinery. Interest is, therefore, an item, and where business is done to any extent with borrowed money, an increase of this kind is not to be overlooked. No matter how accommodating the banker nor how liberal the line of credit extended, this must be paid for, and the increased payments of interest are part of the rising cost of doing business. Even if money is not borrowed, a legitimate item in the cost of doing business—recognized by such authorities as the Federal Trade Commission—is interest on investment.

Greater values in the form of stocks on hand mean higher insurance charges, higher taxes, etc. Supplies of all kinds cost more, whether they are raw materials used in the bakeshop, or accessories needed in the store. Wrapping materials of all kinds have been boosted in price. If the baker is using a horse and wagon, feed and harness cost more, and if he is using a motor truck he is paying more for gasoline, oil and tires than formerly. In fact, you can hardly look in any direction around a bakery today without seeing evidence of the greater expense involved in making and selling the gods.

Help costs more. In fact, high cost of living means the high cost of labor, because employees must have enough to live on, and the increased expenses of maintaining a household are reflected as a matter of course in a bigger payroll. No matter whether you are hiring journeymen for the shop or salespeople for the store, you are paying more for service of this kind than was formerly necessary, because it costs more for everyone of them to maintain himself.

As a general proposition, it is next to impossible to cut down expenses without affecting the successful operation of the business in some vital way. A definite policy of retrenchment, therefore, could mean but one thing—reduced business. And no ambitious baker is willing to decrease the size of his business, especially when conditions are as they are today. The only thing to do is to maintain the pressure, keep up with the procession, absorb all the necessary increases—and then strive for the increased efficiency which is required to get the results.

One thing about holding up promotion work and increasing the volume of business that is interesting to figure out is the effect on overhead. It is interesting of course, that when a business increases, there is a gain due to the profit scored on each additional unit of business. But there is a gain in another way which is especially important in these days of rising costs. That is the gain brought about by cutting down the percentage of overhead.

That is to say, if a concern was doing a business of $25,000 a year at a cost of 15 per cent., and showed an increase in volume to $37,500, without increasing the expense the percentage overhead would fall from 15 to 10. In other words, a 50 per cent. increase in volume would mean a 33 1-3 per cent. decrease in overhead; and the baker would have his direct gain through his larger sales, and his indirect gain through the reduction in the cost of making them.

As a matter of practice, it would be difficult to bring about a gain such as that indicated without increasing the actual amount spent in operating expenses; but it is obvious that the greater the gain, the more the business would be able to stand in the way of expense, and hence the baker would be in the position of spending more to save more; a paradox of business that works out in the experience of every successful tradesman.

It is quite in line for the baker to impress on his help the importance of saving in every legitimate way. For instance, if deliveries have been made unnecessarily, these can be cut down by the simple expedient of urging customers to carry their purchases out with them. Economy in the use of wrapping materials will also help, as this is one point where employees are usually careless, because they fail to realize just what supplies of this kind cost. Everyone should be made to feel that it is up to him to do just a little more than heretofore, and to extend himself to the limit, in order that the business may be able to stand up under all of the increased expenses that have had to be shouldered.

There is no reason why any good baker should falter, or feel that conditions are such as to discourage one. Things are happening fast, and it is not always possible to see the opportunities as readily as the handicaps; but they are there. Decide to do more, and to expand, rather than to do less. That kind of spirit will mean results and will stimulate everybody in the organization to maximum effort.

Above all, keep up your constructive advertising; keep telling the public that "Bread is your best food—Eat more of it."

—‡—‡—‡—

Pennsylvania State Convention

AT the meeting of the Executive Committee of the Pennsylvania Association of the Baking Industry it was decided to change the dates for the 1922 meeting at Bedford Springs to June 5th, 6th and 7th. A very interesting program is being prepared, details of which will be found elsewhere in this issue of THE NATIONAL BAKER.

The Magic Four

EXPERIMENTS and experience has shown that in advertising the line of four words or a group of four pictures is ideal. It is easy to see, understand and remember four words or four pictures. No one has much difficulty in remembering "Say it with flowers." When a slogan consists of more than four words it is not so easy to remember. If a person looks at more than four pictures he is more apt to forget what he has seen than if the number was limited to four.

If the baker is seeking a slogan for his business, he will do well to keep it down to four words. If he is writing an advertisement he will do well to use sentences of four words in every case where these will express the meaning as well as longer sentences. Let us take an example. The baker is going to write an advertisement to place in the newspaper. What he wants to say is the following:

Baked in an absolutely sanitary shop, our bakery products are protected from contamination from the time the raw material arrives until the cooked food leaves our hands, and we do not stop there. We watch it carefully until it reaches you, and we take the utmost care in selecting only the purest products and those best suited for the bread or pastry to be cooked. We take real pride in our plant and those who work in it and invite you at any time to inspect it.

How much of that would stick in the mind of the average reader? The chances are that he would not even read it. Let us put it in this way:

Our shop is sanitary.
We watch every process.
Only pure ingredients used.
Only healthy people employed.
Our plant is our pride.
Come and see us.

We have said in this second case all, or at least all that is essential, that was said in the first. We have used shorter words and shorter sentences. In but one case have we used a sentence of more than four words and in that case the word "our" was repeated.

If these two advertisements were put in the newspaper it is certain that the second would make a much greater and a much better impression than the first. Being a series of short sentences there would probably be some sentence that would catch the eye of the reader even if he did not read them all.

It is necessary to remember that the person reading the paper in which the advertisement appears is busy, and will not read in the advertisements matter that he might read in the news matter. Even in the case of news, the average person reads only the head lines, a half dozen or a dozen words at the top of the column that tell the story.

There is another point to be considered in sifting what one has to say down to four word sentences. These sentences will in many cases have the power of slogans. What a difference there is between the sentence: "We take real pride in our plant and those who work in it and invite you at any time to inspect it," and "Our plant is our pride." "Come and see us." We have substituted two short, compelling sentences for one long one that not likely would make any very great impression.

The baker who tries to write all his advertising in four word sentences will soon find that it is attracting far more attention than it ever did before. He may not be able to shorten all his sentences up to four words. He will find, however, that he is using shorter words and shorter sentences and that he is conveying a clearer meaning. In time his advertisements will become epigrammatic in clearness and a lot of these sentences will stick in the minds of the readers to an extent that longer sentences and longer words never would.

The advertising of the Eastman Kodak Company is conspicuous because of the small number of words that are used. One of the most successful advertisements the company ever ran consisted of a picture with the four words, "The Picture From Home," under it. "Kodak as you go," has sold a great many rolls of films to say nothing about the cameras people have bought because of the desire created by these words to kodak.

It makes no difference whether the advertising is to be done in the papers, on bill boards or on show cards in the window, the briefer the message can be made the closer it will stick. People won't read a long message on a show card. They will read sentences composed of four short words.

In-so-far as possible it is well to use single syllable words. Examine the slogan, "Say it with flowers," one that is said to have accomplished more than any other slogan ever written, and we find that it consists of four words and that there is a total of sixteen letters, or an average of four letters to a word. This is not the slogan that was first considered. The other contained more words and more letters. Every word, even every letter that was taken off that original slogan was probably adding no less than a million dollars to the ultimate value of the slogan.

In selling goods it is not how much is said that counts as much as how little can be said and convey the meaning. When an idea can be expressed in one short simple word it is imbedded upon the mind much better than it would be if dozens of longer words were used.

When selling goods, however, it is not only wise to consider that the ideal is four words, but that it is well to appeal to the four senses, sight, smell, taste and hearing. There is no other industry in which this can be done better than in the bakery industry. When the baker has done his best he has produced a work of art that appeals to the sight, smell and the taste. If added to his art as a baker he has a pleasing voice, he is going to appeal to the hearing when he talks about it.

Perhaps in the past the baker has not exercised as much care as he might have in selecting sales people in the store who have pleasing voices. Anyhow if he has, a lot of other kinds of stores have not. If a person will make the experiment he will discover that his desire to buy is governed to a surprising extent by the voice of the person who is endeavoring to sell to him.

There are some people we like to hear talk. There are others we would rather pay to keep still. There are some with high pitched and harsh voices. There are others with soft, well modulated voices. There are some with musical voices. There are some with voices that are discordant.

Now it stands to reason that if the baker has produced a product that is a work of art, one that appeals to the eye, the nose and the palate, there is going to be a discord in the harmony if one with a displeasing voice tries to sell it. Yet that person with the displeasing voice might be able to do something else extremely well.

Everything that the baker produces should appeal to the sense of sight, of taste and of smell. He can't build up a very large business unless it does. At the same time if he is to sell the maximum volume he needs to complete the quartette and appeal to the ear as well, when trying to sell it.

There are some stores that find it well to introduce a little music occasionally in order to appeal to the ear. In the New York store of John Wanamaker one will at certain times hear the organ playing. At closing time, instead of sending deep voiced, heavy lunged strong men through the store reminding everyone that the store is closed, and it's time to go home, a bugle is played. An appeal is made to the ear. It is hard to say just how much this has contributed to causing people to flock to that store in numbers great enough to enable it to continue to do business way down at Eighth and Ninth streets while all the other stores have had to move up to 34th or 42nd street.

Four words, four pictures, the appeal to four senses, the number four is a magic sales number. As far as building up a business is concerned it is better than the lucky seven. The men who keep this number four in mind are the ones who make their business prosperous. Four is the number we are most accustomed to. The automobile has four wheels, the house four sides, the room four walls, the horse four legs. Perhaps that is one reason why when the number four is used as much as possible in selling, a person finds it so easy to sell.

—‡—‡—‡—

Figures may not lie, but sometimes a shoe dealer uses them to deceive.

A kind word to the cook helps some.

A floating debt isn't a success as a life preserver.

It's a pity we can't correct our mistakes in advance.

Two heads are better than one—in a cabbage patch.

The more you are promised the less you may expect.

Another Bread Weight Bill

A BILL seeking to establish a standard loaf, presented by the Massachusetts Association of Dealers of Weights and Measures, came up for a hearing at the State House, Boston, on January 31st, before the House Committee on Mercantile Affairs.

The New England Bakers' Association, represented by H. V. Keiser, President, Frank R. Shepard, Chairman of the Legislative Committee, Arthur G. Swanson, Treasurer, Walter H. Dietz, Secretary, and George Ochsner, Retail Vice-President, appeared in opposition to this bill. The Ward Baking Company, C. F. Hathaway & Sons, Friend Brothers, and Boston Bakers Cooperative Society were also represented.

Mr. Shepard outlined very forcibly and clearly the reasons why the present law, permitting wrapped bread of any weight to be baked, should be left unchanged. His arguments were substantiated by Arthur G. Swanson, Worcester Baking Co., H. V. Keiser of Dexter's Bakery, Alton Hathaway of C. F. Hathaway & Sons and John Curtin of the Ward Baking Co. and who made a strong impression on the committee.

Two other Massachusetts bills which the New England Association is preparing to take action on are: one, to prohibit the opening of bakeries on Sunday and, another, to prohibit night work in bakeries between the hours of 8 P. M. and 4 A. M.

The action of the New England Association Legislative Committee in watching all legislation, local, state and national, is but one indication of the value of a strong organization.

The new bill as introduced provides as follows:

Section 1. Except as provided in the following section, bread shall not be sold or offered or exposed for sale otherwise than by weight, and shall be manufactured for sale and sold only in units of one pound, one and one half pounds, or multiples of one pound. When multiple loaves are baked, each unit of the loaf shall conform to the weight required by this section. The weights herein specified shall mean net weights, and shall be determined by the average weight of at least six loaves.

Section 2. Unit weights, as defined in the preceding section, shall not apply to rolls or to fancy bread weighing less than four ounces. If any labels are attached to any loaf or unit they shall not be affixed in any manner or with any gum or paste which is insanitary or unwholesome.

Section 3. The director of standards shall prescribe such rules and regulations as are necessary to enforce the two preceding sections, including reasonable tolerances or variations within which all weights shall be kept. The said director, and under his direction the local sealers of weights and measures, shall cause this section to be enforced.

Pennsylvania Bread and Milk Week

THE Bread and Milk Week, January 16th to 21st, as advertised and observed throughout the State of Pennsylvania attracted great attention and was a decided success. The bakers, through the Pennsylvania Association of the Baking Industry, heartily co-operated with the State dairy interests, and the combination "put over" a campaign which attracted favorable attention throughout the State.

President L. J. Schumaker and Secretary Chas. C. Latus were very active on the part of the bakers, and had active assistance from prominent bakers in different parts of the State, particularly in the Pittsburgh District, where the bakers maintain an active, aggressive organization.

Bread and Milk Week was started off by a luncheon by the Executive Committee of the State Associa-

tion of the Baking Industry at Hotel Penn-Harris, Harrisburg, on January 16th, at which Clifford B. Connelley, Commissioner of the State Department of Labor and Industry, was the guest of honor. Bread and Milk were prominent on the menu. On the same date the Rotary Club of Harrisburg also served Bread and Milk at the weekly luncheon, at which the State Secretary of Agriculture, Fred'k Rasmussen, was the guest of honor. The Mayor of Harrisburg issued an appeal to the public to eat more bread and drink more milk.

On Tuesday the 17th the bakers and milkmen of Harrisburg held a fine parade in which over two hundred decorated wagons and automobiles of the two trades took part. There were three bands of music and T. G. Ashbridge, local manager of The Fleischmann Co., proudly led the procession as marshal.

Other cities in the State featured Bread and Milk Week, Pittsburgh and Reading being leaders in the activity. At Reading a large number of Bread and Milk Week buttons were distributed to the School children, and cash prizes were offered for essays on Bread and Milk, and extensive advertising in the newspapers was a feature.

In Pittsburgh, the bakers and dairymen staged a very active week and used large space in the newspapers, featuring same. C. A. Bolen, of The Fleischmann Co., acted as chairman of the joint committee, while Secretary Latus was secretary. All the prominent bakers of the Pittsburgh District were prominent in the week's activities and cash prizes were provided and distributed to the school children for essays on the value of Bread and Milk. These prizes are to be awarded through the Congress of Women's Clubs of Western Pennsylvania, who took an active interest in the campaign.

In Philadelphia President Schumaker, of the State Association, in conjunction with the city's dairy interests, staged an active advertising campaign, using large space in the newspapers and securing editorial support.

The campaign throughout the state was an entire success and reflects great credit on the men and associations who actively supported and participated in the drive. We reproduce herewith several of the advertisements used in various papers in different cities in support of the movement. The illustrated ads were 8½ by 10 inches in dimensions, while the smaller cards, of which there were different copies, were 4½ by 5¾ inches.

The campaign may be repeated and amplified in future years. We hope so.

—‡—‡—‡—

The purchase of three Tacoma wholesale bakeries and their consolidation into a new combined enterprise for the wholesaling of bread in that city has been announced. The plants involved are the Butter-Nut Bread Company, Tacoma Toast & Hardtack Company, and the Steam Baking Company. The new concern will be known as the Butter-Nut Company. L. D. McMichael is president and general manager of the company.

Bakery Standards in Pennsylvania
By Clifford B. Connelley, Commissioner Pennsylvania Department of Labor and Industry.

A DISTINCTLY progressive movement in the application of safety standards to the bakery industry has been attempted in Pennsylvania through the formation of an Advisory Board on Bakeries, consisting of an even dozen prominent bakers of the State.

The first meeting of this Board was held in Harrisburg, on January 16, 1922, and a resolution was adopted, endorsing the policy of the Department in the selection of this committee to co-operate in matters distinctly pertaining to bakeries.

Several suggestions which have been brought to the attention of the Industrial Board were referred to this body for their deliberation and recommendation back to the Board.

The present code, applying to bakeries in Pennsylvania, is being revised to meet modern conditions. Efforts were made about a year ago to sound out the bakers on the subject of wrapping of all bakery products and a tentative ruling was adopted by the Industrial Board. This was the first definite attempt to revise the code, and considerable sentiment was aroused.

Following out the policy of the Department of Labor and Industry of getting as close to the persons affected by these regulations as it is possible to do, it was thought that an Advisory Board, consisting of members of the baking fraternity would be the agents best suited to shape the proposed regulations.

Other questions than the wrapping of bakery products have since been called to the attention of the Board. The Massachusetts Department of Labor and Industries recently requested information on the action of this State on the wrapping of bread and the use of stale bakery products. From another source came the question of ventilation. It was claimed that the present enforcement of the code with respect to bake shop ventilation, makes it impossible in cellar bakeshops for bread to rise adequately. These matters have been referred to the newly organized Advisory Board. It is believed that in this manner some of the harshness of these regulations can be overcome, and at the same time the good features incorporated into public policy.

The personnel of the bakery board is as follows:

L. J. Schumaker, Philadelphia.
R. K. Stritzinger, Norristown.
G. W. Fisher, Huntingdon.
C. C. Latus, Pittsburgh.
Horace W. Crider, Homestead.
Fred C. Haller, Pittsburgh.
Wm. F. Seaman, Hamburg.
Wm. Freihofer, Philadelphia.
R. M. Allen, New York.
Ernest Orthwein, Philadelphia.
C. J. Layfield, Scranton.
J. Fred Schofer, Reading.

The 1922 Loaf—What It Should Contain

By F. C. Stadelhofer, at the Kansas Convention

THE 1922 loaf should contain the heart and soul of yourself. You must strive for perfection and give your idealism full rein. The best and purest of material should be used and a close study made of them, so as to achieve a perfect and harmonious blending of them to get the best testing and most nutritive loaf that can be produced. Since the human taste is naturally at great variance it would be presumptuous for any individual to claim that his opinion should prevail as a standard for the perfect loaf. Nor is it advisable that you should adhere strictly to a set formula. If you want to, and do change your formula at any time, be sure you are improving it and not cheapening it.

A recent conversation with the chemist of one of the largest bakeries in the East confirmed my established conviction that every baker must eventually establish his own standard. This he can best do when he realizes that he is not only in the business for profit, but that he is the purveyor of the most precious food to mankind, "Bread." Expert opinion cannot, and will never, agree on a standard loaf for a thousand and one reasons.

As I am drifting toward the evening of life I give you my opinion as I see it. I do not claim to be right. My observations are based upon practical experiments and experiences over a period of some thirty-five years. Many false opinions and claims are constantly brought forward, based upon actual experiments of absolutely honest men. A pleasant success creates such enthusiasm that one thinks he surely has a perplexing problem solved, only to find out in a short time that it cannot be applied in a general way. I am speaking from personal experiments, and I know I have lots of partners if they are only willing to acknowledge the fact.

At a recent gathering of expert bakers the question of sponge doughs vs. straight doughs came up. After a lengthy debate the opinion was fairly unanimous that sponge bread was better for certain bread on account of peculiar shape, but that straight dough bread was best on account of superior taste and flavor. At this particular time I believe that I cannot go wrong when I make the statement that there is more milk used in the manufacturing of bread than ever before and, therefore, I will include it in the 1922 loaf. There can be no doubt but what the recognition of milk, as a constituent in bread, by the leaders of the baking industry, is due to the fact that it adds materially to the nutritive value of the finished product. I will now proceed to explain what this loaf should contain, according to my idea. I will express myself by giving a formula:

                200 lbs. flour,   100%
                120 lbs. water,   60
                  4 lbs. yeast,   2

(This dough should mature in three to 3¼ hours with 3 punches.)

                3½ lbs. salt,   1.75%
(First punch, 1¾ hours.)
                3 lbs. sugar,   1.5
(Second punch, ¾ hour.)
                6 lbs. malt,   1%
(Third punch, 15 minutes.)
                6 lbs. sweetened condensed
                        milk,   3%
(To div. in 15-30 minutes.)
                3½ lbs. lard,   1.75%

I sincerely hope that my opinion will be thoroughly picked to pieces during the discussion which is to follow. In the meantime, I believe it will not hurt to discuss this formula myself, and dig into a few whys and wherefores.

WHAT YOUR MATERIALS WILL DO

To turn this formula, or any other formula, into good bread it is absolutely necessary that you know your materials and what they will do, and then build your dough accordingly. By this I mean the manner in which it should be mixed. After this is done the next stage is how it should be fermented and brought to maturity and last, but not least, how it should be handled, proved, baked, cooled, wrapped and sold. I will tell you now how I would go at this proposition if I was running my own bakery.

First, I would use at least 75 per cent. of a high patent flour. Reason, most of these are milled from selected wheat. I would judge this flour not absolutely by the amount of gluten contained nor its absorbing quality, but rather on the quality of the gluten, its flavor and aroma in the finished loaf. On the quality of the flour depends the building of the dough. I find that as the flour varies in strength so must I vary the length of time I run my dough in the mixer. For instance, when I have a high quality of gluten I must run my dough a little longer than otherwise. However, if this is overdone, my dough will become too gummy and tough, and if you take this kind of a dough with the usual young proof you will get plenty of spring all right in the oven, but you will also have a bread which is tough when you chew it. I hope you catch my point. You read a lot about the running time of a dough in high-speed mixers and the different opinions run all the way from 500 to 900 revolutions. I claim that no fast rule can be laid down, but I would be careful not to over-develop a dough.

ABSORPTION

Next comes the question of absorption. The amount of water that can be used depends upon the weight of moisture the crumb of the loaf has 12 hours after it is baked. If you use a 64 per cent. moisture for one flour and 58 per cent. for another, see which bread (the crumb) has the most moisture the next day. As a matter of fact, I am inclined to believe that at the present time the question of absorption is degenerating into a harmful stage. I find that breads made with exceptionally high moisture contents are generally flat tasting. The grain of this kind of bread naturally is also influenced by this. The larger concerns in the country have of late adopted as standards for their bread a measurement of cubic inches per ounce of dough. This ranges from five cubic inches to eight cubic inches. It goes without saying that the grain varies with these figures.

One other point I would make about flour upon its arrival in my bakery, I would determine its moisture contents. If this is high, say 12½ or 13 per cent., I would not let it lay too long, as there is always danger of mould or other bacterial diseases. Then store your flour properly.

As to the use of yeast foods I wish to state my opinion clearly. I believe the maximum, where used, should be .33 1-3 per cent. I do not believe in the cut of any yeast, but in a reduction of temperature and a different system of punching doughs. In other words, arrest the process of fermentation at a much earlier stage. As, for instance, on a four-hour fermentation period, fold up your dough the first time in one hour, the second time in two hours later. The third time half an hour later, then to divider in four hours' total time. The addition of these mineral salts depends entirely upon the water you use. Too little attention has been paid to the water used in baking. So long as the water has been bacteria free we have been satisfied, but every baker should be sure of the mineral matter contained in the water and then govern himself accordingly. He can easily get an analysis from the city chemist or from the waterworks chemist.

Yeast, of course, together with the flour, plays the most important part in the baking process, as by and through it we are enabled to bake light bread. I will not go into fermentation, but will quote what Professor Jago had to say at the Toronto convention:

"In bread making the various ingredients are mixed at the desired temperature, and fermentation proceeds. Not only is gas being generated, but the yeast is also modifying the nature of the gluten, which should become softer and more elastic. Some of the

what is going on in his dough during fermentation is far better able to handle it efficiently, to get the best results and to avoid the things which lower quality."

FERMENTATION

There is, so far as bread is concerned, three distinct fermentations with which we are primarily concerned, alcoholic, acetic, and lactic. The first proceeds best at approximately 78 to 82 degrees F. and is the fermentation desired to produce the best bread. Acetic fermentation progresses best at a higher temperature, and if not checked in time produces sour bread. There is also a fourth fermentation found which is by all means to be avoided, namely, Buturic fermentation. This will set in through an extreme high temperature or is brought about through the development of bacterial diseases in a dough, and will produce rope in bread.

Fermentation is the thing which you must study from all angles to become successful producers of a perfect loaf. There are volumes written constantly by excellent men, and you should eagerly read every word of it. How important the power of this knowledge is I can best illustrate by an incident which happened recently in our New York laboratory. Complaint was made by a large baking concern that the yeast was slow. This same yeast and some of the flour they used was sent for and both tried out. At the same time exactly the same trial was made with the same yeast with a standard flour. The dough made with the standard flour matured in the proper time, but the other dough came slightly behind time. The reason was that a toxic action took place with the latter flour.

As to the use of salt I will only say to use only the purest you can get, and use as much as possible. It is the one agent which accentuates the flavor of your other materials used and really produces the best flavor of them all.

The sugars used in the bread differ in so far that beet and cane sugars must be split up first by the action of yeast while corn sugar and glucose are directly fermentable. Malt belongs to the latter class but has the further advantage that, through its diastatic power some of the starches are converted into dextrose. This sacchrification naturally adds to the sweetness of bread and malt, and also produces a delicious aroma in bread. All these sugars are used in varying quantities

Gentlemen, the scientific efforts which are made in your behalf by the American Institute of Baking and other bodies, among them my own firm, surely deserve consideration, and you must help along of your own accord in order to bring your industry up to the point where she rightly belongs. At present you have again a golden opportunity to bring before the American public the fact that for economical reasons the consumption of bread should be increased. I will quote you a passage of my talk to the Arkhahoma Convention at Hot Springs, Arkansas:

BREAD THE BEST AND CHEAPEST

"Cereals are the cheapest food. Before the war cereals furnished the Americans with approximately one-third of their food at approximately one-tenth of the total cost."

Conditions are not far from that today. When the cost of the diet is to be reduced the intake of the lowest-priced food must be increased. The world over with Caucasian people hard times are characterized by increased consumption of cereals. Three-fourths of the cereal consumption in this country is in the form of wheat bread. For the average American, reduction in cost of the diet without reduction in quality is to be attained through increased consumption of bread. For the average American increasing the consumption of cereals means eating another slice of bread with each meal.

In spite of all the hullabaloo of the press who will deny the fact that bread is still not only the cheapest but also the most nutritive food.

Therefore, let us all get together, improve the 1922 loaf, then push it through collective and individual advertising, and let us enjoy the ensuing prosperity to which you are entitled.

—‡—‡—‡—

Activity of the Allied Trades

THE Allied Trades of the Baking Industry, through President Wm. Evans and Secretary C. H. Van Cleef, in January sent out letters of greetings to all bakers holding membership in the various organizations of bakers. This was accompanied by a copy of the constitution and membership roll of the Allied Trades, which shows the firm connections of the different members. The letter adds:

"These men, at this date, are all in good standing and you will find in this booklet, Code of Ethics, which each one of them has obligated himself to live up to in the strictest terms. We consider this Code of so much importance that we are bringing it to the attention of yourself and all other bakers and requesting you to ascertain whether or not the supply men from whom you purchase your goods have adopted and are living up to this Code, as the action of every man reflects on the entire Association.

"We all want to work for the uplifting and bettering of the baking industry, and the supply man who is a member of the Allied Trades is going to do his full share in this great work.

"As evidence of the work being accomplished, we direct attention to the action of Vice-President, John Burns, at the Indiana Convention. He inaugurated closer working arrangements between the Indiana Bakers' Association, and the Allied Trades by having a State Committee appointed consisting of a chairman, who, in this case happens to be W. H. Mohler, past President of the Indiana Bakers' Association. Mohler becomes chairman of this State Committee and there are also five supply men on Mohler's Committee, consisting of a Captain for Indiana, C. P. Taylor, of Indianapolis; Field Captain for Northern Indiana, H. B. Staver, of Ft. Wayne; Field Captain for Central Indiana, John Clark, of Indianapolis; Field Captain for Southern Indiana, Fred Lacy, Terre Haute, and Field Captain for Indianapolis, R. T. Kelly, of Indianapolis.

These men work under the direction of their chairman, reporting to him any matters the bakers wish taken up and handled by the Allied Trades. Chairman Mohler, in turn, works in close connection with C. R. Russ, who is Zone Captain for Indiana of our organization.

"We are going to try to put this plan in effect in each State so as to bring about a closer working arrangement between the bakers and the Allied Trades. President Evans has not completed the appointment of Zone Captains as yet, although he has officially appointed Fred. D. Pfening, of Columbus, Ohio, Zone Captain for Ohio; R. E. Weymuth, of Chicago, Zone Captain for Illinois; D. G. Thompson, of Burlington, Iowa, Zone Captain for Iowa; L. F. Kutler, of Milwaukee, Zone Captain for Wisconsin; F. L. Johnston, of Kansas City, Zone Captain for western Missouri, and C. R. Russ, of Indianapolis, Zone Captain for Indiana. Charles Bobst, of Brooklyn, was appointed Zone Captain at large. Other appointments will be announced as soon as made.

—‡—‡—‡—

Bakers of Fayette county, Pennsylvania, held an interesting meeting on January 31st, at which Horace W. Crider, of Homestead, president of the Western Pennsylvania Bakers' Association, was the principal speaker. Mr. Crider pointed out the benefits of organized effort in the baking trade and urged the members of the craft in that county to take steps to effect an organization for their mutual welfare. It is understood that as a result of the discussion that marked the three and a half hour session, that the bakers of Fayette county will be called together within a short time at which a permanent organization will be effected. C. C. Latus, of Pittsburgh, secretary of the Pennsylvania and Western Pennsylvania Bakers' Association, also attended the meeting.

New England Association Forging Ahead

DURING the past month a committee consisting of C. O. Swanson, Massachusetts Baking Co., Hartford, Conn.; H. V. Keiser, Dexter's Bakery, Springfield, Mass.; O. F. Parker of the Parker-Buckey Co., New Britain, Conn.; and W. H. Dietz of Dietz Bakery, Springfield, Mass.,. toured the state in the interests of the Legislative Committee of Connecticut Bakers and the newly formed New England Bakers' Association.

All bakers present at the meeting gladly pledged their financial support to the Legislative Committee and in each place committees were appointed to solicit all bakers in the territory who were not present, in order that every baker in the state will have an opportunity to support a committee which has proven of such value.

At the meeting at the Hotel Stratfield, Bridgeport, on the afternoon of the 17th the association was not organized, but those present unanimously expressed the sentiment to affiliate with the New England Bakers' Association as soon as the organization could be completed.

At the meeting at the Fleischmann Company's office on the evening of the 17th, the bakers of New Haven and Middlesex Counties unanimously voted to become affiliated with the New England Bakers' Association and elected the following officers: President, L. L. Gilbert, New England Bakery Co., New Haven; Vice-President, C. F. Mory, Mory's Bakery, New Haven; Treasurer, Oscar E. Koehler, Lamond's Home Bakery, New Haven; Secretary, Julius F. Hohl, Hohl's Bakery, New Haven.

The next meeting was held at the Hotel Elton, Waterbury, on the afternoon of the 18th, and there, also, the bakers expressed the desire to join hands with the New England Bakers' Association, electing officers as follows: President, Adolph Reymond, Reymond Bros. Bakery, Waterbury; Vice-President, Otto Pullig, Pullig's Bakery, Torrington; Treasurer, J. G. Troemel, Troemel's Bakery, Torrington; Secretary, F. L. French, Dexter Baking Co., Waterbury.

On Wednesday evening the meeting was held at the Fleischmann Company's office in Hartford and here, too, the bakers expressed a keen desire to have a strong local organization affiliated with the New England Bakers' Association. The following officers were elected: President, O. F. Parker, Parker-Buckey Co., New Britain; Vice-President, G. E. Beroth, Beroth's Bakery, Hartford; Treasurer, John Wittig, Kolb's Bakery, Hartford; Secretary, E. H. Setterlund, Massachusetts Baking Co., Hartford.

After sliding over the ice-bound roads of Connecticut the committee reached New London on Thursday afternoon, where at the meeting in the Crocker House, the bakers of New London County formed an association to become affiliated with the New England Bakers' Association. The following officers were elected: President, Joseph Byers, Byers Brothers, Incorporated, New London; Vice-President, M. A. Barr, Community Bake Shoppe, Norwich; Treasurer, J. C. Ernst, Ernst Bakery, New London; Secretary, A. E. Paquette, Paquette and LeBlanc, New London.

In the evening of that day the committee reached the journey's end, arriving at the Hooker House, Willimantic, where there, also, the bakers were keen for an organization, and after electing officers, unanimously voted to become affiliated with the New England Bakers' Association. The officers elected are: President, William E. Gilman, Blanchette & Gilman, Willimantic; Vice-President, Eugene J. Lescoe, Lescoe's Bakery, Willimantic; Treasurer and Secretary, R. G. Dion, Dion's Bakery, Willimantic.

In each case the above presidents and vice-presidents are wholesale and retail bakers respectively and automatically become the wholesale and retail governors of the New England Bakers' Association for their respective districts.

—‡—‡—‡—

Western Pennsylvania Bakers Meet

AT the annual meeting of the Western Pennsylvania Bakers' Association the following officers were re-elected for the ensuing year: President, Horace W. Crider; vice-president, Ernest R. Braun; treasurer, S. S. Watters, and C. C. Latus, secretary. This marks the eighth term that Mr. Crider has been unanimously chosen as president. He is president and manager of the Homestead Baking Company and is widely known throughout the country in the baking and allied trades.

C. A. Bolen, who since 1884 has been connected with the Fleischmann Company, at whose offices the meeting was held, told of his retirement from active service as district manager, a post he held since 1905. He is now relieved from active duty and placed on the pension roll of the company. Mr. Bolen is well known throughout the state and built up a large and influential business. His successor will be H. C. Elste, who has been connected with the Fleischmann Company for the past thirty years.

S. S. Watters, secretary of the Liberty Baking Company, and a member of the board of governors of the American Bakers' Association, told of the drive for new members and dwelt upon the benefit to be derived from affiliation with the organization by bakers.

President Crider re-appointed the executive committee as follows: E. J. Burry, John Ertl, W. N. Sherman, T. H. Doehla and Chris Stoecklein.

—‡—‡—‡—

Early this month public announcement was made of the merger of the Campbell Baking Company, with plants at Kansas City and nearly a dozen other middle western cities, and Ward & Ward, of Buffalo, New York. Wm M. Campbell will be president of the new concern, the United Bakeries Corporation.

Bakery Accounting—Its Value

Address by D. P. Chindblom at Ohio State Convention.

THE first sure step to business failure is the absence of any reasonably adequate and correct system of accounting. It is by proper accounting that the net result of the operation of a business is known, and without such information there is no way of determining whether or not a business has been successfully conducted. On the other hand, detrimental results from errors of judgment and mistaken policies may be greatly minimized and changes made, before these seriously affect a business, provided correct information is promptly available—in fact—proper accounting furnishes information, which carefully analyzed and considered, will enable the responsible head of a business to avoid many of the mistakes of the misinformed or uninformed.

I have, therefore, made these general comments by way of introduction, not especially to emphasize a need for accounting as a record of what has transpired, but to urge the keeping of this information in such a way that it may be readily interpreted and understood for future guidance.

I wish to say that it is not the receipts or expenditures of a business which in, and of, themselves are important, but the balance between them. Now, that balance is sufficient or insufficient, a profit or a loss, in the measure that we have adequate information as to the factors which cause these receipts or expenditures to be respectively low or high, and then are able to control them.

If a man doesn't know when a selling price is too low, and get down to facts as to the motive back of that price, he may be lead into ruinous competition. Proper accounting will teach a man to distinguish between legitimate price reductions and irresponsible price cutting.

I desire, at this time, however, more particularly to deal with expenditures, which means costs. I repeat that the costs, themselves, are not the important thing for intelligent management to consider. It is rather the factors responsible for these costs and their control that should be thoroughly considered.

To deal with costs in terms of percentage of selling price may be possible in the absence of weight regulations, but even then variations in cost necessarily mean variations in weight and, too often, in quality. Certainly, it means fitting your product to your selling price instead of fitting your price to a uniform quality product, and in any event it is more of an expedient than anything else. Whatever a man's price, or weight, or quality is, it is perfectly obvious that accurate knowledge demands the considering of definite, actual costs.

This, to my mind, has a bearing upon one of the important questions of the day in this industry. Whether or not we believe that the time has come for differences in the price of bread based on quality—that is—whether the consumer can be generally sold on the idea of grades of bread, the fact remains that as never before the legitimate baker has to get his business and his price on the basis of quality competition.

Is it then, I ask, sufficient to simply know that the cost of materials is too high and to instruct the shop to revise the formula accordingly, or is there not a need for knowing why this cost is high and reducing the same by increased efficiency and the elimination of controllable losses? Every time the cost of materials is reduced by efficiency in the handling of these materials, the baker has performed a service, not only for his consumer, but for himself in protecting the quality of his product and, therefore, his competitive standing in the market and his bid for a greater volume of business.

It would surprise many a baker to find the losses which he can control that are responsible for his inability to maintain his quality under the price conditions in his community. Any man who knows anything of bakery costs knows that a five-cent quality loaf is out of the question today as a business proposition between baker and consumer, but many bakers who know this are working as much in the dark in meeting the difficult problem of maintaining quality under proper price conditions, as some of these irresponsible fellows, who cut price regardless of cost or quality.

Here are two bakers buying flour with the same keenness and exercise of good business judgment, but one has heavy, invisible losses as between purchase weights and mixer weights. He fails to get the greatest efficiency, both in the use of his flour and in the quality of his product by reason of low absorption. Unsatisfactory and improper humidity control, or none at all, adds to his costs account of evaporation losses. With increased costs and no knowledge of the extent to which these factors are responsible, what can he do but blindly revise his operations and still further lower his efficiency, measured in comparison to his better informed competitor, both as to quality and costs.

The same principle applies to labor and other shop costs. If a man knows nothing of the efficiency of his employees and their production per hour, and measures everything in total costs, without knowledge of controllable factors, what can he do but assume to lower wages and break down the morale of his organization, whereas proper information and control would show him how to reduce his force and eliminate the slackers to get the necessary efficiency, continuing to reward those whose work is efficient and profitable. On the other hand, when wage readjustments are necessary, he will be able to act intelligently in the best interests of himself and his employees.

It would surprise many to know the cost of certain policies, accepted and countenanced in order to foster and preserve volume of business. Some of these policies may be justified, even without profit, but, at least, the progressive baker should know what they cost and measure their value, accordingly—in other words—what I wish to emphasize, without going into detail, is the principle that costs of material and all other costs should, and must, be reduced, not simply on the basis of arbitrary cuts, but that the baker owes it to his business, to the preservation of his quality and the development of satisfaction on the part of consumers, as well as maintaining the morale of his organization, to know where the leaks are and stop them first. Then the issue is squarely presented and it becomes a question of either meeting the competition of cheap bread, with a cheap product, efficiently made within the limits of its price, based on actual costs; or making a high-grade loaf, in competition with the regular trade, also, efficiently made and based on actual costs.

Personally, I am convinced that in the long run a stable and profitable business can be maintained on quality goods at a fair price. It may be that bakers' bread, on the average, although it has been good, must be even better, and there will probably always be some competition of the ruinous kind which is now being experienced in the trade. It is more than probable, however, that out of the present situation the public may become increasingly solid on the idea that there is a real difference in breads.

In concluding these remarks, I cannot refrain from emphasizing the relationship which exists between the manufacture of a quality product and efficiency in production, through proper attention to controllable factors as a direct cause for high or low costs.

—‡—‡—‡—

On January 24th, the Executive Committee of the Southwestern Association of the Baking Industry held a meeting at Savannah, Georgia, to arrange for the coming convention of the Association in that city. There was a full attendance of members and President J. H. Quint presided. April 17th, 18th and 19th were chosen as the dates for the meeting and the De Soto Hotel will be headquarters. The following were chosen as chairmen of the various committees: Gordon Smith, Program; Peter Nugent, Local Entertainment; W. J. Wood, Local Publicity; O. L. Cook and C. H. Van Cleef, Allied Trades Day; and C. R. Roberts, Membership Campaign. The Southern Association always stages a good convention and a large attendance is expected this year.

Baking Technology

The New Monthly Bulletin of the American Institute of Baking, and its Editor.

FOR their new periodical which is meant to interpret to the baking industry the work of the scientific laboratories of the American Institute of Baking, the American Bakers' Association secured the services, as editor, of I. K. Russell, a New York newspaper man and magazine writer.

I. K. RUSSELL

Mr. Russell, as food editor of the New York *Evening Mail*, handled many of the problems of public contacts with the baking industry.

Women constantly wrote in to him to ask if bakers' bread was made under sanitary conditions, and if it was made with reliable ingredients. The result was a series of articles which set forth the industry to the public in a way to win the respect of many of the leaders in New York of the industry.

Mr. Russell also gained a respect for the modern bakery and its products which made him glad later to become an advocate of baked goods and of the baker, in his public relations.

"All modern civilization," he stated on taking over his new tasks, "is a story of modern machines and the release from drudgery that modern machines have given one section after another of our modern people.

"In old Egypt all but the king and his immediate family of military leaders were slaves. If they wanted a rock from the mountains for an obelisk the king's military chief marshalled 4,000 slaves and led them to the quarries. There with fires and water they cracked open rocks and with sheer muscle power dragged the rocks back to the sacred cities such as Karnak.

"Machines saved man from the drudgery of transportation of materials. In the fields they saved man from the hand reaper and the cradle and the foot-power thresher. In the home the water faucet saved man from hauling water to the kitchen, while the gas range took from his back the drudgery of hauling wood and coal.

"Mother was left in the kitchen as the last person to whom the blessing of modern machines was destined to bring relief. Now that the machine era has come in baking it is foolish to cry it down, futile to roil one's spirit against it, and folly to hope that the kitchen bakery with its back-breaking work for mother will ever come back.

"The pathway for the baker is towards ideal bread ingredients to give a balanced, healthful loaf. And towards sanitary conditions that no mother can find fault with. It is because the American Bakers' Association stands for these ideals and moves to carry the industry along the pathway of its manifest destiny that I am glad and proud to be one of it."

Mr. Russell has been a New York newspaper writer since 1909, and has worked as a political and general reporter successively on the New York *Evening Sun*, the *Times*, and the *Evening Mail*. On the latter paper he took hold of the food problems of New York under Dr. H. E. Barnard, who was its food specialist.

A contact then made with Dr. Barnard has been renewed in their association together in the American Bakers' Association. Mr. Russell was born at Salt Lake City, Utah, in 1879. He enlisted in 1898 as one of the first body of troops to go to the Philippines to support Admiral Dewey. He was present as a member of the First Utah Artillery at the assault on Manila City, August 13, 1898, in an action in which the Tenth Pennsylvania regiment took a conspicuous and gallant part. The Utah artillery supported the Pennsylvania troops' advance and both units became such fast friends that later in Manila they tendered each other complimentary dinners.

On returning from the Philippines in 1900, Mr. Russell entered Stanford University, specializing in biology. He graduated with the firm friendship of David Starr Jordan, the university's president, in 1904. He then entered the newspaper field in Salt Lake City and worked there as a "cub" until he moved on to New York in 1909.

During the war he served the National War Labor Board as a field representative in charge of many acute industrial disputes. Later, upon the occasion of the armistice being signed, he was transferred to the Board of Railroad Wages for which he conducted many industrial inquiries. They worked out ways towards peace and adjustment instead of strikes, which had been threatened in many cases.

At the close of the war era Mr. Russell resumed his newspaper work on the *Evening Mail* and again specialized in food problems, as he considered them the most important problems before the people to-day.

—‡—‡—‡—

THE ninth annual convention of the executives and sales representatives of the Read Machinery Company was held at the home office in York, Pa., during the week of January 1, 1922, and salesmen from all over the United States, one from Paris, France, and one from Toronto, Canada, attended the sessions. The keynote of the convention was the same as former years, "Better Service to the Baker."

An extensive program had been prepared for the instruction and entertainment of the visiting salesmen, and it was carried through successfully and with profit to all. There were a number of sales talks and demonstrations by company executives, including O. R. Read, sales manager; L. A. Hirshon, assistant sales manager, and P. D. Hendrickson, advertising manager. There were several luncheons and a banquet at the Lafayette Club, with President H. Read as the toastmaster.

The men were taken in motors to Glen Rock, Pa., where the new plant, replacing the one recently destroyed by fire, was inspected. Here they were shown the new equipment and the latest machinery designed by the company. The convention was in every way a success.

—‡—‡—‡—

Cake Course at Siebel Tech

THE Special Two Weeks Class in High Grade Cake and Pastry Baking, which started on January 9th, 1922, at the Siebel Institute of Technology proved to be another record class, men coming from all over the United States and Canada, nearly twenty states being represented.

The class roster is as follows: Philip J. Baur, Philadelphia; W. F. Berry, Akron, Ohio; Olaf J. Breivold, Rochester, Minn.; Harry H. Carder, Shinnston, W. Va.; Chas. F. Climie, Alpena, Mich.; D. O. Crites, Huntington, Ind.; Clyde W. Grater, Pittsburgh; Gustave A. Huard, Detroit; Theodore Kleeburg, E. St. Louis, Ill.; Geo. A Lutz, Pittsburg; O. W. McAvoy, Norfolk, Nebr.; R. G. McEwan, Fernie, B. C., Can.; D. A. Nessmore, Peru, Ind.; H. V. Moore, Baker, Oreg.; Leland J. Mott, Auburn, N. Y.; Paul Ohlers, Darby, Pa.; Joseph F. Olson, Milwaukee; Fred C. Powell, Belding, Mich.; H. L. Reinecke, Chicago; Alwin Lorenzel Renouard, Chicago; Wm. Schneider, E. Cleveland; A. F. Schwertman, Davenport, Iowa; F. G. Sims, Nashville, Tenn.; Carl H. Smith, French Lick, Ind.; R. L. Tulley, Kirksville, Mo.; Otto Wallner, New Bedford, Mass.; August Ziegler, Pittsburgh, Pa.

Quite a number of over-enrollments were received and had to be applied for the next Special Two Weeks Cake Course which is scheduled at Siebel Tech. for Monday, February 20th, 1922, and bakers interested in this course should write at once to the Registrar, Siebel Institute of Technology, 900 Montana Street, Chicago, Illinois.

—‡—‡—‡—

D. P. Chindblom, who since his resignation as secretary of the American Bakers' Association has been connected in an executive capacity with the W. E. Long Company, Chicago, was elected as vice-president of this company at the recent meeting of its stockholders and directors. Mr. Chindblom has a wide acquaintance with bakers and their problems and is a valuable member of the W. E. Long organization.

—‡—‡—‡—

John Brinkman of Benwood, W. Va., has bought the bakery establishment of John Kratz, Sixth & Marshall Sts., McMechen, W. Va.

T. Melvin Higgs and Charles A. Moore have purchased the William Offterdinger Bakery on Purdy Ave., Moundsville, W. Va.

The Washington Baking Company, Milwaukee, Wis., opened its third retail bakery recently at 1321 Wells St. This company recently established a retail bakery at 38 State St., Wauwatosa. The main bakery, with a retail store is located at 107 16th St., Milwaukee.

Small Fancy Cakes for Good Trade

WE give herewith a line of goods for fine trade which should be of interest to our readers. Text and photographs should be sufficient guides for any baker of ordinary skill and perseverance. They will be found to be an attractive addition to the usual assortment of the fancy baker.

PETITS FOURS GLACES

The variety in this class is optional, but should be made as varied as possible. The foundation for all should be as follows: 2 pounds butter, 2 pounds sugar, 20 eggs, 2 pounds flour. The usual method of creaming,

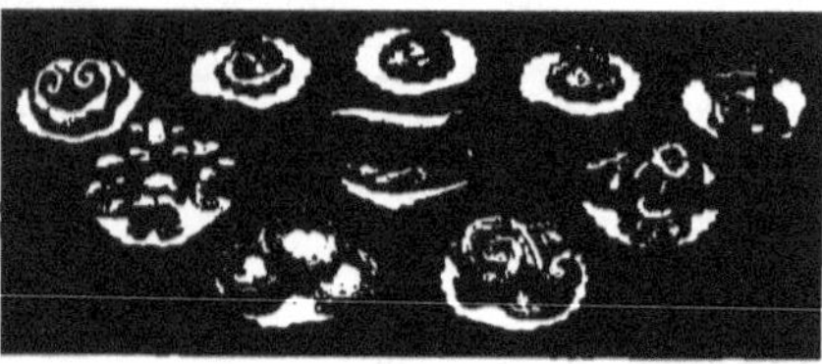

No. 3

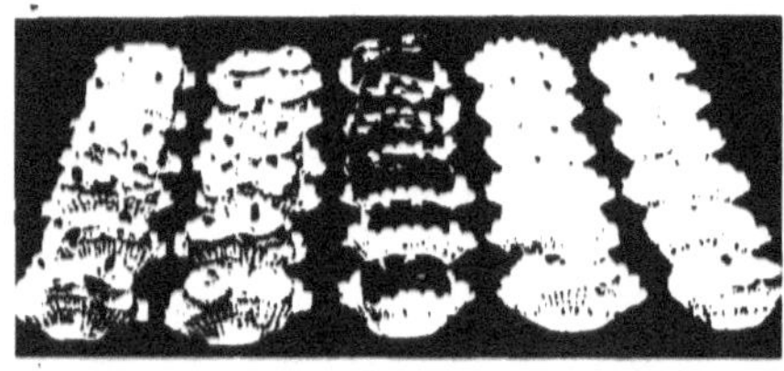

No. 1

lay a sheet of paper on the baking sheet and spread evenly over, bake in a moderate oven. When quite cold cut out the designs exact size. Cover the pieces with apricot puree, and pipe on the top to suit the shape with a very fine star tube, a mixture made of ½ pound ground almonds, moistened with brandy, and 1 pound icing sugar, and when well mixed divide the sugar into as many portions as you wish, and flavor them according to the colors as follows: White maraschino; pink, strawberry or rose; yellow, primrose; green, lilac essence; coffee with essence of coffee, chocolate with melted chocolate, then dip in fondant

the same colors flavored with the same essences, and slightly decorate with fondant to suit the taste. On the top of white place a silver dragee, on the pink a little chopped pistachio, on the lilac a crystallized lilac or small piece of violet, then place in petit four cases. (See Photo No. 1.)

FANCY DROPS

1 pound butter, 1 pound sugar, 1½ pounds flour, 8 eggs beaten up in a bowl as an ordinary cake, then put them in a large bag with a plain round tube, put them on tins, place a strip of angelica on top, or add a few currants or sprinkle cocoanut over and

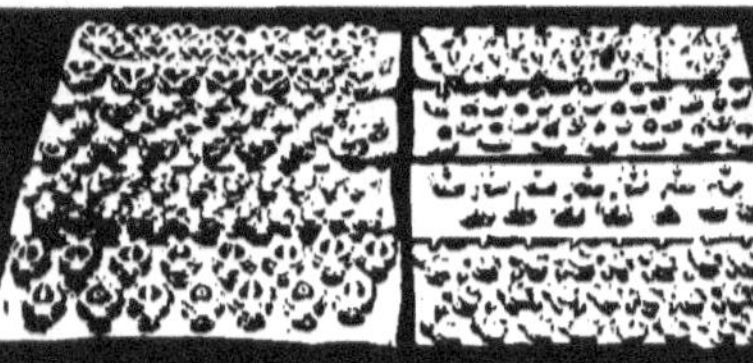

No. 4

bake to a nice brown in a warm oven, and watch very carefully while baking. (See Photo No. 2.)

STRAUSS BISCUITS

Are made from the same foundation. Cut out with a star-shaped cutter, then carefully wash with egg and sprinkle a mixture of chopped almond paste and sugar, place upon clean sheets and bake in a warm oven. (See Photo No. 2.)

FANCY ROUTS

Of which we give a good variety in Photo No. 3, are made as follows: ½ pound pulverized sugar, ½ pound icing sugar, 1 pound ground almonds, mixed into a stiff paste with yolks of eggs and a little orange-flower water. These are made in numerous

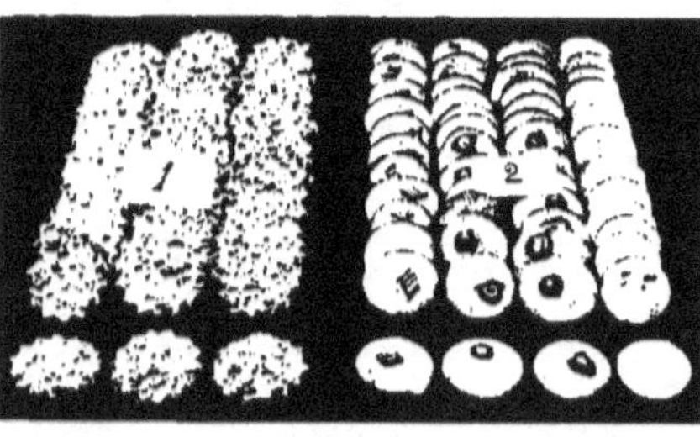

No. 2

designs, a good variety of which is given, and are decorated to taste with royal icing, pistachio, etc.

MACAROON CONFECTS

A difficult biscuit to produce satisfactorily, but notwithstanding is well worth the trouble of trying. Practice and perseverance is always necessary to produce this, which is one of the most attractive dishes of small biscuits. 1 pound ground almonds, 1½ pounds sugar, made into a paste rather stiffer than ordinary macaroon, with whites of eggs. Lay out in various designs upon small sheets of paper in shapes of, say, hearts, harps, lyres, round, triangle, and square. We give a good variety, as will be seen from the photo. The top should be slightly dusted with crystallized sugar before baking; when cold, fondant of two or three different colors should be run across the top, then piped neatly with a very fine round tube. (See Photo No. 4.)

WALNUT MACAROONS

These are made as follows: ½ pound almonds, ½ pound Barcelona walnuts, 2 pounds pulverized sugar. First place your walnuts on a baking sheet in the oven for a few minutes, take them out and rub them between your hands to get the husk off, then grind or thoroughly pound them with the almonds and sugar, using 1 or 2 whites of eggs to make it into a stiff paste; lay out on paper wafer tins, small oval shape, with a bag and tube, sprinkle crystallized sugar over the top, and bake in a slow oven; when cool, sandwich with apricot puree. (See Photo No. 5.)

CHAMPAGNE BISCUITS

½ pound butter, ½ pound sugar, 5 eggs, 1 pound 1 ounce flour, a few caraway seeds. The method for this biscuit is the ordinary creaming of butter, sugar

No. 5

and eggs. When thoroughly mixed they are placed in a bag and run out with a small round tube and are baked in a tin specially made for this purpose, the

1 pound ground almonds, 1½ pounds pulverized sugar, 8 to 10 whites. Put the almonds and sugar with the whites in a clean bowl, beat up well, drop on to wafer paper placed on a baking sheet, with a bag;

No. 6

then place two or three strips of almonds on the top, slightly dust with pulverized sugar, and bake in a cool oven. In order to insure success, it is always advisable to try this mixture before baking. If it is too tight, and does not expand sufficiently, add a little more white of egg, or if too slack, then add a little more almonds, and sugar.

DUTCH MACAROONS

2½ pounds ground almonds, 5 pounds pulverized sugar, 30 whites of eggs. Beat all well together in a clean bowl, lay out on a papered baking sheet with a bag and small tube, about the size of a half-dollar, place in rack or drying cupboard, not too hot, until the next morning, then with a needle draw a line across the macaroon, and bake in a hot oven. When cold, damp the paper, and fasten two together with apricot puree.

ROSE MACAROONS

These are made from the mixture given above, colored pink and flavored with rose essence, and then placed upon wafer paper on tins, slightly sprinkle with coarse sugar slightly crushed. Bake in a slow oven. Cherry macaroons would come from the same mixture, but flavored with cherry and with half a cherry placed on top.

PARISIAN ROUTS

Another variety is made of 1 pound of pulverized sugar, 1 pound ground almonds, rubbed up on the board with about 4 whites, put in a bag, with a star pipe, then pipe in fancy designs and decorate with half almonds, cherries and angelica, set aside until the next day, then bake in a

Dr. Barnard to the Allied Trades

IN a general letter to the members of the Allied Trades, Dr. Harry E. Barnard, manager of the American Bakers' Association, outlined today the new plan of co-operation between the bakers and their friends, to the end that the best work can be done by both for their mutual welfare. The letter follows:

Dear Allied Trades Member:

You have been asking, and properly enough, too, how you could sell the American Bakers' Association when you didn't know very well just what it was. You wanted some samples to show. You wanted conclusive arguments with which to break down the indifference of the self-centered baker who couldn't see how he could get value received for his "dollar a week an oven."

So here is an advance consignment of solid facts, hard boiled reasons why membership in the American Bakers' Association is going to pay, actually *pay* far more than it costs.

Here is the first number of *Baking Technology*. Read it from front to back. Tear out the center pages and use them as examples of how we are helping the baker fight his battles with five-cent bread propaganda.

Then read the fine story Professor Jago writes of the Institute. *That* is something to talk about. And then spread the glad tidings to every baker that 'long about apple blossom time our school for bakers will be going full blast—the best school in the world for training the boys who will use your goods in years to come.

boy who needs our kind of training to enter him at once.

And then tell them that our service laboratories are running overtime analyzing flours, shortenings, milks, all sorts of bread materials, at cost to bakers, at a profit to the Association to non-members.

Then you can speak of the fights we are making for the baker—fights against exorbitant tariffs on frozen eggs, nuts, raisins; fights against excessive freight and express rates; fights against unfair trade practices. We have our fighting togs on now—it should be a joy for every baker to help us win their battles.

And that is but half the story. You know of our Code of Ethics. It is our challenge to unfair, short-visioned business practices, the selfish methods of men who would live at the expense of their fellows.

We enclose an application blank which contains the code of ethics. Read it carefully. It is a good code, isn't it? We tried to make it as strong as your own.

And then read the sanitary code. Is there a single line in that code of cleanliness and decency that your customers will not subscribe to? I think not. Don't lay the blank aside, put it in your pocket and in a day or so send it in to me with a baker's signature on the dotted line. That will be real Allied Trades Service.

Put *From Beer to Bread* in your grip. Look at the pictures once in a while. Fasten in your mind the fact that that splendid building is full of men working for your industry, for your boss, for you. And it is your home, too, as a member of the Allied Trades of the Baking Industry. What else does "allied" mean?

hundred million hungry people are getting better through your efforts—and ours.

Bread, the best food for all mankind. Let's make that challenge good. And if you want to know more of our work; if you want special answers to particular questions, just write us. We'll try to do the rest.

I told you once that we looked to the men of the allied trade "to carry the message to Garcia." I meant it when I said it. I mean it now.

Yours for more and better bread,
(Signed) H. E. BARNARD,
Business Manager and Secretary
The American Bakers' Association.

—‡—‡—‡—

Ohio Convention

THE Ohio Association of the Baking Industry held a very successful convention at Columbus on January 17th and 18th, one of the best ever held in that state, both in point of attendance and in interest manifested by those present. During the past year this Association has had a phenomenal growth, from 31 to 355, owing, mainly, to the active personal work of the new field manager, H. N. Dixon.

President A. G. Beck called the meeting to order, and after a verbal report of the association's activities during the past year, Secretary H. B. Apple and Treasurer H. B. Miller presented their reports, all of which were interesting and instructive, particularly as Ohio now has a standard bread weight law.

The first formal address was on "The Service Ideal in Business," by Galen Starr Ross, Business Manager of the Business Service Club, Columbus. This was a very fine and inspiring address on business ideals and was well worth while. This was followed by a fine talk on "Why Bakers Should Advertise," by J. Adam Payne, of the Fleischmann Company. D. P. Chindblom, of the W. E. Long Co., Chicago, then read a very fine paper on "Bakery Accounting," which appears on another page of this issue of THE NATIONAL BAKER, and should be closely read by every progressive baker. Secretary John M. Hartley, of the Retail Bakers' Association of America, then gave one of his thoughtful and helpful talks.

Field Manager Dixon then presented the report of his work during the past year, which excited unusual interest on account of the practical results accomplished. In a period of only thirty-two weeks he had built up the membership from 31 members in good standing to a total of 350, the dues being on a basis of ten dollars per oven. During this time, Manager Dixon called on 621 bakers in 126 towns. As there are about 600 other towns in the State of Ohio for Mr. Dixon to visit, the scope and importance of his work may readily be imagined.

Mr. Dixon expressed the opinion that there must be something doing besides talk, in the state and local organizations, if the interest and membership is maintained; otherwise, the interest will die out and individual members get tired of doing all the work and being the whole thing. He stated, further, that the number in the organization determines the interest and makes the work easier. He also pointed out the importance of co-operation with the field man by the leading bakers of different communities.

John W. McClinton, of the American Bakers' Association, then addressed the meeting, sketching a few of the more important activities of the major organization and brought greetings from Dr. H. E. Barnard.

At the second day's session there was considerable discussion on the new bread law, which was explained by L. J. Taber, State Secretary of Agriculture, and his assistant, R. M. Black. Many questions were asked these two officials and the discussion became general. One point, apparently in doubt, was settled by Mr. Taber. It was that a twin or split loaf was covered by the name "multiple loaf," and that each half must weigh at least one pound. Mr. Taber expressed a desire to work with the baker in the enforcement of the law, and promised co-operation and not persecution in the enforcement of the provisions of the Act. All bakers in the State of Ohio are required to register.

The election for officers resulted as follows: President, E. D. Kaulbach, of the Bixler Baking Co., Youngstown; Vice-President, N. O. Basford, Marion; Secretary, Wm. H. Schaefer, Cincinnati; Treasurer, Harry M. Miller, Springfield; Executive Committee, Ben S. Weil, Cincinnati, and J. C. Root, Delaware.

—‡—‡—‡—

Rose-colored Spectacles

MANY a salesman saw his market through rose-colored glasses in the first riotous year after the Treaty of Versailles.

It made a pretty and comforting picture. Buyers clamoring for his goods, two sales where one ordinarily grew. What need for sales arguments? What necessity to spend money on advertising?

Good salesmen have long since discarded their rosy spectacles. The pretty picture has proved to be only a mirage. They see their markets in the cold but honest light of reality. Salesmanship is back in the saddle.

The leaders in all lines are getting their names and their products back into the magazines and newspapers. But gone is the short hour of the flowery, generalizing advertisement. Real facts and sound ideas—selling arguments—are the advertising order of the day.

Slowly but surely the man on the road is relearning a lesson he had almost forgotten—not to be discouraged by a buyer's first "No." And in this, advertising is one of the ways the manufacturer and the sales manager are driving the lesson home.

SUPERIOR
Double Chamber Gas Oven

THIS Oven can be operated practically as cheap as a coal or coke Oven, and is more simple to operate. All you have to do is to turn on the gas—no dirt, ashes, or coal pile. With this Oven you have a positive guarantee against fuel shortage.

In the top of the Oven there is a flue running completely around the Oven. This flue gives just enough draft to properly circulate the heat at all times.

Each baking chamber is equipped with two tile hearths and side shields, also a heavy tile bed shelf below the first baking shelf, which insures an even baking temperature on both shelves. Over the burners in the base of the Oven are heavy tile baffle

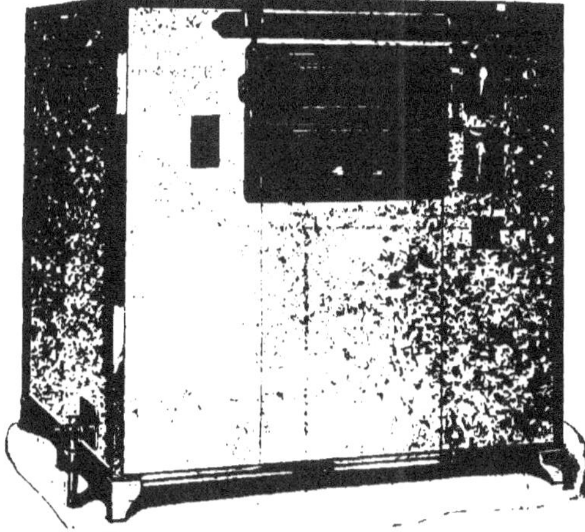

plates which, when once hot, give off a solid baking heat. It requires about forty-five minutes to get the Oven to a baking heat from the cold Oven, but you can bake for an hour, to an hour and a half, after the gas is turned off.

The charging doors in front are equipped with heavy polished re-inforced glass, which makes it unnecessary to open the door to ascertain the condition of the product in the Oven. This is a very important feature, as the baker can see his goods in the Oven from any part of the bakery without going to the Oven and opening the door. **Write or inquire for further information.**

Made in five sizes to meet your requirements.

SUPERIOR OVEN CO.

LEITER BLDG.

CHICAGO, ILL.

Western Office		Eastern Office
SOUTHERN CALIF. SUPPLY CO.		137 HUDSON ST.
Los Angeles, Calif.		New York

The Baker's Score Card

THE Sanitary Code of the American Baking Association has struck a real response in the hearts of government officials charged with the duty of accomplishing baking sanitation.

It has been welcomed as a common standard towards which all health officers in all communities can work.

Similarly the Ideal Score Card for a bakery has also sprung into existence. It was written by Dr. Samuel C. Prescott, head of the Department of Biology and Public Health of the Massachusetts Institute of Technology, and was immediately adopted by the State of Louisiana as the Louisiana official bakery score card.

This adoption followed a visit by Oscar Dowling, president of the State Board of Health of Louisiana, to the new home of the American Bakers' Association at 1135 Fullerton avenue, Chicago.

Dr. Dowling saw the score card as printed in Volume I, No. 1, of "Baking Technology," the official bulletin of the American Institute of Baking. He said it fit every need of Louisiana and as the matter of revising the Sanitary Code was now open and the work was in his hands he would be sure to incorporate this score card in the new code.

Bakery Score Card

Name of Bakery ....Date...:......
Address ....

	Perfect	Allow
1. Above ground	10	....
2. Well lighted	10	....
3. Well ventilated (artificial)	5	....
4. Unconnected by door or hall with living room or with rooms used for other business	5	
5. Screen, 2; free from flies, 3	5	
6. Floor, walls and ceilings clean (deduct 5 for expectoration on floor)	10	
7. Water-tight floor	5	
8. Water closet does not open into room in which food products are handled	5	
9. Basin for washing hands, sanitary plumbing	5	
10. Employees wear clean uniforms, 2; free from disease and clean in person, 3	5	
11. Utensils, mixers, dough troughs and racks clean	10	
12. Protection of raw materials	5	
13. Handling of production, process of manufacture	5	
14. Mechanical mixer	5	
15. Handling final product	5	
16. Bread wrapped in bakery	5	
	100%	

Backing up this score card is the Sanitary Code to which every baker joining the American Bakers' Association is required to comply.

In putting forward both the score card and the Code of Ethics, the American Bakers' Association has made a move to offer all inquiring women a full guarantee that their bakers' bread is of the highest quality baked in ovens, in bakeries as sanitary as any their homes could possibly produce.

Kansas Bakers Meet

KANSAS bakers held their annual convention at the Kansas State Agricultural College, Manhattan, Kansas, January 12th and 13th, with a good attendance of bakers and an instructive program. President A. J. Cripe, Hutchinson, was in the chair, and F. C. Stadelhofer, St. Louis, was the first speaker, his subject being "What's in the 1922 Loaf of Bread?"

Mr. Stadelhofer is a practical man and his talks to bakers are always both interesting as well as instructive, and his talk was enjoyed. It is published in this issue of THE NATIONAL BAKER. Prof. L. A. Fitz, of State College, gave an interesting talk on the "Process of Flour Making," while Frank Rushton, Rosedale, told of the "After Effects of Price Cutting." Mrs. E. B. Keith spoke for the local housewives.

The second day's session was devoted to bakery advertising, and there was an interesting bread contest. In this President Cripe carried off the first and third prizes, while second place went to the Campbell Bread Company, Kansas City. Prof. Fitz and Frank Rushton were the judges.

Election of officers resulted in the re-election of A. J. Cripe as president, and of A. N. Dilly, Council Grove, secretary, and A. E. Jenkins, Salina, as treasurer. A. W. Hyle, Wakeeney, and C. J. Chenoworth. of Junction City, were chosen as vice-presidents. Next year's meeting will be held at Wichita.

—:—:—:—

National Prune Week

NATIONAL Prune Week will be held throughout the United States and Canada February 27th to March 6th. The California Prune and Apricot Growers, Inc., the growers' non-profit co-operative marketing association which sells seventy-five per cent. of the California prune and dried apricot crops, which is fostering the idea of National Prune Week, is asking every baker, grocer, restaurant and hotel and all other distributors who handle California prunes to join hands in making the week a success.

Bakers will be asked to do their part in making the week a success by baking simple and easy prune specialties which can be readily sold. Some of these specialties which the California growers have suggested that the bakers display during the week are prune pies, prune cookies, prune cakes, prune coffee cakes and prune tarts.

Formulas for all of these specialties can be had by writing direct to the California Prune and Apricot Growers, Inc., San Jose, California. The California Prune and Apricot Growers, Inc., will also supply retail bakers with attractive hand lettered window posters for prune bread, prune pie and prune cake and prune coffee cake.

Plans already have been perfected for thousands of window displays of California prunes by retail grocers during the week. Special window trim crews will decorate the grocers' windows in all of the large cities

BUDWEISER Barley Malt—100 per cent pure—is made only from the finest barley and scientifically malted by the most modern methods. It has the advantage of Anheuser-Busch's year of malting experience in developing a diastase of just the right proportion and strength for bakers' purposes.

The result is an extract syrup of barley malt—nothing more nor less—uniformly produced at all times.

The new distributing system makes it possible to secure fresh supplies just as they are needed, without the use of the old contract system.

ANHEUSER-BUSCH SALES CORPORATION
ST. LOUIS, U. S. A.

of the country for the displays to be shown during the week.

Restaurants and hotel dining rooms will be urged to make a feature of prune dishes on their menu during National Prune Week. Special recipes have been mailed by the California prune growers to all the leading restaurants and hotel chefs throughout the country, asking for their co-operation during the week.

National Prune Week will be forcefully called to the attention of the public by extensive advertising campaigns in which such powerful mediums as newspapers, magazines and farm papers will be used to carry large space advertisements announcing National Prune Week, and urging people to eat California prunes every day during that week.

The annual spring newspaper campaigns of the California Prune and Apricot Growers, Inc., announcing National Prune Week will be launched on the morning of February 27th, the first day of National Prune Week. All of the advertising to be run that week by the association will feature National Prune Week and the healthful, economical and appetizing quality of California prunes.

The newspaper advertising campaign will be continued by the California Prune and Apricot Growers, Inc., for four weeks following National Prune Week so that bakers, grocers and other distributors who take part in National Prune Week will be able to extend their sales of California prunes and take advantage of the advertising for several months after National Prune Week ends.

National Prune Week is being held at the time of the year when it is easiest to sell prunes. In February and March there are practically no fresh fruits in the market and people can easily be persuaded to eat high quality dried fruits.

—‡—‡—‡—

Walter Baker & Co. Annual Meeting

AT the annual meeting of stockholders of Walter Baker & Co., Ltd., the following-named directors were re-elected: H. C. Gallagher, Nathaniel H. Stone, William L. Putnam, Ellerton P. Whitney, Rodolphe L. Agassiz, Robert F. Herrick, Thomas N. Perkins, W. Cameron Forbes; treasurer, Henry D. Love; clerk, W. R. Thurber. H. C. Gallagher was re-elected president, Nathaniel H. Stone and W. B. Thurber, vice-presidents.

—‡—‡—‡—

The business of the Syracuse Bread Company, Syracuse, N. Y., a $20,000 corporation, has been merged with the General Baking Company of New York, it was announced on February 2nd. R. Z. Spaulding, of Binghamton, is President of the Syracuse company and is also President of the Russell-Spaulding Co., Binghamton, N. Y.

—‡—‡—‡—

The Richard Baking Company, Southbridge, Mass., has been incorporated with a capital of $30,000 by Edgard Richard, Emile L. Richard and Wilfred Richard.

Charles F. Stehle, St. Louis, Mo., purchased a lot on the southern line of West Florissant Ave., just west of the terminus of the Bellefontaine line, where he will erect a modern bake shop and store room.

Albert W. Davis, one of the pioneer bakers of Atlantic City, N. J., is building a new addition to his bakery at 509 Atlantic Ave., doubling the capacity.

D. Porter Oliver, the Burlington, N. J., baker, has the sympathy of his many friends in the death of his father, Henry Field Oliver, a well known and highly respected citizen of Burlington County.

The Arcadian French Pastry Company, 111 Franklin Street, Jersey City, N. J., was incorporated with capital stock of $50,000 by Herman Berendt Henry Pech and Anton Van Horn.

The New Jersey Bakers' Supply, Inc., at Paterson, N. J., with capital of $100,000 by Henry Schneider, Sophia Schneider and Esther Pantel.

Gerdiner's New Method Bakery, 516 Landis Avenue, Vineland, N. J., is to be remodeled and enlarged and new ovens are to be installed.

The Krasner Bakery, Woodbury, N. J., has bought the interests of the Gigenbach Bakery at Woodbury, N. J.

The Shults Baking Company, New York, has acquired a block of land between 18th and 19th Aves., 52nd and 53rd Sts., Brooklyn, N. Y., and are preparing plans for a huge bakery largely to supply their suburban trade. The plot contains 120,000 square feet.

The Just Rite Baking Company, 431 Lafayette Ave., Hawthorne, N. Y., has been incorporated with capital of $100,000.

The Blackwell Baking Company has been incorporated at Greenville, Ohio, with capital of $25,000 by F. Anketman, J. S. Blackwell, F. Kerwood, J. Matthews, W. A. Zommerman.

L. R. Huth, Punxsutawney, Pa., recently purchased the leading retail bakery business of Carlisle, Pa.

Cornelius Keim, who for many years has been in the baking business at 248-250 N. 3rd Street, Columbia, Pa., is now building a large baking plant at 319-321 Walnut St., that city, to contain all modern improvements and labor saving devices.

The Pryor Baking Company, Penbrook, Pa., is planning to add pastry making to their bread business in the near future. The company is also building a large garage to take care of its motor fleet.

F. L. Schlichenmayer, the well known Philadelphia baker, has just opened his new plant at 15th St., Belfield and Wyoming Aves., in the Logan district of Philadelphia. His son, Otto, is associated with him.

A contract has been issued for the construction of a five-story bakery, 100 feet square, at Hunting Park Ave. & McMichael St., Philadelphia, for the Tasty Baking Company, that city.

W. L. Darby of Chester, S. Car., and B. G. Sanders of Camden, S. Car., are arranging to open up a modern and up-to-date electric bakery at Chester, S. Car.

George Fellers and Hayes Reynolds, Greenwood, S. Car., are preparing to open an electric bakery in the near future on Main Street, same town.

Percy Jones of Hickman, Ky., has purchased the bakery owned and operated by Charles Hurt at Dyersburg, Tenn., which is one of the oldest bakeries in that section.

The Bristol Bakery & Confectionery Company, Bristol, Va., recently purchased the R. L. Knott Bakery on State Street, same town.

Application for a permit to alter their bakery shop by an addition to cost $30,500, was recently made by Nolde Bros., 26th Street, between Broad & Marshall Sts., Richmond, Va.

The Betsy Ann Bakery of Tacoma, Wash., was recently incorporated with capital stock of $40,000 by Edward Hall, Edward Pickert and Napoleon Raquer.

WHAT MAKES BREAD FLAVOR?

If you take a good quality of flour and mix it with water, salt, sugar and milk, it will only have the flavor of wet grain.

Bake this dough. It will have the flavor of cooked grain, not the rich, delicious flavor of Bread.

Now let yeast be used with this same dough, properly fermented and baked. The Bread flavor promptly appears.

BREAD FLAVOR, THEN, IS DUE TO THE YEAST

A further proof is—Bake the yeast alone without any other ingredients, the most important elements of Bread flavor will be produced.

Are You Putting All the Flavor Possible Into Your Bread?

THE FLEISCHMANN COMPANY

Fleischmann's Yeast   *Fleischmann's Service*

To Calculate Dough Temperatures

THE baker has no time for theorizing; in fact, when it comes to calculating heats he must even abandon the most exact figuring on paper and make his calculations mentally, says an English writer. Now, for the practical baker, I question if there is anything of more use to him in carrying through his work than mental calculations, and I have no hesitation in saying that the workers in many other trades would be astonished did they know the amount of mental calculation the average baker finds it necessary to do. But the foundation of any system of memory calculation must be laid on paper first; the principles on which calculations are made must be understood, else the baker will now and again find himself completely at sea when his heats don't work out as he had calculated on. Then again, in making dough, a baker may have to use two different types of machine, or he may go to a new job where a different type of machine is in use, or he may buy a new machine to replace an old one; he may even have to make certain pieces of dough by hand, while other pieces are made by machinery. All these things affect the results of even the most exact calculations; but more, even the proportion of water used to flour affects the results; add to these the varying temperature of the surrounding atmosphere, and we may well cease to wonder why the baker finds it difficult to get exactly what he wants every time. The aim of this article, then, is to show the baker how he may calculate his heats mentally with exactness. But the surest way to impress a fact on a man's memory is to explain why a certain effect is always due to a certain cause, and I will, in the following lines, endeavor to explain why heats vary in spite of the most careful calculation, at the same time pointing out the obvious remedy.

THE CORRECT PRINCIPLE

The principle involved in getting dough at a certain heat is that all substances which may be popularly called warm, part with this warmth when they come in contact with cooler substances, until all are at an equal temperature. If we take a gallon of water at 60 degrees and a gallon at 80 degrees, and mix, the colder water absorbs the heat of the warmer, and rises, as the other falls, until the mixture assumes a certain temperature. In this case the quantities being equal, the mean temperature will be exactly half way between the two, viz.: 70 degrees, but if we take two gallons at 60 degrees, and one gallon at 80 degrees, the mixture will not be 70 degrees, it will be something under 67 degrees, because we have a smaller amount of water at 80 degrees, and of course a smaller amount of heat. Of course, I hear you say, "any fool knows that," and you may be right, but the principle is a thing worth re-

Suppose we repeat the experiment first spoken of, and select from flour at 60 degrees the weight of a gallon of water and mix this into a batter, with a gallon of water at 80 degrees F., what is the resultant temperature? Not 70 degrees, as at first, but well over 73 degrees, and the reason (and mark this well) a given quantity of flour requires less heat to raise it to a given temperature than does an equal quantity of water, or, as in the above case, the same quantity of heat will raise a given quantity of flour to a higher temperature than it will raise water. Now, let us take the second experiment again, and substitute twenty pounds of flour at 60 degrees for the water, and make into dough with one gallon of water at 80 degrees, we are prepared for the result from our last experiment, and so we are not surprised when we find the resultant temperature to be at least 70 degrees, or three degrees above the mixture of the two lots of water, although the temperatures were identical, and this leads us to the important fact which the baker may very easily remember and make use of in memory calculations: one pound of water will part with as much heat as will raise two pounds of flour to a temperature exactly between the two. We can put it the other way, of course, and say two parts of flour will raise one part of water, and so on, but although this is quite correct, we seldom, if ever (as bakers), require to use water colder than flour.

DEPENDENT UPON SURROUNDING CONDITIONS

It must be plain to every baker, even though he has not had practical experience, that after a calculation is made, it will depend upon whether the bakery is comparatively warm or cold, as to whether our calculations work out right or not. If the bakery is cold, it is reasonable to suppose a deal of heat will be lost during the operation of dough making, and this must be allowed for in some way. This leads me to a most interesting discussion, which took place in some of the journals a little while ago, when the "specific heat" of flour was the subject. If the reader will refer back to our experiment with twenty pounds of flour and ten pounds of water, he will see that ten pounds of water lost 10 degrees, which twenty pounds of flour absorbed, and that one rose in temperature exactly as the other fell, in spite of the difference in weight. We made deductions from this fact which are irrefutable—and which the writer proves in practice every day in the year—that one pound of water falling one degree, loses as much heat as will raise two pounds of flour one degree; the amount of heat then required by one pound of flour to enable it to rise one degree is called the specific heat of flour.

Now this is no simple theory. As I said, I practice it every day in the year, but the exact specific heat of

into here. I have already shown, however, that flour takes half the heat which water gives off, so assuming water to be 1, then we may safely call the specific heat of flour 0.5. When we proceed to practice, however, we must make further allowances, due to various causes. In my regular daily practice I like my dough to be not under 80 degrees; my flour varies in temperature, but suppose (as often happens) my flour is 68 degrees, I take 280 pounds of flour and add 14 gallons of water, said water I get at 92 degrees and I never get less than 80 degrees in dough, that is 12 degrees under the temperature I want; 80—68 equals 12, and this added to my desired heat, 80 degrees, makes 92 degrees as the temperature of water to be added. This shows the specific heat as 0.5, or half that of water, but this includes any loss or gain in heat during operation, and is not the actual specific heat, and as proof, note the following: I have often to make small quantities of flour into dough, and this is my practice: Suppose I take sixty pounds of flour at 68 degrees, as I often do, and wet it with thirty pounds of water, I must always allow more heat in water than when using fourteen, twenty-one or twenty-eight gallons, because a small quantity loses heat faster in proportion. In practice, then, the very same flour at 68 degrees wet in small lots is allowed 95 degrees; in this case the half-way heat is over 81 degrees, but I generally find my dough at 80 degrees, which might lead one to Mr. Jago's expressed opinion that the amount of heat a flour takes to raise it is its specific heat, while as a matter of fact it is extra loss in making small lots which makes all the difference, for how could one flour have more than one specific heat?

I have written the foregoing with a purpose, and that purpose is to show clearly, among other things, that if flour requires half the heat of water, or if water parts with heat which raises double its weight of flour, the temperature can only be half way when the proportions are two of flour to one of water, or 280 pounds of flour to 14 gallons. But we don't make all our bread with 14 gallons to the sack; we use 15, 16, 17 or even in some place 18 gallons, and this of course upsets the proportion of two to one, consequently the heat. When I make a dough with 15 gallons to the sack (280 pounds) I never go over 91 degrees, with flour at 68 degrees. When making sack lots I always get 80 degrees in dough, and in making softer doughs or thin sponges, the allowance is still less. We may again say we have arrived at a principle which we must always remember in making mental calculations, and that is, that a less margin of heat must be allowed when the proportion of water is greater than one to two, that is, greater than 14 gallons per sack, and as the proportion increases, the allowance must decrease and vice versa. Here is the general rule, however:

FIGURE BY THIS RULE

Subtract the heat of the flour from the desired heat of the dough; add the result to the desired heat of dough, and the answer is the required heat of the water. For instance, your flour is, say 64 degrees, and you want your dough to be 82 degrees, then 82 minus 64 equals 18 plus 82 equals 100 degrees: 100 degrees of heat in water with flour at 64 degrees will give you 82 degrees in dough. Another way of arriving at the same result is:

Double the desired heat of your dough and subtract therefrom the heat of the flour, the result is the required heat of the water to be added, as for instance in the case just spoken of, you want your dough at 82 degrees. Then 82 degrees plus 82 equals 164 minus 64 equals 100 degrees; thus temperature of the water, same as found by the first method, is 100 degrees. This only applies when the proportions are as two to one; still it is the handiest, most useful, and exact way of

I had better say resuscitated, and my only reason for bringing up the subject here is to show the reader that it is a way how not to do it. In my rule I have said nothing about making allowances for a cold bakery, because that is a different phase of the subject. You make up your mind what heat you want your dough to be, and I tell you how to attain that result in a simple way. All the same, it is a pretty safe rule to follow that having fixed a standard of heat for your dough room, or which is much oftener the case, the dough room having fixed a standard for itself, you may safely ignore a rise or fall of two degrees, but after that it is well to add heat at the rate of one degree in dough for every three in the air of the bakery in inverse ratio; that is, if the shop rises three, drop one in dough, and so on, or vice versa. This rule is much more important when working long doughs or sponges.

In working short processes, it may be even dangerous to follow this plan far; the safest way is to keep doughs well covered. But what the writer referred to is of a different opinion, sometimes at least, because he gives what he calls a "major factor" for a dough lying very little over an hour. This major factor is got by adding together the heat of the shop, the heat of the flour, water and dough. Everything is very simple, say heat of shop is 80 degrees, flour 64 degrees, dough 80 degrees, water 96 degrees, total is 320, and is called the major factor; the universal panacea for getting your dough exactly ready in a given time. Suppose you want to ascertain the heat of water to be added in making dough, add together heat of shop, flour, and dough, and subtract from the major factor, the result is the heat of the water—sometimes. If the variations are not great and the doughs comparatively long, the major factor is all wrong, in which case the author above quoted says you have got to change it; I would therefore ask the baker at least to be very careful in adopting this system.

MACHINERY AFFECTS TEMPERATURE

I referred to machines affecting temperature, but perhaps this is so well-known that it is not advisable to spend much space on it. Certain machines, however, warm up dough very much, in which case it is better, instead of making regular calculations, to fix a standard. Say your flour is 68 degrees, your water

Making the Most of Every Dough

To make the most of every dough that enters your make-up room, requires machine handling with speed and accuracy, a minimum use of dusting flour and without injury to the dough itself. This last is of the greatest importance, and speed and accuracy are of little use if your doughs are killed in making-up. A dead loaf is no seller.

Quality production, quickly and accurately, that's one of the bread baker's greatest problems. DUTCHESS Automatic Make-up Units accomplish this profitably in bakeries all over the country every day. To assure you, we'll be pleased to show you this equipment in operation and have you consult the bakers using it.

"Our Sales Tell the Tale"

DUTCHESS TOOL COMPANY
BEACON, N. Y.

grees, fix 162 as the standard, and proceed as before. The only thing which seems to interfere with all these rules is that flour which is very cold seems to require more heat in proportion than flour which is comparatively warm; at least I have noticed that flour, at, say, 58 degrees, would require 22 degrees full on the water to raise it to 80 degrees, while flour at 74 degrees would run over the heat required, when made into dough with 6 degrees of an allowance. I have read somewhere that the specific heat of flour varies with the temperature, but I am not a theoretical baker, and am not very well versed in these things; the above, however, has been my experience.

—‡—‡—‡—

What Is a Calorie?

THE word calorie is much used now-a-days, especially in all discussions as to the value of certain foods, and the exact meaning of the word is not realized by many, and the question is often asked, just what does a calorie mean?

When fuel is thrown on a fire under a boiler, heat is produced. This heat is required in order that the engine may perform its work. To do work of any kind requires energy. Food used or burned in the human machine produces energy to maintain the normal heat of the body and to do its work. Work done by the body comprises not only that which requires muscular and mental exertion, but also involuntary exertion, such as the beating of the heart, the expansion of the lungs, etc. The chemical process within the body which transforms our food into energy is similar in nature to the process which takes place when fuel is burned over fire—though in the body, the burning takes place very slowly and in every tissue, instead of in one central place. The value of food is determined by the amount of energy it yields to the body; and it also has a building and regulating function.

It was necessary that a unit be established for measuring the amount of heat produced when food was completely burned. The unit chosen or universally adopted as the unit for measuring fuel value or energy value for any kind of food is called the calorie. It represents the same principle in measuring as the inch or foot, the unit of measuring length; the pint or gallon, the unit of volume; and the ounce or pound, that of weight.

The calorie is the amount of heat required to raise the temperature of 1 kilogram of water 1 degree C., or 1 pound of water approximately 4 degrees F. Our requirements of food, so far as the amount is concerned, can therefore be expressed in the number of calories needed for each person per day. It must not be forgotten, however, that the calories

Modern Methods in Shop Control

By J. E. Wihlfahrt, of the Fleischmann Co., at the Canadian Convention

MODERN shop management represents a real constructive force when all of the material is properly selected and everything is so arranged that the entire process of manufacture can be properly timed,

so undue haste with all its evils and consequent resulting damaged bread is minimized. To accomplish this shop reports, showing the schedule and actual running of the doughs and amounts manufactured, are absolutely necessary. Then you are in a position to check up your production against material used, arrest invisible loss, and can compare results; likewise how much work is done in a certain time by one shift or another, and you will learn where the work needs taking up or where it may better be relaxed. The drag may not be due to any fault of the help; the ovens perhaps are laggard, or shortness in equipment, as bread pans, causes delay. By checking up correctly you can estimate the actual loss or gain in time and damaged bread by labor in relative expense.

The invisible loss through fermentation is from 1 to 3 per cent. to total weight of dough and is greatest in overnight sponges, especially where lengthy fermentation is carried on in rooms containing no arrangements for the maintenance of proper moisture in the air. This loss increases in proportion as the process is prolonged.

Additional loss occurs through waste in careless scaling.

It is also well to check all material when received.

Other waste is due to improper firing. Ovens should be fired moderately not more than two hours before baking and thereafter fired slowly each hour, with dampers nearly closed until one hour before last bread goes into the oven.

VALUE OF LABORATORY WORK

Laboratory work represents a protective measure in shop control. Material cannot be judged correctly or used to best advantage without first being properly analyzed and the work regulated through control tests.

How to make it: Use a rich layer cake mixture. For filling, chop uncooked pitted Sunsweet Prunes fine enough to make a paste. Moisten with currant jelly and spread between layers, then ice with flavored water icing. Sprinkle shredded cocoanut on top and sides.

Yes—it's the filling! That's the in-between secret of any layer cake. That's the flavor-secret that explains why some layer cakes go big and others fall flat.

A filling made of Sunsweet Prunes gives your trade a new taste-sensation. It puts novelty into an everyday bakeshop specialty. Easy to make, too—especially when you use Sunsweet Pitted Prunes.

Prepared by a recently perfected process, they are superior to any pitted prunes on the market. They fall apart without extra handling. They do not break apart in the dough. They do not discolor the dough. They are right easy to handle. And—they save labor. No fuss; no bother; no time lost!

Other profitable variations you can make with Sunsweet Pitted Prunes are pies, tarts, coffee cake, fruit slices, etc. Ask your jobber or supply house for Sunsweet Pitted Prunes—and see that you get them.

Also, write for our new formula folder, "I never knew what prunes could do!" Every formula has been proved in the baking and it's free! And, if you ask for it, we'll send along window pasters and other sales-helps that are bringing in new trade to live bakers all over the country.

Simply address Bakery Department, California Prune & Apricot Growers Inc., 192 Market Street, San Jose, California. An association of 11,000 growers.

SUNSWEET *Pitted* PRUNES

This will insure greater uniformity in raw materials and simplify the work of tracing faults to their proper source.

Control tests, whether in the laboratory or on a commercial scale, are quite essential, but to be of real value must be comparative to prevailing shop conditions and to the commercial process used. Then they will present a real precaution. Under such conditions, guesswork can be very much reduced.

It is always well to have the proper information as to fermeutative period of a flour, its absorption quality, or the effect of other batch ingredients on the dough, hence on the finished product.

Some of these tests are quite simple and their proper application can be readily acquired by some one interested in the work; others may be attended to in your own or in commercial laboratories.

Often poor bread is attributed to the wrong cause, hence a discussion of process by the shop personnel is in order, as they really in this instance represent the productive force.

Beginning with the flour handling apparatus, only sufficient flour should be sifted into a storage bin to accommodate one day's work, the principal point being that the flour should be re-sifted directly before the doughing stage, so as to provide from this source the maximum amount of air. The influence of free oxygen, which really means fresh air, is of greatly more importance than is generally realized by the baker. Yeast to do its work requires oxygen, especially for its growth. Without the presence of free oxygen it must derive its necessary supply of oxygen at the expense of the sugar present in the dough; and the latter must first be split up by the action of the yeast, which naturally consumes time.

Therefore, proper aeration of flour directly before mixing, and especially aerating the dough during mixing, either by tilting the machine so dough will take in air, or better through a special device to introduce the air into the dough while being mixed, leads to decidedly better results. Both proper aeration and high-speed mixing increase the moisture-carrying capacity of a dough more or less, according to their efficiency and application. The high-speed machine emulsifies the ingredients to better advantage, and develops the gluten in the dough sufficiently to reduce the length of time for fermentation, thereby increasing the stability of the flour used.

The amount of absorption naturally is further influenced by the character as well as by the moisture content of the flour itself. If stored in the bakery for a considerable time, especially during winter months while the storage room is artificially heated, it may lose considerable of its original moisture content, whereas fresh flour, recently received and stored through the summer months, especially during rainy weather, may contain its maximum amount of moisture. It is well, therefore, to weigh occasional sacks upon receipt and follow again the same practice before the flour is sifted for a day's work; then make your necessary calculations for the difference. This will show up part of the invisible loss.

Next softer flour, from soft red winter wheat, or of the softer spring variety, does not permit the same amount of hydration, as it will slacken more during fermentation. An addition of 15 to 25 per cent. of this type of flour will greatly assist in obtaining a splendid flavor. In such a case, the total time of fermentation must be reduced about 10 per cent. If added, it is far the best to cut your dough over into another trough at first rise, turning it thereafter until matured.

For a slacker dough all machinery must be in good working order. Your rounding-up machines must operate at a higher speed, and this also holds good for your moulder.

Loaves of a properly made dough will rise at a lower temperature with sufficient speed, 88 to 90 degrees Fahr., being the best temperature for the proof-box, and they will be ready in sufficient time to keep up with the speed of the machines provided a corresponding proper amount of motive power has been used, which means yeast. The best amount of yeast depends upon the speed under which we manufacture, and the corresponding baking facilities, which means ovens. Under such conditions the best loaf of bread will be the result. The practitioner who has mastered this is not found among those whose continued object lies in economizing on yeast.

Taking as an example three doughs mixed at a medium speed, set at 90 degrees Fahr. with shop temperature at 80 degrees, using respectively 1, 2 and 3 per cent. of yeast to weight of a strong flour, all other conditions being normal and the same, they would mature approximately in five and one-quarter, three and three-quarters and two and one-quarter hours. The sustained absorption in such doughs without application of air, special high-speed mixing, or addition of milk or other binding products, would be approximately 54, 57 and 60 per cent., being highest with the largest amount of yeast. However, the water available in different localities will influence both absorption and time for fermentation. In some localities the water is so hard as to prolong fermentation considerably. This naturally represents a decided disadvantage. In such cases a slight cut in salt may be desirable.

Salt is not only a very necessary ingredient but regulates the fermentation. It has a binding influence on the dough, and when used in proper proportions helps to produce a finer grain. The best amount of salt is one and three-quarters to two per cent. to weight of flour, and should be regulated in accordance with the amount of liquid used, doughs of higher absorption receiving the maximum amount. Not only has the proper amount of salt a beneficent effect on the eating

The Touch of Quality

It is not the cost of cleaning, nor is it the amount of cleaning done which makes the successful Bakery distinctive and different.   It is in the quality which reflects care, good taste and refinement.

These qualities appeal so strongly to the purchaser of delicate and tasty confections that thousands of bakeries can trace their rapidly increasing trade to the atmosphere of ultra sanitary cleanliness which the use of

so greatly assists in maintaining.

You too will find that this Wyandotte quality cleaning service will give just that needed touch to the quality of your product which means quick sales and added profits.

Order from your supply house.

It cleans clean.

The J. B. Ford Co. SOLE MANUFACTURERS Wyandotte, Mich.

quality of bread, but it also greatly enhances the bloom and keeping quality.

The fermentative period itself, in addition to the existing shop and dough temperatures, is further influenced by atmospheric conditions, especially by the dryness of the air. For the fermenting room, 70 per cent. relative humidity is normal and a difference of 18 per cent. of moisture content in the air affects the total time of fermentation 5 per cent. Best results are obtained by timing all the influences on fermentation and reducing the total time accordingly. *This is especially true when considering a lasting flavor for your bread.*

TO SECURE FINE FLAVOR

Of recent date a good deal of discussion on lack of flavor in bread has taken place. Prolonged fermentation does not supply this want. A drawn-out process, even with sponge and following immediate dough, will not supply the lasting flavor or that delicate eating quality which leads to permanent success. It is not the young dough, deriving its spring for the loaf, but cutting doughs into other troughs at their first rise, which leads to best results.

A liberal amount of yeast not only brings into the dough a large amount of nourishment, but also makes the younger dough a safer process and the desired delicate flavor an actual possibility.

The safest and best motto is to use every batch ingredient upon its own merit. Never substituting one for the other when they are of a decidedly different nature. Take advantage of all opportunities to economize in time and avoid every possible delay.

The following recipes are submitted for those interested:

	Pounds.
Flour	500
Water	280 to 295
Salt	9½
Yeast	9
Sugar	4
Lard	7½
Condensed milk, containing 7 per cent. butter fat	20
Malt extract	5

	Pounds.
Flour	500
Water	285 to 300
Salt	9½
Yeast	9
Sugar	11
Lard	9
Milk powder	6
Malt extract	5

Set dough at 90 degrees Fahr. Allow dough to get three-quarters light, which will require about 2 hours, 30 minutes. Then cut over into another trough. Allow to rise 1 hour more. Now turn your dough and let rise another one-half hour. It is then ready for the scaler. For exclusive handwork take dough at second rise, omitting last one. If 25 per cent. of softer flour is added, reduce fermentative period for first rise to 2 hours, 15 minutes, for second rise to 55 minutes, and for the last rise to 25 minutes, making it a 3-hour, 35-minute dough.

This is as near as I can outline the work; local conditions, equipment and character of flour used play important parts. I believe, however, that a good practitioner will find his way to make the type of loaf desired.

With seven pounds of yeast the foregoing formula would make a four-and-one-half hour dough. The amount of water naturally would have to be reduced. A slice of bread made with a young dough, when exposed to air, will dry out more rapidly unless the dough contains its proper amount of moisture. Hence a tight dough will not produce correct results.

Summing up: Let the control tests be your safety-first appliance, so you can plan securely the schedule for the work, then good and uniform results should be obtained.

Make cool doughs, well aerated and with sufficient yeast to shorten the fermentative period so that the maximum amount of flavor-giving substance is retained in the dough, use sufficient hydration to enable the wheat starch to cook properly during baking and develop the proper grain and texture, but never to the point of producing a wet dough. Also, sufficient salt and ovens of the proper temperature lead to greatest efficiency. (Softer doughs require a slightly hotter oven.)

Such doughs will produce a splendid loaf of bread.

Advanced baking practice, then, means to make bread under sanitary methods, from good material, producing a loaf of good eating quality with a satisfactory amount of nourishment and of pleasing appearance—a loaf of permanent good flavor.

It further means an open door policy, inviting the consumers of your product and making an effort to have them call, to learn correctly the process under which their food is manufactured, to convince them that good bread is the direct offspring of good sense and good material, coupled with good baking.

Nothing is more worthy than making the best bread, and to sell it nothing more important than the confidence of the consumer. Nothing will build this confidence quicker than a uniform, well-flavored, nourishing and appetizing, good appearing product.

—‡—‡—‡—

Many a man likes a woman's style—as long as he doesn't have to pay for it.

—‡—‡—‡—

The things we get for nothing are apt to cost us more than the things we buy.

—‡—‡—‡—

Get on the other side of the fence when you have occasion to argue with a mule.

Information Department

The object of this department is to help our readers, as far as possible, to solve the various difficulties that come up from day to day. We will also answer questions about all kinds of machinery and give every possible assistance in securing detailed information. No names or addresses of manufacturers will be given in these columns. When wanted they will be sent by mail. Address,

INFORMATION DEPARTMENT   **THE NATIONAL BAKER**

J. S., New York: We have your favor of recent date enclosing check for $5 for three years' subscription, for which please accept our thanks. Same is passed to your credit. Your inquiry was referred to our technical editor, who advises as follows:

CHOCOLATE FRIED CAKE

To 1 quart of milk in any fried cake mix, add 4 ozs. chocolate, melted. This must be added to the batch with sugar and shortening, before creaming. The mix will require a little more milk and sugar and a little vanilla will be necessary. Some bakers merely add a little cocoa powder instead of the melted chocolate.

THE USE OF SPICES AND FLAVORS

For Spice cake, using cinnamon, ginger, allspice, cloves, mace and New Orleans molasses, the spices should be mixed in the following proportion: 1 oz. cinnamon, ½ oz. allspice, ¼ oz. cloves; add a dash of vanilla for fruit or wedding cake. Nuts, lemon and orange peel can be added, if desired.

For Cup, Layer and Loaf cake, to a 10 lb. sugar batch, add ½ oz. of lemon emulsion, 1-3 oz. of mace. For Molasses cake use 1 oz. cinnamon, ½ oz. ginger, and a very little lemon flavor. For White Loaf cake use equal parts of lemon, orange and lime essences. For White Pound cake, use rose and almond flavors. For Pound cake, a pinch of mace is all that is required; the butter and sugar, well creamed together, make the best of all flavors.

BREAD TROUBLES

R. C. L., Cleveland, Ohio: We have your favor of the 16th, and duly received the sample loaf of bread. Sorry that you failed to give us the temperatures, which are very important in criticizing bread.

The loaf of bread was a good one, but considering

the high quality of materials you are using, it should
have been better. For one thing, you are using too
much salt (reduce quantity by 25%) and use more
yeast. You do not get the advantage of the amount
of milk you are using. Use enough yeast to have the
dough ready in from three to three and one-half hours
at least. Do not set the dough too warm; a temperature of about 78 degrees is about right. The grain of
the loaf is rather coarse, and this is apparently owing
to the fact that the dough was over-fermented, which
resulted in the sugar in the loaf being turned to alcohol, the smell of which was plainly apparent, and
also results in a loss of sweetness. The loaf had a good
volume and good bloom, and by observing the above
directions we are sure you can greatly improve same.

A quicker fermentation induced by a larger quantity of yeast and less salt will give much better results.
Advise us of your further experience.

C. H., New York: We have your favor of recent
date in reference to a good French and Danish Pastry,
which we give herewith:

FRENCH PASTRY

1 pound bread flour.
2 ounces lard.
1 egg.
Rub gently with hands in fine crumbs.
1 pound of butter with salt washed out in ice
water.
Now pour enough ice water into batch to make it
just as firm as the butter is after being washed in ice
water. Mix very lightly, and make a square on bench
with dough ½ inch thick. Now spread the pound of
butter over it, and sprinkle a little cream of tartar over
it. Fold into a three-layer mass, roll out gently
to its former size. Fold again into a three-layer mass,
gently roll out again. Fold again and put in or near
ice for two hours. Then repeat folding again, then on
ice for two hours more. Then roll twice more; the
last time as thin as you wish. Cut with sharp cutter.

DANISH PASTRY

1 gallon milk.
2 pounds yeast.
2 pounds sugar.
20 eggs.
Salt and mace.

Mix, raise twice, spread on bench, and lay on 3
pounds butter, fold in three layers, and put on ice for
two or three hours. Roll out twice more, same as for
puff paste. Put on ice for two hours. Roll out twice;
last time roll out 10 inches wide, ½ inch thick. Cut
½-inch wide strips, twist them, making any shape;
hearts, rings, crosses or roll or pretzels.

Danish style is to make a large heart 16 inches
long, 12 inches wide, and spreading on it almonds of
nuts of any kind. Also braid rings 14 inches in diameter.

J. W. R., West Va.: Replying to your favor of
recent date, we give herewith recipe for "Fried Cakes,"
which is the standard mix, all others are offshoots.

FRIED CAKES

1 quart sweet milk,
1 pound sugar,
4 eggs,
4 ounces butter and lard,
4 pounds flour,
2¼ ounces baking powder (must be fresh),
Pinch salt, lemon and mace flavor.
Break up sugar, shortening and eggs together.
Add milk, then flour and baking powder.

To make a richer one add 4 ounces powdered milk,
1 egg, 2 ounces sugar, 1 ounce cornstarch, ½ pint milk.
Machine mixes require a little more milk, enough to
flow through machine easily.

There is no cheaper mix than the above. Flour
must be cake or pastry. Bread flour for cake costs
more, as it takes too much shortening. Commercial
manufacturers of doughnuts use powdered milk largely, as it absorbs water, is profitable, and makes a fine
doughnut.

A GOOD CHEAP FRUIT LUNCH CAKE

F. D. C., Vermont: Try the following, as we
think it is about what you want: 1 pound of butter or
lard, 1½ pounds of powdered sugar, 4 pounds flour, 4
eggs, 1 pound of seeded raisins, 1 ounce of good baking
powder sifted in the flour, 1 pound of currants, 1 teaspoonful of good mixed spices, ¼ pound of mixed finely cut peels, 1 quart of milk (more or less), 1 ounce of
good baking powder sifted in the flour. Cream the
butter, sugar, eggs and spice. When creamed add 2-3
of the milk, stir it in, then add the flour, ¾ mix, then
add the fruit and peels and finish mixing, adding the
balance of the milk if needed to form a medium stiff
mass. Bake in papered tins with sloping sides, and in
size to sell at 10 or 15 cents each. Dust the tops with
powdered sugar and sprinkle with water. Bake in a
solid heat. If preferred, this may be baked as a large
cake, in which case use ¼ less baking powder or mix
lighter. In either case this cake should not be removed until nearly or quite cold.

J. F. G., Ohio.: If you make it an invariable practice to oil your machines each day before starting
work, you should have no further trouble in that line.
Only a little oil is required, but use good oil and use it
every day. We give below the two recipes required:

CHEAP NUT CAKE

1 pound of powdered sugar, 10 ounces of butter, ½
pint of eggs, 1¼ pounds of flour, ¼ ounce good baking
powder (full weight), ¾ of a pint of milk, lemon flavor, nut meat. Sift the baking powder in the flour.
Cream the butter, sugar and eggs. When creamed
add the flour and mix, adding milk if needed to form
a mass the same tightness as best pound cake. When
¾ mixed add what your judgment directs of any kind

of nut meat you prefer. Bake in flat cake tin and sell plain or iced, as you choose.

By mixing just a little tighter, and adding a little egg-color, you get a good cheap pound cake—of course, keeping out the nut meat. By adding raisins you get raisin cake, and so on for citron, fruit, cherry, etc.

This mixture also, mixed a trifle slacker than the Nut Cake, and baked in small 5 or 10 cent cake tins, and baked in quicker heat, will give a large and pretty good cake for the money. They may be baked plain or with the additions before mentioned, not forgetting to sugar dust them before baking.

PRUNE CAKE

For this cake you need prunes cut up in about quarters. It may be baked as a flat cake, or as an individual cake in long, narrow and shallow cake tins.

¾ of a pound of powdered sugar, ¾ of a pound of butter or lard, ½ pint of yolks of eggs, 1 pound 2 ounces of flour, ½ pint of milk (more or less), ½ ounce of good baking powder. Mix as directed for cheap Nut Cake. When ¾ mixed add the prune meat and finish mixing, adding milk if needed. When mixed it may be baked in a large flat cake tin, and when baked the bottom iced with a light pink icing, then cut and sold by the pound. Or, it may be baked in long, narrow, rather shallow tins, about 9 inches long. 2½ inches wide and 2½ inches deep, and with nearly straight sides, and not papered out. Some simply bake this

Do You Know What Your Goods Cost?

ONE of the hardest things in bake-shop practice is to keep an accurate account of the cost of each piece of goods, so that the baker will know just how much profit each piece or each dozen pieces will yield, with raw materials at certain prices.

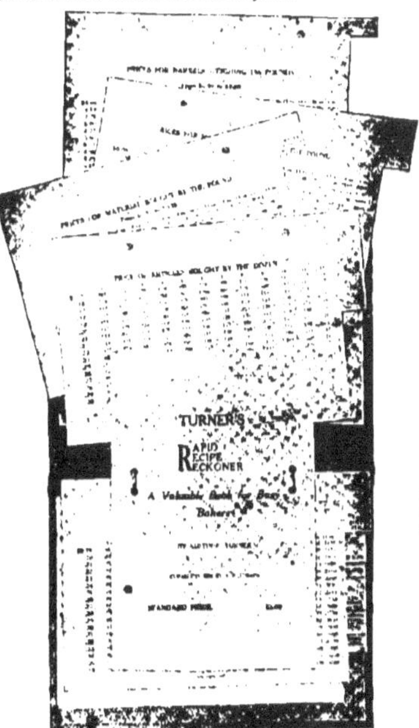

Turner's Rapid Recipe Reckoner

saves a baker all trouble in reckoning up the cost; it is already done for him, and all he has to do is to pick out the desired item at the given price per pound or dozen.

Tables are given of the cost for each ounce of flour at a price per barrel from **$4.00 upward**; and of lard, butter, sugar, eggs and of all other supplies by the ounce or measure at what price you pay in quantities.

Turner's Rapid Recipe Reckoner

simplifies cost accounting so that it is a matter of only a few minutes to get the cost of a batch of any size, and of any class of goods.

The tables are printed on heavy serviceable cardboard, placed in a substantial loose-leaf cover, bound in cloth. It will last a life-time and you can add new sheets or tables, if desired.

In these days of close competition one is needed in every bake-shop, and the cost is but **$2.00**, postpaid. Address

411 Walnut Street
Philadelphia, Pa.

BUILDING RECIPES

WHAT I mean by recipe building, says John Blandy, the English expert, is that there is in every mixture a raw material which is the foundation factor, and if the worker understands its nature and knows its functions when in connection with other ingredients, he will be able to vary these other ingredients in such a way as to make any kind of goods, richer or poorer, as he wills. The agent which influences the finished article in the case of bread is yeast; in cakes or pastry, eggs, fat, baking powder. In wine biscuits and small goods which are required to flow instead of rising, sugar; gelatine for jellies, and temperature for boiled sugar goods. If the behavior of these foundation factors is understood, very little difficulty will be experienced by the workman when making up any quantity or quality of goods.

A GOVERNING PRINCIPLE

The governing principle may be explained by the following data:—An egg will only aerate or raise its own weight of any other ingredient with which it is associated, and therefore, as price is the ruling factor, if the price will not allow of the use of eggs alone as the raising principle, some other agent must be used to assist. A cake may be required, the selling price of which will only permit of the use of one pound of eggs to three pounds of flour, one pound fat, and one pound of sugar; it therefore follows that as there is more than double the weight of eggs in the other ingredients, some other raising, aerating-agent must be employed to co-operate with the eggs to make a light and saleable article. In this case the ordinary baking powder is used, such as cream of tartar and bicarbonate soda. Further, an egg only moistens its own weight of such ingredients as flour, and therefore, if a cake or other moist article is required, some additional liquid must be added.

Applying the same principle to butter and fats will mean that, say for puff paste, one pound to one pound will be necessary; but if two pounds of flour are used to one pound of fat, the difference must be made up with some other aerating power, such as baking powder. In shortbread two-thirds of a pound fat to one pound flour; for cake, one pound fat to one and one-half pound flour, will be the maximum strength of its shortening power. What must be recognized in this connection is that the lighter in bulk required, that the aerating agent must be increased in proportion, and, within limits; this also applies to the quantity of liquid used.

WHAT SUGAR DOES

Dealing with sugar, the governing law to bear in mind is that this ingredient not only sweetens, but when it is subjected to heat its property is to melt and flow; the quantities used, therefore, will decide in this case of sugar confectionery and boiled sugar goods it is not so much the quantity of sugar and water that is employed which will influence the finished production, as the temperature during boiling, to which the mixture is subjected. If the operator places in the boiler fourteen pounds of sugar with five pounds water and a pinch of cream of tartar, and boils this to 240 degrees Fahrenheit, he will get a mass, which, when cool and worked up with a spatula is named fondant. By continuing the boiling a little longer more water will be evaporated, which will bring it to the degree "crack," suitable for drops and hard goods; continue the boiling a little longer and a further evaporation will bring the boiling to the caramel degree for spun sugar, etc. The evaporation of moisture, therefore, is the governing factor in boiled sugar goods.

SOME EXAMPLES

If the principle underlying cake making is understood, no difficulty will be experienced in making any kind of cake. Examples: One pound sugar, one pound eggs, one pound fat, one and one-half pounds flour and one and one-half pounds fruit will make what is termed pound cake. To make a plainer kind, if the flour is doubled to three pounds, what follows? Keeping in mind that an egg will only lift its own weight we have an extra one and one-half pound flour to lift and to moisten, and as *all normal flour requires half its own weight of liquid to moisten it,* three quarter pound of water or milk will be required, and also an extra lifting power in the form of one-half ounce cream of tartar and one-quarter ounce carbonate soda. These additions will insure a light mixture; but to make it palatable, allowing the original weight of eggs and fat to remain, the sweetening purposes of sugar must be increased in weight, and as the principle of the use of sugar in cakestuffs is one-third to each pound of flour, an additional eight ounces of sugar will be necessary to sweeten the extra one and one-half pound of flour. If this principle in cake making is understood and followed, it will be but a simple matter to make cake of any degree of richness to suit both palate and pocket. See how this statement works out. Say we start with a rich Madeira cake mixture: One and one-half pound fat, one and three-quarter pound of sugar, one and three-quarter pound eggs, two pounds flour, with just a pinch of cream of tartar and soda. Cream up in the usual way, and bake in small sizes. By lowering the fat and eggs, and adding moisture, a plainer cake of the same class results: Cream up six pounds of sugar with three and one-half pounds fat and twenty-eight eggs, mix four ounces cream of tartar, two ounces carbonate soda, and twelve pounds flour; mix the whole mixture together with enough liquid, a little yolk coloring and essence of lemon, to make it into a

plain slab cake is required use the same mixture, but being in bulk it should not be so soft, and not being required so light, use less powder. Again, this same mixture, with the addition of fruit, can be made into Genoa or cherry cake.

FURTHER EXAMPLES

To get a clear idea of the simplicity of the principle underlying all recipe building, follow just one or two more examples. Take the sponge cake class. All the varieties of these goods are made from the same kind of materials, the whole of the difference being in the varying quantities of each ingredient. A savoy mould, large size, is made with equal quantities of flour, eggs and sugar, the one pound of eggs lifts the one pound of flour, but when the sponge roll (Swiss, jelly, etc.), is made, something more than merely lifting is required. These good must not only be light but flexible, also to allow for rolling, every additional egg therefore, will increase the flexibility, and in practice the proper quantity is found in double the weight of eggs to that of sugar, say one pound flour, one pound sugar, and two pounds of eggs. The ordinary sponge cake being in lightness and sponginess halfway between a Swiss roll and a savoy mould, three quarter pound sugar and one pound of eggs meets the case exactly, but, except for the differing weights of materials sponge goods are all made, beaten up, in the same way.

THE OLD-FASHIONED BRANDY SNAP

The wine biscuit class offers just as simple an explanation of the science of recipe making. Sugar being one of the chief factors in wine biscuits, its right usage is essential. Sugar not only sweetens, but when subjected to heat, it boils and flows; and therefore the proportions of sugar will govern the shape of the biscuit during the baking. Taking the old-fashioned jumble or brandy snap as a base, it will be quite plain that the sugar element is the governing factor in relation to the degree to which the biscuits will flow out when in the oven; seven pounds syrup, seven pounds coarse moist sugar, seven pounds flour, one-half pound lard, one-half ounce spice and ground ginger. Incorporate the whole together, sprinkle a well-greased baking sheet with water, and lay the biscuits (about the size and thickness of a silver dollar) on it, and put them into a cool oven. In a few minutes they will be seen to boil and spread out quite thin. This is owing to the action of the sugar under heat, the syrup also assisting in this melting and flowing.

Here is another recipe of the same class as jumbles, but their opposite. These do not flow so much because they have egg and ground almonds: One-half pound white of egg, one-half pound fine icing sugar, one-quarter pound ground sweet almonds, one-quarter pound flour. Flavor with six drops noyeau or maraschino liquor. Slightly beat up the whites and mix the whole together. The mixture is run out of a savoy bag on to greased tins, and when baked, while quite hot, are folded into curls like jumbles, and, like jumbles, when cold are quite crisp and brittle.

A plain wine biscuit: Four pounds flour, three pounds sugar, one-half pound butter, one-half ounce baking powder, rubbed together and then add milk to wet into a fairly firm dough. Put a little egg yellow and essence of lemon in the milk. These biscuits retain their shape in the oven, and do not flow. But if one pound of flour is taken away they will flow enough to take away any design there may be in the cutter, and will, of course, be a little richer. Try another recipe with the three pounds flour, two pounds sugar, and one pound fat. Leave out the water, the color, and powder, and wet up with yolk of egg and a rich, high-class dessert biscuit will be the product. Change the quantities of the sugar and butter, *i. e.*, two pounds butter, one pound sugar, and the three pounds flour, and the best Scotch shortbread is the product, and this is the base of a large variety of best wine biscuits, by merely shifting the sugar an ounce or two back or forward, and using a little milk, or yolk of eggs and flavoring and dried fruits.

These few examples with experience in the worker, will go far to help in the building up of new recipes, and this is sadly wanted at the present time. I would suggest too that even the old names of cakes and small goods should give place to an all-round change in name. Here is work for the experienced practitioner, who would be an adept in his calling, and would be more likely to ripen his knowledge than any amount of following old recipes, no matter how clearly and carefully they are written.

A POINT TO REMEMBER

The chief point to lay firm hold of in this question of recipe building, is the law of compensations as to moisture, shortening, sweetening, and aeration, and that the capacity of eggs to raise goods is developed by beating. This is seen particularly in sponge and meringue goods, but applies in all cases. The amount of beating and the mode of mixing in the other ingredients govern largely the behavior of goods during baking.

The character of fat and moisture does not enter very seriously into governing factors or bases. This has more to do with the resulting quality of the article

beaten with the sugar, and the eggs whisked separately, and then the whole of the ingredients lightly and quickly mixed together, but not toughened, in the mixing. Here again, however, there is another proviso, and that is, unless the mixture has also a full quantity of baking powder, when this is the case, the powder is depended upon for the aeration, the fat for shortening, and the mixture should be toughened in the final mixing or the goods are liable to be coarse and crumbly.

—‡—‡—‡—

Information Department

(Concluded from Page 57)

mixture in this tin, and when baked ice the bottom pink and put a piece or two of prune meat on top in the centre. Another plan is to half fill the tin with the mixture, then cover it with a layer of prune meat, letting the meat be a little apart, then add more mixture and bake. When baked, pink ice the bottom and put on a few pieces of prune meat as before directed.

PARISIAN TARTLETS

Three-quarters pound of sugar, one-half pound of currants, three-quarters pound of cake crumbs; one-half pound of butter, one-quarter pound of peel, one-quarter pound of ground rice, one-eighth pint of cream, oil of lemon, two ounces of fine cocoanut. Have some clean patty pans, line each with a good puff paste cut rather thin, and dock well in the center of each. Prepare the above ingredients for filling as follows: Cream up the butter with the sugar to a fine cream, wet the ground rice up with a little milk and add together with the cream. Then add the remaining ingredients, with sufficient milk to form a free cake batter. Spoon out into the patty cases, and bake in a solid oven. When cold, ice the tops with water icing, and decorate as desired.

BELGIAN CAKES

Six ounces of butter, eight ounces of sugar, two ounces of ground almonds, six ounces of flour, eight eggs, orange flower water. Place the eggs and sugar in a round-bottomed bowl, and proceed to beat up to a thick cream over hot water. Wet the ground almonds to a thin paste with white of egg, add a few drops of orange flower water and pour gently upon the sugar and egg batter. Add the flour gently and lastly the

Recipe Department

In this department we will publish new and valuable recipes and want our readers to forward to us any recipe from which they have had good results, or that is not generally known. We wish to make this department as interesting as possible and ask our readers to help us to this end. Address.

RECIPE DEPARTMENT   THE NATIONAL BAKER

COCOANUT CREAM PATTIES

Roll out a sheet of puff paste to one-fourth of an inch in thickness, and cut it into shells with a two-inch fluted cutter. Mark the tops with a small round cutter, just sufficient to break through the surface. Lay the goods on papered tins, and bake them in a moderate oven. When they are cold, remove the centres of the shells, press in the crumbs, and fill the space with the following filling, afterwards squeezing a ball of meringue on the top of each and putting the goods to dry in the oven.

(The Filling)

One pound pulverized sugar, four egg-whites, desiccated cocoanut, lemon flavoring. Whisk the egg whites to a stiff snow; add the flavoring, and then work in sufficient desiccated cocoanut to make a rather soft paste.

COCOANUT SPONGE BALLS

Two pounds flour, one and one-half pounds pulverized sugar, twelve ounces desiccated cocoanut, sixteen eggs, lemon flavoring. Whisk up the eggs to a light froth, add in the sugar and cocoanut, and then whisk again until a stiff batter results. Sift the flour and stir it gently into the batter, and follow with the lemon flavoring. Put the mixture into a savoy biscuit bag, and drop it out, into small cakes the size of a penny, on sheets of white paper. Sprinkle some desiccated cocoanut on the tops, dust the goods over with fine sugar, lay the sheets on baking tins, and bake delicately in a sharp oven. When cold, damp the bottom of the paper, let it lay for a short time, and then take off the cakes and stick two together, while they are damp. Lay these on a papered tray, put them in the oven for a minute, and they should be ready for use as soon as cold.

ALMOND HONEY CAKES

Two and one-half pounds flour, two pounds honey, one pound ground sweet almonds, one ounce baking powder, one-fourth pint cherry brandy, grated rind and juice of one orange. Sift the baking powder with the flour, mix in the almonds and grated peel, and then make a bay; stir the orange juice into the honey, run these into the bay, mix in the brandy, and make all into a stiff paste. Roll out to form a sheet, and cut that into round cakes, one-eighth of an inch thick. Lay the latter on buttered tins, and bake them in a warm oven. While hot, cover the tops with hot-water icing.

ALMOND BISCUIT

Two pounds flour, one and one-half pounds pulverized sugar, one ounce butter, eight ounces ground almonds, one ounce baking powder, one-half pint egg yolk, lemon flavoring. Sift the baking powder with the flour; rub in the butter, mix the sugar, almonds and flavoring, and make a bay. Turn in the egg yolks and work all up into a stiff paste. Roll out to produce a sheet one-eighth of an inch thick; cut into biscuits with a round cutter; place on buttered tins, and bake in a moderate oven. When cool cover the tops with hot-water icing, and while wet sprinkle it with variously colored sugar sands to make as great a variety as possible.

SUGAR ALMOND BISCUITS

Two pounds flour, one and one-half pounds pulverized sugar, one pound butter, twelve ounces ground almonds, eight ounces finely chopped drained lemon peel, one and one-half ounces baking powder, six eggs. Sift together the baking powder and flour, mix the almonds and peel with them, rub in the butter and sugar, form a bay, turn in the eggs, and then make the whole into a stiff paste. Roll this out to form a sheet one-eighth of an inch in thickness, and damp it over with beaten egg white. Now cut this into biscuits with a small round cutter, turn these over on a mixture of equal parts of ground almonds and fine crystal sugar, place the lot on buttered tins, and bake in a moderately warm oven, but do not let the biscuits get too highly colored.

PISTACHIO AND ALMOND CAKE

One pound flour, one pound ground sweet almonds, twelve ounces pulverized sugar, eight eggs, chopped pistachio nuts, crystal sugar. Whip up the eggs to a light froth, add the sugar, and whisk again to a light batter. Mix the flour and ground almonds, and drop them lightly into the batter. Turn that into a paper-lined baking tin about an inch deep, and bake it in a warm oven. When partly cool, spread a layer of hot-water icing on the top, and while wet sprinkle thickly on it a mixture of equal parts of chopped pistachio nuts and crystal sugar. When set, cut into pieces of any desired shape or size.

"ZECOBON" CAKE *

One pound flour, one pound ground almonds, one pound pulverized sugar, one ounce baking powder, one-fourth ounce ground nutmeg, eight eggs. Whisk the eggs and sugar to a light batter, stir in the almonds, sift the nutmeg and baking powder with the flour, and work it into the mixture. Turn the batch into a shallow square tin, previously lined with buttered paper, level the top, and bake in a warm oven. Spread a layer of yellow-colored hot-water icing on the surface of the cake while warm, and when set, cut out to weigh as required.

MOONBEAMS

(The Shells)

Six egg whites, two eggs, juice of one lemon, flour, almond flavoring. Whisk the eggs and egg whites to a light froth, and while doing so beat in the flavoring and lemon juice; then add sufficient flour to make a stiff, tenacious paste. Roll this out to make a sheet as thin as a quarter, and then cut it into rounds with a cutter two inches in diameter. Pinch up the sides of each and form a four-cornered shell, press the corners closely to prevent them falling, and afterwards lay the shells aside to dry.

(The Filling)

One pound ground almonds, one pound pulverized sugar, six eggs, one-half pint water, vanilla flavoring.

Melt the sugar in the water, and boil up in the usual manner. Remove the pan from the fire, gradually stir in the ground almonds, whisk the eggs to a froth, and beat them into the almond mixture. Return the vessel to the fire, and agitate the contents until thick. Again remove it in order to add the flavoring. Stir well, and set aside to cool. Then three parts fill the shells with the mixture, stand them on clean tins, bake in a moderate oven, and while warm, dust over with fine sugar.

DOMINO SQUARES

Roll out a sheet of three-fourths paste one-eighth of an inch in thickness, and cut it into pieces three inches square; place these on clean tins, prick the tops with a docker, and bake in a moderate oven. When cold, spread white hot-water icing on the top of each, and run three strips of vanilla-flavored chocolate icing along the top of one-half of each—leaving the other half of the top to show the plain white icing.

PRIMROSE CAKES

Four pounds flour, one and one-fourth pounds pulverized sugar, one pound butter, two ounces yeast, one quart milk, saffron coloring, lemon flavoring. Make the milk lukewarm, dissolve the yeast in it, work in half the flour, and stand all in a warm position to prove. Rub the butter and sugar into the remainder of the flour, and make a bay. When the sponge has risen turn it into the bay, add the flavoring, and sufficient coloring to make the batch a deep primrose tint.

Mold and work the dough until soft, springy and dry. Break into pieces, shape them; place these on buttered tins, and flatten with the hand. Draw up the edges by making nine notches; mark the centre of each deeply with a small round cutter, and let the cakes prove to the size required. When cool, cover them with a masking of yellow-colored hot-water icing, and run into each of the crevices of the notches a fine line of chocolate icing. A circlé of red jelly piped around the centre of the bun forms a pretty contrast to the other colors, and will heighten the idea of the cakes being representations of the primrose.

ICE CREAM TARTLETS

Roll out a sheet of best puff-paste a quarter of an inch in thickness, mark out rounds with a two-inch fluted cutter, cut the top skin through with a small circular cutter, place the pieces on buttered and papered tins, and then wash each with beaten egg yolk, and bake all in a moderate oven. When quite cold, remove the circle at the top with a pointed knife, press down the inner crumbs, fill the cavity with ice cream, piling it up well in the centre—and place the tartlets in a refrigerator until wanted.

Ice cream of different colors and flavors should be used to give an agreeable variety.

ICE CREAM ECLAIRS

Twelve ounces flour, four ounces butter, twelve eggs, one pint water, chocolate icing, vanilla ice cream. Put the water in a small pan, place that on the fire, add the butter, and when these come to a boil, rapidly stir in the flour. Keep the mixture constantly in motion with a wooden spoon, until the paste leaves the bottom and sides of the pan. Now remove the vessel from the fire, and beat the eggs into the mixture, two at the time, working the spoon rapidly all the while, or the cream will curdle. When all the eggs are in, and the batch is light and smooth, turn it into a bag, and squeeze it out into cakes three-fourths of an inch in width, and four inches long, on buttered tins, and bake in a hot oven. When quite cold, split each cake down one side, fill the cavity with vanilla ice cream, close the cake again, and spread chocolate icing over the tops. Place the cakes in dishes, and put them in a refrigerator until wanted.

ENGAGEMENT DOUBLETS

Two and one-half pounds flour, two pounds pulverized sugar, one ounce baking powder, sixteen eggs, lemon flavoring. Whip up the eggs to a light froth, add the sugar and whisk again to a stiff batter. Sift the baking powder with the flour, and work them and the flavoring gently into the batch. Put the mixture into a savoy biscuit bag, and squeeze out circular cakes, an inch in diameter, on sheets of thin paper; dust the goods with fine sugar, place the papers on baking tins or wires, and bake in a warm oven. When cold, damp the papers, remove the cakes, spread apricot jam on the bottoms, and stick them together in pairs, so that they will represent "twin" cakes or "doublets."

"MIZRAYIM" CRESCENTS

To properly turn out these cakes two mixings will be found necessary:

First Batch (Brown)

Two pounds flour, one pound butter, one pound pulverized sugar, three ounces ground almonds, one and one-half ounces ground cinnamon, grated rind of two lemons, four eggs. Beat the sugar and butter to a cream, and add the ground almonds and grated peel; whisk the eggs and work them into the mixture; sift the cinnamon with the flour and incorporate that with the other ingredients. Then mold and work the paste on the table until it is smooth, dusting it well while doing so.

Second Batch (White)

One pound ground almonds, one pound pulverized sugar, eight egg yolks. Mix together the sugar and almonds, add the egg yolks, and make a stiff paste, which should be molded until quite smooth.

Cut the cinnamon paste in halves, roll one piece out to produce a sheet one-eighth of an inch thick, then work the almond paste into a sheet exactly the same size, making each as square as possible. Next roll the remaining half of the cinnamon paste into a sheet the same thickness as the others; damp the first with water, place the almond paste sheet on the top of it, afterwards slightly dampening the surface, and then put the second sheet of cinnamon paste over this. Cut the whole into crescents, lay them on buttered tins, and bake in a moderate oven. When cold, pipe the top edges of these crescents (which show three thicknesses) with red currant jelly.

FRUIT AND RICE ECLAIRS

One pound rice, twelve ounces pulverized sugar, eight ounces butter, one pint egg yolks, one-half pint fruit pulp (stoneless), one-half pint water. Boil the rice until it is quite soft, beat it until smooth, and then mix it with the sugar. Put the water, fruit pulp and butter into a clean copper pan, and place the vessel on a moderate fire. Stir the contents until they boil, and add the rice and sugar. When these are thoroughly incorporated, remove the pan from the fire, let the mixture get partly cool, and then gradually work in the egg yolks with a large spoon. Beat until cold, and afterwards put the mixture into a savoy biscuit bag, and squeeze it out into cakes four inches long and one inch wide. These should be laid on buttered tins, and baked in a sharp oven. While warm, pass a thin palette knife under the cakes to free them from the tin, and when cold split them open at one end, spread some jam or preserve inside, and after reclosing, cover the cakes with clear, white, hot-water icing, and then dust with rather coarse sugar sands—red on some, green on others, and chocolate on a few more, to give variety to the whole.

Business Chances

MACHINERY FOR SALE

1—20-inch Thomson Moulder Extension, new.
1—Thomson Zerah Baller.
1—Hubbard Oven, No. 11½.
1—Bennett Oven, No. 115.
1—Bakerite Oven.
1—2½-bbl. Day Dough Mixer.
1—2-bbl. Read Dough Mixer.
1—1½-bbl. Read Dough Mixer.
1—1-bbl. Read Dough Mixer.
2—Union Bun Rounders.
2—Day Dough Brakes.
1—No. 3 Day Clipper Beater.
3—Day Wood Flour Sifters.
2—Triumph All-Steel Flour Sifters.
1—2-bbl. Triumph Dough Mixer.
2—Wood-Proof Closets, for public view bakery.
2—Steel-Proof Closets, for same.
1—1½-bbl. Peerless Dough Mixer.
1—Giant Cake Mixer and Motor.
1—Triumph Mixer and Motor.

Cake Machines, Bread Racks, Troughs and Equipment of every description ready for immediate shipment, new or rebuilt. Rebuilt machines guaranteed same as new ones.

J. H. BAST & CO.
649 W. Pratt St.   Baltimore, Md.

MISCELLANEOUS

TURNER'S RAPID RECIPE RECKoner simplifies cost accounting so that it is a matter of only a few minutes to get the cost of a batch of any size, and of any class of goods. The baker is saved all the trouble in counting up the cost; it is already done for him. Tables are given of the cost of each ounce of flour at a price per barrel from $4.00 upward, of other materials from $0.01 to $0.60 by the pound, and the cost of each ounce. One is needed in every bake-shop, and the cost is but $2.00 postpaid. For sale by THE NATIONAL BAKER, 411 Walnut Street, Philadelphia, Pa.

MACHINERY FOR SALE

FOR SALE—FOR A VERY LOW price you can secure the following slightly used equipment:
Two Yankee Reel Ovens, $100 each.

DOUGH MIXERS
1 Dutchess, 4 bbl. J. H. Day, 3 bbl.
1 Rockwell, 4 bbl. 2 Rockwell, 8 bbl.
J. H. Day, 2 bbl. Double Jacketed.
1 Century, 3 bbl.

CAKE MACHINES
Read
1 Little Giant   1 Champion
1 Hobart with D. C. Motor attached
Dutchess Two-Pocket Divider
Dutchess Roll Dividers
Bread and Pan Racks
Proofing Closets   Troughs
Work Tables   Bread Pans
1 Day Egg Clipper   Shipping Boxes
Sheet iron pans for the following ovens: Yankee, Barker and Federal.
Dough brake, A-1 condition
2 Doughnut Fryers with trays

I. KALFUS COMPANY
176 Stanton St.   New York City

MACHINERY WANTED

PRINTING MACHINES WANTED —New, rotary 2 color, for producing first-class printed bread wrappers. Must be complete with casting box, etc. State full particulars and location for inspection. Box 8, care THE NATIONAL BAKER, 411 Walnut St., Philadelphia.

BAKERIES FOR SALE

FOR SALE—MODERN EQUIPPED wholesale bakery with good established business, owns corner lot, 200 x 125, upon which bakery is situated; also 15 automobile trucks, 5 ovens, and two 7-room dwelling houses. Located in Jacksonville, Florida, a city of 100,000 population. An exceptional opportunity for any one interested in a wholesale bakery. For further information communicate with Morgan F. Jones, Receiver, 104 Law Exchange, Jacksonville, Florida.

BAKERIES FOR SALE

FOR SALE—BAKERY AND ICE Cream Parlor. Good business. Established 40 years. Death of owner selling reason. Town 16,000. For price and particulars address Mary K. Storck, 226 Gilman Ave., Marietta, Ohio.

FOR SALE—ONLY BAKERY IN thriving tobacco and college town. Hubbard three deck oven. Hobart cake machine. Baking outfit complete. Cheap for quick cash sale. Ill health reason for selling. Address Blackstone Bakery, Blackstone, Va.

FOR SALE—ESTABLISHED 33 years, modern equipped wholesale bakery doing excellent business. For further particulars address E. T. Reese, 207 Pearson St., New Castle, Penna.

FOR SALE—CASH AND CARRY bakery, best location in a good Ohio town of 10,000. Baking outfit complete—price cheap, if taken at once. Address B. 20, care THE NATIONAL BAKER, 411 Walnut St., Philadelphia, Pa.

FOR SALE — BAKERY, ICE cream parlor, candy, cigars, cigarettes, tobacco and light grocery in growing Michigan industrial city of 5,000 population. Splendid farming territory surrounding. All cash business. Century cake mixer, Bennett oven, first class soda fountain, 2 cash registers. Complete bakery and store outfit. Good lease. Sell at real bargain. Price $3,800. Must sell on account of disagreement of partners. City Bakery, Sturgis, Mich.

FOR SALE—BAKERY WITH two Petersen ovens, dough mixer, Hobart cake machine, bun divider and accessories, all in good condition. Steam boiler, motor. A bargain and an old established business. Building for rent with rooms above. H. D. Odom, Realtor, Louisville Ky.

A Classified List of Goods Needed by Bakers

Automobile Trucks—
Republic Truck Sales Corp., Alma, Mich.

Almond Paste—
Henry Heide, Inc., New York.

Bakery Advertising—
L. B. Nordhem Co., N. Y.
Schulze Advert. Service, Chicago.

Bakers' Institute—
Siebel Institute, Chicago.

Bakers' Machinery—
Champion Machine Co., Joliet, Ill.
J. H. Day Co., Cincinnati, O.
Dutchess Tool Co., Beacon, N. Y.
Freymark Steam Generator Co., St. Louis.
Jaburg-Miller Co., New York.
Peerless Bread Mch. Co., Sidney, O.
Read Machinery Co., York, Pa.
Reeves Pulley Co., Columbus, Ind.
Syracuse Steam Generator Co., Syracuse, N. Y.
Thomson Mch. Co., Bellevue, N. J.
Thomas Mills & Bro., Philadelphia.
Union Machinery Co., Joliet, Ill.

Bakers' Pans—
J. W. Allen & Co., Chicago.
Jaburg Bros., New York.
Jaburg-Miller Co., New York.
Edward Katsinger Co., Chicago.
The Aug. Maag Co., Baltimore.
Thomas Mills & Bro., Philadelphia.

Bakers' Tools—
J. W. Allen & Co., Chicago.
Jaburg Bros., New York.
Jaburg-Miller Co., New York.
Edward Katsinger Co., Chicago.
The Aug. Maag Co., Baltimore.
Thomas Mills & Bro., Philadelphia.
Union Steel Products Co., Albion.

Books for Bakers—
Malsbender's Recipe Book.
Turner's Rapid Recipe Reckoner.

Bread Labels—
Mirror Printing Co., Kalamazoo.
National Binding Mch. Co., N. Y.

Bread Wrapping and Sealing Machines—
National Bread Wrapping Machine Co., Nashua, N. H.
Lambooy Label & Wrapper Co., Kalamazoo, Mich.
Union Machinery Co., Joliet, Ill.

Cash Registers—
National Cash Register Company.

Chocolate—
Walter Baker & Co., Ltd., Dorchester.

Cooking Oil
Corn Products Ref. Co., New York.
Patent Cereals Co., Geneva, N. Y.

Dough Mixers and Kneaders—
Champion Machinery Co., Joliet, Ill.
J. H. Day Co., Cincinnati, O.
Read Machinery Co., York, Pa.

Eggs-Desiccated—Egg Products—
Joe Lowe Co., N. Y.

Flour—
Atkinson Milling Co., Minn.
Big Diamond Mills Co., Minn.
Commander Mills, Minneapolis.
Empire Milling Co., Minneapolis.
W. J. Jennison & Co., Minneapolis.
Russell-Miller Milling Co., Minn.
Updike Milling Co., Omaha.
Washburn-Crosby Co., Minneapolis.

Food Colors—
National Aniline & Chem. Co., N. Y.

Fruit Growers—
California Associated Raisin Co.
California Prune & Apricot Growers.

Honey—
Arthur A. Beals, Oto, Iowa.

Ice Cream Tools and Supplies—
J. W. Allen & Co., Chicago.
Atlas Mfg. Co., New Haven.
Chr. Hansen's Lab., Little Falls, N. Y.
The Aug. Maag Co., Baltimore.
Thomas Mills & Bro., Philadelphia.

Malt, Extract and Dry—
American Diamalt Co.
Anheuser-Busch, Inc., St. Louis.
P. Ballantine & Sons, Newark.
Freihofer Baking Co., Philadelphia.
Malt Diastase Co., N. Y.
Stein-Hall Mfg. Co., Chicago.

Milk, Powdered and Condensed—
Consolidated Prod. Co., Lincoln, Neb.
I. H. Nester & Co., Philadelphia.

Ovens—
Bennett Oven Co., Battle Creek.
Duhrkop Oven Co., New York.
Hubbard Oven Co., Chicago.
Meek Oven Mfg. Co., Westport, Conn.
Middleby Oven Co., New York.
Middleby-Marshall Co., Chicago.
Standard Oven Co., Pittsburgh.
Superior Oven Co., Chicago, Ill.

Oven Lights and Doors—
Dutchess Tool Co., Beacon, N. Y.
Chas. Robson & Co., Philadelphia.

Papers (Parchment and Waxed)—
Lambooy Label & Wrapper Co., Kalamazoo, Mich.
Menasha Ptg. & Carton Co., Menasha, Wis.
Waterproof Paper & Board Co., Cincinnati.

Pie Machinery—
Edwin E. Bartlett, Nashua, N. H.
J. H. Day Co., Cincinnati, O.
Union Machinery Co., Joliet, Ill.

Potato Flour—
Falk American Potato Flour Co., Pittsburgh, Pa.

Pyrometers—
Hubbard Oven Co., Chicago.
Philadelphia Thermometer Co.
Chas. Robson & Co., Philadelphia.

Shipping Boxes (Wood and Paper)—
A. Backus, Jr., & Son, Detroit.
Rob't Gaylord, Inc., St. Louis.

Shortening—
Corn Products Refining Co., N. Y.
Procter & Gamble Co., Cincinnati.

Stoves for Bakers and Confectioners—
Edward Katsinger Co., Chicago.
Thomas Mills & Bro., Philadelphia.

Sugar and Sugar Syrups—
American Sugar Ref. Co., N. Y.
Corn Products Ref. Co., New York.
Franklin Sugar Ref. Co., Philadelphia.

Supplies—
J. W. Allen & Co., Chicago.
Jaburg Bros., New York.
Joe Lowe Co., N. Y.
Stein-Hall Mfg. Co., Chicago and N. Y.
Ward Baking Co., New York.

Thermometers—
Phila. Thermometer Co., Phila.

Vermin Exterminator—
Berg & Beard Mfg. Co., Brooklyn.

Washing and Cleaning Material—
J. B. Ford Co.

Yeast—
The Fleischmann Co., New York.

INDEX TO ADVERTISEMENTS

                    Page

American Diamalt Co. 14
Anheuser-Busch Sales Corp......... 43
American Sugar Refining Co........ 47

Baker & Co., Ltd., Walter 57
Ballantine & Sons, P. 15
Bartlett, Edwin E................. 39
Bennett Oven Co. 4
Berg & Beard Mfg. Co............. 62
Big Diamond Mills Co. 4
Business Chances 65
California Associated Raisin Co..... 11
California Prune & Apricot Growers 51
Carter, Rice & Co., Corporation..... 13
Commander Mills 55
Corn Products Ref. Co. 9

Day Co., The J. H................. 6
Duhrkop Oven Co. 18
Dutchess Tool Co. 14, 49

Empire Milling Co. 16

Fleischmann Co., The 45
Ford Co., J. B.................... 55

Freihofer Baking Co. 59
Freymark Steam Generator Co...... 47

Heide, Inc., Henry 63
Hubbard Portable Oven Co. ......Cover

Jennison Co., W. J. 16

Katsinger Co., Edward ....Cover

Lambooy Label & Wrapper Co. 4

Maag Co., The Aug. ....Cover
Malt Diastase Co. 16
Malsbender, M. 13
Meek Oven Co. ....
Menasha Printing & Carton Co. 55
Middleby-Marshall Oven Co........ 8
Middleby Oven Co., N. Y.......... 15
Mills & Bro., Inc., Thomas 61

National Bread Wrapping Mach. Co. 13

Philadelphia Thermometer Co. 4
Procter & Gamble Co. 6

Read Machinery Co. 7
Reeves Pulley Co. 6
Republic Truck Sales Corp. 3
Robson & Co., Charles 13
Russell-Miller Milling Co. 10

Siebel Institute 17
Standard Oven Co. 6
Superior Oven Co. 41

Thomson Machine Co. 7
Turner, A. R. 57

Union Steel Products Co...... ...
Union Machinery Co. 5

Ward Baking Co. 22
Washburn-Crosby Co. ....Cover
Water-proof Paper & Board Co. 4

KLEEN-KRUST
RIVETLESS
REG U S PAT. OFF
"STEEL-SHOD"
BREAD PANS
(Patented Jan. 21, 1913; Jan. 16, 1917.)

The Appearance of the Loaf
is of Prime Importance--

Flanges Prevent
Pans from Spread-
ing.

—it goes a long way in creating
a demand for your bread. If
you would turn out loaves of
exceptional uniformity—clean,
spotless loaves—you will bake
in Kleen Krust Rivetless "Steel-
Shod" Bread Pans.

Extra Heavy Steel
Rod Used in Binding
Pans Together.

Steel Shod Ends
Protect the End
Pans.

With Covers for
Pullman or
Sandwich
Loaves

Entirely Different from Any Other Pan on the Market

Their construction, the most rigid and sanitary ever devised, entirely eliminates strapping, therefore neither dirt nor grease can collect.

The outer face of the end pans is protected by a sheet of steel which
acts as a piece of armor-plate. This steers the peel underneath
the pans, eliminating all danger of battering the end pan.

Kleen-Krust Rivetless "Steel-Shod" Bread Pans are manufactured under letters patent granted by the U. S. Government. We are sole manufacturers.

The advantages of Kleen-Krust Rivetless "Steel-
Shod" Bread Pans go a long way toward creating a
demand for your bread by improving the appearance
of the loaf. In order that you may find out these
advantages for yourself we will forward a sample
set of open Pans for immediate practical use in
your oven room.

Specially Adapted for Traveling Ovens

We have issued a New Catalog illus-
trating and describing our Kleen-
Krust Rivetless "Steel Shod" Bread
Pans and Kleen-Krust Rivetless
Pullman or Sandwich Bread Pans.
Catalog mailed on request.

UNIFORMITY

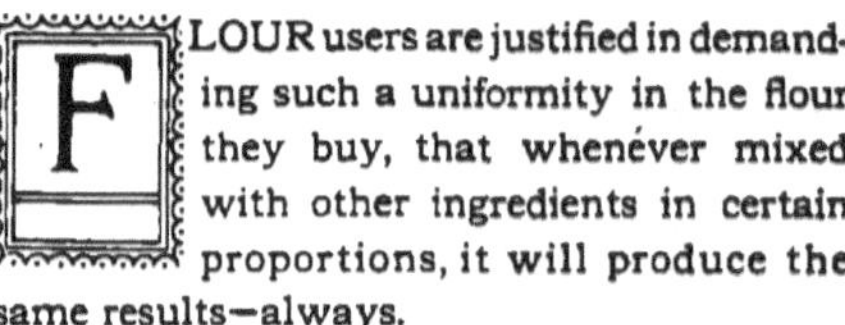

FLOUR users are justified in demanding such a uniformity in the flour they buy, that whenever mixed with other ingredients in certain proportions, it will produce the same results—always.

To supply this uniformity Washburn-Crosby Company maintains a complete scientific elevator and mill control.

Streams of tested wheat from all sections of the great spring wheat territory flow continuously through mammoth distributing elevators to all of the Company's mills.

Each day's grind in every mill is governed by a standard formula prepared in the Company's laboratories and is made up of tested wheat containing the vital flour elements in exact proportions.

This is one of the various accurate processes which assure the uniformity of Gold Medal Flour.

VOL. XXVII.   ENTERED AT THE PHILADELPHIA POST OFFICE AS SECOND CLASS MATTER   No. 314

THE NATIONAL BAKER

PUBLISHED MONTHLY BY
THE NATIONAL BAKER PUBLISHING CO.
411 WALNUT STREET
B. F. WHITECAR, Pres. and Editor

PHILADELPHIA, PA., MARCH 15, 1922

Price per Year, U. S.
and Canada $2.00
Foreign Countries $3.00

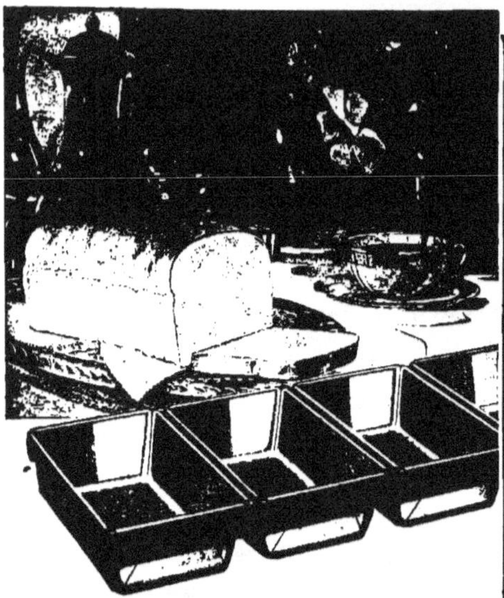

Wholesome Pure Bread
Makes Pleased Customers

SAVORY, sweet loaves that tempt the appetite with their golden-brown crust, and smooth, firm sides. Bread whose rich, nut-like flavor whets the taste. That is the kind of bread people like, and people buy.

That is the kind of bread that may always be expected of Ekco Everstay Strapped Sets. Their unique construction helps bake loaves that please customers. All supply houses carry stock sizes for prompt shipment.

STOCK SIZES

Single and Double Loaf

Pan No.	Top Inside	Bottom Outside	Depth	Capacity Ounces
06	8 x4	7¼x3¼	2½	12–13
06A	8 x4	7⅝x3⅝	2¼	12–14
07	8½x4½	7⅝x3⅝	2¾	16–18
07A	8¼x4¼	7¼x3⅝	2½	15–17
08	8¾x4¼	7½x3¼	2½	16–18
017	9½x4½	8⅜x3½	2¾	16–20
017A	9¼x4¼	8⅜x3⅝	2½	16–20
044	9 x4½	8⅜x3¾	2½	16–18
045	9¼x5¼	8½x4¼	2¾	20–24
046	10¼x4¾	9⅝x4¼	2½	24–26
047	9¾x5¼	8¾x4¼	2¾	24–26
047A	9 x5	8¼x4¼	2½	24–26
048	9½x5½	8½x4½	3	24–28
055	9½x5	8¾x4¼	3	24–28
056	10 x5	9⅜x4½	3	24–30
027	9½x4½	8½x3½	3½	18–22
027A	9¾x4¾	8½x3½	3	20–24
084	7¾x7¾	7½x7¼	2	24–28
085	8 x8	7¼x7½	2¾	24–32
088	8½x7½	8 x7	2½	32–36
088A	8 x7	7½x6½	2½	24–32
086	8½x8½	7½x7¾	2½	32–36
086A	8¼x8¼	7⅝x7¼	2¾	32–36
087	8⅜x8¼	8 x8	2¾	36–44
089	9 x8	8⅝x7½	2½	32–36

There's an Ekco Guaranteed Product for Every Baking Need

Ekco Layer Cake Pan

Drawn from a single piece of heavy tin. The straight sides do away with wasteful trimming and allow even icing. The rolled edge gives great strength and lasting ability. Specify Ekco.

EDWARD KATZINGER CO.

131 N. SANGAMON STREET - CHICAGO, ILL.
Dept. K DREXEL BLDG. - PHILADELPHIA, PA.

Largest Manufacturers of Bake Pans in the World

Republic Rapid Transit, with Panel Body and Fore-Door Open Cab, Cord Tires, Electric Starter and Lights. Price on application

Increase Your Profit-Margin by Cutting Delivery Costs

Other body types include

Carry-All
Canopy Top
Stock Rack
Screen Enclosed
Tank Body
Open Express
Double Deck
Platform Stake
Bus Body
Police Patrol
Grain Body
Bottlers' Body
Dump Body

The one sure way to prevent delivery costs from eating up small profit-margins is to install the Republic Rapid Transit.

This truck cuts cost—it is the lowest priced truck of its capacity and class; it is the lowest in operating and upkeep expense.

Republic Rapid Transit enables you to make more and quicker deliveries daily. It gains the good-will of customers. Instead of subtracting from, it *adds to bakers' profits.*

Send for Vocational Catalog showing how Republic Trucks save time and money for bakers.

The Republic Line: ¾, 1, 1½-2, 2½-3, 3½-4 tons capacity.

REPUBLIC TRUCK SALES CORPORATION
ALMA, MICH.

REPUBLIC
RAPID TRANSIT ©

Republic has more trucks in use than any other exclusive truck manufacturer

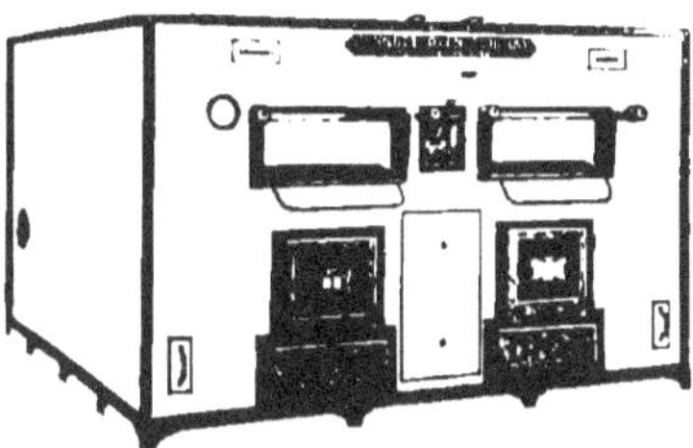

Bennett Ovens Make Busy Bakers

ARE you worrying along with an old style oven? Are you turning down new business because you cannot turn out the goods?

Install a modern, efficient Bennett Oven and you will be able to handle an increased demand on a profitable basis. Others are doing it. So can you.

Bennett Ovens Are Better Ovens

BENNETT OVEN CO.,   Ave. C & 22nd Street, Battle Creek, Mich.

The perfect bread-baking qualities of the Standard Oven builds business for the baker—and then he needs more Standard Ovens.

STANDARD OVEN COMPANY

1835 OLIVER BUILDING,   **PITTSBURGH, PA.**

THE RIGHT SPEED AT THE RIGHT TIME—that is the only solution for getting superior quality and maximum production of your pastry at the least expense.

"The Reeves" Variable Speed Transmission does this very thing to absolute perfection; you can get any variation at any time without even stopping your machine.

Some decided improvements have been made in the construction of "The Reeves" Transmission, such as—

Two Keys Full Length of Shaft.
Larger Roller Thrust Bearings, Etc.

which tends to give larger wearing surface, greater carrying capacity and longer life. SKF Ball Bearings are furnished for main boxes if desired.

Write for Bulletins T-1040 and T-1056 for Complete Description.

REEVES PULLEY COMPANY
COLUMBUS, INDIANA.

"DAY" Universal Moulder

With Adjustable Drum
For Different Length Loaves

Height Reduced — Unequalled Capacity — Silent Chain Drive

Again "Day" takes the lead in offering you the latest improvements in dough moulder construction. The new "Day" Universal Moulder embodies many exclusive features and has been pro-nounced by bakers who have seen it as the acme of perfection in moulders.

Adjustable Drum permits moulding of loaves for different length pans from 6 inches to 10 inches. No need for two or more moulders. Large feeding and sizing rolls reduce punishment to dough. Requires little flour. Alemite lubrication throughout.

Mixers, Rounders, Dividers, Proofers, Troughs and Racks

The J. H. DAY COMPANY
CINCINNATI, OHIO

New York   Boston   Chicago   San Francisco
Philadelphia Kansas City St. Louis Buffalo
Milwaukee Minneapolis Atlanta Pittsburgh Columbus

BAKE BETTER BREAD

Increase Your Profits

Model C—Double Oven—This is but one of the types we make. Our catalog describes many others. Our line comprises a size and style to meet your particular requirements.

Every baker knows that the better bread he bakes, the more sales he will make and the greater will be his profits.

Regardless of how good the quality of the materials used in the mixture and how careful you are in the various steps of preparations, unless you have a reliable oven you cannot assure yourself of a quality loaf that will satisfy your customers, and hold your trade.

But why take such a chance?

With a Middleby-Marshall Oven you will be absolutely sure of your product being properly baked regardless of whether it be bread or cake.

For all 'round work, Model C. Double oven, pictured above, cannot be equalled. The purchase of this oven is not an expense, it is an investment. Repeat orders are constantly being received from bakers everywhere who are using this oven with the greatest satisfaction.

Let us tell you more about this All 'Round Continuous Baking Oven. Upon request we shall be glad to send you our catalog free. Write for it today. You will be glad you did later.

MIDDLEBY-MARSHALL OVEN CO.

Largest Builders of Ovens in the World

760 W. Adams St.   **Chicago, Ill.**

Branch office and factory at   Address all correspondence to
St. Louis, Mo.   main office at Chicago

Saving
$10,000
annually

ONE BAKERY turning out over 150,000 loaves of bread daily is saving $10,000 annually through the use of REFINED CERELOSE—a new product; and there are many other bakers saving likewise in proportion to the number of loaves they turn out.

After exhaustive experiments with REFINED CERELOSE, both in the laboratory and in a practical way in their bakery, these bakers are obtaining as good a quality loaf in every respect, i.e., volume, color, moisture and texture as can be obtained with cane sugar at a cost of approximately one cent per pound less.

Keen competition which exists today in the bread baking industry, costly advertising about quality, together with an attempt to sell bread, generally, at five cents per loaf in face of the still high cost of labor, makes it necessary for every baker to do his utmost to cut his cost of production.

Here is an opportunity to save approximately one cent per pound on sugar by using REFINED CERELOSE—a new product—and still maintain your high standard of quality.

Sample of this product cheerfully sent upon application.

Corn Products Refining Co.
17 Battery Place, New York City

OCCIDENT

Extra Strong High Patent Flour

The enviable reputation of Occident as "First Among Flours" has been earned on genuine merit.

Russell-Miller Milling Co. Minneapolis Minnesota

Branch Offices:

Pittsburgh, Pa.	Park Bldg.	Boston, Mass.	Board of Trade Bldg.
Philadelphia, Pa	Lafayette Bldg.	Seattle, Wash.	Maritime Bldg.
Syracuse, N. Y.	Seitz Bldg.	San Francisco, Cal.	Merchants' Exch.
New York City	Produce Exchange	Des Moines, Iowa	122 S. W. 7th St.
	Los Angeles, Cal.	660 Santa Fe Ave.	

Again Millions Will Get Their Favorite Bread for

Raisins Are Now

40% Cheaper

RAISINS for *less money* offer you the opportunity to build up a large new trade on popular Seeded Raisin Bread.

Millions are clamoring for it—now you can bake it for them, *at a profit* well worth your while.

And these are *finer* raisins to do it with—raisins that make an even *more delicious* loaf than you ever made before.

Your mix with *seeded* raisins costs *less* than formerly —a combination that is hard to beat.

Begin at once. There is no question about the profit. It's sure. *The demand is waiting*—you know that. Meet it.

SUN-MAID RAISINS

Raisin bread is a "food of the ages." It has always been wanted—and always will be. It is nothing new— but a *constant* profit-maker for the baker who makes it well.

Indeed, you can well establish a reputation for yourself by making your shop *headquarters for good raisin bread.*

Start it Now

Now is the time to open up this trade. Raisins are 40% cheaper. Jump right in—before someone else lays the foundation for the trade *you* can have. Use the delicious Bakers' Seeded Sun-Maid Raisins.

Sun-Maid Raisin Growers

Membership 13,000   DEPT. E-603, FRESNO, CALIFORNIA

Free

The coupon below is for your use, no matter what position you hold in any bakery, large or small.

If your raisins, *no matter from whom purchased*, have deteriorated or lost quality for any reason, if you have an unused stock of raisins, *ask us for* suggestions to help remove the difficulty—no matter what it is. We maintain a Bakers' Service Department which will supply free formulas for mixes on request.

Short Cuts That Many Use

Here are ways that many bakers use to easily and quickly separate these Bakers' Seeded Sun-Maids:

Dip hands in hot water—the raisins quickly come apart, or

Mix an equal weight of flour with the raisins, working flour through with the hands, or

Dip hands in lard—which works like hot water, or

Place raisins on sheet pan in the oven for a while. That will separate them, and will also cause the white sugar-spots, if any, to disappear, the sugar going back into the raisins, restoring them to the same condition in which they left our California packing plant.

Use Bakers' Seeded Sun-Maids for your raisin bread and you'll be delighted with results.

Baker's (Seeded) Sun-Maids

Delicious Raisin-Bread Raisins

Bakers' Seeded Sun-Maid Raisins are especially for bakers' use in bread, cakes, cookies, snails, "race tracks," pie, etc., are selected, washed and sterilized, to make them perfect raisins for your use.

Now cheaper by 40% than formerly. Rely on price and other information given you by our own representatives who will call on you.

Bakers know that Seeded Raisins absorb 10% more water.

Sun-Maid Raisin Growers
Dept. E-603, Fresno, California.

Please send me free formulas for mixes for raisin products that you have found to be practical sellers through large and small bakeries.

Name

Street

City   State

Hot Cross Buns

The baker's opportunity to develop a profitable straight-through-Lent success

The tremendous success of Hot Cross Buns last year has proved the possibility of lifting them from a two-day novelty to an all-season success.

Last season we set ourselves the task to create the habit of eating Hot Cross Buns straight through Lent.

The public responded strongly—and is all ready to respond again.

We're just as ready with all the trade-aids you need to put over the idea big and strong.

—Newspaper Advertising
—Window Posters
—Movie Slides
—Publicity Stories

Ask the Fleischmann representative.   He'll supply you.

Department of Sales Promotion

The Fleischmann Company

Fleischmann's Yeast   *Fleischmann's Service*

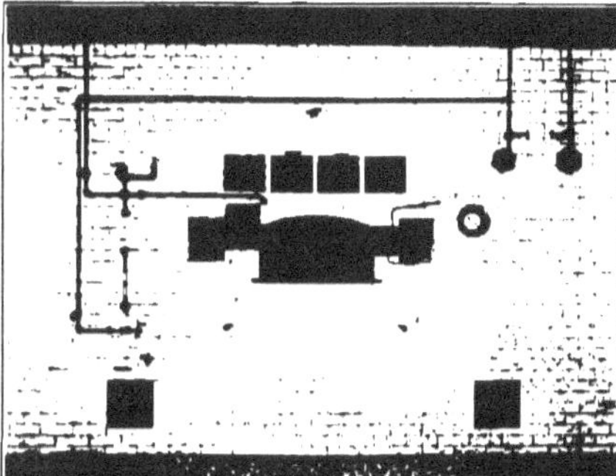

DUHRKOP OVENS

Mean

Oven

Satisfaction

This is proven by the fact that 90 per cent of our business is REPEAT ORDERS.

Ask for our list of DUHRKOP USERS--Note those in YOUR VICINITY.

DUHRKOP OVEN COMPANY

PARK ROW BUILDING   **NEW YORK, N. Y.**

DUTCHESS

Roll Dough Dividers, Oven Lights, Oven Doors, Fire Doors, Etc.

Make your work easy, accurate and profitable with a DUTCHESS Roll Dough Divider. These great labor and material savers are built in two sizes—a heavy floor machine, and a lighter machine for bench use. They can't be equalled for making rolls. Each machine cuts 36 pieces of equal weight at one operation. Don't waste your time breaking off rolls in the old fashioned, slow, wasteful one-at-a-time method. Save your time and material. Use a DUTCHESS

New Prices Effective May 2nd, 1921
Stand Machine $180.00

Bench Machine $80.00

For That New Oven

Insist on DUTCHESS Fixtures and you may be sure that they will give you lasting dependable service. They are made only of the best grade of grey iron castings, carefully fitted, no leaky joints, and resist the effect of heat and hold their shape.

Ask Your Supply House

✓ *Experience*

We can tell you, as hundreds of satisfied users have told us, that Diamalt makes better bread at less cost. But you will never really know the worth of Diamalt until you have tried it. Personal experience is most impressive.

So try Diamalt and know from personal experience that it saves sugar and that it gives more bread from a given batch of dough and larger loaves. Good bread, too, nice and solid instead of being full of large holes. And of better flavor.

The American Diamalt Company

Home Office, 419 Plum St., Cincinnati, Ohio

1182 Broadway, New York City
327 South La Salle St., Chicago
424 Bankers Investment Bldg.
San Francisco

(When addressing advertisers kindly refer to THE NATIONAL BAKER)

The Test of Time

is the surest test

OP Malt Extract

has stood this test and has not been found wanting.

Prudent bakers do not experiment—they place full reliance in

OP MALT EXTRACT

Malt-Diastase Company

79 Wall Street, NEW YORK

Warehouses: CHICAGO, PHILADELPHIA　　Laboratories, BROOKLYN, N. Y.

THE NATIONAL Baker

PUBLISHED ON THE FIFTEENTH OF EACH MONTH

AT

411 WALNUT ST., PHILADELPHIA

BY

THE NATIONAL·BAKER PUBLISHING CO.

B. F. WHITECAR, PRESIDENT AND EDITOR
W. W. GALE, SECRETARY AND TREASURER

MEMBER OF THE AUDIT BUREAU OF CIRCULATIONS

SUBSCRIPTION RATES

UNITED STATES, ITS POSSESSIONS AND CANADA ..$2.00 per year
FOREIGN COUNTRIES .... 3.00 per year

PAYABLE IN ADVANCE

ADVERTISING RATES ON APPLICATION

Make all remittances payable to the order of
The National Baker Publishing Company

*Changes for displayed advertisements must reach this office
by the 5th of the month*

VOL. XXVII	MARCH, 1922	No. 314

CONTENTS

American Bakers' Association 27
Bakers' Prices and the Public 24
Baker's Success 46
Bread Wars 23

Cake Recipes—
  Orange Sponge Squares... 58
  Marshmallow Roll 58
  Marshmallow Cocoanut
    Squares 58
  Marshmallow Roll 58
  Jelly Roll 58
  Tea Rusk 62
  Tea Biscuits 62
  Jelly Cake 62
  Rye and Raisin Ginger-
    bread 63
  Chocolate Jumbles 63
  Cocoanut Jumbles 63
  Milk Jumbles 64
  Wafer Jumbles 64
  Cinnamon Jumbles 64
  Mignons 64
  Genoese Pastry 64

Color in Bread 52
Council of Baking Meets.... 28
Dear Wheat—Cheap Bread. 38
Folklore of Bread and Cake 32
Fruit Cake Points 54
Illinois Convention 36
Information Department:
  Thirty Gallon Dough 59
  Cheap Lunch Cake 60
  Ants, To Get Rid of..... 60
  Jellied Cocoanut Buns.... 60

Butter Sponge Cake 60
Lemon Pie Filling........ 60
Patty Cakes 60
Fried Pies 60
Jelly Doughnuts 60
Hot Cross Buns 64
Is Your Heart in Your Work 26
Laboratories Ready for
  Service 30
Legal—
  Partners Should Register
    Names 40
Motor Delivery for Smaller
  Baker 36
New England Convention... 34
New Jersey Bread Weight
  Law 31
Norfolk Bakers Organize... 48
North Carolina Baker...... 37
Nutrition in Bread 58
Pennsylvania Convention.... 38
Publicity for Bread........ 30
Reduce Your Labor Costs.. 31
Salt in Baking 55
School of Baking of A. B. A. 44
School of Baking Starts.... 38
Stop the Leaks 24
Sugar Situation 42
Texas Convention 48
Trade Items 50
Work Horses and Their Care 36
Your Business Owes You a
  Proper Salary 25

Bread Wars

BREAD wars between opposing bakers are a form of madness which occasionally afflicts the trade in different parts of the country, and the results are usually disastrous to those who take part in them and the profit to the public is negligible. They are usually started by some' baker who either is ignorant of his costs or who hopes to secure a larger amount of trade at the expense of his competitors.

Ordinarily such price wars are indefensible from any standpoint. They create heartburnings and trade animosities, the effects of which endure for years. The baker who recklessly slashes prices seldom if ever profits from his action. He forces his competitors to meet his prices and they in turn cut prices below that of the man who started the merry (?) game. The result is that everyone loses money and trade; the public, for a time, get cheaper bread, then they get poorer quality bread; then they bake their own bread, and the bakers are just about where they started, but in every case with a much diminished bank account and an abiding "grouch."

Who profits from these senseless bread wars? The baker doesn't, the grocer doesn't, the public doesn't. To be sure, the local newspapers do profit, for each price-cutting baker rushes into advertising publicity and spends his good money recklessly to increase his sales—and on every sale he loses money.

Do the newspapers commend the bakers for selling bread at a lower cost—or below cost? Not so that you would notice it. They usually accuse the price-cutting baker of having taken inordinate profits previously. Rather poor reward!

The above reflections were inspired, in part, by the disastrous bread war that has been raging in Kansas City and vicinity. The Campbell Baking Co. announced a heavy cut in bread prices, and their competitors, claiming that they had not been given adequate notice of the cut, went the Campbell Company one better and cut below their prices, and chaos reigns in that territory. It is claimed, and apparently with good reason, that the several large bakeries in that city are losing thousands of dollars every week.

Win M. Campbell, president of the Campbell Baking Co., is also president of the American Bakers' Association and is widely known throughout the country. At the meeting of the Board of Governors of the Association at Chicago on February 18th, Mr. Campbell presented his resignation, which was accepted. There was nothing else to do.

We understand that Mr. Campbell denies intent to start a bread war, but it is a fact that despite repeated requests to do so he has declined to give any explanation of his actions. Considering Mr. Campbell's high position in the baking trade, and the fact that his fellow-bakers throughout the country had deemed him worthy of the honorable position of president of their trade organization, and considering further that the American Bakers' Association had adopted a Code of Ethics designed to adjust trade misunderstandings, his friends are greatly disappointed, and justly so, that his actions should have created a situation fraught with so much danger to the baking trade in general and to the Association in particular.

There are, of course, two sides to every story, but, again considering Mr. Campbell's late official position, we believe the baking trade will agree that he owes it to the bakers of the country to give his side of the story. If he was right in his actions at Kansas City there need be no fear but that his fellow-bakers will do him justice. If he was wrong, it would be the act of a man to say so. In either event his late official position places the obligation upon him of submitting his side of the controversy to the judgment of the baking trade. If he is the strong man his friends claim him to be, he will do so.

—‡—‡—‡—

Bakers' Prices and the Public

THERE are always a number of people, in no way associated or familiar with the baking trade, who arrogate to themselves the right of fixing for the baker the price at which he should sell his bread. No regard is paid to the amount of trade done, the cost of his raw materials, labor or fixed charges, such as rent, taxes, delivery costs, etc. These people affect to believe that bread can be made and sold at a lower price than then prevails, and, *"presto,"* why isn't it?"

Such solicitude for and by the public does not induce criticism of any other merchant or manufacturer; *they* may set selling prices according to their costs, or otherwise, and the public pays. But the baker is always a fair mark for criticism no matter what his costs may be, and these costs are frequently at the business danger line.

Of course, the baker is the object of solicitude of these busybodies, who affect to know so much, because the quotation of the prices of wheat and flour are so freely published, and because bread is the first consideration of so many people. The production of bread, however, is not a monopoly, far from it. No tradesman has greater present and potential competition. The baker must sell at a fair price or many of his customers will return to home baking; he must give good value or the housewife will turn the flour into bread instead of the baker. He cannot profiteer to any extent without inviting certain and effective competition. He must be "good." No baker has held or can hold up prices beyond a fair level for any length of time; the odds are too strongly against him.

Those who complain of the price of bread in proportion to the price of flour, too often lose sight of the fact that there are certain fixed charges which must be met, and which in the aggregate make up a considerable total. Flour is but one item, and constitutes less than half the cost of a loaf of bread delivered at the home, and flour is the only material which shows a reduction in price, and the very people who noted the low price of flour in January know nothing of its greatly increased cost since that time, and care less.

But, people must have something to talk about, and certain newspapers must have something "snappy" to bring before their readers. So they go after the baker. Everybody wants the high cost of living reduced—except where it touches their own business. Hands off then, but the baker has always been fair game and is so today.

—‡—‡—‡—

Stop the Leaks

CAREFULLY weigh everything that comes into your shop. Mistakes will occur, and money can be saved in this way. This policy also makes fair competition, as it insures against any possibility of getting a low price which is made up by short weight; wholesale houses always carefully check goods. There is no reason why retail bakers should not.

Insist on absolute cleanliness; nothing so mars the appearance of a shop as to have it untidy, and showcases and glasses should be scrupulously clean and neatly arranged, all goods being placed so as to be out of the way of flies.

Have intelligent people to wait on customers; better to pay a few dollars a week more and get help with brains, to be pleasant and know what people want and how to give it to them.

Always lend your ear to salesmen who visit you. They are walking encyclopedias of their particular line, and they can sometimes post a baker in five minutes more than he can otherwise learn in a month.

Prevent, as far as possible, all wastage; see that the butter tubs are well scraped, and that no eggs go back in the chaff. An ounce of sugar, of butter, or a few ounces of flour don't seem much to waste; but little things like that very soon run away with a five-dollar note, and in the course of a year amount up to a considerable sum, especially at present prices.

Keep your stock in a salable and neatly arranged condition. No matter how small, always fix that window so that it will look full. A full window attracts trade and gives your shop a lively appearance.

Never allow your accounts to become mixed. Every baker should so arrange his accounts as to be able to tell at a glance how he stands. No great amount of bookkeeping is necessary, but clear knowledge of your affairs is indispensable.

—‡—‡—‡—

Any number of men when considering or discussing a trade association will say: "What are *they* going to do now?" How much better it would be to say: "What are *we* going to do now?" And then jump in and help do whatever is to be done, or at the very least contribute of your means and advice to help make the Association a success!

Don't Fool Yourself—Your Business Owes You a Proper Salary

IF today there is one thing more important than another it is an intimate knowledge of the business. This does not mean merely knowing how to bake. It means knowing costs. People are demanding more for their money, and the only way that more can be given is by knowing more about costs. Every little while people are accusing business men of making undue profits, and especially the baker.

It is rather significant that the small business men, those who are usually making the smallest profits, are the ones who suffer most from this agitation against profiteering. The manufacturer and the big business man can present facts and figures to show that he is making little or no profit. Yet the individuals connected with these concerns may be making vastly more than the little man.

The president of a big concern may be drawing a salary of anywhere from twenty-five to more than a hundred thousand dollars a year, while the little fellow may not be making twenty-five dollars a week, yet the public will be more certain that he is profiteering than it is that the big fellow is. The reason for this is simple.

Big concerns have complete bookkeeping systems. They can show that they are not making undue profits, and they do show that this is the case. But profits do not begin until all expenses have been met, and these expenses include all the salaries.

On the other hand, the small man may not be paying himself a salary out of the business, at least not an adequate salary. He takes a smaller salary than he could get if he was working for someone else, and makes up the difference out of which he may call profits, but which, in fact, are not profits at all. He really does not know his business well enough so that he can show that he is not making an undue profit.

It is important in these days that a man know what his real profits really are. He will do better to draw out of the business each week or charge up against it at least as large a salary as he could draw from some other company. He is actually justified in giving himself a higher salary than he could earn elsewhere, because he is obliged to burden himself with more care and worry than he would if he was working for someone else.

If every baker did this in practice, many a one would find that he is making no profit at all. As a matter of fact, the business would owe him some money at the end of each year. If members of his family work in the business he should pay them just as much as he would have to pay any outsider. They may be worth more than an outsider and, if they are, they should be paid more.

Not until this is done can he realize just where the business stands. Not until this is done can he realize

just where the business stands. Not until then will he be as well acquainted with it as he should be.

To take an example, suppose that a man has five thousand dollars invested in a retail bakery. He devotes all of his time to it, his wife helps out some, and a son in school works during his spare time. Let us suppose that this man could earn, say, forty dollars a week, if he worked for someone else. He is trying to build the business up, however, so he draws out only thirty dollars a week for his own labor and that of his wife and son. He leaves the rest in the business. At the end of the year there is a profit of one thousand dollars.

This is a return of 20 per cent. on his investment of five thousand. It looks as though the business was doing mighty well, but as a matter of fact that man hasn't made any profit at all. He has instead gone behind to the extent of $1,460.

In the first place he should have had a salary for himself of not less than forty-five dollars a week. He could earn forty dollars by working for someone else, and he certainly puts in enough extra time running his own business to entitle him to five dollars a week more. Since he has underpaid himself to the extent of fifteen dollars a week, the business owes him 52 times $15 or $780. It would cost him at least another fifteen dollars a week to hire others to do the work that his wife and son are doing. This makes another $780 that the business owes him. He is surely entitled to an 8 per cent. return on his investment before any profit is considered. He wouldn't invest his money in any other manufacturing enterprise where it would be subject to such risks for a less return. There are even times when the bank charges him 7 or 8 per cent. for loans.

Eight per cent. on $5,000 is $400 more that the business owes him. Then he has overlooked the matter of depreciation of his machinery and equipment, and the fact that some of it will have to be renewed before it is worn out, because it will be out of date. When he figures out just what this means each year he discovers that it amounts to the tidy sum of $500. This means that the business owes him the sum of $780; $780, $400, and $500 or a total of $2,460, and there is only a thousand dollars with which to pay it. He hasn't made any profit after all, and the people surely have no cause to accuse him of profiteering.

On the other hand, if a certain kind of committee should investigate his business they would find that according to the way he has been keeping his books he has made undue profits and that he ought to reduce his prices to a point such that he would make only $400 a year instead of the thousand that he appears to have been making. In other words this committee would insist that he cut prices until he would actually be losing $1,860 a year.

It is perfectly proper for a man in business to economize and put as much money as possible back into the business. In fact it is wise for him to do this.

The more a man saves, the more he will have in the end. It is wrong, however, for him to fool himself into believing that he is making more profit than he is, for he will find it far too easy to fool his customers in the same way and they may insist that he reduce prices to a point where he will not be making these "huge" profits.

When a man starts in business it often happens that for the first few years the business cannot pay him an adequate salary, then it grows and becomes more prosperous and is not only able to pay him a proper salary but to show a profit. But what about the back salary that he has given to the business? He wouldn't have given it to any other business.

Surely the only fair way is to charge that back salary up to the business and either consider it as so much additional investment or collect it from the business later. Until it is accounted for no real profit can be actually made.

Only when all these costs have been considered does a man know enough about his business to enable him to ascertain just what it is costing to do business. He doesn't know what a loaf of bread is actually costing to produce, what a cake costs or for that matter what any other work costs.

After he has adjusted this salary and the overhead expense so that everything is accounted for, then he is in a position to find out just what the costs are in each department and to determine whether or not he will be able to give greater value for the money, or if he must charge more for certain goods. He is in a position to cut down here and cut down there to reduce costs.

No man can be asked to work for less money when he is working in his own business, in which he has risked his own money, than he would work for any other person. Yet there is a surprisingly large number of men who are doing this very thing and a lot of them don't realize that they are doing so.

These men should get acquainted with their business and every baker in the community who knows his own costs should make it his business to do all he can to have these others correct theirs. There are a surprisingly large number of men who think they are making money and a greater percentage than larger concerns, because they don't have to hire all their help! They have a strong and willing wife and several children who can help out, so they are making a profit! As a matter of fact they are only making a living, and that's altogether a different thing.

—:—:—:—

W. H. LaFever, Jr., has been recently appointed by the Thomson Machine Company to represent them exclusively in the States of Arkansas, Oklahoma and Texas. Mr. LaFever is well known to the baking industry in the South, and has had a practical training which particularly adapts him for such a position.

Is Your Heart in Your Work?

IT FREQUENTLY happens that when someone has made a conspicuous success of his business his advice is sought on the subject of how others may go and do likewise. Usually, when the interview with the great man is published it reads rather disappointingly; and the effect is as though he were concealing something, holding back the real "secret of success," which must have guided him unerringly to place and power.

Some years ago, at a Tri-State Convention of bakers, Hugh Chalmers, one of the world's greatest salesmen, gave an inspiring address on the "Road to Success." He said that no man could tell another man how to succeed; all he could do was to indicate a few "sign posts" which pointed the way.

As a matter of fact, there is no royal road to business success, and no "secret," which, once mastered, will enable anybody to get to the top of the ladder without working. The most successful baker the writer knows puts in more time at his store than any of his employees. That isn't because he feels that he is tied to the treadmill, or anything like that; but he is so intesely interested in the great game of business and likes his work so much that he gives it all of the time he can spare from his family.

This, after all, is one of the things which determines whether or not a man is going to be successful, in the bakery or any other line of trade; that is, he must like it. There may be isolated cases where men have gone into certain lines when they had an utter distaste for the work, and were inspired only by the idea of getting rich. Such men, as suggested, may have succeeded in a few instances, but the number is certainly very small compared with the list of failures who have arrived at that point on account of their lack of liking for and interest in their work.

It isn't simply a matter of dollars and cents. Life is too short, after all is said and done, to justify anybody in spending his days at work which is distasteful to him. The thing to do is to find out what you are best fitted for, and go do that thing. If it means a few dollars less a day or week than the other thing, let them go; for what is a little money compared with a lifetime of enjoyment? The man who is fitted for a certain task, whether it is selling boots or baked goods, will like it, and the job will grow on him, and become a part of himself. If he doesn't like it, his distaste for it will grow, and his work will be a burden hanging around his neck and destroying the delights of living.

There is a cue in this for the baker who would be successful. He can't be so unless he has able lieutenants and sergeants and privates in the ranks; unless, in other words, his shop and store are well manned with those who are capable of producing the goods and dealing with his trade in the best possible way. They, too, must like their jobs, and while paying them a sufficient amount of money is one of the surest ways of stimulating interest, that isn't the whole thing.

The boss can make a bakeshop the most interesting place in the world for his employees, especially the youngsters, if he will but go to the trouble of visualizing for them the mighty industrial forces represented by the goods which he is handling. He is dealing wth foodstuffs—the one essential to the existence of the human race. The vast array of men and machinery, land and laborers, needed to place a single barrel of flour in the bakery, for example, is enough to make anyone with even a slightly imaginative mind realize that the baker is playing a part in a great industrial drama, which might well be styled, "Feeding the World." The baker can suggest to his helpers the possibilities of the business, the importance of making a better loaf, of making a more attractive store, and in that way assist them to get out of the dull routine of ordinary affairs. There is no reason why the bakery trade should not be just as interesting to the young fellows who are starting to work as selling automobiles and sporting goods, which attract because of their inherently appealing qualities.

There is no reason why the baker who really takes an interest in making his help take an interest in the business should not succeed in the big way represented by the creation of an enthusiastic and capable organization.

Trade papers devote a great deal of space, and properly, to the technique of business; to such things as salesmanship, window displays, advertising, etc. This is part of the necessary equipment of the business man, and yet, as a matter of fact, knowledge of these things never made anybody successful. They are the minutiæ of business, which every business man should know, and knowledge of them will make a successful man more successful, or a failure perhaps less of one; but it is the man himself, the big idea dominating his work, which determines whether or not he assays 100 per cent. in his particular calling.

The successful business man does not need to look at his bankbook to find out if he has arrived. He knows himself, and he knows whether he has succeeded. Many times a man fails before reaching substantial, dollars-and-cents success; but because he knows his business, because he has the man-power back of his knowledge, and because he is confident of his own ability to grasp the problems of life and overcome them, he is potentially always a success. That kind of man can't be downed.

The bakery trade is one of great detail. A man who is running a retail shop has got to keep his mind on many items of business, and the danger here is that in thinking of little things he may forget the big ones. Please don't. It is part of your job to keep your head clear, your brain active, and your mind's eye fixed on the big ideal of success, represented by the larger things back of the daily routine of business—the things, in short, which make the wheels of business go 'round.

American Bakers' Association

A MEETING of the Board of Governors of the American Bakers' Association was held at Association headquarters, 1135 Fullerton Avenue, Chicago, on February 10th, to consider many important business matters. The meeting was called to order by President Win M. Campbell, who made a short statement in reference to the bread war in Kansas City, following which he tendered his resignation as president and withdrew. The resignation was accepted.

Vice-President Alex. L. Taggart, of the Taggart Baking Co., Indianapolis, Ind., took the chair and became Acting President. The minutes of the previous meeting were approved, as were the revised constitution and by-laws.

The Board then adjourned, and a meeting of the American Bakers' Foundation was called and the trustees elected the following officers of the Foundation: Chairman, A. L. Taggart, Indianapolis; Vice-Chairman, L. F. Bolser, Minneapolis; Secretary, Dr. H. E. Barnard, Chicago; Treasurer, H. W. Zinsmaster, Duluth. These, with J. F. Livingston, Chicago; E. D. Strain, Battle Creek, and Wm. Freihofer, Philadelphia, constitute the Executive Committee.

Dr. Barnard made a full report on the work done in preparing the headquarters' building for the needs of the Association and of its child, the American Bakers' Institute. The work planned will, including an addition, cost approximately $30,000, which was approved. The Institute will be incorporated as a separate institution.

The Secretary-Manager also reported that it was expected to open the School of Baking on May 15th, the first class to consist of thirty-six pupils, with provisions to be made for the admission of one hundred students, to be divided into three classes of four months each.

The following resolution, presented by W. E. Long, was unanimously adopted:

WHEREAS this Association, by vote of its Executive Committee, has adopted a form of membership application blank embodying all conditions for membership set forth in the by-laws; and

WHEREAS one of these conditions of membership is full compliance with the Code of Ethics affecting trade practices;

Now therefore be it resolved that whenever any complaint from a member shall be lodged with the Business Manager of the Association, charging a violation of the Code of Ethics in respect of unfair trade practice, the Business Manager shall at once refer such complaint to the Industrial Relations Committee;

Further resolved that upon receipt of such complaint the Industrial Relations Committee shall forthwith institute an investigation of all conditions bearing on such situation and after hearing all the evidence shall make report to the Board of Governors at its next meeting following such investigation, setting forth its findings and conclusion upon the facts;

Further resolved that upon receipt of such report the Governors shall then determine whether the membership of the concern involved shall be suspended or cancelled.

Chairman of the Industrial Relations Committee, S. F. McDonald, made a full report of the work undertaken by his committee in adjusting differences between bakers in Danville, Ill.; Belleville, Ill.; Seattle, Wash.; Fort Wayne, Ind.; Fort Worth, Texas, etc. There is every indication that the work of this committee will add greatly to the usefulness of the Association.

Counsellor E. N. Rabenold reported on the work of the Public Relations Committee, in the absence of Chairman Tipton, and with special reference to the legislative situation in New York, New Jersey, Maryland, Massachusetts, etc. Counsel E. H. Hickok reported on the express rate situation and, on his suggestion that a special committee be named to investigate the situation and, if necessary, appear before the Interstate Commerce Commission, S. F. Donald, Memphis; Ralph D. Ward, New York, and C. N. Power, Pueblo, were appointed for that purpose.

A communication was received from the Bakery Equipment Manufacturers' Association as to a possible exhibition at Chicago this year during the annual meeting of the American Bakers' Association. Such an exhibition was approved.

Council of Baking Meets

THE Council of Baking and affiliated organizations met at the Hotel La Salle, Chicago, on February 17th, with President B. B. Grenell, Chicago, in the chair. There was a general discussion as to the best methods of rendering service to the baking industry. One method devised was to aid in preventing the conflict of dates between various Association meetings, which has created considerable confusion in the past.

It was also decided to do all possible to close exhibits at the various conventions while the Association meetings were in session. The following resolution was adopted:

"We believe that every baker should know the cost of every piece of goods he sells and we deprecate the action of any baker who sells below cost plus a reasonable profit, and we, therefore, recommend that the two bakery organizations discuss the matter with their members to the end that disastrous trade wars be prevented."

A further resolution approved and promised the support of the Council of Baking and Affiliated Organizations on any action which may be taken by the American Bakers' Association to obtain a legal decision regarding the sale of bakery products below cost of production.

An Association Pledge Fulfilled—School of Baking Starts May 15th, 1922

THE constitution of the reorganized American Bakers' Association pledges the Association to encourage the education of the baker. This pledge will be fulfilled by the American Institute of Baking.

To this end the Institute will conduct a school which will meet every need of the operative baker, the baking chemist and technologist, and the graduate in science who wishes to enter the baking industry.

In order to accomplish its aim, the School of the American Institute of Baking will be so organized that instruction will be given along three lines.

1. It will give training to fit bakers to be better foremen and superintendents.

2. It will train men to act as control chemists in the baking or milling laboratory, in the purchase and use of the ingredients of bread, etc.

3. It will afford opportunity for men of considerable chemical and baking experience to engage in special problems of scientific research in the laboratories of the School and Institute.

As soon as work is well under way in these courses, college graduates and others are invited to get in touch with the School of Baking for the purpose of arranging for special work in the nature of postgraduate investigations which will give them an insight into the baking industry, and lead to positions of considerable desirability.

All of the regular courses will be followed shortly by similar courses which apply to the manufacture of cake as well as bread.

It is indeed a task to take an empty building and fit it on short notice for as pretentious an undertaking as has been just outlined. In our case, however, the bakers are very fortunate in the nature of the building which their association has taken over. It already contains classrooms and laboratories which can be used just as they are. In fact, if new ones were to be installed, they could not be better than those already available. We need, then, only to install a school bakery and to make slight modifications of facilities already at hand before the school is opened.

That it is the bakery which must be installed new, is indeed fortunate because it is here that we find the most vital point in the whole course of study in the regular bakers' course. Professor William Jago, of England, has already recognized its importance in his article on the American Institute School of Baking. He emphasizes the prime importance of the institute bakery, and he is very anxious to have the proper type of equipment and the proper policy of operation decided upon. This is of course logical as the entire instruction will center on the practical work in the shop.

However, actual shop practice, except for preliminary training in fundamentals, should be received in outside shops. If the student has not had the benefit of previous experience before coming to the School of Baking, he will pick up the details of shop practice in the school bakery and then round out his manual ability through assignments to commercial shops about the city where he will come into contact with the conditions existing under competitive manufacture. The bakery of the School of Baking will be run almost entirely on the bases of experiment, demonstration of the effects of varying conditions and ingredients, and research.

The output of the bakery has not yet been determined. Sufficient bread will be produced so that the runs will be on a commercial scale, and normal conditions of bread manufacture will be preserved throughout. In fact, the school bakery will be equipped as if the purpose were to turn out commercial bread, and equipment in triplicate will be installed so that there will be three bakeries in one, and by the rotation of the use of this equipment, experience in the operation of all will be available.

Whatever the details of the courses are, certain fundamentals will be included and instructions in the following subjects will be given.

SUBJECTS FOR INSTRUCTION

1. **Commercial Manufacture of Bread.**
   Receiving, handling, and storage of ingredients.
   Measuring, weighing, and blending ingredients.
   Mixing practice and dough room practice.
   Making up practice, both machine and hand.
   Proofing practice, both automatic and otherwise.
   Oven practice.
   Cooling practice.
   Wrapping bread.
   Shipping and sales practice.
   Experimenting with variations, both proper and improper, in formulas and manufacturing processes. Every dough will be an experimental one.

2. **Experimental Baking Laboratory.**
   The various "recognized" methods of conducting the experimental baking test.
   Experimenting with variations in formulas and manufacturing processes; with different flours used alone and blended; with different sugars; different shortenings; yeast foods, etc., etc. This work will parallel the work done in the school bakery, but because of the smaller size of the doughs and the larger number which one man can run at one time, a greater range of work will be done.
   Control of the ingredients and processes used in the school bakery.
   Baking bread with flour manufactured in the experimental mill of the school.
   Problems of research connected with the investigation of new methods of manufacture.
   Demonstration of various principles and practices.

3. **Chemical laboratory of the School of Baking.**
   Training in simple analytical procedure.
   Routine testing of flours, sugar, milk, salt, yeast, water, etc., according to special A. I. B. methods of analysis.

Investigations of the nature and properties of the various ingredients of bread doughs.
Studies of malt products, etc., with special reference to the action and control of enzymes.

4. **Special work and lectures.**
   The relation between the employer and the employee.
   Bonuses, strikes, social features, etc.
   Legal relations of the baker.
   Weight laws, wrapping laws, sanitary laws, material standards, business law, leases, workmen's compensation laws, etc., etc.
   The nutritive value of bread.
   Bookkeeping and cost accounting for the baker.
   Electrical information of interest to the baker.
   Mechanical information of interest to the baker.
   Refrigeration machinery of interest to the baker.
   Temperature and humidity control in bake shops.
   The microscope and its use by the baker.
   Flour mixtures, determination of strength of yeast, examination of molds, bacteria, etc.
   Fuels and their relation to combustion with special application to the firing of bake ovens.
   The manufacture and properties of all materials handled in a bakery.
   The metric system of weights and measures.
   Water and its treatment.
   Bleaching of flour.
   Baker's machinery, its use, care, installation, etc.
   Blending flour.
   Yeast foods.
   Records in use in the shop.
   Special commercial shop problems, met with by foremen and superintendents on the job. How to solve them.
   Bread troubles, and their solution.
   Rope, what it is, how to prevent it, how to eliminate it, how to prevent its recurrence. Sour bread.
   The five fermentations, and their control.
   Special lectures by prominent men on problems of the hour.

WHEN CLASSES START

The first class for bakers will start on Monday, May 15th, and continue for four months, closing September 2d. In order to do justice to all the men enrolled, the number to be admitted has been set at 36. All who apply after this number has been accepted may take the work during the second term for 1922, which will be from Monday, September 4th, until December 23d.

THE FACULTY

A faculty of nationally known men with previous experience in the training of bakers is being collected. In addition to the full-time members of the faculty of the Baking School, all members of the staff and advisory committees of the American Institute of Baking are available for special lectures, and men of prominence who from time to time pass through Chicago will be called on to address the class on problems of the day. In this way and by shop visits throughout the course as well, the class will receive the latest information of interest to them.

THE COST

Tuition for the course has been set at $300.00 for the four months bakers' course. Other special courses will be given at terms to be arranged for in each case. It is figured that the total cost to a visiting student, in addition to his tuition, will be about $100.00 per month.

Applications for enrollment are now being received. Those who desire to be with us at the start should secure their places soon by writing to Peter G. Pirrie, Principal, The American Institute School of Baking, 1135 Fullerton Avenue, Chicago.

—‡—‡—‡—

Laboratories Ready for Service

American Institute of Baking Examines in New Home Wide Variety of Baking Materials and Technical Supplies.

THE American Institute of Baking has greatly extended its research and technical service for the baking and allied industries since its removal to the new location in Chicago.

In addition to the equipment formerly used in Minneapolis it has now consolidated the laboratories and other scientific facilities of the Wahl-Henius Institute with its own. This improvement in resources makes it possible to announce that the Institute is now ready to examine the widest variety of baking materials, products and miscellaneous technical supplies in its new analytical and bacteriological laboratories.

Analytical and other control work, special investigations and consultations can now be carried on under more favorable conditions than was possible under the old arrangements at Minneapolis.

The new experimental baking, flour or cereal laboratory will be of unusual interest to the baker, not only in special details of equipment such as ovens, fermentation and proofing cabinets, but in its exceptional resources for the complete examination of flour and other cereal products and foods.

The examination of flour is one of the most important services that the Institute can give the baker. A thorough knowledge of the flours that are purchased for the bakery can only be attained by constant laboratory supervision. This not only applies to the grade and baking value of the flour and how it should be handled to make good bread, but to its relative freedom of infection from organisms, molds and bacteria. The attention of both the baker and the miller is called to the facilities which the Institute now possesses for the examination of flour.

It has been suggested that the Institute can be of efficient help to both industries in cases of disagreement on analytical results such as moisture, protein, ash, gluten, etc.

How many bakers realize that they can use the Institute for the analytical control not only of baking materials and products but for such miscellaneous raw material as coal, coke, oils, gasoline, soaps, washing compounds, trough and divider grease, boiler compounds, sweeping compounds, paraffin paper and other material of a technical nature?

If the baker submits such products to the Institute laboratories he will soon learn the value of this work as measured in dollars and cents. It is only by the strictest supervision of raw materials, processes and products that uniformity can be attained and uncertainty eliminated from the shop.

Not only can the laboratories be of service to the baker in the examination of such materials, but it can also test and standardize the thermometers, hygrometers and pyrometers of the dough room and oven.

Many bakers who are troubled by dough room problems will find that the difficulty lies in the use of a thermometer in inaccurate readings.

The Institute was founded by practical bakers for research and education in baking. No matter how ample its scientific facilities and organization may be, it will fall short of the purpose of its founders, if its resources are not used by every baker who is in need of technical help.

—‡—‡—‡—

Good Publicity for Bread

THE Millers' National Federation is reviving their campaign for a greater consumption of bread, and their advertising matter could be used with advantage by the bakers.

One of their circulars is as follows:

EAT MORE BREAD!

CALCULATIONS of Relative Food Value of the following articles were made by AMERICAN INSTITUTE OF BAKING, Chicago, Illinois; the Retail Prices used are those quoted on February 6, 1922, by Mr. Sol. Westerfeld, Grocer, Chicago. (Formerly Secretary of Retail Grocers' Association):

Commodity	Retail Price	10 Cents Will Purchase
Round Steak	....25 Cents per Pound	.. 356 Calories
Lamb Chops	.....35 " " "	.. 307 "
Premium Ham	...45 " " "	.. 363 "
Potatoes	.... 4 " " "	.. 738 "
BREAD	...... 9 " " "	.1330 "
Milk	.............12 " " Quart	... 517 "
Eggs (Fresh)	....43 " " Dozen	... 197 "

(Note the high standing of bread)

Copies of this circular were sent to every member of the Federation, the idea being to secure the publication of the matter in local newspapers. It would be a very good idea for bakers to take this copy to their local editor and request that same be published on the newspages as information for the public. It is good publicity for bread, and that means good advertising for the baker.

Reduce Your Labor Cost by Providing Effective Tools

MORE than ever before is it necessary for the baker to watch his labor costs and to do everything possible to increase the productive value of his men by providing the right sort of labor-saving tools. This is the day of machinery; it is the modern method of increasing output and profits by eliminating the hand process, which is too slow and costly for these progressive, stirring times.

Hand labor, of course, can never be done away with in the bakeshop. There are many important operations which can only be performed successfully by the trained hand, but the number of these different operations is decreasing yearly, as the bakery engineers become more familiar with the labor problems of the bakeshop and devise and build tools to successfully meet them.

Of course, the baker with a moderate size retail business is limited as to the number of power-driven tools he can profitably operate, but one important fact escapes the attention of many otherwise progressive bakers. That is: machinery produces in a shorter time and at a cost much below that of hand labor, and greatly increases the output. Thus it saves the time of the master baker which he can devote to the office or trade-building end of his business and the enlarged output compels an increase of sales. The baker thus has more time to devote to that end of the baking business which is so often neglected by men who are expert in the *practical* side of the trade.

The present high cost of labor bears hard on the trade, but the shop with a full modern equipment of labor and time-saving tools is the one best adapted to meeting the strain and, in fact, is about the only one which will show a profit under present conditions.

Another view: Bakers have frequently been heard to denounce the journeymen as a class, and complain of the inconveniences caused by their constantly changing jobs. The average journeyman baker is by no means perfect, but the "boss" is frequently responsible for the desire of the journeyman to "keep moving." We have conversed with journeymen, good workers, and admitted to be such by their employers, who were expected to turn out first-class goods with half an equipment. They would indignantly point to the sparse supply of utensils and ask how any man could be expected to keep up his name and use such tools. Usually in such cases the employer is not a practical baker, and cannot appreciate the handicap under which a man works with insufficient equipment. In many cases, however, the master is his own journeyman, and even he "putters" along doing without half a dozen articles that he should have. Unfortunately, some bakers cannot realize that their time should be worth something, and they forget that the journeyman could do perhaps twice as much with a suitable equipment. Money exchanged for tools is invested, not spent, and yields good returns. The journeyman would not be so anxious to move elsewhere, after a week or a month, if he has reasonable encouragement in the matter of utensils, providing other matters are satisfactory.

—:—:—:—

New Jersey Considering Bread Weights Law

COMPULSORY standardization of bread into loaves of a pound, pound and a half, or multiples of a pound, as provided in Assemblywoman Laird's House bill 112, was opposed by the bakers of New Jersey when the House Miscellaneous Business Committee gave a hearing on the measure at the State Capitol, Trenton. E. N. Rabenold, counsel for the American Bakers' Association, asked that House bill 182, introduced by Assemblyman Corio, of Atlantic, requiring regulation of the baking industry as to sanitation, etc., and for marking the weights of bread sold, whatever they might be, be substituted for Mrs. Laird's bill, which was drawn up by the Weights and Measures Department. House bill 182, he said, is revised draft of Senate bill 97, introduced on request by Senator White, of Atlantic.

Counsellor Rabenold, as the bakers' representative, asserted that the industry should be allowed to determine the size of the loaf, and to sell bread in other ways, as by weight, so long as the public was told what it was getting. He said that it took a change of $2.40 a barrel of flour to make a difference of a cent in the price of bread. "We want to be able to pass on to the public in increased weight smaller fluctuations than that," he said.

A. W. Swartz, Assistant Superintendent of Weights and Measures, whose department is responsible for the Laird bill, Mrs. L. G. Peloubet, chairman of the legislative committee of the Federation of Women's Clubs, and Henry Hilfres, secretary of the New Jersey Federation of Labor, spoke in favor of the bill.

—:—:—:—

The New England Bakers' Association is making excellent progress. At a meeting at the Hotel Stratfield on March 8, Division No. 5, comprising the bakers of Fairfield County, formed an association with the following officers:

President—E. E. Malpass, Soderholm Baking Co., Bridgeport.

Vice-President—Peter Sorenson, Bridgeport.

Secretary—Julius Roth, Adams-Roth Baking Co., Bridgeport.

Treasurer—H. C. Hideroth, Stamford, Conn.

The state of Connecticut is now fully organized, with six divisions functioning, and having members from every nook and corner in the state.

—:—:—:—

The Washington Bakeries have been incorporated at Seattle, Wash., with capital of $300,000 by Moritz Thomsen, G. E. Rasmussen, Harry Mosier, D. E. Skinner and G. W. Skinner.

Folklore of Bread and Cakes

THE folklore of bread and cakes gathers very largely round the three important events of births, deaths and marriages. In Sicily, when a birth is to take place, as a preventive against evil, some wise woman places in the *bed* some bread and salt; whilst in Bavaria any iron article takes the place of the salt. In the Vosges (Eastern France) district, they have a most curious marriage custom. If amongst the guests there is one of them pregnant, after the ceremony is over, she takes a small piece of bread and, after having made the sign of the cross over it, or blessed herself, she presents it to the new-made wife, saying: "May it be as profitable to you as it has been to me!" Women in such a condition in Lower Brittany send as an expression of their good wishes to those who are similarly situated, a little gift of white bread and new bread.

"Traditions et Superstitions de la Boulangerie" is a book containing many curious facts. Its author is not a baker, but a French literary antiquary and authority on folklore, M. Paul Sebillot. The work is a perfect wealth of legends and traditions connected with baking. From this book we gather, says Edward Conner, in the Practical Baker & Confectioner, London, that in all countries the first feeling after the dough is made is an earnest desire to keep it from the influence of evil spirits. This is done in many ways, the most frequent being to cut a cross upon the dough, or only sign one above it with the finger. The original notion of this may have been to stamp it with the symbol of our common religion and as a tribute to God, whose highest gift is acknowledged in many places to be that of bread, from the pure and dependent prayer taught by His Son for the gift of our daily bread to the simple custom of the peasants of Brittany, who will not play cards on the same table-cover on which bread has been laid; for they say, the game of cards is that of the devil, the gift of bread is that of God, and to place the devil in God's place would be sin. They explain to visitors that the reason why they cross the dough (hot-cross bun fashion) is to keep in remembrance the miracle of the feeding of the multitude, as before Christ broke the bread He signed the cross upon it. Crossing the dough was also intended to keep away evil spirits. The same spirit came out in the baking bread, which is not yet entirely obsolete in many parts of the Highlands of Scotland, when a sixpence is put under the churn in making butter, or a cross made of rowan twigs placed over the door. In Scotland, it was the custom some years ago, when the good wife baked cakes, to leave the last as an offering to the fairies, while it was deemed very unlucky to count the cakes or scones in making, as the fairies did not like that, and if such were done the cakes would not last as long as they ought to have done. In other parts of Scotland, unless the first cake of a baking was hallowed by being crossed the whole baking could be claimed by the fairies.

From the very commonest of bread of various descriptions it is perfectly discernible how it came to be so much employed in the folklore of different countries. From the use or abuse of it grew inevitably, the proverbs which are traced in every tongue. "Dry bread at home is better than roast meat abroad." "You can't eat your cake and have it." "Eaten bread is soon forgotten." "Better eat grey bread in your youth than in your age." These are but a few of the proverbs.

BREAD AT EASTER TIME

Customs connected with bread and cakes center round special seasons of the year, natural events, and traditionary customs. The simplest, and most feasible explanation of the cross on Good Friday buns is that as buns were used in connection with a religious observance the bakers crossed them with the mark of the cross, which bulked so largely in the minds of the worshippers during the celebration of Passion Week. During the observance of Holy Week the Church in early times was far stricter in the matter of feasts than she is now. Only a certain amount of bread could be eaten, and that was duly marked off in the dough by two lines to show its length and breadth. These loaves were sold in some churches, and were carried from place to place by pilgrims, and so the custom was continued of crossing the bread used on Good Friday, long after the occasion for it passed away. This is the new account of the cross upon the bun according to Canon Donlevuy, of Edinburgh.

It used to be a common belief that bread baked on Good Friday never grew mouldy, and the same belief has extended to hot cross buns, one writer suggesting that the spice preserves them. A piece of the bread which was baked on Good Friday was carefully preserved far on into the year, and it was considered a sovereign remedy against the house getting on fire. Others preserved a piece of it for whooping cough and for presentation to cattle to cure them from certain diseases. In Normandy, bread baked the night before Christmas conferred the same advantage, and preserved the possessor of it from the ravages of storms and the rage of mad dogs. But the belief as regards Good Friday bread was quite different in Asia Minor. There no one would make bread at all on Holy Friday, being under the belief that the water so used would change into the blood of Christ, and when the bread was eaten a deadly sin would be committed.

It was the custom at one time in England for cakes sold at Christmas to bear an image of Christ stamped upon the dough, these cakes were largely given away as gifts by the bakers to their customers. At Perigueux (France) there is the custom for servants every New Year's Day to throw a bit of bread into the well of the house to keep it from drying up, and no matter how great the drought of summer may be, if this little ceremony has been performed the water will always be assured.

A pretty little custom used to take place on Beltanes Bay in Scotland. Early in the morning the mother presented to each of her children a fairly large round oatcake. With this the little ones trooped to meet their friends, all supplied with cakes and cheese, and other provisions necessary for children to spend a hunger-causing holiday in the open air. They made their way to some sloping hill; once on top crosses and circles were cut upon each cake. Each child next took his or her own cake and all stood in a row at the top of the hill. At a given shout the cakes are let go and trundle down the hill. Down after them scampered the children. If the cake fell with the cross uppermost it was a sign that its possessor would live another year, but if the circle was on top the child would die. Three times the children ascended the hill with their cakes and went through the same performances; whichever symbol showed itself the oftenest was taken as the right prognostication.

Older people held their celebrations of Beltane's Day as well as the children. In the wild stretches of Glenorchy and Lorne, the housewife used to bake on Beltane morning a cake for the evening's entertainment, which had to be eaten within doors. In the Island of Mull it had a large hole cut in the middle, through which every cow in the byre was milked. Three people baked it with a variation, making it of a triangular shape instead of a round one.

In the North of England there used to be prepared what was called a "Groaning Cake," a slice of which was given to all those who came to see the new-born child. There used to be a custom in the Highlands of Scotland of taking a new-born child and tying it up in a sheet along with bread and cheese, and tie them all on to the swinging hook that hung over the open fire, and turn it three times to keep the evil spirits away from the child. In Asia Minor, if a careful mother has to leave her child before he is 40 days' old she places beside him or her a bit of bread, a pair of scissors, and a little image of Christ.

In Switzerland, as in Scotland, the party returning from the church after a christening, give a piece of bread to the first person they meet to ensure happiness to the child. In some parts of France the bread is carefully preserved by the tender mother, who looks at it periodically with great anxiety, for if it turns mouldy the child will turn ill and probably die, but if it remains dry and hard the child will enjoy good health. There is no end, so to speak, about the folklore of bread and cakes.

—‡—‡—‡—

Success depends upon more than one thing in the bakery business. Are you a good baker? Can you increase the sales on bakery goods? Are you managing the bakery as well as it should be? The answers to these questions have to do with success.

—‡—‡—‡—

The coming man usually turns out to be a bill collector.

Pennsylvania Program

THE Executive Committee of the Pennsylvania Association of the Baking Industry held a meeting on Friday, March 10th, at the Manufacturers' Club, Philadelphia, to arrange a tentative program for the annual convention to be held at Bedford Springs, Pa., on June 5th, 6th and 7th.

Those present were President L. J. Schumaker, Philadelphia; Vice-President, R. K. Stritzinger, Norristown; Secretary, C. C. Latus, Pittsburgh; Treasurer, Geo. W. Fisher, Huntingdon; Harry S. Long, Lebanon, and Chas. E. Gunzenhauser, Lancaster, and a number of local bakers. Fred. P. Siebel, President of Siebel Institute, Chicago, was an interested visitor.

A detailed report was made of the recent Bread and Milk campaign in Pennsylvania and posters, newspaper advertisements and editorial references to the campaign from 79 cities and towns within the state were shown and excited much interest and favorable comment.

Elaborate arrangements for the Bedford Springs convention have been made and there is every prospect that this meeting will surpass in interest any previous convention in the Keystone State. Some details appear on another page of this issue.

The tentative program as so far arranged is as follows:

MONDAY, JUNE 5TH, 1922

10 A. M.   Registration.
Noon.   Business Session, Report of Officers.
2 P. M.   Golf Tournament, Bakers vs. Supply Men; Fine Prizes.
9 P. M.   Masked Ball; Wonderful Prizes.

TUESDAY, JUNE 6TH

9.30 A.M.   Opening Convention.
Invocation, R. T. White, Altoona.
Address of Welcome, Judge Thos. F. Bailey.
Response, President L. J. Schumaker.
Address, Dean C. B. Connelley, Commissioner of Labor and Industry.
Address, Dr. H. E. Barnard, Secretary-Manager American Bakers' Association.
Address, Fred H. Frazer, Vice-President General Baking Co.
Introduction of Associate Members and Visiting Delegates.
Nomination for Officers.
2 P. M.   Afternoon Amusements, Sports and Special "Stunts."
8.30 P.M.   Reception and Dance.

WEDNESDAY, JUNE 7TH

9.30 A. M.   Convention Called to Order.
Address, Hon. Jas. Foust, Pure Food Commissioner.
Address, Fletcher Stites.
Address, Mrs. John S. Sloan, President Congress of Women's Clubs.

Address, W. T. Smedley, Secretary Retail Merchants' Association.

Discussion (in Executive Session), Problems Affecting the Bakers.

Election of Officers.

1 P. M. Adjournment.

2 P. M. Baseball Game Between Bakers and Associates.

8 P. M. Dancing and Awarding Prizes.

A large attendance is anticipated and assurances are given that the Bedford Springs Hotel can easily accommodate all who attend. The entire hotel will be at the disposal of the convention.

—:—:—:—

Reduced Fares for Pennsylvania Convention

THE Trunk Line Association has granted a special rate of fare from all points in Pennsylvania to Bedford, Pa., for the Pennsylvania Bakers' convention at the Bedford Springs Hotel, June 5 to 7 next. The certificate plan, similar to that used to the Chicago convention last September, will be used. By this plan the ticket purchaser buys a ticket from his home town to Bedford, pays one-way fare, and at the same time asks for a certificate. This certificate when validated at the convention will entitle the holder to half fare rate home. This is the first time in the history of the association that state convention fares will be reduced. This is due to the persistency of L. J. Schumaker, president of the association. This special rate will be available for bakers and their friends who will flock to Bedford Springs in great numbers.

—:—:—:—

C. C. Latus, secretary of the Pennsylvania Bakers' Association, attended the second annual convention of the West Virginia Association of the Baking Industry at Clarksburg on March 1 and bore the greetings of the Keystone State Bakers to their brethren of the Mountain State. Mr. Latus spoke at the banquet on "Organization." Louis Storck, of Parkersburg, was elected president; P. C. Beseler, of Huntington, vice-president, and W. I. Grayson, of Huntington, secretary-treasurer.

—:—:—:—

On March 4th the plant of the Sunville Baking Co., Pueblo, Colorado, was damaged by fire to the extent of $3,000. C. N. Power, former president of the American Bakers' Association, is president of this company. Extensive improvements are to be made when the plant is rebuilt.

—:—:—:—

Not many years ago when machinery was mentioned, some small bakers looked upon the proposition as extravagence, but nowadays so many small shops are using machinery to advantage and producing so much better goods than formerly, and at such a saving in labor cost, that the value of power-driven tools in *all* bakeshops is generally conceded as beyond question.

New England Bakers' Association

THE first bi-monthly meeting of the New England Bakers' Association was held at the Hotel Bond, Hartford, Conn., on Wednesday, March 1st, beginning with a luncheon at 1 P. M. George D. Beroth, of Hartford, retail Governor of the Association for Connecticut, introduced George B. Chandler, State Compensation Commissioner of Connecticut, who congratulated the bakers on the wonderful progress their industry had made in recent years and extended a hearty welcome to the visitors.

In having as the two principal speakers for the meeting those two orators of our industry, Victor Friend, of Melrose, Mass., and F. H. Frazier, vice-president of the General Baking Company, the bakers were especially fortunate. Mr. Friend strongly advocated the standard loaf, expressing the belief that it would have prevented a recent bread war in his territory. He urged support of the Association and in making his report as temporary Chairman of the Legislative Committee, gave concrete evidence of its work and effectiveness in opposing and preventing unfavorable legislation.

Mr. Frazier did not view the standard loaf law as a panacea because his company experienced the same unfavorable conditions in districts where it was in operation as well as where it was not on the statute books. He foresaw a bright future for the New England Bakers' Association and felt that it is in a position to do more good for the bakers of New England than any other. But he also pointed out the absolute necessity for a National Association to represent the entire industry.

George Ochsner, retail Governor for Massachusetts, brought the good news that the Boston Co-operative Retail Bakers' Association would probably affiliate with the New England Bakers' Association, bringing with it a membership of several hundred.

President Keiser appointed the following committee to propose for honorary membership, men who had performed some signal service to the industry and association in New England: Victor Friend, Chairman; D. F. Phelps, M. Calderwood, Sr., E. J. Arnold, George West, Romeo LaForme, L. L. Gilbert.

The sentiment of the meeting was to work in close harmony with the Allied Trades, and the president appointed the following committee to take the matter under consideration and report at the next meeting on Ways and Means to bring this about: Frank Eighme, Chairman; W. S. Verity, E. C. Campbell, B. S. Ferguson, R. H. Dietz.

C. O. Swanson, Chairman of the Conn. Legislative Committee, made a plea for funds to meet the indebtedness of $4,800 incurred in opposing a recent bread law. Delinquents in Connecticut please heed this plea.

E. H. Shields, of The Fleischmann Company, outlined a Bread and Milk Campaign and told of its success in Pennsylvania. By unanimous vote it was left to local divisions of the Association to determine what action each would take. It was voted to adopt a certificate of membership bearing the seal of the Association in colors for display in the offices and windows of the members. There were 86 present. Thanking you for your co-operation,

        (Signed)   W. H. DIETZ, *Secretary*.

—‡—‡—‡—

The Moisture Content of Bread

IN a recent address before the American Chemical Society at its annual meeting in New York City, Dr. H. E. Barnard, Secretary-Manager of the American Bakers' Association, made the following sensible and seasonable remarks about the moisture content of bread:

"The value of any material is measured by the work it will do. This is as true of paper money as of loaves of bread. Squeeze the water out of marks or rubles or bread and the solid substance remaining does the work. In money, the basic substance is gold; in bread, dry material. Foreign exchange rates measure money values, but bread values are still determined by misleading labels. "This loaf weighs sixteen ounces," says the label. What of it? How much is that in terms of well-nourished children, in ability to pitch hay or to run the marathon of the day's work? Does the 16 ounces mean dry material? Is it the weight of the loaf fresh from the oven or is it the weight of the loaf at the time of sale? In all probability it is none of these. It doubtless represents the desire of the baker to comply with a law or ordinance which tells him his bread must be sold by weight, and so he does the best he can to remain a law-abiding citizen. If the loaf is newly baked it is probably overweight and legal; if it is over 24 hours old it is underweight and illegal, unless it has been wrapped in a heavy, airtight wax paper, in which case it has lost little moisture and is still legal. But if the wrapper is broken or removed, it lost weight and becomes illegal unless the day is dull and humid, then it gains weight and remains legal. All of which, while of importance to the baker who is trying to stay out of jail, is of no interest at all to the consumer who gets the same amount of bread no matter whether the loaf is fresh or stale, wrapped or unwrapped.

"The fact is, the label which is intended to tell the truth usually tells the opposite, simply because it is impossible to attach a uniform label to loaves of bread which from the moment they leave the oven are subject to conditions which cannot be controlled.

"United States Department of Agriculture Bulletin 13, issued many years ago when H. W. Wiley was the illustrious chief of the Bureau of Chemistry, contains perhaps the best series of bread studies ever made. This report covers the entire bread field as it was twenty or more years ago. It tabulates a great mass of analytical data on bread. It shows the differ-

ence between types of bread with respect to their fat, protein, ash, crude fibre and moisture content. The data are calculated back to a moisture-free basis—except for the moisture data. They are, as they are. It is the moisture in the bread at the time of the analysis.

"The moisture content of ten samples of bakers' bread of Vienna bread bought on the market at Washington is 38.71 percent; of seven rye breads, 33.42 per cent; of nine Graham breads, 34.80 per cent. But what do these figures mean? Was the bread fresh from the oven or stale? Was it wrapped so its original moisture content was intact or was it unprotected against evaporation? Was it analyzed in the summer when the air was moist and vaporation slow or in the winter when conditions were the reverse? Was it analyzed on a rainy day when the crumb perhaps gained in weight during the process of analysis, or on a day when rapid loss took place?

"The tables are silent. The analytical data tell us only that certain loaves, analyzed in a certain way, gave certain results; beyond that, nothing. And so, today, when we need to know what the moisture content of bread may be supposed to be, we find, in the best study of bread available, no facts that are helpful. The analytical data are inadequate. We turn to the reports of scores of studies of bread, we study hundreds of analyses; we tabulate masses of data, and then we find—nothing

"How often a chemist looking for facts finds the same shadowy data supporting them. Of course his path is plain. If the data are not complete they must be determined before he can go ahead. And when his results are tabulated and printed it may be that he will be more careful in setting down the data than his forerunners have been."

The above is respectfully referred to those legislators who appear to believe that Standard Weights are the cure for all bread troubles.

—‡—‡—‡—

Enforcement of the St. Louis ordinance prohibiting the sale of bakery goods on Sundays will be suspended until the Missouri Supreme Court passes on its validity. Circuit Judge Hamilton, on March 2d, issued an order that the ordinance should not be enforced pending action by the higher court on an appeal from his decision of several weeks ago, in which he held it valid.

—‡—‡—‡—

Why is it that a reformer seldom begins on himself?

It is easier to promise bread than it is to provide butter.

If a man has sense his dollars will take care of themselves.

Better a close-mouthed friend than one who is close-fisted.

A good scare is of more benefit to some men than good advice.

Motor Delivery for the Smaller Baker

Often Brings Possibilities of Business Extension Which Make It a Good Investment. Points to Watch in Buying a Motor Delivery Wagon.

IT is fair to assume that if the larger bakers must take advantage of every business economy and progressive method in order to make their business profitable, it behooves the smaller baker to do likewise. There are many ways of doing this, but one of the most important and the one in which possibly the greatest single saving can be accomplished is by means of the motor truck. The advantages of motor truck delivery are many, and the possibilities presented for enlarging the territory in which a baker can give better service are great.

The baker who uses two or three horses for delivery purposes quite frequently feels he does not have sufficient hauling to keep a motor truck busy the entire day. Business timidity is causing him to deny himself the advantages of motor truck delivery. He overlooks the fact that he has a special need for a truck because of the truck's capacity for expanding his business. The motor truck is the most formidable weapon to seize upon in an effort to make his business a bigger business.

Instead of looking upon the motor truck as an extravagance, he should look upon it as an investment and set about to arrange his business so that he could use the truck to the best possible advantage.

In this day of standardized goods one baker has very little advantage over another, either in the quality of his goods or the prices. But one point wherein he can excel is in the service he gives. If he can give the better service, without increasing the cost of that service, he has an advantage over his competitor.

Complaints on the service given by the retail bakers of this country far outnumber the complaints on goods. Purchasers either see the goods before buying or they know them by reputation, but the service that goes with the goods is often an unknown quantity. Poor service and a successful baker never go hand in hand. The baker who reduces complaints on his delivery service to a minimum is the man who knows how to catch the trade and keep it. It is the store that gives the best service that usually gets the big end of the trade.

Therefore, before a baker decides that his present volume of business is too small to keep a truck profitably employed, he should carefully investigate the possibilities of new trade that would result from his installation of a better service.

After the smaller baker has thrown aside his timidity and is able to see that the motor truck is the modern weapon for increasing his business and reducing his delivery cost, the important questions which confront him are: Which truck is best adapted to my business—will do my work at the lowest cost—and can be bought at a reasonable price? He naturally wants a truck that will give him *service*. In other words, what he wants is the truck that will carry the load the greatest distance at the least expense.

A commercial motor car to give the best service should be simple in construction and operation. The power plant should be designed for commercial work. A power plant that might be used with fair success in a pleasure car would not come up to the requirements of a commercial car motor.

It seems reasonable that the simpler a motor is the less liable it is to get out of adjustment, the easier it is to care for, and the more cheaply it is repaired if it should get out of order. Therefore, in purchasing a commercial car look well to the motor.

The prospective purchaser should also consider the reputation of the manufacturer back of the car, and the possibility of the manufacturer being in business five or ten years hence. The manufacturer's responsibility does not terminate with the sale of a motor truck. His responsibility is just commencing because spare parts should be furnished promptly in case of necessity. The proximity of branch houses, where spare parts are kept on hand, to the prospective purchaser naturally influences the promptness with which a car can be placed in service again after accident or any mishap. When the owner of a truck is furnished with repair parts promptly and finds a convenient place for whatever assistance he may need in taking care of his truck, it is a feature not to be overlooked.

About price. The output of any factory governs the price to a great extent. It might therefore be well for the prospective purchaser of a motor truck to inquire of the maker, how many of your motor trucks are in use? How many were manufactured last year?

Remember always the real worth of a motor truck lies in the service it gives, and the service a truck gives depends upon the skill of the manufacturer and the facilities he has for turning out a high-grade product.

—‡—‡—‡—

Work Horses and Their Care

They Should Be Given Plenty of Good Feed and Wholesome Water—Regularity of Meals—Different Treatment for Horses Kept in the Stable and Those Hard Driven.

THERE are few days of idleness for the work horse, and, consequently, he has a hearty appetite and a good digestion. Regularity in work brings regularity of feeding, and these naturally conduce to comfort and long years of usefulness. Professor W. A. Henry, of the Wisconsin University, says the work horse should be supplied with about two pounds of provender daily for each hundred pounds of weight. Of this amount from 10 to 18 pounds, according to the severity of the labor performed, should be grain in some form. The heavy feeding should come at night, when the animal has time for masticating and digesting his food.

The morning meal should be comparatively light, consisting mostly of grain with some chaffed hay. It should not possess much bulk, and should be in condition to be easily and rapidly consumed, so as to be well out of the way when the animal is led from the barn.

In many stables the noon meal is omitted, but most horsemen hold that some grain should be given at noon. In any case the amount of feed given at midday should not be large.

For horses taxed to the limit of their endurance, all grain should be ground and fed upon moistened chaffed hay. Food thus prepared is more rapidly masticated, and consequently remains a longer time in the stomach. A little long hay may be supplied the animal to be consumed at leisure after the stomach is well filled.

ORDER OF FEEDING AND WATERING

Horses should receive their regular and largest supply of water previous to feeding, and it may be well to supply a limited quantity after feeding. Horses heated and fatigued may be given eight or ten quarts of water, even if cold, the balance of requirements being supplied after they are rested and cooled. On the road a few quarts may be given, no matter how much the horse is heated, but never give a large quantity at one time. On journeys give water every few miles. Water the horse often, so that he will drink only a small quantity at a time.

Water first, then feed ground grain sprinkled upon a small allowance of moistened chaffed hay. Do not overfeed with hay or many ills will result—staring coat, labored breathing and quick-tiring being the least serious. Give each horse a definite allowance of hay, and never as much as he will consume. Feed regularly and uniformly.

Plenty of oats and good hay will supply energy and spirited action, but a horse is better nourished by several kinds of grain and forage plants than by one or two only.

For horses which are out of the stable during the day and worked hard, all grain, with the possible exception of oats, should be ground. For those at extremely hard work all grains should be ground and mixed with chaffed hay. For horses not working, oats or corn should not be ground, nor need the hay or straw be chaffed.

SOME STANDARD FEEDING STUFFS

It seems that chemists fail to find the stimulating principle in oats. On account of their palatability it is claimed that some oats should be included in every ration. New oats are unfit for horse feed, it is said by some authorities, as they have a tendency to soften the horses, causing them to sweat easily.

Next to oats, corn is the commonest grain for horses. It should be ground for working horses. It is best suited for animals at plain, steady work.

In protein and carbohydrates barley lies between oats and corn, and has less oil than either. When the horses' teeth are good, and the work not hard, it may be fed whole. If ground it forms a pasty mass in the mouth.

Wheat mixed with corn, oats or bran is superior to either alone for work-horses. Fed exclusively on wheat, horses are apt to go "off feed" and suffer other digestive derangements.

Whole wheat has no advantage over the same weight of bran and shorts in the ration, but two parts ground wheat and one part bran make a good ration, fed with hay. The "bran mash," made by scalding bran with hot water, is fed once or twice a week as a laxative in most countries.

—‡—‡—‡—

North Carolina Bakers Organize

THE North Carolina Bakers' Association was formally organized at Greensboro, N. C., on February 21, at a meeting of some 50 representatives of the baking and allied businesses. Officers were elected, enthusiastic talks were made, and by unanimous expression the young organization was most successfully launched.

W. L. O'Brien, of Winston-Salem, was elected president; R. W. Miller, of Greensboro, was elected vice-president, and M. J. Paschall, of Durham, secretary and treasurer. A board of governors was also elected as follows: R. A. Grant, of Asheville; Fred Stout and B. Strebb, of Raleigh; J. L. Sally, of Statesville; H. O. Miller, of Charlotte, and C. E. Wendlinger, of Wilmington. The three officers are also members of the board of governors.

Meetings were held at the O. Henry hotel morning and afternoon, and in addition the entire group had luncheon together at the hotel. The attendance was large and representative, and the enthusiasm and interest shown by all present in the birth of the organization were enough to insure its growth and well-being.

A meeting of the bakers of the state was held there in November, at which time it was decided to form a regular association, and the February meeting is the outgrowth of the first preliminary gathering. It was the first state convention.

Much of the time was spent on details of organization, but several strong talks were made, notably those by Ben B. George, of Cincinnati, of the Proctor and Gamble company; by J. L. Skelton, of Morristown, Tenn.; by H. O. Miller, of Charlotte, and Charles E. Wendlinger, of Wilmington.

Through the new organization the bakers hope eventually to raise the standard of the loaf of bread in North Carolina. They think that through association many petty jealousies and much price-cutting and lowering of the standard of the bread may be eliminated, and that a healthy spirit of co-operation may be encouraged throughout all the bakeries of the state.

Illinois Convention

OSCAR STRAND, president of the Illinois Association of the Baking Industry, recently sent a timely and sensible letter to the members of that association on the evils of price-cutting, which is apropos at the present time. The letter was as follows:

"FEBRUARY 23, 1922.

"We hear and read so much in the newspapers and trade journals about bread wars being waged in different places, that we wonder what is coming next. It seems to me that some bakers have gone mad. If they would stop and think for one minute what the outcome of these bread wars will be, I do not believe they would plunge into them so hastily.

"Bakers throughout the country have worked very hard for years to bring the baking industry to the high standard it now holds, with the result that it ranks as one of the leading industries of the world. It looks to me like we are now tearing down the very thing that all of us have worked so hard to build up. If these bread wars continue for any length of time it will certainly lower the quality of our goods, for I am sure there is no baker today that can make a real quality loaf of bread, wrap it, sell it for 5 cents and make a legitimate profit. Especially when the price of flour is going higher every day and overhead expenses still considerably above normal.

"I wish to say right here that if there is any baker to be found who has a system whereby he can manufacture a loaf of bread, at profit, for a nickel, I would very much appreciate receiving the details of his method.

"There is no commodity housewives can buy today where they get as much value received for their money as they do in bakery goods. I do not believe the housewife is complaining about prices on bakery goods, so why should we give our products away.

"Now, fellow-bakers, I would stick by quality and a price that will allow you a fair profit, for I do not think the bread wars will last very long. Do not cut your prices unless absolutely forced to. I would sell a little less and make a profit rather than 'cut' and go out of business. It is almost a crime, it seems to me, that this price-cutting should have got started just because of one or two men. There is no doubt but that this will have a tendency to keep the smaller baker from recognizing our Association, for surely bread wars are not what the organization advocates or stands for. However, we should not let this come between us and our organization, for, in my opinion, this only goes to demonstrate that we are in need of a stronger and better Association than ever before. If one man commits suicide, it is no reason for all of us to do so, and likewise no baker should be against the Association merely because one or two men have been unfair, Until we get a real strong organization—an organization that we will all stand back of and co-operate with

—we cannot expect anything else but more or less trouble,

"I wish to take this opportunity to urge all bakers in the state of Illinois, and any in other states that can possibly come, to be at our state convention, which will be held in Danville, Illinois, the 18th, 19th and 20th of April. There are things coming up at this time that I think we should all be interested in, and especially in placing a bill before the legislature—the kind of a bill we want, and not the kind of a bill that they will put over on us whether we want it or not, unless we defend ourselves. Just such bills have been put over on the bakers in other states, therefore it is up to us to wake up and not let them slip over anything on the Illinois Association. Our full program for the convention will be published in a later issue.

"(Signed)   OSCAR STRAND,

"Monmouth, Illinois.   President."

—‡—‡—‡—

Dear Wheat—Cheap Bread
From the American Miller.

THE Farmers' National Council, which would seem from its name to represent something of size and quality, is going to demand of Congress the revival of the U. S. Grain Corporation. It wants it revived with a government guarantee $2.50 per bushel as the minimum price of wheat. And in palliation of its demand it declares that "the standard 14-ounce loaf of bread can be sold for five cents by preventing profiteering between the wheat farmer and the consumer."

If all wheat were sold at $2.50 per bushel that would mean that there would be 5.75 cents worth of wheat in a pound of flour and a little over 3½ cents worth of wheat in a 14-ounce loaf of bread. That would leave 1½ cents to cover all the costs of milling, the cost of the package, railway and other transportation and handling, the labor of the baker and the cost of selling, not to mention profit, for there would be none. The loaf would cost five cents before it left the mill as flour. It would cost more than ten cents before it left the bakery, still without profit. In their figuring the Farmers' National Council have not only eliminated "profiteering," but profit, overhead, transportation and labor. Evidently they think all activities apart from farming should be philanthropic.

The Farmers' National Council that demands a government guaranteed minimum price of $2.50 per bushel for wheat, also demands that cheap flour and five-cent bread be made from that same wheat. This would be a humorous situation if it were not such old stuff; and it is wrong to laugh at the aged.

—*American Miller.*

—‡—‡—‡—

The general advance in cost of materials during the past few years has caused small bakers to look more closely to bakeshop costs of production, and in doing so it has been noticed that hand methods are slow and costly.

LEGAL

No. 117.—A Warning.—Names of Partners Must be Registered in Some States

I WANT to warn the readers of these articles of a danger which in cases recently brought in several states has cost business men a lot of money. It is the failure to obey state statutes requiring the names of a partnership to be registered. Most states now have such acts in one form or another, and the courts are giving them a most unexpected and in many cases a disastrous application.

The statutes in question provide in substance that when anybody adopts an assumed or fictitious name to do business under, he must register it in some public office or be guilty of a misdemeanor. The act was aimed, I believe, solely against the suspicious concerns who hide behind such names as the Regal Tire Company, the American Mercantile Company, and so on. When you come to sue such concerns, it is a very difficult job to find out who to name as defendant. Very often they are not incorporated, and therefore cannot be sued under their trade names. You must sue them as John Jones, trading as the Regal Tire Company, or John Jones and William Brown, trading as the Regal Tire Company, and if you don't do that, your suit is bad.

To prevent the concealment of identity on the part of the real factors in a business concern, the registration laws were passed, and every honest business man considered them good things. It soon developed, however, that the courts had a totally different idea of the application of these laws than the business world had. The courts believed that they applied to such concerns as the Regal Tire Company, of course, but they also held that they applied under certain conditions to partnerships like Moore & Smith and John Smith & Sons, and furthermore, that if such partnerships did not register their names *they could not sue in the courts to recover claims due them.*

These decisions have fallen like bombshells among business people, for regularly constituted partnerships like John Smith & Sons never dreamed the registration act would apply to them at all.

In Pennsylvania a case has just been decided which shows the damage which can be done by the line of decisions I refer to. The decision I am about to discuss is typical of those which have been handed down in certain other states. In the Pennsylvania case there was a partnership consisting of three members, Moyer, Carpenter and Miller, which traded under the name of Moyer & Carpenter. It had a claim against one Kennedy, and failing to collect it, brought suit. Kennedy raised the point that Moyer & Carpenter was an "assumed or fictitious" name, that it had not been registered and that therefore Moyer & Carpenter could not

sue under that name. Both the lower court and the Appeal Court upheld this view, and the case—doubtless an attempt to collect a perfectly honest debt—was thrown out and the debt is forever lost. The court in a nutshell held that "Moyer & Carpenter" was assumed and fictitious because it implied that there were but two partners, while there were three. "The plaintiffs were therefore," goes on the decision, "engaged in an unlawful business. It was not only forbidden, but declared to be a misdemeanor. The account against the defendant was contracted in the prosecution of that business; it was a part of the business in which they were engaged and for which the firm was organized. It had been the declared law of this commonwealth for more than a hundred years that an action founded on a transaction prohibited by statute cannot be sustained, although it be not expressly declared in the statute that the contract is void. This was the rule of the common law in England and the principle has been firmly established in this state."

In another recent case a man founded a business, ran it under his own name for several years and then gave his son an interest. The business was still run under the father's name without registration. A claim of several hundred dollars accrued against a rascal who when sued to recover it raised the point that the father's name alone was assumed or fictitious under the law, because there were two partners. The father's counsel was obliged to advise him that this view would probably be sustained by the court. Therefore the case was compromised at great loss.

All states do not go this far. New York State, for instance, has been very fair, holding that the object of the registration act was not to aid dishonest debtors in avoiding just debts, therefore the application of the law would not be carried that far. But the court of any state which has a registration act is liable to follow the other view, with the result, as I have pointed out, of losing perfectly just claims to which, on the merits, there would be no defense whatever.

My advice to every reader of this article who trades under a firm name, therefore, is (1) to at once find out whether his state has an act requiring such names to be registered, and (2) to register his firm name under it if necessary. It has been held that where there are only two partners, John Brown and William Smith, for instance, the firm name Brown & Smith does not have to be registered, because it discloses the family names of both partners.

—‡—‡—‡—

The Tolleston Baking Company, Gary, Ind., has been incorporated with capital of $15,000 by Casimir Paxera, Alex Norvaish, Joseph Gurskis.

K. D. Wetherby recently opened his new modern bake shop in the Loomer Bldg., Main Street, Derby, Conn.

Hilger's Bakery was recently opened at 18-20 West Avenue, Lockport, N. Y.

The Sugar Situation

From "Facts About Sugar"

WHEN the price of sugar was mounting high under the influence of the post-war shortage, members of the sugar trade, whose memories should have extended back over a generation or more, were predicting that sugar never again would sell at the levels prevailing prior to the war. Yet, before the end of 1921, prices had fallen to the lowest point touched in twenty years. Now, these same prophets can see ahead nothing but low prices and over-production.

In support of this view they assert that the world's appetite for sugar has suffered a serious diminution. During the period of scarcity that attended the war, they argue, many persons got out of the habit of eating sugar and now are content to do with a much smaller quantity than they formerly were accustomed to consume. Children have grown up without the opportunity to acquire the sugar habit. Not for many years, if ever, according to their reasoning, will the world be able to absorb the 18,500,000 tons of sugar which it consumed in the year before the world war.

To appreciate the fallacy of these assertions, it is only necessary to look back at the growth of sugar consumption during the past two decades. At the beginning of the present century the world's production—and consumption—was about 8,500,000 long tons. Twenty years ago, in 1901-2, it exceeded 10,000,000 tons for the first time in history. Prices were low in 1902, the lowest, in fact, that had been known. Cuban raw sugar in bond declined almost to one and a half cents a pound. Predictions were plentiful that production would have to be cut down as the only alternative to complete ruin for producers, but by 1905-6 the world was producing and finding a market for some 14,000,000 tons, or 40 per cent. more than the output five years earlier.

The crop year 1910-11 was the first in which production exceeded 15,000,000 long tons, and never since then has it fallen below this figure. The largest output in any one year up to the present time was reached with the 1913-14 crop of roundly 18,700,000 long tons. From that time until 1920 there was a gradual decline, due to the war, which brought production again below 15,500,000 tons in the latter year. Although there was a small increase last year, the world's output is still below that of 1910-11.

In the matter of sugar supply we are today just about where we were ten years ago, while in the preceding ten years consumption increased almost 100 per cent. To argue that the growth in the demand for sugar which had been under way for a century and more has been permanently checked, and that we shall be satisfied henceforth to remain on the basis of 1911 and 1912, is to defy all the teachings of past history and human experience.

The existence of a million-ton sugar surplus in Cuba at the end of last year is a fact that naturally has bulked large in the minds of the American sugar trade, but it was due to special and wholly temporary conditions. One of these was the glutting of the United States market with a million tons which had to be absorbed during 1921 and lessened buying demand correspondingly. A second influence was the depletion of Europe's purchasing power, aggravated by highly unfavorable exchange conditions.

Of these two factors, limiting absorption during the past year, the first already has been entirely removed and the second has been greatly modified. Moreover, prices have declined to a level at which Cuban sugars are being rapidly distributed and are able to meet competition from any other part of the world. The particular problem created by the accumulation of sugar in Cuba appears to be in a fair way to solution during the present year.

As concerns the world situation, the question is not whether the demand for sugar will regain the proportions it had attained before the war, but within what time this lost ground will be made up and the progress interrupted by the outbreak of that conflict resumed. Not yet has the world's consumption regained its full normal volume, nor is it likely to do so within the present year, but a big stride in that direction undoubtedly is being taken.

It is noteworthy that in Europe, where the enforced decline in consumption has been greatest, renewed activity and optimism as to the future of the industry are the outstanding features of the situation. European refiners are improving the equipment and increasing the capacity of their plants. Producers are going forward with plans for increased output. Every important manufacturer of sugar machinery and equipment is busily occupied with orders.

In other parts of the world the same signs of activity and progress appear. Very extensive plans are under way for improvements in Java mills that will require the investment of millions of dollars. India is stirring with ambitious plans for the modernization of its vast sugar industry. South Africa and South America are interested in the improvement of their milling equipment. It is not in reason to believe that the United States and Cuba, which have led the way in important developments and improvements in sugar production heretofore, are not going to take part in carrying the industry forward to meet the new and enlarged demands which the world will soon be making on it.

—‡—‡—‡—

The Huber Baking Company's plant at Chester, Pa., has been sold to the Freihofer Baking Company of Philadelphia. The Chester plant, which was built during the war, is a thoroughly modern bakery, but has not been in operation for about eight months.

The Anheuser-Busch distributing organization makes it possible for bakers to secure fresh supplies of BUDWEISER BARLEY MALT just as it is needed. With one of these distributors close at hand, it is unnecessary—and inadvisable—to use the old-fashioned contracting system.

ANHEUSER-BUSCH SALES CORPORATION

ST. LOUIS, MO.

(DISTRIBUTORS)

Aberdeen, S. D.—Ward-Owsley Co., Inc.
Atlanta, Ga.—Bessire & Co., Inc.
Augusta, Me.—Holmes Swift Co.
Baltimore, Md.—Anheuser Busch Branch
Brooklyn, N. Y.—Anheuser Busch Ice & Cold Storage Co.
Brooklyn, N. Y.—Jabург Bros.
Brooklyn, N. Y.—High Grade Malt Co.
Buffalo, N. Y.—High Grade Malt Co.
Chicago, Ill.—Anheuser Busch Agency
Cincinnati, O.—Hilker Bros. & Co.
Cleveland, O.—Bruce & West Mfg. Co.
Cleveland, O.—Wm. Edwards Co.
Columbus, O.—The Central Ohio Supply Co.
Detroit, Mich.—Hilde Bros., Anheuser Busch distributor
Detroit, Mich.—E. B. Gallagher & Co.
Detroit, Mich.—Bakers' Supply Co.
Duluth, Minn.—Wright Co.
Evansville, Ind.—Besse & Co.

Ft. Smith, Ark.—J. Foster & Co.
Grand Rapids, Mich.—Wolverine Spice Co.
Houston, Texas—J. S. Waterman Co.
Indianapolis, Ind.—Besatte & Co.
Jacksonville, Fla.—Atlantic Distributing Co.
Kansas City, Mo.—Tri-state Beverage Co.
Kansas City, Mo.—S. W. Nagle Co.
Los Angeles, Calif.—Crane Commercial Co.
Louisville, Ky.—Bessire & Co., Inc.
Memphis, Tenn.—Uberdebrunn Co.
Newark, N. J.—A. H. Weidman
New Orleans, La.—J. S. Waterman Co.
New York City, N. Y.—Jabург Bros.
New York City, N. Y.—High Grade Malt Co.
Omaha, Neb.—J. J. Nagle Co.
Peoria, Ill.—Leisy Brewing Co.

Philadelphia, Pa.—Jos. A. Lewis
    Also leading Bakers' Supply Houses
Pittsburgh, Pa.—W. I. Knorr Co.
Portland, Ore.—Blumauer & Hoch
Quincy, Ill.—Anheuser Busch Agency
Richmond, Va.—W. H. Harris Grocery Co.
San Francisco, Calif.—Tillman & Bendell, Inc.
Seattle, Wash.—Schwabacker Bros. & Co., Inc.
Salt Lake City, Utah—W. H. Britz Co.
St. Joseph, Mo.—Anheuser Busch Agency
St. Louis, Mo.—All Bakers Supply Houses
St. Paul, Minn.—Anheuser Busch Agency
Syracuse, N. Y.—Bruce & West Mfg. Co.
Tampa, Fla.—Consumers Ice Co.
Toledo, Ohio—E. B. Gallagher & Co.
Washington, D. C.—Anheuser Busch Agency
Wheeling, W. Va.—Bernard Wiesner

The New School

Of the American Institute of Baking, by Peter G. Pirrie, Principal.

ON my arrival in Chicago at the new home of the American Institute of Baking at 1135 Fullerton Avenue, I found a building, almost ideal for its purpose, in which Dr. H. E. Barnard and his associates already had matters well under way as far as the service and research departments were concerned, and into which it was up to me to install and get into operation a complete baking school designed to fit closely into the needs of the baking industry.

The space available for this purpose is both adequate and efficiently distributed throughout the building. Class rooms and chemical laboratories are already completed, and with the addition of a few items of equipment will shortly be available for use.

Work is also proceeding at present on the experimental bakery. This room has a north exposure, and is exceptionally well lighted, consequently well fitted for its purpose of testing the various ingredients of a loaf of bread, and judging the experimentally baked loaves.

In order to make this particular phase of the work efficient in proportion to its importance, individual equipment will be installed for each student, so that there will be no interference due to two different men finding it necessary to use the same oven at the same time, but under conditions which are proper for neither.

These class rooms, experimental baking rooms, and school laboratories so far mentioned, occupy the entire third floor of the building and, rather than being in any manner crowded, so much space is available that it is planned to install a specially equipped microscopical laboratory on this same floor for students' use.

One of the interesting features of the brewing institute which is now to be the home of our new school for bakers was the small model brewery installed in a separate four-story building adjacent to the main building. All machinery formerly installed here, and given over to the manufacture of beer, has now been removed and is leaving behind an excellent location for the bakery. This bakery is to be installed just as if it were for the purpose of turning out commercial bread, with the exception that all equipment will be in triplicate. In other words, instead of there being one mixer, one rounder, etc., there will be three of each particular machine all the way through, and these machines will be used intermittently, so that the benefit of experience on all will be available.

Just exactly what the output of the bakery is to be has not yet been determined, however, the main point is that this volume of production will be so chosen that it will not interfere in the slightest with instruction. Sufficient bread will be produced so that will be no possible criticism due to the smallness of the doughs or other than normal conditions of bread manufacture. All through the operation of this school bakery the fundamental conditions, as explained so well by Professor Jago, will be kept in mind, and the object be experiment, demonstration of the effects of variation of conditions and ingredients, and research. There will, of course, be instruction in the technique of bread manufacture (shop practice), but the idea is that the plant will be run *not for the purpose of making bread for sale* but for demonstration of processes and principles.

The courses of study at the American Institute's School of Baking will be divided into three general groups. The aim is to supply education of the type desired by any man in the baking industry. It will, however, be realized that it will be impossible to have sitting next to each other in the same class a man who is trained to be a better foreman or superintendent, and a man who is to be expected to direct the activities of chemists engaged in industrial research.

Then, in addition to these two men, we have the baking chemist, who must be so trained that he is able to personally do the laboratory work necessary to control the purchase of any materials, and the progress of the bread through the plant.

Consequently there will be at least three distinct and separate courses of study available for applicants for admission. There will be the course for bakers, designed to equip men previously experienced in the baking industry for positions as foremen and superintendents. There will be a course for baking chemists, designed to equip men with or without previous baking experience for positions in chemical laboratories. There will also be opportunity for men of considerable previous chemical and baking experience to engage in special problems of research in the laboratories of the school and institute.

The basic length of the main course will be four months, and the first class will start probably at the end of April. The second class will start about the middle of August. Each course will last for 112 days. Facilities will be provided for the admission of not more than forty-eight men.

It is anticipated that there will be an unusual demand for enrollment, and every effort is being made to take care of these men when they arrive for their period of training.

Peter G. Pirrie has returned to Chicago to resume his position on the staff of the American Institute of Baking, under Dr. Harry E. Barnard, as principal of the new School of Baking. He comes to Chicago from Minneapolis, Minn., where he has been well known to bakers as the Head of the Baking Department of the William Hood Dunwoody Industrial Institute, and as the chief of the Technical and Service Departments

The Sévigné Wrapping Machine

Your Hunt
For
Machine Supremacy
Will End With
SÉVIGNÉ

National Bread Wrapping Machine Co.
Nashua, N. H.

The Baker's Success

*By F. G. Atkinson, Vice-President Washburn-Crosby
Co., at the Southern Illinois Convention, Carbondale*

THE first question I asked myself after receiving
the invitation to write a paper for your Convention was, "What can I say that will help our co-
laborers in the world's work, the bakers who are located
in medium-sized towns, to make their business more
nearly perfect in a financial way?" Hence let us make
the title of this paper read, "The Baker's Success."

Most large successful bread factories in the United
States made their start in a small way, which illustrates the fact that it is better to start one's own business in a conservative manner and add thereto as
conditions and financial ability may permit. It is always a nice question to settle as to how big a bite a
person should take in starting a new business, or when
the time comes to enlarge on what he already has.

As a good business man has already said: "It is
a mistake to bear the United States." He meant, of
course, that business men in this country should look
toward growth and success rather than to figure on
things going backward. If, therefore, a man decides
to start a bake shop with one oven, he would be perfectly justified, if he is financially able, to provide room
throughout the establishment for a fifty or one hundred per cent increase. The chances are nine in ten,
if for no other reason than that population is bound
to increase, that he will need the extra room and facilities within a short time; thus taking it for granted
that the individual has the business capacity to successfully carry on a business in a business-like manner.

When a business is fairly well established, then the
main thing for the owner to figure on is how to maintain satisfactory profits. The bakers here present
probably in their respective communities have a fair
share of the bread and bakery goods business of their
neighborhood. They should study well and long before making radical moves. The safe and sane rule
to guide one when it comes to the enlargement of a
plant is, "Is the demand from the public for my quality
of products so insistent that there is no question but
what I ought to add more facilities?"

You all know how to produce good bread, but the
question is, "Are you producing that quality of bread
and quality of other products that the people of your
vicinity really want?" The baker who hits that nail
on the head most squarely is the one that runs his shop
with regularity, care and good judgment, and consequently is in a position to make money. Sometimes
such a baker does not make money because his shop is
being run extravagantly. By this I mean he may be
spending money needlessly. For instance, some bakers make a quality of loaf, the ingredients of which
are too expensive, the idea being to produce a high
quality loaf, whereas if scientific methods were used

in the production of the bread, so many different ingredients might not be necessary. Wonderful flavor
and a handsome looking loaf of bread can be produced
simply by watchfulness during the period of fermentation. Let me say right here that nineteen out of twenty
bakers who have trouble with poor bread, can put the
blame on over-fermentation rather than under-fermen-
tation. It is common knowledge in the business that
carelessness during fermentation period can easily
break down the quality of the finished product.

When a baker graduates from the store class to the
wagon or truck class, he should pay particular attention to the routing of his wagons or trucks; watch
and work for a low cost of distribution, distributing
being very costly even at the best.

KNOW YOUR COSTS

This reminds me of the importance of having some
statistical records, for it is just as necessary in a moderate sized bakery to have a first-class accounting
system as in the larger factories. If any baker has
reason for feeling dissatisfied with his accounting or
statistical departments, then he should get hold of
some reliable auditing firm, who can provide him with
a simple and reasonable system. The next thing on
the program would be to engage a young man or young
woman having brains, and who would be earnest, and
preferably a stenographer and typist. Weekly or
monthly statistical records should come out with regularity, and should be studied by the master baker
carefully. It is always a good thing to have a monthly
review of your business, paying particular attention
to cost of production and distribution.

A careful and well developed selling program con-
tributes to success. The man at the head of the business should personally know almost every channel
through which his bread is being distributed. Such
a contact puts him in a position to judge as to how
much of his product should go through each channel.
If his monthly records show a falling off, then something should be done, each specific case having attention, and where necessary some special advertising indulged in. Advertising is very expensive, and exceedingly costly if not followed up thoroughly. In fact, a
baker, except on special occasions, should hesitate a
long while before entering in on some advertising program, for advertising eats up money very rapidly, and
is of mightily little worth unless backed up by good
quality and the proper selling and distributing
methods.

Every baker that is doing good work on quality, and
stands well with the grocers and consumers in his community, is doing much toward increasing the consumption of bread manufactured in the bake shop. For
years it has been my observation that the percentage of
bakery goods used in a town depends very largely
whether there be one or more bakers in a town who are
setting a high standard of quality. The facts of the
case are that if a community is going to be a large

consumer of bakery goods it is the baker himself that has the say, for high quality means big consumption, just as medium or low quality means a restricted use of bakery bread and more home baking.

I understand that the Beechnut people who have made a tremendous success in the distribution of their foodstuffs and other articles, have their various factories scrubbed out completely every 24 hours. This certainly is a good example to follow, for cleanliness is the first requisite of success in the selling of foodstuffs. By maintaining a clean bake shop, you not only have something big to talk about to the consumer, but you also set a standard for your employees. They will take pride in everything that pertains to the company they work for, just to the extent that the company takes pride in its business.

Once in a while, and there have been more of them than usual lately, you will find a baker who is striving to give the public something for nothing. It cannot successfully be done. I am one of those people that believe the housekeeper is willing to pay full value for a handsome, wholesome, well-baked, nutritive loaf of bread. If bread is to continue as the staff of life, it should be a good staff, something that the children will thrive on.

VALUE OF CONVENTIONS

I take it that these conventions and associations of bakers are organized for two or three special purposes. For instance, each baker attending a convention wants to learn something that will help him produce a better quality at a lower cost. Second, he likes the social atmosphere of these gatherings. Third, in a specific way he would like to discover how to make his business more successful financially. It goes without saying, therefore, that bakers as a rule are good fellows. Hence the social side of the convention is easily taken care of.

On the commercial side at these conventions the beneficial features will just naturally take the form of endeavors to help one another to make a fair margin of profit. How foolish then it is for any baker or group of bakers, after attending an association meeting, to go home and permit themselves to be drawn into a price war. These present days are peace days; hence why not keep the peace commercially?

Immediately there develops in any neighborhood a tendency on the part of some ill-advised person to precipitate a bread war, the remaining bakers in that district should get togther for the purpose of working up an atmosphere of opposition to such an unworthy program. The united efforts of such a group can often produce the desired results.

The public is getting its bread at a fair price. Therefore, no baker is justified in selling his product below cost. Bankers certainly are justified in scrutinizing very closely business statements submitted by their customers who indulge in the very questionable practice of price cutting. Bakers attending conventions should say, "We are standing together. Let us keep together and give our best efforts toward the stabilization of fair prices."

It pays a manufacturer well to buy nothing but first-class raw materials. He makes less mistakes and his goods appeal more strongly. He cannot produce good goods except the foundation in the shape of raw materials be all right. In the buying of flour a baker can waste or make considerable sums of money. The flour to buy is a standardized article. It is a great thing to have everything in a bake shop all set in place to make bread automatically, but, of course, this cannot be done unless the base article is running uniform.

As regards the kind of flour to buy, I would refer you to an article by John C. Summers entitled, "The Science of Bread Making," which appeared in the *Northwestern Miller*, issue of January 25, 1922. Just one point in that article I would like to emphasize, and that is, where a baker is buying his flour on an analysis basis, he should not look for a product having an ash below .44 per cent. Some of the very fine and glutenous streams in a mill are being eliminated from the flour when a mill's product show an ash less than .44. In fact, we believe shops having high powered, rapid mixers, can use profitably a flour having even a higher percentage of ash than that specified. The yield of loaves per barrel would be benefited, at the same time color of loaf well maintained.

We have often read of the man who has "too many irons in the fire." The statement has usually been coupled with some person who has failed in business. Let us all keep this in mind, for a baker is always tempted to gradually add a number of new products to his manufactured list. Sometimes the number will run as high as forty or fifty. I wonder if such a development in ordinary sized shops is not dangerous. Will not a baker make more money in the long run if he confines himself, say, to ten or a dozen leading articles found in bakers' showcases, and does his levelest toward making each one of these a masterpiece? Sometimes one department in a business loses money, hence is a drag on every other department. Each item, therefore, manufactured in a bake shop should be scrutinized closely from the profit and loss standpoint, and anything showing up badly should be eliminated. It requires a very efficient organization to properly and profitably manufacture more than a dozen different articles. I am speaking now of those shops that are of medium size, and not of those large institutions that can afford to have a well-organized department for each article produced.

One of the early big successes in the bakery business of the United States was that achieved by Mr. John E. McKinney, formerly of St. Louis, Mo. Some of the things I have told you about in what has been read was taught me some twenty-five years ago by Mr. McKinney.

—‡—‡—‡—

Norfolk Bakers Organize

Retail bakers in Norfolk, Virginia, have organized an association to standardize trade practices and promote co-operation between different establishments and cleanliness in all operations of baking. The name of the association will be the Tidewater Retail Bakers' Association.

Organization was perfected on February 6th, with W. T. Andrews, president; W. R. Floyd, vice-president; C. E. Bennett, secretary-treasurer. Only Norfolk firms were present at the organization meeting, but bakers from nearby cities will be asked to join. The scene of the organization meeting was the office of The Fleischmann Company, and Milton Carlough of the New York office of the company made an address.

—‡—‡—‡—

Texas Convention

THE Executive Committee of the Texas Association of the Baking Industry at a meeting held at the Southland Hotel, Dallas, Texas, chose the city of Houston for the convention of 1922, and set the dates as May 16th, 17th and 18th, and selected the Bender Hotel as convention headquarters.

The Texas Association usually has a very fine meeting and a good attendance, and this year will doubtless prove to be no exception. A fine program is being prepared, and an invitation is extended to all bakers and others interested in the baking industry to be present; they will be made heartily welcome.

Making the Most of Every Dough

To make the most of every dough that enters your make-up room, requires machine handling with speed and accuracy, a minimum use of dusting flour and without injury to the dough itself. This last is of the greatest importance, and speed and accuracy are of little use if your doughs are killed in making-up. A dead loaf is no seller.

Quality production, quickly and accurately, that's one of the bread baker's greatest problems. DUTCHESS Automatic Make-up Units accomplish this profitably in bakeries all over the country every day. To assure you, we'll be pleased to show you this equipment in operation and have you consult the bakers using it.

"Our Sales Tell the Tale"

DUTCHESS TOOL COMPANY
BEACON, N. Y.

Trade Items

T. B. Marquis, recently opened the National Bakery at 118 North First Ave., Phoenix, Ariz. The bakery is modern and sanitary in every respect, the entire process of baking being carried out in full view of the public. Mr. Marquis is also successfully operating similar bakeries at Tucson, Ariz., and El Paso, Texas.

Hubbs & Butler, bakers of Walnut Ridge, Ark., are preparing to remove their plant to the new McCarroll Bldg., same town.

The Square Deal Baking Company has been incorporated at De Land, Fla., with capital stock of $20,000, by A. D. Brown, Joseph Larweth and Frank Halman.

The Geo. McMahon Bakery has been incoprorated at 2409 Madison Street., Chicago, Ill., with capital of $20,000 by Arthur Martin, Hugh Lammie and George McMahon.

The T. H. Buster Baking Company, Quincy, Ill., are building an addition to the rear and right of their plant at 1034 Main Street.

The North Side Bakery has been incorporated at Indianapolis, Ind., with capital of $30,000 by James M. Gossard, Lee A. Boulware, Oliver P. Swank.

Geo. F. Hilborn, Portland, Me., has leased the factory building on Forest Avenue, where he plans to start a bakery.

After thirty years in the Atlantic Block, Beverly, Mass., Carl Klink has opened his bakery in a new location in the Butman Block, Cabot Street, which is one of the most attractive stores on the street, and a plant with every modern equipment.

The Edgerly Baking Company, Brookline, Mass., has been incorporated with capital of $50,000 by John H. Edgerly and Howard S. Edgerly, and John A. Edgerly.

Peter's Bakery of Lowell, Mass., has been incorporated with capital stock of $5,000 by Peter Couremblis, George Panagotopoulos and Argero Couremblis.

John Kawa, North Adams, Mass., has purchased the bakery business of Joseph Wotkiewicz at 9 Hoosac Street, same place.

John Wendall Swint, well-known baker of Winthrop, Mass., died suddenly on February 21st of heart disease. Mr. Swint was connected with the baking business for many years, both in Winthrop and East Boston, and was one of the early members of the National Association of Master Bakers. He is survived by his wife, three daughters and a son.

Extensive alterations are to be started on Hausold Brothers' Bakery and Restaurant at Third and Washington Streets, Hoboken, N. J.

Excavation work on the new bakery for George Simi, corner of Virginia and Fourth Streets, Reno, Nevada, is finished, and the building is to be started in the near future.

The Portsmouth Baking Company, Portsmouth, N. H., have purchased the business and bakery of James Flynn at 75 State Street, Portsmouth, N. H.

The Holbrook Pie Baking Company of Albany, N. Y., was recently incorporated with capital stock of $10,000 by Robert C. Poskanzer, N. M. Medwin and Charles F. Murray.

The American Baking Company recently took possession of the M. E. Conn wholesale bakery at 21 Schuyler Street, Amsterdam, N. Y., having leased this large and modern equipped plant. Robert Hyman is sales manager.

Papers of incorporation were recently filed at Buffalo, N. Y., by the Old English Baking Company, capital stock $10,000. The incorporators are: Henry Das, Harry S. Read and Dirk Das.

A large and modern equipped bakery is to be erected for D. Linehan and Brother at Sagamore Street and Lawton Avenue, Glen Falls, N. Y., to replace the plant on Oak Street, which was recently destroyed by fire.

The Malone Baking Co., Malone, N. Y., has been incorporated with capital stock of $10,000.

The North Side Baking Co., New Rochelle, N. Y., has been incorporated with capital stock of $100,000 by M. Shumofsky, C. V. Breese, J. J. Casey.

The Breatlin Bakeries, incorporated at Brooklyn, N. Y., with capital of $50,000 by Edwin C. Morsch, Hazel E. Nelson and Stephen J. Rudd.

Dahl Bros., incorporated at Syracuse, N. Y., with capital of $30,000 by F. & S. Dahl, F. Crump.

J. D. Ginakes & Thomas Stramus will open a bakery and confectionery business at Grafton, N. Dak.

The Holland Bread Co., 443 W. Third Street, Dayton, Ohio, has purchased property on S. Ludlow Street, near Bayard, where it will erect a modern bakery at a cost of more than $200,000. The company is also operating bakeries at Columbus, Toledo and Youngstown.

The Achbach-Williams Baking Company, St. Mary's, Ohio, has been incorporated with capital stock of $10,000 by G. Edward Achbach, Ruth E. Achbach, Guy F. Williams, Mabel Williams, Donald Kirsch.

The Hull & Fought Baking Company has been incorporated at Toledo, Ohio, with capital of $10,000 by Robert Hull, Burton E. Fought, George W. Pearson, Martha Enright and Dennis N. Maloney.

Harry B. Burt, the baker and confectioner, Youngstown, Ohio, has purchased a new and handsome store at 325 W. Federal Street, which will be newly equipped throughout.

W. B. Caum, proprietor of Caum's Cafe, Twelfth Avenue, between Eleventh and Twelfth Streets, Altoona, Pa., recently opened a first-class pastry department in connection with the dining-rooms. M. Rom, a pastry chef of many years' experience, is in charge.

A new brick fireproof structure is to be built by the Leopold Bakery, Haynes Street, Johnstown, Pa., to replace the former one which was recently destroyed by fire.

Owen & Rastetter, formerly managers of Federal Bakeries at Pittsburgh, Pa., are opening a new bakery at 105 Miller Avenue, Clairton, Pa.

It is reported that the Drennan Cake Company will operate a large cake bakery at Front Street and Talbot Avenue, Memphis, Tenn., for the manufacture of cakes. The company's home office and factory are at Chicago, Ill.

Articles of incorporation were recently filed at Nashville, Tenn., by Miss Ramsey's Bakery, capital stock $10,000, by Mindle Ramsey, Stella Ramsey, Mollie R. Porter, Lee S. Ramsey and Sue May Ramsey.

Rudolph Inkel, an expert St. Johnsbury, Vt., baker, has bought the bakery and business of T. R. Woodard at Morrisville, Va., and already taken possession. Mr. Inkle expects to move to Morrisville in the early summer.

The Princeton Home Bakery has been incorporated at Princeton, W. Va., with capital stock of $10,000 by C. D. Radford, W. L. Ryan, A. L. Bowling, J. H. Gadd, L. G. Bowling.

William Edwards and Carl Poppe have bought the half interest owned by Joe Keppel in the Hoquiam Baking Co., Hoquiam, Wash.

Color In Bread

THAT color in the crumb of bread is assessed far too highly for its own sake goes without saying, says an English writer, but possibly color is sought after more because it is a grand reflection of other things in bread; although the seeking from this point of view may be more or less of an unconscious affair. After all, color, as color, affects the bread but little, although the commercial value of color in flour and bread is a very important affair indeed. In making bread of good color a great many things come in for attention, but it is possible that many details do not get the consideration they deserve. In his age of scientific bakers the older ideas are brushed aside if the holder of such ideas or opinions is unable to explain the reason for his views.

When I use the word mechanical, it is in its broader sense and not merely in the technical sense of bread making by machinery, interesting as that sense or aspect is; and I have no hesitation in saying that this aspect, as distinct from the chemical or biological aspect, is not well understood, nor are the main facts appreciated at their true value. Some bakers do put a proper value on this, to be sure, but a great many do not worry about it; the chemical and the "life" idea appeals more to them. Like everything connected with bread making, the physical aspect is closely related to the chemical and biological; for we know that the aeration of dough by a mechanical appliance whitens it, bleaches it, clears it; and this not only because the air distends the dough and makes it closer in texture when the dough is pushed down, but the air itself (or, to be more exact, the oxygen of the air) has a whitening effect on the dough. But I am inclined to believe that the mere mechanical action of the air has a good deal to do with the results obtained, for several reasons, chief of which may be mentioned the undoubted fact that the resultant loaf looks well "cleared," with a bright and shining texture, as distinct from what might be called bleaching, mere whitening, as may be said to be the case more or less with flour that has been bleached. Also if free oxygen (the oxygen of the air) accomplishes this by simple chemical means (oxidation) we might safely expect such an aerating apparatus to have the same effect at any time during the fermentation of the dough, but this is not so. It is only when the fermentation of dough has made considerable progress that aeration has any effect on the final color of the loaf, and this I say with complete confidence, although on the American market there is a kneading machine, the feature of which is to aerate the dough as it is being made. However, I do not want to give credit to manipulation alone and say that free oxygen has no chemical action on dough, because I believe it has; but I want my friends to believe that a great deal depends upon the manipulation of the dough, not only so far as texture is concerned, but also so far as color is concerned.

We know, of course, that the good color of a loaf of anything which is white, depends upon the amount of white light reflected back; it must therefore be our task to make the crumb of a loaf of such a nature that it will reflect back the maximum of white light, and that all parts of the cut surface will reflect evenly. If anyone doubts that unevenness in color is due to a mechanical defect in a loaf, let him cut a slice from a defective loaf and hold it up between himself and a light; in nineteen cases out of twenty he will find, if he cuts the slice evenly and about half an inch in thickness, that where the loaf is cloudy in color there also is it more dense; there will be no trouble in seeing this. I do not, of course, insinuate that a proper fermentation of the dough is not also necessary. We get "muddiness" in bread through immaturity, but we also notice a want of brightness should dough be made too tight—a mechanical defect again. And not only that, but if the loaf has been heavily (but properly) moulded, either by hand or by a machine—and a machine can mould more heavily and more thoroughly than the hands of man can—and then allowed to recover properly before putting into the oven, the loaf will be distinctly whiter and clearer than if moulded in an offhand kind of way. In this case there can be very little free oxygen present, but the final thorough moulding seems to properly place the particles, so that good color is got when the loaf is cut.

You may take it from me, then, if you were not already aware of the fact, that the mechanical or physical aspect of fermentation requires from the baker a great deal of attention. It is most important that dough should be well made, but it is equally important that the fermenting dough should be cut back at exactly the right time—that it should be scaled not only when fermentation has reached the proper stage, but also when there is a certain amount of proof on the dough. After handing up, it is again absolutely necessary that the pieces of dough should have sufficient proof to enable the baker to mould them properly without harassing himself. This proving of pieces should in very few cases be less than of twenty minutes' duration, and if the pieces are singled out, as in a prover, half an hour is seldom too much. If care is not exercised at this stage "muddiness" results. All this clearness and brightness, as I have already tried to explain, is completely different from, and more natural than, the improved color got by the use of nascent oxygen.

—‡—‡—‡—

The Stroehmann Baking Company of Wheeling, West Virginia, a million dollar corporation, with plants also at Ashland, Ky., and Huntington, W. Va., has been absorbed by the United Bakeries Company of Buffalo, N. Y., according to announcement. The purchasers, the Campbell Baking Co., and the Ward Brothers interests, already operate twenty-two plants. While the purchase price was not announced it is reported to have been near the million dollar mark.

Interesting Points On Fruit Cake

*By Professor Fred Knab, Siebel Institute of
Technology*

(Read at the Southern Illinois Master Bakers' Convention
at Carbondale, Illinois, February 8, 1922.)

PROBABLY there is no one item that plays a more important role in cake baking, than *fruit cake* and yet, strangely, it is the one item that has been given the least attention, probably because it is a so-termed "Seasonal" article, and therefore made only by some bakers during this particular season.

However, with the ever-increasing demand for sweet goods, there is no question that Fruit Cake is certain to become a staple article with the progressive baker, and this being true, it seems that too much cannot be said on this subject.

This is especially true when we consider that the consumer is daily becoming a connoisseur of articles of quality, and certainly to produce fruit cake of quality, special care must be given, not alone to the nature and character of the materials but particularly also to the mixing and the baking.

Many are the instances that have been brought to my attention where fruit cake, when cut, crumbles—and strange to say, in many cases the baker has never given any thought as to what might be the cause of this. On the contrary, he has insisted that his was the best fruit cake that could be made.

While, as stated, the quality of the materials employed is important, yet, irrespective of their quality, if the mix is not what I term "built up" right, the results will be no different than a building in which the best of materials have been employed but the contractor has failed to carry out the plans correctly. There will be crumbling in both instances.

A correctly "built-up" Fruit Cake, properly baked, should, in my opinion, when sliced ¼ inch thick, cut like bacon or cheese, leaving a nice, smooth surface, with little or no crumbs. I have before me a fruit cake that was baked about a year ago and on cutting it, it gives nice, smooth slices without crumbs.

The formula, although important in itself, does not make so much difference, since one can use a little more or less of one ingredient—or of another, but I have found in practice the following formula gave the most satisfactory results:

FORMULA FOR FRUIT CAKE

10 pounds brown sugar
10 pounds butter
5 quarts eggs
1¼ quarts light molasses
10 pounds citron
10 pounds orange peel
10 pounds currants
10 pounds raisins
10 pounds figs
10 pounds dates
10 pounds almonds
11 pounds flour
5 or 6 quarts hard cider (or 4 quarts cider and 2 quarts brandy)
6 ounces baking powder
8 ounces cinnamon
12 lemon gratings and juice of same.

All of the fruit required, after being thoroughly cleansed and washed, should be cut in pieces, not too coarse, and then be mixed with the liquid portion of the formula, such as either cider or brandy—and allowed to stand for three days, so that the fruit may absorb as much of the liquid as possible.

This mix should be prepared and allowed to stand either in a wooden bowl or pail and not in metal receptacles, as the latter would tend to impart a bitter taste.

It is right here I find the greatest number make their first mistake in mixing the fruit with the liquid, just at the time they are ready to make the mix. This results in the batter becoming too thin and does not effect the proper binding, while during the baking process, this liquid matter would bake out to a greater extent and in consequence of which the cake would have a tendency to become dry and crumble, almost immediately after it has been baked.

On the other hand, if the fruit has been allowed to absorb the liquid by proceeding as indicated above, the action will be different in the baking process: firstly, not as much moisture will be baked out, and secondly, the moisture which is retained by the fruit is gradually imparted to the cake as the moisture of the cake itself escaped, and thereby permeating the flavor of the fruit more thoroughly throughout the cake.

Probably some will criticize this formula because of the absence of ginger, allspice, nutmeg, etc., but this has been purposely omitted because here a serious mistake is made with fruit cake by having present therein flavors that are foreign to it. *Fruit Cake* should, as its name indicates, possess a *fruit flavor*—and not the flavor of spices. The only flavor that is excepted to this is cinnamon, which by virtue of its character has the tendency of bringing out the fruit flavor more prominently.

The butter and sugar indicated in the formula should be rubbed up well, after which the eggs are added gradually and then the lemon grating and juice—as also the cinnamon—should be added, then the molasses and last the flour (sifted together, with the baking powder) which will make a nice, smooth batch when the fruit is worked into it.

Now then as to the preparation of the tins with paper and the forming of the cake, these I take it are minor details which are so well-known to the baker that they need no special emphasis on my part.

Too often an error is made by too hot an oven, which means quick baking. One of the secrets (if I may use that term) in making fruit cake, is that the same is baked slowly, for which purpose the oven should have a temperature of from 280 to 300°F.

Many bakers have found it an insurmountable problem to bake large fruit cakes, weighing over five pounds, without having them raise extraordinarily high in the middle. This difficulty can readily be overcome by surrounding the pan with a water-soaked piece of cloth (usually a sugar bag will serve that purpose) being tied around the outside of the tin. The raising of the cake will consequently also be more even, and effect a nice thin crust on the top and sides.

By allowing the fruit cake to be exposed to the air for three or four days before packing into boxes, the tendency of their turning mouldy is minimized.

—‡—‡—‡—

Salt in Baking

By Dr. C. B. Morison, American Institute of Baking, at Kansas Convention

COMMON salt, or sodium chloride as the chemists term it, is a most important and essential baking material. Salt is one of the most widely distributed compounds in nature and is found in most all rocks, the soil, natural waters, lakes, rivers and the sea. Great deposits of salt occur in many parts of the world. Sea water contains it to the extent of 3 per cent. and the waters of the Dead Sea and the Great Salt Lake, several times this amount. The United States possesses important salt producing deposits in Kansas, Michigan, New York, Louisiana, Colorado and other states.

The modern manufacturer of salt has succeeded in so improving processes that the baker can be assured of a uniform supply of high-grade salt at the present time. Analyses of cooking and table salt made by the writer some years ago showed several brands of salt that contained nearly 100 per cent. of sodium chloride. Recent analyses corroborate this condition.

If the baker is in doubt of the purity of his salt, simple analytical tests can be easily made to establish the presence of excessive moisture, insoluble matter, calcium and magnesium compounds. Salt intended for use in bread-making should be free from such objectionable impurities. It should not contain coarse particles or lumps that resist rapid solution.

The American Institute of Baking, in the pursuance of its registration of approved baking materials, will examine the various brands of salt sold for use in baking.

EFFECT ON FLAVOR OF BAKED GOODS

Salt is used to advantage in baking for several purposes. Its effect in bringing out flavor is well known to the practical baker. The influence of salt in stimulating the palate, particularly in relation to the recognition of small quantities of sugar, has been demonstrated by experiment. This not only applies to sweetness but to other flavors. Rye and other coarser types of bread than wheat bread made from high-grade patent flours, require in general more salt than the latter. If the baker uses salt judiciously he can often improve the flavor of his bread. Bread made without salt is flat and tasteless. An excess of salt is as bad as too little in its influence on flavor.

The use of salt exerts other important influences on successful bread-making apart from its effect on a desirable flavor. The use of a proper and carefully controlled amount of salt can be added to the dough batch for the regulation of fermentation.

The retarding influence of salt on gas production by yeast can be easily demonstrated in yeast sugar solution. Amounts of salt of about 1.5 per cent. and over materially decrease gas production. This retarding action of salt on alcoholic fermentation is also marked in other types of enzyme action. The baker takes advantage of this action of salt in controlling fermentation and an intelligent application of the effects of salt in the dough batch will solve many troublesome problems. The following table shows the effect of salt in retarding the total time of fermentation. The doughs were constant in composition with the exception of the addition of varying amounts of salt, and fermented under uniform conditions.

Effect of Salt on Time of Fermentation

Dough.	Per cent. salt.	Total time of fermentation.
1	0.00	140 minutes
2	0.50	175 minutes
3	1.00	200 minutes
4	1.50	220 minutes
5	2.00	230 minutes
6	2.50	250 minutes
7	3.00	325 minutes

INFLUENCE ON GLUTEN

There are other important effects of salt in bread-making which are involved in the problem of modifying the physical properties of gluten. The tenacity, viscosity or plasticity and other qualities are all influenced by the presence of salt. For example, the weak glutens of flour are appreciably strengthened by the addition of suitable concentrations of salt to the dough batch. This action is familiar to the baker under the term "binding" or "tightening" effect of salt. The reason for this action of salt in modifying the physical properties of the proteins has been the subject of much study and research by the physical chemist, and it is only in recent years that much light has been shed upon this very interesting but complex problem. The baker should thoroughly study the characteristics of his flour, and govern the amount of salt to be added after fermentation and baking tests. For this reason it is not good practice to arbitrarily state the amount of salt that should be added to a dough batch to produce the best results. While it is common practice in this country to use in general from 1.5— 2.0 pounds of salt per 100 pounds of flour, it should be clearly understood that the proper amount of salt is determined by the character of the flour, the formula, the fermentation period and the flavor of the finished loaf, and also the quality of the water in relation to mineral contents should not be neglected.

—‡—‡—‡—

National Biscuit Company Prosperous

THE National Biscuit Company, for the year ended Dec. 31, 1921, reports net earnings after taxes of $5,677,461, which after allowing for the regular dividends on the preferred stock was equal to $13.48 a share on the $29,,236,000 of common stock outstanding. In 1920 the company reported earnings of $5,543,120, or $13.02 a share after preferred dividends.

The income account for 1921 and 1920 follows.

	1921	1920
Net earnings	$5,677,461	$5,543,120
Preferred dividends	1,736,315	1,736,315
Common dividends	2,046,520	2,046,520
Surplus	$1,894,626	$1,760,285
Previous surplus	21,089,097	19,328,812
P & L surplus	$22,983,723	$21,089,097

Roy E. Tomlinson, President of the company, in his remarks to stockholders, in part pointed out that "the only indebtedness is for raw materials and other incidental items incurred so recently that the accounts could not be audited and paid before the close of the year." He further pointed out that it was the practice of the company to buy raw materials only as they are needed.

"The new Bethune Street bakery in New York City," he said further, "has shown great production facilities. A class of product has been baked there which has found ready sale. The new warehouse and manufacturing building at Marseilles, Ill., has been in use since last May for cartons and paperboard containers.

"Contract has been made for a new bakery in Buffalo on a piece of land located on the Belt Line tracks, having an area of about 141,000 square feet. This new bakery in time will take the place of the present bakery in Buffalo, which is located in a leased building."

—‡—‡—‡—

Worcester Bakers Organize

THE New England Bakers' Association continues to grow. At a meeting in Worcester, Mass., on February 6th the bakers of Worcester County assembled at the office of The Fleischmann Company and formed a local organization, unanimously voting to affiliate with the New England Bakers' Association.

The following officers were elected:

President—John Calder, Calder's Bakery.
Vice-President—George Brown.
Treasurer—Carl W. Swanson, Swanson Bakery.
Secretary—Harry N. Brown, Worcester Baking Co.

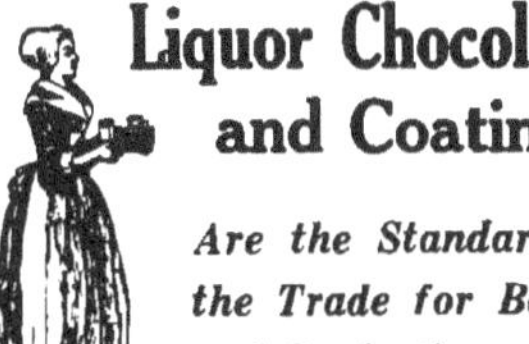

WALTER BAKER & CO.'S
Liquor Chocolates and Coatings

Are the Standards of the Trade for Bakers' and Confectioners' Use

Registered.
U. S. Pat. Off.

Sweetened and unsweetened; light, medium and dark, whatever the difference of color or flavor, all are *absolutely pure,* smooth and uniform to work.

The taste and appearance of bakings and confections depend largely upon the coating.

Send for Samples and Prices.

Walter Baker & Co. Ltd.
Established 1780　　　DORCHESTER, MASS.
57 Highest Awards at the Expositions of Europe and America.

Malzbender's
Practical Recipe Book
Second Enlarged Edition
In German and English in parallel columns

Written by a well known Baker, Pastry Chef and Confectioner of many years' experience in Europe, U. S., and Canada.

PART I. "BREAD"
15 recipes for Sponge, Straight Dough, Home-made, Quaker, Genuine French, Rye (sponge and yeast), Hot-Cross Buns, English Muffins, Breakfast Muffins, all kinds of Rolls, Buns, Vienna, Sweet Goods, Salt Rising Bread.

PART II. "CAKES"
305 recipes for common, plain up to the high grade Fancy Cakes, wholesale and retail. All kinds of Coffee Cakes, Christmas Goods, Dresdener Stollen, etc.

PART III. "PASTRY COOKING"
110 latest up-to-date recipes for Puddings (warm), Frozen Puddings, (Crèmes), Sauces, Ice Creams, Water Ices (Sherbets), Soufflés.

PART IV. "CONFECTIONERY"
80 recipes for making up-to-date Candies, Chewing Gum, Preserves, Candied Fruits, Canning Fruit, Preparing of Jellies, Cordials, Syrups, Wines, Liquors; all kinds of up-to-date Soft Drinks.

PART V. "DECORATING"
Instructions for decorating cakes in European and American Style.

Over 500 Recipes　**Price $2.00**　*Unique in its line*

Send your order to-day to

The National Baker
411 Walnut Street, Philadelphia, Pa.

Do You Know What Your Goods Cost?

ONE of the hardest things in bake-shop practice is to keep an accurate account of the cost of each piece of goods, so that the baker will know just how much profit each piece or each dozen pieces will yield, with raw materials at certain prices.

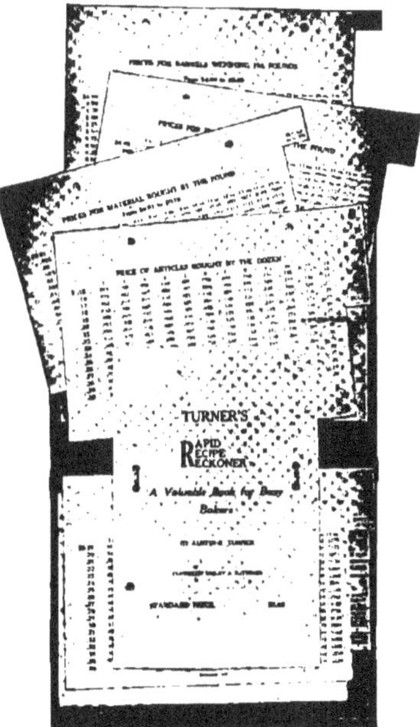

Turner's Rapid Recipe Reckoner

saves a baker all trouble in reckoning up the cost; it is already done for him, and all he has to do is to pick out the desired item at the given price per pound or dozen.

Tables are given of the cost for each ounce of flour at a price per barrel from $4.00 upward; and of lard, butter, sugar, eggs and of all other supplies by the ounce or measure at what price you pay in quantities.

Turner's Rapid Recipe Reckoner

simplifies cost accounting so that it is a matter of only a few minutes to get the cost of a batch of any size, and of any class of goods.

The tables are printed on heavy serviceable cardboard, placed in a substantial loose-leaf cover, bound in cloth. It will last a life-time and you can add new sheets or tables, if desired.

In these days of close competition one is needed in every bake shop, and the cost is but $2.00, postpaid. Address

The National Baker　411 Walnut Street
　　　　　　　　　　　　Philadelphia, Pa.

I am sending you a few recipes which I hope will meet with your approval. I am using them in the shop where I am cake foreman, and they prove to be good sellers. CARL ALM, Minneapolis.

ORANGE SPONGE SQUARES

1 qt. whole eggs,
½ qt. yolks,
1 lb. granulated sugar,
1 lb. 4 X sugar,
1 lb winter wheat flour,
1 lb. spring wheat flour.

Put eggs and sugar in machine bowl and put on high speed and beat up good and stiff, then put in a little orange flavor and mix in flour (previously sifted) carefully and fill baking sheet (18 x 24 x 1), and bake in a good solid heat (to dry out). When baked, cut sheet in half and spread custard (flavored orange) on one half and put the other half on top. Now ice the whole top with orange icing, rich yellow. Let dry a few minutes and cut in 9 pieces. Then on top put 3 slices of orange diagonally on each piece and ice with a good white icing. These cakes are nice in appearance and good eating.

MARSHMALLOW ROLL

First Part.

2 lbs. sugar.
10 oz. cocoa.
1 qt. boiling water.

Second Part.

2 lbs. sugar.
1 lb. shortening.
1 oz. soda.
¾ qt. milk.
4 lbs. flour.
1 pt. eggs.

Mix second part as for any other cake, and then add first part to it and mix thoroughly. This makes 4 pans—18 x 24 x 1; bake in brisk oven and turn on sugared sacks when baked.

Now make marshmallows as follows:

Boil 5 lbs. granulated sugar, ½ lb. glucose and 1 qt. water to 158 degrees F. Pour this boiling syrup in a thin stream into 1 qt of egg white, which has been beaten very stiff, while sugar is boiling. Usually start your machine on high, when sugar reaches 140 degrees Fahr. After all sugar is in, let it stand a few minutes until very light and stands up on point of finger. Spread marshmallow on sheets and roll like jelly roll. Ice chocolate and cut each roll into 4 or 5 pieces to suit your trade. These rolls are delicious and good sellers.

MARSHMALLOW COCOANUT SQUARES

2 lbs. 4X sugar.
1 lb. shortening.
½ qt. white.
½ qt. milk.

2½ lbs. flour.
1 oz. baking powder.
Almond flavor.

Cream sugar and shortening very light and add whites, little by little, and then flavor. Now add milk, flour and baking powder (sifted), mix well, and spread on baking sheet regular size, 18 x 24 x 1. When baked, cut in half and spread marshmallow on one half, put other half on top and cut each into 9 pieces. Ice each square with marshmallow and cover sides and top with long shredded cocoanut.

A very nice cake and has proven a good seller. Price is usually 30 cents per square.

L. C., New Jersey: We have your favor of recent date requesting recipe for Jelly and Marshmallow Rolls, which we give herewith:

JELLY ROLL

Whip up one pound of sugar, 12 eggs, and a pinch of salt until quite stiff; take out beater and sieve in on the mix 1 pound spring wheat flour; do not stir, but lift it up gently until well mixed. Flavor vanilla and spread on paper. Some add a few ounces of milk and ½ ounce of baking powder.

MARSHMALLOW ROLL

You can use the above or this one: 2 pounds of sugar, add 1 pint hot water, 2 pounds cake flour; mix good, 1 quart of egg yolks, and pinch of salt. Beat up good; flavor lemon and mace.

—‡—‡—‡—

The Nutrition in Bread

THE nutritive value of bread depends not only on its chemical composition, but also on its digestibility which, in its turn, seems to depend largely on the lightness of the loaf. It is the gluten in a flour which gives it the power of stretching and rising as the gas from the yeast expands within it, and hence of making a light loaf. Rye, barley and oats have less gluten than wheat, and corn has none, and therefore wheat, despite its higher cost, yields the most nutriment for a given sum. It was the absence of gluten or the reduction in its quantity and quality which made "War Bread" so tasteless to most people.

It is true that of the various kinds of wheat flour those containing part of the bran—entire wheat and graham flours—hold more mineral matters than fine white flour, but they do not yield more digestible protein, as was for a time supposed and by food faddists claimed. In fact, government experiments prove that they yield less. It is safe to say that, as far as known, for a given amount of money white flour yields the most actual nourishment, with the various food ingredients in the best proportion.

As compared with most meats and vegetables, bread has practically no waste and is very completely digested. As a food it is invaluable, and well deserves its title of "the staff of life."

Information Department

The object of this department is to help our readers, as far as possible, to solve the various difficulties that come up from day to day. We will also answer questions about all kinds of machinery and give every possible assistance in securing detailed information. No names or addresses of manufacturers will be given in these columns. When wanted they will be sent by mail. Address,

INFORMATION DEPARTMENT   **THE NATIONAL BAKER**

THIRTY-GALLON STRAIGHT DOUGH, NO. 1

We give herewith two formulas for a thirty-gallon straight dough. Either should answer your purpose. They may be slightly altered to suit conditions:

Two hundred and fifty pounds of water, 470 pounds of flour, 4 pounds of oil, 4 pounds of sugar, 4 pounds of yeast, 5 pounds of malt extract, 6 pounds of ceraline, 4 pounds of milk powder, 5½ pounds of salt.

First, take about 20 pounds of water at 120 degrees and make a mush with the ceraline and malt extract. This should be kept warm and allowed to stand about 30 minutes in order that the malt may have a chance to do its best work.

Dissolve the milk powder and put it in the mixer with water, sugar and salt.

When batch is ready dissolve yeast thoroughly in the mush, mix and put in the mixer. The mixer should run from 20 to 25 minutes, according to the speed. A machine running about 24 revolutions to the minute should mix for 25 minutes.

Don't put in the oil until the mixer has run 6 or 8 minutes, or until the flour is dissolved.

Have the dough as near 83 degrees as possible when it leaves the mixer, and the shop 70 degrees. This dough should be ready to cut over in from 3 to 3½ hours. A good test for the first time up is to draw the hand edgewise across the dough. If it settles quickly around the crease made by the hand it is ready to put down the first time. This should be watched carefully, as it is the critical time in a straight dough.

This dough should be ready for the bench in 5 hours, if conditions are right. If it is too rich in milk or shortening, it can be cut, but we would not advise cutting the malt or yeast. The flour may have to be cut or increased a little, according to its strength, as no set rule can be laid down for different flours. Do not steam too much in the proof box; just enough to keep from crusting. Do not give too much proof; make the bread do its work in the oven.

THIRTY-GALLON STRAIGHT DOUGH, NO. 2

Two hundred and forty pounds of water at 77 degrees, 360 pounds of flour, 4½ pounds of yeast, 5 pounds of sugar, 2½ pounds of malt extract, 7½ pounds of lard or other shortening.

Room where dough stands should not be below 80 degrees, nor above 90 degrees, to get good results. Too much proof should not be given before it goes into the oven; it will come up good in the oven.

Dough should not be over 80 degrees when it comes out of the mixer.

First, knock down or cut over in 2 hours, no matter how little it may have come.

Second, 1¾ hours later.

Third, ¾ of an hour later.

Fourth, ¾ of an hour later, making a total of 5¼ hours, and, if necessary, it can stand longer but must be kept down. It should not be taken in less time than given above, 5¼ to 5½ hours.

If no malt extract is used, use that same amount more of sugar.

H. McK., Toledo: The sample of cake submitted would indicate that poor material had been used. We would suggest your following this recipe:

CHEAP LUNCH CAKE

Three pounds sugar, eighteen ounces lard, fifteen eggs, three quarts milk, five pounds and four ounces flour, one ounce soda, two ounces cream of tartar.

Compound these after the manner of making wine cake by creaming up lard and sugar, then adding the eggs, milk and soda, and lastly flour with cream of tartar; do not mix more than necessary. The mixture may then be baked in molds or it may be spread into sheets, and when baked, sandwich same with jelly, lemon filler or the like; ice the top or spread jelly over it and sprinkle with shredded cocoanut and cut up into pieces to suit your trade.

The above may be used in a number of different ways, and should please your customers.

GETTING RID OF ANTS

C. E. R., Ohio: We have your favor of the 26th, in relation to getting rid of black ants. One remedy is to soak a sponge in a thin syrup of sugar, place it where the ants can reach it, and they will swarm through it; then take the sponge, and immerse in scalding water, then soak the sponge again in syrup, and repeat the operation.

Try and find the nest of the ants. When found, fill with scalding hot water. If you can thus kill the "queen ant," the others will leave. Or if you can place a broad band of lard around the nest, or at some other convenient point; the ants cannot cross the lard.

We do not give you any poisonous remedies, as they are hardly safe to use in a bakery.

JELLIED COCOANUT BUN

These are good for the quick lunch counter trade. For them you need scalloped pattypans about one inch in depth and in size to sell at five cents each.

One pound of lard or butter and lard, one and one-fourth pounds of powdered sugar, one ounce of good baking powder, two pounds of flour, four eggs, one pint of milk (more or less). Sift the baking powder in the flour, cream the butter, sugar and eggs, add the milk, give it a stir around, then add the flour with the baking powder in it and half mix, then add a fair showing of shredded cocoanut and finish mixing, adding what more milk may be needed to form a mass the same tightness at best pound cake, or a little slacker. Then with a spoon nearly half fill the pattypans with the mixture, hollow it a little in the middle and put in a teaspoonful of some good fruit jelly, then put on a top of the mixture, to three-fourths fill the pattypan; dust them with powdered sugar and sprinkle them with water; then bake in a solid heat to take on a nice rich brown. Some bake these a rich egg color. These may be made in any size pattypan.

BUTTER SPONGE CAKE

One pound of sugar, ten eggs, ten ounces of butter, half a pint of milk, two teaspoonfuls of baking powder, one and a half pounds of flour. Beat the sugar and eggs together a few minutes, as if for sponge cake;

melt the butter and beat it in; add the milk, then the powder, and then the flour, and stir up well. Flavor if desired. Bake twenty-five minutes at good heat.

LEMON PIE FILLING

G. A. F., Iowa.—25 gal. water, 90 lbs. sugar, 7½ lbs. starch or 7 lbs. flour, 10 qts. eggs, 20 oz. butter.

Mix sugar and starch or flour together. Beat eggs smooth, add to sugar, add lemons, juice and grated peel. Mix in butter. Add water; small quantity at first, then the rest, keeping mass free from lumps by adding a little more flour. The whites of eggs can be separated, whipped stiff and put on top of pies after being baked. Then returned to oven, and browned slightly. This can be cooked like Cream Puff filler and put on baked crusts, decorated with whipped whites, and returned to oven for browning. This amount can be enlarged indefinitely, but must be used in a day or two.

Salt must never be omitted; always using enough to bring out the flavor.

For making it a little cheaper, butter may be omitted, and more flour and water added. Always taste the mass to see if it has proper tartness.

If lemons ever get scarce so you cannot get them, use a little saturated solution of citric acid, with lemon-oil.

PATTY CAKES

G. M. A., Conn.—Take good puff paste, roll it out not quite ¼ of an inch thick, and cut out for large size patties with a 3-inch cutter. Put on wet baking pans a little distance apart. Mark the center with a smaller cutter of 1 inch diameter, and set in a cold place to rest for 15 to 20 minutes.

Before baking wash the patties with an egg-wash and bake in a brisk heat of about 400 to 450 degrees Fahr. in an empty oven without steam.

In washing the patties, care should be taken that the wash does not run down the sides of the paste (only the top should be washed). The running down prevents the paste from rising evenly in the oven during baking.

When the patties are baked, lift the top carefully and take out the soft inside paste to make room for the filling.

FRIED PIES

J. W. B., W. Va.: Fried Pies are made from any Fried Cake mixture, rolled out quarter-inch thick, cut out with a 4 to 4-inch cutter. The edge is washed with an egg wash, that is egg whipped, so it will spread well. Place any jam or fruit preserve in center, fold over, press edges with fingers; fry in a somewhat cooler fat than for fried cake, as being larger they will take longer to fry through. These were called French Fried Pies many years ago.

JELLY DOUGHNUTS

B. D. H., Maine: To make a jelly doughnut take any roll dough, add some sugar, 1 ounce to 1 pound, or

(Concluded on page 64)

Recipe Department

In this department we will publish new and valuable recipes and want our readers to forward to us any recipe from which they have had good results, or that is not generally known. We wish to make this department as interesting as possible and ask our readers to help us to this end. Address.

RECIPE DEPARTMENT   THE NATIONAL BAKER

TEA RUSKS

These are fine rusks and their makers should find ready sale for them.

2 pounds of flour (more if needed), ¾ pound of powdered sugar, 4 eggs, ¼ ounce of salt, ¾ pound of lard or butter, 1 quart of milk, 1 ounce of good baking powder, a good flavor of lemon. Whisk the eggs into the milk; add the sugar, salt and flavor, and let it dissolve. Then sift the baking powder into about ½ pound of flour; then rub the lard into the 2 pounds of flour; make a hole in it, add the milk with the sugar, eggs and flavor in it and stir all together. Add the flour with the baking powder in it and finish mixing, adding what more flour may be needed to form an easy working dough. Well and fully mix, then turn it on your board, break it up in pieces in size to sell at ten cents per dozen; ball them up round, and good and clear, place them half an inch apart, or a little less, on a buttered baking pan with an inch high rim to it, flatten them a little, wash them with egg and milk wash, but do not let it run down the sides. Let them lay out of the oven from five to ten minutes, then bake in a good solid heat. In the baking they should run together, thus forming good sugar rusks. Any left over ones may be cut n two and dried and sold as sweet rusks.

TEA BISCUITS

3 pounds of flour (more if needed), ¾ ounce of salt, ½ pound lard, 2 ounces of good baking powder, 1 quart of milk. Divide the flour in two parts; in one part rub the lard, in the other sift the baking powder and add the salt to the milk. Make a hole in the flour, with the lard in it, add the milk and salt; stir it around, then add the flour and the baking powder in it and finish mixing, adding what more flour may be needed to form an easy rolling dough. Mix thoroughly, turn out on your board, roll in a sheet a full half inch in thickness and cut up with a plain round cutter, in size to sell at ten cents per dozen. Pan them to just touch, wash with milk and bake in a quick heat. Cutting them up is the usual method, but I prefer balling them and setting them close enough together on the pans that when they are flattened a little they will touch and when baked come out a square, high biscuit.

Just a word about baking powder. Baking powder is more easy and certain to rise than soda and cream of tartar; but if it is not good, better use soda and cream of tartar in the usual manner. The amount of baking powder here stated (2 ounces) is only approximate, and it is supposed to be good baking powder.

JUMBLES

This jumble mixture is supposed to hold the shape in baking given to it by the bead it passes through:

1 pint of water, 2¼ pounds of granulated sugar, ¼ ounce of ammonia, 4½ to 5 pounds of flour (more if needed), 6 eggs, 1¼ pounds of butter or lard, ¼ ounce of salt, what flavor you choose. Dissolve the sugar in the water, whisk the eggs and add them to the water and sugar, together with the salt. Rub the butter in the flour, make a hole; add the sugar, water and eggs; add the ammonia; give it a stir in, then draw in the flour; give it a shake up, then add the flavor and finish mixing, adding what more flour may be needed to form a rather tight dough, but one that will pass through the jumble forcer fairly easy. Then work them off in the usual manner. Jumble mixtures, to hold the impressions of the bead after baking, must be fairly tight. It is difficult to pass the mixture through a tube, consequently it needs to be passed through the jumble forcer. The star bead is generally used for jumbles. If you wish to make mixture a little richer in butter do so; that will not affect its holding the impression of the bead.

A GOOD CHEAP JELLY CAKE

1¼ pounds of powdered sugar, 10 ounces of butter and lard, 5 eggs, ¾ pint of milk (more or less), 1½ pounds of flour, 1 ounce of good baking powder. Sift the baking powder into the flour; cream the butter, sugar and eggs. When creamed, add the milk, give it a stir around, then add the flour and baking powder and finish mixing, adding more flour if needed to form a medium slack mass. Bake this mixture in the usual jelly cake tins and in the usual manner. When baked put them two or three together, with some good fruit jelly between, press them together a little, dust with powdered sugar, and they are ready. These jelly cakes are usually sold plain; still it is in order to ice them in white or cream-colored icing, either egg or water icing.

Sometimes they are meringued, but that is rarely done except for party trade.

This same jelly cake mixture, baked in a ½-inch thick sheet and when baked put two together with jelly between, then meringued and cut up into 5 cent squares, and a scroll of jelly piped on the meringue or a large dot of jelly in the center and a glace or preserved cherry or a dot of plain water icing put on it, forms an attractive and saleable article.

RYE AND RAISIN GINGERBREAD

4 pounds flour, ½ ounce ground ginger, ½ pound lard, ⅛ ounce carbonate of soda, ½ pint water, ½ pound rye flour, 1 pound stoned raisins chopped medium fine, ⅛ ounce cream of tartar, 1 pint molasses. Sift the soda, acid and flour together, then add the rye flour. Mix together; make a hole; add the molasses and water mixed together; also add the spices; work all together, drawing in enough flour to form a medium stiff batter; then add the lard in a half melted condition; work it into the batter; add the chopped raisins and draw in the balance of the flour and finish mixing, adding more flour, or molasses and water to form as soft a dough as you can, so you can handle it well. Then lay it on a level baking pan in a half-inch thick sheet, wash with a mixture of molasses and water, and bake in a solid heat. When baked and cold cut it up with a sharp knife into pieces to sell at what price you choose, say five-cent pieces, and wrap each piece in white or yellow tissue paper and tie with colored string.

CHOCOLATE JUMBLES

2 pounds powdered sugar, 1 pound of lard, 3 pounds and 4 ounces of cake flour, 10 eggs, 1 pint of milk or water, 1 pennyweight of soda, ½ a pennyweight of ammonia, 2 pennyweights of cream tartar, 4 ounces of chocolate. Cream sugar and lard in the usual manner, add eggs and milk, then mix in the chocolate; the latter may consist of powdered or the so-called liquor chocolate. The powdered chocolate can be mixed in dry, while the other has to be first melted in order to become liquid. Then mix in the other ingredients. Do not work the mixture more than necessary. Fill in bag with large-sized star tube and dress up rings (upon previously greased and flour-dusted baking tins) of such size to sell at ten cents per dozen, sprinkle them with granulated sugar, shake off the surplus sugar by quickly turning the tin upside down, then bake in moderate oven. Chocolate bars or sticks of any shape whatever your fancy dictates can be made of this mixture and finished different ways—that is, some left plain, others sprinkled with cocoanuts, chopped almonds or peanuts, etc.

COCOANUT JUMBLES

2½ pounds powdered sugar, 1½ pounds shortening, 4½ pounds of flour, 16 eggs, a scant quart of milk, 1 ounce of soda, 2 ounces of cream tartar, a pinch of mace. Rub up sugar and shortening in the usual way, adding the different ingredients as for wine cakes, and finish in the same manner. Then fill the mixture in bag with plain round tube and dress the cakes upon

---

HENRY HEIDE'S

Genuine Almond Paste

Insures success in baking

MACAROONS and ALMOND PASTE CONFECTIONS

On the market since 1875

Marshmallow Cake Filler

An excellent and convenient Filler for

LAYER CAKES, JELLY ROLLS, TARTS, Etc.

WRITE FOR BOOKLET

HENRY HEIDE, Inc.,   Manufacturer

Spring, Hudson and Vandam Streets   New York City

similarly prepared tins as for the foregoing recipe; dust them richly with cocoanut and bake in good heat.

COCOANUT JUMBLES—II.

1 pound of powdered sugar, 12 ounces of shortening, 3 eggs, 1½ pounds of flour, ⅛ of an ounce of ammonia, a pinch of mace. Mix this together with enough milk to form a medium stiff dough. Roll it in thickness as you would for sugar cakes, cut out with jumble cutter and lay them upon shredded or desiccated cocoanut; press them down so that enough cocoanut will adhere to the cakes, then place them in clean baking pans and bake in moderate oven.

MILK JUMBLES

2 pounds of powdered sugar, 1½ pounds of shortening, 10 eggs, 1 pint of milk, 4 pounds of flour, 2 pennyweights of soda, 4 pennyweights of cream tartar; flavor with vanilla or mace. Mix up shortening and sugar together to a fairly creamy consistency; gradually add the eggs, stir in the milk, then mix in the other ingredients with as little handling as possible, so as not to get the mixture tough. Fill in bag with star tube and dress the cakes upon clean baking pans; bake in hot oven.

WAFER JUMBLES

1 pound of powdered sugar creamed with 1 pound of good washed butter, 5 eggs creamed in, mixed with 1 pound 2 ounces of cake flour, flavored with vanilla. Fill in bag with small plain tube and dress rings upon very clean baking tins of any suitable size, not too close together, as this mixture will spread to a considerable extent, running very thin; then bake in a cool oven until the cakes have a nice yellow color; remove them from the tins while yet hot.

CINNAMON JUMBLES

3 pounds of sugar, 2 pounds of shortening, ½ ounce of ammonia, 2 pennyweights of soda, 4 pennyweights of cream tartar, 10 eggs, 1 pint of milk, enough cinnamon to suit your taste; mix this together in the usual manner. Roll it on the table about 1/6 of an inch in thickness, cut out with jumble cutter, lay them on baking tins, brush them over with milk and bake in medium heat.

FRENCH CINNAMON JUMBLES

2½ pounds of sugar, 2 pounds 12 ounces of cake crumbs, 1½ pounds shortening, 3 pounds 14 ounces of flour, 8 eggs, 1 ounce of ammonia, 1 pennyweight of soda, 1 spoonful of cinnamon. Mix this together with enough milk to form a pretty stiff dough, then roll out in thickness as for sugar cakes, cut out with round jumble cutter and lay them upon granulated sugar; place them on baking tins, sugar side up, and bake in medium heat.

MIGNONS

Work together ½ pound sugar, ½ pound butter, ¾ pound flour, ½ pound fine pounded almonds, one small pinch soda, six yolks of eggs, one pinch cinnamon, a little vanilla extract; roll out to the thickness of a

pencil and use a suitable cutter; wash with white of egg; dust with shredded almonds and crushed cut-loaf sugar, bake in sharp oven, on greased pan.

GENOESE PASTRY

These are a delicious, good looking, also useful, form of pastry. To make them, take best puff paste, pin it out ¼ inch in thickness, then double it and pin it out into sheet ⅛-inch in thickness and some 12 to 15 inches in length; roll this sheet up to form a roll 3½ to 4 inches in diameter, wet the edge to make it stick, then flatten it down to about an inch in thickness, then with a very sharp smooth-edged knife cut the flat roll up into a ¼-inch thick slices and pan them the cut side down, having first turned them over into powdered sugar, making them take up as much sugar as possible. Pan them an inch apart and bake in as quick heat as possible to bake without burning, giving them a high color and the sugar a glaze. When baked they are ready for sale or for use for ornamental purposes.

Another style of these is to bake in a slow heat, one that will fully bake but not color them. When baked they are water iced in one or more colors if desired, but said colors should be restricted (apart from plain white) to cream, pink, orange and chocolate.

—‡—‡—‡—

Information Department
(Continued from page 60)

4 ounces to quart of liquid, 3 eggs, pinch of mace for flavor. Proof good, cut round, same as for buns. Proof again and fry.

HOT CROSS BUNS

H. L. A., Maryland: Here are two formulas for Hot Cross Buns, furnished by courtesy of The Fleischmann Company: 50 pounds flour, 24 pounds water, 3 pounds sugar, 3 pounds lard, 1 pound malt, ½ pound salt, 1½ pounds yeast, 3 pounds condensed milk (or 1 pound milk powder, and 1 pound additional sugar), 12 pounds raisins or currants, 3 pints eggs, 2 ounces cinnamon, 1 ounce mace—101 pounds, 3 ounces.

This is a 3½-hour process, mixing at 82 F. and allowing for three risings to full proof.

This formula should yield 80 dozen buns.

(For larger batches increase all ingredients proportionately.)

25-MINUTE DOUGH

One hundred pounds flour, 52 pounds water, 7 pounds sugar, 7 pounds lard, 1 pound salt, 6 pounds yeast, 5 pounds condensed milk, 25 pounds raisins or currants, 3 quarts eggs, 4 ounces cinnamon, 2 ounces mace—209 pounds.

Temperature after leaving the mixer 87 degrees.

Dough will be ready in from 25 to 30 minutes. It should then be made up in the usual way. The time can be varied according to the room, but is not to be increased more than 10 minutes.

Business Chances ·

MACHINERY FOR SALE

1—20-inch Thomson Moulder Extension, new.

1—Thomson Zerah Baller.

1—Hubbard Oven, No. 11½.

1—Bennett Oven, No. 115.

1—3½-bbl. Day Dough Mixer.

1—3-bbl. Read Dough Mixer.

1—1½-bbl. Read Dough Mixer.

1—1-bbl. Read Dough Mixer.

2—Union Bun Rounders.

1—Day Dough Brake.

1—No. 3 Day Clipper Beater.

3—Day Wood Flour Sifters.

2—Triumph All-Steel Flour Sifters.

1—2-bbl. Triumph Dough Mixer.

2—Wood-Proof Closets, for public view bakery.

1—1½-bbl. Peerless Dough Mixer.

1—Triumph Mixer and Motor.

Cake Machines, Bread Racks, Troughs and Equipment of every description ready for immediate shipment, new or rebuilt. Rebuilt machines guaranteed same as new ones.

J. H. BAST & CO.
649 W. Pratt St.　　　Baltimore, Md.

MISCELLANEOUS

TURNER'S RAPID RECIPE RECKoner simplifies cost accounting so that it is a matter of only a few minutes to get the cost of a batch of any size, and of any class of goods. The baker is saved all the trouble in counting up the cost; it is already done for him. Tables are given of the cost of each ounce of flour at a price per barrel from $4.00 upward, of other materials from $0.01 to $0.60 by the pound, and the cost of each ounce. One is needed in every bake-shop, and the cost is but $2.00 postpaid. For sale by THE NATIONAL BAKER, 411 Walnut Street, Philadelphia, Pa.

MACHINERY FOR SALE

FOR SALE—FOR A VERY LOW price you can secure the following slightly used equipment:

Two Yankee Reel Ovens, $100 each.

DOUGH MIXERS

1 Dutchess, 4 bbl. J. H. Day, 3 bbl.
1 Rockwell, 4 bbl. 2 Rockwell, 3 bbl.
J. H. Day, 2 bbl. Double Jacketed.
1 Century, 3 bbl.

CAKE MACHINES

Read

1 Little Giant　　　1 Champion
1 Hobart with D. C. Motor attached
Dutchess Two-Pocket Divider
Dutchess Roll Dividers
Bread and Pan Racks

Proofing Closets　　　Troughs
Work Tables　　　Bread Pans
1 Day Egg Clipper　　　Shipping Boxes
Sheet iron pans for the following ovens: Yankee, Barker and Federal.
Dough brake, A-1 condition
2 Doughnut Fryers with trays

I. KALFUS COMPANY
175 Stanton St.　　　New York City

MACHINERY WANTED

PRINTING MACHINES WANTED —New, rotary 2 color, for producing first-class printed bread wrappers. Must be complete with casting box, etc. State full particulars and location for inspection. Box 8, care THE NATIONAL BAKER, 411 Walnut St., Philadelphia.

WANTED—UNION BREAD WRAPping Machine, portable, in good condition. Address W. D. Estlow, 36 East Main Street, Norristown, Pa.

OVENS WANTED

WANTED — TO BUY SECONDhand oven for cake use; would buy hearth-fired oven. Address 58 West Louther Street, Carlisle, Pa.

BAKERIES FOR SALE

FOR SALE — A GOOD, GOING bakery, doing about $400 per week, all over the counter. Located on main street of city. Equipped with elegant fixtures, large size Middleby Oven, Cake machine, etc. Everything complete. Price $2,700. Exceptional opportunity. Address Rudolph J. Huss, 170 E. Front Street, Plainfield, N. J.

FOR SALE—ESTABLISHED 33 years, modern equipped wholesale bakery doing excellent business. For further particulars address E. T. Reese, 207 Pearson St., New Castle, Penna.

FOR SALE—CASH AND CARRY bakery, best location in a good Ohio town of 10,000. Baking outfit complete—price cheap, if taken at once. Address B. 20, care THE NATIONAL BAKER, 411 Walnut St., Philadelphia, Pa.

FOR SALE — BAKERY, ICE cream parlor, candy, cigars, cigarettes, tobacco and light grocery in growing Michigan industrial city of 8,000 population. Splendid farming territory surrounding. All cash business. Century cake mixer, Bennett oven, first class soda fountain, 2 cash registers. Complete bakery and store outfit. Good lease. Sell at real bargain. Price $3,800. Must sell on account of disagreement of partners. City Bakery, Sturgis, Mich.

FOR SALE—BAKERY WITH two Petersen ovens, dough mixer, Hobart cake machine, bun divider and accessories, all in good condition. Steam boiler, motor. A bargain and an old established business. Building for rent with rooms above. H. D. Odom, Realtor, Louisville Ky.

A Classified List of Goods Needed by Bakers

Automobile Trucks—
Republic Truck Sales Corp, Alma, Mich.

Almond Paste—
Henry Heide, Inc., New York.

Bakery Advertising—
I. B. Nordheim Co., N. Y.
Schulze Advert. Service, Chicago.

Bakers' Institute—
Siebel Institute, Chicago.

Bakers' Machinery—
Champion Machine Co., Joliet, Ill.
J. H. Day Co., Cincinnati, O.
Dutchess Tool Co., Beacon, N. Y.
Freymark Steam Generator Co., St. Louis.
Jaburg-Miller Co., New York.
Peerless Bread Mch. Co., Sidney, O.
Read Machinery Co., York, Pa.
Reeves Pulley Co., Columbus, Ind.
Syracuse Steam Generator Co., Syracuse, N. Y.
Thomson Mch. Co., Bellevue, N. J.
Thomas Mills & Bro., Philadelphia.
Union Machinery Co., Joliet, Ill.

Bakers' Pans—
J. W. Allen & Co., Chicago.
Jaburg Bros., New York.
Jaburg-Miller Co., New York.
Edward Katzinger Co., Chicago.
The Aug. Maag Co., Baltimore.
Thomas Mills & Bro., Philadelphia.

Bakers' Tools—
J. W. Allen & Co., Chicago.
Jaburg Bros., New York.
Jaburg-Miller Co., New York.
Edward Katzinger Co., Chicago.
The Aug. Maag Co., Baltimore.
Thomas Mills & Bro., Philadelphia.
Union Steel Products Co., Albion.

Books for Bakers—
Malzbender's Recipe Book.
Turner's Rapid Recipe Reckoner.

Bread Labels—
Mirror Printing Co., Kalamazoo.
National Binding Mch. Co., N. Y.

Bread Wrapping and Sealing Machines—
National Bread Wrapping Machine Co., Nashua, N. H.
Lambooy Label & Wrapper Co., Kalamazoo, Mich.
Union Machinery Co., Joliet, Ill.

Cash Registers—
National Cash Register Company.

Chocolate—
Walter Baker & Co., Ltd., Dorchester.

Cooking Oil—
Corn Products Ref. Co., New York.
Patent Cereals Co., Geneva, N. Y.

Dough Mixers and Kneaders—
Champion Machinery Co., Joliet, Ill.
J. H. Day Co., Cincinnati, O.
Read Machinery Co., York, Pa.

Eggs-Desicated—Egg Products—
Joe Lowe Co., N. Y.

Flour—
Atkinson Milling Co., Minn.
Big Diamond Mills Co., Minn.
Commander Mills, Minneapolis.
Empire Milling Co., Minneapolis.
W. J. Jennison & Co., Minneapolis.
Russell-Miller Milling Co., Minn.
Updike Milling Co., Omaha.
Washburn-Crosby Co., Minneapolis.

Food Colors—
National Aniline & Chem. Co., N. Y.

Fruit Growers—
California Associated Raisin Co.
California Prune & Apricot Growers

Honey—
Arthur A. Beals, Oto, Iowa.

Ice Cream Tools and Supplies—
J. W. Allen & Co., Chicago.
Atlas Mfg. Co., New Haven.
Chr. Hansen's Lab., Little Falls, N. Y.
The Aug. Maag Co., Baltimore.
Thomas Mills & Bro., Philadelphia.

Malt, Extract and Dry—
American Diamalt Co.
Anheuser-Busch, Inc., St. Louis.
P. Ballantine & Sons, Newark.
Freihofer Baking Co., Philadelphia.
Malt Diastase Co., N. Y.
Stein-Hall Mfg. Co., Chicago.

Milk, Powdered and Condensed—
Consolidated Prod. Co., Lincoln, Neb.
I. H. Nester & Co., Philadelphia.

Ovens—
Bennett Oven Co., Battle Creek.
Duhrkop Oven Co., New York.
Hubbard Oven Co., Chicago.
Meak Oven Mfg. Co., Westport, Conn.
Middleby Oven Co., New York.
Middleby-Marshall Co., Chicago.
Standard Oven Co., Pittsburgh.
Superior Oven Co., Chicago, Ill.

Oven Lights and Doors—
Dutchess Tool Co., Beacon, N. Y.
Chas. Robson & Co., Philadelphia.

Papers (Parchment and Waxed)—
Lambooy Label & Wrapper Co., Kalamazoo, Mich.
Menasha Ptg. & Carton Co., Menasha, Wis.
Waterproof Paper & Board Co., Cincinnati.

Pie Machinery—
Edwin E. Bartlett, Nashua, N. H.
J. H. Day Co., Cincinnati, O.
Union Machinery Co., Joliet, Ill.

Potato Flour—
Falk American Potato Flour Co., Pittsburgh, Pa.

Pyrometers—
Hubbard Oven Co., Chicago.
Philadelphia Thermometer Co.
Chas. Robson & Co., Philadelphia.

Shipping Boxes (Wood and Paper)—
A. Backus, Jr., & Son, Detroit.
Rob't Gaylord, Inc., St. Louis.

Shortening—
Corn Products Refining Co., N. Y.
Procter & Gamble Co., Cincinnati.

Stoves for Bakers and Confectioners—
Edward Katzinger Co., Chicago.
Thomas Mills & Bro., Philadelphia.

Sugar and Sugar Syrups—
American Sugar Ref. Co., N. Y.
Corn Products Ref. Co., New York.
Franklin Sugar Ref. Co., Philadelphia.

Supplies—
J. W. Allen & Co., Chicago.
Jaburg Bros., New York.
Joe Lowe Co., N. Y.
Stein-Hall Mfg. Co., Chicago and N. Y.
Ward Baking Co., New York.

Thermometers—
Phila. Thermometer Co., Phila.

Vermin Exterminator—
Berg & Beard Mfg. Co., Brooklyn.

Washing and Cleaning Material—
J. B. Ford Co.

Yeast—
The Fleischmann Co., New York.

INDEX TO ADVERTISEMENTS

	Page
American Diamalt Co.	14
Anheuser-Busch Sales Corp	48
American Sugar Refining Co.	47
Baker & Co., Ltd., Walter	57
Ballantine & Sons, P.	15
Bartlett, Edwin E.	39
Bennett Oven Co.	5
Berg & Beard Mfg. Co.	63
Big Diamond Mills Co.	4
Business Chances	65
California Associated Raisin Co.	11
California Prune & Apricot Growers	51
Carter, Rice & Co., Corporation	45
Commander Mills	59
Corn Products Ref. Co.	9
Day Co., The J. H.	8
Duhrkop Oven Co.	18
Dutchess Tool Co.	14, 49
Empire Milling Co.	16
Fleischmann Co., The	12
Ford Co., J. B.	58
Freihofer Baking Co.	55
Freymark Steam Generator Co.	47
Heide, Inc., Henry	68
Hubbard Portable Oven Co.	Cover
Jennison Co., W. J.	16
Katzinger Co., Edward	Cover
Lambooy Label & Wrapper Co.	4
Maag Co., The Aug.	Cover
Malt Diastase Co.	16
Malzbender, M.	57
Menasha Printing & Carton Co.	
Middleby-Marshall Oven, Co.	8
Middleby Oven Co., N. Y.	16
Mills & Bro., Inc., Thomas	61
National Bread Wrapping Mach. Co.	45
Philadelphia Thermometer Co.	4
Procter & Gamble Co.	6
Read Machinery Co.	7
Reeves Pulley Co.	8
Republic Truck Sales Corp.	3
Robson & Co., Charles	13
Russell-Miller Milling Co.	10
Siebel Institute	17
Standard Oven Co.	8
Superior Oven Co.	41
Thomson Machine Co.	7
Turner, A. R.	57
Union Steel Products Co.	
Union Machinery Co.	4
Ward Baking Co.	33
Washburn-Crosby Co.	Cover
Water-proof Paper & Board Co.	13

THE NATIONAL Baker

KLEEN-KRUST
RIVETLESS
REG. U.S. PAT. OFF.
"STEEL-SHOD"
BREAD PANS
(Patented Jan. 21, 1913; Jan. 16, 1917.)

The Appearance of the Loaf
is of Prime Importance--

Flanges Prevent
Pans from Spread-
ing.

—It goes a long way in creating
a demand for your bread. If
you would turn out loaves of
exceptional uniformity—clean,
spotless loaves—you will bake
in Kleen-Krust Rivetless "Steel-
Shod" Bread Pans.

Extra Heavy Steel
Rod Used in Binding
Pans Together.

Steel Shod Ends
Protect the End
Pans.

With Covers for
Pullman or
Sandwich
Loaves

Entirely Different from Any Other Pan on the Market

Their construction, the most rigid and sanitary ever devised, entirely eliminates strapping, therefore neither dirt nor grease can collect.

The outer face of the end pans is protected by a sheet of steel which
acts as a piece of armor-plate. This steers the peel underneath
the pans, eliminating all danger of battering the end pan.

Kleen-Krust Rivetless "Steel-Shod" Bread Pans are manufactured under letters patent granted by the U. S. Government. We are sole manufacturers.

The advantages of Kleen-Krust Rivetless "Steel-
Shod" Bread Pans go a long way toward creating a
demand for your bread by improving the appearance
of the loaf. In order that you may find out these
advantages for yourself, we will forward a sample
set of open Pans for immediate practical use in
your oven room.

Specially Adapted for Traveling Ovens

We have issued a New Catalog illus-
trating and describing our Kleen-
Krust Rivetless "Steel Shod" Bread
Pans and Kleen-Krust Rivetless
Pullman or Sandwich Bread Pans.
Catalog mailed on request.

Showing Rigid Con-
struction of Cover.

Style No. 87
Made of extra heavy tin with loose

THE AUGUST MAAG CO.
509-11 W. Lombard St.

VOL. XXVII. ENTERED AT THE PHILADELPHIA POST OFFICE AS SECOND CLASS MATTER No. 315

THE NATIONAL Baker

PUBLISHED MONTHLY BY
THE NATIONAL BAKER PUBLISHING CO.
411 WALNUT STREET
B. F. WHITECAR, Pres. and Editor

PHILADELPHIA, PA., APRIL 15, 1922

Price per year, U. S.
and Canada $2.00
Foreign Countries $3.00

Hot Cross Buns
—Sell Them Now

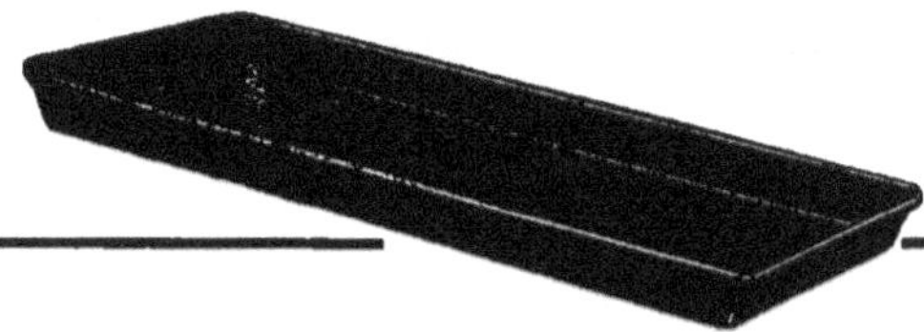

Stock Sizes
EKCO Velvediron
Bun Pans

All sizes made one-piece folded end, heavily wired, sanitary style. Flared-to-nest pans suggested. They save room when not used.

Flared-to-Nest Sizes

No.	Gauge.	Top Outside
100	27	12x26x1
200	26	18x26x1
300	24	18x26x1
350	22	18x26x1

Straight Side Sizes

No.	Gauge	Top Outside
190	26	17½x25½x1
290	34	17½x25½x1
390	22	17½x25½x1
80	26	19¾x27¼x1
180	24	19¾x27¼x1
280	22	19¾x27¼x1

ALWAYS a tempting dish, there's no reason for confining your Hot Cross Bun sales to one day or one week. When you display buns and cookies now you create the desire, and you are building an all-year-round demand.

There's Parker House, Crescent, Vienna—rolls of all kinds—crisp, tasty, flavory. Teach your customers to get them fresh from the bakery each morning for breakfast.

Leading supply houses can furnish you with Velvediron Pans in the sizes you need.

EDWARD KATZINGER CO.

131 North Sangamon St.

Drexel Building, Dept. K.

CHICAGO, ILL.

PHILADELPHIA, PA.

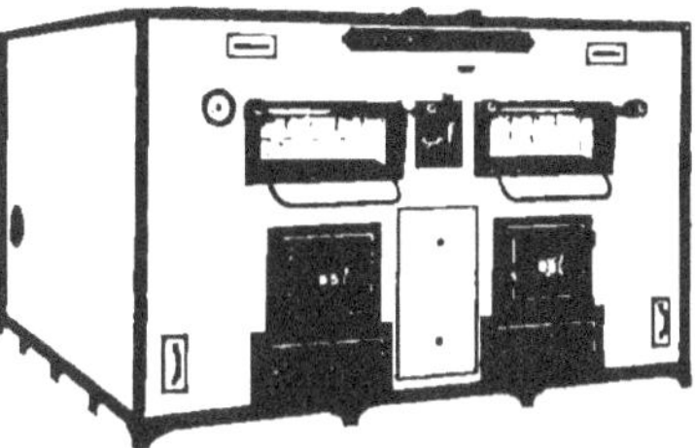

Bennett Ovens Make Busy Bakers

ARE you worrying along with an old style oven? Are you turning down new business because you cannot turn out the goods?

Install a modern, efficient Bennett Oven and you will be able to handle an increased demand on a profitable basis. Others are doing it. So can you.

Bennett Ovens Are Better Ovens

BENNETT OVEN CO.,   Ave. C & 22nd Street, Battle Creek, Mich.

The "Standard" Meets Every Bakeshop Requirement

The baker using but one oven must have a good one if he is to succeed in business.

That's why the Standard Oven scores every time.

STANDARD OVEN COMPANY

1835 Oliver Building   PITTSBURGH, PA.

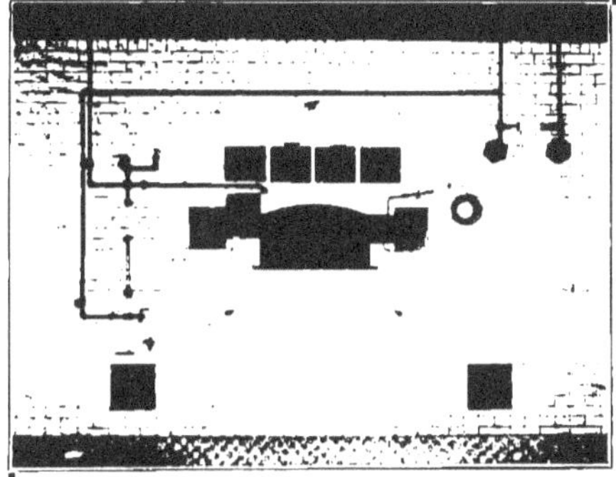

DUHRKOP OVENS

Mean

Oven

Satisfaction

This is proven by the fact that 90 per cent of our business is REPEAT ORDERS.

Ask for our list of DUHRKOP USERS--Note those in YOUR VICINITY.

DUHRKOP OVEN COMPANY

PARK ROW BUILDING   NEW YORK, N. Y.

NEW WIDE MOUTH OVEN DOOR 10½"x40"

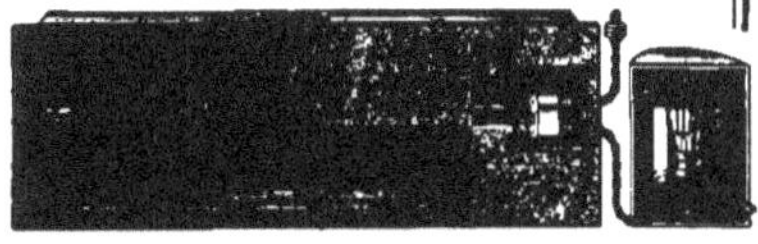

Fig. 1 F

With light controlled by opening and closing door. Flue opening in top.

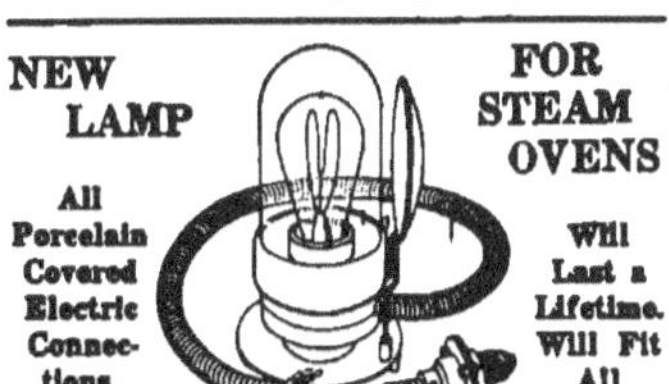

CHAS. ROBSON & CO.
8th St. & Washington Ave., Philadelphia, Pa.

THE WATERPROOF PAPER & BOARD Co.
BREDRAP
DESIGNERS AND MANUFACTURERS
CINCINNATI, OHIO
U. S. A.

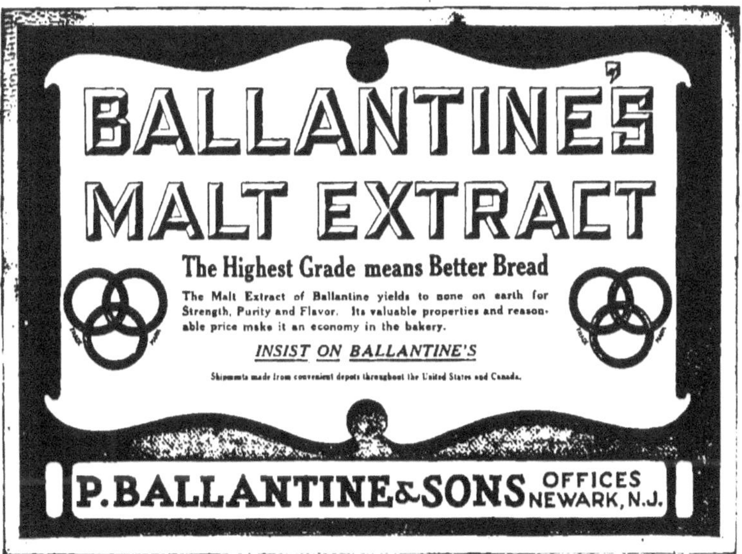

BALLANTINE'S
MALT EXTRACT
The Highest Grade means Better Bread
The Malt Extract of Ballantine yields to none on earth for Strength, Purity and Flavor. Its valuable properties and reasonable price make it an economy in the bakery.
INSIST ON BALLANTINE'S
Shipments made from convenient depots throughout the United States and Canada.
P. BALLANTINE & SONS
OFFICES
NEWARK, N.J.

The Test of Time

is the surest test 

OP Malt Extract

has stood this test and has not been found wanting.

Prudent bakers do not experiment—they place full reliance in

OP MALT EXTRACT

Malt-Diastase Company

79 Wall Street, NEW YORK

Warehouses: CHICAGO, PHILADELPHIA   *Laboratories,* BROOKLYN, N. Y.

"SWEET CREAM"
"VERY BEST"
- QUALITY FLOURS -
W·J·JENNISON C? MINNEAPOLIS, MINN.

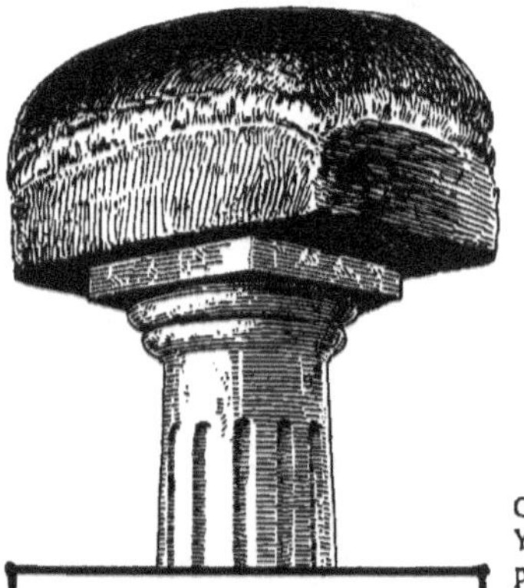

Every Loaf
is a Masterpiece

when you use

YEAST FOOD

Patented in U. S. A. and Foreign Countries

One of the most desirable features of ARKADY YEAST FOOD is its ability to standardize your product—to make every loaf uniform in appearance, bloom, texture and flavor. One loaf is just as good as another and every loaf as good as bread can be.

If you want to leave less progressive competitors far behind, you can do it with ARKADY YEAST FOOD. And at the same time greatly reduce production costs.

ARKADY is sold in 50 pound drums and in sacks of 180 pounds. Price 13c per pound. In lots of 900 pounds and over, 11c per pound. Both prices f.o.b. New York and subject to change without notice.

Write for literature, or, better still, order a trial shipment of this wonderful yeast nutrient and prove its merits yourself—in your own shop.

Here Is a Typical Arkady Loaf

1. Full expansion with the top pulling, but not pulled loose from the sides.

2. Golden brown crust with perfect bloom, the inner texture is smooth, fine and silky with the dough cells finely divided.

3. The texture does not crumble when the loaf is cut, but remains firm. The color of the crumb is creamy white, the flavor sweet and suggestive of the nutty flavor of wheat.

4. Finally, it has good keeping qualities and will remain sweet and palatable for several days.

Research Products Department

WARD BAKING COMPANY, NEW YORK

THE NATIONAL Baker

PUBLISHED ON THE FIFTEENTH OF EACH MONTH

AT

411 WALNUT ST., PHILADELPHIA

BY

THE NATIONAL BAKER PUBLISHING CO.

B. F. WHITECAR, PRESIDENT AND EDITOR
W. W. GALE, SECRETARY AND TREASURER

MEMBER OF THE AUDIT BUREAU OF CIRCULATIONS

SUBSCRIPTION RATES

UNITED STATES, ITS POSSESSIONS AND CANADA ..$2.00 per year
FOREIGN COUNTRIES .... 3.00 per year

PAYABLE IN ADVANCE

ADVERTISING RATES ON APPLICATION

Make all remittances payable to the order of
The National Baker Publishing Company ·

*Changes for displayed advertisements must reach this office
by the 5th of the month*

VOL. XXVII　　　APRIL, 1922　　　No. 315

CONTENTS

British Wheat Subsidy..... 24
Cake Recipes:
　Theresias 62
　Valencias 62
　Rarebit 62
　Cinderellas 62
　Casino Cakes 62
　Mazarines 62
　Ghibelines 62
　Wine Sticks 62
　Lady Grays 62
　Mozarts 63
　Amourettes 63
　Othellos 63
　Cardinal Cakes 63
　Berlingoes 63
　Aristocrats 63
　Windsor Tarts 64
　Marshall Cake 64
　Haselnut Bars 64
　Chocolate Tarts 64
　Dewey Tarts 64
　French Orange Cake..... 64
　Spice Cake 64
Exposition of Bakery Goods 28
Fancy Meringue Biscuits... 62
Filling Baking Prescriptions 25
Good Ventilation 30
Home-Town Business 23
Indiana Bakers Meet....... 28

Information Department:
　Phosphate Baking Powder 59
　Bread From Kansas Flour 59
　Royal Icing 59
　Pralines 60
　Egg Icing 60
　Vienna Icing 60
　Water Icing 60
　Raisin Bread 60
　Angel Cake 60
　Devil's Food Cake....... 60
Keeping Track of Stock and
　Tools 27
New England Bakers...... 29
Officers of Trade Associations 38
Operation Problems 44
Pie Crusts and Fillings..... 56
Potomac States Meeting.... 52
Practical Cake Making Sug-
　gestions 54
Raisin Week 54
Reduce Fire Hazards....... 32
Rye Bread 50
School-Trained Baker 31
Show Window 30
Siebel Institute 34
Southeastern Convention
　Program 28
Variations in Flour........ 33

Home-Town Business

THERE was a time when a great many of the smaller towns had no such thing as a professional baker, with his own shop, making and selling bakery goods of all sorts to the public. And it was in that time that the big city wholesalers managed to get a hold on the small-town trade which in many cases they have since retained, much to the disgust and displeasure of the bakers in these towns. The latter put forth the argument that the business in their home towns belongs to them, and they are inclined to resent the fact that out-of-town bakeries come in and sell bread.

Certainly it is true, in a certain sense, that the business in a given locality belongs to the business men there located; but this is not true in the sense that they have any exclusive and enforceable claim upon it. This is so far from being the case that the tremendous success of several enormous mail-order houses, selling about everything on earth, is one of the notorious facts of modern American business; and yet the success of these great houses, as well as of any concern which has proved its ability to go into a town at a distance and grab business from under the noses of local men, is, to a great extent, due to the local men themselves.

This does not mean, of course, that the local men do not want the business, because they undoubtedly do want it. Many a small town has been all but ruined by the inability of the local merchants to hold the trade of their home people, and by the consequent decay of local business, from the bank to the baker—although not so often the baker as others, it should be said. But it is a homely and truthful old saying that "it isn't what you want that makes you fat"—it's what you get; and merely wanting the business, and the mere fact that home business ought, on fundamental principles, to stay at home, will not keep it there. The home merchant, including the baker, must do something more.

Why do small-town grocers buy bread of out-of-town wholesalers? And why do small-town residents buy of their grocer bread and other bakery goods made elsewhere? Well, there are several reasons; among them that suggested at first, that the out-of-town concerns obtained a hold on the business in the first place, when there was no local baker, and that they have been able to retain it notwithstanding local competition. And where there has been a local baker, the quality of the in-coming bread has frequently been so superior to the local product that the trade which should have remained with the local baker, has gone to his out-of-town competitor, thus enabling him to retain the trade as against the presumably warm competition of the home-town baker.

To make no invidious comparisons—because it is everywhere acknowledged to be wholly legitimate for an honorable business house to seek trade wherever it can get it, as long as its methods are what they should be—let the baker turn his attention to the troubles of his friend the general merchant, and see what he suffers from the competition of the mail-order house. This merchant, in numerous small towns, and in many not so small, loses, in the aggregate, an immense amount of business to the big mail-order concern; and where he sticks to old-fashioned methods, he continues to lose it, whereas in the rapidly-increasing number of cases where he adopts the same vigorous measures followed by his big competitor, he gets all that is coming to him, in a literal sense.

In the past few years small-town merchants have received a liberal practical education on the subject of fighting the mail-order house, and they have benefited from it. They have had it forced upon their attention that if they are content to sit around and bewail their hard luck, and hope that people will stop buying out of town, they will continue to have hard luck to wail about; whereas if they go after business energetically with products of quality, and along up-to-date lines, they will get it, and can adopt a cheerful "I-should-worry" attitude toward all competition whatsoever. Which, of course, is the sensible attitude for any business man who is conducting his business properly.

The home-town man, in any case, no matter what his business is, has the inestimable advantage of being on the ground. That means that he has a personal knowledge of and personal contact with his customers, involving an appreciation of their wants, and a hold upon their patronage, which should be of the utmost value to him. The mail-order house, the outside competitor of any sort, has nothing of this advantage. The outsider has only the modern way of going after business, which, of course, is not his exclusive property any more than air and sunshine are exclusive property. These things are free to everybody who will avail himself of them; and if the small-town man permits the outsider to come in and get his business by reason of superior merchandising and much better quality, he has only himself to blame.

This, obviously, applies quite as forcibly to the baker as to anybody else. It is the complaint of merchants in various lines that they are handicapped in meeting mail-order competition by the ability of the big houses to undersell them, and the baker may make the same complaint; and both complaints have some ground. The greater volume of business handled by the larger concerns certainly gives them an advantage in the matter of cost of production; but, on the other hand, the cost of transportation and handling tends to equalize this advantage, as far as prices are concerned, leaving in the hands of the home-town man, baker or merchant, the advantages of his location, already referred to.

With these to go on, it remains entirely in the hands of, the local man to utilize to the fullest the fact that he is on the ground, in order to get the trade

to which, from the business standpoint, he is entitled; but his "title" is better and more certain if his bread is as good or better than the bread shipped into his town. He has a perfect right to use every proper means to impress upon his home people that there is a certain duty resting on them to support local business; but aside from this, he should rather go after business in the approved manner of the up-to-date concern, and land it on the merits of his goods, rather than merely because he is a local man.

As stated at the outset, the home man has no actual right to home business, although he has a good case in his claim upon it. He must convince the public that he has good products, and that his prices and service are right. Once he has done this, he will get the business, and he need not worry about the competition of outsiders; and, of course, the way to do this is to live up to the best standards, and to tell people about it. A program along that line will leave little cause for complaint.

Making good bread, alone, will not suffice. Modern methods require that the successful merchant, be he baker or shoedealer, must use printers' ink, aggressively and steadily, if he is to get his share of the business of his locality.

Make better bread and tell the public about it—now and hereafter.

—‡—‡—‡—

The British Wheat Subsidy

DURING the war it was a mystery to many people, and to a number of newspapers, who should have known better, how it was that the price of bread was lower in Great Britain than it was in this country, and these people and newspapers naturally accused the American baker of profiteering.

It was explained time and time again that the British Government was paying a subsidy on all bread made by the bakers, in order to keep the price of this very necessary food at the lowest possible figure—nine pence for a four-pound loaf. But many of these American objectors could not, apparently, get it through their heads just what the word "subsidy" meant and why it should be paid at all.

In Great Britain, and in fact in all Europe, bread is literally the "Staff of Life," and every possible effort is made, to keep its cost down to the irreducible minimum. A rise in the price of bread inevitably means trouble for the rulers of that country where the rise occurs. Many a government has fallen because they could not or would not keep down the price of bread to its old level of cost. Great Britain was no exception. A considerable advance in the price of bread would have caused the people to murmur and become greatly dissatisfied; there was a possibility of many of them opposing a war which increased the cost of bread; the British Government thought it could not afford to take this chance, and in consequence took control of all food supplies. They purchased wheat in the markets of the world for a price and sold it to the bakers at a lower price, absorbing the loss and charging same to war expenses.

Few realized the enormous amount of money involved in this wheat subsidy; but in the report of the Royal Commission on Wheat Supplies, recently issued, it is stated that "the cost to the nation of the bread subsidy was approximately £102,500,000." At the normal rate of exchange this means $786,500,000. A sizable bill for the British Government to pay in order to sell bread to its people at a low price in time of war and blockade. However, they probably feel that it was worth it.

Some idea of the magnitude of the task with which the Royal Commission was confronted when they started upon their duties of controlling the wheat supplies may be gathered from the statement that the total cereal importations of the United Kingdom alone were 10,000,000 tons per year. Prior to the war the standard extraction of flour was about 72 per cent. This was gradually raised until by February, 1918, the required extraction was 95 per cent., and even this high percentage could be used only with a considerable addition of other grains.

. There was more or less growling in this country over the character of the "war bread" offered the public, but our bread was cake in comparison to the only bread permitted the British public, and it was a crime over there, heavily punished, to offer even this bread until it was at least 24 hours out of the oven, and a wilful waste of bread meant a still heavier fine and imprisonment.

"The original instruction given by the Food Controller to the Commission was that the War Cabinet had ordered that the price of the four-pound loaf was to be reduced to the uniform level of nine pence. The decision being one of policy, the Commission was charged only with its administration, and was in no way responsible for the inception of the measure. The first point considered was whether it would be possible to differentiate between the use of flour for the loaf and its use for other purposes. The Food Controller reported that it was not administratively possible to confine the subsidy to the nine-penny loaf, and it was accordingly decided by the Cabinet that all flour, except flour used for certain precluded purposes, should be subsidized at the uniform price. Several efforts were subsequently made to devise means of confining the subsidy to the loaf only, but the administrative difficulties were always found to be insuperable."

All flour was sold to the bakers at the uniform price of 44 shillings, 3 pence per sack of 280 pounds. The average cost of this flour to the British Government was 60 shillings, 7 pence per sack. A loss of 16 shillings, 4 pence on every sack of flour, either of home manufacture or imported. In one year the flour importations reached the great figure of 11,000,000 sacks. On April 12, 1920, control of bread prices was withdrawn.

Few of us, in this country, realize our blessings.

Filling｜Baking Prescriptions

WHAT has the baker to do with filling prescriptions? He has this to do. Physicians are today prescribing food perhaps to even a greater extent than they are prescribing medicine. Drug stores have been forced to sell merchandise in order to make money. The prescription department of many a drug store is not an especially profitable department. Some of them would be just as well off, possibly better off, if they did not have any prescription department at all.

This is partly due to the fact that drugs are not being relied upon so much today as diet. In addition, people are very much interested in diet. Anybody from a humorist to a medical authority who writes a good and interesting article, story or book on dieting can count on big sales. The Waldorf-Astoria in New York City has instituted a scientific diet service. Probably no innovation any hotel has made has proved so popular as this one has.

A large baking company making a genuine wholewheat bread is selling a quarter of million loaves a year. Dairy companies specializing in health foods find a good demand for their products.

Yet, after all is said, these people, these concerns are merely filling prescriptions. They have not created any demand. The medical profession has created the demand.

Since they are doing this it would seem like good business policy on the part of the baker to co-operate with the physicians to the greatest possible extent. Just what such co-operation may mean is illustrated by the experience of a man who started a dairy farm.

This man set out to make his farm please the physicians. Every hygienic and sanitary precaution that would appeal to medical men he put into force on his farm. After he had made it just as perfect as he knew how, he invited physicians and health officials to visit the place.

They did this. They were pleased. They did not hesitate to endorse what he had done. This man had no market for his milk. He would have to sell it for more than the market price, but after he saw how well pleased the medical men were he did not worry. They created the market for him. They recommended the milk, and soon there was a demand for all that could be supplied. To a very considerable extent this man was merely filling prescriptions.

When a physician places a patient on a diet he must take into consideration what the patient can get in the way of food. Many a patient cannot follow a diet strictly because he cannot find just the food that he should eat. That is the reason why the service now being offered by the Waldorf-Astoria is creating the enthusiasm that it is. It makes it easier for people to follow the doctor's orders.

A great many of the things that the doctor orders could be supplied by the baker. Some bakers have facilities for one thing, some for another. All could to a limited extent at least sell those articles of food that the physicians are recommending.

In the past the baker has not connected his business with the medical profession. In the future the more he co-operates with that profession, the more profitable business he is pretty certain to secure. A larger profit can usually be made upon the special foods.

Usually such health foods as' are carried are stocked without any special reference to what the physicians are doing. They are handled more as patent medicines have been handled, rather than as an aid to the physician. When this is done, a great amount of co-operation from the physicians cannot be expected.

On the other hand, however, if the baker talks the matter over with some of the leading physicians of his community, if he familiarizes himself with the diets they are prescribing, if he learns as much as he can about these diets and the number of people that should be following them, then he is placing himself in a position where he can expect some aid and support from the physician. Unless the present tendency changes there is every evidence that sooner or later dealers in food products will have to work more along this line or new stores specializing in diets will be established.

In the past most of the work that has been done by restaurants, bakers and dealers has been to cater to some fad or cult. Sooner or later it is going to be necessary to co-operate with the physicians and do as much as possible to make it easy for patients to follow the diet directions that the physicians have given them.

The baker can play a very important part in this co-operation. He is in a position to prepare at least some of the food. It is much easier to instruct a patient to buy what is needed at a certain place than it is to teach them how to prepare it themselves.

At the present time, many a physician who prescribes diets is in much the same position he would be if he was prescribing drugs and there was no drug store at which prescriptions could be filled. He naturally would have to make the drugs the simplest possible. Today diets have to be simpler than they would be if it was easier to get diet foods.

Physicians can give information that will indicate just about what the market will be. He can give information that will indicate just what new lines it will be profitable for the baker to add to his stock. He can and will help the baker sell if the baker can gain his confidence and can show that he is endeavoring to work with him.

In the case of the diets that are most popular the baker may find it worth while to prepare menus, have them printed and distribute them to the customers. The physicians will usually help him in preparing these menus. He himself can make or at least sell the cereal part of these menus and recipes may be given for the vegetable and meat parts so that they can easily be prepared in the home.

The more he does along this line the more impressed his customers will be with the service that he is rendering, the more confidence they will have in him and the more they are going to patronize him. More important, however, he is raising his business far above the plane of the ordinary baker. He will be considered a man of greater intelligence. He will be a man whose advice will be more likely to be sought. His business will be more upon the plane of the druggist.

Besides, if he renders all the co-operation that he can, the physicians are going to say more and more good words for him and that will not hurt the business to say the least. In order to secure the co-operation of the physicians, however, it is necessary to be frank with them. It is necessary to show a willingness to render real service. It is necessary to watch the quality. It is also necessary to allow them to inspect the plant and the processes as often as they wish. In fact they should be encouraged to do so.

A physician considers it his right to go behind the prescription counter in a drug store and watch the druggist compound prescriptions. He would hardly consider himself justified in sending any person to a store where this right was not accorded him.

If the bakery is kept in a condition such that it appeals to the physician, then he is going to patronize that bakery himself and encourage his friends to do so for products that have nothing whatever to do with special diets. If physicians could be persuaded to visit the bakery, even if no special diet products were being made, it would be a good thing for the baker if the bakery was so conducted as to please the physicians. What they say now has a great deal of influence with people in regard to food and where it should be bought.

They, however, would not be likely to visit a bakery that did not make something that was rather vitally interesting to them, and diet foods are. Therefore, if the baker does make any diet foods he will find that one of the advantages is the greater interest that the physicians take in his business. This interest has a real advertising value for everything that is produced and sold in the bake shop.

When business is none too good, anyhow, is one of the best times to start a diet food prescription department, where people can have prepared for them or can buy the very products that their physicians advise them to eat, and to which physicians can send their patients to get food. The idea is sufficiently new to make an appeal. This is demonstrated by the experience of all those who have done anything along this line. If the idea is carried out in the right way it can be made a real source of profit and good advertising.

Keeping Track of Stock and Tools

SOME of the advantages to be had from perpetual inventory or stores control are pointed out in a bulletin just issued by the Fabricated Production Department of the Chamber of Commerce of the United States.

"When capital," says the bulletin, "is in the form of cash, it is carefully protected, its receipt and disbursement safeguarded, its custodians held to a strict accounting, but once this capital is converted into materials there is a tendency to become lax, to lose sight of the value of the investment, to husband the capital less diligently, to tolerate practices that are wasteful, inefficient and needlessly expensive.

"There is something at fault with business methods when material is purchased far in excess of production requirements, when material becomes obsolete before it is even processed, when production lags for the lack of material or is throttled by the uneven flow of material through the departments, when a careful check of material receipts is not provided, when material is not protected or kept accessible for use, when foreman and workmen help themselves without authorized requisitions and material is consumed without any record for cost purposes.

"To those firms and organizations who are not satisfied that their material investment is at an efficient minimum, who suffer periodically from shortages of material, who are unable to make monthly profit and loss statements, who fret at the prospect of the annual physical inventory, who are not adequately conserving their material investment by giving it the best of physical care, to such the perpetual inventory is recommended.

"The perpetual inventory will show the past and present consumption of material, and will allow for a revision of the quantities of material carried to comply with present market and production conditions, will indicate the items that are slow moving, overstocked and non-standard. The perpetual inventory ties up here with the problem of standardization. In fact, the standardization policy cannot proceed far without the information and data supplied by the perpetual inventory system.

"An efficient stores or perpetual inventory system, and that alone, will provide for:

1. Sufficient material to meet production requirements so that production shall at least not be checked by a lack of necessary material.

2. A minimum investment in inventories which is of supreme importance at the present time.

3. An orderly and accessible arrangement of material and the physical safeguarding of material from the elements and theft.

4. The elimination of the burdensome and inaccurate annual physical inventory.

5. A monthly closing by giving the amount and value of material on hand at any time.

6. Is an invaluable record in case of fire loss.

7. A safeguard against the accumulation of obsolescent material.

"A material control system takes on an increased importance where there are numerous parts entering into production, the lack of any one of which is sufficient to check operations and throw the production program out of balance. Parts must not only be physically available in the store-room, but must converge to the point and at the time desired in production. An undue accumulation of material in the course of production will serve to interrupt the flow of production. The costliness of the sluggish movement of materials is not generally recognized, but an enterprise is impoverished by it as an individual suffering from a weakened circulation.

"Economy of material investment, particularly of parts, cannot be determined on a strictly interest charge basis. There is something bigger at stake—the most economical use of production facilities. A three months' supply of a specific part may be a high enough level to meet the usual demand, but a six months' or a year's supply may be fabricated far more cheaply and permit of greater plant output. Economy demands that work be put through in adequate lots.

"The control of material does not end with the store-room or its record; it is genuinely a factory problem. To a large degree, the success of a stores control system will depend on the co-operation of foremen and workmen. In particular, the foreman can directly help the control of materials by avoiding congestion in the departments, by protecting material in the departments against breakages and theft by assisting in the proper distribution of material to their men, by seeing that the men get the quantity of material ordered, by ascertaining that the correct number of finished pieces are produced from the quantity of material drawn or the equivalent in scrap presented, that material is skilfully handled in the departments and when processed that it is promptly and properly transferred.

"The foreman can prevent the irregular accumulation of material in this department. Who does not know the factory with its miscellaneous material smuggled away in assembly rooms or containers, or strewn under work benches and around machines, and even thrown into waste cans, all of which unnecessarily increases the investment in inventories.

—:—:—:—

The National Association of Wholesale Pie Bakers will hold its fifth annual convention at the Hotel Statler, Detroit, Mich., Tuesday and Wednesday, May 23d and 24th, and subjects of interest to pie bakers will be discussed and acted upon. Jos. C. Hutchison, Philadelphia, is president and Jas. J. Regan, 3240 Walnut Street, Philadelphia, is secretary.

Bakery Exposition at Chicago

THE annual meeting of the Bakery Equipment Manufacturers' Association was held at the Hotel Sherman, Chicago, on March 27th and 28th, at which time it was decided to hold a large exhibition of bakers' machinery, tools, equipment and supplies, during the week of September 11th to 16th, during the annual convention of the American Bakers' Association. The exhibition will be held on the Municipal Pier, which is splendidly adapted for that purpose.

Felix Notz, of the American Oven & Machine Co., is chairman of the Exposition Committee, the other members being Arthur Fosdyke, of the Superior Oven Co., and C. W. Helm.

—‡—‡—‡—

Indiana Bakers' Association

THE first Zone Meeting for 1922 was held in Indianapolis, March 25th, at the Claypool Hotel. The meeting was opened at 8:30 P. M. by E. L. Cline, Commissioner for Zone 10, with a few welcoming remarks. C. P. Ehlers, Secretary-Manager of the Indiana Association, outlined the proposed campaign of the Allied Trades for a drive for members for the Indiana Bakers' Association. C. R. Russ, captain of the committee for the state, said that no direct appeals had been made as yet, and asked the members of the Allied Trades to stay for a meeting after adjournment of the bakers' meeting, and plans would be made for more active work.

Fred Lacy, of Terre Haute, reported that a great many bakers in the section of the state covered by him were under the impression that the Association was an instrument for adjusting prices, and as they (the Association) did not do this, felt that the Association had failed in its undertaking.

Mr. Cline asked every supplyman present to carry the information to bakers throughout the state, that the Association in no way was responsible for prices; that the Association was in a position to render invaluable service to its members, such as interpretations of the Indiana Bakers' Law, listing of used machinery, purchasing of labels, etc. He urged the members of the Allied Trades to preach "Better Bread" wherever and whenever possible, as it was only by having the majority of the people eat bakers' bread, that would bring about success.

Other speakers of the evening were: H. E. Schortemeier, E. K. Quigg, John Clark, V. C. Vanderbilt, Russell White and O. E. Patterson.

The question of giving premiums was brought up, and although a number of bakers throughout the state are indulging in this practice, Mr. Ehlers informed those present that the State Attorney General had handed down the opinion that this was a violation of the lottery law.

Meeting adjourned at 9:30 P. M.

MEETING OF ALLIED TRADESMEN

Mr. Russ met with the Zone Captains and other allied tradesmen after the Zone Meeting was over, and outlined their plans for the coming year, which were, that each captain should make a monthly report to him, and that they would have a meeting here in Indianapolis every three months, or oftener if they thought it advisable. The Captains and other Allied Tradesmen asked Secretary Ehlers for some ideas and pointers on how to interest the bakers in the Association, and what the Association had to offer them. He replied by showing them what the Association has been doing in the past for the good of the bakers, and that the Association could do many more good things providing the membership was large enough, and the funds sufficient to carry out the work that could be outlined by the Advisory Commission. When the meeting adjourned all thought that they had derived a great deal of good from this meeting, and would be able to carry the message of "Quality" back to the bakers with more enthusiasm than they ever had done before.

—‡—‡—‡—

Southern Convention Program

THE eighth annual convention of the Southeastern Association of the Baking Industry will be held at the DeSoto Hotel, Savannah, Georgia, on April 18th-20th, with the following program:

TUESDAY, 18TH

Convention called to order by the President, J. H. Quint. Prayer by Dr. William Hoppe, Savannah.

Welcome by the Hon. Murray M. Stewart, Mayor of Savannah.

Response by C. R. Roberts, Knoxville, Tenn.

Report of Officers.

Address by Alex. W. Taggart, 1st Vice-President American Bakers' Association, Indianapolis, Ind.

Address by Elwood M. Rabenold, General Council American Bakers' Association, New York, N. Y.

"The American Institute and Its Relationship to the Baker," by Dr. H. E. Barnard, Manager-Secretary American Bakers' Association.

Discussion led by T. A. McGough, Birmingham, Ala.

"Baking Technology," by I. K. Russell, of the American Institute of Baking.

Discussion led by A. Geilfus, Spartanburg, S. C.

WEDNESDAY

Allied Trades Day

Meeting called to order and chair turned over to President George E. Dean.

Address, "Our Program—Its Purposes."

A Two Act Playlet—"The Human Side of Selling," written and directed by Ben B. George, Bakers' Products Division, Procter & Gamble Co.

"Memoirs of an Old Traveling Man," speaker to be announced.

"Salesmen of the New Day," by B. B. Grenell, Chapman-Smith Company, Chicago.

"What the Allied Trades Hope to Accomplish," by C. H. Van Cleef, Secretary-Treasurer Allied Trades Association.

Five-Minute Discussions—"My Impressions of Salesmen That Call on Me," by Gordon Smith; William Barr, Cameron & Barr Co., Chattanooga; T. A. McGough, McGough's Bakery, Birmingham; J. L. Skelton, Skelton's Bakery, Morristown, Tenn.; William Craig, Craig's Bakery, Columbus, Ga.

Round Table Luncheon.

THURSDAY

Election of officers.

"Up-to-Date Ideas on Quality Bread," by J. E. Wihlfahrt, The Fleischmann Co., New York.

Discussion led by J. L. Skelton, Morristown, Tenn.

"Making and Selling Bread on Quality Rather Than Price," by Ben J. Poelman, Meridan, Miss.

Discussion led by Roger Grant, Asheville, N. C.

"Quality Bread," by John T. Kern, President Peter Kern Baking Co., Knoxville, Tenn.

Discussion led by John Cureton, Greenville, S. C.

"Better Bread from Better Ingredients," Frank Emmons, Chemist Washburn-Crosby Co., Minneapolis, Minn.

Discussion led by William Condon, Charleston, S. C.

Installation of new officers.

Adjournment.

ENTERTAINMENT

(Tentative Program)

Monday Evening—Get-together Dance at DeSoto Hotel.

Tuesday Afternoon—Rotary Luncheon for All Rotarians, DeSoto Hotel, 2.15 P. M.

Tuesday Afternoon—Auto Ride for Ladies.

Tuesday Evening—Dance at DeSoto Hotel.

Wednesday Afternoon—Boat Ride.

Wednesday Evening—Street Dance.

Thursday Afternoon—Bijou Party (Vaudeville).

Thursday Evening—Banquet.

—‡—‡—‡—

New England Bakers' Association

THE second bi-monthly meeting of the New England Bakers' Association will be held at Worcester at the Hotel Standish, Main Street, opposite the Y. M. C. A., on April 26th.

Harry N. Brown, of the Worcester Baking Co., secretary of the Worcester Division of the New England Bakers' Association, is chairman of the committee on arrangements, and we can all be assured of a real, live meeting. His first request is, that all who come to Worcester by rail notify him of their arrival and automobiles will be provided to transport them from the station. There will not be an idle moment, not even during the luncheon, music and entertainment being provided.

As there is a large number of questions to be brought before the meeting, the number of speakers will be limited to three. Albert Klopfer will speak on the value of trade organizations, and A. S. Martin, of New Bedford, whose subject has not yet been decided

upon. C. O. Swanson, president of the Massachusetts Baking Co., will talk on "How to Meet Labor Conditions."

Reports will be heard from the associate membership committee and from the honorary membership committee, and will be acted upon at the meeting.

The old Massachusetts Master Bakers' Association has had a very successful employment bureau, and it will be left for this meeting to decide whether the New England Bakers' Association shall take it over and render the same service to all bakers of New England. This question is very timely on account of the present labor situation.

A committee has been appointed to draw up a Code of Ethics governing methods and principles members should employ in their relations with one another. The meeting will take action on this report. This is also a very important subject, as adherence to these principles will prevent many of the demoralizing and destructive situations bakers find themselves in today in various sections of the country.

Addenda to the constitution governing local divisions will be submitted to the meeting for action, and an invitation to the Pennsylvania State Convention will be acted upon.

The New England Bakers' Association is an association formed for the benefit of all bakers, retail as well as wholesale, and for this reason all New England retail bakers are especially urged to make an effort to attend.

—‡—‡—‡—

C. I. Corby, National Councillor

CHARLES I. Corby, of the Corby Baking Company, Washington, D. C., has been appointed new National Councillor to represent the American Bakers' Association in the Chamber of Commerce of the United States.

The National Council of the Chamber of Commerce of the United States consists of one representative each from the more than fourteen hundred commercial and industrial organizations making up the National Chamber's membership. It serves as an advisory body to the National Chamber's Board of Directors. The Council holds a special meeting preceding the annual convention of the National Chamber to pass on the program and to select a nominating committee. A councillor occupies a position of liaison officer between the National Chamber and his own organization on important questions.

The Chamber of Commerce of the United States is the strongest commercial organization in the world. Its object is to encourage trade and commerce; increase the efficiency of American business organizations; to obtain uniformity and equity in business usages and laws and to get proper consideration and concentration of opinion on questions affecting the financial, commercial, civic and industrial interests of the country at large.

Good Ventilation Aids Good Work

A WELL-ventilated shop is absolutely necessary if you want intelligent work from your men, and if all master bakers realized this important fact in hygiene there would be much less growling about the stupidity of the shop hands. A close, poorly ventilated bake-shop becomes filled with foul, semi-poisonous gases quicker than most any other work-shop, owing to the fact that the fermenting doughs are constantly throwing off carbon dioxide, which is not good for men to breathe undiluted. This gas, particularly in the heated, nearly stagnant air of many shops, has a depressing effect upon the men mentally, and no man of sluggish mentality can do good work. Poor ventilation is largely responsible for poor and unsatisfactory work.

The great importance of fresh air is but little understood by many bakers. One reason being the fear of drafts and their influence on the fermenting doughs. The consequence being that the air in the shop is not changed to any appreciable extent and becomes unwholesome, with severe depressing effect upon all who are compelled to breathe it for hours at a time.

The lack of light and ventilation is one of the principal reasons why boards of health start crusades against basement bakeries, yet it is possible, in most cases, to secure proper ventilation in a basement shop at a comparatively small cost, if the proprietor of that shop would only appreciate the great importance of pure, clean light and air.

While inspecting a fair-sized, well-appointed bakery lately, the proprietor pointed to a machine bolted to the ceiling, near an open window, saying to the writer: "There is the best machine in this shop." It was an "exhaust" fan, driven by a small motor and drawing out of the shop all the heated gases and foul air, which, being lighter than pure air, respond quickly to the suction of an exhaust fan. The result being that the air in this shop was pure, sweet and of even temperature.

The proprietor said that since installing the fan they had had very little trouble with the doughs, ascribing their success to the fact that they could maintain a *steady, even temperature.* He further said that it had a noticeable effect upon the workmen; they seemed more alert and got through with the work more quickly and with fewer mistakes than formerly. And this was not a basement shop, but one well located on the ground floor of a large building.

This baker was well within the mark in stating that an exhaust fan was his best machine, for proper temperature and pure air are of vast importance in the bakeshop, and those who have given serious thought to bakery problems realize this fact. As this baker further expressed it: "Ventilation is economy and actual experience has shown that a healthy, cheerful and comfortable employee will do more and better work than one who works with an effort and a feeling of languor and dullness, these being a few only of the ill effects of overheated or dust-laden air. Windows, doors, ventilators and similar efforts at natural ventilation frequently all fail to cool the bakeshop, but an exhaust fan is a perfect mechanical ventilator and never fails to remove the foul and heated air, giving place to fresh and invigorating air, which your employee must have to render you efficient service."

Fresh air is essential to the restoration of the human organism—it livens the spirit and keeps up the muscle. A man usually works as he feels. If his mental attitude is adverse to his working conditions or his personal treatment, he cannot very well work to his highest efficiency.

—:—:—:—

The Show Window

A STORE window offers the cheapest advertising a retail baker can employ. Windows are often preferred to newspaper space, because the results are quicker and surer, because showing an article will sell it more quickly than a printed description. Then, too, it is already an asset, as the rent is being paid just the same whether the window is used or not.

The neighborhood baker is judged largely from the appearance of his window. Hence, the window should always have a fresh appearance and with this in view they should be re-dressed regularly with strong, attractive, appetizing displays. The window displays need not necessarily be elaborate, for some of the most effective are simple and inexpensive.

A great many bakers don't "work" their windows as they should, and as a natural result the windows do not work for them.

The windows must be kept alive. They must be made to tell a distinct, mouth-watering story to the people who pass by and look in. You can't make a lively window without putting things there which will attract attention and cause people to keep watch of the windows for interesting things.

A Western grocer adopted a simple plan for a lively window attraction which brings him very good results. About Thursday of each week he puts a big placard in his window saying:

"Watch this window about 6 o'clock Saturday afternoon. Don't miss it." Then at 5 o'clock Saturday the curtains of the window are drawn, and the merchant puts into the window some especially attractive bargains. It may be a choice line of sundries at 10c. each; it may be a display of bananas at a low price or in the berry season of berries at a low figure. It is bound to be something which will move fast and attract instant attention. People have learned to watch for his Saturday night window, for it always holds something especially attractive.

The above hint can be modified and used to advantage by many retail bakers, and will add materially to your list of transient customers.

The School-Trained Baker

*In an Era of Machine Methods He Is Giving Modern
Bakeries Intelligent Direction*

THE Baking Industry is in a state of progressive growth. An old art is being performed in a new way. Hand methods are yielding to the machine, uncertain guesses are becoming predetermined certainties, and where once was much lack of control there now exists a demand for standardization and rigid adherence to schedule.

Such conditions demand intelligent and trained direction, which is not a usual outcome of practical experience alone, no matter how extended or varied. This does not mean that practical experience is to be discounted. Nothing has greater value than familiarity with trade problems through personal contact. But modern industrial conditions require more than average ability, and the foreman or superintendent who does not supplement his fund of practical knowledge with an understanding of the technical and scientific side of his trade will soon find himself outmatched by his trained competitor, who wins out in spite of his lack of long years of apprenticeship.

The Baking Industry is rapidly accepting the help and guidance of the mechanical engineer, the food chemist, the sanitary expert and the industrial technologist. It is not concerned simply with turning out the best bread under existing circumstances, but rather is it desirous of baking the best bread which can be turned out under any circumstances.

In order to accomplish these results men whose minds have been trained along these special lines must be available. Such men are rarely if ever the product of the commercial plant, and those exceptions who do not succeed in grasping and understanding the required new information while on the job, do so at an unnecessarily great effort and at a great loss of time. It is far more efficient to take the promising baker out of the shop and send him to an institution designed for the specific purpose of training him to fit better than ever into the needs of the trade. Such an institution is the School of the American Institute of Baking.

Here, in a few months, properly qualified men of previous experience are trained to return to their work *fitted to make better bread*. It *must* not be lost sight of in all this discussion of the application of science to industry that no good would result if it did not make it possible to produce better, more uniformly and more economically, the bread the sale of which constitutes the backbone of the industry.

But to produce this bread today requires not only the manual ability of the apprentice but also a full knowledge of the effect of variation of conditions and ingredients; knowledge of the nature, qualities and uses of the many materials found in bread mixes; knowledge of the latest developments in machinery and processes; knowledge of simple methods of testing to assure uniformity and to discover changes during storage; and information regarding industrial relations, laws, records, shop troubles and a thousand and one other matters, all new and in process of development, but nevertheless intimately tied into the baking of bread. The baking foreman and superintendent must know all these things, and all of them he may learn in his School of Baking.

Assisting the production man in the bread industry are two other men who must be trained to work hand in hand with the practical superintendent, but whose work is nevertheless of such a nature that special instruction along particular lines is required. These men are the control chemist, who acts in connection with the purchasing and control of materials, and the research chemist, whose function is the investigation of special problems of scientific research in baking laboratories. Sometimes the production superintendent and the control chemist may be one man, but this is not usual. More often they are distinct individuals, and in practically all cases the research man must be especially trained.

In conclusion, then, we find that the School of Baking supplies three men greatly needed by the industry. These are (1) the Production Superintendent, trained to go back into his trade equipped with knowledge to make better bread and to understand more fully the new commercial conditions; (2) the Control Chemist, to assist in and control the purchase and use of ingredients and processes; (3) and the Research Chemist, trained to attack and solve the new and unknown problem.—*Baking Technology.*

—‡—‡—‡—

Coming Conventions of Bakers

April 17-20. Southeastern Association. Annual, Savannah, Georgia; headquarters, Hotel De Sota.

April 18-20. Illinois Association. Annual, Danville, Ill.; headquarters, Plaza Hotel.

May 16-18. Texas Association. Annual, Houston, Texas; headquarters, Hotel Bender.

May 23-24. Wholesale Pie Bakers. Annual, Detroit, Mich.; headquarters, Hotel Statler.

May 10. Southern Illinois. Annual, Marion, Ill.

June 5-8. Pennsylvania. Annual, Bedford Springs, Pa.; headquarters, Bedford Springs Hotel.

June 20-21. Potomac States. Annual, Baltimore, Md.; headquarters, Hotel Rennert.

—‡—‡—‡—

Ivan B. Nordhem. who conceived the Rotary Prosperity Campaign and successfully carried this to its completion, has opened offices at the Bryant Park Studio Building, Suite 70, Fortieth street and Sixth avenue, New York City. Now that the country is at work again and determined that prosperity will be brought back. Mr. Nordhem has shouldered another big responsibility and this time in the interest of his old friends, the bakers. It is said that he has a big improvement in scientific, sanitary baking which Mr. Nordhem believes will greatly advance the baking industry.

Reduce the Fire Hazard

THE best and cheapest fire insurance policy is fire prevention—reduction of the fire hazard to a minimum. Few investments pay a larger rate of interest than time and money spent to prevent a fire from starting. Some men are so constituted that as long as they can secure what they consider to be ample fire insurance protection they take little thought towards the reduction of the fire hazard on their own premises. They argue, apparently that if a fire should occur, the insurance companies will foot the bill. "We should worry!"

As a matter of fact, even if your bakery should be insured to the full amount of money invested, a fire would mean a heavy money damage to you through loss of business, and in other ways, now fully appreciated by those who have passed through this unprofitable experience.

So, we repeat: "Few investments pay a larger rate of interest than time and money spent to prevent a fire from starting."

Be prepared to check a fire if it does start; have a number of requisites for fighting fire. Fire extinguishers cost little and serve well; in fact, they are about the only sure way of putting out a fire caused from grease, oil or gas. Hand grenades may also be placed along the bakeshop walls. Several pails should be hung up, marked "Fire," and these should be kept filled and used only for putting out a fire; if you use them for other purposes they will likely be out of place should a fire occur. Sand or salt is a good thing for handling some fires. Salt thrown in the firebox when the chimney is burning has a tendency to quiet the fire. A reel of hose placed near a waterstand may some time be needed. Flour will smother some fires. It is well to have a ladder on the roof, or outside wall, so that ready access can be gained to the chimney should it burn out.

Any baker can take precautions against having a fire. Grease, oils, kerosene, gasoline, etc., should be kept in a safe place. If you must keep a large supply of kerosene or gasoline, have an underground tank from which to pump what you need from time to time. Don't allow the bakeshop floor or other woodwork to become saturated with grease; scour it with cleanser. Use matches which must be struck on the box—they are the safest and the cheapest in the long run.

The bakeshop chimney should be cleaned frequently —just how often depends on the amount of baking and character of fuel used. Soft coal soon clogs a chimney so it does not draw well, and where it is left uncleaned for a time it is likely to cause a fire.

Keep rubbish cleaned up. Sometimes old boxes are thrown back of the shop or old sacks stacked in a corner, but the aim should be to keep the premises clear of everything of this kind. Much depends upon a baker's instructions to his men as to how clean the premises are kept.

The bakery store is as safe from a fire as any store. However, it pays to be careful. Everything should be kept picked up. Do not use combustible carpets or rugs on the floor. A burning match may ignite them. See that electric wiring in store and window is well insulated. There should be no accumulation of paper or rubbish under counters. If there is a ventilation grate in the walk in front of window, keep it cleaned out, for a cigar stump might fall through it and cause a fire.

Make a daily inspection of the premises and see that everything is kept so that the possibility of a fire may be avoided. Nearly every baker knows what might cause a fire and has merely to look around the bakery and have things kept cleaned up, or have some responsible person do this for him.

It costs nothing to get local officials, such as insurance men, fire chief, etc., to look over the bakery for fire hazards. They may be able to see that which you have overlooked. A fire, at any time, is a bad thing, and the aim should be to prevent having one. It is a most profitable sort of prevention.

—‡—‡—‡—

To Study Trade Associations

WASHINGTON.—Appointment of a committee to study and report on the subject of trade associations was announced April 4th by the Chamber of Commerce of the United States. The committee will direct its inquiry with a view to determining in what manner trade associations can render the greatest service to business and the public. It held its first meeting at the headquarters of the Chamber on April 5th.

Members of the committee are:

Philip H. Gadsden, chairman, Philadelphia; president, American Electric Railway Association and formerly member of Federal Electric Railways Commission; vice-president, United Gas Improvement Co.

Thomas S. Adams, New Haven, Conn.; secretary, National Tax Association; professor of political economy, Yale University.

Fred R. Babcock, Pittsburgh; formerly president, National Wholesale Lumber Dealers' Association and of the Pittsburgh Chamber of Commerce; president, Babcock Lumber Company.

Charles J. Brand, Pittsburgh; formerly chairman, Cotton Distribution Board, and chief of Bureau of Markets, Department of Agriculture; vice-president and general manager, United Fruit Growers, Inc.

Henry S. Dennison, Framingham, Mass.; formerly director of planning and statistics, War Industries Board, and president of the Taylor Society; president, Dennison Manufacturing Company.

James R. Maccoll, Pawtucket, R. I.; formerly president, National Cotton Manufacturers' Association and chairman executive committee, World Cotton Conference; treasurer, Lorraine Manufacturing Company.

J. D. H. Morrow, Washington, vice-president, National Coal Association.

Alfred Reeves, New York; secretary, National Automobile Chamber of Commerce.

George Rublee, New York; formerly member of Federal Trade Commission and delegate to Allied Maritime Transport Council.

Variations In Flour

FEW people realize the wide differences that exist in the quality of the numerous kinds of flour on the market. The quality of a flour for bread-making purposes is dependent upon even granulation of the particles of the flour, color, and the quantity and quality of the gluten. The production of flour of even granulation is entirely a milling problem. The color of a flour is influenced by the nature of the wheat used and by the milling process, but it is practically under the control of the miller.

What is known as strength in flour is almost entirely dependent upon the inherent qualities of the wheat; or, in other words, on amount and quality of gluten. As the gluten content of wheat varies very widely in different varieties and in wheat grown in different localities and in different seasons, it is probable that the wheat delivered at the mill differs very widely in the qualities required for the production of a strong flour.

Millers soon become familiar in a general way with the quality of flour that may be made from certain varieties of wheat, or from the wheat grown in different localities, and generally mix or blend the stronger with the weaker wheats, and in this way produce a grade of flour of fairly uniform quality throughout the year. But without accurately conducted tests, experienced as the miller may be in judging flour by feel and by doughing tests, he cannot be absolutely sure of the result.

Owing to differences in climatic conditions, and possibly to other influences, wheat grown in one season may produce flour of a very different quality from that of another. One year the flour may be characterized by low yield of bread; another by poor expansion in the loaf, slow fermentation, etc.—all of which are due to inherent qualities of the wheat and entirely beyond the control of the miller.

Because of these variations in the strength of flour, the problems of the baker are increased. If flour was always of the same nature and strength, the making of bread would be a comparatively simple matter; but, where the flour differs so widely in quality as it is very apt to do, especially at the time of the change from the old to the new wheat, the problem is not a simple one. This is at least partly due to the fact that comparatively little is known about the make-up of the different parts of a flour.

We do know that flour contains carbohydrates, fat, ash materials and gluten, and that we are probably correct in stating that the strength of a flour is in some way dependent upon the quantity and quality of the latter substance; but there are still many points in connection with the gluten and carbohydrate content of a flour that we do not understand. Two fresh, sound flours may be equal in color and in quantity of gluten, and yet act altogether differently when baked.

Some of the causes of this difference may be explained as a result of a chemical examination, but the fact remains that there are many peculiarities about the way a flour "works" that cannot be fully explained by the scientific knowledge possessed today. It may seem strange that a material that is so generally used, and in such enormous quantities, has not been more fully studied; but frequently the most common things around us are, after all, the least understood.

—‡—‡—‡—

Bakers' Lunch Club

MEMBERS of the Allied Trades of the Baking Industry and a number of Chicago bakers recently organized the Bakers' Lunch Club, with headquarters in the Celtic room, Hotel Sherman, Chicago. The idea in forming this club was to have a meeting place for both local and out-of-town bakers and the supply trade, where the midday meal can be taken and trade topics discussed. A table is reserved in the Celtic room each day from 12.30 to 2 P. M., and up to the present the attendance has been good. W. E. Long, of the W. E. Long Co., is president; Arthur Katzinger, Edward Katzinger Co., vice-president; W. D. Bleier, Joseph Baker Sons & Perkins Co., Ltd., secretary, and H. N. Weinstein, Malt-Diastase Co., treasurer.

—‡—‡—‡—

Large profits await the man who can show how to move goods from the producer to the consumer with less effort. The present cost of distribution, especially of food products, is far too high.

—‡—‡—‡—

Figures do not lie, but estimates are often misleading.

It's easier to set a good example than to hatch it out.

Men who ask favors are seldom willing to grant them.

Give some men rope enough and they will rope you in.

Men may be brighter than they look, but they seldom look it.

The photographer who can make unnatural pictures gets the most patronage.

Unless a man has a little egotism in his make-up he'll never amount to much.

Some brands of reform make the world better, and some make it more uncomfortable.

The average man has to sprint occasionally in order to keep up with his running expenses.

The poorer the sermon the longer it is.

Many are called, but few want to get up.

And the easier the job the harder it is to land.

A liberal-minded man isn't always liberal handed.

And one touch of weather makes the whole world talk.

Envy provides the mud that failure throws at success.

There is one bad habit that most of us are addicted to. We talk too much.

Some men would work if given a chance, but there are others who refuse to take chances.

A man never knows what he can do until he tries. But it isn't always expedient to try.

Spring Semester at Siebel Institute

THE general recognition that is extended to the Siebel Institute of Technology as an educational Institution for the baker is perhaps best evidenced by the fact that during January and February, forty-five men and women enrolled for the Special Cake Course and twenty students were enrolled for the Regular Three Months' Course in Baking Technology.

As the list of the members of the Special Cake Course in January has appeared in the February issue, we are confining ourselves to giving below the names of the members of the Regular Three Months' Course and the February Cake Class as follows:

Mrs. Daisy Albrecht,	Rockford, Ill.
Wm. Austermeuble,	Chicago, Ill.
Jerry Blecha,	Chicago, Ill.
Mrs. Anna Buffington,	Crawfordsville, Ind.
Grant A. Butler,	Highland Park, Mich.
C. E. Dahl,	Lansing, Mich.
Geo. David,	Newport, R. I.
Mrs. J. R. Dippel,	Milwaukee, Wis.
Lloyd Dreas,	Allentown, Pa.
Earl Dutro,	Davenport, Iowa.
Fred Emmerling, Jr.	Pekin, Ill.
Mrs. Bert Fisher,	Waukesha, Wis.
Mrs. Floyd Fisher,	Jefferson, Wis.
Erltchoff B. Franson,	Ishpening, Mich.
A. H. Garter	Brooklyn, N. Y.
Ernest Haas,	Liberty, N. Y.
E. R. Hall,	Beaver, Pa.
Earl L. Heller,	Cass City, Mich.
Geo. A. Huffman,	Elkhart, Ind.
R. H. Kaufman,	Lacon, Ill.
Lawrence J. Kilroy,	Chicago, Ill.
Robb H. Kittelberger,	Hot Springs, Ark.
J. J. Kmetz,	Streator, Ill.
August Linn,	E. Cleveland, Ohio.
J. S. Love,	Fresno, Calif.
Josephine B. Mahon,	Evanston, Ill.
H. V. Moore,	Baker, Oregon.
Geo. Mueller,	Ft. Wayne, Ind.
Walter L. Sheets,	Lansing, Mich.
Geo. A. Smith,	Shelby, Mich.
Anna Socatch,	Chicago, Ill.
Norman Spacek,	Cedar Rapids, Mich.
Mrs. John Waters,	Chicago, Ill.
Walter P. Watson,	York, Pa.
Hoy Windsor,	Greentown, Ind.
Stanley S. Wisniewski,	Chicago, Ill.
Mike Yuhas,	Chicago, Ill.

The accompanying view was taken in the model bakery at the Siebel Institute and portrays the February Special Cake Class in session.

—:—:—:—

Sugar Production

The annual report of the American Sugar Refining Co. states that the production of sugar for 1921 in the United States, its possessions and Cuba, to be as follows:

	Long tons
United States Beet	960,000
Louisiana and Texas Cane	157,000
Hawaii	508,000
Porto Rico	437,000
Philippines	252,000
Santo Domingo & Hayti	191,000
Virgin Islands	4,000
Cuba	3,936,000
Total	6,434,000

The production in the above territories in 1898 was only 1,156,000 tons; in 1913 it was 4,288,000 long tons.

Willett & Gray's estimate of the sugar production of the entire world for the current year is 16,488,560 long tons.

The report of the American Sugar Refining Co. states "We have drawn $11,706,689.81 from Sundry Reserves in order to meet losses on Accounts Receivable of $4,206,689.81, and losses on Raw Sugar Purchased in 1920 and received in 1921 of $7,500,000."

TRADE ITEMS

A modern bakery has recently been opened on Eufaula street, Eufaula, Ala.

R. E. Blackwood, Dora, Ala., recently opened a bakery there.

A new bakery is to be opened at Pacific Grove, Calif., by the New England Bakery Co.

D. E. Fauve, proprietor of the French Bakery, Riverbank, Calif., has purchased a lot of ground, upon which he will begin the erection of a two-story modern building, and will conduct a grocery and bakery in the lower floor.

A new sanitary bakery shop has been opened under the name of Gellen's Holland Bakery at 2081 University Ave., Berkeley, Calif., by J. E. Gellen, who formerly conducted a bakery in Oakland Calif. Mr. Gellen will offer a full line of baked goods.

Work and rebuilding the plant of the Sunville Baking Company, Pueblo, Colo., of which C. N. Power is president, is now under way. Extensive improvements will be made, and the plant will be enlarged.

K. D. Wetherby has opened a new modern bakery at Derby, Conn.

Hessler & Damon have purchased the interest and good will of Kelly's "Ye Old Time Bakery" at Fair Haven, Conn., and will continue the business under the name of "Hessler's Old Time Bakery."

Charles O. Gardner, formerly of Jersey City, N. J., has opened up a model bakery in the new Burr Building, Montauk avenue and Bank street, New London, Conn.

Meyer and Wartz, bakers of Norwich, Conn., have incorporated; authorized capital stock of $10,000.

The J. S. Elliott Baking Company, Macon, Ga., have purchased the lot on the corner of Madison Ave. & N. Liberty St., next to Madison Avenue Christian Church.

B. E. Brantley formerly with the Tifton Bakery, Tifton, Ga., has opened a first-class bakery in the Morse Bldg., on Main St., Tifton, to be known as the City Bakery.

The Standard Bakeries have taken over the plant of the Waycross Bakery, Waycross, Ga., and will make alterations and improvements.

The American Bakeries Company has closed a contract for a $100,000 bakery at Macon, Ga. The plant to be located on Plum street between Third street and Broadway. It will have every modern appliance.

Fred Muecke and Howard Redin have opened a new bakery at the corner of E. State and Seventh Sts., Rockford, Ill., and will carry a full line of bakery goods, specializing in fancy pastries and cakes.

The Smith Baking Co., 6848 S. Ashland avenue, Chicago, Ill., has been incorporated with capital of $20,000 by J. T. Smith, A. M. Hoopes and Maurice J. Nathanson.

Carl Holmberg and Josef Carlson, two well-known Rockford, Ill., business men, will open a home bakery at 519 Fourth avenue, Moline, Ill., and baked goods made according to Swedish methods will be a feature of the new shop.

The Brudi National Bakery has been incorporated at Fort Wayne, Ind., with capital of $50,000 by Henry E. Brudi, Martinc C. Brudi, Harry M. Wenker.

The Grecian Bakery has been incorporated at Indiana Harbor, Ind., with capital of $30,000 by John Counelis, James Alexopoulos, Steve Gavros.

The Taggart Baking Company, Indianapolis, Ind., has bought a large tract of land along the Monon railway, between 23rd and 24th Sts., and will later build a large plant for their wholesale business

John Ford, well known baker of Shelbyville, Ind., has purchased the Killoren & Sutherland Bakery on E. Washington Street, and is now ready for business.

The Ideal Baking Company, Terre Haute, Ind., has increased its capital stock from $25,000 to $100,000.

Keanley & Dietzen, Connersville, Ind., are remodelling and enlarging their bakery and installing new ovens, additional capacity being needed to take care of increasing business.

The Tolleston Baking Company, Gary, Ind., have been incorporated with capital of $15,000 by Casimir Pazera, Alex Norvaiah, Joseph Gurskis.

Mitchell & Son have opened a well-equipped bakery and store at Peru, Ind.

William E. Cyr, Van Buren, Me., has bought the bakery business of Christy Brothers.

Ben Michaud is making repairs to the interior of his bakery on Sweden street, Caribou, Me.

G. Fred Eliot and Wendell Higgins recently purchased of Charles F. Ireland his interest in C. F. Ireland & Co., bakers, Dexter, Me. The new firm will be known as the Dexter Baking Company.

L. P. Belanger, Millinocket, Me., will soon open a new bakery on Spruce street.

U. G. Flickett, of Brewer, Me., has purchased of Mr. and Mrs. McIntire the Newport Bakery, Newport, Me., and has taken possession.

L. C. Schneider, 622 Arlington avenue, Baltimore, Md., plans erecting a bakery.

The Delmarvia Baking Company has been organized at Salisbury, Md., by W. P. Hobbs, Dr. J. McFadden Dick, A. M. Walls, O. Straughn Lloyd, John A. Price.

Elmer E. Skedd has purchased the Irving Home Bakery in the Commercial Block, Beverly, Mass., and has taken possession. Mr. Skedd formerly owned the same business.

A new bakery is being established in the Miller Building, Danvers, Mass.

The Bread Shop Company has been incorporated at Rockport, Mass., with capital of $20,000 by Harrison P. Wires and Charles E. Breen, and Frank S. Amaseen.

A permit was recently issued to E. Papy to make alterations and repairs in the bakery at the rear of 257 Park street, Holyoke, Mass., at an estimated cost of $750.

Albert H. Reed, who recently purchased the old Bullock Bakery property at Manchester, Mass., is making extensive repairs and improvements on same, and expects to be ready for business at an early date.

The Bakery Finance Corporation will build a new plant for the Grocers' Bread Company of Springfield, Mass., in that city, to cost about $125,000.

An exclusive bakery is to be opened soon by Miss Juanita Hart in the new building at 3940 Troost avenue, Kansas City, Mo.

Bernard Nuessell, 3728 Fairview avenue, St. Louis, Mo., is planning the erection of a new bakery, but a number of neighbors object, claiming that same interferes with building restrictions. The case will be thrown into court.

The Quality Shop Bakery recently opened a branch store in conjunction with the North Asbury Lunch Shop on Fifth avenue, near Main street, Asbury Park, N. J.

The Hudson Baking Company has been incorporated at

665 Newark avenue, Jersey City, N. J., with capital of $100,000.

Frederick Linderman, formerly connected with the Hot Loaf Baking Co., New York City, has taken over the management of the bakery at 511 Palisade avenue, Jersey City, N. J.

Hausold Brothers, Hoboken, N. J., are planning extensive alterations to their bakery and restaurant at Third and Washington streets. Their branch bakery will be consolidated with the main plant.

Charles Zeh, formerly employed at the Max Linder Bakery, 587 Bergenline avenue, W. Hoboken, N. J., recently purchased same.

Hampel's Bakery, Baldwinsville, N. Y., has been incorporated with capital of $10,000 by A. A. Hampel, F. R. and E. K. Paneltz.

Work has been started on the construction of D. Linehan & Brothers Bakery at Lawton avenue and Sagamore street, Glens Falls, N. Y., which will replace the bakery in Oak street, recently destroyed by fire. The new plant will be modern and up-to-date in every way.

Charles B. Everett, baker and grocer of 255 Wall street, Kingston, N. Y., has purchased of Mannie Morgenstern The Popular System of Bakeries, which include two stores, one on Wall street and the other on Broadway and Cedar street.

Construction has been begun on the new plant of the General Baking Company, which occupies almost the entire block on 144th street between Walton and Gerard avenues, Bronx, Greater New York. This will make the sixth plant of the company in the Metropolitan district.

L. W. Comstock, who has conducted a confectionery and bakery business at 201 Irving avenue, Port Chester, N. Y., for several years, has removed the same to his new store at the corner of Westchester avenue and Grove street, Port Chester, N. Y.

J. S. Robinson and Don Ledford will shortly open a bakery at Belmont, N. C. A ten-pound cake is to be awarded to one of the ladies of the community who selects the most appropriate name for the new bakery.

E. M. Raper's new bakery, which is to be on Martin street, Elizabeth City, N. C., will be called the Star.

Harold J. Hoppstetter, formerly of the Hoppstetter Baking Company, Zanesville, Ohio, has purchased a large four-oven bakery in the East End of Cleveland, and has taken charge.

The Standard Baking Company has been incorporated at Cleveland, Ohio, with capital of $5,000 by A. W. Hatman, D. F. Klein, E. M. Chaloupka, I. F. Werley and Evelyn M. Goldsmith.

It is reported that the Ward Baking Company will build an immense new plant at Cleveland, Ohio, to cost about $1,500,000, and to be located on 2½ acres between Perkins and Windsor avenues, from E. 40th street to the Pennsylvania Railroad tracks.

The Hull & Fought Baking Company of Toledo, Ohio, has been incorporated, with capital of $10,000, by Robert Hull, Burton E. Fought, George W. Pearson, Martha Enright and Dennis N. Maloney.

Edgar M. Gambill and Henry Walter have bought the City Bakery at Skiatook, Okla., from C. A. Benedick.

Repairs will be started at once on Pace Brothers Bakery, 16 River street, Bradford, Pa., which was recently damaged by fire at a loss of $1,000.

A new bakery will be erected on Main street, Fogelsville, Pa., by George Peters, of Allentown, Pa., and Oscar Werley, of Fogelsville.

Excavation work has been started for the erection of the new one-story brick bakery on W. Walnut street, Hazleton, Pa., for Jacob Block, formerly of Shenandoah, Pa.

G. W. Williams, who for several years successfully operated the Nu Bakery in West Hazleton, Pa., recently became the owner of the property where same is located, and plans

to make considerable improvements and to increase the capacity of the bakery.

A five-story manufacturing building will be built by the Tasty Baking Company at Hunting Park avenue and McMichael street, Philadelphia, Pa., at a cost of $150,000.

W. T. Eagan and G. B. McGlasson, formerly with the Bake-Rite Bakery, have opened the New Mark Bakery at 902 Houston street, Shamokin, Pa.

Articles of incorporation have been filed by the Rhode Island Biscuit Company, Providence, R. I., with capital of $150,000. The incorporators are: Charles W. Proctor, James C. McDonald and Fred S. Stuart.

The Greenville Bakery Company has been incorporated at Greenville, S. C., with capital of $50,000 by W. J. Cole and H. L. Eaton.

The Walker Bread Company has been incorporated at Fort Worth, Texas, with capital of $155,000 by H. C. Walker, J. H. Wright and L. H. Wright.

Millie J. Drury, of the Home Bakery, Williamstown, Vt., has bought the stock and good will of same, and will continue the business.

The Princeton Home Bakery has been incorporated at Princeton, W. Va., with capital stock of $10,000 by C. D. Radford, W. L. Ryan, A. L. Bowling, J. H. Gadd, L. G. Bowling.

The Washington Bakeries has been incorporated at Seattle, Wash., with capital of $300,000 by Moritz Thomsen, G. E. Rasmussen, Harry Mosler, D. E. Skinner and G. W. Skinner.

Theodore Anderson, Andrew Fotopolus and George Kiskaris have organized a corporation which is to engage in the bakery business in South Cheyenne, Wyo.

Frank Saxonmeyer and son, Jack Saxonmeyer, of Saugatuck, Conn., are to begin a bakery business in the Saxonmeyer Block in Riverside avenue, near Bridge street, Saugatuck, Conn.

Wm. B. Drexler, the Main Street baker, Ansonia, Conn., has opened a wholesale bakery on Lester Street, which will be conducted in connection with the retail bakery.

The Fowler Bakery Shop is soon to open in Fairfield, Conn.

Raymond Copsy, Ozark, Ark., has bought the Sanitary Bakery from Arrington & Jeffers.

N. J. Ooury, Jacksonville, Fla., is installing a bakery in addition to his grocery, which is to be located on Hendricks Avenue in the rear of the grocery.

H. C. Cummock and George Kellogg have purchased the business interest of Harry Morrow in the Weiser Bakery, Weiser, Idaho.

B. E. Allen recently purchased the Thomas Bakery at DeWitt, Iowa, and has taken possession.

—‡—‡—‡—

Nebraska Bread Law Contest

A BRIEF of 138 pages has been filed with the supreme court of Nebraska by bakers seeking to prevent operation of the standard weight bread law passed by the last legislature. Hearing will be held April 17th.

The first hearing was in the district court at Lincoln, where the law was upheld and an appeal taken to the supreme court.

State Representative E. A. Smith, author of the bread bill, stated that recent tests made by him in Omaha showed nearly all bakers observing standard weights, notwithstanding their resistance of the new law.

The law requires weights of half pound, one pound and one and a half pounds or units thereof.

"I wish I knew of some institution that could help me analyze my market; study my competition, my equipment and my organization, and tell me what I must do to speed up my growth and stabilize my business."

THERE IS one concern that is organized to render such a service to baking institutions— the W. E. Long Co.

For 22 years, this organization of specialists has been counselling and serving many of the leading bakers of the country. Through constant study of every problem connected with bakery management and operation, a staff of experts has been developed, and consistently trained in the particular lines of work.

Here is offered expert counsel on questions of policy; the establishment of correct operating principles in all departments; the instruction of your shop superintendent in the latest technical phases of baking and correct shop practice; the training of your accountant in right methods of accounting and cost-finding; the organization and training of your sales force and the planning and handling of your advertising.

If you are interested in such a service, we shall be pleased to arrange an interview with you and go further into detail.

THE W. E. LONG CO.

Scientific Service for Bakers

Advertising — Accounting — Laboratory — Purchasing

155 No. Clark St., Chicago, Illinois

Baking Trade Organizations--National, Sectional and State

THE following list of National, State and Group State Associations of bakers has been carefully compiled and corrected to February, 1922, as far as possible. We would appreciate your calling to our attention any errors or omissions. Trade Associations are valuable to their membership in proportion to the support given them and to the use made of them. Keep in touch with your Association, the Secretary of which will willingly reply to all requests for information. You are requested to co-operate.

AMERICAN BAKERS' ASSOCIATION
President—(Vacant.)
1st Vice-President—A. L. Taggart, Indianapolis. .
2nd Vice-President—Harry D. Tipton, New York.
Treasurer—H. W. Zinsmaster, Duluth, Minn.
Business Manager and Secretary—Dr. H. E. Barnard, 1135 Fullerton Ave., Chicago.

RETAIL BAKERS' ASSOCIATION OF AMERICA
President—Eugene Lipp, Chicago.
1st Vice-President—Jos. Poehlmann, Milwaukee.
2nd Vice-President—J. J. Machetchek, St. Louis.
3rd Vice-President—Chas. Schulz, Los Angeles.
Treasurer—George Geissler, Joliet, Ill.
Recording Secretary—L. F. W. Meese, Minneapolis.
Corresponding Secretary—John M. Hartley, Chicago.

COUNCIL OF BAKING AND AFFILIATED ORGANIZATIONS
Composed of Presidents and Secretaries of the
American Bakers' Association.
Retail Bakers' Association of America.
Bakery Equipment Mfrs.' Association.
Allied Trades of the Baking Industry.
National Association of Bakers' Supply Houses.
Millers' National Federation.
Flour Clubs.
President—B. B. Grenell, 1017 W. Washington St., Chicago.

ALLIED TRADES OF THE BAKING INDUSTRY
President—Wm. Evans, Chicago.
Vice-President—John W. Burns, Louisville.
Secretary-Treasurer—C. H. Van Cleef, 419 Plum St., Cincinnati.

MIDWEST BAKERS' ASSOCIATION
President—Harry E. Howland, Fargo, North Dakota.
Vice-President—Sidney Drew, Sioux Falls, South Dakota.
Treasurer—H. K. Geist, Grand Forks, South Dakota.

NEW ENGLAND BAKERS' ASSOCIATION
(Conn., Maine, Mass., N. H., R. I., Vt.)
President—H. V. Keiser, Springfield, Mass.
General Vice-President—Frank Eighme, Providence, R. I.
Treasurer—Arthur G. Swanson, Worcester, Mass.
Secretary—W. H. Dietz, Mass. Baking Co., Hartford, Conn.

PACIFIC NORTHWEST ASSOCIATION
(Wash., Oreg., Mont., Idaho, Brit. Col.)
President—Wm. P. Matthael, Tacoma, Wash.
Treasurer—N. F. Burger, Billings, Mont.
Secretary—Mortimer Miller, Chamber of Commerce Bldg., Tacoma, Wash.

PENINSULA BAKERS' ASSOCIATION
(Delaware and Eastern Shore of Maryland and Virginia)
President—C. W. Phillips, Salisbury, Md.
Vice-President—Joseph Schaeffer, Cape Charles, Va.
Treasurer—A. L. Hudson, Georgetown, Del.
Secretary—R. L. Phillips, Cambridge, Md.

POTOMAC STATES ASSOCIATION
(Va., W. Va., Md., N. C., D. C.)
President—T. F. Bayha, Wheeling, W. Va.
Vice-President—Frank E. Smith, Cumberland, Md.
Treasurer—J. J. Mattern, Richmond, Va.
Secretary—Glenn O. Garber, Market St. at 5th, Frederick, Md.

RETAIL BAKERS' ASSN. OF THE EASTERN STATES
President—Max Strasser, New York.
1st Vice-President—Leonhard Metz, Newark, N. J.
2nd Vice-President—Joseph Schaefer, Philadelphia, Pa

Treasurer—Martin Keidel, Brooklyn, N. Y.
Secretary—Wm. Cordes, Jersey City, N. J.

SOUTHEASTERN ASSOCIATION
President—J. H. Quint, Savannah, Ga.
Vice-President—B. C. Dorsey, Jacksonville, Fla.
Treasurer—J. B. Everidge, Columbus, Ga.
Secretary—Harry Crawford, Mobile, Ala.

TRANS-MISSISSIPPI ASSOCIATION
(Iowa, Kansas, Missouri, Nebraska.)
President—Charles W. Ortman, Omaha, Neb.
Vice-President—John Hasten, Springfield, Mo.
2nd Vice-President—C. F. Altstadt, Waterloo, Iowa.
Treasurer—Elmer Zimmerman, Hannibal, Mo.
Secretary—T. F. Naughtin, 913 S. 13th St., Omaha, Neb.

BAKERY EQUIPMENT MFRS. ASSOCIATION
President—Geo. E. Dean, Albion, Mich.
Vice-President—E. L. Parsons, Belleville, N. J.
Treasurer—Jos. C. Emley, New York City.
Secretary—Bruce M. Warner, Schofield Bldg., Cleveland, Ohio.

PIE BAKERS' ASSOCIATION
Chairman—Jos. C. Hutchison, Philadelphia.
Vice-Chairman—Albert Schulteis, Washington, D. C.
Secretary-Treasurer—W. J. Regan, 3240 Walnut St., Philadelphia.

PROGRESSIVE MASTER BAKERS
President—J. W. Lloyd, Martinsburg, W. Va.
Vice-President—Frank Smith, Cumberland, Md.

BREAD AND CAKE MANUFACTURERS' ASSOCIATION OF CANADA
President—Dent Harrison, Montreal.
1st Vice-President—Jas. MacIntosh, St. Catharines.
2nd Vice-President—Wm. Strachan, Montreal.
Secretary—H. E. Trent, 208 Simcoe St., Toronto.
Treasurer—A. W. Carrick, Toronto.

ALABAMA
President—T. A. McGough, Birmingham.
Vice-President—Gordon Smith, Mobile.
Treasurer—James Toole, Montgomery.
Secretary—O. L. Cook, Birmingham.

ARKANSAS
President—George Reigler, Little Rock.
Vice-President—J. H. Fisher, Blytheville.
Treasurer—T. W. Phillips, Hot Springs.
Secretary—P. F. Lenea, Little Rock.

CALIFORNIA
President—G. W. Banzhaf, San Francisco.
Secretary—W. M. Foley, 523 Merc. Exchange Bldg., San Francisco.

SOUTH CALIFORNIA (Wholesale)
President—T. J. Van de Kamp, Los Angeles.
Vice-President—Albert Gordon, Los Angeles.
Treasurer—C. P. Brower, Los Angeles.
Secretary-Chairman—Wm. Francis Ireland, 314 Coulter Bldg., Los Angeles.

SOUTH CALIFORNIA (Retail)
President—Raymond Keyser, Los Angeles.
Vice-President—Richard T. Walsh.
Treasurer—Adam Kullman.
Secretary-Chairman—Wm. Francis Ireland, 314 Coulter Bldg., Los Angeles.

COLORADO
President—L. D. Ward, Denver.
Vice-President—P. C. Johnson, Boulder.
Treasurer—E. R. Tabor, Colorado Springs.
Secretary—F. E. Coddington, Denver.

CONNECTICUT
President—W. J. Travis, Bridgeport.
Vice-President—Henry Brueggerstrat, Hartford.
Treasurer—B. L. Marsh, Stamford.
Secretary—H. L. Pardee, 149 York St., New Haven.

FLORIDA
President—John Seybold, Miami.
Vice-President—Frank H. Allen, Tampa.
Treasurer—J. B. Arnot, Jacksonville.
Secretary—J. W. Carpenter, Jacksonville (Box 97).

GEORGIA
President—J. B. Quint, Savannah.
Vice-President—George Mau, Atlanta.
Treasurer—J. B. Everidge, Columbus.
Secretary—F. R. Nugent, 312 W. Bryan St., Savannah.

IDAHO
President—S. J. Keyes, Boise.
Secretary-Treasurer—A. J. Stephan, 922 Front St., Boise.

ILLINOIS
President—Oscar Strand, Monmouth,
　　　sident—Eugene Lipp, Chicago.
Treasurer—George Geissler, Joliet.
Secretary—Geo. M. Chapman, 618 West Lake St., Chicago.

SOUTHERN ILLINOIS
President—J. G. Stager, Cairo.
Vice-President—F. H. Opdyke, West Frankfort.
Treasurer—Frank Theobald, DuQuoin.
Secretary—D. P. Young, Box 157, Carbondale.

INDIANA
President—Eugene K. Quigg, Richmond.
Vice-President—A. W. Wilkinson, Rushville.
Treasurer—J. A. Dietzen, Franklin.
Secretary-Manager—C. P. Ehlers, 617 Merchants Bank Bldg.,
　　Indianapolis.

IOWA
President—Guy Stark, Leon.
Vice-President—James Johnson, Boone.
Treasurer—J. F. Brems, Cedar Rapids.
Secretary—C. O. Schweickhardt, Burlington.
Educational Secretary—R. H. Holbrook, Ames.

KANSAS
President—A. J. Cripe, Hutchison.
Vice-President—A. Hyle, Wakeeney.
Treasurer—A. E. Jenkins, Salina.
Secretary—A. N. Dilley, Jr., Council Grove.

KENTUCKY
President—J. Nill, Louisville.
Vice-President—A. Roth, Newport.
Treasurer—W. L. Traxel, Maysville.

Secretary—J. H. Stehlin, 1455 S. Preston St., Louisville.

LOUISIANA
President—Wm. Sehrt, New Orleans.
Vice-President—A. H. Vories, New Orleans.
Treasurer—Lars Jensen, New Orleans.
Secretary—Leon Salmon, 4914 Prytania St., New Orleans.

MARYLAND
President—George E. Mubly, Baltimore.
Vice-President—Chas. W. Rheinhardt, Baltimore.
Treasurer—Adolph H. Schlag, Baltimore.
Secretary—H. C. Benner, 944 S. Clinton St., Baltimore.

MASSACHUSETTS
President—A. H. Hathaway, Cambridge.
Vice-President—H. P. Dion, New Bedford.
Treasurer—Geo. A. Sanderson, Charlestown.
Secretary—C. A. Merry, Boston.

Treasurer—C. H. Bailey, Minneapolis.
Secretary—R. T. Beatty, Miller Bldg., Minneapolis.

MINNESOTA (Retail)
President—Charles Holz, St. Paul.
Vice-President—E. A. Swanson, Glenwood.
Secretary—E. C. Jerabek, St. Paul.
Secretary—L. F. W. Meese, 324 E. Hennepin Ave., Minneapolis.

MISSISSIPPI
President—Ben. J. Pollman, Meridian.
Vice-President—Harold Martin, Gulfport.
Treasurer—Miss Minna Wolff, Meridian.
Secretary—Thula Allen, Meridian.

MISSOURI
President—J. D. Bondurant, Kirkville.
Treasurer—H. C. Strieder, St. Louis.
Secretary—Otis B. Durbin, 1012 Baltimore Ave., Kansas City.

SOUTHEAST MISSOURI
President—E. F. Schorle.
Vice-President—G. H. Arthur.
Treasurer—Carl Bauer, Cape Girardeau.
Secretary—Max J. Wielpuetz, Cape Girardeau.

MONTANA
President—Eddie O'Connell, Helena.
Vice-President—Dave Nichols, Billings.
Treasurer—W. C. Schustrom, Livingston.
Secretary—R. W. Osenbrug, 107 Olympia St., Butte.

NEBRASKA
President—C. E. Masterman, Lincoln.
Vice-President—Otto Wagner, Omaha.
Treasurer—Charles W. Ortman, Omaha.
Secretary—E. B. Ransom, 20th and Cuming Sts., Omaha.

NEW HAMPSHIRE
President—Andrew Weber, Laconia.
Vice-President—J. J. Harrington, Littleton.
Treasurer—O. Cote, Sr., Manchester.
Secretary—L. S. Bergeron, Rochester.

NEW JERSEY
President—Richard F. Mayer, Paterson.
Vice-President—Jesse N. Barber, Trenton.
Treasurer—Richard H. Hanschka, Newark.
Secretary—Louis Rose, 26 Lombardy St., Newark.

NEW JERSEY BAKERS' BOARD OF TRADE, INC.
President—Leonhard, Metz, Newark.
Vice-President—A. Mulley, Paterson.
Treasurer—Wm. Cordes, Jersey City.
Secretary—A. Lang, 106 Lillie St., Newark.

NEW YORK (Wholesale)
President—Harry D. Tipton, New York City.
Vice-President—E. St. John Taylor, New York City.
Treasurer—F. W. Dawdy, Elmira.
Secretary—Chas. A. Hagaman, 883 Madison Ave., Albany.

NEW YORK
President—Max. Strasser, New York.
1st Vice-President—Chas. G. Spiedel, Buffalo.
2nd Vice-President—John Ramsey, Syracuse.
3rd Vice-President—Carl Blutau, Rochester.
Treasurer—Julius Zink, New York City.
Secretary—Rudolph Zink, 630 Courtland Ave., New York City.

NORTH CAROLINA
President—W. J. O'Brien, Winston-Salem

SUPERIOR
Double Chamber Gas Oven

THIS Oven can be operated practically as cheap as a coal or coke Oven, and is more simple to operate. All you have to do is to turn on the gas—no dirt, ashes, or coal pile. With this Oven you have a positive guarantee against fuel shortage.

In the top of the Oven there is a flue running completely around the Oven. This flue gives just enough draft to properly circulate the heat at all times.

Each baking chamber is equipped with two tile hearths and side shields, also a heavy tile bed shelf below the first baking shelf, which insures an even baking temperature on both shelves. Over the burners in the base of the Oven are heavy tile baffle

plates which, when once hot, give off a solid baking heat. It requires about forty-five minutes to get the Oven to a baking heat from the cold Oven, but you can bake for an hour, to an hour and a half, after the gas is turned off.

The charging doors in front are equipped with heavy polished re-inforced glass, which makes it unnecessary to open the door to ascertain the condition of the product in the Oven. This is a very important feature, as the baker can see his goods in the Oven from any part of the bakery without going to the Oven and opening the door. **Write or inquire for further information.**

Made in five sizes to meet your requirements.

SUPERIOR OVEN CO.

LEITER BLDG.

Western Office		Eastern Office
SOUTHERN CALIF. SUPPLY CO.	**CHICAGO, ILL.**	137 HUDSON ST.
Los Angeles, Calif.		New York

OREGON

President—W. B. Heusner, Portland.
Vice-Presidents—E. F. Davidson, Harry Korn, Bert Frans, A. Danlen.
Treasurer—H. F. Rittman, Portland.
Secretary—Burt Holcomb, Portland.

PENNSYLVANIA

President—L. J. Schumaker, Philadelphia.
Vice-President—R. K. Stritzinger, Norristown.
Treasurer—Geo. W. Fisher, Huntingdon.
Secretary—C. C. Latus, 623 Pittsburgh Life Bldg., Pittsburgh.

WESTERN PENNSYLVANIA

President—Horace W. Crider, Homestead.
Vice-President—Ernest R. Braun, Pittsburgh.
Treasurer—Sam'l S. Waters, Pittsburgh.
Secretary—C. C. Latus, Pittsburgh Life Building, Pittsburgh.

RHODE ISLAND

President—E. J. Arnold, Saylesville.
Vice-President—Daniel F. Joy, Providence.
Treasurer—A. H. Liddle, Providence.
Financial Secretary—F. W. Palmer, Providence.
Secretary—R. C. Carr, Providence (Box 237).

SOUTH CAROLINA

President—A. Gellfuss, Spartanburg.
Vice-President—W. J. Condon, Jr., Charleston.
Treasurer—A. Schnell, Charleston.
Secretary—J. A. Cureton, Grenville.

SOUTH DAKOTA

President—William Owsley, Aberdeen.
Vice-President—F. P. Drew, Chamberlain.
Secretary-Treasurer—C. W. Anthony, Sioux Falls.

TENNESSEE

President—Chas. Evers, Nashville.
Vice-President—J. A. Winkelman, Memphis.
Treasurer—Charles Mitchell, Nashville.
Secretary—R. W. McFadden, Nashville.

EASTERN TENNESSEE

President—J. L. Skelton, Morristown.
Secretary—John P. Kern, Knoxville.

TEXAS

President—Henry C. Walker, Fort Worth.
Vice-President—Julius Schepps, Dallas.
Treasurer—Joe Schepps, Dallas.
Secretary—Fred W. Pflughaupt, 507 Hoefgen Ave., San Antonio.

WASHINGTON

President—W. C. Hutchinson, Seattle.
Vice-President—Leo Loevinstein, Yakima.
Secretary-Treasurer—Mortimer Miller, Chamber of Commerce Bldg., Tacoma.

WEST VIRGINIA

President—H. J. Sayer, Huntington.
Vice-President—S. W. Helner, Huntington.
Secretary-Treasurer—P. C. Beseler Huntington.

WISCONSIN

President—Joe Poehlmann, Milwaukee.
Vice-President—C. L. Sorensen, Racine.
Treasurer—J. T. Fischer, North Milwaukee.
Secretary—Joseph Pinzer, 2425 Hadley St., Milwaukee.

—❖—❖—❖—

Frangipanni means broken bread. The Frangipannies were famous nobles in Rome in the eleventh and twelfth centuries. There is a legend that this family was ennobled by a Pope in reward for the lavish generosity with which its founder distributed food in a great famine. Among the Italians and French the word is used as a designation for a kind of confectionery—this luxury is attributed to one of the Frangipanni nobles.

Keep Track of Your Business

THE National Association of Credit Men sometime since issued a circular in which were listed a number of questions designed to encourage merchants and manufacturers to keep track of their business expenses. The circular stated that he who could answer all the following questions the way they should be answered has a satisfactory working knowledge of his business.

Read these questions over carefully, and see if you can qualify. They are as follows:

Do your accounts show your total cash sales and total charge sales separately, yearly or monthly?

Do you keep a "purchase account" which shows you the total amount of goods bought?

Do you discount your bills?

Do you know how much money you save yearly by discounting your bills?

How often do you take stock?

Do you make allowance in your inventory for depreciation, or dead stock?

Do you make allowance for depreciation of store fixtures, horses and wagons, tools, etc.?

Do you figure it at cost or selling price?

Do you consider the stock you carry too large or too small for the amount of business you are doing?

Do you carry fire insurance?

Are your stock and fixtures fully covered?

Do you know the percentage of your gross profit to total sales?

Do you know the percentage of your expenses to the total sales?

Do you keep an exact account of all your expenses?

Into how many separate accounts are your expenses subdivided?

Do you own the building in which you do business?

If so, do you charge a fixed amount for rent as an expense?

Do you charge your own salary as an expense?

If not, do you charge all your living expenses to the business?

Do you provide for losses for "bad accounts" in fixing your selling price?

Are the goods taken out of your store for your family use charged as a business expense?

How often do you make up a "profit and loss" statement?

Do you know the total amount that you owe at least once a month?

Do you know the total amount that is due you at least once a month?

—❖—❖—❖—

"Too many men with small businesses sit around envying men with big businesses, wishing they could sit at a mahogany desk and rest their feet on an inch-thick rug, forgetting that the prosperity of every business, large or small, rests on the activity of individual salesmen who are out turning the door-knobs of prospective customers."

The use of BUDWEISER Barley Malt means a better loaf of bread at a lower cost, for *pure* malt gives a healthier fermentation by energizing the yeasts, and its maltose content reduces the quantities of sugar necessary. Full development of gluten means greater nutrition value.

BUDWEISER Barley Malt—100% pure—develops a bigger volume with a finer texture and a better flavor—and the richer appearance and golden bloom of the loaf will mean a steadily growing volume of business.

Fresh supplies are constantly available from Anheuser-Busch distributors without the need of a contract.

ANHEUSER-BUSCH SALES CORPORATION
ST. LOUIS, U. S. A.

Operation Problems

Paper by Gerald Billings, Read at Convention of Ohio Association

IT is not often that the production manager is fortunate enough to get in on the building of a baking plant and have it designed around the operation, so the problem is how to fit the operation to the plant. A survey of conditions must be made.

The first detail to consider is the sales demands. Often they are so incompatible with the economical operation of the plant, that they seriously handicap the production manager in turning out his product on time. Often they are so incompatible with the economical

In some of the plants that I have been privileged to inspect I found that the salesmen are permitted to order their product as they would a sandwich at the corner restaurant. Little do they consider the time it takes to mature a dough, bake-off, cool, check, and deliver—a matter of six and one-half to eight hours. It takes time to bake the first loaf as well as the last. And the difference in time between the first and the last baking may be eight hours, twelve hours, or eighteen hours.

The production man must get his sales demands in advance, preferably twenty-four hours in advance. Then he can schedule the flow of raw material and meet the demand of the full capacity of his baking units.

The ovens collectively will bake a given amount, allowing the difference in large and small pan bread, hearth breads, etc. The capacity of each unit must be determined on the basis of quantity per hour, so that the production manager can figure an average tonnage per hour. When this is determined and when the mixing, dividing, moulding and panning equipment is checked, the time for delivery can be divided and the size of doughs designed to meet the schedule.

After these details are recorded a time study is put on each operation to get the required capacity per man.

ACTUAL TIME AND MOTION TIME

Two times must be taken. One is termed "Actual" and the other "Motion" time.

To take an actual time, time the operator over quite a long period on the actual operation. This does not include delays, but should include all time which he actually puts on the operation. Never ascertain an actual time for less than 100 counts, and 500 counts are better.

Motion time is the time required to perform the actual operation under good conditions. If the motion time is taken and the operating conditions are not good, disregard the time which you obtain. To get a motion time to put on the recording sheet it will be necessary to take an average of at least ten motion times taken by the watch under good operating conditions.

The success and corrections of the data depends entirely upon the close attention and judgment of the man using the watch and his attending strictly to business when he is getting his times.

RECORDING TIME

In recording the times obtained to the sheet, all time should be figured to a basis of 1,000 loaves and recorded as such on the sheet. The times in the detail note book should be left exactly as set down when taken from the watch.

The note book should be numbered consecutively by pages, beginning with the first book and carrying through as many books and as many pages as are required. The front of the page should be used for getting down the actual data taken from the watch and to set down data figures ready to post to the data sheet. All figuring and scribbling will be done on the back of the sheet. A separate sheet will be used for each study taken.

In recording data obtained on the data sheet the entries will be made of the actual and motion times under the proper number, the names or numbers of the man on whom the study is taken and the rate at which he is working. It would be well to list all men on the payroll and assign to each a number and use this number in referring to the men in this work.

A skeleton including all items which are manufactured and showing all operations on each item should be made on the data sheets and the data sheets bound together in a book. This will then form an outline showing what data must be obtained and will serve as a working basis.

This operation is controlled by the actual time of the divider instead of the action of the man. In timing all other operations the action of the man only will be timed. Take notice that in timing the operation of mixing, removing the mixer and placing in the trough, only the time actually used by the man is required, and not that of the machine.

OPERATIONS ON A DOUGH

1. Preparing mix.
2. Mixing, removing from mixer and placing in trough.
3. Place in divider, scaling and placing in proof box controlled by machine.
4. Placing in moulder.
5. Placing in pans and pans to rack.
6. Placing in peel.
7. Peeling into oven.
8. Peeling out of oven.
9. Dumping pans and placing pans on truck.
10. Placing bread on rack.

Wrapping department:
1. Removing from rack to bench.
2. Wrapping.
3. Placing to rack or box.

FILLING OUT TIME SHEETS

In making out this skeleton and filling time sheets in the book, first comes the item which the sheet is supposed to represent. Then number all the sheets of the item that may be used consecutively, beginning with one.

The Sévigné Wrapping Machine

Your Hunt
For
Machine Supremacy
Will End With
SÉVIGNÉ

National Bread Wrapping Machine Co.
Nashua, N. H.

For example, Betsy Ross Bread may require five sheets or more. Show items on five sheets, Betsy Ross Bread, Number 1, 2, 3, 4 and 5. Place the sheets consecutively according as the successive operations follow one another.

The operations performed in producing each item of manufacture will be determined. A series of stop-watch studies will be taken on each operation. In order to get a fair figure several studies will be taken on each man. This will give a number of studies on each operation. In order to get a fair figure, studies on the same operation will be taken on several different men, likewise several studies will be taken on each man.

This will give a number of studies on each operation, taking into consideration the productive abilities of the different men and the variation in ability of each man.

Time studies will consist of two parts: A study of each individual motion making up the operation and a study of the complete time in making the operation a number of times in succession.

The average motion time and the least motion time should in each case be determined and a total operation time arrived at by taking the difference between the sum of the average and the least time for each elemental operation. This synthetic operation time should be compared with the studies made by timing the complete operation repeated a number of times.

A comparison will show the synthetic time to be less than the operation time of the complete cycle of motions. Dividing the synthetic time by the time of the cycle of motions will give the efficiency of the man at the time the studies were taken. If this efficiency is very low, there is something the matter with either the man, the condition under which the operation is being performed, or with the motion studies.

A low efficiency may show that the operator was obliged to wait between the various motions or between the various successive operations; because of the speed equipment or because he was obliged to wait for another employee.

Where the low efficiency is the result of conditions beyond control of the operator and where it is not practical to change the conditions, it will be necessary to use as a basic time the operation of the complete cycle of motion. In all other cases the synthetic or motion time should be taken as the basic time. The cycle times are always a good check on the accuracy of the motion and very often the judgment of the time-study man will

Up to this point, if the above has been carried out there will be several studies per thousand units on each of several men for the operation and differing somewhat. At this point the productive abilities of the various men being compared becomes a factor in further determination of the rate. The time-study man must determine from his experience in watching the different men on the operation and in comparing the different men on different operations which men have a productive ability of 100 per cent. and which are below and above that figure. The man 100 per cent. efficient is usually taken as the steady, conscientious, but not necessarily fast worker.

Comparing the other men with this one it can be determined whether they are over or under 100 per cent. productive ability. If the operation study man has before him times per thousand units, taken on four different men on the same operation, he can determine from his observation and from the results of the four studies which of the four men is the 100 per cent. man, or if all of them are above 100 per cent., he can determine how much they should be reduced to get 100 per cent. standard.

To get uniform results it is necessary to have very definite control on all mechanical equipment, human efforts required, temperatures, analysis of raw material, and the ability to interpret analysis, proof box control, sufficient pans for turn over, oven heat control and well-defined standard shops practice. This combination in connection with energetic supervision on the part of production manager and foreman insures uniform product.

There are three factors entering into the formation of a successful bakery organization. Administrative, manufacturing and sales. These three factors are closely allied and harmony must prevail to insure perfect execution.

There is a definite, fixed plan for each department. The detail of the manufacturing department can be worked out as follows: A man makes two distinct steps to reach a given end. First, he acquires knowledge concerning the thing in question. Second, he applies that knowledge to the accomplishment of some definite purpose.

The aim of organization literally defined is: First, to systematically unite individuals into a body purposed to work together for a common end. Second, to unite in reciprocal and concrete relations and duties. Third, to

ends, just as a human body has, and it is governed by similar conditions. It must also be directed by a specific intelligence and must have internal avenues of correspondence to keep it alive, and, like a living organism, must adhere to the eternal economy of things and show a profit by its activities or it cannot progress.

Departmental division is a necessity oftentimes not well understood, and means much more than a mere division of authority. It is necessitated by the fact that different methods of procedure in the manufacture and marketing of goods require widely varying experience with the authorities that govern them so that the division of a business into departments is controlled by two elements: viz., the character of the labor it is necessary to employ; and the character of the material processed. Therefore, in order to know the proper division of a manufacturing business into departments, it is necessary to first trace the essential processing of material from a raw state to a finished product by progressive steps, and then lay off the departments along this line of travel in accordance with its differences in the elements above designated.

THE PRODUCTION MANAGER

The office of production manager has a path of authority extending under the general manager as far as the manufacturing section goes, and sub-authorities under him of chief engineer, assistant superintendent, the chief shop clerk, under whom the business is again divided into sub-authorities as the occasion demands.

THE SUPERINTENDENT

The superintendent, under the direction of the production manager, has full charge of the manufacturing end of the business. Independent of the regular workings and the department organization of the factory, the superintendent has directly under his charge all time-keeping and all inspection of work in the factory, which is in no way under the charge of any department or foreman of departments.

The superintendent is responsible for all requisitions made for material, machinery and supplies, for all requirements and requisitions for the arrangement of allotment of work throughout the factory and their execution on time in accordance with the production manager's orders.

He has sole responsibility for the class, character and quality of labor employed throughout the factory and has the discipline under which this labor is maintained. He has full and complete authority in the appointment of all foremen and assistants employed under his charge.

As the superintendent is the connecting link between the manufacturing department and the commercial end of the business, he should be prepared for conference on any matter pertaining to the whole business at a moment's notice. To do this his office must be constantly posted and up-to-date regarding all conditions of materials, supplies and work under his charge in order that he may estimate the raw material and time required to execute any order.

THE ENGINEER

The engineer, under the direction of the superintendent, is responsible for the condition, operation and maintenance of all primary power units, such as boilers, pumps, engines and all their auxiliary machinery, all motors used for driving apparatus and machinery throughout the factory. He has charge of all firemen, oilers and watchmen, and is responsible for all plumbing and sanitary arrangements. He is responsible for all supplies relative to the units under his charge, such as fuel, oil and waste, and make requisition on the superintendent for same. The engineer is responsible for the appurtenances used for the moving of machines around the factory, looks into the condition of trucks, bread racks, etc.

THE CHIEF FACTORY CLERK

The chief factory clerk acts as receiving clerk, under the direction of the superintendent, and has charge of all goods received by the factory, must check over entire receipts in detail and hand memo of receipts to superintendent. The latter immediately forwards them to the main office for checking against original invoice accompanying them.

Under no circumstances is the consigner's invoice to be given to the receiving clerk to check from this, as this too often leads to check marks on the invoice without a count of goods.

The chief factory clerk is responsible to the superintendent for a correct billing of all manufactured goods. This clerk is independent of the factory count.

THE SHIPPING CLERK

The shipping clerk, under the direction of the superintendent, has charge of all shipments made by the factory and is responsible for the direct acquisition of all data relative to means of transportation. He is responsible for all material used for packing purposes and making of shipments and must render requisitions for them to the superintendent. He is held responsible for all errors in shipments and for all delays after goods have been delivered to his department. All shipments must be made in accordance with written instructions and requisitions, and must be correctly written on shipping clerk's name. The shipping clerk has no authority outside of his department.

The checkers work under the direction of the chief clerk. Their duties are counting and assorting.

THE SHOP FOREMAN

The shop foreman acts as assistant superintendent. To him is assigned detail of the shop work, under the direction of the superintendent. He prepares the programs for the layout of shop work and looks after all details pertaining to process work, spots his labor, and is responsible to the superintendent for a proper check on raw materials used, as well as check on the finished product. Maintains discipline.

The foreman may have two senior assistants: one covering the night shift (senior assistant) and one the day shift (junior assistant). In addition to the assistants there should be a cadet training for the advanced

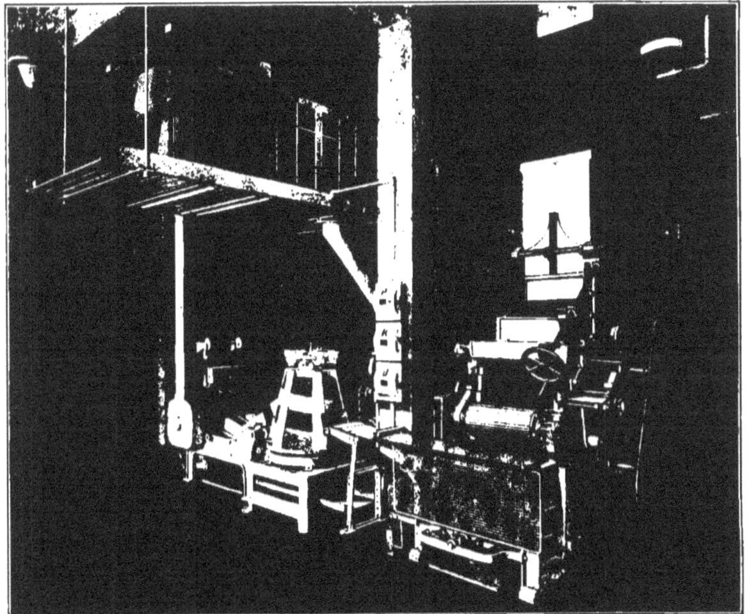

A DUTCHESS Automatic Make-up Unit recently installed in one of Baltimore's leading bakeries — it includes a divider, rounder, proofer and moulder and has a capacity of 48 loaves per minute with 9 minutes proof.

If it's a question of quality — bread produced economically by dependable machinery, we can supply the equipment.

Just as it is relied on for steady every day profitable operation in the best bakeries in the country, just so will it perform for you.

"Our Sales Tell the Tale!"

DUTCHESS TOOL COMPANY

BEACON, N. Y.

positions. A man sometimes called a minute man or "wild man." This man is a graduate mixer and head oven man.

It is good policy to have a confidential rating for all men in advanced positions. Head mixer is considered senior and head oven man junior. In plants operating day and night shifts the senior offices are held by the night man.

Advancement is made by seniority when possible. It does not always follow that the senior man is fitted for the position, but in the spirit of fairness he is given a tryout. A new position is always backed up by the wild man.

LABOR PROBLEMS

I think it opportune to say here a few words in regard to the policy and attitude of any administration toward labor. It should be borne in mind that labor as a whole does not work from choice but from necessity, and this effect is obtained only by employing incentives. While the incentive of wage is the first consideration it does not by any means, as many suppose, cover the whole question. Absence of any other incentive than this simply makes it impossible to progress or modernize a business in any way. In addition to this we should bring to bear upon labor such incentive as will result in the use of their heads as well as their hands, by way of promotion, personal credit or financial reward.

The men in a company who are in charge of departments or have authority in any way should be led to distinctly understand what their possible promotion may be and what personal credits will be allotted them for achievement of any kind. Other labor throughout the factory should have such incentives applied to it as will make them understood that suggestions for improvements in any way will be a subject of financial reward.

A workman may be dense and plebian in his personal make-up, at the same time he may acquire an experience in certain operation or operations after months or years of service that will point out a new method of processing that will very materially result in a reduction of costs of production, and no incentive is so strong in any factory as the one that makes this man understand that if he can do this, he will be suitably rewarded in hard cash.

MEANS OF COMMUNICATION

Every man in every factory should be made to understand that provisions are arranged whereby communication on any subject of this character will not first have to pass through his and several other foremen's hands with the probability of never reaching headquarters. He must be provided with means whereby his suggestion can reach the management direct and he be made to understand that it will be given consieration by the management, first, in the shape of an immediate acknowledgment, and second, in the shape of action either for or against by some committee that may be provided for such work. If any one doubts the efficiency of such an arrangement, let them try it for sixty days and they will marvel at the amount of brain stored up in their business that they have never taken advantage of.

PLAN OF WAGE PAYMENT

In connection with a system of wage payment, known as the differential time bonus by which employees are paid an increased hourly wage based on the time of performing the work in comparison with a standard time, detailed operation and time studies are necessary for determining the standards.

Time standard per thousand for the items manufactured will be determined. The standard time for the production of a pay period will then be determined by taking the total of the production figures for the various items manufactured multiplied by the time standards for each item.

All employees participating in the scheme will then be paid an increased hourly wage based on the efficiency shown by dividing the standard time by the actual time from the payroll.

—‡—‡—‡—

Rye Bread

RYE flour differs from wheat flour in that its gluten has not the same elasticity; however, rye flour contains the most protein. At the same time, it cannot be said that the best rye bread is made entirely from rye flour, for it bakes into the best loaf when the rye flour is mixed with a percentage of wheat flour in the bakeshop. It is altogether questionable whether a miller could turn out a suitable rye flour with the proper percentage of wheat flour mixed in, for the reason that all bakers do not want the same percentage mixed. However, on account of rye bread being of a dark color a baker should not mix much of a third or fourth grade wheat flour, but rather some medium grade with more life in it.

Some folks seem to think that rye bread is a ration for poor people, and such it might be if some bakers were handling it, but as a matter of fact, rye flour is second in importance as a breadstuff, and when rye bread is properly made, as by a German baker, or a Yankee baker with German ideas, it is preferred by many folks to wheat bread. It is not a "poor man's" bread in our country by any means, for a cheaper bread could be made from low-grade white flour, or flour made from barley or oats, were "poor people" so poor that they couldn't buy anything else. It costs nearly as much to make a good loaf of rye as of white bread, although most bakers give a larger loaf.

—‡—‡—‡—

And still many bright young men hesitate to accept the statement that many good positions in bakeries are open to men who know how. The bakery trade is "hungry" for well-qualified bakers—the demand is far greater than the supply.

The American Institute School
OF
BAKING
TECHNOLOGY

Teaches
How to Make
Better Bread

Equipment Includes
A Three Oven Shop
With Three Machines of each kind

FOUR |MONTHS REGULAR COURSE STARTS MAY 15

Instruction Includes:—

The Problems of the Foreman and Superintendent Baker.
Baking and Chemical Tests of Flour, Malt, Milk, etc.
Fermentation, Yeast, Yeast Foods, etc.
Shop and Other Records.
Business and Legal Relations of the Baker.
Manufacture of Bread, etc., Under Commercial Conditions.

ENROLLMENT IS LIMITED
So That
Each Student Gets Individual Attention
and Individual Equipment.

Courses Also Given in

Baking and Milling Chemistry
Industrial Research

COURSES IN PREPARATION FOR
SWEET GOODS SCHOOL.

Fancy Meringue Kisses

OWING to the simplicity of these sweets, they usually receive in most places a sort of indifferent study or attention, yet owing to their volume in a parcel of mixed cakes, such as is cus-

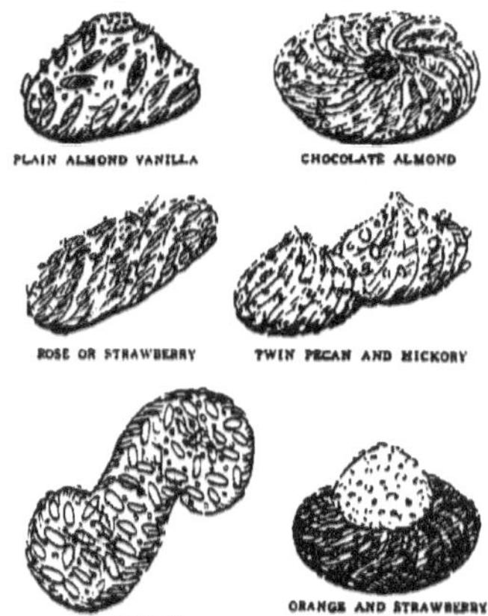

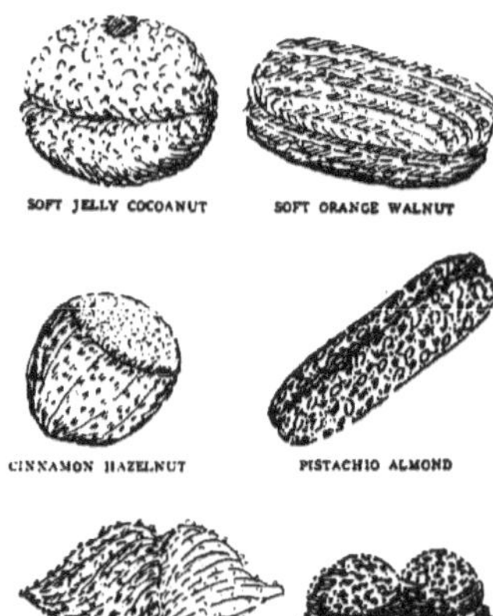

The various names indicate what kind these shapes are, hence a detailed account is uncalled for here.

—:—:—:—

Potomac States Meeting

THE Executive Committee of the Potomac States Association of the Baking Industry met at the Hotel Rennert, Baltimore, Md., on March 14th, with the following members present: President, Theo. F. Bayha, Wheeling, West Va.; vice-president, Frank E. Smith, Cumberland, Md.; treasurer, Jacob J. Mattern, Richmond, Va.; secretary, Glenn O. Garber, Frederick, Md., and J. A. Singer, Staunton, Va.; J. W. Stohlman, Washington, D. C.; H. O. Miller, Charlotte, No. Car.; C. W. Reinhard and F. A. Mueller, of Baltimore.

Arrangements for the 1922 convention were presented and discussed, and the dates, June 20th, 21st and 22d, were selected for the Baltimore meeting and Hotel Rennert chosen as headquarters. Among those speakers of national prominence whom the Entertainment Committee hope to have on the program are Daniel P. Woolley, of The Fleischmann Co.; Prof. Harry R. Snyder, of the Russell-Miller Milling Co.; Ben R. Jacobs, Washington, D. C.; Henry J. Hahn, of Jaburg Bros., New York; Chas. E. Meade, Baltimore; E. C. Baum, of the Joe Lowe Co., New York.

—:—:—:—

"It costs money to keep books and to maintain a cost system. It costs money to make an investigation of market conditions. It costs money to get down to the basic facts of production difficulties. But until the facts are marshalled, the problem cannot be understood, and to solve a problem without understanding it is impossible."

tomarily called for, it is certainly to the advantage of the fancy baker as well as the consumer that they should be as attractive in looks, as well as varied in taste or flavor, as the baker's genius can possibly produce, with all the various flavors, such as lemon or orange zest, mace, cinnamon, chocolate, strawberry extract, rose oil.

The latter is put into meringue thus: Mix one pound of sugar, which has been colored with carmine to a pronounced rose pink, four drops of real oil of rose. Keep in a tight Mason jar and use to each pound of sugar eight whites of eggs, two tablespoonfuls of the rose sugar. Then there is the blanched and shredded almond, the chopped almond, walnut, hazelnut, pistachio, cocoanut, the sugared anise seed, pearled and smooth, and lastly the crushed and evenly grated cut-loaf sugar.

When nuts are sprinkled over the kisses, sprinkle the sugar after. The first six kisses are baked on well-dusted pans, and are of light meringue paste, of nine whites of eggs, eighteen ounces of sugar and should be baked quite crisp in a very cool oven.

The next six kisses of heavy meringue, of six whites of eggs and one pound of sugar, and baked on dampened and papered boards in a moderately cool oven, so that in fifteen to eighteen minutes they get a stiff, but not too brown, a crust. It is always well to have the damper on the oven controlled to a degree, as the rushing current of air will help to crush the kisses.

Practical Cake-Making Suggestions

TOO often bakers who have written books have forgotten the basis from which all cakes and cookies are made. While there are many formulas and methods of making sweet goods, there is only one base from which the cake baker can work. Let us start from the fundamental base of equal proportions—a pound cake mixture. Here we have a base of one pound sugar, one pound butter, one pound flour, one pound eggs. Starting from the above, we can deviate from it to cheapen it in whatever proportion best suits the baker, according to the price he is to receive. Let us assume, for instance, that the above cake is sold for fifty cents per pound. But if eggs are quoted at forty cents a dozen, and it takes ten eggs to make a pound, where before it only cost eighteen cents to buy the same, why should the baker not cheapen this mix just a little? Why not use just about one pound of milk and one pound more of flour to this mix and still get the same price for it? But here is the hitch: This mixture in the first place had no leaven in it, relying only on the beating in of the eggs to give the cake a light appearance and spring in the oven. But with the addition of a liquid, the eggs would lose this lightening tendency, so there must be added to it a leaven, such as baking powder, or cream of tartar and soda. This would also change the appearance of the cake a little, but not much.

I say to any baker that with just a little study he can throw away all formulas and make his own, if he will adhere to the principle that the richer the cake, the more it costs to make it. If he wanted to make a cheap cookie that should run flat, it would only be needed to add two and one-half times as much sugar to the base of shortening, and also add milk and flour to equal the weight of shortening, sugar and eggs and milk to the equal weight of shortening. In other words, if sugar were two and one-half pounds, butter one pound, and eggs one pound, I would add three and one-half pounds of milk and four and one-half pounds of flour for a soft cookie, such as cup, spice, fingers with nuts or sugar on them, or slices baked on paper, just as ladyfingers would be, except they are not beaten in the same way as sponge cake mix would be.

Many bakers, if they would, could use a drop cake mixture in ten or fifteen ways. For instance, if he had a batch of cup drop cookies to make he could just as well make a spice cookie, chocolate drop, or a few fingers could be run through a bag, and be iced with a banana icing, and called banana slices. This same batch would make a cheap sheet cake, which could be jellied, and over the jelly a frosting, then over the frosting a few nut meats could be spread; cut up in diamond slices, and sold for fifteen or twenty cents a dozen.

The same is true of flat cookies, if white cookie mixture is used, after sugar cookies, cocoanut, raisin and currant cookies are made and the end of such a batch has been worked so that it will not spread, because if it is tough it could be cut up in squares of about one and one-half by three inches, and iced so that it would be a new shape, and frosted in chocolate, pink or any other way to suit the baker.

Out of a frosted cream mixture, a soft one, bakers can make ginger bread, frosted creams, molasses drop cakes, spice drops, and spice sheet cake, which could be used as a block in block cakes. If a three-layer block cake, it could be three colors, and iced with a thin, transparent water icing, and wrapped in wax paper to keep it fresh for at least a week. It ought to be cut up like an ice cream brick. Out of a wine cake mix all kinds of ribbon cakes, loaf cakes, cup cookies and layer cakes can be made.

All large cake batches should be creamed up before adding the eggs, and then eggs should be added slowly, rubbing them in. In cookie mixture there is no need to do this. All sponge goods should have the eggs and sugar beaten up; all fruits, such as raisins, currants or citron, should be mixed into a batch with the flour, except where several kinds of cake are to be made from one batch. In such cases the fruit should be floured before adding to mixture.

A cake mixture should never be overworked after flour and milk have been added. It makes the mixture tough, more so in cookie batches than in soft cakes. Soft wheat flour should always be used, because of its lack of gluten, which is just the reverse from the flour used for bread. All substitutes should be dissolved before being added to a cake mixture. Fresh egg substitutes should be dissolved the night before using. Dry milk can be rubbed into the mixture with the sugar, shortening and eggs, but would give better satisfaction if it were dissolved in water; this, of course, is optional with the baker who uses it.

In molasses mixtures the leavening should be soda; in all other kinds baking powder, or cream of tartar and soda can be used. As an example of what can be done, I will give a few formulas and what can be done with them, the balance is left to the baker who wants to know and is willing to experiment, spend a little time and money for his own good.

Six pounds powdered sugar or soft A.

Three and one-half pounds butter.

One and one-half quarts egg whites or whole eggs, or one-half substitute, if cheap cake is desired.

One and one-half quarts milk or five ounces milk powder.

Nine pounds soft wheat flour, six ounces baking powder.

Out of the above mixture layer, sheet, loaf cakes of several kinds can be made. If whites are used it will make white kinds of cake; then if yellow is desired a little egg color can be used; then a chocolate color or cocoa can be used with spices. The white cup cookies, and yellow, as well as the chocolate spice cakes can be made from this mix. Ribbon block cake, spice loaf, and many others can also be made. It is not an expensive batch, and is a very good one. Out of the same batch the baker can make all kinds of soft fingers, by using a bag run on dusted pans or paper.

Out of a jelly roll mixture:

Three pounds sugar.

One quart eggs, half substitute, if desired.

One quart milk, or three ounces milk powder and one quart water.

Four and one-half to seven pounds flour.

Three ounces baking powder.

Here we can make a jelly roll, by placing two flat sheets together we can make slices of all kinds, with preserve layer in centre and different kinds of icings to suit, spread thin. Filling with apricots ground to a pulp, or any other kind of fruit in the same manner. Then ice top same way and cut in slices, one and one-half inches wide, three inches long. This mixture can also be cut into strips to use for charlotte russe, cup and for soft sponge layer cakes.

—‡—‡—‡—

Raisin Week

THE last week in April—that's the time to turn special attention to raisin bread and raisin pie and scores of other raisin delicacies, because during that week, which has been proclaimed "Raisin Week" by the California raisin industry, people will be more interested in those products than in anything else you bake.

The event is receiving national publicity. The entire raisin industry of California has inaugurated this movement to increase your raisin business at a definite time when you can be prepared to take care of it. Over ten thousand of the biggest raisin producers of the Golden State urge you to get into the swim and derive the profit from it that is yours.

Turn your attention to raisin pie and raisin bread. You know of the steady increase in sales these specialties have enjoyed lately—prepare yourself from April 23d to 29th to take care of even a larger one. Throughout those days people will be thinking raisins—with window displays and possibly a few other advertising specialties you can draw them into your store; the sale of raisin specialties will take care of itself.

It is planned to make this big event a national one. For years the prosperous city of Fresno, situated in the very heart of the San Joaquin Valley and known as the Raisin Capital of the World, has celebrated its Raisin Day much as New Orleans celebrates its Mardi Gras. The tremendous success of the event, and the marked increase in sales in the very locality where raisins are the most abundant, has led progressive men behind the industry to foster this national Raisin Week and Raisin Day, and back it up with advertising messages to all retailers and strong publicity support to the consumer.

Thursday—the climax of the week—will be known as Raisin Day, and special effort toward raisin sales will certainly prove profitable on that one day alone. But remember the week—April 23d to 29th, and enjoy the raisin business that you can easily have.

Pie Crusts and Fillings

A NICE flaky pie crust can be easily produced, providing the manipulator takes the proper precaution in the mixing. Of course, flour and shortening are factors to be considered, too. It is a mistaken idea by some bakers to think that a good strong flour will produce the best of crust, or that the more the dough is worked the better it will turn out. With shortening it is different; good butter or lard, or both, will make a better crust than a compound or oil, providing the mixture is properly manipulated. A soft wheat flour with a good color is needed. Success depends not so much on the amount of shortening added to a given amount of flour, but rather on the mixing of same, which must consist of as little handling as possible. The bottom crust of a pie can stand more handling and needs less shortening than the top; for that reason a rich bottom crust takes longer in the baking, and, in fact, it is a difficult matter to accomplish a thorough baking without endangering the filling as well as the top. This point we will touch upon later and will now proceed with the crust proper:

To four pounds of flour add from two and a half to three and one-fourth pounds of shortening and break it up with the flour, seeing that it is not broken up too finely; little lumps of shortening should be plainly visible through the mixture. Those are the basis of forming the leavening and make a flaky crust. This done, add as much cold water (all ingredients should be kept cold) as it will readily take to form an easy working dough. This must be done with very little handling, and not even mixed thoroughly, as the mixture has to undergo some more handling before being spread upon the pie. The dough must now be removed from the bowl, divided or broken up into the required sized pieces and then rolled down for topping; by that time it will be fully mixed. The mixture must be short, in which lies the secret of a flaky crust. It is quite true that this mixture will be a trifle harder to handle than a tougher one, but it will repay you for the little extra trouble it may take. Crust intended for top should not be made ahead or left standing for a day or two, for the longer it stands the tougher it will get and it will lose its leavening qualities. Crust or scrap which is left over should be turned into the bottom crust by the addition of some more flour and water. According to the nature of the shortening a corresponding amount of salt must be added. So much for the crust.

Now a few instructive points in reference to filling will not be out of order. The first sign of spring in the pie-baking trade is the appearance of the time-honored rhubarb pie. The preparation of rhubarb needs little description, as there is only one way of preparing it properly. Remove the bark or skin from the stalk, cut it up into convenient sized pieces, place in kettle with water and stew until tender. This re-

quires very little time, and precaution should be taken to prevent it from becoming too soft. When done, drain, add enough sugar to give it the necessary sweetness and it is ready for use.

Next in order come the different berries. It goes without saying that almost any of them will do duty as a pie filling. Most of the berries are used in their raw state, with the necessary amount of sugar added. Some are stewed with the sugar and an addition of cornstarch in order to absorb the moisture and make the filling more binding. The apple pie, which, no doubt, is the king of all pies, is in demand all the year round. In all cases apples for pies should be stewed, be they green, canned or dried. A few slices of lemon added while being stewed will greatly improve their flavor; also a stick of cinnamon will add to their aroma. In fact, lemon is a great flavor improver in most fruit. Some makers add a little allspice, mace or ground nutmeg; this, of course, is a matter of taste, and the workman must trust to his own judgment, bearing in mind that in pie filling the principal point is the proper sweetness. No matter in how fine a crust a pie may be enveloped, or how nicely it may be baked, when it lacks the proper sweetness it is not agreeable eating, to say the least. It must also contain a certain amount of juice and moisture.

Now the next order in this line would be the baking, which can be stated very briefly. The pie must be baked top and bottom alike—a nice light brown color—remembering that it is the bottom of the pie that has to be looked after; it is much easier to have a nicely baked top than a thoroughly baked bottom. The top heat in the oven can readily be regulated by closing or opening the door and damper. Owing to the downward pressure of the filling in the pie a good solid bottom heat is needed. This rule especially applies to the baking of open pies, such as pumpkin, custard, etc. If the bottom heat is too slack, the moisture in the pie will soak through the bottom crust, making a thorough baking impossible, and it is a hard task to remove the pie from the plate. Now you will comprehend the essential points of pie making. A nice flaky crust, a sweet juicy filling, and last, but not least, a well-baked bottom.

CUSTARD, COCOANUT, RICE PIES, ETC.

Pies of this kind are baked in deep pie plates or dishes of any size; large sized plates are suitable for lunch and restaurant trade. The plates are lined with ordinary pie crust, pressed above the edge of the plate, then with the fore-finger and thumb working up a rim diminishing towards the end and cut off the surplus crust. Some bakers notch the rim, but this is left to the judgment of the workman. It should be remembered that the crust at the bottom of the plate should always be pressed very thin. By doing this the pie will bake more thoroughly, enabling the bottom heat

to penetrate crust and custard, preventing a raw and soggy bottom. The fillings for those pies are numerous, and I will give a few pointers on same, starting with custard, which is the principal factor in the filling for this line of pies.

Custard is somewhat expensive, but to be good it should be nice and smooth, rich in flavor, not too yellow in color and free from all watery substances.

A good custard should consist of eggs, sugar, milk and flavor only, of the following proportions: eight eggs with four ounces of powdered sugar mixed in, one quart of fresh sweet milk and the necessary flavor, beaten thoroughly.

Cheap grades of custard can be obtained by using less eggs, and adding a proportionate amount of cornstarch, or similar ingredients, which will tend to jelly during the process of baking. By using such ingredients it lessons the tendency of the custard to become wavy, a detriment to the appearance of a nice custard. To avoid curdle (cornstarch and other ingredients are not advisable to use in good custard) and bake a perfect custard, the heat should be from three hundred and fifty to three hundred and eighty degrees, according to size of dishes or plates the custard is baked in. The surface, when baked, should be even in color; a nice yellow, no blisters, but a level thin skin should cover the top.

Those pies, or rather shells, are filled in the oven with the so-called pie dipper, which is attached to a stick or pole. All pies in this line should not be filled full at one time, or at the start; by doing so it will often burst the rim of the pie, which renders it useless, besides being a source of loss. Filling four-fifths at the start, or first time, ought to be sufficient; after a while when the dough of the rim has acquired a solid crust, the filling may be repeated until full to the top, thus avoiding all danger of bursting the rim.

Cocoanut pie is obtained by simply adding shredded, grated or desiccated cocoanut in suitable proportion to the custard. Rice pie is made in the same way. Well-cooked rice, in proportion to suit the taste, is placed in the bottom of the pie and the custard poured over it, or enough rice may be mixed with the custard and filled in the above described manner.

CHEESE CAKE

The pans for cheese cake may be lined with sweet dough or coffee cake dough. I will here give two formulas for making them: Three pounds of cheese passed through a sieve, one pound of sugar beaten up with six egg yolks, a good pinch of cinnamon and the rind of one lemon added; then rub six ounces of butter with the cheese, and mix in the sugar and yolks. Now beat up ten egg whites to a stiff snow and mix thoroughly. Should the cheese be too dry and the mixture become too stiff, add enough sweet milk to make it of an easy running consistency. Fill in pans up to the rim and bake in medium heat. Some bakers, before baking, prefer brushing the surface slightly with

egg wash and sprinkling thinly with currants also dusted over with a dash of cinnamon; this is left to the fancy of the operator. It must be remembered that this cake should have a well baked bottom; to ascertain this the cake may be raised on one side and examined. This is one of the finest cheese cakes possibly made.

CHEESE CAKE, ANOTHER FORMULA

Two pounds of cheese passed through a sieve. Put in a bowl and add half a pound of powdered sugar, four eggs, three ounces of butter, and two ounces of cornstarch, or four ounces of flour, mixed well together, flavor with cinnamon, lemon, vanilla, or mace. Vanilla and lemon may be used together. The mixture should be of a running order, adding sufficient milk to make it so. Cheese cake when baked should have the appearance of custard; it should be nice and smooth when cut. Cheese cake can be altered or cheapened to suit prices and trade. Less butter and eggs may be used and a proportionately large amount of cornstarch or flour and milk added.

Care should be taken in selecting a good cheese for this cake. Hard, sandy and dry cheese is as good as useless, for you never get the "grit" out of it, and it will not absorb the milk or moisture. All cheese cakes, when baked, are sprinkled over with powdered sugar.

—‡—‡—‡—

"Make better bread and don't worry about the price," E. L. Cline of the Taggart Baking Company told members of the Indiana Bakers' Association at their meeting at the Claypool Hotel, Indianapolis, on March 25th.

"When the government limited baking materials during the war," he said, "the bake shops got all the baking because they were able to produce better bread with the limited materials than the housewives. The bakers should get rid of the fantastical idea now that they will make money by saving a penny on expenses. The best idea is to buy the best material, make the best bread and let the price take care of itself."

—‡—‡—‡—

"The fellow who doesn't advertise is like the man who threw a kiss to his sweetheart in the dark—he knows what he wants to do, but nobody else does."

Statement of the ownership and management of THE NATIONAL BAKER, published monthly at Philadelphia, Pa., required by Act of August 24, 1912.

Publisher, THE NATIONAL BAKER PUBLISHING COMPANY.

Editor, Benj. F. Whitecar, 411 Walnut Street.

Business Manager, Benj. F. Whitecar, 411 Walnut Street.

Stockholders, Benj. F. Whitecar, 411 Walnut Street; W. W. Gale, 4711 Windsor Avenue; C. McD. Harvey, 40th and Walnut Streets.

(Signed) BENJ. F. WHITECAR, *Business Manager.*

Sworn and subscribed before me this Thirtieth day of March, 1922.

(Signed) J. HENRY ERBER, *Notary Public.*

Information Department

The object of this department is to help our readers, as far as possible, to solve the various difficulties that come up from day to day. We will also answer questions about all kinds of machinery and give every possible assistance in securing detailed information. No names or addresses of manufacturers will be given in these columns. When wanted they will be sent by mail. Address,

INFORMATION DEPARTMENT　　　　**THE NATIONAL BAKER**

PHOSPHATE BAKING POWDER

H. K., Baltimore: We have your favor in reference to baking powder, and submitted same to our expert, who says your proportions are not right, and suggests the following:

44½ ounces Phosphate.

14½ ounces Starch.

20¼ ounces Bicarbonate of Soda.

(Suggest that you make a small lot, before making a large amount.) Further, it is better to use granular phosphate in preference to powdered phosphate, also the starch should be super-dried to expel the moisture, because ordinary starch carries a per cent. of moisture, which spoils the recipe.

QUALITY BREAD MADE FROM KANSAS FLOUR

One barrel flour, 14 gallons water, 3½ pounds salt, 2 pounds sugar, 2 pounds malt, 5 pounds condensed milk, 5 pounds lard, 2¼ pounds yeast.

Temperature mixed, 80 to 82 degrees.

Let lay 3 hours; punch.

Let lay 45 minutes; punch.

Let lay 30 minutes; bench.

Round on bench before panning and give ¾ proof for oven.

Note—In case the water is soft and the dough should come up in 2½ hours to its full height, punch at that time and make the rest of the time for punches the same. This will shorten the fermenting period ½ hour; that is, instead of 4¼ hours it will be 3¾ for fermentation in trough.

J. H., Wisconsin: We have your favor of March 31st, and in regards to "Egg Powder," would say that there are several different kinds of "Egg Powder" used in different ways. We believe it would be safer for you to get details from the manufacturer of the powder you use, as all of these manufacturers have worked out formulas to suit the peculiarities of their powder.

Referring to your request for recipes to use up cake crumbs, would say that we mail you under separate cover a copy containing a number of good recipes to use up cake crumbs, which we trust will answer your purpose.

We do not exactly know what you mean by a bread or cake pudding. If you mean for family style, we can give you one, but do not know of a pudding of this sort to be sold over the counter.

ROYAL ICING

M. H., Tenn.: The royal icing is used for icing and for ornamenting. It dries rapidly if exposed to the air, and should be kept well covered with a damp cloth at all times, in a cool place.

For ornamenting it is beaten with the whites of eggs until it retains its shape if drawn to a point. For icing it is only beaten to the consistency of a cream, so it runs smooth.

The sugar should be run through a very fine sieve before using, to prevent lumps clogging in the cornet in decorating.

Much acid makes a coarse icing, and very little should be used in piping; or none at all if a tough icing for fine thread lining is required.

Make the icing pretty strong at the beginning and work up white and light, then add a little more of the whites until it is of the proper consistency.

Take from three to four whites of eggs to one pound of XXXX powdered sugar, a small pinch of cream tartar, or one drop of acetic acid, put in a china bowl and beat with one or two small spatulas (one in each hand), and treat as directed above.

PRALINES

Take three pounds of granulated sugar, and one and one-half pints water. Let come to a boil, and throw into it two pounds of shelled sweet almonds. When the almonds begin to crackle in the syrup, take the pan off the fire and stir with a spatula until the sugar grains and gets sandy. Put the dry sugar and almonds in a coarse sieve and sift off the sugar and break the almonds apart, if they form lumps. Return the sugar to the pan and add about one pint of water, and a few drops of carmine for color. Let boil to the low crack, or 254° Fuhr., and put in the almonds; stir again until grained. Repeat this once or twice more, and they are then ready.

Pecans, peanuts, walnuts and filberts are made into pralines like the almonds.

Orange and lemon peel; also rose leaves, violets and orange flowers are made into pralines in the same manner.

EGG ICING FOR PIPING

Put into a bowl the whites of six fresh eggs and whisk them with one pound of icing sugar; then add a quarter of a teaspoonful of cream of tartar and a mite of blue; beat these well in and then add another pound of icing sugar, adding it gradually and beating it in until the icing acquires the proper consistency for piping. To make the icing for other use than piping, eight eggs will be required, instead of six, to the two pounds of sugar.

VIENNA ICING

One-half pound best fresh butter, three-fourths pound icing sugar, two yolks of eggs, one glass of rum. Wash the butter free from salt and dry it on a cloth, put it in a clean dry basin, and rub to a cream with a wooden spoon; then add the yolks of eggs, beating well; sieve the sugar and mix into the butter, lastly mixing in gradually the rum, or any other kind of spirit that may be preferred. To color, simply mix in the kind of vegetable color required. It is best to make up just the quantity required for use, as if kept it will go rancid. Should any be left over it can be used up the next day by beating it up again to the cream.

WATER ICING

Taking about two pounds of fine icing sugar, add one-fourth ounce of tartaric acid, and then stir in sufficient *boiling water* to make it a soft paste; beat it up well with a wooden spoon in the same way that you would ordinary cake icing; color and flavor as directed, and use as required. You can make it stiff or soft by adding either more water or sugar, as desired.

M. Mc. H., Penna.: We give herewith two methods of making Raisin Bread; your present method cannot give good results:

RAISIN BREAD

Fifteen gallons water, two and one-half pounds salt, five pounds sugar, three pounds lard, three pounds compressed yeast, one hundred and fifty pounds California raisins, one barrel patent flour. Temperature of dough eighty-five degrees, temperature of room eighty-five degrees. Let dough stand three hours, turn and let stand one hour. Medium oven.

RAISIN BREAD, NO. 2

Sponge Dough—Set a soft sponge of nine gallons of water and twelve ounces of compressed yeast. Temperature eighty-seven degrees. Let stand three hours or until sponge begins to drop. Add six gallons of water and break up, then add five pounds of sugar, two and one-half pounds of salt, two and one-half pounds of lard, one hundred and fifty pounds of raisins. Patent flour enough to make medium dough according to flour. Let dough stand one hour, then mould into loaves. Do not let this dough raise too much in the pans before baking.

ANGEL CAKE

M. H. B., Minn.: For these cakes the pans should be free from grease and the cake should stick to the pan when baked. After baking, the pans are turned upside down on the table and left to cool. This prevents the cakes from shrinking. When cold loosen the sides or run a knife blade around the sides, knock the pan on the table and the cake should drop out.

Small 1 and 2-pound cakes should bake in from 15 to 20 minutes in a heat of 300 degrees.

A. One quart whites, 2 pounds sugar, 14 ounces flour, 2 ounces cornstarch, ½ ounce cream of tartar, vanilla.

B. One quart whites, 1¾ pounds sugar, 18 ounces flour, 2 ounces cornstarch, ½ ounce cream of tartar, vanilla.

Mix flour, starch and two-thirds of the sugar, sift together. Beat whites firm; beat in one-third of the sugar and cream of tartar, add flavor and mix lightly but fully the other flour and sugar; fill mold three-fourths full and bake.

These mixtures may be colored pink and flavored with rose, strawberry or raspberry, and iced in different colors and flavors.

DEVIL'S FOOD LAYER CAKE

Put ½ pound bitter chocolate and 1 pound sugar in double kettle on the fire and add gradually 1 pint of milk; stir till it thickens and stir smooth; cream 1¼ pounds sugar and ¾ pound butter and ¾ pint yolks. Add ¾ ounce soda and 1 pint sweet or sour milk. Then add the cooled chocolate mixture, vanilla, and 2 pounds flour. Bake in square or round layers. Ice and fill with a boiled icing or ice chocolate. Decorate with nuts. These cakes may be baked as a loaf cake, or on paper and rolled up like jelly roll.

ESTABLISHED 1864
THOS. MILLS & BRO., Inc.
MANUFACTURERS OF
BAKERS', CONFECTIONERS' AND ICE CREAM MACHINERY AND TOOLS
1301-1311 NORTH EIGHTH STREET :-: :-: PHILADELPHIA, PA.
ALL SIZES OF TUBS AND CANS IN STOCK
COMBINED ICE CREAM FREEZER AND BREAKER
EGG WHIPS
LARGE ASSORTMENT OF INDIVIDUAL ICE CREAM MOULDS
PEELS AND SWAB POLES
ALL SIZES OF TIN, STEEL AND RUSSIA IRON PANS
ALL STYLES
OF BRUSHES
ALL SIZES OF PIE PLATES
PATENT BEATING MACHINE
ICE CREAM REFRIGERATORS, HARD WOOD OR MARBLE FRONTS
WE ISSUE THREE DISTINCT CATALOGS—CONFECTIONERS' BAKERS' AND ICE CREAM

Recipe Department

In this department we will publish new and valuable recipes and want our readers to forward to us any recipe from which they have had good results, or that is not generally known.   We wish to make this department as interesting as possible and ask our readers to help us to this end. Address.

RECIPE DEPARTMENT   THE NATIONAL BAKER

Fancy Mixed Cakes

THE public will take more notice of the baker who offers occasional varieties in his line of goods than the one who keeps the same humdrum style year in and year out. In these times of rapid changes people are ever on the hunt for something new, and the one who can please their palates is held in highest esteem. In most shops, ladyfingers, macaroons, kisses and sugar cakes constitute the whole variety with probably a gingersnap or brandy wafer change occasionally. The recipes given here have been collected from various parts of Europe and America. They have all been tested by the writer, who vouches for their correctness.

THERESIAS

Beat, on a slow fire one-half pound of sugar, five eggs, to a very stiff broth, get it just so that you can stand the heat with your finger, then beat it until cold, add grating of one lemon, one-half teaspoon of cinnamon, one-quarter teaspoon of allspice, one strong pinch of mace, one pinch of cloves; then add six ounces chopped almonds, six ounces of flour; spread this on oblaten wafers and cut to suit into oblong squares, set on papered pans, place a thin small piece of citron on top of each, then bake in a moderate oven.

VALENCIAS

Beat five eggs, four yolks, six ounces of sugar on a slow fire until quite warm, and to a very stiff froth; beat until cold; then add the zest (grating) of one orange, finally six ounces of flour, two ounces of almond meal; bake this into a sheet three-quarters of an inch thick, on papered pans; when cold cut into blocks one and one-half inches long, three-quarters of an inch wide; dip these into lukewarm orange juice frosting, richly tinted; then place on each a liberal pinch of fresh sugared orange grating; on each side of it run a little currant jelly and a zigzag dash of royal icing.

RAREBIT

Mix ten ounces of butter, four ounces of sugar, juice of two lemons, one egg, three yolks, one pinch of ground cardamom, ten ounces of flour to a stiff dough; roll it out one-eighth of an inch thick, then with two-inch scalloped cutters cut from it rounds; set the half of them on a papered pan, wash the edges with a small brush and white of egg, and place in each center a little ball of currant jelly through which some chopped raisins and figs have been mixed. If dried pears are handy they are better tasting than raisins. Place the tops, which have been forked, on it firmly and wash

with egg; when baked place a little pink and white ton on the centre.

CINDERELLAS

Beat one-half pound of sugar, eighteen yolks very light and stiff; add a pinch of salt, a pinch of ground anise seed, one pinch of cardamom, twelve ounces of flour; dress up like ladyfingers on greased and flour dusted pans, besprinkle freely with granulated sugar and bake rather quick. They will rise about one-quarter of an inch.

CASINO CAKES

Mix one-quarter of a pound of sugar, six ounces of butter, twelve ounces of flour, two eggs, one tablespoon of rum, one grated nutmeg, one small pinch of carbonate of soda the size of a pea; mold the small cakes as shown, set on greased and slightly dusted pans, wash with egg and bake in a rather sharp oven to a rich brown.

MAZARINES

Combine into dough one-half pound of sugar, four eggs, ten ounces of flour, five ounces of chopped almonds, two ounces of orange peel, one small pinch of soda, one-half teaspoon of cinnamon, a good pinch of ground cloves, allspice and cardamom; roll it out to the thickness of a pencil, cut it out into one and one-quarter inch square diagonals, wash with milk thinly and dust with granulated sugar. When done put on top a leaf formation of pink and white royal icing.

GHIBELINES

Mix six ounces of sugar, six ounces of butter, eight yolks of eggs, four ounces of pounded almonds, three ounces of brown crisp toasted bread passed through a coarse flour sieve, two ounces of chopped almonds, a little mace, cloves, eight whites of eggs beaten stiff; bake these in small greased and dusted cone-shaped molds; when done, coat them with white pearl icing and put a pink top of stiff light royal icing with a star tube.

WINE STICKS

Beat one-half pound of sugar and five eggs, very stiff, add ten ounces of flour, a good pinch of mace, a small pinch of salt; dress up on waxed pans, three inches long and one-quarter inch wide, dust with sugar and let them stand three or four hours to get evenly crusted, then bake in moderate oven.

LADY GRAYS

Stir six ounces of sugar, fourteen yolks of eggs, four ounces of butter, very light; beat twelve whites of eggs very stiff, add three ounces of flour, three ounces of starch, two ounces of currants, two ounces of finely chopped orange peel, one tablespoon of rum; bake this mixture in small cup moulds; when done, dip each into lukewarm lemon water icing, then put a good sized dot of pink royal icing, with star tube, on top.

MOZARTS

Grind one pound of almonds, eight eggs, very fine, add one pound of sugar, one-half pound of flour, two ounces of finely chopped orange peel, two ounces of citron, the grating of two lemons, spread this on ob-laten wafers, cut into strips three inches long and three-quarters of an inch broad, put a long piece of angelique in the middle; when baked, glace over with a little sugar, boiled to the thread, with a small brush. In a half hour or so it will turn white.

AMOURETTES

Beat nine whites of eggs very stiff, add eight ounces of sugar, four ounces of flour, two or three drops of oil of rose; spread this a scant one-quarter inch in thickness on oblaten wafers, cut up into pieces three inches by one and one-half inches, set on papered pans, let stand in a warm place for an hour or so, then bake in a very moderate oven; when done decorate with a little green stem and a leaf of royal icing. Next put into a paper cone one-third of pink, one-third of red, one-third of white royal icing, with a small leaf tube in the end of the cone; form a little rose with a mere circular twist of the hand.

OTHELLOS

Beat seven whites of eggs very stiff, add one pound sugar, one-half teaspoon of ground cinnamon and a little ground allspice; dress up on greased and flour-dusted pans with a medium sized star tube, sprinkle with shredded almonds and dust with sugar, bake in a cool oven; when done dip each into dark rich fond-ant chocolate icing, set them for a minute in the oven, which will help them to retain their gloss.

CARDINAL CAKES

Mix one-half a pound of commercial almond paste with five whites of eggs, add a tablespoonful of very finely chopped orange peel; spread this on a piece of scrap puff paste, rolled out to about three-sixteenths of an inch thickness; let this stand for about one-half an hour in the ice-box, then cut it out with suitable oblong cutters, bake in a moderate oven; when done, with a cornet put a little currant jelly on them in some sort of a design.

BERLINGOES

Work up one-half a pound of sugar, one-half a pound of butter, two whites and two whole eggs, one pound flour, four ounces starch, vanilla flavor and a pinch of mace; divide this dough into eight parts, roll it to about the thickness of a cigar, then with a length-wise, small grooved roller dent the dough stems as shown; cut these up into three and one-half inch lengths and form rings on papered pans; bake in a rather sharp oven. The ends of rings must be joined with a little egg wash.

ARISTOCRATS

Make a dough of one and one-quarter pounds of chopped almonds, one pound of sugar, five ounces of

---

butter, three eggs, one gill of rosewater, a pinch of cinnamon and a little red coloring, so as to give the dough a rich pink color. Make three to four long rolls out of it, about one and one-half inches thick, and flatten evenly on greased and dusted pans to one-half inch thickness; wash with egg and bake in a moderate oven. When done, cut while warm into one-half inch bars on the slant, dip one cut side into lukewarm thin rosewater and lemon juice icing, so that the pink of the cake can be seen through it.

WINDSOR TARTS

Roll out puff paste scrap dough to one-eighth of an inch thickness, cut from it four-inch discs with a scalloped cutter, lay these into tartlet moulds, place a bit of raspberry jam on the bottom, then mix one-half a pound of fine crushed brown almonds with ten ounces of powdered sugar into eight whites of eggs beaten stiff, add a pinch of cloves, one-half a table-spoonful vanilla extract, one-half an ounce of melted chocolate. Fill each mould three-quarters full, dust with a little sugar and form a little slender cross over it; when done, put a few preserved cherries on them.

MARSHALL CAKE

Mix one pound of butter, one-half a pound of sugar, one and one-half pounds flour, one pinch of salt, one pinch of cardamom, one gill of rosewater and plain water enough to make a stiff dough; this is handled exactly like pie crust, do not work it too much, especially in summer. Roll it out into two strips a scant one-quarter of an inch thick, four inches broad; prick these well and evenly with a fork, then bake to a rich brown; while hot set together with raspberry jam and coat with thin rum and water icing, into which a little lemon juice has been mixed. Cut up into one and one-quarter inch bars and place a half cherry in centre, with probably a dash of royal icing or an angelica leaf.

HAZELNUT BARS

Grind with orange flower water one-half a pound of shelled and lightly browned hazelnut kernels, very fine and rather stiff, however, do not get them oily by too dry grinding; now mix this up with one-half pound of butter, three-quarters of a pound of sugar, one-half a pound of flour, four yolks of eggs, a small pinch of nutmeg and cinnamon and pinch of salt; roll this dough into lengths one-quarter of an inch thick, set two together with a touch of the eggwash and then cut to suitable lengths and set on greased and thinly dusted pans; wash with eggs and sprinkle with fine crushed cut-loaf sugar.

CHOCOLATE TARTS

Make a custard of two ounces of chocolate, a pinch of cinnamon, two ounces of finely chopped lemon peel, four ounces of sugar, two ounces of ground rice or cornstarch, one pint of milk, and five eggs; beat the eggs, and gradually mix all the ingredients together, then stir over a slow fire until it thickens as an or-dinary custard (but don't let it boil or curdle), let cool, then fill into patty-pans lined with puff-paste, and bake at good heat.

DEWEY TART

Roll out a thin round bottom of sweet dough, cut it into the proper size and shape, place it on a stout baking sheet, then fill with currant jam, leaving about an inch and a half free all round; now beat three whites of eggs very stiff, add four ounces of sifted powdered sugar and two and a half ounces of blanched, shredded and dried almonds, one ounce of citron, cut fine and a pinch of ground cinnamon; place this mixture on the space left free, forming a ring, and dust with fine sugar. Grease a band of paper, lay it around the ring to keep it in shape, and set a tin ring around the whole cake. Fill the centre of the cake with the following mixture: Pound in the mortar until very smooth two and a half ounces of blanched almonds with a little water, place in a bowl and stir with four ounces of sugar, seven yolks of eggs; then beat five whites of eggs very stiff, and mix it with the almonds and sugar, also one ounce and a half of flour. Bake at slow heat. When cold, ice the almond part with lemon fondant icing and decorate to suit your taste.

FRENCH ORANGE CAKE

Ten ounces powdered sugar, sixteen egg yolks, fifteen egg whites, six ounces flour, two ounces corn-starch, four ounces melted butter, cream up sugar and egg yolks until light. Beat up the egg whites to a staunch froth, add to above the flour and cornstarch and mix with as little handling as possible. Lastly add the melted butter. Bake in cake hoops or layer cake pans in moderate heat. Now make the following preparation for filling: Grate the rind of two oranges, add ten ounces of powdered sugar, six egg yolks and two whole eggs, the juice of two lemons and two oranges, one glass of wine. Place this over a slow coal fire, constantly stirring, until it becomes thick and creamy—not allowing it to boil. When cold spread this mixture between the layer, cutting up another orange in thin slices and covering the filled layer with it. Trim the sides with a sharp knife and cover the cake with an orange-colored and flavored fondant or water icing. Previously have two oranges peeled; the slices divided without bursting the delicate skin, and dried in the air; then dipped in caramel sugar, cooked to three hundred degrees and the top decorated with same, tastefully arranged.

SPICE CAKE

One quart molasses, one pound shortening, two and one-half pounds crumbs, six ounces sugar, ten eggs, one scant quart water, two and one-half pounds flour, one and one-third ounces soda, two-thirds ounce cream tartar, a good flavoring of ground spices. When well mixed drop in well-greased muffin pans and bake in medium hot oven. When cold, ice the tops with chocolate icing. This mixture may be baked in sheet form, the top iced over and then cut into pieces to sell to suit the trade.

Business Chances

"WANT" and "FOR SALE" advertisements inserted in THE NATIONAL BAKER for three cents a word, payable in advance. Stamps accepted in payment.

HELP WANTED

WANTED — GOOD ALL-AROUND Foreman in Bakery. Would have to be a thorough bread man. Our output is from 5,000 to 6,000 loaves a day and we operate five ovens. Write: Jefferson City Baking Co., Jefferson City, Mo.

MACHINERY FOR SALE

1—20-inch Thomson Moulder Extension, new.

1—Thomson Zerah Baller.

1—2½-bbl. Day Dough Mixer.

1—2-bbl. Read Dough Mixer.

1—1½-bbl. Read Dough Mixer.

2—Union Bun Rounders.

1—Day Dough Brake.

3—Day Wood Flour Sifters.

2—Triumph All-Steel Flour Sifters.

1—2-bbl. Triumph Dough Mixer.

2—Wood-Proof Closets, for public view bakery.

1—1½-bbl. Peerless Dough Mixer.

Cake Machines, Bread Racks, Troughs and Equipment of every description ready for immediate shipment, new or rebuilt. Rebuilt machines guaranteed same as new ones.

J. H. BAST & CO.

649 W. Pratt St. Baltimore, Md.

MISCELLANEOUS

TURNER'S RAPID RECIPE RECKoner simplifies cost accounting so that it is a matter of only a few minutes to get the cost of a batch of any size, and of any class of goods. The baker is saved all the trouble in counting up the cost; it is already done for him. Tables are given of the cost of each ounce of flour at a price per barrel from $4.00 upward, of other materials from $0.01 to $0.60 by the pound, and the cost of each ounce. One is needed in every bake-shop, and the cost is but $2.00 postpaid. For sale by THE NATIONAL BAKER, 411 Walnut Street, Philadelphia, Pa.

MACHINERY FOR SALE

FOR SALE—FOR A VERY LOW price you can secure the following slightly used equipment:

Two Yankee Reel Ovens, $100 each.

DOUGH MIXERS

1 Dutchess, 4 bbl. J. H. Day, 3 bbl.

1 Rockwell, 4 bbl. 2 Rockwell, 3 bbl.

J. H. Day, 2 bbl. Double Jacketed.

1 Century, 3 bbl.

CAKE MACHINES

Read

1 Little Giant 1 Champion

1 Hobart with D. C. Motor attached

Dutchess Two-Pocket Divider

Dutchess Roll Dividers

Bread and Pan Racks

Proofing Closets Troughs

Work Tables Bread Pans

1 Day Egg Clipper Shipping Boxes

Sheet iron pans for the following ovens: Yankee, Barker and Federal.

Dough brake, A-1 condition

2 Doughnut Fryers with trays

I. KALFUS COMPANY

175 Stanton St. New York City

OVENS FOR SALE

MUST SELL TWELVE-PAN, TWO-deck oven to make room for large single-deck Hubbard. Address Box 10, care THE NATIONAL BAKER, 411 Walnut Street, Philadelphia.

OVENS WANTED

WANTED — TO BUY SECOND-hand oven for cake use; would buy hearth-fired oven. Address 58 West Louther Street, Carlisle, Pa.

BAKERIES FOR SALE

FOR SALE — A GOOD, GOING bakery, doing about $400 per week, all over the counter. Located on main street of city. Equipped with elegant fixtures, large size Middleby Oven, Cake machine, etc. Everything complete. Price $2,700. Exceptional opportunity. Address Rudolph J. Huss, 170 E. Front Street, Plainfield, N. J.

FOR SALE—ESTABLISHED 33 years, modern equipped wholesale bakery doing excellent business. For further particulars address E. T. Reese, 207 Pearson St., New Castle, Penna.

FOR SALE—CASH AND CARRY bakery, best location in a good Ohio town of 10,000. Baking outfit complete—price cheap, if taken at once. Address B. 20, care THE NATIONAL BAKER, 411 Walnut St., Philadelphia, Pa.

FOR SALE — BAKERY, ICE cream parlor, candy, cigars, cigarettes, tobacco and light grocery in growing Michigan industrial city of 8,000 population. Splendid farming territory surrounding. All cash business. Century cake mixer, Bennett oven, first class soda fountain, 2 cash registers. Complete bakery and store outfit. Good lease. Sell at real bargain. Price $3,800. Must sell on account of disagreement of partners. City Bakery, Sturgis, Mich.

FOR SALE—BAKERY WITH two Petersen ovens, dough mixer, Hobart cake machine, bun divider and accessories, all in good condition. Steam boiler, motor. A bargain and an old established business. Building for rent with rooms above. H. D. Odom, Realtor, Louisville Ky.

A Classified List of Goods Needed by Bakers

Automobile Trucks—
Republic Truck Sales Corp, Alma, Mich.

Almond Paste—
Henry Heide, Inc., New York.

Bakery Advertising—
I. B. Nordham Co., N. Y.
Schulze Advert. Service, Chicago.
W. E. Long Co., Chicago.

Bakers' Institute—
Siebel Institute, Chicago.

Bakers' Machinery—
Champion Machine Co., Joliet, Ill.
J. H. Day Co., Cincinnati, O.
Dutchess Tool Co., Beacon, N. Y.
Freymark Steam Generator Co., St. Louis.
Jaburg-Miller Co., New York.
Peerless Bread Mch. Co., Sidney, O.
Read Machinery Co., York, Pa.
Reeves Pulley Co., Columbus, Ind.
Thomson Mch. Co., Bellevue, N. J.
Thomas Mills & Bro., Philadelphia.
Union Machinery Co., Joliet, Ill.

Bakers' Pans—
Jaburg Bros., New York.
Jaburg-Miller Co., New York.
Edward Katzinger Co., Chicago.
The Aug. Maag Co., Baltimore.
Thomas Mills & Bro., Philadelphia.

Bakers' Tools—
Jaburg Bros., New York.
Jaburg-Miller Co., New York.
Edward Katzinger Co., Chicago.
The Aug. Maag Co., Baltimore.
Thomas Mills & Bro., Philadelphia.
Union Steel Products Co., Albion.

Books for Bakers—
Malzbender's Recipe Book.
Turner's Rapid Recipe Reckoner

Bread Labels—
Mirror Printing Co., Kalamazoo.

Bread Wrapping and Sealing Machines—
National Bread Wrapping Machine Co., Nashua, N. H.
Lambooy Label & Wrapper Co., Kalamazoo, Mich.
Union Machinery Co., Joliet, Ill.

Cash Registers—
National Cash Register Company.

Chocolate—
Walter Baker & Co., Ltd., Dorchester.

Cooking Oil—
Corn Products Ref. Co., New York.

Dough Mixers and Kneaders—
Champion Machinery Co., Joliet, Ill.
J. H. Day Co., Cincinnati, O.
Read Machinery Co., York, Pa.

Eggs-Desiccated—Egg Products—
Joe Lowe Co., N. Y.

Flour—
Big Diamond Mills Co., Minn.
Commander Mills, Minneapolis.
Empire Milling Co., Minneapolis.
W. J. Jennison & Co., Minneapolis.
Russell-Miller Milling Co., Minn.
Washburn-Crosby Co., Minneapolis.

Food Colors—
National Aniline & Chem. Co., N. Y.

Fruit Growers—
California Associated Raisin Co.
California Prune & Apricot Growers.

Honey—
Arthur A. Beals, Oto, Iowa.

Ice Cream Tools and Supplies—
Atlas Mfg. Co., New Haven.
Chr. Hansen's Lab., Little Falls, N. Y.
The Aug. Maag Co., Baltimore.
Thomas Mills & Bro., Philadelphia.

Malt, Extract and Dry—
American Diamalt Co.
Anheuser-Busch, Inc., St. Louis.
P. Ballantine & Sons, Newark.
Freihofer Baking Co., Philadelphia.
Malt Diastase Co., N. Y.
Stein-Hall Mfg. Co., Chicago.

Milk, Powdered and Condensed—
Consolidated Prod. Co., Lincoln, Neb.
I. H. Nestor & Co., Philadelphia.

Ovens—
Bennett Oven Co., Battle Creek.
Duhrkop Oven Co., New York.
Hubbard Oven Co., Chicago.
Meek Oven Mfg. Co., Westport, Conn.
Middleby Oven Co., New York.
Middleby-Marshall Co., Chicago.
Standard Oven Co., Pittsburgh.
Superior Oven Co., Chicago, Ill.

Oven Lights and Doors—
Dutchess Tool Co., Beacon, N. Y.
Chas. Robson & Co., Philadelphia.

Papers (Parchment and Waxed)—
Lambooy Label & Wrapper Co., Kalamazoo, Mich.
Menasha Ptg. & Carton Co., Menasha, Wis.
Waterproof Paper & Board Co., Cincinnati.

Pie Machinery—
Edwin E. Bartlett, Nashua, N. H.
J. H. Day Co., Cincinnati, O.
Union Machinery Co., Joliet, Ill.

Potato Flour—
Falk American Potato Flour Co., Pittsburgh, Pa.

Pyrometers—
Hubbard Oven Co., Chicago.
Philadelphia Thermometer Co.
Chas. Robson & Co., Philadelphia.

Shipping Boxes (Wood and Paper)—
A. Backus, Jr., & Son, Detroit.
Rob't Gaylord, Inc., St. Louis.

Shortening—
Corn Products Refining Co., N. Y.
Procter & Gamble Co., Cincinnati.

Stoves for Bakers and Confectioners—
Edward Katzinger Co., Chicago.
Thomas Mills & Bro., Philadelphia.

Sugar and Sugar Syrups—
American Sugar Ref. Co., N. Y.
Corn Products Ref. Co., New York.
Franklin Sugar Ref. Co., Philadelphia.

Supplies—
Jaburg Bros., New York.
Joe Lowe Co., N. Y.
Stein-Hall Mfg. Co., Chicago and N. Y.
Ward Baking Co., New York.

Thermometers—
Phila. Thermometer Co., Phila.

Washing and Cleaning Material—
J. B. Ford Co.

Yeast—
The Fleischmann Co., New York.

INDEX TO ADVERTISEMENTS

	Page
American Diamalt Co.	14
Anheuser-Busch Sales Corp.	43
American Sugar Refining Co.	47
Baker & Co., Ltd., Walter	57
Ballantine & Sons, P.	15
Bartlett, Edwin E.	39
Bennett Oven Co.	5
Big Diamond Mills Co.	4
Business Chances	65
California Associated Raisin Co.	11
California Prune & Apricot Growers	51
Carter, Rice & Co., Corporation	45
Commander Mills	59
Corn Products Ref. Co.	9
Day Co., The J. H.	6
Duhrkop Oven Co.	13
Dutchess Tool Co.	14, 49
Empire Milling Co.	16
Fleischmann Co., The	12
Ford Co., J. B.	58
Freihofer Baking Co.	55
Freymark Steam Generator Co.	47
Heide, Inc., Henry	63
Hubbard Portable Oven Co.	Cover
Jennison Co., W. J.	16
Katzinger Co., Edward	Cover
Lambooy Label & Wrapper Co.	4
W. E. Long Co.	37
Maag Co., The Aug.	Cover
Malt Diastase Co.	16
Malzbender, M.	57
Middleby-Marshall Oven Co.	8
Middleby Oven Co., N. Y.	15
Mills & Bro., Inc., Thomas	61
National Bread Wrapping Mach. Co.	45
Philadelphia Thermometer Co.	4
Procter & Gamble Co.	6
Read Machinery Co.	7
Reeves Pulley Co.	6
Republic Truck Sales Corp.	8
Robson & Co., Charles	18
Russell-Miller Milling Co.	10
Siebel Institute	17
Standard Oven Co.	5
Sun-Maid Raisins	11
Superior Oven Co.	41
Thomson Machine Co.	7
Turner, A. R.	57
Union Steel Products Co.	
Union Machinery Co.	4
Ward Baking Co.	32
Washburn-Crosby Co.	Cover
Water-proof Paper & Board Co.	13

KLEEN-KRUST
RIVETLESS
REG. U.S. PAT. OFF.
"STEEL-SHOD" BREAD PANS
(Patented Jan. 21, 1913; Jan. 14, 1917.)

The Appearance of the Loaf is of Prime Importance--

Flanges Prevent Pans from Spreading.

—It goes a long way in creating a demand for your bread. If you would turn out loaves of exceptional uniformity—clean, spotless loaves—you will bake in Kleen-Krust Rivetless "Steel-Shod" Bread Pans.

Extra Heavy Steel Rod Used in Binding Pans Together.

Steel Shod Ends Protect the End Pans.

Entirely Different from Any Other Pan on the Market

With Covers for Pullman or Sandwich Loaves

Their construction, the most rigid and sanitary ever devised, entirely eliminates strapping, therefore neither dirt nor grease can collect.

The outer face of the end pans is protected by a sheet of steel which acts as a piece of armor-plate. This steers the peel underneath the pans, eliminating all danger of battering the end pan.

Kleen-Krust Rivetless "Steel-Shod" Bread Pans are manufactured under letters patent granted by the U. S. Government. We are sole manufacturers.

The advantages of Kleen-Krust Rivetless "Steel-Shod" Bread Pans go a long way toward creating a demand for your bread by improving the appearance of the loaf. In order that you may find out these advantages for yourself, we will forward a sample set of open Pans for immediate practical use in your oven room.

Specially Adapted for Traveling Ovens

We have issued a New Catalog illustrating and describing our Kleen-Krust Rivetless "Steel Shod" Bread Pans and Kleen-Krust Rivetless Pullman or Sandwich Bread Pans. Catalog mailed on request.

Showing Rigid Construction of Cover.

Style No. 87
Made of extra heavy tin with loose fitting covers. Covers wired and

THE AUGUST MAAG CO.
509-11 W. Lombard St.

Republic Rapid Transit, with Panel Body and Fore-Door Open Cab, Cord Tires, Electric Starter and Lights. Price on application

LEADERSHIP

Unequaled Service

Other body types include

Carry-All
Canopy Top
Stock Rack
Screen Enclosed
Tank Body
Open Express
Double Deck
Platform Stake
Bus Body
Police Patrol
Grain Body
Bottlers' Body
Dump Body

Quality : Price : Service

The real worth of a motor truck is in the service it gives—and its Service depends upon the manufacturer's skill and facilities for turning out a high-grade product.

Republic Rapid Transit enjoys a reputation for Unequaled Service. It is a quality product at a very low price—the crowning achievement of nine years devoted exclusively to truck manufacture.

For bakers who require speedy, dependable delivery service, Republic Rapid Transit is admittedly the most economical equipment.

The Republic Line: ¾, 1, 1½-2, 2½-3, 3½-4 tons capacity.

**REPUBLIC TRUCK SALES CORPORATION
ALMA, MICH.**

REPUBLIC
RAPID TRANSIT©

Republic has more trucks in use than any other exclusive truck manufacturer

Bennett Ovens Make Busy Bakers

ARE you worrying along with an old style oven? Are you turning down new business because you cannot turn out the goods?

Install a modern, efficient Bennett Oven and you will be able to handle an increased demand on a profitable basis. Others are doing it. So can you.

Bennett Ovens Are Better Ovens

BENNETT OVEN CO.,   Ave. C & 22nd Street, Battle Creek, Mich.

Battery of Three Standard Ovens

Front Furnace with two large charging doors in each oven.

STANDARD OVEN CO.

1835 OLIVER BLDG.   PITTSBURGH, PA.

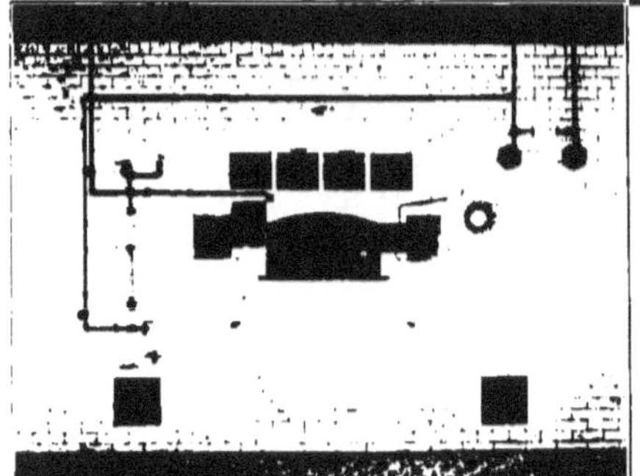

DUHRKOP OVENS

Mean

Oven Satisfaction

This is proven by the fact that 90 per cent of our business is REPEAT ORDERS.

Ask for our list of DUHRKOP USERS--Note those in YOUR VICINITY.

DUHRKOP OVEN COMPANY

PARK ROW BUILDING **NEW YORK, N. Y.**

The Thomson Loaf Moulder
With Extender Attached

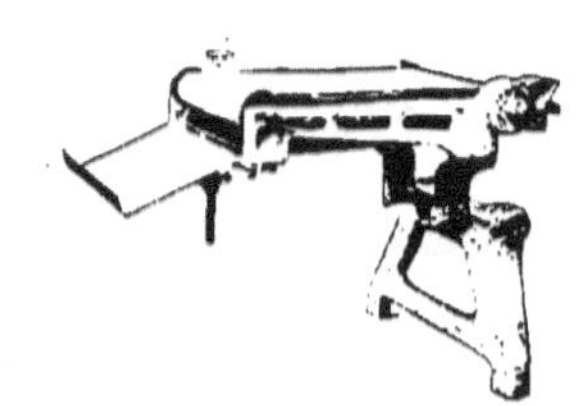

There would not be a very large number of Bakers using Thomson equipment if it were not for the fact that it fills a long felt need. The unprecedented demand for Thomson equipment is very gratifying to us, its builders. We like to assign as a reason for this, the inherent goodness of our equipment and the fairness of our policy, because Thomson equipment is designed and produced by a group of farseeing, capable men.

"Take it up with Thomson"

THOMSON MACHINE CO.
BELLEVILLE **NEW JERSEY**

(When addressing advertisers kindly refer to THE NATIONAL BAKER)

READ THIS IMPORTANT LETTER ABOUT

Refined Cerelose

Corn Products Refining Company   Chicago, February 4th, 1922
   17 Battery Place, New York City

Gentlemen:

   In accordance with your instructions we have examined the sample of H. P. Cerelose submitted
to us by your Mr. Kirkland with a view to determining its value as compared to cane sugar for
bread making.

   The sample was analyzed chemically with the following results:

$$\text{Moisture} \quad . \quad , \quad . \quad . \quad . \quad . \quad . \quad . \quad . \quad . \quad . \quad . \quad . \quad 8.84\%$$
$$\text{Reducing Sugar calculated as dextrose} \quad . \quad . \quad 87.10$$

   The rate at which it is fermented by yeast in comparison with the rate of fermentation of cane
sugar was determined first in a solution of the sugar to which had been added small amounts of
mineral nutrients. The weight of gas evolved in six hours from the cane sugar solution was 1.162
grams. The weight of gas evolved from the corn sugar solution was 1.187 grams. This test was
supplemented by one in which the volumes of gas evolved from doughs prepared in the ordinary way
for bread making was determined.

   In these tests the amount of gas produced was measured every half hour for a period of six hours.
The rate of evolution of gas was substantially the same for both the cane and corn sugars, and the
average of experiments showed a total of 1153 c. c. of gas produced by the corn sugar dough, and
1150 c. c. of gas produced by the cane sugar dough during the total fermentation period of six hours.

   The relative hygroscopicity of the corn sugar and of cane sugar was compared by placing the
two in thin layers in a chamber where the atmosphere was kept saturated with moisture. Under
these conditions the cane sugar absorbed much more rapidly than the corn sugar.

   Change in the moisture content in the two sugars under ordinary atmospheric conditions at a
room temperature of approximately 70 F., was also determined, and we found no material variation
between them. The facts in regard to both these hygroscopicity tests have been platted in the form
of curves which are attached herewith.

   The important tests in connection with this investigation were naturally the baking tests. These
were made first on a small scale in the laboratory, the tests being made on doughs prepared from
exactly the same raw materials and in exactly the same fashion with the exception that in one case
sugar was used as in our regular testing formula, and in the other exactly the same weight of corn
sugar was substituted for it. These tests were repeated in the laboratory on successive days, and we
were not able to detect any difference either in the rate of fermentation or in the resultant loaves.

   However, since we are convinced that final and reliable results on baking problems of this type
cannot be obtained by the laboratory alone, the tests were repeated on 50 and 100 loaf batches in two
commercial bakeries, and in both cases the rate of fermentation was substantially identical and the
finished loaves were of substantially the same quality.

   We are, therefore, of the opinion that H. P. Cerelose of the quality submitted to us for this test
can be substituted satisfactorily, pound for pound, for cane sugar in ordinary bread-making operations.

                              Very truly yours,

CSM*C   THE MINER LABORATORIES
                                                per CARL S. MINER

HERE is an opportunity to save approximately one cent
per pound on sugar by using REFINED CERELOSE—a new
product—and still maintain your high standard of quality.
Sample of this product will be cheerfully sent upon application.

Manufactured Both in Pearl and Powdered Form

CORN PRODUCTS REFINING COMPANY
17 Battery Place, New York City

Extra Strong High Patent

The aim of the Occident Millers has always been to produce a flour of the highest quality.

That is why this company operates more than 140 elevators spread throughout the spring wheat belt, ten mill elevators and one huge terminal elevator—a combined wheat storage capacity of 9,500,000 bushels.

Unusual for a daily flour capacity of 13,000 barrels, but all-important to the production of a better flour.

Costs More — Worth It!

OCCIDENT

Russell-Miller Milling Co. Minneapolis Minnesota

Branch Offices:

Pittsburgh, Pa.	Park Bldg.	Boston, Mass.	Board of Trade Bldg.
Philadelphia, Pa.	Lafayette Bldg.	Seattle, Wash.	Maritime Bldg.
Syracuse, N. Y.	Brix Bldg.	San Francisco, Cal.	Merchants' Exch.
New York City	Produce Exchange	Des Moines, Iowa	112 S. W. 7th St.
	Los Angeles, Cal.	658 Santa Fe Ave.	

Birmingham, Ala. American Trust Bldg.

Raisins 40% Cheaper

means a new opportunity in—

—millions want it daily

Start it Now

Don't wait too long with your raisin bread!

Raisins are now 40% cheaper than formerly. That means a new opportunity for you—a good reason why you should lose no time in again featuring raisin bread.

Another good reason—here are even *finer* raisins that will make a *better bread*. Use the delicious Bakers' *Seeded* Sun-Maids—the raisins with that real raisin flavor.

We are constantly advertising raisin bread. Most all women see this advertising. They will come to *you* for it, because we tell them that the neighborhood bakers have it, and that they make it *best*.

Raisin bread enjoys a permanent popularity. It has been the favorite bread for ages and ages, just as it is the favorite loaf of today. The demand for it is constant—and always large.

So with better raisins today, 40% cheaper, you can now realize larger profits with seeded Raisin Bread. Start baking it regularly—now!

SUN-MAID RAISINS
Delicious *Raisin-Bread* Raisins

'Bakers' Seeded Sun-Maid Raisins are especially for bakers' use in bread, cakes, cookies, snails, "race tracks," pie, etc., are selected, washed and sterilized, to make them perfect raisins for your use.

Now cheaper by 40% than formerly. Rely safely on prices and other information given you by our own direct representatives who will call on you.

Bakers know that Seeded Raisins absorb 10% more water.

California Associated Raisin Co.
Membership 13,000 Growers
Dept. E-6-1 Fresno, Calif.

Free

The coupon below is for your use, no matter what position you hold in any bakery, large or small.

If your raisins, no matter from whom purchased, have deteriorated or lost quality for any reason, if you have an unused stock of raisins, ask us for suggestions to help remove the difficulty—no matter what it is. We maintain a Bakers' Service Department which will supply free formulas for mixes on request. Use coupon below.

Free Service to Busy Bakers

Write us about your difficulties, if any, with any variety of raisins—see our offer below. We will gladly place at your disposal, without charge, the resources of our Bakers' Service Department, composed of practical bakers familiar with *your* problems and methods that have solved the same problems for others.

We came in contact with one baker not long ago who found that placing the raisins on a sheet pan in the oven for a while caused the white sugar-spots, when there were any, to disappear quickly, the sugar going back into the raisin, and thus restoring it to the same condition in which it left our California packing plant.

That is but an instance of the various helpful little hints we pick up all along the line, and incorporate in the service we offer you.

California Associated Raisin Co.,
Dept. E-6-1, Fresno, California.

Please send me free formulas for mixes for raisin products that you have found to be practical sellers through large and small bakeries.

Name...

Street..

City.....................State.......................

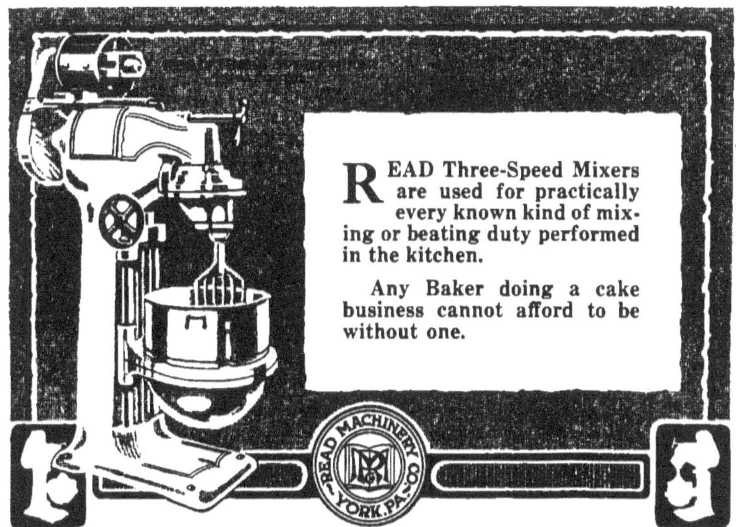
READ Three-Speed Mixers are used for practically every known kind of mixing or beating duty performed in the kitchen.

Any Baker doing a cake business cannot afford to be without one.

READ MACHINERY CO.
YORK, PA.

NEW WIDE MOUTH OVEN
DOOR 10½"x40"

Fig. 1 F
With light controlled by opening and closing door. Flue opening in top.

NEW LAMP FOR STEAM OVENS

All Porcelain Covered Electric Connections.
Fig. 1 S

Will Last a Lifetime. Will Fit All Ovens.

CHAS. ROBSON & CO.
8th St. & Washington Ave., Philadelphia, Pa.

ZEBRA TAPE
VENTILATED YET TAPABLE
Perfect Bredrap

Once you apply the tape, the paper will tear before it loosens. Furthermore, no matter how humid or rainy the weather, or how warm the bread, this wrapper prevents premature mould.

THE WATERPROOF PAPER & BOARD co.
BREDRAP
DESIGNERS AND MANUFACTURERS
CINCINNATI, OHIO
U.S.A.

DUTCHESS

Roll Dough Dividers, Oven Lights, Oven Doors, Fire Doors, Etc.

Make your work easy, accurate and profitable with a DUTCHESS Roll Dough Divider. These great labor and material savers are built in two sizes—a heavy floor machine, and a lighter machine for bench use. They can't be equalled for making rolls. Each machine cuts 36 pieces of equal weight at one operation. Don't waste your time breaking off rolls in the old fashioned, slow, wasteful one-at-a-time method. Save your time and material. Use a DUTCHESS

New Prices Effective May 2nd, 1921
Stand Machine $169.00

Bench Machine $30.00

For That New Oven

Insist on DUTCHESS Fixtures and you may be sure that they will give you lasting dependable service. They are made only of the best grade of grey iron castings, carefully fitted, no leaky joints, and resist the effect of heat and hold their shape.

Ask Your Supply House

The Test of Time

is the surest test 

OP Malt Extract

has stood this test and has not been found wanting.

Prudent bakers do not experiment—they place full reliance in

OP MALT EXTRACT

Malt-Diastase Company

79 Wall Street, NEW YORK

Warehouses: CHICAGO, PHILADELPHIA   *Laboratories,* BROOKLYN, N. Y.

Be a Bakery Superintendent

No matter what your present job may be, there is always room for better men at higher wages—AT THE TOP.

Experts are scarce. Cheap help is plentiful enough. Employers want CAPABLE people in their employ—men who know their business thoroughly. To such they will pay big wages.

You cannot know too much about the Baking Industry.

The Siebel Institute of Technology

has a plan whereby you can earn while learning greater proficiency in baking.

Their Home Study Course in Scientific Baking enables you to train yourself for a better paid position in the Bakery business. *You owe it to yourself to make more money.*

It is easy to learn these simple lessons which have been written for your benefit by TWENTY LEADING AUTHORITIES in the Baking Industry.

Your Home Study is rendered still more interesting by practical laboratory work which you do at home in your spare time with the FREE LABORATORY OUTFIT, included with the Home Study Course.

If your pay ranges from $30.00 to $50.00 a week—or even higher—the Siebel Home Study Course will show you how to command *much more*. It will help you to attain greater efficiency—greater earning capacity—and *more money*.

Therefore send TODAY—without obligating yourself—for full particulars by filling out and mailing the accompanying coupon to the

835 Montana Street   CHICAGO, ILL.

SIEBEL INSTITUTE OF TECHNOLOGY, Dept. "NB."
935 Montana Street, Chicago, Illinois.

Please send me full particulars of the Siebel Home Study Course in Scientific Baking, FREE.

Name ....

Address ....

Town ....

State ....

Position I Now Hold...

Arkady bakers have many advantages over those who have not yet adopted that great bread-improving and money-saving yeast nutrient. For with the aid of

they are able to turn out a loaf of far better texture, bloom and flavor.

They need buy only half as much yeast as the non-user.   ARKADY really *makes* the rest of the yeast in the dough itself.

ARKADY bakers save over two months' supply of sugar every year, because It conserves 20% of the sugar from fermentation loss.

They save a whole week's supply of flour every year because ARKADY also conserves 2% of the flour from destruction by fermentation.

ARKADY has become a standard ingredient in the making of bread. Over 15,000,000 loaves of bread a day are ARKADY-baked in America alone.

When will *you* decide to make bread the modern ARKADY way? Why not order a trial shipment to-day?

ARKADY is sold in 50-pound drums and 180-pound sacks. Price 13c per pound. In lots of 900 pounds or over, 11c per pound. Both prices f.o.b. New York, and subject to change without notice.

Write for the ARKADY book.

RESEARCH PRODUCTS DEPARTMENT

WARD BAKING COMPANY, NEW YORK

PUBLISHED ON THE FIFTEENTH OF EACH MONTH

AT

411 WALNUT ST., PHILADELPHIA

BY

THE NATIONAL BAKER PUBLISHING CO.

B. F. WHITECAR, PRESIDENT AND EDITOR
W. W. GALE, SECRETARY AND TREASURER

MEMBER OF THE AUDIT BUREAU OF CIRCULATIONS

SUBSCRIPTION RATES
UNITED STATES, ITS POSSESSIONS AND CANADA ..$2.00 per year
FOREIGN COUNTRIES .... 3.00 per year

PAYABLE IN ADVANCE

ADVERTISING RATES ON APPLICATION

Make all remittances payable to the order of
The National Baker Publishing Company

*Changes for displayed advertisements must reach this office
by the 5th of the month*

Vol. XXVII   MAY, 1922   No. 316

CONTENTS

Advertising for the Smaller Bakeries 29
American Bakers' Association 30
Bread of Life............. 32
Business Value of Optimism 27
Cake Recipes:
  Fruit Cookies 56
  Sugar Cookies 56
  Ginger Cookies 56
  Wine Cookies 56
  Sponge Cake 56
  White Loaf Cake........ 56
  Raspberry Fingers....... 56
  Butter Snaps 56
  Madagascars 56
  Fig and Raisin Cake..... 56
  Fluted Lemon Cake...... 58
  Cocoanut Cakes 58
  Russian Loaf Cake...... 58
  Crumb Jumbles 55
Chicago Convention 40
Coming Back to Bread..... 28
Copyright Designs for Bread Wrappers 42
Flour Wisdom 29
Have Good Tools.......... 25
Importance of Good Credit 31
Improving Rye Bread...... 55

Information Department:
  Devil's Cake 62
  Swiss Buns 62
  Bread Troubles 62
  Crumb Cakes 62
  Milk Bread 62
  Cheap Pound Cake...... 63
  Anise Drops 63
  Vanilla Wafers 63
  Angel Cake 63
  Maple Mousse 64
  Dark Rye Bread......... 64
  Sugar and Glucose Icing. 64
New England Convention... 39
Overhaul the Equipment... 25
Pennsylvania Convention Program 35
Pie Bakers to Meet........ 42
Power and Lighting for Bakeries 44
Proposed Pennsylvania Regulations 48
S. S. Watters Tendered Dinner 36
Trade Items 59
Up-to-Date Ideas on Quality Bread 52
Wheat Stocks and Prospects 54
Western Pennsylvania Bakers 36
Why Do Business On Sunday? 23

Why Do Business on Sunday?

CONSIDER the retail baker. He works hard on Monday, works hard on Tuesday, works hard all the rest of the week up to Saturday, when he and all his employes buckle down and work harder. Then comes Sunday, ordained from Creation as a day of rest, but in many cases the poor old baker on that day puts in the hardest and the longest licks of all the week. Pretty nearly all the rest of the world rests, or worships or plays, but the retail baker toils. It is time he heard of Sunday closing. The baker has been the industrial goat long enough.

The trend of the times is toward shorter hours of labor, especially since the war. The tendency is a positive one, and gaining strength as it goes. In virtually all of the cities retail business on Sunday is suspended, except, in cases like the baker's, with industries administering to the requirements of the public stomach. Not only do most workers get their Sundays off, but in many cases they get their Saturday afternoons off as well, and their evenings throughout the week.

The principle involved is a simple one and means only that the retailer must train his trade to do all its buying on week days. These are numerous enough and long enough; and, except in unusual cases, the baker, as have his brothers in other retail lines, can train his customers to provide on Saturdays for their Sunday wants. His customers have their Sundays off and, once they get the idea in their heads that the baker is seeking for himself what others enjoy, they can be depended upon to respond. The baker does not want to be classed as an industrial reactionary, and he will have no one but himself to blame if he fails to climb aboard the Sunday-closing band wagon.

The master and the employes of a certain bakery in a busy town used to boast that they began work at 7 o'clock on Sunday morning and they never finished until 11 o'clock at night. They were proud of it. It meant that the house was doing a big business and making money. It was an illustration of the point to which the American scramble for the almighty dollar was leading the workers of the land. The owner of the shop had a friend in business downtown, while his was a neighborhood bakery. The downtown friend went into the Sunday-closing movement which the merchants on his street organized, and thereafter his shop was closed on Sunday.

The neighborhood baker was not pleased with long Sunday hours after that. He missed his friend on that day, for his friend was in the country, or at church or at a ball game, according to the season and the humor in which the Sunday morning found him. Then he determined to see if he could not afford to close up shop on Sunday. He went over his books carefully and noted the names of the people who were given to Sunday ordering of bread and cake and pies or ices. He watched the shop on Sundays to see also who went for supplies on the Sabbath. .He found that everything except the ices could just as well be delivered or called for on Saturday evening or Saturday night as on Sunday. He figured that the profit he made on the ices alone was not sufficient to justify keeping open on Sunday, and made up his mind that he and his employes were going to get their Sundays off.

HOW IT WORKED

Having figured that the Sunday-closing scheme would work, he determined to give his trade a month to get used to the idea and prepared a circular in which he set forth to the customers his reasons for wanting to close on Sundays. He was by no means a highly educated man, but was wise enough to realize it. His advertising he had written for him, the ad writer using information the baker furnished for the copy. To the ad writer he took this problem and together they framed up a statement of the situation, which put the case squarely before the housewives of the whole neighborhood.

The trade was told that in most of the other retail businesses in town there was no such thing as Sunday service. People were accustomed to laying in on Saturday everything they would need for Sunday, and that was accepted as a matter of course. It was set forth that everything the bakers made and sold, except the ices, could be delivered to the homes in which they were to be used on Saturday as well as Sunday, and it was announced that Blank's bakery would, on June 1st, adopt a policy of Sunday-closing. The store would not be opened at all for business, though certain deliveries would be made on Sunday morning, provided the orders for such supplies were left at the shop before closing time on Saturday night.

The circular was sent out first of May, along with the monthly statements of the shop. Collectors carried these bills around for Blank, who figured that he was in a position to profit more by using collectors than by sending out statements in the mail. Each collector carried the shop's circulars, folded neatly and enclosed in envelopes and addressed to the people at whose houses they were to be left, and involved only a little more work and time when the collector stopped in at the other houses on the block. By this means the baker made sure that every home in the whole neighborhood was advised of his plan a month in advance.

In addition such advertising as the baker did during May contained a statement to the effect that after the first of June his bakery would be closed on Sunday. A Sunday-closing campaign was on in town at the time, aimed at reaching some of the obstinate downtown merchants who had refused to observe the agreement entered into by the other retailers, while the grocers in town had announced a Thursday half holiday through the summer months. This enabled the baker, through the good offices of a newspaper man he happened to know, to get a "story" in each of the city newspapers, featuring the fact that Blank's bakery was the latest Sunday-closing recruit.

Neatly printed placards in the shop, attached also to the delivery wagons, and similar devices stamped on the bottoms of the paper plates that were used in putting up goods, as well as on the bottoms of the candy boxes and the paper sacks, throughout the mouth contained the same announcement. The big cards were done by a sign painter at a small cost, while the small ones were made by a rubber stamp and ink pad. In addition to these means of acquainting the customer with the purpose of the baker, special attention was given to the Sunday orders. With each of them the drivers of the wagons and the clerks in the store were instructed to deliver one of the original circulars, with a word to the cook in the kitchen or to the child who came forward for the order that there would be only one or two other Sundays when such purchases could be made.

It worked like a charm. The baker and his clerks helped out a bit for the first few Saturdays by suggesting to every caller and to every person who telephoned an order in that there would be no Sunday deliveries unless orders were received that night, and that the shop would not be opened at all on Sunday. Some little complaint was made because the baker declined to deliver ices after Sunday mid-day, though he guaranteed that special orders for Sunday night suppers could be delivered at noon on that day and the ices so well packed that they would keep perfectly until they were to go on the table. One or two of the employes, with sometimes a little assistance from the baker himself, were able to put up and send out in a few hours on Sunday morning the orders that had been received on the night before.

The delivery wagons were easily able to take care of the deliveries, for, with all the orders in, deliveries could be routed in such a way that no driver had to cover the ground more than once. It got to the point where deliveries could be taken care of so well in three hours that the men did not report till 9 o'clock and got away by noon or very shortly afterward. They loaded their wagons as they left and this meant that the shop employes who reported on Sunday morning were able to get away in time, if they chose, for Sunday school. By rotation of the Sunday morning assignment the new plan worked out so that each man and each girl had only a little work to do every third Sunday, whereas previously Sunday had been about the busiest day for everybody.

BUSINESS DID NOT SUFFER

The baker's business did not suffer a bit, either. Here and there he offended a customer by declining to make an afternoon delivery, as he used to on Sunday, but the volume of this business was not big enough to cause any hole in the net receipts. His gross receipts fell off lightly at first, but the decreased outlay meant a bigger net return. The morale of his whole force was improved, everybody felt better, and the chronic grouches became optimists. Besides being a humanitarian move, Sunday-closing with this baker proved to be a good business.

Throughout the country are hundreds and hundreds of neighborhood and downtown retail bakers situated in much the same position as was this baker. They keep a seven-day week, with Sunday one of the hardest days of all. Work gets to be monotonous and the baker and his employes become mere automatons. They bake and sell mechanically, get into a rut. This results in an attitude toward business which probably explains more than any other one thing the unfavorable condition of many of the shops. The baker's own initiative is worn down by the constant grind. He gets used to seeing trash accumulate and doesn't have the time nor the heart to overhaul his place. The first thing he knows, unless he has a business big enough to sit back and watch it, his shop deteriorates and his business decreases.

A good day of rest, or of freedom from the grind that cannot be escaped through the week, will send the baker and all his employes back to the shop on Monday fresh and rested. They will work better and faster for the rest and take a renewed interest in the shop and everything about it. Instead of getting into a rut, they will be in the best possible position to get out of it and keep out of it. Everybody is entitled to his one day of rest in the week provided he gives honest and reasonable services on the other six days.

It probably will be a long time before the baker will be able to confine his week's work to the first five days, but there is no good reason why he should not have his Sundays off.

—‡—‡—‡—

Have Good Tools

BAKERS have frequently been heard to denounce the journeymen as a class, and complain of the inconveniences of their nomadic traits. The average journeyman baker is by no means perfect, but the "boss" is frequently responsible for the resistible desire of the journeyman to "keep moving." We have conversed with journeymen, workers, and admitted to be such by their employers, who were expected to turn out first-class goods with half an equipment. They would indignantly point to the sparse supply of utensils and ask how any man could be expected to keep up his name and use such tools. Usually in such cases the employer is not a practical baker, and cannot appreciate the handicap under which a man works with insufficient equipment. In many cases, however, the master is his own journeyman, and even he "putters" along doing without half a dozen articles that he should have. Unfortunately, some bakers cannot realize that their time should be worth something, and they forget that the journeyman could do perhaps twice as much with a suitable equipment. Money exchanged for tools is invested, not spent, and yields good returns. The journeyman would not be so anxious to move elsewhere, after a week or a month, if he has reasonable encouragement in the matter of utensils, providing other matters are satisfactory.

Overhaul the Equipment

THERE is a certain large baking company that since the war has been receiving many complaints about its bread. The bread is not uniform in quality. Some batches are very good. Some are not so good. Some cause a great many complaints.

In the case of this company the cause is traceable largely to labor. The war called some of its employes to the colors. Some left to earn higher wages in the munition plants. Since then it has not been possible to get the labor force back to the efficient basis it was before the war.

The chances are that in all industries this trouble will be experienced for some years to come. Talk to nearly any manufacturer or any dealer and if you can win his confidence he will tell you that it is hard to find the dependable quality in many lines that existed before the war.

The manufacturer in many cases does not find it easy to secure the kind of raw material that he was able to get before the war. He has more trouble also to keep the quality of his own goods up to the pre-war standard. It is the working force that often gives him the most trouble.

Even today many a person who has been trained in one line is working or seeking work in another. Take a single example. A man who all his life had worked in a store secured work in a machine shop during the war. Since then he has been out of employment at times but he is still working or seeking work in a machine shop. He has not gone back to the store.

In addition to this there were some four million young men who would have spent the six months to the two or more years that they were in the service learning some trade or business if it had not been for the war. After the war many of these started out in a line entirely different from that which they had begun to learn at the outbreak of the war.

The method that the large baking company previously mentioned is adopting to overcome these conditions is to install baking machinery that is automatic in its operation, machinery that maintains the same temperature in the oven, that keep the humidity and the temperature of the proofer and dough room uniform. It is installing machinery that requires less skill and experience on the part of the operator to turn out a uniform product.

Now this machinery costs money. In some cases the operating cost, the fuel and the electric power costs more than was true of the old machinery yet it is saving money. It saves labor and it saves selling expense.

Let us suppose that a baker installs new equipment that increases the actual cost of each loaf of bread one-third of a cent. The bread costs more to make but it is of absolutely uniform quality. The probability is that the labor cost would be reduced to an extent that would off-set the increased cost of operating the machinery, but we will assume that the labor cost is not reduced, that the cost of each loaf of bread is actually increased by one-third of a cent.

At first sight it would seem that this would reduce or eliminate the profits. The cost has been increased and consequently if the selling price is not also increased, and this cannot very well be done, the profit margin is reduced.

The cost of making the bread, however, is only a part of the total cost of turning that bread into money. After it is made it must be sold.

If the bread is of absolutely uniform quality, people are going to get into the habit of buying it and they are going to continue to buy it simply because they can depend upon it. They are going to tell their friends and neighbors about it and the sales work these people do because the bread is uniform in quality is going to be worth real money to the baker.

On the other hand if the bread varies in quality, if the batch turned out today is of the very best quality, the bread turned out tomorrow is not quite so good due to a lower oven temperature or something wrong elsewhere in the shop, if the bread day after tomorrow is still poorer, and then the next day the quality jumps up to standard again, there is going to be trouble. People will become disgusted with the bread. They will either patronize some other baker or will bake in their own homes.

It costs a great deal of money to sell bread under such conditions. It may cost much more than the third of a cent a loaf that will have to be spent to bring the bread up to a uniform standard of quality.

If the trouble being experienced is due to labor, then either better labor will have to be secured or machinery installed that will in so far as possible require no expert operation. It is quite possible that considerable difficulty will be experienced for some time to come in always securing exactly the class of labor that is desired.

This is always the case after an upheaval. Millions of young men were killed during the war. These were not Americans to be sure, but their taking off will affect America. We can no longer draw upon Europe for well trained and skilled men to the same extent that we did before the war, because there is no longer the surplus of such men in Europe there was before the war.

It is in many cases necessary to rely upon machinery more than upon human beings to perform exact operations. This means that it will be well for the baker to look to his machinery. If he can procure something better for the purpose than he has now, this is the time to make the change.

Today the manufacturers are more willing to sell upon favorable terms than they will be when business once more becomes active. The machinery can be installed now with less interference with the conduct of the business than it can when the demand for the goods produced increases.

More important than all this, however, is the fact that if the baker now overhauls his present machinery and puts it into condition to make his output uniform, or installs new machinery that will make it more uniform, he is preparing at once for more and better business. Now is a good time to create a reputation for dependability.

As business picks up it is going to pick up fastest for those bakers who have served their customers best. It is going to pick up fastest for those bakers who in spite of all obstacles have been able to keep their products a uniform quality.

It is going to pick up fastest for those bakers who, when they have found it impossible to secure the right kind of labor have substituted the machinery that will do the work. Money spent on the right kind of machinery, now, is pretty certain to be spent where it will do the most good.

Of course there is the argument that at the present time business is not good enough to go to this expense. This seems like a perfectly good argument. But there is another side. Today everybody is looking for business. Under such conditions the buyer can buy at the greatest advantage. He can get the service that he desires. He will be given more attention than he would be given if business was better and orders were merely being filled rather than sought.

When business gets better everyone who has been waiting will begin to buy. As a matter of fact buying is already starting. The railroads are beginning to turn the deficits of the past into profits. They are using these profits to buy new equipment. Railroad after railroad is placing large orders. This increases the demand for iron, wood, and other material that not only enters into the construction of what the railroad buys but into the construction of the machinery that the baker buys.

These orders will give employment not only to the people working in the factories filling the orders but in many other factories as well. The wages earned will be spent and business will improve. Then everyone will increase their purchases and within a few months everyone will be buying.

The baker who wants to get his plant into shape to profit by the return of prosperity cannot afford to delay starting even by a single day.. If he does, it is bound to lose profits that could be his if he will start at once. Now is the time to bring the shop thoroughly up to date, to buy the new machinery that sometime during the coming year or two will be needed.

—‡—‡—‡—

The Freihofer Baking Co. opened their large new plant at Twelfth and Chestnut streets, Chester, Pa., on April 28th, with a general celebration, at which the people of Chester were invited. There was music, dancing and refreshments, and a large number of people took advantage of the opportunity to see a modern, automatic bakery in operation. This plant was built by the Huber Baking Co., who ran it for some time. It has been brought up to date in every respect.

The Business Value of Optimism

THERE is no greater monument to optimism than the western half of the American continent. It began to be settled before there were any railroads. People crossed the plains in wagons to reach it, and because that original optimism has never waned that part of the country has continued to grow and prosper.

Today there are 60 automobiles in the Pacific Coast States for every native born white man over the age of 21. It is optimism more than anything else that has made this possible. There are other parts of the world with at least almost as many natural advantages as can be found here, but there most certainly is no other part of the world where there is so much optimism.

What optimism has done for the West it will do for any industry, in fact it has done so for at least two industries. The automobile industry is an industry of optimists, and the number of cars in use has risen from about 300 in 1895, to nearly ten million now. The moving picture industry is another industry of optimists, from practically nothing, twenty-five years ago, it has grown to be the fifth largest industry in the country.

In the case of this industry it is quite possible that the optimism of the West proved contagious, for much of the production takes place on the Pacific coast. One thing is certain, however, this industry could never have grown to the size that it has, had it not been for the optimism displayed by those connected with it.

What optimism has done for the West, what it has done for the automobile industry, what it has done for moving pictures, it will also do for the bakery business. Let every baker be as optimistic about the bakery business as every Californian is about his state and the bakery business simply can't help growing and prospering. The very optimism would make it do so.

It would be a bad thing for California to have a lot of people living there who thought it had a rotten climate. It is equally a bad thing for any business to have a lot of people in it who think it is a rotten business. The fact that there are men in the bakery business who think it is a bad business is making the growth of the bakery business slower than it otherwise would be.

No one wants to patronize a man who considers his business is a bad business, a rotten business, if they can get just as good value by spending their money with someone else. They do like to spend money with an optimistic man, just as everyone who receives a letter in the East from a friend living in the West wants to go West.

It is optimism that does it. The first essential for real success in the bakery business is a firm belief, a belief that cannot be shaken that the bakery business is the best business in the world and that it has the greatest future. The moment that one is able to acquire this attitude of mind, he is bound to make rapid progress. As a matter of fact no business depression, no set back, no obstacles, no matter how great it may be will be able to hold him back.

Just what optimism has done in individual cases is illustrated by the business experience of a man who, beginning life on a barren farm, went to work in a store and saved enough money to start a store of his own. For a time he prospered but it was not many years before there came a business depression and it required all his optimism to keep him in business during the depression. He, however, did succeed in borrowing the money that he absolutely had to have in order to avoid bankruptcy.

He saved from the business enough money to tide him over the next business depression only to lose it at the very beginning of that depression and again his optimism was put to the test. This time he survived.

Instead of reverses causing him to be discouraged his optimism caused him to profit by them, and as a result he is a rich man today. That man has no more ability and in some respects has less ability than many other men who failed. The only respect in which he is greatly superior to them is in his optimism.

There is a man, who with no previous experience in the business, bought a little bake shop. Everyone who knew anything about that shop and the community it served explained to him that he could not possibly succeed there. They showed him that he had simply thrown his money away.

But he was an optimist and did not listen to them. Within a surprisingly short time he had built up a very profitable business and now has more money than any of the pessimists who told him he had thrown away his money.

There is something about optimism that is contagious. Let a person enter a store that is owned by an optimist and in spite of himself he will spend more money than he intended to spend. That atmosphere of optimism makes it so easy to spend money that he simply can't help doing so.

If John Wanamaker was not an optimist the sales in his store would not begin to total the volume that they now total. Probably no man in the retail business has tried more new things than has this man, and the main reason why he has tried them is because he is an optimist. It has been said that no newspaper advertising is more effective than that this merchant uses, and here again we find the value of optimism. Other concerns that have closely approached the advertising in form have never secured the same results, largely because they have not backed that advertising with the same degree of optimism.

The automobile industry has been the first to recover in this business depression, not because people were more inclined to buy automobiles than they were cake, but because there were a few optimistic men in the industry who started out and sold cars. Once these men had demonstrated their optimism in a practical way, it was only a short time before other men were infected with optimism and the Industry rapidly approached normal, while some other industries were and are still waiting for conditions to pick up.

People don't base their judgments upon facts and figures, they don't go to places they have learned about from careful study. They go to those places they hear talked about in the most optimistic and enthusiastic manner. People don't buy what they need most. There is scarcely a person who does not need things he don't buy more than he does those things he does buy.

People spend money with those stores that are owned by optimists. They buy the commodities they hear talked about with the greatest enthusiasm and optimism.

Just a little more enthusiasm and optimism on the part of the bakers is going to make more people buy bakery products. Just a little more enthusiasm and optimism on the part of those who work for bakers is going to increase sales for the simple reason that these people are going to talk with more enthusiasm and optimism.

A certain concern found it necessary to increase sales. Apparently everything was being done that could be done to increase those sales. A little investigating, however, showed that one thing had been neglected. No determined effort had been made to make the employes enthusiastic about the goods and optimistic about the industry. Steps were taken to imbue these employes with enthusiasm and optimism and nothing more was needed to increase sales.

No matter whether it is a nation, a portion of a nation, a city, an industry or an individual concern in that industry, optimism will increase the prosperity. The Chinaman and the Russian are each a good deal of a fatalist. They are not actively optimistic. To a great many the mere word Russia suggests anything but optimism. The dyed-in-the-wool westerner is an active optimist. He goes around spreading optimism broadcast and look at the difference between Russia, China and our own country. Many a business does not need more capital, a better location or more customers. All that it needs is OPTIMISM.

—‡—‡—‡—

Modern drainage, a liberal use of paint or whitewash, a good system of lighting and intelligent care will keep any shop clean and sweet, whether it is located above or below ground. A clean shop unquestionably means more business and a better paying business than an ill-kept shop. A clean shop is reflected in the store, likewise a dirty shop, and your customers soon get to know which sort you keep and increase their patronage or drop you as the case warrants.

—‡—‡—‡—

The Potomac States Convention will be held at the Hotel Rennert, Baltimore, Md., June 20th-22nd, and Secretary Glen O. Garber advises that a large and interesting program is in preparation.

Coming Back to Bread

IT has been an economic axiom that when times are hard people eat cheaper foods. They buy poorer cuts of meat, they eat less fruit, they turn to bread and cheap vegetables. But the war upset a lot of things and even economic laws were badly bent. Last year, in spite of dull business, lowering wages, cheap corn and wheat, and bread prices approaching pre-war levels we have eaten, not more bread, but decidedly less bread than when it was high and when unparalleled prosperity imposed no economic need for cheap food.

People may be eating more carefully than when there seemed to be no limit to the contents of the family purse, but it is to be doubted if they are actually eating fewer food units. That is, the food intake stands about level year in and year out. It is said that the German abdomen suffered a marked reduction during the lean years of the war when food was scarce and high. But even then the food actually consumed was but little less than usual. The difference lay in the fact that the German heavyweight consumed his own fat which he had been piling up as a surplus for years instead of taking it in the form of sausage and other comestibles.

The probable explanation of lessened bread consumption lies in the fact that at last we are practicing the lessons in thrift we learned so well in the meatless and wheatless days.

But there is a serious flaw in the logic which would have us eat less bread or counsel us to economize in our purchases at the bakery.

Of all the foods flour and sugar are the cheapest, the most concentrated, the least wasteful. There are no bones in a loaf of bread, there is no waste in cake or cookies. And bread and cakes, made of flour and sugar and the cheapest and best of fats, furnish far more food, with no cost to prepare or serve, than can possibly be found in any other form.

In the months ahead which we must meet with shrunken purses it would be well for our housekeepers to study carefully the relative food values of meats, fruits, preserves, the fancy groceries which cost so much more than staples and which furnish so little except variety and flavor, pastries and bread.

There is a way to meet living costs, an easy way, a wholly safe and comfortable and satisfactory way. That way is to get back to bread and milk, back to toast as a breakfast food, back to lunches of bread and meat, bread and jam, bread and cheese, back to great piles of evenly sliced bread on the dinner table. We can double our bread consumption and be the better fed; we can cut our food bill fifty per cent. and still be well nourished. The answer to every wail over the cost of living, whether it is raised by social workers, by economists or by politicians is EAT MORE BREAD.—*Baking Technology*.

—‡—‡—‡—

Some men would rather steal a poor living than earn a good one.

Advertising for the Smaller Bakeries

WHILE posters and wall and window cards are of undoubted value in any campaign to advertise bakery products, particularly bread, yet they are not as effective as newspapers, coming more under the heading of "General Publicity."

While general publicity is a factor in the successful advertising of any goods, it does not have the effect that good, reason-why advertising copy has; that is, advertising that tells the customer the merits of your goods and why he or she should buy your product rather than that of another firm.

Most bakers can use the local papers to better advantage as a medium through which to reach the consumers. In getting up copy for the newspapers you should consider that every word costs, and make each word carry its message to the consumers. Say you wish to advertise a good loaf of bread, a loaf that is above the average and should be preferred by the housewife; sit down and figure out why this loaf is better than the average, why it should appeal to the housewife; then pick out the strongest reasons and use them to make up a series of interesting advertisements, advertisements that carry with them conviction enough to make the first sale easy. After that, of course, the loaf itself must carry out your claims and make the consumer wish for more.

It is not necessary to mention all the good points of a loaf in every advertisement. You can feature one point in each advertisement, following it up with a strong appeal for the first purchase. The next advertisement may feature another good point, and so on.

In getting out a circular, always remember that any remember that it is the housewife who is your greatest competitor and who must be convinced that you can make better bread than she can, at a saving to her of time, trouble and money. While the men eat the bread and may comment on its goodness, it is the housewife, after all, who has the final word in buying. Once you convince her you have a loaf of real worth, the rest is easy.

Another way you can advertise your goods is to get out circulars for distribution. Don't make the mistake of using a poor grade of paper and having the work done in a slipshod, careless way. Such advertising is really a waste of money. It may be read in a few instances, but the very cheapness of the circular will create a bad effect that more than overbalances the money saved on the printing.

First, get up an attractive advertisement of your goods, written to appeal to the tastes of those who will read it. Make it sound good, so that it will make the reader wish for a bite of the delicious cake, jelly roll or other goods advertised. Don't be satisfied with your first attempt at writing this copy. Revise it several times, if necessary, until you have a finished piece of work that will be sure to appeal.

Then go to the printer and get him to show you several kinds of good paper stock on which to print it. Pick out one that will agree with the color of ink that you wish to use. Then instruct the printer to set it up in an attractive style and tell him that you must see a proof of it before it is printed. It might be well to have him notify you just as he is going to put the job on press, so that you can see how the colors harmonize when it is printed. Then a change can be made in the color to suit, if not just right, and by being there before it is run off, you will be sure to get what you wish.

In getting out a circular, always remember that any extra time or expense that is gone to will be more than repaid by the additional impression it will make on the consumer. Shun cheap printing in advertising.

Still another way is to distribute samples. While this means an added expense and takes nerve on the part of the advertiser to carry to a successful conclusion, it is a very good way to introduce your goods into the homes of non-consumers.

Vanity is too frequently the besetting sin of business men. They labor under the delusion that if they advertise during the few busy months the public will keep them in mind for the remainder of the year. They overlook the fact that when the mightiest of earth pass away, people cease to talk or think of them after a week. In order to be in the public mind one must keep his name or his business before the public. Advertising loses one-half of its efficacy when put out spasmodically.

—‡—‡—‡—

Flour Wisdom

IT seems unnecessary to point out to the baker that his advantage lies in buying a good quality of flour and paying a reasonable price for it. He may "shop" about and hammer down prices, and possibly he may occasionally get some standard flour at less than its value, but, in the very nature of things, a miller cannot continue to sell at a loss and, sooner or later, is compelled to furnish flour to fit price. Competition excuses him.

It is no more reasonable for the baker to expect the miller to furnish a standard quality of flour at cost or less, than it is for the public to expect the baker to make and sell a standard loaf of bread at five cents when it costs him that much or a trifle more to produce it. The baker could not continue business under such conditions and must either make poorer bread or offer a smaller loaf.

The baker of to-day takes a broad view of things or he drops out of the running. It is a well-established principle among the progressive, successful men in the bakery trade, that a superior quality of bread made in a sanitary bakery induces larger consumption. It must also be apparent to such bakers that to obtain good flour, the essential of good bread, it is necessary to pay a fair price. Quality should always be the first and foremost consideration and price secondary.

American Bakers' Association

A. L. TAGGART ASSUMES DUTIES OF ACTING PRESIDENT

AS A RESULT of action by the Executive Committee of the American Bakers' Association at a meeting held April 25th at the Association's new home, 1135 Fullerton avenue, Chicago, A. L. Taggart, of Indianapolis, has assumed the duties of Acting President of the bakers' organization. Mr. Taggart

served for some time as first vice-president, and has been keenly interested in building up the National organization and the American Institute of Baking. His choice as the organization's executive head settled much doubt on the part of bakers as to the status of Association affairs from an executive standpoint. In becoming Acting President Mr. Taggart made the following statement:

"While I have always been interested in association accomplishments I have never been actively connected with the actual workings of the executive offices. At this time I find myself in the position of many others, as I am an individual baker with a limited organization and therefore more closely tied to the details of my work than many others who have the time to devote to association affairs.

"A survey of the present situation convinces me that we are now prepared to concentrate all our efforts on our immediate tasks. Among these we find awaiting us the work of building up the American Institute and the School of Baking, and of making these activities accomplished facts before the convening of the National convention in Chicago in September.

"I have become familiar with the personnel and the activities of the American Institute and I am convinced that the work under way deserves the absolute confidence and support of the entire baking industry.

"We have all wasted too much time in the past in finding points on which to disagree and fall out. And now that, in taking charge at this particular time. I have 'jumped on the horse in the middle of the stream,' can I not count on the whole-hearted support of all members of the baking industry in a search for a basis on which we can all unite and work together for the common upbuilding of our industry?"

SCHOOL OF BAKING OPENS MAY 15TH

A special meeting of the Executive Committee of the American Bakers' Association was held in the offices of the Association, 1135 Fullerton avenue, Chicago, on April 24th and 25th, to prepare for the formal opening of the School of Baking on May 15, 1922.

Dr. H. E. Barnard, the Director of the American Institute of Baking, which will operate the school, reported that satisfactory progress is being made upon the two-story addition being constructed to the rear of the Institute building, in which will be installed two ovens, a Duhrkop and a Roberts Portable Oven, for use in the school. The funds for this construction work, together with other physical improvements to the Institute building for the school operations, have been provided by the American Bakers' Foundation, which appropriated $15,000 for these purposes. An additional appropriation of $15,000 was also made by the Foundation to equip and modernize the Institute building proper.

The school will be in the immediate charge of Peter G. Pirrie. Sixteen students for the first term have already been enrolled, and there are seventy-two additional applicants. The first class will be limited to thirty-six. The tuition to students sent by members of the American Bakers' Association will be $225 for the four months' term; for other students the tuition will be $300.

The Executive Committee confirmed the selection of the week of September 11th to 15th for the next annual convention of the Association, at which time the Bakery Equipment Manufacturers' Association will hold an extensive exhibit upon the Municipal Pier in Chicago.

In view of the desire to have the School of Baking in full operation, showing maximum results, for this convention, and develop the activities of the Institute to the farthest possible extent by that time, it was the unanimous sense of the Executive Committee that the entire efforts of the American Bakers' Association and its officers and committees from now until the next convention should be directed to strengthening and promoting this work of the Institute and the School, other activities to be undertaken or furthered only in so far as this may be possible through the office of the Association with the existing personnel and without increase of administrative expense, so that all the resources of the Association may be concentrated for the next five months upon the Institute activities.

AMERICAN INSTITUTE INCORPORATED

The General Counsel to the Association reported that, pursuant to the action taken by the Board of Governors at its last meeting, the American Institute of Baking was incorporated under the laws of the State of Illinois as a membership association, not for pecuniary profit. This incorporation of the Institute as a separate legal entity was deemed advisable in order to enable the Institute as an educational body for scientific learning, to deal more effectively with its own peculiar problems. The American Institute of Baking will continue, however, to be operated under the auspices of American Bakers' Association and under the control of that Association, the Board of Directors of the Institute being at all times composed of the same individuals or corporations who constitute the Board of Managers of the Association. Membership in the American Bakers' Association will carry with it active voting membership in the Institute and the only way to secure active membership in the Institute will be through membership in the Association.

The Executive Committee of the Association recognized, however, that there are many individuals and corporations, not engaged in the baking business and, therefore, ineligible for membership in the American Bakers' Association, who nevertheless are most keenly interested in the work of the Institute and who desire to express their active support to the work. It was the sense of the Committee that opportunity should be afforded such persons to become subscribers to the Institute, including "Baking Technology," at $10.00 per year.

The Executive Committee further voted its approval that the American Institute of Baking might accept support for its work from any individual or corporation, non-member of the Association, to be known as Contributor.

Dr. Barnard outlined a plan for establishment of fellowships in research work, such fellowships to be open to college and university graduates in chemistry who desire to continue their studies with a view to entering more largely upon the problems of the baking industry. The Committee voted to establish initially two such fellowships, each with a stipend of $500. It is hoped that these fellowships may multiply from special funds made available to the institute by special contributions or donations.

The Executive Committee further approved the purchase by the Institute of the entire laboratory equipment of Wahl-Henius for $5,000, payment for which will be made entirely through service rendered to Wahl-Henius Institute by the analytical laboratories of the Institute of Baking.

—‡—‡—‡—

The Importance of Good Credit

IT IS surprising the number of bakers who make a habit of neglecting to pay their supply bills when due; who "hang up" their supply account until they get good and ready to pay. They make a serious mistake. If a bill of goods is bought on thirty days' time it is due thirty days from the date of the bill, and the baker who holds such accounts for forty, fifty or sixty days is *not* saving money, as he may fondly imagine, but is seriously injuring his credit, which is and should be worth much more to a business man than his monthly balance at the bank.

Make no mistake, the man of slow pay, who ignores his financial obligations, is known and marked. If it is believed that he will pay sometime, the jobber may take a chance, but such a baker does not buy his supplies at the lowest market price. He may think that he does; therein he makes a mistake. The jobber who can collect his outstanding accounts quickly and turn his money over frequently is the one who can sell at a small margin of profit, which is a decided advantage to his customers.

All jobbers have at times "bargains," goods which, for good business reasons, they have been able to buy below the regular market price, and consequently can afford to sell at a reduction from the usual figure. Almost without exception these bargains are offered to those of their customers who are known as prompt pay. They favor the people who favor them; this is human nature. Men will, for the sake of holding their trade, submit to injustice at the hands of their debtors, but it doesn't make them feel good just the same, and when favors are to be shown in the way of special low prices, they go at once to those of their customers who promptly and cheerfully pay their just accounts.

The man who is known to discount his bills can pick and choose among the various supply dealers; you never hear of him being "owned" by any one house. He buys at the lowest price and has a chance at any special offering of goods which may be on the market, consequently he can sell at as low, or at a lower price than any of his competitors and make a fair profit on all of his goods. He can sell at a lower price and yet make a larger profit than can his competitor who is slow pay. Whereas, a man whose credit is poor, who pays his bills at uncertain intervals, who fails to keep his promises to pay, cannot expect to buy goods as cheaply as the man who discounts every bill and who fulfills every promise he makes to his creditors.

Holding fast to your money is not always economy. If you have it, or can borrow, pay your bills promptly. Take advantage of every discount; let your jobber know that you are in the market for any special offerings, when he needs "spot cash." After a year under this new method, compare your bills with those of the previous twelve months and you will never more be known as "slow pay." Bakers in general should give this matter more serious consideration. It is a matter of profit in many ways to the small baker as well as the large one.

—‡—‡—‡—

The Bureau of Foods of the Pennsylvania Department of Agriculture has given a clean bill of health to the chocolate coated ice cream bars sold in Pennsylvania. Since March 10th, agents of the Bureau have collected 90 samples sold in thirty cities and towns of the State.

These samples were submitted to the six chemists of the Bureau for analyses. Director James Foust, of the Bureau, has announced that the reports of the chemists showed that each of the ninety samples was entirely free of paraffin, cocoanut fat or adulteration of any kind.

Early in the year it was reported that a few dealers were substituting paraffin in the coating of the ice cream bars. A crusade instituted by the Bureau of Foods has resulted in the industry turning out a product that may be purchased without fear.

The Bread of Life

*By Ellwood M. Rabenold at the Southeastern
Convention*

THE symbolism of bread as life-giving and life-sustaining is very old. The spiritual relationship is recorded by Buddhist, Mohammedan and Hebrew prophets and disciples. The biological relationship is entablatured with the cartouches of the Pharoahs in the tombs of the pyramids. The symbolism is true today. The feeding of an entire nation of old in its forty-year journeying through the wilderness, by miraculous bread, is repeated in the salvation of millions abroad through the administration of our relief organizations, in distribution of bread-producing flour. From these unnumbered peoples, expressing human nature's primal instinct of persistence in being, their prayer for life has been a prayer for bread.

Under war conditions the Italian people derived ninety per cent. of their nourishment from bread. It is estimated that sixty per cent. of the French diet is bread. Great Britain with restricted meat supply increased greatly her consumption of bread during war times.

QUALITY REPLACES QUANTITY

The world conflict emphasized as never before the significance of bread for saving humanity and stabilizing civilization. Several European nations in order to avoid riots subsidized the wheaten loaf and charged the loss up to the cost of the war.

This intensive need of the world for quantity under war conditions having been somewhat relieved, the emphasis now is upon quality. And quality is judged today not merely by wholesomeness of ingredients, or proper fermentation, or taste, but rather by nutritiveness. The test is—how far does your bread sustain human life?

This necessarily involves a study of the chemical elements composing the human organism.

"Each human body is now recognized to be a chemical factory in which the most complicated chemical and physical changes are continuously taking place. When these reactions are normal from day to day, we are in good health. When they are abnormal they are a direct cause of disease, as in gout, diabetes, goiter and other serious diseases. Moreover, when abnormal, these fundamental chemical reactions lower the natural resistance of the body, especially to invading disease germs, and they thus lead indirectly to infection, disease and death."

How far does your bread assist those normal reactions that mean good health?

"Life in all its forms, be it vegetable, animal or human, is the highest expression of the transformation of matter and of energy. When we plant seeds in the fertile soil, the first stage of development consists in the transformation with the aid of water of the food, starch, proteins, fats, stored in the seed itself, into

rootlets, striking down into the soil below, and into stem and stalk, striking upward to reach finally the free air above. From the soil the rootlets absorb water and mineral salts—potash, lime, sulphates, phosphates, nitrogen in the form of nitrates and ammonia; from the air above the growing plant absorbs and transforms with the aid of the energy of sunlight carbon dioxide, the waste products of all animal life and of our cities' furnaces. From these simple ingredients thus taken from soil and air, the plant manufactures an infinite variety of new chemical substances, including carbohydrates (starches, sugars, gums, cellulose, wood), proteins, fats and oils, alkaloids (quinine, strychnine, morphine), dyes, and innumerable other substances. We have here in our growing plants tremendously intensive and infinitely varied *chemical laboratories* on the output of which all animal life and in particular all human life is finally dependent for its very existence.

"Human life, quite obviously, is also dependent in its every instant on the chemical transformation of matter; from our inception to our return to dust, we are transforming carbohydrates, fats, proteins, salts, water; every breath we draw, every motion we make involves chemical combustion. The assimilation of our food, its proper utilisation, its proper elimination, every single function indeed of our life is dependent on definite chemical and physical processes—relations so profound, in fact, that even the ultimate questions of life, of paramount moment to the race, are based on them, the fertilisation of the seed, the enlivening of the ovum—so like the kindling of a flame—the problems of heredity, of transmission of race and character from generation to generation."

How far does your bread, constructed from the berry of the wheat plant, contribute to these chemical and physical processes of life?

DEMANDS OF THE BODY

"The body demands an impressive variety of materials for its healthy sustenance. In its blind effort to contribute these, a part of humanity has been inclined to overeat, with its resultant ills of functional disturbances. Another large proportion of humanity has been well nourished in quantity, but undernourished in regard to particular units of sustenance—with the resultant diseases of undernourishment, beri-beri, pelagra and rickets.

"Recent work has shown that while the human body can construct a considerable number of its needs from the common ingredients of all foods, there are other vital, specific needs which must be supplied to it in finished form or else starvation of vital parts and disease and death follow in the midst of what otherwise would be plenty. It will be the duty of chemists to furnish a complete statement of such specific needs, to show just how they can be satisfied, to help out perhaps, indeed, by showing how certain rare and difficult units can be manufactured artificially.

"Indeed, co-operation between medicine and chemistry has already scored important victories in this field: Diseases such as scurvy and beri-beri have been found by physicians and chemists to have their source in the lack of certain minute but vitally important principles—hence called vitamines—found in some but not in all foods, and with these discoveries and the results of the analysis of a great variety of foods properly brought home to the practitioner the world over, these diseases should vanish from the face of the earth."

How many of these vitally important principles does your bread contain?

These questions must be answered. Human happiness in large measure is dependent upon the way in which you answer them. The physician often strives with devotion and sacrifice to alleviate suffering, check the ravages of disease and rally the fluttering pulse, only to face defeat because of undernourishment and malnutrition in a wasted body. His answer to the questions is perforce negative, defensive. It is your privilege to make your answers affirmative, offensive. You can assist in constructing a sturdier, stronger manhood and womanhood, in proportion as you understand the chemistry of your bakeshop in relation to the chemistry of life. The bloom of your loaf may be reflected in the ruddy cheek, the alert eye and the mobile body, vivified and fortified against attack of germ and bacillus, according as you build into your loaf more and more of the chemical elements that sustain life. You will elevate civilization as you increase nourishment, for nations grow only if well fed.

To accomplish this you must join forces with the chemist, the physicist, the bacteriologist, the pharmacologist, the pathologist, the experimental biologist and the medical practitioner, to make "analysis of the constituents of our body cells, of the components of the blood, of tissues, together with analysis of the components of our foods—so that we may have complete knowledge of the body in health and of what it needs to preserve its health."

CO-OPERATION AT EVERY HAND

Generous foundations are contributing millions to Johns Hopkins and to Harvard for establishing schools of public health; and the Public Health Service of the United States Government is extending its co-operation and encouragement everywhere. It is your great privilege to join in this work, in the study and practice of preventive medicine, with a true professional spirit, setting before yourselves the common task, to accomplish "that ultimate complete mastery of science over life, which will give man the wisdom to maintain health and increase the life span of the greatest number."*

I venture to go further. This is not only your privilege; it is your very solemn responsibility. You are the greatest food purveyors to mankind. Your

architects and engineers are rushing to increase your production. Your artists and litterateurs splash color and rhyme, dazzling the eye and the mind, to stimulate sales. Your ubiquitous yeast associate calls upon all to eat more bread. To what purpose? Merely that people shall gorge and stuff for your greater pecuniary profit? Not so. You are increasing your capacity for service—greater than that of any other industry, and when you invite human beings to rely more and more upon the product of your ovens to supply their life energy, you cannot avoid increased responsibility to make that service real and constructive. You cannot content yourselves with mere mechanical production. Your product is not an end in itself. No test applied to it is sufficient excepting the test of life.

In the assembling of your ingredients, in their commingling, in the fermentation and the baking, you are building chemical agencies which shall enter, harmoniously or inharmoniously as you determine, into the chemical fabric of the human body. Would you check life? Would you stunt growth? Would you blight existence? Would you by a year, or a day, or an hour, or even by a minute, shorten the existence of any human being? You cannot be sure that you avoid any of that unless you know—really know the effect of your handiwork upon human life. On the other hand, if you can be shown that by close attention, greater knowledge, finer perception of your processes and your raw materials, you may add to the span of life, develop the manhood and womanhood of your community, help combat disease so that all men may have life and life more abundantly—would you not do it?

The baking industry has caught this vision of its relationship to science. It has established the American Institute of Baking for this very purpose; it has called men of learning and devotion in this cause; it has established relations with eminent scientists, to study foods and foodstuffs and raw materials, to weigh their value in terms of nutrition, in terms of life, and give you the benefit of their findings, their scientific researches, their chemical insight, for the betterment of your business, the enriching of your product, the enlarging of your contribution to the public in your immediate community, and for the broadening of the permanent satisfactions of your calling. Are you supporting this Institute?

The Acting President of the national association, which is sponsoring and maintaining the Institute, is here with you. Will you not show him some visible and tangible sign that you uphold his hands? The director of the institute whose professional life and work and hopes and fears are bound up in it, is here with you. What heartening stimulus will you give him to carry back to his associates? The editor of the journal which publishes the results of the institute's researches is here with you. What sentiments of yours, what fervor, what reaction from you shall be reflect to the baking industry of the country?

---

*The quotations are taken from a report entitled "The Future Independence and Progress of American Medicine in the Age of Chemistry," prepared by a group of scientists and published by The Chemical Foundation. Inc.

Last evening, in the verdancy of this springtime, fresh blossoms suffusing the air with an anaesthetic aroma, as shadows lengthened and birds nestled, and stars began to peep and blink in your southern skies, the world seemed very much at peace and at rest. But you and I know that through the calm atmosphere there were waves eddying, carrying the radio music of operas, lectures of deep thought and pronouncements of political moment, all of which we could have for our edification.

So in your industry, the American Institute of Baking is today a broadcasting station, sending forth with vibrancy the scientific knowledge which shall make you truly great in the service of humanity. Will not you, each of you, set up an aerial to catch this knowledge, to enliven your business, to rejuvenate your minds, attuning your thought to the common thought which shall infuse into your handiwork more and more life-giving and life-sustaining substance and enable you to demonstrate that physical man *can* live by bread alone. Then you will have realized the highest goal of the baking industry. Your product will in fact be Bread of Life.

—‡—‡—‡—

Indiana Bakery Law

IN A circular letter recently sent to the members of the Indiana Bakers' Association, Secretary-Manager C. P. Ehlers, issues the following warning:

During the past few months I have received numerous complaints that bakers throughout the state are violating certain sections of the Indiana Bakers' Law, as well as the laws pertaining to premiums, lotteries, drawings, etc.

Now there isn't any question in my mind but that every baker in the state of Indiana knows when he is violating any of the laws, and even if he does not, *ignorance is no excuse*, for the Indiana Bakers' Association has, in its various bulletins, given the interpretations of the Indiana Bakers' Law, and we have always been ready and willing to give you any information that you may want.

One baker (let us call him Jones) says, "Smith, my competitor, takes back stale bread and I have a right to do it also." Still another baker says, "Smith and Jones are taking back stale and have never been prosecuted, I will operate on the same basis." And in a short time the entire community is affected by such unfair and unlawful practices.

It may happen to you or anyone else, who is violating the law, as it did to one baker who was using a stock wrapper without his name or the name of his bakery printed thereon. This baker was arrested and brought into court where he at once let out a loud yell that he was being unduly persecuted, as he had never been warned beforehand. The truth of the matter is, this same baker had received numerous letters from this Association telling him of the Indiana Bakers' Law and its requirements, and had been warned by

the State Food Inspectors at least three or four times, but at each warning he merely said, "They never have done anything to me, and I don't believe they ever will." These inspectors are on the job constantly, and are willing to aid you in every way possible, but if you do not respect them and their work, they have the power to enforce the law, and in some cases this may prove unpleasant.

My advice to any baker who is contemplating putting on a campaign which borders on lottery is, take this matter up first with L. L. Miller, State Food and Drug Commissioner, who will give you his decision promptly. "Lottery" has many interpretations, for instance, putting a thimble, money or other prize in bread is considered lottery; giving premiums, the conducting of drawings; all of these come under the lottery law.

—‡—‡—‡—

Wheat Stocks and Prospects

THE Government report of farm reserves of wheat showed 131,136,000 bushels of wheat on farms, March 1st. Private estimates of statisticians were practically the same. Kansas showed the largest amount, with 18,000,000 bushels. North Dakota came next with 14,000,000 bushels and Nebraska third with nearly 11,000,000 bushels. None of the other states showed as much as 7,000,000 bushels, although Ohio, Illinois, Minnesota and Oklahoma approximated that figure. The total farm reserve of wheat March 1st of last year were 217,937,000 bushels.

Stocks of wheat in country mills and elevators on March 1st, were estimated by the U. S. Department of Agriculture at 72,504,000 bushels. This was the smallest quantity in the records of the Department on that date for 10 years, with the exception of March 1, 1918, when the mills and elevators had only 66,000,000 bushels. The average for the past five years has been in the neighborhood of 91,000,000 bushels.

The winter wheat outlook has changed greatly, especially in Kansas and the Southwest, through the spring rains which did not come too late, as was feared. It is still early to figure on damage done to the crop. Some injury is reported in Ohio and the green bug is reported in Oklahoma. In most of the Soft Winter wheat territory the outlook is excellent, but any forecast of the harvest would be premature.—*American Miller.*

—‡—‡—‡—

The Franklin System very recently opened a bakery in the Palmer Building, Chambersburg, Pa.

All who attend the Pennsylvania Association Convention at Bedford Springs, June 5th to 7th, can secure special rates. On buying ticket, ask for a certificate. This, when validated at Bedford, will entitle the holder to half-fare back home. Ask for a certificate, not a receipt. Those who desire hotel reservations should write direct to the Bedford Springs Hotel, Bedford, Pa.

Convention Program, Bedford Springs, Pennsylvania

Monday, June 5th

10 A. M.: Registration.

12 o'clock Noon: Business Session. Reports of Officers and Executive Committee. Appointment of Committees.

1 P. M.: Luncheon.

2.30 P. M. Golf Tournament

Ralph D. Ward and A. R. Tucker in charge. Bakers vs. Supply Men. Unusually Attractive Prizes.

8.30 P. M.: Grand March, Masquerade and Dance, Direction of George P. Reuter, of New York. (Valuable Prizes for costumes, unique, elaborate and comic.)

For the Ladies

10 A. M.: Ladies Reception in Hotel Parlors—Ladies' Reception Committee in charge, Mrs. George W. Fisher, chairman. All ladies who register with active members Monday evening and remain until Wednesday evening are eligible for a number of costly prizes.

Tuesday, June 6th

9.30 A. M.: Opening of Convention.

Invocation: Rev. J. W. Royer.

Address of Welcome: Hon. T. F. Bailey, Huntingdon.

Response: Pres. L. J. Schumaker.

Address: Dean C. B. Connelly, Commissioner of Labor and Industry of Pennsylvania.

Address: "The Baking Industry," Dr. H. E. Barnard, Chicago, Secretary and Business Manager, American Bakers' Association.

Address: "Co-operation," Fred H. Frazier, New York, vice-president General Baking Company.

Address: Robert L. Corby, N. Y. C., vice-president Fleischmann Co.

Address: "What Does a Show Window Mean?" Carl Goettmann, Joseph Horne Co., Pittsburgh.

Introduction of Associate Members.

Introduction of Visiting and Fraternal Delegates. Nomination of Officers.

Afternoon

2.30 P. M.: Amusements, Direction of George W. Fisher.

Three Legged Race, Direction of R. R. Sanborn, Pittsburgh.

Sack Race, Direction C. H. Ruhl, Penbrook.

Potato Race, Direction S. S. Watters, Pittsburgh.

100-Meter Race, Direction Louis J. Baker, Pittsburgh.

Fat Men's Race (handicapped according to weight) Direction R. C. Jobe, Millersburg.

Quoit Pitching Contest: Direction Ernest Orthwein, Philadelphia.

Trap Shooting Contest, Direction J. Fred Schofer, Reading.

Swimming Race (in pool) for men and women, Direction Mr. and Mrs. Harry S. Long, Lebanon.

Valuable Prizes for Winners.

8.30 P. M.: Reception and Dance, R. K. Stritzinger and Mrs. George W. Fisher and committees in charge.

Stag Pinochle Game: Direction Chas. S. Sharpe, of Hubbard Oven & Mfg. Co.

For the Ladies

10 A. M.: Five Hundred and Bridge Tables in Hotel Parlors. Valuable Prizes for winners.

Wednesday, June 7th

9.30 A. M.: Convention Resumes.

Address: Hon. James Foust, Director Bureau of Foods, Department of Agriculture of Pennsylvania.

Address: "The Club Woman and The Baker," Mrs. John S. Sloan, Pittsburgh, President, Congress of Women's Clubs of Western Pennsylvania.

Address: "Organization a Business Builder," William Smedley, Philadelphia, Secretary, Retail Merchants Association of Penn.

Some of the prizes to be awarded at the Pennsylvania Convention

Ladies' Attendance

All ladies registered with Active Members of the Association before 8 P. M. on Monday, June 5th, will receive a card for their signature, which is only valuable if kept until the dance on Wednesday night, when it may be deposited in the proper container. Three cards will then be drawn and the winners will receive the following prizes:

1st—18-carat White Gold Ring with Diamond and Sapphire Setting, donated by Midland Milling Co. through A. D. Acheson & Co.

2nd—Gold Mesh Bag, donated by Petersen Oven Co.

3rd—Beaded Bag, donated by Thomas J. Furthy, Jr., & Co.

Special Awards

To the oldest Pennsylvania Master Baker (Active Member) present.

17-jewel Hamilton Gold Watch, appropriately engraved, donated by Joseph Bakers Sons & Perkins Co., Inc.

＊＊＊

To the youngest Pennsylvania Master Baker (Active Member) present.

11 volumes of Treatises on Baking Technology, etc., donated by Henry H. Ottens Mfg. Co., Inc.

＊＊＊

To the Active Member of the Association who travels the longest distance to the convention, figured as the crow flies:

Leather Suit-case, donated by Procter & Gamble Co.

Golf Tournament

Direction of Ralph D. Ward and A. R. Tucker

Home Club Handicaps Apply Prizes

16 Bronze Medals, donated by Duhrkop Oven Co.

To be awarded to the winners of the individual matches between 16 Active Members and 16 Associate Members of the Association.

＊＊＊

Sterling Silver Loving Cup, donated by Julius Fleischmann.

To be awarded to the Active Member shooting the low net medal score of the Active Members.

＊＊＊

Sterling Silver Loving Cup, donated by George S. Ward.

To be awarded to the Associate Member shooting the low net medal score of the Associate Members.

＊＊＊

Sterling Silver Cigarette Humidor, donated by The Hammersley Mfg. Co.

To be awarded to the Visiting Baker from another State or country shooting the low net medal score.

Masquerade Dance

Direction of George P. Reuter

All novelties and favors donated by Malt Diastase Company.

Prizes

Ladies' Most Elaborate Costume

Gold Wrist Watch, donated by Samuel Knighton & Sons

Ladies' Most Unique Costume

Gold Wrist Watch, donated by Larabee Flour Mills Co.

Ladies' Best Comic Costume

Platinum Front Bar Pin with Diamond, The J. H. Day Co.

Men's Most Unique Costume

Platinum Front Cuff Links, donated by Eagle Roller Mill Co.

Men's Most Elaborate Costume

Sterling Silver Cigarette Case, donated by Pillsbury Flour Mills Co.

Men's Best Comic Costume

Platinum, Diamond and Pearl Scarf Pin, donated by Richardson Brothers

Ladies' Card Party

Direction of Mrs. George W. Fisher

Bridge Prizes

1st—Set of 16 Duplicate Boards, donated by Russell-Miller Milling Co.

2nd—Deluxe Set of "Par Auction," donated by John C. MacAlpine.

3rd—Gold Eversharp Pencil, donated by A. Backus, Jr. & Sons.

"500" Prizes

1st—Silver Chocolate Set, donated by Commercial Truck Co.

2nd—Chest of Stationery, donated by Coated Paper Products Co.

3rd—Two pair of Silver Salt and Pepper Shakers, donated by The Diamond Crystal Salt Co.

—‡—‡—‡—

Western Pennsylvania Bakers

AN INTERESTING talk on "The Telephone" was delivered at the April meeting of the Western Pennsylvania Bakers' Association in the Fleischmann Building, Pittsburgh, Saturday evening, April 5th, by C. H. Lehmann, assistant to the president of the Bell Telephone Company. Mr. Lehmann told of the inception of the telephone and its great growth throughout the country. He predicted that the day was not far distant when anyone could go to a telephone and ask to be connected with an ocean liner in mid-ocean. Following his talk a number of the bakers asked numerous questions of Lehmann relative to the operation of the telephone system, which he answered in a satisfactory manner.

Barney Rosenthal, of the American Diamalt Company, was elected to associate membership. F. M. Grout, of the bakery division of the Pillsbury Flour Mills Co., was a visitor at the meeting. Horace W. Crider presided. After adjournment of the meeting, Harry C. Elste, district manager of the Fleischmann Company served a delightful buffet luncheon, with Adam Ziegler, the Fleischmann consulting baker, as official dispenser of refreshments.

—‡—‡—‡—

S. S. Watters Tendered Dinner

S. S. WATTERS, secretary and general manager of the Liberty Baking Company, of Pittsburgh, was tendered a testimonial dinner at the Pittsburgh Athletic Association in honor of his completing 29 years in the baking industry. The dinner was a surprise affair. A. P. Cole, vice-president of the Jesse C. Stewart Company, was the toastmaster. Letters and telegrams, congratulatory in nature, from prominent bakers from all sections of the country were read by C. C. Latus, secretary of the Western Pennsylvania Bakers' Association, of which body Mr. Watters is the treasurer. He is also a member of the board of governors of the American Bakers' Association.

Horace W. Crider presented Mr. Watters with a keepsake from Canada, with an appropriate address. Richard Meyers, a prominent baker of Paterson, N. J., sent a handsome floral piece to Mr. Watters in honor of the anniversary. All of the 23 guests present made brief remarks congratulating Mr. Watters and extolling him as a good friend and business competitor.

New England Convention

THE New England Bakers' Association held a splendid meeting at the Hotel Standish, Worcester, Mass., on Wednesday, April 26th, with a fine attendance of members; about one hundred and fifty bakers answering roll call.

Hugh V. Keiser, President, was in the chair and Secretary Dwight E. Babcock, of the Chamber of Commerce, welcomed the visitors and A. S. Martin, New Bedford, was the first regular speaker and gave an able address on co-operation in business, showing how it helped develop men in the trade.

At the last meeting a committee consisting of Frank Eighme, B. S. Ferguson, R. H. Dietz, W. S. Verity, and E. C. Campbell was appointed to consider the question whether or not members of the allied trades should be admitted as associate members. This committee now reported in the affirmative, and that dues for such membership be placed at ten dollars per year, and that extra representatives of associate members be charged three dollars each.

Vice-president Frank R. Shepard, then reported in behalf of the Legislative Committee, stating that several bills obnoxious to the bakers had been withdrawn, while others had been satisfactorily amended. D. F. Phelps, for the committee on Honorary Membership,

*Needn't Take Our Word for It!

Hundreds of bakers could tell you how Diamalt has lowered costs and increased profits for them.

Then, after you try Diamalt, your customers will tell you how much better they like the big, brown loaves of better flavor and lasting freshness.

And you will see for yourself how Diamalt saves sugar and helps to produce more bread from a given amount of dough because of smaller evaporation.

*No, you needn't take our word for it!

The American Diamalt Company

Diamalt

Home Office

419 Plum Street   Cincinnati, Ohio

1182 Broadway, New York City
327 So. La Salle St., Chicago, Ill.
424 Bankers Investment Bldg., San Francisco, Cal.

recommended the following to be Honorary Members: Geo. A. Sanderson, Boston; S. Bergeron, Rochester, N. H.; Dudley Page, Lowell, Mass.; Jas. A. Ferguson, Boston; F. W. Calderwood, Portland, Maine, and Albert Klopfer, New York, and same were unanimously elected.

C. O. Swanson then spoke on "Labor Problems Affecting the Baker," and pleaded for fair consideration of this great question. It was decided to send a delegation of three members to the Pennsylvania Convention at Bedford Springs, Pa., June 5th to 7th.

After full discussion it was decided to take over the labor bureau conducted in the past by the Eastern Massachusetts Association, and a plea was made for a paid secretary-manager.

E. H. Shields, Jr., of The Fleischmann Co., outlined the preparations being made for New England Bread and Milk Week, June 5th to 10th, and urged the bakers to get behind it and make the campaign successful.

—‡—‡—‡—

New England Bakers' Association

ANOTHER very active division of the New England Bakers' Association was formed in Pittsfield, Mass., at a meeting at the American House on Tuesday, April 18th.

After President Keiser, of the New England Bakers' Association pointed out the purpose and ideals of the organization the following officers were elected:

President—Harold Lloyd. Lloyd's Bakery, North Adams.

Vice-President—Justin E. Aubry, Federal System of Bakeries, 159 North street, Pittsfield.

Secretary—Ralph T. Lloyd, Lloyd's Bakery, North Adams.

Treasurer—C. I. Rigley, 84 Columbus avenue, Pittsfield.

Each member pledged himself to bring a new member to the next meeting, so that the prospects are that the membership will soon be doubled.

At a very enthusiastic and well attended meeting of the bakers of Essex County at the Colonial Restaurant, Lowell, Mass., on April 25th, Division 10 of the New England Bakers' Association was organized and the following officers were elected: President, Robert Friend, Friend Bros., Melrose, Mass.; Vice-president, Edward Scalley, Lowell, Mass.; Treasurer, Clayton B. Stoddard, Lowell, Mass.; Secretary, D. C. Bibeau, N. E. Bakery, Lawrence, Mass.

Announcement of a Great Event

THE Twenty-fifth Annual Convention of the Baking Industry and the National Retail Bakers' Association Convention will be held together on the Municipal Pier, Chicago, the week of September 11th. The Second National Exposition of the Baking Industry will be held under the auspices of the Bakery Equipment Manufacturers' Association at the same time and place.

This triple announcement is of supreme importance not only to every wholesale and retail baker, but to the entire supply trade which will be equally represented.

A great era of prosperity and development awaits the entire baking industry. How soon it comes depends largely on the alertness of every member to take advantage of such opportunity as is offered by this coming Convention and Exposition.

Certain it is that at it will be gathered every baking expert and technologist of note in the country. Its all-star official list will embrace speakers of world-wide fame. Men who have made spectacular successes in their own individual fields. And not only will the official program prove of absorbing interest, the Mile-Long Municipal Pier will be the focal center of exhibits worth crossing a continent to see.

Atlantic City Surpassed

This is the age of mechanical marvels. Wonderful advances have been made within the last two years. Great as the attractions of Atlantic City were voted two years ago, they sink to nothing beside those planned for this coming event. Among the exhibits will be complete bakeries in operation, demonstrating the baking of Bread from start to finish. Every latest development of modern baking machinery will be displayed. The moving picture will lend its aid with fascinating films. Completely equipped laboratories will demonstrate their marvels.

Entertainment Free

In addition to the educational features, an entertainment program unsurpassed has been planned—and this is free to all bakers. You don't have to be a member of any association to enjoy it. Come anyway. The big city of Chicago with its string of parks, boulevards, notable bathing beaches and Big Pier is yours for the week.

Plan a Summer Vacation

—

baker large and small in the industry should attend. Naturally the baking industry needs you and your attendance; but that is secondary, beside the great personal opportunity offered to you in this Convention and Exposition.

—‡—‡—‡—

Bakers' Delivery Car Equipped With Wireless

The Kolb Bakeries, Philadelphia, Pa., have placed in service a large Autocar motor truck equipped with a wireless outfit for radio telephony, said to be the first vehicle equipped for this purpose, and the car is receiving much attention.

The wireless outfit in the Kolb Autocar is complete in every detail, and is a highly interesting indication of the successful operation of wireless telephoning under conditions which only a few months ago would have seemed impossible. The ground is accomplished by connecting a wire to the frame of the Autocar. The apparatus inside the truck is a complete radio receiving outfit, having a detector with three stages of amplification and a magnavox horn attachment, by means of which radio concerts can be heard by a large number of people. The entire apparatus is mounted on a separate set of cushioning springs, which protect it from sudden jars when the truck is in motion.

It is possible to receive radio messages just as clearly when the Kolb Autocar is in motion as when it is standing still. It is now literally possible for the Kolb Bakery to telephone to anyone of the several broadcasting stations in Philadelphia and ask that station to notify the driver of their wireless Autocar that they wish to get in touch with him and the driver, no matter where he might be, if he had the head-piece over his ears and was tuned in, would get the message and, while he could not reply by radio, it would be possible for him to get in touch with his home office by an ordinary telephone immediately. This gives Kolb's Bakery a degree of control over their delivery service which has hitherto been impossible for any firm to achieve.

—‡—‡—‡—

Copyright Designs for Bread Wrappers

FOR a number of months the problem of copyrighted bread wrapper designs has been causing more grief in the waxed paper business and in the baking business, than nearly all of the rest of the work put together. This does not apply to those cases where the baker owns his own copyrighted design, himself, because that ownership gives him the right to place orders for his own bread wrappers wherever he wants to. But when waxed paper manufacturers copyright designs and attempt to hold the right to manufacture those wrappers to the exclusion of every other manufacturer the real trouble begins. There are as many designs as there are ideas. They may have good designs and all that sort of thing but the copyrights do not mean much besides trouble to them and to the baker.

The members of the Waxed Paper Manufacturers' Association have grown tired of threatened law suits, etc., over copyrights and registered trade marks of questionable value. The whole problem is a nuisance so far as the waxed paper manufacturer is concerned and he has been trying to find a way out. The result is the following official announcement:

"Members of the Waxed Paper Manufacturers' Association wish to state to the baking trade their policy in reference to copyrighted designs. It has been brought very forcibly to the notice of the Waxed Paper Manufacturers' Association that waxed paper manufacturers not members of the Association, have originated designs for bread wrappers, which under the present copyright and patent laws, they are allowed to copyright. Such designs copyrighted by a waxed paper manufacturer become his property and he can control the printing, waxing and manufacture thereof.

"Members of the Waxed Paper Manufacturers' Association wish to declare themselves to the effect that any design originating with a manufacturer belonging to the Association, even though copyrighted by him, may be printed by any waxed paper manufacturer, thus insuring to the baker who uses such designs free and unlimited competition in the purchase of such wrappers."

The above action, of course, does not affect those wax paper manufacturers not members of the Association.

—‡—‡—‡—

Pie Bakers to Meet

THE fifth annual convention of the National Association of Wholesale Pie Bakers will meet at the Hotel Statler, Detroit, Mich., on May 23rd and 24th, and the following interesting program has been prepared:

MAY 23RD

10.00 A. M. Address of Welcome by Hon. James Couzens, Mayor of Detroit. Regular order of business. Address—"The Pie Industry," Albert Schultels. Address—"Standards for Pie Fillings." Dr. L. E. Sayre, member of Federal Committee on Definitions and Standards and Referee in the subject of Standards for Pie Filling.

4.00 P. M. Executive Committee Meeting.

5.00 P. M. Assemble for auto ride to boulevard and Bell Island Park arriving

7.00 P. M. At the Bell Island Casino where a chicken, frog, and fish banquet will be served.

MAY 24TH

10.00 A. M. Regular order of business. Address—"Egg Products," A. V. Harris. Address—"Electric Vehicle Transportation," C. A. Sweet. Address—"Dehydrated Fruit," C. A. Clark. Address—"Washington Flour," Otis B. Durbin.

BUDWEISER Barley Malt—100 per cent pure—is made only from the finest barley and scientifically malted by the most modern methods. It has the advantage of Anheuser-Busch's years of malting experience in developing a diastase of just the right proportion and strength for bakers' purposes.

The result is an extract syrup of barley malt—nothing more nor less—uniformly produced at all times.

The new distributing system makes it possible to secure fresh supplies just as they are needed, without the use of the old contract system.

ANHEUSER-BUSCH SALES CORPORATION
ST. LOUIS, U. S. A.

Power and Lighting Economies in the Bake Shop

By Q. H. Cook, C. E. (Siebel Institute of Technology)

POWER and lighting costs are not the greatest items entering into the general expenses of a bake shop, but still they are not so small that they can be handled carelessly or disregarded. There is always a tendency in every industry toward concentrating all attention upon reducing the major expenses and of neglecting possible savings in the smaller items, and under these conditions the power and lighting charges often assume excessive proportions without being detected by the management. When competition is keen, and the margin of profit is small, we must look to every item upon our cost record, and among these entries it is strongly suggested that due attention be paid to the power consumption and lighting charges.

Light and power naturally come under one head since they are both directly related to fuel consumption. This is true whether the power is generated on the premises or purchased through a meter from a local electric service corporation, for in either case the light and power are purchased in terms of fuel consumed. Carelessness in handling the machinery or in maintaining it in proper working condition are two of the greatest causes of excessive power demands. Improper arrangement of the lights, unnecessary use of the lights, or dark, heavy painted interiors increase the cost of the lighting service. All this demands a frequent checking up by the management, and strict laws laid down for the "conservation of energy." Installation and the arrangement of the equipment have a permanent effect upon the consumption of power, hence all possible care should be taken in laying out the plant to avoid unnecessary complication in the transmission system.

FRICTION THE GREATEST FACTOR

Machine friction or resistance offered to motion is the one greatest factor in power consumption. To reduce friction to a minimum means that the machinery should be properly lubricated with the proper oils or greases and that the shafting and machinery should be in perfect alignment. It is not sufficient to "douse" the bearings at irregular intervals with any sort of oil that may be at hand. Lubrication should be performed systematically at regular intervals with an oil that is especially adapted to the bearings in question. A test made along these lines will rather surprise you if your millwright has been negligent in taking care of the oiling systems. Frequently, it is possible to cut down the power demand by 20 to 30 per cent. by proper attention to the lubrication and lubricant, and as excessive friction always means excessive wear on the working parts, a similar saving is made in preserving the wearing surfaces and prolonging the life of the machine.

Right from the start I wish to call your attention to the fact that buying oils on the basis of price does not pay. A poor oil is expensive at any price, no matter what it may cost per gallon, for it does not properly reduce the friction and does increase the wear tremendously. It not only fails to provide a proper liquid support for the shafts in the bearings, but it decomposes into objectionable compounds and wastes away rapidly. Any reputable oil company will make investigations and recommend the proper oils for use on the various machines. No one oil will fit all conditions and the selection of the oil should be left to those experienced along these lines. As a general rule, heavy machines working at a high temperature require a heavier or more viscous oil than light machinery working normally at lower temperatures. As the temperature increases, the oil thins out and has less supporting value for the shaft, thus allowing the shaft to rub in the bearings and cause friction and wear. On the other hand, if the oil is too thick, then it causes a viscous drag and will not enter the bearing clearance properly. All this must be taken into consideration.

If shafting gets out of alignment it will bind in the bearings and cause heavy rubbing that no lubricant can diminish. Misalignment is a very common cause of friction and wear in lineshafts and is very frequently neglected by those in charge. All buildings settle somewhat in the course of time, and in settling, throw the shafting and bearings out of line. All bearings supported directly from the building should be checked up at least every six months and should be readjusted if even slightly out. This is not a difficult matter and is quickly performed. Large, heavy machines, particularly those supported on the floor without foundations also get out of line and must be corrected by means of thin shims placed under the legs or other supports.

There is always a tendency toward installing unnecessary shafting and bearings in cases where the machinery is driven from line shafts. It should be noted that every bearing used consumes power and adds to the liability of binding, sticking, and getting out of line. Line shafts should be short and compact, with only enough bearings to properly support the shaft without undue deflection. High speed shafts should be particularly short, since they use up power rapidly through bearing friction and the "windage" caused by stirring up air currents. Any shaft running over 350 revolutions per minute should be carefully taken care of and should be kept well lubricated at all times. As an example, a two-inch shaft in a certain mill, running at 400 R. P. M., consumed 7.3 horsepower at full load when improperly lubricated and out of alignment. With these conditions corrected, the loss was reduced to 0.87 horsepower.

In cases where only a part of the machinery is being used it is often advisable to cut off the idle length of shaft by loosening the coupling halves. There is no use in paying for the power consumed by idle shafting. Where the distribution of the machinery along the shaft is such that the shafting section cannot be uncoupled, then the belts of the idle machines or their

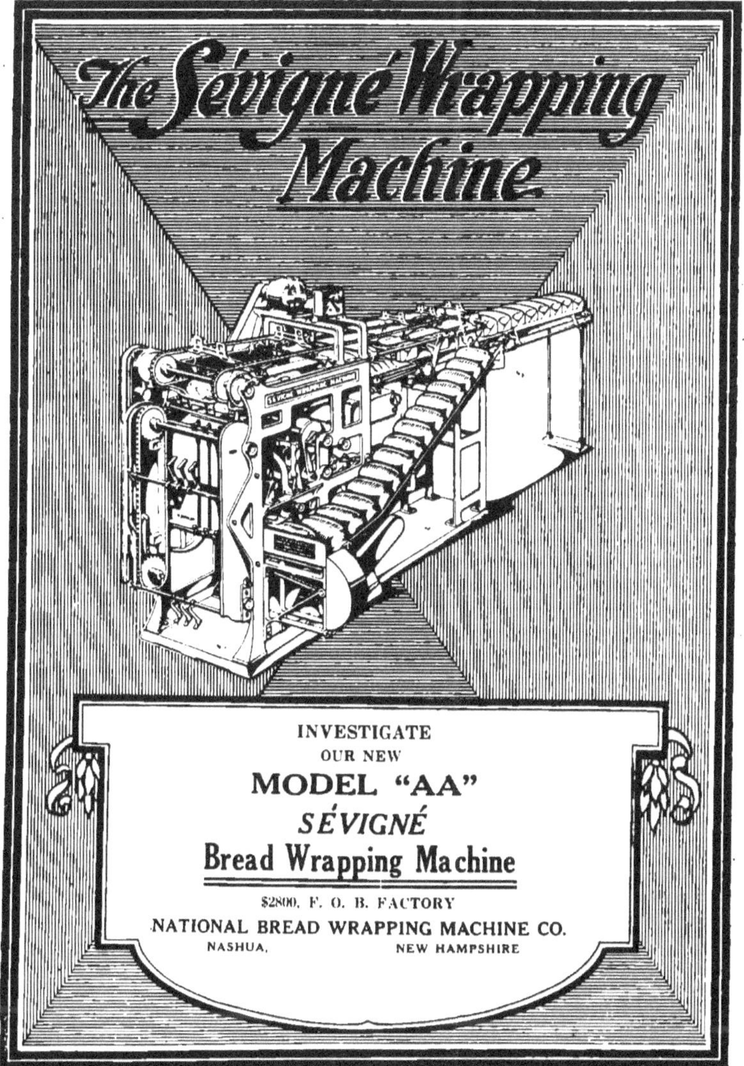
The Sévigné Wrapping Machine
INVESTIGATE
OUR NEW
MODEL "AA"
SÉVIGNÉ
Bread Wrapping Machine
$2800. F. O. B. FACTORY
NATIONAL BREAD WRAPPING MACHINE CO.
NASHUA,　　　NEW HAMPSHIRE

countershafts should be thrown out. In this way, it is possible to effect considerable economies in medium to large shops. All of this waste shows up on the meter and is paid for, and at the end of a year's time, the power bill may take the profit off of a great many loaves of bread.

BELT SLIPPING

In every belt-driven installation there is a great amount of power lost by belt slipping, this loss varying from two to 20 per cent. When a belt slips the loss of power is indicated by heating at the pulley surface or by a screeching or squeaking noise, and this by the way does not improve the belt nor the pulley. The loss of power is due to the fact that the belt drags the full load at a higher speed than would be the case were it traveling at the speed of the pulley rim, and in traveling faster, develops or absorbs more foot-pounds of energy. Belts to be efficient should be kept tight, not tight enough to produce undue friction in the bearings, but tight enough to prevent more than two per cent. of slippage. The belts, wherever possible, should be run as near the horizontal as possible, with the slack side uppermost so that the belt strands will wrap around the greatest percentage of the pulley circumference. Belts in which the slack strand is at the bottom or with vertical belts, the strands hang away from the pulley, and in this way reduce the frictional contact area and promote slipping.

Electric motors are provided with slide rails and adjusting screws by which slack in the belts may be easily and quickly taken up, but with ordinary classes of machinery the only remedy is to take a piece out of the belt and then relace it. Another cause of slippage is found in poor alignment between the machine pulley and the lineshaft pulley, a condition which results in the belt running off center and which reduces the "embrace" or belt grip. For the best results, the belt should run truly in the center of the pulley, and should run without wavering or "galloping" from side to side. Still other causes contributing to slipping belts are short belt centers, that is, very short distances between the centers of the pulleys, or else combinations of very small and large pulleys connected by a single belt. If one pulley is very much smaller than the other, then there will be very little belt wrap or embrace around the small pulley, and slipping will be the result. Where there is to be a high speed ratio or increase of speed between two shafts, it is usually better to employ two sets of pulleys and two belts, dividing the speed ratio between them.

All belts should be kept soft and pliable so that they will conform to the surface of the pulleys, and so that the amount of surface contact will thus be at a maximum. Neatsfoot oil applied sparingly or belt compounds or dressings will keep the belt in good condition, but care should be taken that no rosin or other sticky substance is used. Rosin is likely to burn the belt and does not remedy the primary trouble.

MACHINERY ALIGNMENT

In the course of time wear will take place in the various parts of the machinery, particularly in the bearings and gearing, and the parts will thus get out of line. This may or may not increase the power consumption, but it is always safest to take up the wear whenever it becomes noticeable. When toothed gears are in mesh, a dropping shaft may cause the teeth to mesh too deeply which in turn will cause hard running and wear. If the shaft drops away so that the teeth are pulled apart or partly out of mesh, then the motion will be irregular and noisy because of the increased side play or backlash between the teeth. This will sooner or later reflect trouble into other parts, although in itself may not be the cause of power loss. Bevel gears must be given special attention since they cause end thrust and friction under all conditions, and a very high degree of friction should they become out of line.

Machine lubrication is usually given more attention than that of the lineshafts, but in any case the proper lubricant must be used in the proper quantities. When the machine is driven individually by an electric motor, see that the driving motor gear is running in proper mesh with the driven gear or that the chain belt is running true and with the proper degree of tension. "Cocked" chains on motor drives are the cause of unlimited trouble and expense and at the first suggestion of whining or humming, they should be gone over and corrected. Chains and gears require careful lubrication, the chains requiring oil while the gears demand either a heavy oil or a semi-fluid grease. Special gear grease should be used—not cup grease—so that the grease will not "track" nor be thrown off by centrifugal force. With heavy stiff greases, the gear teeth cut a groove or track straight through the grease and after the first greasing has disappeared no more will find its way into the tooth spaces.

One cause of trouble on belt-driven machines is the adjustment given to the belt shifters or clutches. A dragging shifter fork will eat up a surprising amount of power and further will chew up the belt. Slipping clutches consume power in the same way as slipping belts. Where tight and loose pulleys are used, make sure that the alignment of the machine is such that the belt runs centrally on the loose pulley and that the edges do not overhang and engage with the tight pulley. The latter causes a great deal of drag when the machine is idle and wears the belt. Further, be sure that the loose pulley is well lubricated at all times and that it runs freely, for a sticking, binding loose pulley on a high speed machine often uses almost as much power as the machine itself when running.

ELECTRIC MOTORS

There is not much to do with the electric motors except to keep them clean and well oiled. See that the wire connections are kept tight and that no metallic contact is made by any casing or adjacent body with the current-carrying parts of the motor. Current leakage in the wiring or due to faults within the motor itself are a direct loss of power that will be registered

(Concluded in June issue)

How to make it: Use a rich layer cake mixture. For filling, chop uncooked pitted Sunsweet Prunes fine enough to make a paste. Moisten with currant jelly and spread between layers, then ice with flavored water icing. Sprinkle shredded cocoanut on top and sides.

Yes—it's the filling! That's the in-between secret of *any* layer cake. That's the flavor-secret that explains why some layer cakes go big and others fall flat.

A filling made of Sunsweet Prunes gives your trade a new taste-sensation. It puts novelty into an everyday bakeshop specialty. Easy to make, too—especially when you use Sunsweet *Pitted* Prunes.

Prepared by a recently perfected process, they are superior to any pitted prunes on the market. They fall apart without extra handling. They do not break apart in the dough. They do not discolor the dough. They are right easy to handle. And—they save labor. No fuss; no bother; no time lost!

Other profitable variations you can make with Sunsweet Pitted Prunes are pies, tarts, coffee cake, fruit slices, etc. Ask your jobber or supply house for Sunsweet Pitted Prunes—and see that you get them.

Also, write for our new formula folder, "I never knew what prunes could do!" Every formula has been proved in the baking and it's free! And, if you ask for it, we'll send along window pasters and other sales-helps that are bringing in new trade to live bakers all over the country.

Simply address Bakery Department, California Prune & Apricot Growers Inc., 192 Market Street, San Jose, California. An association of 11,000 growers.

SUNSWEET *Pitted* PRUNES

Proposed Pennsylvania Regulations

L. J. SCHUMAKER, a member of the Advisory Board on Bakeries, which is rendering a valuable service to the State Industrial Board, has explained the bakers' stand on three important questions which have been brought to the attention of the Pennsylvania Industrial Board of the Department of Labor and Industry. The questions affect sanitation, weight, and disposal of stale bread products. Mr. Schumaker, who is also President of the Pennsylvania Association of the Baking Industry, outlined the bakers' viewpoint at the request of the Secretary, Fred J. Hartman, of the Industrial Board, to satisfy the request of E. C. Whittemore, of Cumbridge, Massachusetts.

It is unwise, he says, to force on the public something which it does not want and for that reason the regulations which would require the wrapping of all bakery products is not favored. Certain kinds of bread, such as hearth bread and rolls, cannot be wrapped without destroying the flavor, he adds.

"It is the consensus of opinion of the leading bakers of the State," declares Mr. Schumaker, "that, while the wrapping of bread and cake at the bakery is in many places desirable, yet the sanitation and cleanliness of the bakery, of the delivery wagon and of the driver are as important as the wrapping; and furthermore, that the wrapping of hearth bread and rolls is not practical. The eating qualities of hearth bread depend upon a crisp crust, which is destroyed shortly after the loaf is wrapped or sealed. We have, accordingly, taken the position that the public should be allowed to choose which kind of bread or cake it prefers, wrapped or unwrapped. The wrapped loaf offers the baker far better opportunities for advertising and for identifying his own product and it is, of course, preferred by the baker, but we are serving the public and must consider their interests, and believe it unwise to attempt to force on the public anything which they do not favor."

The second point treated by Mr. Schumaker is the desirability of scaling bread to uniform weights. Any interference along this line would be unfair because of fluctuation in prices of flour, butter, eggs, and other ingredients of a loaf of bread, Mr. Schumaker believes.

"The writer some years," he continues, "was greatly in favor of having all bread scaled to uniform weights similar to the requirements of the Food Administration during the war. In fact, the writer was responsible for a bill which passed the Legislature of this State, but which was later vetoed by the Governor, which bill specified uniform weights to be scaled by all bakers. Since the enactment of this bill was vetoed by the Governor, the writer has had further opportunity to confer with a great many bakers throughout this and other states and has definitely come to the conclusion that we were wrong in expecting the bakers to scale uniform weights. The price of flour fluctuates from month to month, just as do prices of butter and eggs;

but the public is not educated to a fluctuating price on bread as they are to fluctuating prices in butter, eggs, lard, etc. Accordingly, the only way in which the baker can avoid either over-charging the consumer when flour is low, or losing money himself when flour goes up, is to vary the weight of his bread.

"It is true that radical changes in the prices of wheat and flour have caused the baker to make radical changes in the price of his bread, but I am referring to the ordinary changes of from fifty cents to one dollar per barrel in flour which means to the baker a change in the cost of the pound loaf of from an eighth to a quarter of a cent a loaf, which may seem small, but comes close to being the actual net profit per loaf on the sales of our largest bakers. Bread being one of the few foods that is eaten practically three times a day, is very closely observed by the buying public who are quick to notice whether they are getting large or small loaves and whether the loaf is loose or compact. I am of the opinion that competition takes care of this feature very satisfactorily and that it is a matter in which it is unwise for us to attempt to interfere."

Third, regarding the return of stale bread, Mr. Schumaker states that "he has always been opposed to the return of stale bread, and, while it is impossible to do anything by way of State legislation, we tried for several years to convince the boards of health in Philadelphia and Pittsburgh that the return of stale bread should be prohibited as a health measure. This we were unable to accomplish. The grocer's profit on the sale of a loaf of bread is quite small, and if on Saturday he has a number of loaves remaining which he cannot return, he may lose the entire profit of his Saturday's bread business because this bread will be too hard to sell to his customers on the following Monday. Some bakers have advocated the return of stale bread on Monday morning only, thus taking care of this situation. This has been tried, but is not practical, as grocers would carry over their stale bread from the previous days of the week and put it altogether on their returns Monday morning. If it were possible to enforce a rule that no bread could be returned to the baker, it would be an excellent measure. It would enable the baker to give more bread for the money, as the average baker's losses from stale returns amount to considerable, and I believe that once the practice was generally observed it would soon become a matter of course and there would be no objections to it; but the grocer has been so accustomed to buying his bread practically on consignment that it is very difficult to convince him that it is anything but a hardship on him to permit him to return to the baker any bread unsold from the day's delivery. In some of our communities in Pennsylvania there are very few returns of stale bread, as the bakers and grocers have exchanged views on the subject and have come to the conclusion that they are all better off not to have returns of stale bread."

A Brief Statement of the Publishers' Case

NO country can live and grow without information highways. In many ways it is more important to provide the means for the dissemination of intelligence than for the transportation of material commodities.

For this reason the government has always recognized the necessity for low postal rates on newspapers and periodicals. During the war, however, the publications of the country were loaded with increases on the carrying charges in the mails. These increases were provided for in the Revenue Bill of 1917 and now amount to four times the pre-war charges.

While paying this excessive special tax, the publishers have been paying all other taxes of what ever kind, levied upon industry as a whole, and have had to stand and are still suffering under high costs for labor, paper, and other essentials.

It is significant, too, that this special tax on the circulation of publications, is a tax ou a *process* of the industry. It is a recognized principle of taxation that taxes should be levied on the products of industry and not on the processes. Publishers have been paying on both processes and products.

The case is not dissimilar to taxation of traveling salesmen or labor-saving machinery. Indeed the advertising pages of publications may be likened to traveling salesmen. How foolish and futile to make it difficult to get the orders which are the life blood of industry.

Every interchange of commodities must be preceded by an interchange of ideas, of information, of proposals and acceptances, and this important function of our publications needs support and encouragement at this time to build up and restore national prosperity.

We would abhor the idea of taxing schools, yet but 7 per cent. of our boys and girls go beyond the grammar grades. The rest of their education must come from reading, and yet the present law is in effect a tax on this source of education which is depended upon by 93 per cent. of the people to take the place of higher education.

As a result of these exorbitant postal changes, publishers have had to increase subscription rates greatly, or have ceased soliciting subscriptions from sections of the country where the high postal rates would make it unprofitable. In still other cases publishers have tried to absorb the additional costs and numbers of them have fallen by the wayside in the attempt.

In 1918 the Federal government collected from the publishers $11,712,068.18 and in the last fiscal year this had grown to $25,496,719.94. During the current year it is estimated that the publishers will pay to the government for carrying their papers the huge sum of $33,000,000.

This, too, notwithstanding the fact that the high rates have forced out of the mails an enormous tonnage of newspapers and magazines which now go by express,

baggage, motor truck, freight or by water for less than Uncle Sam will carry them.

Unfortunately some of the most necessary publications cannot be shipped in bulk lots and cannot escape the back-breaking postal charges. Among this class of papers are the business and technical papers going to retailers, factories, and professional men; the farm papers which are raising the standards of agriculture; the religious papers which promote the spiritual life of the country; the fraternal publications which bind together groups of men and women for their common good; the educational papers which carry the light of new knowledge into the humblest homes, and many others of similar kind.

The burden falls heaviest upon the smaller papers of the country. The big papers with a million or more of readers can afford to develop their own systems of transportation. It falls heavily, too, upon the readers who most need the enlightening force of good reading.

In spite of all this the publishers are most modest and moderate in their appeal. All that is asked is the repeal of the last two increases, those which went into effect in 1920 and 1921, retaining the rates in effect just prior to these increases.

This will not affect the zone system in the least, neither will it affect the present free-in-county privilege enjoyed by the smaller weeklies and dailies.

The rates asked for in the bill now proposed in Congress, would still give the government approximately *175 per cent. more than the pre-war rates,* and would not relieve the publishing industry of one cent of the other Federal Taxes now paid by other industries.

Here is another very important consideration—the special or super-taxes which the War Revenue bill imposed upon some ten other industries have either been taken off or materially reduced. Is it fair that the publishing industry, of all industries, should be singled out as the sole exception and compelled to stagger along under special war taxes to defray war expenses?

This seems all the more unfair, when it is remembered that the newspapers and periodicals of the country did not go over the top for pay, during the war; that they did not profiteer; that they were in no sense a war industry. On the contrary they volunteered space and services to the value of millions of dollars.

In a word what the publishers are asking, would amount in dollars and cents to a gross reduction in rates of about $8,000,000 as against total post office receipts of about $500,000,000.

Furthermore, the effect of lowering the rates would attract back into the mails enough tonnage to largely compensate for the apparent or bookkeeping loss.

The American Institute School

OF

BAKING TECHNOLOGY

Teaches
How to Make
Better Bread

Equipment Includes
A Three Oven Shop
With Three Machines of each kind

FOUR MONTHS REGULAR COURSE STARTS MAY 15

Instruction Includes:—

The Problems of the Foreman and Superintendent Baker.
Baking and Chemical Tests of Flour, Malt, Milk, etc.
Fermentation, Yeast, Yeast Foods, etc.
Shop and Other Records.
Business and Legal Relations of the Baker.
Manufacture of Bread, etc., Under Commercial Conditions.

ENROLLMENT IS LIMITED
So That
Each Student Gets Individual Attention
and Individual Equipment.

Courses Also Given in

Baking and Milling Chemistry
Industrial Research

COURSES IN PREPARATION FOR
SWEET GOODS SCHOOL.

TEAR OUT AND MAIL TO US FOR INFORMATION NOW

PETER G. PIRRIE, Principal, American Institute School of Baking
1135 Fullerton Avenue, Chicago, Ill.

PLEASE SEND INFORMATION ABOUT COURSES TO

Name...
Street and No...
City...
State...

Up-to-date Ideas on Quality Bread

By J. E. Wihlfahrt, at the Southeastern Convention

QUALITY Bread means more than mere appearance of the loaf. To deserve this term it must be real nutritious and of pleasing flavor as well as be attractive to the eye.

The public not only demands quality bread, but fresh bread as well. If the bread is lacking in quality, then other food will take its place.

A high standard quality loaf should not be too sweet, be of fair expansion, good interior development, with color creamy white, good appetite appealing flavor, while the outer color should be of an even golden brown. The loaf itself must be well baked, devoid of sogginess and after baking should become soft and remain so for at least two days. If the loaf has a hard crust, the consumer, in the great majority, will consider it stale, and the sales of such bread will suffer accordingly.

FERMENTATION

The causes for successful as well as faulty bread production are often traced directly to the fermentation.

Of course, good material in proper quantities are needed, as well as their correct incorporation into dough.

This term, fermentation, when applied to the manufacture of bread, means the production of a more digestible form of food.

Prolonged fermentation means excessive invisible loss for both sponge and straight doughs. If the temperature at which it is carried on is at a high point at the beginning of the process, the dough will rise in temperature to a point producing maximum viscosity and greatly increased slackening of the dough.

Correct fermentation means to make a dough with proper hydration and at the same time one at a minimum point of viscosity, carried on at a low temperature so as to obtain the maximum baking value from all material used.

This maximum efficiency can only be obtained by using an adequate amount of yeast to moderate the time needed for correct maturing of the dough. This leads to increased nutrition, better quality, greater keeping quality and increased yield.

If we collect samples from various stores, it is striking how little real good bread we find. Comparison of samples collected bring home many interesting facts. Unless you practice this, I advise that you send to the store and secure a sample of every type of bread, inclusive of your own. You will observe that the loaf which sells best is not always the one most pleasing to the expert's eye, which proves that the consumer has his own way of deciding what suits best. You may gain many points by combining your efficiency with such judgment.

When you get the samples, arrange them according to the type of loaf, next weigh, then cut the samples and compare them carefully and make notations.

This may induce you to adopt more effective methods which lead to a pronounced advantage in the competition always just ahead.

We hear so much about ideal ways of storing and conditioning flour, ideal shop conditions, temperature control, careful manipulation of our raw material and efficiency of their incorporation.

All this is very well, but let us investigate the reason why some bakers get such very low absorption, for which they blame the flour, or let us discuss the conditions why the bread picked from the market does not show a greater keeping quality or with other words, a better market value?

The public does not demand cheap bread, but good bread of good keeping quality, which will remain fresh until consumed.

A dough may be properly made, carefully nursed through its different stages of fermentation and the loaves proved at moderate temperature with a minimum amount of yeast and by giving it sufficient time at low temperature a fairly successful loaf results at a cost of decreased yield. This, however, is by far in the great minority. What the bakers are doing, is to set their doughs at the higher temperature, 81 to 82 degrees and even higher, and when the loaves are moulded and panned they get what resembles a Russian bath in the proof box, or are raised under conditions undoing all preceding efforts. I find some of them to be over 100 degrees and as high as 120 degrees and more. Very seldom at the more suitable temperature of 88 to 90 degrees F. This common evil has very detrimental effects on the final products and its keeping quality. The work should be so regulated that no such unsatisfactory practice becomes necessary.

CONDITIONS HAVE CHANGED

In days gone by the higher temperatures may have given you results up to 95 or 100 degrees. Remember general conditions have changed, while efficiency is increasing all around you.

For instance, if a baker is using only 1 per cent. of yeast to weight of flour and sets his dough at 82 degrees F., with shop at 80 F., such a dough would mature around 85 to 86 F. The average time of fermentation would be 4¾ hours. His absorption should be not less, and most probably would be at the low point of 54 per cent.

The same dough set at 78 degrees F., otherwise the same conditions, would carry absorption at about 56 per cent., but the time of fermentation would have to be extended one hour, or to a total of 5¾ hours.

Comparing this with a dough containing 3 per cent. of yeast and temperature of dough at 78 F., the proper comparative absorption would be 60½ per cent., while the time for fermentation would be reduced to 2½

A Growing Demand

The growing demand for "Bakers' home made bread" has only been made possible by a high order of sanitary and scientific production.

An important factor in sanitary and scientific production of pure and wholesome bread is the sweet, safe, distinctive, sanitary cleanliness which always follows the use of

Knowledge of this fact has enabled thousands of bakers the country over to depend upon this cleaner to accomplish results which are greatly assisting to hasten the day when a majority of families will eat "Bakers'" bread exclusively.

This efficient and economical cleaner is so pure and purifying, providing as it does a sweet, wholesome, faultless, sanitary cleanliness, that your baking processes and display rooms are always protected from insanitation, and your product displayed under the most attractive conditions.

Wyandotte Sanitary Cleaner and Cleanser is quick and easy in its action and is entirely harmless to the hands.

Indian in Circle

Order from your supply house.

In every package

The J. B. Ford Co. _{SOLE} MANUFACTURERS Wyandotte, Mich.

hours. Such a dough would mature at about 81 degrees F.

With 4 per cent. of yeast and dough at 78 degrees F., the absorption can easily be carried further or would be proper at 62½ per cent., while the fermentative period would be reduced to 1¾ hours.

In the short process dough the relative periods of turning and punching of dough comes much closer together and while the dough drops softer from the mixer this extra moisture is sustained, the dough tightening up through the punching and turning at shorter intervals, while during baking the better development of the gluten fully sustains the necessary weight. Such increased efficiency can only be obtained by applying a more vigorous fermentation, not through increased temperatures which results in a dry, crumbly and ill-keeping product.

As time is a necessary factor, the baker using diminished amounts of yeast works his doughs at increased temperatures and naturally so in order to save time. This practice materially decreases the production from a given weight of flour, as the following will show. The comparison is a fair one, and is based on oven efficiency in the application of both formulas.

Of course, total production in reference to yield is further influenced by the character of flour used, by proper and modern mixing of the dough and by the character and amount of batch ingredients added. Also by proper aeration of the flour and of the dough itself during mixing, as the oxygen of the air acts as a direct stimulus to the process of fermentation.

A RELIABLE FORMULA

A high standard product or quality loaf may be made over the following formula:

Use		or Use
600 lbs.	Flour	600 lbs.
363 lbs.	Water	371 lbs.
12 lbs.	Salt	12 lbs.
18 lbs.	Yeast	18 lbs.
30 lbs.	Sweetened Cond. Milk	
	Milk Powder	10 lbs.
12 lbs.	Shortening	12 lbs.
5 lbs.	Sugar	15 lbs.
5 lbs.	Malt Extract	7 lbs.

1,045 lbs. Total Weight of Dough 1,045 lbs.

This formula shows 60½ per cent. absorption with condensed milk and 61.83 per cent. for the formula with milk powder. Therefore, the absorption is figured irrespective of water contained in the milk.

The dough should drop from the mixer at 78 degrees F.

With shop conditions at 80 F. and otherwise normal conditions prevailing, the dough would mature in 2½ hours.

The turning point of the dough would be as follows:
First rise, 1 hour, 30 minutes.
Second rise. 40 minutes.
Third rise, 20 minutes.

Total time for machine work, 2 hours, 30 minutes. (For hand work take dough one-half hour sooner.)

The ingredients total up 1,045 pounds.

This dough under normal conditions will lose not more than one-third of one per cent. during the fermentative period and if scaled carefully will produce 923 full pound loaves of unwrapped bread, or, practically 154 loaves for every 100 pounds of flour used.

If 4 per cent. of yeast were used, the hydration of the dough at the low temperature of 78 degrees F. may easily be carried to 62½ per cent. producing 18 pounds additional dough or 16 full pounds of baked bread. The proper time for fermentation would be 1¾ hours (for hand work, 20 to 25 minutes less).

This same formula under exactly the same conditions with a total of 6 pounds of yeast or 1 per cent. only to the weight of flour, dough set at 82 degrees F. as is still practiced in many bakeries, would carry not more than 54 per cent. absorption and produce a total of 992½ pounds of dough. It would require 4¾ hours to mature. I will give you the formula for comparison, showing a difference in water, salt and yeast.

600	lbs.	Flour.
324		Water.
10½	lbs.	Salt.
6	lbs.	Yeast.
30	lbs.	Sweetened Condensed Milk.
12	lbs.	Shortening.
5	lbs.	Sugar.
5	lbs.	Malt Extract.

992½ lbs. total weight of dough.

Such a dough will lose, even under most favorable conditions, one per cent. of its weight during fermentation. The net yield would be 873 one-pound loaves, or 145½ for every 100 pounds of flour.

Comparison shows the following:

Total flour used, 600 pounds.

Yield with 1 per cent. of yeast to weight of flour, 873 loaves.

Yield with 3 per cent. of yeast to weight of flour, 923 loaves; increase, 50 pounds.

Yield with 4 per cent. of yeast to weight of flour, 939 loaves; increase, 66 pounds.

In addition to this nominal increase in pound loaves we must also consider the great saving in time.

No mention is made here of invisible loss other than through fermentation, such as shrinkage in weight in flour and other raw material before it is used up. This naturally remains the same for either process. This shrinkage is more or less checked according to efficiency in managing supplies in storage and when used.

The fact is, the larger amount of yeast makes possible a much reduced temperature for fermenting the dough as shown in the formulas. This produces a dough with viscosity at a minimum.

Remember what you need is a dry dough, one that will tighten up during fermentation and not a stiff dough, which will unduly heat and slacken as the work proceeds.

OTHER ADVANTAGES

Increased yeast means a quicker fermentation and a bolder loaf from a younger dough. The ripening of the dough also proceeds at a more rapid pace during the time the individual loaves stand in proof, prior to baking.

The gluten is mellowed at a more rapid pace—with other words, the ripening effect on the dough is greater than the comparative gas production.

The increase in salt corresponds to the increased hydration, this together with the extra yeast naturally adds materially to the bulk of the dough.

No better way exists to produce more quickly and efficiently the proper acidity value in a dough than by using a liberal amount of yeast, which also results in a great saving in time and brings into the dough an immense amount of additional nourishment.

Summing up: Greater profits through increased sales with greater security in one's established trade represents the net returns for marketing a Quality Loaf.

—‡—‡—‡—
Improving Rye Bread

THE rye bread sold over the counter varies widely, says the *American Miller*. In German localities. a dark loaf is the favorite. Where there is a distinctive Jewish population, the rye loaf is whiter. Where the population is cosmopolitan in character, the rye loaf may have almost any character, generally edging away from the dark loaf, however.

There are two reasons for this: Many bakers have the mistaken idea that a whitish rye loaf will attract new consumers; and the rye flour itself contains little or no insoluble gluten, and requires wheat flour to make a satisfactory loaf. Rye flour is usually sold in three grades, Pure Dark Rye, Medium Dark and White Rye. The latter is equivalent to short patent wheat flour. It possesses much less absorption capacity than the dark rye flours. It is an unsolved mystery why bakers buy White Rye Patent and then mix it with wheat flour, for it costs much more, and is without that distinctive rye flavor on which increased consumption of rye must be based.

The dark ryes have the rye flavor. A large rye milling firm recommends a blend of Dark Rye and second clear wheat flour as the best for making rye bread with the real flavor of both rye and wheat. The loaf will hold moisture longer. The whitish rye loaf is without distinctive characteristics to recommend it. The rye-eating peoples do not prefer the dark loaf because it is dark, but because it has the rye flavor; and it cannot have the flavor if the flavor is largely eliminated from the rye flour and then further diluted with wheat flour, with a resultant loaf that is not attractive from any standpoint, whether compared with the dark rye loaf for flavor or the wheat loaf for color.

Recipe Department

In this department we will publish new and valuable recipes and want our readers to forward to us any recipe from which they have had good results, or that is not generally known. We wish to make this department as interesting as possible and ask our readers to help us to this end. Address.

RECIPE DEPARTMENT   THE NATIONAL BAKER

LIGHT FRUIT COOKIES—(CHEAP)

4 pounds light brown sugar, 2 pounds lard compound, 8 eggs, 1 quart good milk, 8 pounds soft flour, 2 pounds California seeded raisins, 2½ ounces ammonia (dissolved in milk); a little lemon.

From this mix you should get 38 dozen and the material is low. It will be found a splendid seller.

SUGAR COOKIES—(CHEAP)

4 pounds light brown sugar, 2 pounds compound lard, 2 quarts good milk, 8 pounds soft flour, 4 ounces ammonia, egg color and vanilla.

Stir up the sugar and lard; stir in the milk with the ammonia dissolved in the same, then mix in the flour. Spread sugar over the top and run over with a rolling pin. Right here it may be well to say that more can be made out of any cookie mix by putting in about twice as much of the raising material and rolling it very thin and not count on its spreading any.

GINGER COOKIES

2½ pounds granulated sugar; 1 pound lard, 4 eggs, ½ pint molasses, ½ pint milk, 2 ounces ginger, 1 ounce cinnamon, 3½ pounds flour, 2 ounces soda.

Mix up the same as any other cookie. It will run, and is a little richer than the ordinary molasses cookies; is a fine eater and a good seller. It will keep well.

WINE COOKIES

2 pounds granulated sugar, 1 pound compound lard, 5 eggs, 1 pint good molasses, 1½ ounces soda, 1 ounce allspice, 1 ounce cloves, 4½ pounds soft flour, 1 pound cleaned currants.

Stir up the sugar and lard; stir in the eggs, then the molasses and spices; mix the soda in the water, and stir all in the mix. Now sift the flour on top and put the currants on the flour; mix all together. This will make 12 dozen splendid cookies.

FINE SPONGE CAKE

2 pounds granulated sugar, 1 quart eggs, ½ pint water, 2 pounds and 6 ounces soft flour, a little salt and vanilla.

Beat up the sugar and eggs and water thoroughly until it stands; mix in the flour. You will have some sponge cake, the best you ever ate. You can bake it in any shape desired in a moderate oven.

WHITE LOAF CAKES

ter and lard, 1 pint egg whites, 1 pint skimmed milk, 2 pounds and 2 ounces soft flour, 1 ounce baking powder, vanilla.

Thoroughly rub the butter, lard and sugar; beat in the egg whites a few at a time; stir in the milk. Sift in the flour and baking powder. Take five single 1-pound bread moulds and line them neatly with paper; put in each 15 ounces. Bake in moderate oven.

RASPBERRY FINGERS

3 pounds of flour, 3 pounds of sugar, 3 eggs, ¼ of a pint of water, raspberry jam. Whisk the eggs and sugar to a light froth, add the water, and continue the whisking to a stiff batter. Sift the flour and stir lightly in. Put the mixture into a bag, squeeze it out on thin sheets of white paper into cakes as long and as wide as the middle finger. Dust the tops with icing sugar, place the papers on tins or wires, and bake in a hot oven. When cold, dampen the papers, remove the fingers, and stick them in pairs with thick raspberry jam.

BUTTER SNAPS

5 pounds of flour, 5 pounds of brown sugar, 2½ pounds of butter, 2 pounds of chopped orange peel, 1 ounce of ammonia, 1 ounce of ground cinnamon, 2 ounces of molasses, ½ pint of water. Rub the butter into the flour, sift the sugar and cinnamon, breaking all lumps, and mix it with the flour. Make a bay, turn in the molasses; powder and dissolve the ammonia in the water, stir it into the molasses, work the chopped peel into it, and make up a stiff dough. Roll out sheets a quarter of an inch in thickness, cut into cakes with an inch cutter, and place them an inch apart, on well-greased tins. Wash over with water, and bake in a hot oven.

MADAGASCARS

1 pound of flour, 6 ounces of powdered sugar, ⅓ ounce of ammonia dissolved in 1 gill of milk, 6 ounces of butter or lard, 3 yolks of eggs, a good flavor of lemon. Rub the butter in the flour; make a hole; add the sugar and yolks; cream them, adding the flavor; then add the milk; stir it in, then add the flour and mix, adding milk if needed, to form an easy working dough. When mixed roll it into a sheet one-eighth of an inch thick, and cut it up with a pound scalloped cutter about three inches in diameter. Pan them two inches apart; wash them with egg and milk wash. Then take a cream puff mixture—dough, not filling—

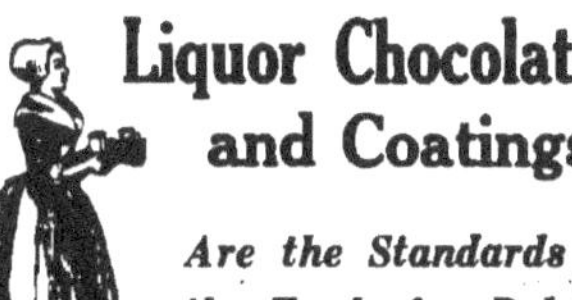

WALTER BAKER & CO.'S
Liquor Chocolates and Coatings

Are the Standards of the Trade for Bakers' and Confectioners' Use

Sweetened and unsweetened; light, medium and dark, whatever the difference of color or flavor, all are absolutely pure, smooth and uniform to work.

The taste and appearance of bakings and confections depend largely upon the coating.

Send for Samples and Prices.

Walter Baker & Co. Ltd.
Established 1780　　DORCHESTER, MASS.

57 Highest Awards at the Expositions of Europe and America.

Malzbender's
Practical Recipe Book

Second Enlarged Edition

In German and English in parallel columns

Written by a well known Baker, Pastry Chef and Confectioner of many years' experience in Europe, U. S., and Canada.

PART I. "BREAD"
15 recipes for Sponge, Straight Dough, Home-made, Quaker, Genuine French, Rye (sponge and yeast), Hot-Cross Buns, English Muffins, Breakfast Muffins, all kinds of Rolls, Buns, Vienna, Sweet Goods, Salt Rising Bread.

PART II. "CAKES"
305 recipes for common, plain up to the high grade Fancy Cakes, wholesale and retail. All kinds of Coffee Cakes, Christmas Goods, Dresdener Stollen, etc.

PART III. "PASTRY COOKING"
110 latest up-to-date recipes for Puddings (warm), Frozen Puddings, (Crèmes), Sauces, Ice Creams, Water Ices (Sherbets), Souffles.

PART IV. "CONFECTIONERY"
80 recipes for making up-to-date Candies, Chewing Gum, Preserves, Candied Fruits, Canning Fruit, Preparing of Jellies, Cordials, Syrops, Wines, Liquors; all kinds of up-to-date Soft Drinks.

PART V. "DECORATING"
Instructions for decorating cakes in European and American Style.

Over 500 Recipes　**Price $2.00**　*Unique in its line*

Send your order to-day to

The National Baker

411 Walnut Street, Philadelphia, Pa.

Do You Know What Your Goods Cost?

ONE of the hardest things in bake-shop practice is to keep an accurate account of the cost of each piece of goods, so that the baker will know just how much profit each piece or each dozen pieces will yield, with raw materials at certain prices.

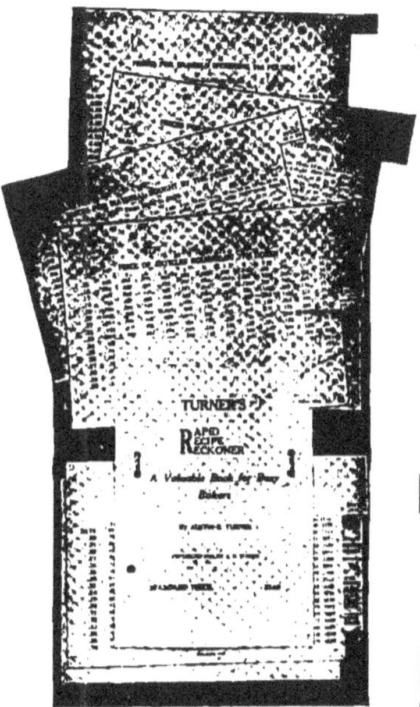

Turner's Rapid Recipe Reckoner

saves a baker all trouble in reckoning up the cost; it is already done for him, and all he has to do is to pick out the desired item at the given price per pound or dozen.

Tables are given of the cost for each ounce of flour at a price per barrel from **$4.00 upward**; and of lard, butter, sugar, eggs and of all other supplies by the ounce or measure at what price you pay in quantities.

Turner's Rapid Recipe Reckoner

simplifies cost accounting so that it is a matter of only a few minutes to get the cost of a batch of any size, and of any class of goods.

The tables are printed on heavy serviceable cardboard, placed in a substantial loose-leaf cover, bound in cloth. It will last a life-time and you can add new sheets or tables, if desired.

In these days of close competition one is needed in every bake-shop, and the cost is but **$2.00**, postpaid. Address

411 Walnut Street
Philadelphia, Pa.

tube. Put it in a bag with half plain round tube, same as used for lady or sponge finger and with it run a ring of the dough round on top of the pieces on the tin, keeping it a quarter of an inch from the edge and arranging to leave a fair size hole in the middle; wash them, same as for cream puffs, and bake. When baked put a little fruit jelly of any kind in the well; then add a good boiled custard to stand a little above the top edge and sprinkle pink sugar on it, also place half of a split almond in centre of each. If preferred dispense with the colored sugar and put on a cone of meringue on the custard, and sprinkle it with fine chopped almonds. These are supposed to sell at five cents each.

FIG AND RAISIN CAKES

½ pound of butter or lard, ¾ of a pound of sugar, 1 pound of flour, ¼ ounce of good baking powder, sifted in the flour, ¼ of a pound of figs and ¼ pound of seeded raisins, chopped fine, 2 eggs, egg color, 1½ gills of milk. Mix in the same manner as for wine cake, using more or less milk, as may be needed. When mixed, spread it half an inch thick on a level and greased and papered baking pan. Dust with powdered sugar and bake. When baked and cold, cut up into squares, to sell at what price you choose. Another way to cut these up is to cut them in pieces twice the length of their width, or into larger squares, then cut each square from corner to corner, thus making triangular or three-cornered pieces.

Those wishing to make a change in these may mix it a little slacker and bake it in small-drop-cake or medium-sized patty pans, to sell at ten cents or twenty cents per dozen, as they choose.

These squares may be sold plain or water-iced. The mixture may also be run thinner in layer-cake tins, and put two together when baked with charlotte russe filling between, then sold plain or water-iced, as you choose.

FLUTED LEMON CAKES

1½ pounds flour, 1½ pounds pulverized sugar, 1½ pounds lard or butter, 2 ounces corn-flour, 1 ounce baking powder, 10 eggs, ½ pint milk, grated rind and juice of 3 fresh lemons, essence lemon. Beat the shortening and sugar to a glossy cream, adding the eggs gradually while beating. Stir in the lemon juice and a few drops of essence, then add the milk. Sift the baking powder with the flour and work it in, then mix the grated rind with the corn-flour and stir it well in. Have some small fluted tin pans well buttered and dusted with icing sugar, place a strip of lemon peel at the bottom of each pan, then three parts fill them with the batter. Place them on baking tins and bake carefully in a warm oven. Remove the cakes from the pans while warm.

COCOANUT CAKES

10 pounds flour, 6 pounds stale cakes (pounded to dust), 6 pounds fine crystal sugar, 3 pounds lard, 3 pounds desiccated cocoanut, 1 gallon golden syrup, lemon flavoring. Rub the lard into the flour, mix in the cake dust and the sugar and make a bay. Turn in the syrup, add the flavoring, and color the batch to a deep golden tint, stir well, and make all up to a soft dough. Break off pieces of about one and one-half ounces each, roll them round in the palms of the hands, and place them on well-greased tins. Do not put them too close together, as they will spread a good deal. Flatten the balls, first dipping the hand in cold water. Bake delicately in a warm oven.

RUSSIAN LOAF CAKE

This cake forms an easy and profitable way to dispose of stale cake, but not too many fine crumbs should be used. Cut the stale cake in squares, discs and slices of irregular sizes and shapes, place them in a kettle or bowl. Make a small boiling of syrup, to which add some jelly and a good flavoring of rum, or any suitable extract; slowly pour the syrup over the cakes, shaking them so as to evenly distribute the liquor and until well saturated, so they form a binding consistency. Previously have a frame lined with a thin sponge cake sheet, place the mixture in the frame, heaped full, press down and place another sponge cake sheet on top. Lay a sheet of paper on top, then a board or tin, and a weight on top of it so as to press it down and keep in shape. When entirely cold and firm, ice it over with a lemon-flavored water icing and cut into suitable sized slices. In place of being iced the cake may be enveloped in a coat of meringue mixture, liberally sprinkled with shredded cocoanut, then push in a hot oven long enough to acquire a nice yellow color.

FRENCH GINGERNUTS OR CRUMB JUMBLES

2 pounds crumbs, 1 pound granulated sugar, 1 pint molasses, ½ pint water, 1 ounce soda, a flavoring of ground cinnamon and ginger, ½ pound shortening, and enough flour to form an easy-rolling dough. Place all the dry ingredients into a bowl, break up the shortening with it, then add the molasses and water and mix. Roll down to one-third of an inch thickness, cut out round and throw them on coarse granulated sugar, place them on baking pans (sugar side uppermost), then pipe a dot of jelly in the middle of each cake and bake in moderate heat. Some bakers prefer icing in place of jelly. In this case it is applied after the baking, when a little hollow is pressed in the middle and the icing dropped in. For variety's sake different colored icing may be used. If crumbs are used which contain a large amount of sugar, less sugar is added to the mixture or vice versa. These cakes are sold at 10 cents per dozen.

—‡—‡—‡—

Many a so-called strong-minded person is merely stubborn.

The people we envy always envy some other fellow higher up.

TRADE ITEMS

The Quality Bakery has been opened by Jack Foster at Safford, Ariz.

L. E. Burtch will open a new bakery at Mena, Ark.

Coston & Smith have bought the City Bakery at Fort Morgan, Colo.

Mary Suppa, Bridgeport, Conn., will erect a one-story concrete bakery building at 1788 Stratford avenue.

The Goetz Bakery Co., Inc., New Haven, Conn., has been granted a permit to rebuild three of its buildings on State street, which were recently damaged by fire. The cost of repairs will be $20,000.

The Mt. Carmel Bakery Co. has been incorporated at New Haven, Conn., by Mary A. Alling, Levi W. Alling and Chas. J. Stanley.

Morris Sachs, of New York City, has bought the premises and bakery business of Harry Kurtz, at 5 Bouton street, Norwalk, Conn., for $14,000.

Albert Spector, of Ansonia, Conn., has purchased the Elite Bakery at Shelton, Conn.

August Leske has sold his bakery business on Beach avenue, Tarryville, Conn., to a Meriden bakery firm.

The Polt Bakery, Torrington, Conn., has been sold to Joseph Negri and John Seagliorini.

G. R. Pierson, proprietor of the Arcadia Bakery, W. Oak street, Arcadia, Fla., recently bought out the O. L. Shobe Confectionery adjoining his present store, and will operate same in connection with the bakery.

The Liberty Baking Company will open a modern baking plant about July 1st at Lake Wales, Fla., D. A. Walker, proprietor.

W. H. Bazemore's Bakery has been opened on Madison street, Dublin, Ga.

Harold I. Rathbun is successor to W. E. Green in the Glasford Bakery, Glasford, Ill.

G. A. Weisenbach, proprietor of the Mattoon Steam Bakery, Mattoon, Ill., has sold the fixtures and good will to the owner of the building, Fred Messmer, who will continue to manufacture the same fine line of bread and fancy cake, and will overhaul and enlarge the plant and install new machinery and ovens.

Everett Holcomb, a leading baker of Paris, Ill., who retired a short time ago, has returned to the baking business at the same place, where he will continue to manufacture a complete line of baked goods.

C. R. Spencer, baker of Arcadia, Ind., is remodeling his bakery and installing new fixtures.

Peter White, 110 N. Main street, Goshen, Ind., is making extensive improvements to his bakery.

Jocup's Model Baking Company, Indiana Harbor, Ind., is enlarging its plant there.

The City Baking Company of Indianapolis, Ind., of which organization William Elwarner is president, and R. L. White is secretary and treasurer, opened their immense new plant at the corner of 16th and Bellefontaine streets, last month, with a general celebration. The new plant cost over $300,000.

Mr. Rahm, of 903 College avenue, Terre Haute, Ind., has

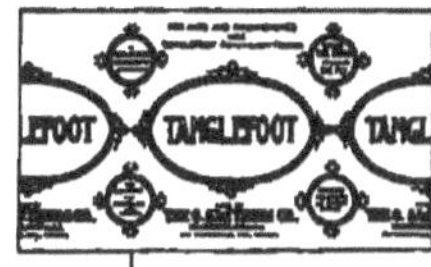

A Valuable Impression

A pleasing impression upon customers is of value. You can create one and at the same time save your goods from damage by spreading sheets of **TANGLEFOOT** in your show windows, especially over Sunday.

TANGLEFOOT will then be at work for you and will not only catch the flies, but attract the attention of people who pass your store to your efforts to keep your stock clean and fresh. For 1922 **TANGLEFOOT** has been considerably reduced in price.

Remember **TANGLEFOOT** *catches the germ as well as the fly, and that poisons, traps or powders cannot do it.*

retired after 30 years' continuous service. The business will be continued by O. C. Davis, who will run a first class shop.

A. J. Miller, Indianapolis, Ind., will soon open a new bakery at 1959 Ashland avenue.

The Tasty Bake Shop, 2967 N. Illinois avenue, Indianapolis, Ind., was recently opened by Ralph W. Hackleman, formerly of Ft. Worth, Texas. A complete and first class line of baked goods will be made.

Ort Waltz is successor to Clarence Culp in the Kewanna Bakery at Kewanna, Ind.

A new bakery has been opened at Inman, Kan., by H. C. Schattenberg.

A bakery department is to be installed at the Dibble Grocery Store, Sixth avenue and Quincy street, Topeka, Kan. Mrs. J. E. DuBreuil will be in charge.

William Brown Martin will open a new bakery at 914 State street, Bowling Green, Ky.

A new bakery has been opened at Burnside, Ky., by Joseph Nance, costing $4,000.

B. J. & H. F. Linneman are successors to Teekin & Steplin in the Winchester Bakery, Winchester, Ky. They will improve the bakery and install new machinery.

The Delhi Bakery has been recently opened at Delhi, La.

The new plant of the Maine Bakery Company, 254-256 Minot avenue, Lewiston, Me., will shortly be opened for business. Messrs. Philippe J. Couture and Armend Dufrense, the proprietors, have made a model shop of this new plant.

Leon Miller has opened a new bakery store at Mapleton, Me.

The Service Baking Corp. has been incorporated at Boston, Mass., with capital of $100,000 by Francis J. Mahoney, Dwight L. Allison and Frederick W. Banker.

Councillor Albert Pierce recently opened his new retail bake shop establishment on North street, Salem, Mass., and will carry a complete line of baked goods.

The Orville Bakery has been opened at Central Lake, Mich.

A new bakery has been opened on Main street, Cheboygan, Mich., by Bert Picco & Co., cost $4,000.

A bakery is to be started by Paulsen & Paulsen in the W. G. Johnson Bldg., Henning, Mich.

Carl A. Swanson, Glenwood, Minn., is remodeling and enlarging his bakery there.

B. N. Smith has purchased the Loyal Bakery of John P. Rowe at Bayard, Neb.

Chas. B. Wollner sold his bakery business at 23 Main street, Mt. Holly, N. J., to Walter & Bauer.

The name of the Skinner Baking Company, Omaha, Neb., is to be changed to that of the Quaker Baking Company, and the new officers of the concern are: John E. Hoffman, president; A. Louie, vice-president and manager; H. V. Jeffrey, secretary and treasurer; Bert Francis, assistant manager.

The Norris Baking Company, one of the oldest industries of Concord, N. H., has been recently organized with James H. Welch as president, and Giuseppi Nardini as treasurer and general manager.

The Star Cake Bakery Company has been incorporated at 747 Broad street, Newark, N. J., with capital of $125,000 to do a general bakery business.

William J. McDonald and Walter S. Stewart, an experienced baker, have purchased the interest of W. H. Allen in the Perfect Bake Shop, Fourth and Central streets, Albuquerque, N. Mex., and will make same the retail sales department of their bakery, transferring the manufacturing plant to 202 E. Central avenue, where a retail salesroom will also be conducted.

The Pure Food Bakery and Delicatessen at 113 Court street, Binghamton, N. Y., recently held a very successful opening. Mr. Becker is the proprietor, and carries a complete stock of the very best baked goods.

Extensive renovations are being made to the Cornwall Bakery, Main street, Cornwall, N. Y., of which Frank Ziegler is proprietor.

The Uffelman Baking Co. has been incorporated at Cincinnati, Ohio, with capital of $50,000, by Edward L. Uffelman, Christ Uffelman, Jr., Bernard Kasper, Christ Uffelman, Sr., George F. Eyrich, Jr.

Harry Caplan, 12,117 Kinsman Rd., Cleveland, Ohio, is erecting a new addition to his bakery building.

Frank Showalter has purchased the bakery of F. B. Kane at Billings, Okla.

E. L. Whittaker has bought the City Bakery of C. L. Chasteen, at Stratford, Okla.

George Harris has bought out the interest of Mr. Monaghan in the bakery firm of Harris & Monaghan, Pittston, Pa., and has moved into a new fire proof building at 1093 Wyoming avenue, Exeter, Pa., where he will conduct a wholesale business of fine baked goods.

Ernest F. Gunn, baker, of Glenside, Pa., will erect a one-story and basement building at Paxson avenue and Mill Road.

Application was made to the Governor of Pennsylvania on April 24th for a charter for the Crystal Baking Company of Reading, Pa. The proposed incorporators are C. T. Mantis, Christ Mantis, Charles Parella, Vincent Rosatto, and Arthur K. Stern, all of Reading.

The partnership formerly existing between John L. Orth and Paul R. Boaman, of Reading, Pa., in the pretzel baking business, has been dissolved and a new partnership to be known as the Quality Pretzel Company has been formed with Mr. Boaman, William L. Quinlan and Charles E. Brown as the new partners.

Fred Gilbert, 289 Wyoming avenue, Wyoming, Pa., is successor to Geo. S. Frantz.

Philip Schad & Sons have leased the Farmers Pub. Co. Bldg. at Milbank, S. D., and will open a bakery there in a short time.

The Stude Baking Company, of Houston, Texas, have increased their capital stock from $10,000 to $30,000.

Andrews & Krone are successors to the Farmers Bakery at Hillsboro, Texas.

R. Q. Travers has opened an up-to-date bakery at 105 S. Fifth street, Waco, Texas.

A. A. Duenwald, proprietor of Duenwald's bakery and delicatessen store at 312 S. 11th street, Tacoma, Wash., will shortly open a new store at 917 Broadway, which will be modern and up-to-date in every respect.

The Quality Bakery has been opened at Alderson, W. Va.

Hoyt's Consumers Cracker & Biscuit Company has been incorporated at Los Angeles, Calif., with capital stock of $50,000.

The Weiser Bakery, of Weiser, Idaho, has been incorporated with capital stock of $10,000, by George B. Kellogg, H. P. Cummock and Edward Romph.

C. S. Ray and T. A. Belcher have purchased the F. A. O. Hammill Bakery at 703 N. Main street, Pueblo, Colo., and the name will be changed to that of The Bonafide Bakery. The entire interior has been redecorated and painted, and they are planning on operating a thoroughly modern and up-to-date bakery.

Fire recently damaged Eddy's Steam Bakery, 900 Second avenue, North, Helena, Mont., to the extent of about $6,000. The loss is fully covered by insurance, and will not prevent the resumption of business, as three of the ovens remained untouched.

George J. Stover, an experienced baker of Pittsburgh, Pa., has purchased the Hancock Baking Company's plant at 409-11 Madison avenue, Elmira, N. Y., at a cost of $30,000, and has taken possession.

Stelle Frangk, of the Pastry Shop, Poughkeepsie, N. Y., recently bought of Frank J. Slater the property at 518 Main street, which is 54 feet by 107 feet, and same will be improved before being used for business purposes.

ESTABLISHED 1864

THOS. MILLS & BRO., Inc.

MANUFACTURERS OF

BAKERS', CONFECTIONERS' AND ICE CREAM MACHINERY AND TOOLS

1301-1311 NORTH EIGHTH STREET :•: :•: **PHILADELPHIA, PA.**

ALL SIZES OF TUBS AND CANS IN STOCK

COMBINED ICE CREAM FREEZER
AND BREAKER

EGG WHIPS

LARGE ASSORTMENT OF INDIVIDUAL
ICE CREAM MOULDS

PEELS AND SWAB POLES

ALL SIZES OF TIN, STEEL
AND RUSSIA IRON PANS

ALL STYLES

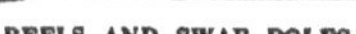

OF BRUSHES

PATENT BEATING MACHINE

ALL SIZES OF
PIE PLATES

ICE CREAM REFRIGERATORS, HARD
WOOD OR MARBLE FRONTS

WE ISSUE THREE DISTINCT CATALOGS—CONFECTIONERS' BAKERS' AND ICE CREAM

Information Department

The object of this department is to help our readers, as far as possible, to solve the various difficulties that come up from day to day. We will also answer questions about all kinds of machinery and give every possible assistance in securing detailed information. No names or addresses of manufacturers will be given in these columns. When wanted they will be sent by mail. Address,

INFORMATION DEPARTMENT　　　　THE NATIONAL BAKER

BREAD TROUBLES

S. R., New York: Received your loaf of bread, and same is too young, shown by surface of loaf covered with tiny blisters, which is undeveloped gluten. Your bread is dark all through, which shows you have either set dough too warm or are using bleached flour. The coarseness and holes in loaf are by a young or over-heated dough. Try this: 1 pound of flour, 8 pounds condensed milk, 3 pounds sugar, 1 pound lard (not compound), 3 2-3 pounds salt, 3 2-3 to 4½ pounds of yeast. Temperature of dough 78 to 80 degrees. Time to bench, 3½ hours. Your loaf shows the proof too warm. Never get it warmer than 96 degrees.

DEVIL'S CAKE.—SPICE CAKE

R. N. L., Washington: Answering your favor of the 7th, a good Devil's Cake may be made from an ordinary chocolate cake mixture or a spice cake mixture about as follows: 1 quart molasses, 1 pound lard, 5 eggs, 1 quart water, 2 ounces soda, 3 pounds crumbs, 1 pound sugar, 1 ounce mixed spices, 3 pounds flour, 4 ounces currants, 4 ounces chopped peel. Rub the crumbs through a coarse sieve. Dissolve the soda in water. Cream sugar and lard; add molasses, spices, water and soda, and mix in the crumbs and flour. Add more water if required to make a soft mixture.

This can be made in several layers if you wish, with chocolate filling between and all iced with a good chocolate coating. Actually a Devil's Cake is a *dark mixture* and you can make pretty near anything that your trade will pay for.

SWISS BUNS

Swiss Buns are rather elaborate. We give you herewith a fine recipe. It can be cheapened as your experience may suggest: 1 pound of sugar, 1½ pounds flour, 1 ounce baking powder, 5 eggs, ½ pint milk. Sift the baking powder in the flour; beat the sugar and eggs together, and add the flavor and flour. Mix the milk afterwards.

Spread the mixture with the palette knife on the paper very thin, and bake in 400 to 450 degrees Fahrenheit. When done, turn at once over on a paper dusted with sugar. Wet the paper, remove it quickly and spread the cake over with a soft preserve or jelly, and roll up. Roll it up tight, so it keeps its shape in the paper.

A better mixture is made with sixteen eggs to the pound of flour and sugar; beaten up warmed, and made and rolled as described above.

Lately some bakers and caterers are making a variety of fancy rolls in this manner. In place of using a plain jelly or jam, cream fillings and cream icings are used, and the rolls are iced with almond and cream icings and rolled in chopped nuts, which makes a very rich looking roll. Fill the roll with the creams, and ice when cold with chocolate, vanilla, or caramel icing; or spread with a light jam or jelly, and roll in cocoanut; or fill with nut or almond cream, or icing; spread the outside with a thin almond icing and roll in chopped nuts. These fancy rolls are sold as Swiss Roll, Paris Roll, Princess Roll, etc.

MILK BREAD, NO. 1

R. M. N., Penna.: 40 pounds flour, 2 gallons water, 1 gallon milk, 12 ounces salt, 8 ounces sugar, 8 ounces malt extract, 8 ounces lard, 8 ounces yeast. Temperature, 82 degrees mixed. Let stand 3 hours—punch. Let stand 1 hour—punch. Let stand 45 minutes—bench. Ball on bench before panning; give three-quarters proof in pans for oven. Have oven about 475 degrees or medium solid heat. To make a plain top loaf give good proof in pans for oven. The three-quarters proof is for a burst or cut loaf. Watch time and temperature closely.

MILK BREAD, NO. 2

12 gallons water, 10 pounds cream of maize, 2 pounds lard, 3 pounds sugar, 1½ pounds dry milk, 1¼ pounds yeast, 3 pounds salt, 140 pounds flour—3 parts spring patent, 1 part winter. Dough should have a temperature of 82 to 84 degrees and must not be too stiff. Let come up well first time (3 to 3½ hours). Let dough come up second time, knock down, let recover. Bring to bench and scale.

CRUMB CAKES

F. R. B., Minn.: In reply to your request for "a recipe for crumb cake" we wish to say that the name crumb cake is being applied to many cakes where crumbs which accumulate in the shop from time to time are utilized. However, we will gladly help you with two recipes, which should answer the purpose: 1 pound of sweet crumbs, 1 pint of molasses, ½ pint of water, 8 ounces of sugar, 8 ounces of lard, 1-2 ounce of soda, the same weight of cream of tartar, spices to suit, flour. Mix all together, adding enough flour to form an easy rolling dough. Roll it down into a sheet, cut out with round cutter, place them upon granulated sugar and lay them upon baking tins, sugar side uppermost. Then bake in moderate heat.

Another method: 1½ pounds of sweet crumbs, 1 pound of lard, 4 eggs, 1 ounce of soda, ½ ounce of cream of tartar, 2½ pounds of flour, 1 quart of molasses, 1 quart of water, spices to suit. If crumbs are not sweet enough, add a sufficient amount of brown sugar. Mix this together, which should form a slack dough, then drop into whatever size muffin or cake pan you choose (previously greased) and bake in medium heat. If desired, you may add sultana raisins or currants.

A GOOD, CHEAP POUND CAKE

F. L. A., Penna.: The following should answer your purpose:

1 pound of powdered sugar, 1 pound of washed butter, 8 eggs, 1 pint of milk, 2 pounds of cake flour, 1 ounce of baking powder, a little egg color, flavor with mace, vanilla or lemon. Cream sugar and butter in the usual way and gradually add the eggs, stir in the milk and flavor, sift in flour and baking powder together and mix thoroughly, then fill in pans and bake in moderate heat. The same formula holds good for raisin or citron cake. When the batch is entirely finished, then the fruit is added, but before the raisins and citron (the latter cut up into slices) are mixed in the batch they should be floured thoroughly to prevent settling to the bottom of the cake during baking; the oven damper should be kept closed till the cake has raised and takes color. This cake generally sells by the pound and is baked in sheets or cards, which consist of wooden frames. It is certainly the best method of baking this cake, as it does not get a hard crust on the sides and raises evenly. This method of baking should be followed for all cakes in this line, as plum cakes, molasses fruit cakes, lady cakes, etc. The above mixture may be altered at will to suit trade; that is, cheapened by adding more flour and milk and taking less eggs and butter or lard, but a proportionate amount of raising powder must be added. Lard or any shortening may be substituted for butter.

ANISE DROPS

N. O. F., Baltimore.: The recipe for Anise Drops is as follows: 1 pound of sugar, 1 pound of flour, 8 eggs, ½ ounce of anise seed, lemon extract. Beat the sugar and eggs together on a slow fire, same as for sponge cake. When light, add the seeds and flavor. Lay out with bag and tube on greased and dusted pans in drops the size of a silver quarter, and let dry, for three or four hours, until a crust is formed, and bake in a cool oven. The cake may be made in several colors and flavors.

VANILLA WAFERS

The recipe for the vanilla wafers is as follows: Use 1 pound and 2 ounces of butter, 8 eggs, 1 pound of flour, vanilla flavor, 1 pound of XXXX powdered sugar. Cream butter and sugar, add eggs, flavor and flour. Dress on greased pans in rings or in the form of an 8; or use a forcer, which is a very handy machine. Bake on very straight, smooth pans, lightly greased, and take off the pans while warm.

ANGELS' CAKE

G. B. N., New York: These cakes are famous everywhere, but especially in the United States. There are a great many recipes for them, but we consider the following to be the best:

(a) Cream 2 pounds of butter with 4 pounds of fine white sugar; beat 16 whites into 1 pint of new milk flavored with vanilla essence; sift 2 ounces of baking powder with 4 ounces of flour; make dough, adding flour a little at a time, working with large fork. Bake in two-inch deep square tins. Make vanilla royal icing; sprinkle with grated cocoanut.

MAPLE MOUSSE

We have your favor of March 9th, enclosing $2.00 for renewal of subscription to THE NATIONAL BAKER, for which we thank you. Same has had attention this date.

R. H. D., Maine: In reference to your request for formula for "Maple Mousse," would advise that it is made as follows:

Mousse is a frozen whipped cream. Its composition and manufacture being as follows: The cream to be used in making mousse must be of such richness that it will whip to a stiff froth. The richness of the cream as well as the method of making may have to be varied somewhat with different flavors.

The flavors which may be used are vanilla, coffee, caramel, almond, pistachio, maple and various fruit flavors. When the extract flavors are used, the directions for whipped cream may be followed until the mousse is ready to pack.

The freezing is accomplished without agitation by packing the whipped cream in a mould or a can surrounded by equal parts of ice and salt. To obtain good results it will be necessary in many cases to use gelatin, particularly where fruit is used quite liberally.

Maple flavoring may be made by using maple extract and enough caramel syrup to give the desired color, but Maple Ice Cream lacks the fine quality of the ice cream flavored with maple sugar or maple syrup. The best quality of maple is made by substituting two pounds of maple sugar or a quart of maple syrup for two pounds of the granulated sugar. Two ounces of vanilla and two or three ounces of caramel should also be used to bring out the flavor and a light brown color.

Referring to your favor of March 21st, we herewith give you good recipe for Dark Rye Bread, which we trust you will find satisfactory.

DARK RYE BREAD

Set a sponge with all rye flour having 1/10 of mass consisting of sour rye dough left over from day before. Let sponge fall ¾ inch. Add ¼ of amount of rye used of wheat flour. Mix, let rise a little. Ball up, proof 20 minutes. Mould in your style. Proof, bake. There is a light rye flour and a dark one; use either or both till the bread is dark enough to suit you.

ANGELICA AND CHERRY CAKE

One and one-half pounds flour, one pound pulverized sugar, one pound butter, eight ounces preserved cherries, six ounces drained angelica, one ounce baking powder, one-fourth pint milk, eight eggs. Beat the butter and sugar into a light cream, adding the eggs two at a time while doing so. Mix in the milk, sift the baking powder with the flour, and work them into the cream. Next add the cherries and angelica (previously cut into very small pieces), blend all well together, fill into a paper-lined rim, dust the tops with fine sugar, and bake in a moderate oven.

SUGAR AND GLUCOSE ICING

J. W., Pennsylvania: A wholesale cake manufacturer who wants a recipe for cake icing made partly from glucose.

There is only one icing to our knowledge which can be made partly from glucose, or, in other words, sugar and glucose together; that is, the so-called fondant or French cream. Composed of 80 per cent. of sugar and 20 per cent. of glucose, with the necessary addition of water. We may state right here, that 20 per cent. of glucose is about all that can be added to make a good icing, and if less is added the icing will be so much the better. The formula would be about as follows:

20 pounds of granulated or confectioners' sugar, 5 pounds of glucose and 3 quarts of water. Place this in a copper kettle and set it on a good fire, stirring until it is dissolved. When it starts to boil, wash down all the sugar that may adhere to the sides of the kettle and cover up for about 5 or 7 minutes (according to the size of your batch), and cook to the soft ball, or 238 degrees on the thermometer. While the boiling is going on, get your marble slab ready by having cleaned and sprinkled with cold water and the edges framed in order to keep the sugar from running over. Then pour your batch on the slab and again sprinkle the surface of the sugar with cold water and let it stand to cool off, but not to a dead cold. For larger batches it requires two men to do the turning. This is done by means of two especially constructed spatulas; the sugar being worked to and fro, through the whole batch, and always toward the centre of the slab. When worked long enough it will become white and creamy. At that stage throw it in a heap as quickly as possible, scraping the slab clean. Then cover up the batch with a damp cloth and a bowl, or something like it, over the whole, and let it "steam" for about a half of an hour. Then uncover it and work the batch with the palm of your hand, it will then become soft and smooth.

If you do not desire to use it right up, place it in a stone crock or tub and keep it covered with a damp cloth. Before this icing is applied, place as much as you intend to use in a pan and over a slow fire, or in a hot water bath, warm it up slightly under constant stirring; do not let it get hot or any part of it, else it will grain and become lumpy. When heated, or rather warmed, to the proper temperature and it should prove to be too thick for the icing intended, then stir in enough water until it has reached the proper consistency.

Business Chances

"WANT" and "FOR SALE" advertisements inserted in THE NATIONAL BAKER for three cents a word, payable in advance. Stamps accepted in payment.

MACHINERY FOR SALE

1—20-inch Thomson Moulder Extension, new.

1—Thomson Zerah Baller.

1—2½-bbl. Day Dough Mixer.

1—2-bbl. Read Dough Mixer.

1—1½-bbl. Read Dough Mixer.

2—Union Bun Rounders.

1—Day Dough Brake.

3—Day Wood Flour Sifters.

2—Triumph All-Steel Flour Sifters.

1—2-bbl. Triumph Dough Mixer.

2—Wood-Proof Closets, for public view bakery.

1—1½-bbl. Peerless Dough Mixer.

Cake Machines, Bread Racks, Troughs and Equipment of every description ready for immediate shipment, new or rebuilt. Rebuilt machines guaranteed same as new ones.

J. H. BAST & CO.

649 W. Pratt St.   Baltimore, Md.

FOR SALE—FOR A VERY LOW price you can secure the following slightly used equipment:

Two Yankee Reel Ovens, $100 each.

DOUGH MIXERS

1 Dutchess, 3 bbl.   J. H. Day, 3 bbl.
1 Champion, 4 bbl.   2 Rockwell, 3 bbl.
2 Read, 1½ bbl.   1 Read, 5 bbl.
1 Peerless, 1½ bbl.
1 Champion Sifting Machine, 3 bbl.
1 Read Sifting Machine, 5 bbl.

CAKE MACHINES

Read   1 Champion
1 Hobart with D. C. motor attached
Dutchess 6-Pocket Divider
Dutchess Roll Dividers
Bread and Pan Racks
Proofing Closets   Troughs
Work Tables   Bread Pans
1 Day Egg Clipper   Shipping Boxes
Champion Dough Brake, A1 condition, motor drive
2 Doughnut Fryers with trays

J. KALFUS COMPANY
119-127 Ridge Street
New York City

BAKERIES FOR SALE

FOR SALE—GOOD BAKERY IN town of 10,000 population, together with wagons, horses and all tools. Only bakery in town or in the towns around it. Address Baldowski Bros., 72 West Main Street, Miners Mills, Penna.

FOR SALE—BAKERY IN GOOD, live town of 1,500; two railroads, one running east and west and the other running north and south. Nearest bakery in county 14 miles. Town contains brick plant employing 70 men daily. Everything in first-class condition and sanitary. Priced at a bargain. Half cash and balance in five years. For further particulars write City Bakery, I. T. Mains, proprietor, St. Elmo, Ill.

FOR SALE — BAKERY, DOING good business, equipped with No. 11½ Hubbard Oven, dough mixer, moulder, bun divider, steam boiler, tank, etc. Good opportunity. Write Maloy Baking Co., corner Second and Oak Sts., London, Ohio.

FOR SALE—BAKERY IN CITY OF 80,000. Full Meek gas equipment. New brick oven. Peerless 1½ bbl. mixer, doughnut machine, dough roller, one truck. A wholesale and retail trade. Cash. Address Sanitary Bakery, Wichita, Kans.

FOR SALE — WHOLESALE BAKery in town of 16,000 population. Equipped with bread and cake mixer, bread moulder and wrapping machine. Also sell property. Wm. H. Fox, 312 E. Broad Street, Millville, N. J.

FOR SALE—MODERN BAKERY— Marshall-Middleby Oven, gas-oven, Read bread mixer, Read cake mixer, Union cookie machine, fried cake machine, bread wrapper. All in first-class condition, and now doing good business. Selling out on account of ill health. Address Dan Deegan, Geneva, N. Y.

SITUATION WANTED

MISCELLANEOUS

TURNER'S RAPID RECIPE RECKoner simplifies cost accounting so that it is a matter of only a few minutes to get the cost of a batch of any size, and of any class of goods. The baker is saved all the trouble in counting up the cost; it is already done for him. Tables are given of the cost of each ounce of flour at a price per barrel from $4.00 upward, of other materials from $0.01 to $0.60 by the pound, and the cost of each ounce. One is needed in every bake-shop, and the cost is but $2.00 postpaid. For sale by THE NATIONAL BAKER, 411 Walnut Street, Philadelphia, Pa.

OVENS FOR SALE

MUST SELL TWELVE-PAN, TWOdeck oven to make room for large single-deck Hubbard. Address Box 10, care THE NATIONAL BAKER, 411 Walnut Street, Philadelphia.

A Classified List of Goods Needed by Bakers

Automobile Trucks—
Republic Truck Sales Corp, Alma, Mich.

Almond Paste—
Henry Heide, Inc., New York.

Bakery Advertising—
I. B. Nordhem Co., N. Y.
Schulse Advert. Service, Chicago.
W. E. Long Co., Chicago.

Bakers' Institute—
Siebel Institute, Chicago.

Bakers' Machinery—
Champion Machine Co., Joliet, Ill.
J. H. Day Co., Cincinnati, O.
Dutchess Tool Co., Beacon, N. Y.
Jaburg-Miller Co., New York.
Peerless Bread Mch. Co., Sidney, O.
Read Machinery Co., York, Pa.
Reeves Pulley Co., Columbus, Ind.
Thomson Mch. Co., Bellevue, N. J.
Thomas Mills & Bro., Philadelphia.
Union Machinery Co., Joliet, Ill.

Bakers' Pans—
Jaburg Bros., New York.
Jaburg-Miller Co., New York.
Edward Katzinger Co., Chicago.
The Aug. Maag Co., Baltimore.
Thomas Mills & Bro., Philadelphia.

Bakers' Tools—
Jaburg Bros., New York.
Jaburg-Miller Co., New York.
Edward Katzinger Co., Chicago.
The Aug. Maag Co., Baltimore.
Thomas Mills & Bro., Philadelphia.
Union Steel Products Co., Albion.

Books for Bakers—
Malsbender's Recipe Book.
Turner's Rapid Recipe Reckoner.

Bread Labels—
Mirror Printing Co., Kalamazoo.

Bread Wrapping and Sealing Machines—
National Bread Wrapping Machine Co., Nashua, N. H.
Lamhooy Label & Wrapper Co., Kalamazoo, Mich.
Union Machinery Co., Joliet, Ill.

Cash Registers—
National Cash Register Company.

Chocolate—
Walter Baker & Co., Ltd., Dorchester.

Cooking Oil
Corn Products Ref. Co., New York.

Dough Mixers and Kneaders—
Champion Machinery Co., Joliet, Ill.
J. H. Day Co., Cincinnati, O.
Read Machinery Co., York, Pa.

Eggs-Desiccated—Egg Products—
Joe Lowe Co., N. Y.

Flour—
Big Diamond Mills Co., Minn.
Commander Mills, Minneapolis.
Empire Milling Co., Minneapolis.
W. J. Jennison & Co., Minneapolis.
Russell-Miller Milling Co., Minn.
Washburn-Crosby Co., Minneapolis.

Food Colors—
National Aniline & Chem. Co., N. Y.

Fruit Growers—
California Associated Raisin Co.
California Prune & Apricot Growers.

Ice Cream Tools and Supplies—
Atlas Mfg. Co., New Haven.
Chr. Hansen's Lab., Little Falls, N. Y.
The Aug. Maag Co., Baltimore.
Thomas Mills & Bro., Philadelphia.

Malt, Extract and Dry—
American Diamalt Co.
Anheuser-Busch, Inc., St. Louis.
P. Ballantine & Sons, Newark.
Freihofer Baking Co., Philadelphia.
Malt Diastase Co., N. Y.

Milk, Powdered and Condensed—
Consolidated Prod. Co., Lincoln, Neb.
I. H. Nesler & Co., Philadelphia.

Ovens—
Bennett Oven Co., Battle Creek.
Duhrkop Oven Co., New York.
Hubbard Oven Co., Chicago.
Meek Oven Mfg. Co., Westport, Conn.
Middleby Oven Co., New York.
Middleby-Marshall Co., Chicago.
Standard Oven Co., Pittsburgh.
Superior Oven Co., Chicago, Ill.

Oven Lights and Doors—
Dutchess Tool Co., Beacon, N. Y.
Chas. Robson & Co., Philadelphia.

Papers (Parchment and Waxed)—
Lamhooy Label & Wrapper Co., Kalamazoo, Mich.
Menasha Ptg. & Carton Co., Menasha, Wis.
Waterproof Paper & Board Co., Cincinnati.

Pie Machinery—
Edwin E. Bartlett, Nashua, N. H.
J. H. Day Co., Cincinnati, O.
Union Machinery Co., Joliet, Ill.

Potato Flour—
Falk American Potato Flour Co., Pittsburgh, Pa.

Pyrometers—
Hubbard Oven Co., Chicago.
Philadelphia Thermometer Co.
Chas. Robson & Co., Philadelphia.

Shipping Boxes (Wood and Paper)—
A. Backus, Jr., & Son, Detroit.
Rob't Gaylord, Inc., St. Louis.

Shortening—
Corn Products Refining Co., N. Y.
Procter & Gamble Co., Cincinnati.

Stoves for Bakers and Confectioners—
Edward Katzinger Co., Chicago.
Thomas Mills & Bro., Philadelphia.

Sugar and Sugar Syrups—
American Sugar Ref. Co., N. Y.
Corn Products Ref. Co., New York.
Franklin Sugar Ref. Co., Philadelphia.

Supplies—
Jaburg Bros., New York.
Joe Lowe Co., N. Y.
Stein-Hall Mfg. Co., Chicago and N. Y.
Ward Baking Co., New York.

Thermometers—
Phila. Thermometer Co., Phila.

Washing and Cleaning Material—
J. B. Ford Co.

Yeast—
The Fleischmann Co., New York.

INDEX TO ADVERTISEMENTS

	Page
American Diamalt Co.	39
Anheuser-Busch Sales Corp.	43
American Sugar Refining Co.	15
Baker & Co., Ltd., Walter	57
Ballantine & Sons, P.	14
Bartlett, Edwin E.	
Bennett Oven Co.	5
Big Diamond Mills Co.	4
Business Chances	65
California Associated Raisin Co.	11
California Prune & Apricot Growers	47
Carter, Rice & Co. Corporation	45
Commander Mills	39
Corn Products Ref. Co.	9
Day Co., The J. H.	7
Duhrkop Oven Co.	8
Dutchess Tool Co.	14, 19
Empire Milling Co.	16
Fleischmann Co., The	13
Ford Co., J. B.	63

	Page
Freihofer Baking Co.	55
Freymark Steam Generator Co.	47
Heide, Inc., Henry	63
Hubbard Portable Oven Co.	Cover
Jennison Co., W. J.	16
Katzinger Co., Edward	Cover
Lamhooy Label & Wrapper Co.	4
W. E. Long Co.	37
Maag Co., The Aug.	Cover
Malt Diastase Co.	16
Malzbender, M.	57
Middleby-Marshall Oven Co.	8
Middleby Oven Co., N. Y.	15
Mills & Bro., Inc., Thomas	61
National Bread Wrapping Mach. Co.	45

	Page
Philadelphia Thermometer Co.	4
Procter & Gamble Co.	7
Read Machinery Co.	13
Reeves Pulley Co.	7
Republic Truck Sales Corp.	3
Robson & Co., Charles	13
Russell-Miller Milling Co.	10
Siebel Institute	17
Standard Oven Co.	5
Sun-Maid Raisins	11
Superior Oven Co.	41
Tanglefoot	59
Thomson Machine Co.	6
Turner, A. R.	57
Union Steel Products Co.	
Union Machinery Co.	4
Ward Baking Co.	13
Washburn-Crosby Co.	Cover
Water-proof Paper & Board Co.	13

VOL. XXVII. ENTERED AT THE PHILADELPHIA POST OFFICE AS SECOND CLASS MATTER No. 317

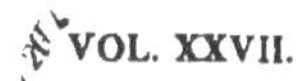

THE NATIONAL BAKER

PUBLISHED MONTHLY BY
THE NATIONAL BAKER PUBLISHING CO.
411 WALNUT STREET
B. F. WHITECAR, Pres. and Editor

PHILADELPHIA, PA., JUNE 15, 1922

Price per year, U. S.
and Canada $2.00
Foreign Countries $3.00

People Will Walk Blocks for Hubbard Baked Goods---Use HUBBARD OVENS

HUBBARD OVEN AND MFG. CO.
303 Wool Exchange, NEW YORK CITY

HUBBARD OVEN COMPANY
1146 Belden Avenue, Chicago

HUBBARD OVEN COMPANY
303 Scarritt Arcade, Kansas City, Mo.

BIG
DIAMOND
FLOUR
BIG DIAMOND MILLS CO. MINNEAPOLIS MINN.

THERMOMETERS
STANDARD OVEN THERMOMETERS
MADE TO FIT ANY OVEN
Dough Tasting Thermometers
Vacuum Pan Thermometer
Long experience has gained for us an invaluable fund of knowledge on the subject of Thermometers. Write for information and Prices
THE PHILADELPHIA THERMOMETER CO.
54 No. 9th St.   Philadelphia, Pa.

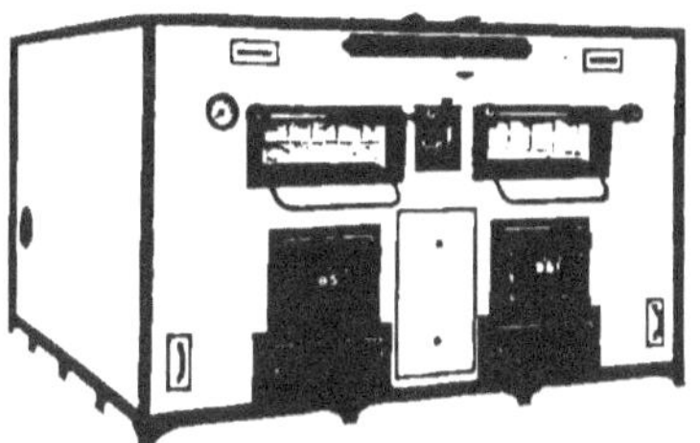

Bennett Ovens Make Busy Bakers

ARE you worrying along with an old style oven? Are you turning down new business because you cannot turn out the goods?

Install a modern, efficient Bennett Oven and you will be able to handle an increased demand on a profitable basis. Others are doing it. So can you.

Bennett Ovens Are Better Ovens

BENNETT OVEN CO., Ave. C & 22nd Street, Battle Creek, Mich.

Battery of Three Standard Ovens

Front Furnace with two large charging doors in each oven.

STANDARD OVEN CO.
1835 OLIVER BLDG. **PITTSBURGH, PA.**

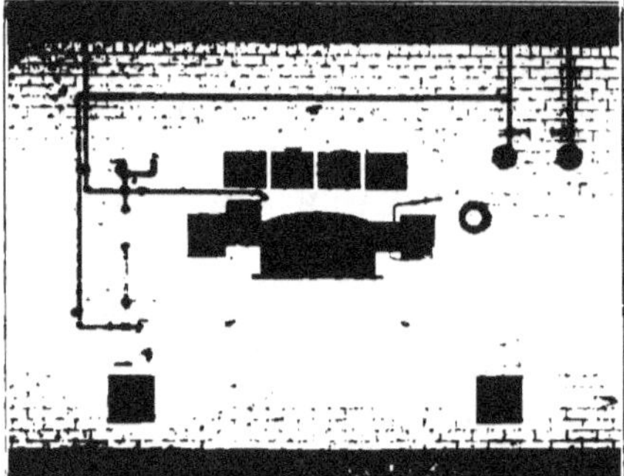

DUHRKOP OVENS

Mean

Oven

Satisfaction

This is proven by the fact that 90 per cent of our business is REPEAT ORDERS.

Ask for our list of DUHRKOP USERS--Note those in YOUR VICINITY.

DUHRKOP OVEN COMPANY

PARK ROW BUILDING   **NEW YORK, N. Y.**

THE baking industry instinctively couples the development of labor and time-saving equipment with the name Thomson.

For over a quarter of a century Thomson has utilized every known principle of construction in building the automatic bakeshop equipment that bears its name.

Its present high place in the esteem of the bakers today is the result of the conscientious endeavor and manufacturing genius of the Thomson engineers who have persistently bent their efforts toward producing better equipment.

Today the steadily-increasing demand for Thomson equipment is due to the recognition of its superb qualities and consistent performance.

You—like hundreds of other far-sighted men who have placed their equipment problems before Thomson engineers—will reap the benefit of their long experience if you simply

"Take it up with Thomson"

THOMSON MACHINE CO.

BELLEVILLE   **NEW JERSEY**

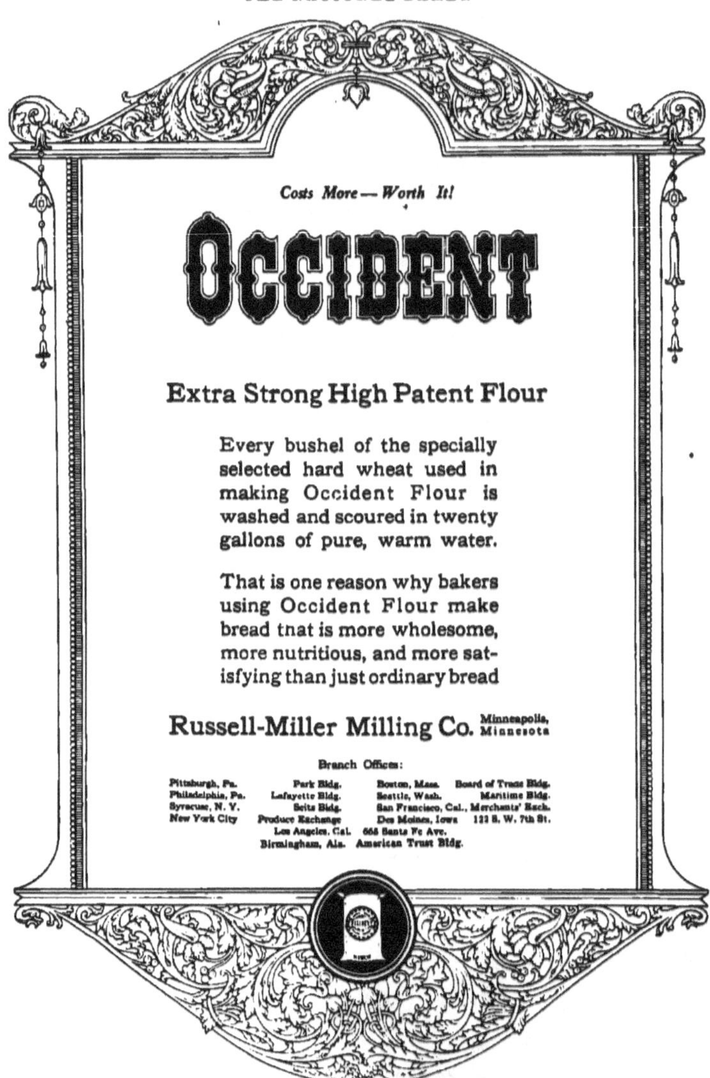
Costs More — Worth It!

OCCIDENT

Extra Strong High Patent Flour

Every bushel of the specially selected hard wheat used in making Occident Flour is washed and scoured in twenty gallons of pure, warm water.

That is one reason why bakers using Occident Flour make bread tnat is more wholesome, more nutritious, and more satisfying than just ordinary bread

Russell-Miller Milling Co. Minneapolis, Minnesota

Branch Offices:

Pittsburgh, Pa.   Park Bldg.   Boston, Mass.   Board of Trade Bldg.
Philadelphia, Pa.   Lafayette Bldg.   Seattle, Wash.   Maritime Bldg.
Syracuse, N. Y.   Seitz Bldg.   San Francisco, Cal., Merchants' Exch.
New York City   Produce Exchange Des Moines, Iowa   122 S. W. 7th St.
                      Los Angeles, Cal. 663 Santa Fe Ave.
                      Birmingham, Ala. American Trust Bldg.

Great *Raisin Bread* Campaign!

in the interest of bakers *everywhere*

THE Sun-Maid Raisin Growers are now running a tremendous advertising campaign on *Raisin Bread*. It embraces the entire country.

This advertising is appearing in newspapers in every state in the Union—*increasing Sun-Maid sales for you.*

Advertisement after advertisement arouses consumer interest in this delicious Raisin product. Start baking *more* Raisin Bread now. Get in quick—make your bakery the headquarters in your neighborhood for this product thousands will want. It is a profitable business.

5,314 Newspapers!

Over 5,000 newspapers in this country will carry this *localized* national advertising on Raisin Bread. The leading papers in *your* territory have it. Probably never before has Raisin Bread been so attractively and *thoroughly* advertised in your neighborhood. Best of all—*every one* of the

150,477,736 Advertisements say—
"Ask Your Baker or Grocer"

We *urge* your customers to come to you for your own delicious bake of Raisin Bread. The product is *yours.* If it's good, this advertising will create a demand which will *continue* to build Raisin Bread sales for you.

Bake more Raisin Bread. Let this great advertising campaign and our Bakers' Dealer Service aid you to increase this *profitable* business.

Sun-Maid Raisin Growers
Membership 13,000
DEPT. E-606, FRESNO, CALIFORNIA

SUN-MAID RAISINS

Short Cuts That Many Use

Here are ways that many bakers use to easily and quickly separate these Bakers' Seeded Sun-Maids:

Dip hands in hot water — the raisins quickly come apart, or

Mix an equal weight of flour with the raisins, working flour through with the hands, or

Dip hands in lard—which works like hot water, or

Place raisins on sheet pan in the oven for a while. That will separate them, and will also cause the white sugar-spots, if any, to disappear, the sugar going back into the raisins, restoring them to the same condition in which they left our California packing plant.

Use Bakers' Seeded Sun-Maids for your raisin bread and you'll be delighted with results.

Bakers' (Seeded) Sun-Maids

Delicious Raisin-Bread Raisins

Bakers' Seeded Sun-Maid Raisins are especially for bakers' use in bread, cakes, cookies, snails, "race tracks," pie, etc. They are selected, washed and sterilized, to make them perfect raisins for your use.

Bakers know that Seeded Raisins absorb 10% more water.

Be Ready for This Opportunity

*In 4,000 cities of the country, 47,000
street-cars will carry this June street-
car message of Bakers' Bread.*

To tired housewives, this bright Summer scene spells coolness
and freedom from drudgery. The last clause, "Buy Bakers'
Bread—it is BEST when made with Fleischmann's Yeast," presents a happy solution of her housekeeping problem.

Summer is the best time in the world to cash in on your appeal
to the housewife. This attractive card at just the psychological
moment makes her ready for your Bread.

Fleischmann's Service will show you how to be ready for her—
how to link up your own advertising with the national Fleischmann advertising—how to solve your delivery, sales and production problems.

Call the Fleischmann representative—he's ready for you.

The Fleischmann Company

Fleischmann's Yeast   *Fleischmann's Service*

The Test of Time

is the surest test

OP Malt Extract

has stood this test and has not been found wanting.

Prudent bakers do not experiment—they place full reliance in

OP MALT EXTRACT·

Malt-Diastase Company

79 Wall Street, NEW YORK

Warehouses: CHICAGO, PHILADELPHIA   *Laboratories,* BROOKLYN, N. Y.

Many men have spent half their lives learning the Bakery business and they are still learning, without any guarantee that they are acquiring the right kind of knowledge.

Today it is possible to get into a well-paid position in the most important industry, by a much shorter route.

You can quickly get a better job—no matter what your present job may be—by acquiring a thorough knowledge of Scientific Baking.

Hundreds of successful bakers ascribe their success to the application of the fundamental scientific principles taught by the

Siebel Tech Home Study Course in Scientific Baking

YOU can also get started on the road to greater efficiency and increased earnings by taking up the study of the simple lessons provided by this Course. You will be surprised to note how soon after you start the Course your work will show a decided improvement which will become more apparent and effective as you continue your spare time training.

A FEW MINUTES' STUDY EACH DAY WILL ENABLE YOU TO FINISH THE COURSE WITHIN A SHORT TIME!

Fill out the enclosed Coupon and send it in TODAY. It will not obligate you in any way, but will mean a great deal to your future success.

SIEBEL INSTITUTE OF TECHNOLOGY
(Established 1872)
935 Montana Street   Chicago, Illinois

SIEBEL INSTITUTE OF TECHNOLOGY, Dept. "NB."
935 Montana Street, Chicago, Illinois.

Please send me full particulars of the Siebel Home Study Course in Scientific Baking FREE.

Name ....

Address ....

Town ....

State ....

Position I Now Hold...

IN THE RACE
FOR TRADE

Arkady Bakers
Always Win

Arkady bakers have many advantages over those who have not yet adopted that great bread-improving and money-saving yeast nutrient. For with the aid of

YEAST   FOOD

Patented in U. S. A. and Foreign Countries

they are able to turn out a loaf of far better texture, bloom and flavor.

They need buy only half as much yeast as the non-user.   ARKADY really *makes* the rest of the yeast in the dough itself.

ARKADY bakers save over two months' supply of sugar every year, because It conserves 20% of the sugar from fermentation loss.

They save a whole week's supply of flour every year because ARKADY also conserves 2% of the flour from destruction by fermentation.

ARKADY has become a standard ingredient in the making of bread.   Over 15,000,000 loaves of bread a day are ARKADY-baked in America alone.

When will *you* decide to make bread the modern ARKADY way?   Why not order a trial shipment to-day?

ARKADY is sold in 50-pound drums and 180-pound sacks.   Price 13c per pound.   In lots of 900 pounds or over, 11c per pound.   Both prices f.o.b. New York, and subject to change without notice.

Write for the ARKADY book.

RESEARCH PRODUCTS DEPARTMENT

WARD BAKING COMPANY, NEW YORK

THE NATIONAL Baker

PUBLISHED ON THE FIFTEENTH OF EACH MONTH

AT

411 WALNUT ST., PHILADELPHIA

BY

THE NATIONAL BAKER PUBLISHING CO.

B. F. WHITECAR, PRESIDENT AND EDITOR
W. W. GALE, SECRETARY AND TREASURER

MEMBER OF THE AUDIT BUREAU OF CIRCULATIONS

SUBSCRIPTION RATES
UNITED STATES, ITS POSSESSIONS AND CANADA ..$2.00 per year
FOREIGN COUNTRIES .... 3.00 per year

PAYABLE IN ADVANCE

ADVERTISING RATES ON APPLICATION

Make all remittances payable to the order of
The National Baker Publishing Company

*Changes for displayed advertisements must reach this office
by the 5th of the month*

VOL. XXVII   JUNE, 1922   No. 317

CONTENTS

A B C for Bakers.......... 38
Announcement 26
Apple Specialties 50
Bakery Delivery Motor..... 27
Better Bread 32

Cake Recipes:
Almond Cakes 54
Cherry Cakes 54
Sponge Goods 54
Sponge Biscuits 54
Sponge Sandwiches 54
Savoy Fingers 54
Sponge Moulds 54
Drop Buns 54
Rock Cakes 55
Fermented Buns 55
Short Paste 55
Genoese Cake 55
Swiss Almond Tarts...... 56
Lightning Cake 56
Lemon Snaps 56
Layer Cake 56
Oatmeal Cookies 56
Molasses Cookies 56
Sugar Cakes 56

Different Flours — Different
    Treatment 42
Ferments and Fermentation. 44
Indiana Bakers' Meeting.... 28
Information Department:
    Sandwich Buns 58
    Whole Wheat Bread..... 58
    Salt Rising Bread........ 58
    Bread Troubles 58
    Cake Filling 59
    Sponge Cake 59
    Puff Paste 60
    Pie Troubles 60
    Frosting for Pies........ 60
Legal—At the Mercy of Your
    Driver 35
New England Bakers....... 28
Pennsylvania Convention.... 29
Potomac States Convention. 31
Power and Lighting Econo-
    mies 60
President Schumaker's Ad-
    dress 30
Puff Paste 52
Retail Advertising 26
Sales Plans 38
Value of Appearance....... 23
Who Pays for Advertising? 36

The Value of "Appearance"

THE man who said that "It's the little things that count," probably had in mind, more than anything else, the thousand and one details which go to make up the appearance of a man, a store or a city, or anything else, and which, neglected, resulted in a general ensemble which is far from attractive. At any rate, it is certainly true that "little things" count rather more in this connection than in most others, and that they can do harm far beyond what anyone would dream who had not considered the matter carefully.

For example—a baker example, at that—there is a member of the trade running a nice, prosperous little shop in a good residence neighborhood, with a trade which ought to be a good deal better than it is. The reason why the business refuses to grow beyond a certain point has escaped him, because, while he is a good baker, and a fairly good business man, as bakers go, he does not possess the happy but rare faculty of being able to stand off, so to speak, and look at himself. If he could do this, it is possible that he would find out the trouble which has kept off a big volume of business, and has prevented him from attaining more than a moderate success.

Now, this baker, as indicated, is a good one, as far as the active and actual work of the trade is concerned; he turns out bread and rolls, cakes and pastries, which those who have tried them swear by. Once a customer of his, and the consumer is pretty sure to be converted to permanent buying; and this means a great deal in the success of a baker, as a matter of course. But there are a great many of the people passing his shop, morning and evening, on their way to the car going to work or going home as they return from their labors, who will never get a chance to see how good this baker's products really are, because they do not intend to sample them. They do not like the baker's looks.

He is a fine, round, healthy specimen of manhood, with a genial smile for the youngsters who pass by and occasionally drop in for a penny bun or roll. He is evidently an optimistic soul, who doesn't believe in looking for trouble in any form—his pleasant face shows that; but, still, there are many customers who are impressed in a distinctly unfavorable manner by his looks, as he stands now and then in the door to get a look at things in general and a short relief from the work of the shop. He is certainly entitled to this short respite from his hot, hard work, but at the same time this has worked against him in the minds of many of the fastidious suburbanites who pass him; because this excellent baker has cultivated a scorn of appearances which shows his independence, perhaps, but does not speak well for his business judgment.

On the warm days of last summer, and of other summers, this was especially in evidence. Baking is warm work, at the best, and both the baker and his assistants were inclined to get down to first principles in the matter of clothing, naturally. Moreover, being of a large and well-fed type, the baker perspired a good deal, which was also natural. These things are a part of the work; but this does not mean that it is a good idea to exhibit them, in detail, to the public.

However, this baker made it a practice, all summer, as he has done for a long time, to take his regular breathing spells at the front door of his shop, one of his favorite times being at about half-past five in the evening, when the people were coming out from the city to their homes; and he did not attempt to conceal the fact that he was very hot, nor that he dressed accordingly. Therefore, people passing, all of them possible customers, saw lounging comfortably in the doorway a large man, approaching something like fatness, perspiring freely, clad lightly in an old undershirt, open at the throat and with short sleeves, and an old pair of trousers.

Of course, there were a good many people who thought nothing of this, save to reflect sympathetically on the hardship of having to work in a heated shop, before a big oven, in such hot weather; but there were even more who did not like to contemplate eating bread and fancy goods handled by this large man, who did not give an impression of scrupulous regard for sanitation, to say the least. Many a woman, and not a few men, passing and seeing the baker in this way, gave their imaginations free rein, and picturing him handling all of the highly appetizing goods shown in his shop, refrained from buying.

This, of course, was a great injustice to the baker; for, aside from turning out excellent goods, he had a sensible regard for the desirability of cleanliness, and his small shop was really a model in this respect. Of course, he could not dress himself up like a soda fountain clerk for work in the shop, nor can any baker; but, all the same, the unfair impression of his methods which so many people obtained was his own fault, for the simple reason that he permitted himself to be seen in what might be called his "undress uniform." His business suffered by it, and will continue to suffer as long as he shows himself in the shop or in front of it in the abbreviated undershirt and the old trousers in which he works.

He has several alternatives. He could simply slip on a light-weight white jacket, for wear in front of the store, in combination with white trousers—many bakery salesmen wear this uniform on their rounds; or he could decide that he will not appear outside the shop, not even in the retail section, at all. It would obviously be much better to have a neat girl to wait on customers, at a small salary, than to make a bad impression on even a few of them by doing it in person —in an undershirt.

In this connection, there is a Greek confectioner in the same town, who is branching out into the bakery business in a very enterprising manner, from whom this baker could take a lesson or two with considerable profit. The methods used in the Greek's shop, behind the scenes, as it were, unseen by the public, once brought him into sharp conflict with the local pure food department; but in front there has never been the slightest ground for fault-finding on the part of the public.

The several boys who sell the goods are always dressed in immaculate white, giving an impression of spotless cleanliness which, if the customers only knew it, would not at all be borne out by a look into the place where the cakes and candies are made. But that is exactly the point—that the shop, as a rule, is not seen by the public. It might be said, in fact, that in ninety-nine cases in a hundred the customer has never been in a bakeshop, and probably never will be. What he sees is the front of the shop, and by that he must judge the whole business. And if the baker himself, as in the case referred to, conveys an unfavorable impression, however innocently, the business of the shop must suffer accordingly. There is no way of getting away from it. The fact should be understood, and the baker should act in view of it, thus saving himself the loss of a good deal of possible business.

The same point was illustrated rather amusingly not long ago in the case of a wholesale concern which had completed a big new plant, and was rather proud of it. The management thought it would be excellent advertising for its bread to have the public make a tour of inspection through the plant and see how things are done in a large modern bakery. The invitation was accordingly extended, with a considerable blaring of trumpets through the newspapers, and on a given day, with everything about the plant in apple-pie order, as the management thought, visitors began to arrive to look over what was truly advertised as being the most up-to-date bakery in the city.

The men were all working, as usual, in all departments, busily engaged in supervising the operations of the mixers and other machinery, and, finally, in wheeling the bread to the ovens and placing it in them for baking; and the superintendent, who conducted the first group of visitors through, was busily explaining, with no small pride, how systematically everything was done, when he was shocked at a question from a small lady who was in the group.

"Do those men work that way—dressed that way, I mean—all the time?" she asked, in a horrified tone, as she observed the comparative undress of the busy and unconscious bakers.

The superintendent saw the point at once, but hurriedly explained that the work was hot, that the men were perfectly clean, and that their clothing was clean, and so forth; but he saw that not only the visitor who had asked the question, but a number of others in the group, were very unfavorably impressed by this. He made up a good deal of this lost ground, he felt, in the delivery department, where the long row of wagons, with their white-jacketed drivers, brought forth admiring exclamations from the visitors, but, at

ANNOUNCEMENT

The National Baker Publishing Co. announces to its readers the merger of The National Baker with the Bakers Weekly, New York, this consolidation being effective July 1st.

B. F. Whitecar, who has filled the position of Managing Editor of The National Baker for the past twenty-five years, and is in full touch with bakery conditions throughout the country, will be a member of Bakers Weekly staff, and through this connection be in a position to serve our subscribers with the same zeal and fidelity as before.

All subscriptions for The National Baker have been absorbed by the Bakers Weekly, and commencing July 1st all subscribers will receive a copy of the paper weekly until their paid for subscriptions have expired. The subscription price to the Bakers Weekly is only $2.00 per year, the same as has been the subscription price to The National Baker, but instead of receiving but one publication a month subscribers will now have a copy once a week.

Bakers Weekly by sending subscribers a copy every seven days will give up-to-the-minute information, thus presenting an advantage over a monthly publication in this respect.

Our readers through this merger will have the benefits given all Bakers Weekly readers; that is, the FREE use of the Laboratory maintained for ascertaining the cause of baking troubles—the question box and many other departments not available before the consolidation.

In taking formal leave of our long-prized subscribers and advertisers we do not do so completely, as Mr. Whitecar will take his old relations with them into his new position, and thus keep up the intimate contact which has been his aim and pleasure to enjoy for so many years now gone by.

THE ASSOCIATE EDITOR.

the same time, he felt that he was on ticklish ground, and looked forward with alarm to the rest of the day, with a constant stream of visitors all looking askance at open undershirts.

Being a man of resource, however, he arose to the occasion. He got his first group out as soon as possible, and hurriedly investigated the resources of the delivery department. He found that he could secure several dozen freshly laundered drivers' jackets, kept in reserve for the men on the wagons, and he promptly had them brought out. Then he went through the plant, distributing them.

"Slip 'em on, boys," he directed, to the amazed bakers. "I hate to ask you to do it, but the visitors insist, and there's nothing else for it."

And all through the rest of that long day, therefore, the sweating men worked in the neat-looking, close-fitting jackets, expressing among themselves their opinions of the view of the admiring visitors. At that, the superintendent was absolutely right. He decided to take no further risks of making a bad impression on visitors, and all of them went away with nothing but words of praise for the new plant and its employees.

It cannot be emphasized too often that for the baker, who is slowly but surely forging ahead in his fight for the right to make all of the bread and cake and pastries consumed in the average household, the appearance of scrupulous cleanliness, as well as its actuality, is all important. He should give no one any opportunity to criticise him on this point, for it means almost the certain loss of business; whereas proper care will be a powerful aid in his efforts to get and hold the trade of the ordinary family.

—‡—‡—‡—

Retail Advertising

THE best goods ever shown in a bakeshop will not bring the volume of trade which will make the business profitable unless the purchasing public knows the goods are there. Further, the mere announcement that the goods are in stock will not accomplish everything, though it may be admitted that this is important. There must be a campaign planned. One must begin the work of building up trade, which is a long, though not necessarily a difficult process. One must offer good reasons why the public should buy of him, either because his goods are of better quality than those made by some other baker, or else they must cost less.

The selling of bakers' goods is in reality a contest in which the baker is ranged on one side and the purchaser on the other, the purchaser attempting to secure goods at low figures and the baker attempting to sell for higher prices than the purchaser wants to pay. The winner will generally be the baker, who, if he maintains his position, will be able to secure his price upon substantially his entire line. It is quite likely that he will feel the onslaughts, however, and will often be forced to retreat for a short distance, but if he per-

sistently fights it out on the line of fair dealing and good goods he will finally build up a profitable business.

But how will the public know what you are doing? Surely, if you sit in your doorway all day long, possible purchasers who will visit you will not make your fortune. The chances are that the bulk of the passers in your street will go by without giving your shop more than a passing thought. They may not even look at it. If they do, they will not bestow upon it a second thought, much less will they stop to buy. This inertia must be overcome and there is only one way to do it; advertise.

Perhaps this subject seems hackneyed, but it is not. The advertising end of a retail business is far more important than is usually admitted, and the advertising is a matter which requires more than merely a passing consideration. If you expect to win you must make your advertising reflect the characteristics of the store. You must see that your advertisements tell the truth, and that your stories can be backed up by actual facts. If you do this you have accomplished much in the fight for better business. Conditions are substantially the same in all sections of the country. In some localities the outlook may vary, but the principles apply with equal force everywhere. It is a difference in detail, not in methods.

Advertising can be done in two ways: using the newspapers, carrying a reasonable amount of space regularly, and supplementing this with window displays. These two features will create business and will help hold what you have. Without them, your trade will be comparatively light; with them, you will unquestionably obtain your share. You cannot safely neglect either one. You can do business in some fashion without either of them, but you will find it difficult. In great cities, newspaper advertising must be replaced with something else, such as circularization, personal solicitation and similar tactics, but the same principle prevails. You must attract attention to your wares, otherwise your customers will be limited to your acquaintances. They will know you have good goods, but no one else will. Consequently, whatever is obtained through advertising makes for increased profit. You will have the steady growth of your trade as evidence that your advertising campaign is paying, and paying well.

In dressing your windows emphasize the desirable qualities of your goods and their appearance as strongly as you can. In this way you will impress the public with your ability to make the goods they want, and you will also impress them with the fact that you are progressive, a reputation which is well worth obtaining, even at the expense of a considerable investment of money and time.

Once begun, keep it up. You can't advertise in one issue of a paper and drop out of the next and make a favorable impression. You will be forgotten in the meantime. It is the constant hammering, the steady determination to create a favorable impression upon those who may be buyers that will win in the long run. It is the persistent effort to do business, no matter what may be the difficulties in the way, and making this determination clear, that will bring about the changes which will build up your business.

Advertise your goods thoroughly; keep them up to the standard of quality guaranteed in your advertisements, and you will succeed in establishing a trade which should grow rapidly; and the time to begin all this is now. Not next month or next year, but now. The floater will go where he is invited and if he is well treated, may become a permanent customer. The situation will, therefore, resolve itself into seeking business through advertising, and then exerting yourself to hold it over the counter. It is a double effort which must be exerted, but the results are usually so good, and the effect of good work, in this direction, is so satisfactory that the baker who fails to undertake the work of advertising will make a mistake. It is time to consider this carefully and the sooner you plan your campaign the better it will be for you. Business depression, indifference, desire to go elsewhere, all alike will succumb to vigorous attractive advertising.

—‡—‡—‡—

The Bakery Delivery Motor

SINCE many bakers now have an automobile delivery or motor truck and many more are getting them, a few pointers are here given regarding the care, handling and general usefulness of this efficient, up-to-date vehicle.

Generally, it is best to keep the car in a shed or small building which is used only as a garage. A cement or a brick floor is much better than a wooden floor. A sinkhole leading to the sewer is also a handy arrangement, as the water-tank or engine jacket can easily be drained, or the woodwork of the car washed, and the water drained. The gasoline storage tank should be underground, outside the shed. A cupboard for accessories and car tools, and a small work-bench fitted with a vise, are convenient in making small repairs. Keep the shed locked. Pilfering of car parts might be practiced in your neighborhood.

One of the principal things in caring for a motor is to keep the working parts cleaned and well lubricated. The engine is a very rapid running piece of mechanism which necessarily requires wiping and plenty of lubrication. This attention should be given the machine every morning or evening. The lubrication, in fact, should be careful, frequent and complete.

Compression—the packing of the gas in the engine cylinder preparatory to ignition, which moves the piston and starts the wheels—is one of the chief functions which gives the motor its power, consequently the compression should be perfect, which is readily accomplished by keeping the valves clean, preventing any foreign substance from lodging in them, such as a piece of straw, which would leave a valve partly open and interfere with perfect compression—and by properly handling the carburetor, or gas chamber, so that the cylinder will receive the required volume of gas.

Some merchants keep their delivery motors in a public garage, or club together and hire a regular gas engine machinist to take care of the several machines. This is a very efficient way and relieves the baker or the chauffeur from this responsibility. Considering that some motors are run from early morning until evening, they are not apt to always get the cleaning they deserve if the work is left to a man who has worked hard all day or who is about tired out.

However, these remarks are not intended to convey the impression that taking care of one is a serious task, but to emphasize the necessity of seeing that the machine *gets the necessary amount of attention daily,* though it may require merely a looking over and a slight cleaning of working parts. Of course, it is understood that the body of the car should be washed regularly, the same as is done with any well-kept delivery wagon.

Usually, the baker gets complete instructions regarding the handling and caring for the car at the time he buys one, as well as a book of parts and pointers treating upon the care of the machine, all of which are understandable by the average automobile novice.

Delivery motors, today, have attained a high degree of perfection, having gone first through years of experimenting, followed by numerous improvements, particularly as regards the motor and mechanism. The first cars are considered makeshifts in comparison with those now in use, and while the future may bring added improvements to delivery motors, yet the cars now in use are of a well-tried, useful kind, with adjustable mechanism which can be handled by an ordinary man.

Care should be taken by the driver to not start the motor with a roar, and then rush back to the throttle lever to slow the engine down. Giving the crank a turn or two is usually sufficient to start any motor car. Should the motor refuse to start easily with the throttle partly open, surmount the difficulty by switching off the ignition and opening the throttle wide, giving the crank a couple of turns, and then placing the throttle partly off, and the ignition on, when by giving the crank a turn the cylinder is filled with gas and the motor is ready to start as soon as the spark passes the gap. Most cars now, however, are provided with "self-starters," a great improvement.

Running a car fast, over a poor road, jouncing it up and down, is, of course, harder on the car than where the driver picks his way over ruts. A careful driver, in fact, is the man to have at the wheel, for a careless one can and will do considerable damage to a car. The driver of a motor can usually get plenty of pointers, and should, therefore, quickly acquire easy handling of the motor on the road.

Most bakers will remember that a few years ago a motor delivery was somewhat of a curiosity, while today the streets are filled with them, so great has become the demand for quick and efficient delivery service, and among these horseless wagons are not a few bakery delivery motors, delivering bread, cake and ice cream post-haste to different sections of the city. Some cities have excellent paving for motor deliveries, and as a result, cars may be seen by the hundreds passing up and down the streets, yet motors are much used on unpaved streets and country roads.

The quickness with which some bakers discarded the horse for the motor was rather surprising in bakery circles, but it has been considered a wise move by those who are using them, and many more motor deliveries will be in service within the next year or two, as an efficient, economical means of delivering bakery goods.

—‡—‡—‡—

Indiana Bakers' Meeting

INDIANA is to be congratulated on the number of wide-awake, progressive men engaged in the baking industry within her state. C. P. Ehlers, Secretary-Manager of the Indiana Bakers' Association, called a joint meeting of Zones 6 and 7, to be held in Marion on Wednesday, May 24th.

In arranging the date, he did so with many misgivings, as he tried to select a time when he could get together, at least, twenty or twenty-five bakers. This, he thought, would be a good-sized crowd for this time of year, taking into consideration the business conditions, weather, etc. Can you imagine his surprise and joy to have thirty-eight bakers assemble in Marion on the aforesaid date?

And the meeting was a success from start to finish. Every man present made some kind of a speech, and after everybody had had his say, it helped to clear up a number of misunderstandings that had previously existed. Why can't all bakers get together every so often and have these friendly meetings?

Among the principal speakers of the day were President Quigg, of Richmond; Secretary Ehlers, of Indianapolis; Messrs. Mohler, of Kokomo; Middleton, of Marion; Singer, of Muncie; Cline of Indianapolis, and others. QUALITY BREAD came in for a goodly share of the discussions, and it was the unanimous opinion of all that only by the manufacturing of BETTER BREAD could the baker hope to get and keep the housewives' trade.

J. C. Blakesly, of the Muncie *Evening Press*, presented a co-operative advertising campaign which was met with great favor, voted on and endorsed by the members present at the meeting. This campaign, no doubt, will be started within a short time. Others interested in this kind of advertising will do well to get in touch with this office or Mr. Blakesly.

The Indiana Association expect to hold these Zone Meetings throughout the state, and it is to be hoped that all will be as successful as the meeting just held in Marion.

An A B C Creed for Bakers

Advertise constantly and truthfully.
Believe in myself and in the baking industry.
Cater to the best trade and cause my products to deserve it.
Devote my time and my energies to improving my product.
Endeavor to imbue my employes with loyalty.
Fulfill promptly the promises I make.
Give my best efforts every day.
Have respect for others; conduct myself so that others respect me.
Invent new means of increasing the efficiency of my employes.
Join hands with fellow-citizens in making my town a better town.
Keep my product up to the standard originally established for it.
Learn the territory in which I propose to do business.
Make at least one new friend every day.
Note the progress of other bakers; equal or exceed it.
Overlook nothing that honorably promotes the welfare of my business.
Prepare for adversity—but forestall it.
Qualify myself to supervise the larger business I am building.
Right the mistakes I make; make none.
Subscribe to trade journals; read them.
Tackle my biggest problems with confidence.
Utter nothing derogatory to fellow-bakers; the golden rule still exists.
Value my self-respect more than the adulation of others.
Work with a view to serving the public as well as myself.
Xanthippe lost her temper; I control mine.
Yield only when wrong, then yield gracefully.
Zealously guard the interests of my customers from January 1 to December 31.

—‡—‡—‡—

The Progressive Master Bakers' Association held their annual banquet and meeting at Cumberland, Md., May the second, at the Fort Cumberland Hotel. The following were elected as officers: President, Frank E. Smith, Cumberland, Md.; Vice-president, C. Z. Eby, Waynesboro, Pa.; Secretary, E. B. Clark, Hagerstown, Md.; Asst. Secretary, C. V. Wilkes, Hagerstown, Md.; Treasurer, A. B. Fogel, Cumberland, Md.

—‡—‡—‡—

New England Bakers' Association

The next bi-monthly meeting of the New England Bakers' Association will be held at Burlington, Vermont, on Monday, July 10th. This will give bakers an opportunity to spend a most enjoyable week-end. The great feature of this meeting is that it will be held aboard a boat on beautiful Lake Champlain. George West, of the Vermont Baking Company, White River Junction, Vt., is the chairman in charge of arrangements. Detailed program will follow shortly.

(Signed)   W. H. DIETZ, *Secretary.*

Pennsylvania Association, Fourteenth Convention, Bedford Springs, Pa., June 5th to 7th, 1922

BEDFORD SPRINGS, an ideal spot among the mountains of Pennsylvania, was the gathering place of the largest number of bakers who have yet answered the call of the State Association at its annual convention. This was the fourteenth meeting of the Keystone organization of bakers and it was in every way a notable and successful gathering of men prominent in the trade throughout the state.

President Schumaker and Vice-president Stritzinger, with an able convention committee, had worked very hard in preparing the program and the results justified their efforts. Everyone praised both the program for the meetings and the ample arrangements for the pleasure and entertainment of the bakers, their ladies and members of the allied trades. This was one convention where the registrations of bakers exceeded those of the associate members, while many ladies were in attendance.

Bedford Springs was an ideal location for the convention, surrounded as it is by tree-clad mountains and in its best June dress. Its location on the Lincoln Highway made it easily accessible to motorists and many members used that method of conveyance.

At the opening session President L. J. Schumaker called the meeting to order and after the singing of "America" a message was received from Governor Wm. C. Sproul, to which suitable acknowledgment was made, and Judge T. F. Bailey welcomed the visitors to the Springs.

The President then delivered his annual address, followed by those of the Secretary and Treasurer. The report of the latter shows that there are $2,500 in Liberty Bonds and over $1,000 cash in hand.

The following committees were appointed:

Auditing Committee—C. H. Ruhl, Penbrook; John Schoeller, Norristown.

Nominating Committee—E. R. Braun, Pittsburgh; John Haller, Altoona; Wm. F. Seeman, Hamburg.

Resolutions Committee—J. Fred Schoefer, Reading; John B. Sloan, Johnstown; L. H. Michel, Philadelphia; Albert Klopfer, New York City; C. C. Latus, Pittsburgh.

REPORT OF SECRETARY C. C. LATUS

The past year since we last met at Scranton, was one of unusual activity in the office of the secretary. Immediately following the Scranton convention, the question of compulsory bread wrapping was brought up in a rather forcible manner. However, happily, through the prompt co-operation of the officers of this association and some of the active members, a meeting was arranged in Harrisburg with the Industrial Board, with the pleasing result that a satisfactory solution of the problem was arrived at to the entire satisfaction of the bakers. In this connection, it is fitting to state that the Bakers' Advisory Board was named by Dean Connelly, Commissioner of Labor and Industry, so that today the bakers of Pennsylvania have a semi-official board to whom all problems affecting the baking industry of the state can be referred and a satisfactory adjustment arrived at. I would most strongly urge every member of this association to promptly inform the secretary, or your nearest officer or executive board member, if at any time you are confronted with problems, legal or otherwise, for which you hope to find a solution.

Pennsylvania is now recorded as having launched the first state-wide bread and milk week campaign ever held in the United States. The influence of this campaign has been most far reaching, and while one cannot point out definitely the exact increase in sales of bread and bread-stuffs during that week, we wish to most emphatically state that the bread and milk week campaign has been conducted in at least forty of the sixty-seven counties of the state and has left a lasting impression, especially upon the younger generation.

Some 18 months ago a formal invitation was received by this association to participate in the International Bakers' Exposition at Leipsic, Germany, July 1st to 10th, 1922. The acceptance to the invitation was so pronounced that it is a pleasure to state that on June 10th, a party of more than 100 bakers from various sections of the country will sail to participate in this international bakery event. This association will be represented by at least a half dozen members, including the secretary.

Your secretary is pleased to report that, as a result of special trips made to different counties of the state, local bakers' organizations have been organized or reorganized and strengthened. It is a pleasure to note the increased interest and activity that many bakers in the state are taking in association affairs, especially in their own localities. The value of organized effort in the baking industry of Pennsylvania has been amply demonstrated, and needs no further comment. The successful and progressive baker is a firm and consistent believer in association work and association activities. Our records show active members as of January 1, 1922, 136; associate members, 134.

Since we last met at Scranton, your secretary has traveled more than 2,800 miles, during which he attended 38 meetings of different kinds, including executive, committee, county, and city meetings. The value of publicity needs no recommendation on my part. The press of the state has been most liberal and generous in giving excellent space, detailed accounts of different meetings held, and other association activities. The press is a close ally of the baking industry, and every baker should make his home town editor his friend.

Get to know the reporters of your city, and invite them to your bakery to inspect it, following with a luncheon, if you please, of your own bakery products, and you have turned the trick. There have been more than 70 columns of newspaper space devoted to recording the doings of bakers of the entire state since we last assembled in convention. However, this does not include the tremendous publicity given during the Bread and Milk Week Campaign. To the officers and executive committee, so prompt to respond to any letters or telegrams sent, I wish to return my sincere thanks.

The first address was delivered by Fred. J. Hartman, Secretary of the Pennsylvania Industrial Board, who gave a splendid account of the harmonious co-operation of the bakers of the state with the department, to the benefit of the public and our great industry.

Dr. H. E. Barnard, Secretary-Manager of the American Bakers' Association then briefly reviewed the work of the American Institute of Baking and invited the bakers to take advantage of its facilities. Fred H. Frazier, Vice-president of the General Baking Co., then gave a fine address on "Co-operation" and Robert L. Corby, Vice-president of the Fleischmann Co., reviewed the scientific work so far undertaken on behalf of the baking industry and predicted much greater advances for the future.

Secretary Marinelli, of the Italian Master Bakers' Association, asked the support and co-operation of the State Association in improving the condition of the Italian bakeries and a committee was appointed to this end. Greetings were then extended by visiting representatives of other associations, including the Canadian organization.

The opening address at Wednesday's session was by Mrs. John S. Sloan, of Pittsburgh, President of the Congress of Women's Clubs of Western Pennsylvania, followed by Secretary Wm. Smedley of the Retail Merchants' Association of Penna. Then followed an "Experience Meeting" in which many speakers participated. One good result was that the bakers in the Lebanon Valley were induced to meet together under the chairmanship of Fred C. Haller, to reconcile their differences which had disorganized their trade in that locality. This "get together" meeting was a success and it is believed the results will be of the best.

Following a short talk by Julius Fleischmann, S. S. Watters, Pittsburgh, of the Board of Governors of the American Bakers' Association, gave a short account of the great work undertaken by that organization and asked for the support and co-operation of every baker. This was followed by a stirring address from I. R. Russell, editor of Baking Technology, the scientific monthly issued by that association.

The election for officers resulted as follows: President, Raymond K. Stritzinger, Norristown; Vice-president, Fred C. Haller, Pittsburgh; Treasurer, George W. Fisher, Huntingdon; Executive Committee, C. I. Layfield, Scranton, and J. Fred Schofer, Reading.

President Schumaker was presented with a handsome gold watch as an appreciation of his earnest and effective work during the year.

—‡—‡—‡—

President Schumaker's Address

AT ASSOCIATIONAL meetings, where members get together only once a year, custom has established an annual address by the president —a review of the past, a statement of the present and a look into the future.

The work of this association for the past year has been notably marked by the activity of the executive committee, the co-operation of associate members, and

a spirit of determination to make this association of service to our civil authorities as well as to the bakers themselves, an influence to be recognized by the leading business bodies of the State and a credit to the industry at large. Special mention is due our trade journals. Their representatives have always been ready to attend any meetings where their presence was desired. Their columns have been freely open to this association and they have been quick to spread any news which they felt would be helpful to the association and the industry, all of which has been an inspiration to the officers of your association and has urged them to strive to the utmost to be worthy of the trust you placed in them.

If this convention meets with success, it is due to a vice-president who has worked untiringly throughout the year; a secretary who has been constantly on the job; a treasurer whose long experience in associational work has been most helpful; an executive committee who never failed to furnish a quorum when meetings were called.

The action of the Department of Labor and Industry in appointing a Bakers Advisory Board from members of the association has been a distinct recognition and has given this association new opportunities for usefulness.

Our secretary will present to you the details of the year's work; our treasurer will give you a report on our finances, but the proceedings at this convention, which bring to a climax the work of the association for the past twelve months, will disclose to you from day to day, better than any words of mine in a formal address, just what has been attempted, what has been accomplished and what possibilities await us in the coming year.

I hope each one will read with care the history of the Pennsylvania association as printed in our convention program. Scan the names of the men who worked diligently that this association might grow to its position of size and influence, and then ask yourself these questions: "To what extent am I responsible for the successes or failures of the work of this association?" and "How much am I going to do in the future for this association?"

The growth of the baking industry depends upon our being able to prove to the housewife that a baker who works at his trade six days a week can and does make better bread, cakes and pies than the woman in the home who bakes only a few hours a week, and that these products can be produced and sold to the consumer at a lower actual cost than they can be in the home—and this result can be accomplished satisfactorily only through the work of the bakers' associations, it cannot be done with any great degree of success by individual bakers. It requires the strength and influence of the entire industry.

It has been gratifying to observe the formation of local associations throughout the state. These will accomplish great good. They have the full support of the State association. It is expected that in the coming year the Secretary of the State association will from time to time, attend meetings of all these local associations and will assist in the organization of others and that at our State convention one year from now each local association will be represented by one or more delegates who will give a formal account of their work.

Let me plead for—

A closer relationship among the bakers of the state.

A bigger and stronger state association.

More local associations.

Support of the trade papers.

A strengthened industry.

A constructive co-operation that will take "Baking Day" off the housewife's calendar.

—‡—‡—‡—

The Human Motor

AT LEAST 19/20 of what we pay for in food is actually used as gasoline to drive the engine, not as spare parts to mend breaks, so we, too, often, telephone to the butcher shop for an expensive "new tire," when what we really need is another "gallon of oil" from the bake shop. A nutritious food is one that drives the bodily engine.

When all is said, then, our bodies are simply human motor cars. They are built of flesh and bone instead of steel and leather. They run on bread and butter instead of gasoline. They have a million cylinders in place of six, and the least of their parts is more complex in its structure than all the automobiles that ever came out of Detroit. But at bottom, they are explosion engines, which our souls, sitting at the steering wheel under our hats, guide through seventy years of work—and then, let us hope, change for an improved model.—E. T. Brewster and Lilian Brewster in "The Nutrition of a Household."

Potomac States Association Convention

ELABORATE and extensive plans are being made for the seventh annual convention of the Potomac States Association of the Baking Industry to be held in Baltimore, Md., June 19th, 20th, 21st and 22nd. Not the least important phase of the convention will be the entertainment features. Plans have been completed for royally entertaining delegates and visitors while they are in Baltimore, and the indications are that the social and sightseeing features of the convention will be long remembered by those who participate.

Chas. E. Meade, ex-president of the association, is chairman of the committee on arrangements. The Hotel Rennert has been selected as hotel headquarters, where all the meetings will be held in the big assembly room.

Attractive entertainment features have been planned, which will include a banquet and an all-day boat ride on Chesapeake Bay, and a sightseeing trip for the ladies to the many points of interest in and around Baltimore.

Leading bakers from Delaware, Maryland, District of Columbia, Virginia, West Virginia and North Carolina are boosting hard for a hundred per cent. attendance at the Baltimore convention.

If you are a member of the association, you cannot afford to miss this convention. If you are not a member, the officers want you to come anyway, and join them in the association work. If there ever was a time when the bakers should meet in convention, exchange ideas and discuss the problems they have to meet, it is now.

Let us all lay aside our business duties for the week of June 19th to 22nd, inclusive, and go to this convention, which will probably be the largest attended in its history, and the committee guarantees that you will cash in several hundred per cent. on your investment of time and money.

There is going to be a good time. Bring the good lady along, and enjoy some of Baltimore's historical scenery. The committee hopes to have the pleasure of shaking hands with you at the convention.

Official business program, seventh annual convention of the Potomac States Association of the Baking Industry to be held at Baltimore, June 19th-22nd, headquarters Hotel Rennert.

Monday, June 19th, 7 to 9 P. M., arrival of delegates and registration in hotel lobby.

9 P. M. meeting of Executive Committee.

Tuesday, June 20th

Opening of convention 9.45 prompt.

Convention called to order by President T. F. Bayha.

Song, America, leader George E. Mahly, Baltimore.

Invocation, Rev. Julius Hofmann, Baltimore.

Address of Welcome, Mayor Wm. F. Broning.

(Continued on page 34)

Better Bread From Better Ingredients

By F. W. Emmons, of the Washburn-Crosby Co., at Southeastern Convention

THIS subject was suggested through correspondence with some of our baker friends throughout the country. The problems encountered by them may be of interest, and of the same nature as those encountered by some of those present.

The one difficulty found most often when bread is not up to its usual standard has to do with fermentation. This seems to be the most troublesome factor in bread making, and the most difficult for the baker to overcome. In our experience, we have found that at least 90 per cent. of the difficulties encountered by bakers are caused by improper fermentation.

OVER-FERMENTATION

In visiting bakeries the writer finds baker after baker fermenting too much. The overfermentation may not be sufficient appreciably to affect the physical appearance of his loaf, but it has gone beyond the proper point so that the flavor of the loaf is impaired.

There seems to be an especial dread of too young a dough, to such an extent that it is generally allowed to ferment until it is too old.

Many bakers expect to obtain flavor in bread through the addition of various ingredients. Generally, if a better quality is desired, the first thought is to use more sugar, milk, or some such ingredient. There are proper amounts of these ingredients; if these amounts are exceeded, a poorer quality of bread is obtained, for the reason that the dough is loaded down with extra material to be carried, the formula is thrown out of balance, and variations are required in the temperature and the time of risings in order to obtain satisfactory results.

The addition of large quantities of these ingredients seems only to cover up the wheaten flavor which the baker has been trying to develop.

If you add enriching material to an improperly developed dough, you are not improving the quality, but merely trying to hide the imperfections which are in the loaf. In other words, you are just sending good money after bad.

The best flavored bread is obtained by using a normal quantity of the ingredients desired, with especial care as to the method of fermentation. The wheaten flavor is brought out properly only by the exercise of great care in the fermentation of the dough.

Formerly bakers had a tendency to overferment their doughs by using too high a temperature. This, of course, was especially true in the summer time. We have found many bakers who could not afford to use ice in their doughs during the hot weather, and the bread certainly suffered in appearance.

Nowadays bakers are holding their temperatures down to the proper point more consistently. We do find many, however, who allow too long a time for rising.

Bakers are quite generally using three and one-half hour straight doughs, while several years ago a five-hour dough was considered standard. With the increased amount of yeast used, as well as yeast foods, it is a very simple matter to allow a dough to ferment too much. An over-development is obtained, which, while it may give volume to the loaf, certainly has the effect of at least a loss of flavor.

The shortening of the time of rising has had the effect of opening another avenue wherein difficulties may arise. In fermenting a dough there is a certain point where the development of the dough is at its best. When a long time fermentation is used—as for instance, five hours—the variation from this point, either on the young or old side, may be relatively quite wide. On the other hand, when a short time dough is used —three hours, for example—the permissible variation in time is appreciably shortened.

In other words, the time of variation from the ideal, which may be allowed in a short time dough, is much less than in a longer time dough. The doughs must be taken more nearly at the proper time in order to obtain a good loaf.

SPONGE DOUGHS

A peculiar situation is found sometimes where a baker is using a sponge dough, such as the popular sixty per cent. sponge. After the dough is mixed, it is allowed to stand fifteen to twenty minutes and then "made up." If the sponge is overfermented by reason of too long a time or too high a temperature, an unusual condition develops wherein the baked loaf has a gummy crumb. Customers complain that the bread is not baked. We have found that bakers were not successful in trying to overcome this by harder baking, and were unable to locate the difficulty. This condition is clearly the result, not of insufficient baking, but of too much fermentation in the sponge.

Nowadays sponges are made quite stiff. If a sponge is ready it can easily be held until its proper time, merely by punching in the same manner as you would punch a straight dough. This keeps down the further development of the sponge by not allowing an increased action of the carbon dioxide and alcohol upon the gluten. By frequent punching the dough is relieved of the bulk of gas and so is affected only to a small extent.

We are not convinced that the sponge is the most satisfactory way of making bread. When we analyze the fermentation of a sponge we find that sixty per cent. of the flour is fermented for a period longer than is normal in a straight dough. Then forty per cent. or the remainder of the flour is added, and the only fermentive action it receives is the fifteen to twenty minutes it is allowed to stand before "making up" and the time of the proof in the pans. It does not seem possible that the overfermenting of part of the gluten and underfermenting of the remainder can give the proper development to the gluten as a whole. Unless just the proper point is reached in the fermentation, which hardly seems possible in a sponge, a decided loss in flavor is noted.

Sponges do, however, have their advantages, as for instance, the ability during some years to obtain better volume of loaf with a possible loss of flavor, and better control in the shop. This seems to be the point most generally emphasized in a discussion of the relative merits of the sponge and the straight dough.

TEMPERATURE

The temperature is probably referred to more often in a discussion of baking than any other factor, and it merits even more emphasis than it receives.

How many of us have really analyzed the reason we use a temperature of 80 degrees or possibly slightly less. Yeast grows faster and better at 86 degrees than at any other temperature, but unfortunately other bacilli begin to develop at 86 degrees; therefore, to eliminate these bacilli, the temperature is kept below the point at which they develop. Also, if higher temperatures are used, and gluten has a tendency to soften and become slightly sticky. There is, therefore, a loss of absorption as well as a poorer texture in the finished loaf.

Probably temperature is as responsible for a good or poor loaf as any other single factor. If a temperature of not over 80 degrees is used, and other conditions are not too far out of balance, you are practically assured a good loaf.

The time required for fermentation is another rather difficult factor to determine. While the baker can tell something as to when a dough is ready by its "feel" and general appearance, he is not sure; especially when he has a different temperature to contend with every day.

Time also is a factor as judged by the method of punching the dough. The reason we allow a dough to rise is to give the carbon dioxide and alcohol developed by the yeast an opportunity to come in contact with the gluten and act upon it. When this action has continued to the proper point of development we say a dough is ready.

During the rising this action may become too strong, and we relieve the dough of the gas by what the baker calls "punching." When we wish to obtain a certain action upon the gluten by the carbon dioxide and alcohol, we accomplish this by eliminating the gas at certain periods in order to control the development of the gluten—in other words, by "punching."

Flour has to a certain degree a standard factor of fermentation. If a flour has 11.50 per cent. gluten, it will require five hours' fermentation, with one per cent. of yeast, one and three-quarters per cent. salt and a temperature of 80 degrees. With two per cent. of yeast, it will develop properly in three hours.

With flours containing a larger or smaller amount of gluten, the time required will be more or less in proportion to the amount present. This is taken on the basis that the quality is the same in all cases. As an example, if you have a flour containing 10.50 per cent. gluten and you change to one containing 11.50 per cent., it will be necessary to make some changes either in your formula or methods of handling.

FORMULA

We have always contended that there is no formula for bread making. One baker can obtain a certain result with a specified formula, while another uses the same formula, carries out the operation in as nearly the same manner as possible, and obtains an entirely different loaf. Of course, this is due to the varying conditions under which different bakers work. They may have the same machinery and methods of handling, but there are always the little things that cannot be controlled.

It is these little details that may make or mar a loaf in a great many instances—such things as not rounding the loaf after it comes from the divider, not allowing the proper time of rest between the rounder and moulder, using too large pans for the amount of dough used, improper proofing in the pans, and not having the oven in the proper condition for baking the particular character of bread desired.

If you build your loaf around the proper amount of yeast, salt, water, and flour, using the other ingredients to obtain certain desirable characteristics, you are on the road to the result you are after in a good quality loaf.

In the examination of a loaf, one should be particularly interested in the amounts of flour, yeast, salt and water, the time of risings, and the temperature. The other ingredients used may be taken into consideration only in reference to some particular characteristics desired in the loaf. These can be varied to a considerable extent without a decided change in flavor or character of loaf.

FLOUR CHARACTERISTICS

As flour represents in quantity the largest amount of any ingredients in bread-making, it might be well to speak of some characteristics not generally known or considered by the average baker.

We all know of the changes we find on passing from the old crop wheat to the new, and the difficulties we encounter in baking the first of the new crop under ordinary conditions. Of late years this has been quite generally overcome by the gradual introduction of the new wheat into the old, instead of jumping all at once from old to new wheat flour. It is not generally known, however, that there is a change taking place in wheat the year around.

Flour is generally stored before baking to allow it to age. This ageing process goes on in the wheat as well as in the flour. There is a continuous change taking place in wheat, whether in its original form or in the form of flour. Just as you have noted the lack of ageing in the first flour from the new crop, we have found that the fermentation period shortens as the flour becomes older. In fact, we found this shortening of the time to be about five minutes per month or one hour during the year. This means that a flour having a fermentation period of five hours in the fall will need only four hours the next summer.

Have you ever noticed how fast your doughs ferment in July and August? And again when you get on to the new wheat flour, how the fermentation period is lengthened.

This rapid fermentation in the first case is due to the ageing process which has taken place in either the wheat or flour. We do not know just what takes place during this change. In fact, it is the miller's problem, just as determining when a dough is ready is the baker's problem. Neither of these problems is thoroughly understood. The miller is studying his problem and the baker must also study his.

CHANGING CONDITIONS

For the baker to counteract this shortening of the fermentation period it requires a change either in time or in the ingredients of his formula.

Generally the shortening is not noted by the baker until suddenly his doughs appear too old. He has not made changes to eliminate the gradual shortening, and after three or four months, or in December, he notices his bread is not up to the usual standard. It just means that the time required for fermentation has shortened fifteen to twenty minutes. He has not considered this and may think his difficulties caused by any one of many things.

He will notice the same thing again after three or four months, or in April or May. This same condition will appear again in midsummer.

There are two methods of overcoming this: the baker may shorten the time of risings, which he usually dislikes to do on account of the rearrangement of his shop system; or he may change the amounts of some of the ingredients of his formula in order to adapt it to the shortened fermentation period.

I have merely called attention to a few of the causes of poor quality in bread. There are many things which will cause poor bread which have not been mentioned in the above, but in merely giving a short digest, these should give an opportunity for discussion which would be helpful to all.

—‡—‡—‡—

Articles of incorporation were recently filed by the Weiser Bakery, of Weiser, Idaho, with capital stock of $10,000 by Geo. U. Kellogg, H. P. Cummock and Edward Romph.

(Concluded from page 31)

Response, Vice-president Frank E. Smith.
President's annual address.
Reports of Secretary, Treasurer and Committees.
Greetings from members and other Associations.
Standing Introduction.
Address, The Standardization of Bakers' Materials, Dr. B. R. Jacobs, Director of National Cereal Products Laboratories, Washington, D. C.

Afternoon session, 2 o'clock

Address, A Talk on Bakery Problems, Professor Harry Snyder, Chemist, Russell-Miller Milling Co., Minneapolis.

Address, subject to be selected, Ellwood M. Rabenold, New York City, counsel for the American Bakers' Association.

Address, subject, The Necessity of Advertising, Daniel P. Wooley, New York City, vice-president, The Fleischmann Co.

Nomination of officers.
Suggestions for next Convention City.

Wednesday, June 21st

Entire day given over to a boat ride on Chesapeake Bay.

Thursday, June 22nd

Morning session, 9.45 prompt.

Address, A Practical talk on Cake Baking, More Cakes, Better Cakes. E. C. Baum, sales manager, The Joe Lowe Co., New York City.

Address, What the American Bakers' Association is doing for the Baking Industry, Isaac Russell, Chicago.

Address, subject, Organization, Charles E. Meade, Baltimore.

Short talks by bakers.
Election of officers.
Installation of officers.
Adjournment.

Official entertainment program, seventh annual convention of the Potomac States Association of the Baking Industry to be held at Baltimore, June 19th-22nd, headquarters Hotel Rennert.

Monday evening, June 19th

Informal reception and dance. Refreshments.

Tuesday morning, June 20th, 10.30 o'clock

Sightseeing trip for ladies only.

Tuesday evening, 7 o'clock

Annual banquet and dance.

Wednesday morning, June 21st, 10.00 o'clock

Place, Pier 18, Light street Wharf.

What's doing? Steamer Annapolis leaves for an all-day boat ride down the beautiful Chesapeake Bay to Annapolis, arriving there at 1 P. M., where the bakers and their friends will be conducted through the United States Naval Academy grounds by guides.

Leave Annapolis at 3 P. M., for a sail down the bay to Tolchester Beach, where there will be plenty of bathing and amusements.

Leave Tolchester Beach at 7.30 P. M., for a sail up the bay, arriving at Baltimore at 10.30.

Luncheon and dinner will be served on the boat.

Plenty of eats and drinks.

Plenty of music.

Plenty of dancing.

Lots of fun and a good time for all. Bring the ladies and be on time, 10.00 A. M.

Thursday, June 22nd

Go-as-you-please.

LEGAL

No. 118.—At the Mercy of Your Driver

SOME time ago I made the observation that the business man who used a delivery truck, particularly a motor delivery truck, was to a considerable extent at the mercy of his driver. A motor truck is an agency for damage, and the driver can do a lot of damaging things with it which his employer will have to pay for. Some employers protect themselves against this by insurance, but a surprising number do not.

I have just read the report of a case which shows how these things work out. A retail merchant in Cleveland, Ohio, used several delivery trucks. He had given strict orders to all of his drivers not to allow boys to have anything to do with the trucks. One day one of the machines had finished its work and was heading for the garage. On its way it encountered a fourteen-year-old boy who asked for a lift. The driver good-naturedly gave it, and the boy climbed up and stood on the running board. And then, being in a hurry the driver cut across on the wrong side of the street, at much too rapid a speed, ran into a wagon and there was a bad smash. The boy was seriously hurt, and his father sued the *owner of the truck* for $10,000.

The owner thought there was nothing at all to the case. He went into court and vigorously defended on the ground (1) that the boy's injuries were his own fault; he had no business to stand on the running board of a moving truck, and (2) that even if this were not so he, the owner, wasn't responsible because he had told the driver not to let boys ride and the driver had disobeyed him. The boy's injuries were the result of the driver's disobedience, for which, of course, the employer wasn't liable. The lower court sustained this defense and threw the case out, but on appeal the decision was reversed and the higher court sent the case back for trial. The trial hasn't occurred yet, therefore we don't know what the verdict will be, but it is bound to be something, because the court has said

the employer was liable, and the only thing to determine now is for how much. The chance is that the merchant who did his utmost to prevent this thing from happening will be let in for a damage verdict of several thousand dollars. Of course, he can sue the driver who got him into this mess, and possibly in one case out of ten thousand he might recover something. He would be certain to get a judgment against the driver, whatever that might be worth.

The decision of the court in this case is in substance this: That granting the boy was a trespasser on the truck, and had no right there (that is, no right from the owner), nevertheless it is a well-known rule of law that even a trespasser must not be injured by wilful or wanton acts of negligence. When the driver drove his truck on the wrong side of the street at excessive speed, he was guilty of a wilful or wanton act of negligence, and as same was done while he was driving on the business of his employer, the employer was responsible for the boy's injuries which resulted. It is true that when somebody becomes a trespasser on your premises or your truck you aren't liable to him for anything that happens to him because of your simple failure to use ordinary care, but you are liable to him for anything that comes from wilful and wanton negligence.

Some of the judges filed an opinion saying they didn't regard the boy as a trespasser at all, since he was allowed to ride by the driver who was in charge of the truck. This view was even worse for the driver's employer, for it would have made him liable for the result of any negligence on the driver's part, even though not wilful or wanton.

I quote the following from the decision:—

When an employer places such an instrumentality (a delivery truck) in the possession and control of an employe in the conduct of his business, and voluntarily substitutes the management and supervision of the employe for his own, the law holds him for what the employe does while using the instrumentality in the course and scope of his employment. And we hold in this case that when the young boy, clinging to the running board of the truck in a precarious position, of which the driver had knowledge, was injured by the wanton and reckless acts of the driver, while in the course and scope of his employment, the employer is liable.

There is no doubt about it—a careless or reckless driver can let his employer in for a lot of unpleasant and expensive things. Some employers have gone so far as to compel their drivers to furnish bonds, and I have heard some talk to the effect that certain insurance companies intended to refuse to insure against drivers' negligence unless they were bonded. The other day I noticed another case in which the driver of the truck, thinking he was doing the right thing, shooed a boy off his truck while it was in motion. The boy fell and was hurt, and the employer was held responsible. The court said the driver ought to have slowed up before the boy got off. In another case the driver invited the boy to ride, but made him get off while the car was in motion. This boy was hurt also and the employer was held responsible on the same ground.

The wise owner of a delivery truck which is not to be driven by himself will get for himself all the protection he can possibly get against these possibilities.

(Copyright, 1922, by Elton J. Buckley, Phila., Pa.)

—:—:—:—

Who Pays for Advertising?

I HAD an idea that the old theory that the consumer pays for advertising had been exploded. Because I am an advertising man and have thrashed this matter out so many times I believed that everyone knew that this belief was false, says Arthur S. Ballard, in *Dough*.

Last week I received a decided shock. A large baker—an intelligent and successful business man—was talking over the matter of advertising with me. In the course of our conversation he said, "If we do any advertising we will have to raise the price of our products. Somebody has got to pay for it. We cannot spend all the money we are contemplating without getting it back somehow."

Believe me, I was flabbergasted. Here was a leading figure in his community, a clever merchandising man, and a man of vision who had never been put right on that idea.

I felt that if this man believed that the public pays for advertising, there are probably hundreds of other bakers who are laboring under the same delusion. For that reason I am writing this article. In it I will try to explain to you as I did to him, just why advertising is beneficial to the public, to the manufacturer, and to the distributor.

Let us suppose that you are a baker. You are producing 3,000 pounds of bread a day, or approximately 900,000 pounds a year. We will assume, just for the sake of comparison, that your total costs are 7c per pound, and that you are selling this bread to the retail grocer for 8c, who in turn sells it for 10c to the consumer. That means that with this production you are earning a profit of $9,000 over your salaries and expenses every year. Now, let us say that you are contemplating an advertising campaign in which you are going to spend $9,000. You prepare a forceful campaign. I do not believe that it is necessary to go into great length to convince you that advertising does stimulate sales. There are too many thousands of proofs with which you come in contact every day to necessitate this.

Now we'll start our campaign. Provided it is properly prepared it will stimulate sales. In the course of a short time you will find that the demand created by your advertising allows you to raise your production.

As your production increases, naturally your costs decrease and your selling costs are greatly lowered. As your advertising goes on you will find that your production can be constantly increased and at the end of the year you will find that you can produce 12,000 loaves a day and sell them, even including the cost of the advertising, for at least the same percentage if not a lower percentage of costs than when you were producing 3,000. Therefore, you can readily see that this advertising cost need not be charged to the consumer. In fact, in most instances, you will find that the advertising manufacturer can give the consumer a better product due to his decreased cost where volume is maintained, at the same price, and often the consumer can purchase the same article for less money than he could before it was advertised and sold in quantity.

Consider any national advertiser. We will take Ivory soap for example. Do you believe that Ivory soap, which actually tests, as they claim, 99.44 pure, could be sold for 10c if it were not produced in volume, and do you believe that it could be successfully produced in volume if advertising had not created a demand for this soap? This is a concrete example of a quality article selling at a decidedly low price made possible by the power of advertising. Advertising is like a snowball started at the top of a hill. Its effect increases as it goes along.

Now let us consider the effect of the manufacturer's advertising from the standpoint of the distributor.

Let us suppose that you are a grocer selling bread along with your other lines. To begin with, you have a fixed overhead required to handle your present business, which cannot be cut down. We will say that it cost 17% to do business. That is the cost of your rent, depreciation, supplies, salaries, expenses, etc. Now you are handling bread. We'll call it Golden Wheat. For this bread you are paying 8c a loaf and are selling it for 10c. That means of course a close profit of 20% on your sales cost. You are selling 50 loaves of bread a day. This allows you $1.00 profit on the loaves. Now the manufacturer begins a strenuous advertising campaign. This campaign creates a demand for the bread, and as a result, you sell 100 loaves instead of 50 as before. Your profit, then, is $2.00. You have earned double the amount that you were earning heretofore, and because of this increased turnover with the same fixed overhead your selling costs are lowered. Therefore, as the volume increases on your merchandise, your overhead is lowered and your profits consequently increase. This is one way in which the manufacturer's advertising helps the distributor. As the manufacturer advertises, the dealer's turnover naturally increases.

Now comes the consumer. You may ask how you, as a consumer of clothing, hats, food, etc., are benefited by the advertising of the manufacturers of these products. Earlier in the article I pointed out just how

A Scientific Service to Bakers

—TO systematize the operations of a bakery—

—TO find the cost on every variety of goods made—

—TO establish standards for costs—for materials—for labor —for wrapping—for delivery, and for overhead—

—TO set standards for all ingredients and keep the buyer informed as to the exact value of each kind of material he purchases—

—TO establish correct principles for selection of employees and develop their ability through systematic training—

—TO measure your costs and your quality each month by comparison with the costs and quality of scores of other plants—

—TO make an analysis of your shop, your equipment, your organization — and report our observations and recommendations—

—TO make a careful study of your market, your competition, and determine your possibilities for growth—

These are a few of the things we are prepared to do for you under a contract for service such as we have made for years with many of the most successful and fastest growing bakery institutions in the country.

The W. E. Long Company is an organization of experts giving their whole time to a study of bakery operation and management. The Departments of Accounting, Laboratory and Shop Management, and Sales Promotion and Advertising have special corps of men who devote their time and expert knowledge to each particular phase of bakery operation.

We solicit the interest of wide-awake bakery owners or managers who wish to associate with a large group of leading bakers forming our present clientele.

THE W. E. LONG CO.

Scientific Service for Bakers

Advertising　　　　　*Accounting*　　　　　*Laboratory*

155 N. Clark Street, Chicago

it is possible for the manufacturer to offer to the consumer either a better product at the same cost, or the same product at a lower cost. But how do I know, you may ask, that the manufacturer will give us this quality? "How do I know but that he'll conduct a tremendous campaign and sell an article that is worthless? There is one born every minute, you know. And again how do I know but that he'll create a demand for a good article and then cut out the quality after becoming well known?"

Now here's just how you know that. A business, to be successful, must be permanent. The initial shot in most cases is not what the manufacturer is after. He cannot afford to spend a great deal of money merely to sell you one of his products. For example, take the manufacturers of toilet articles such as shaving creams, soap, etc. In many instances, they spend as high as $1.00 to place a $0.50 article in your hands. But they are doing this knowing that it is a quality article and that once you have tried it you will be inclined to repeat your order. Mr. Lincoln was right when he said, "You can fool some of the people some of the time, but you can't fool all of the people all of the time." For that reason if a manufacturer is to have repeat orders, he must maintain a high standard of quality and if he is not to have repeat orders, he may just as well stop advertising, for his money will be wasted. Advertising can, and does, put over articles that have merit, but there are few—very few—advertising campaigns, and none to my knowledge, that have put over permanently articles without merit. For that reason, advertising benefits the consumer in that it forces the manufacturer to maintain a higher standard of quality than if his goods were unknown and allows the consumer to buy this at a reasonably fair price.

—‡—‡—‡—

The Koeppel Bakery, Nebraska City, Nebr., has recently been taken over by Oscar Lucas, an experienced baker of many years.

F. Frasch, who for many years conducted a bakery at Fourteenth street and Bergenline avenue, West New York, having sold same, has opened a new shop at Woodcliff, N. J., and will keep a fine line of baked goods.

A. Vidulich will open a bakery and confectionery store at 50 Park street, Amsterdam, N. Y.

J. Frank Shellenberger, the well-known candy manufacturer and retailer of Philadelphia, has opened a handsome new and modern bakery at 6th and Bay avenues, Ocean City, N. J., where he will specialize in fine pastry, also carrying a line of his candies. Mr. Shellenberger has also opened an attractive store on the Ocean City Boardwalk.

The new plant of the Travis Baking Company was recently opened on North Hamilton street, Poughkeepsie, N. Y. The bakery is a model of its kind, and is in every sense a daylight one.

The Waynesville Bakery has been incorporated at Waynesville, N. C., with capital of $2,500 by Sam Rosenbaum, J. H. Smathers and C. B. Russell.

The Franklin System will open a bakery in the Palmer Bldg., S. Main street, Chambersburg, Pa.

Sales Plans

An address by Wallace A. Cook, of The Fleischmann Co., at the Southeastern Convention

I AM going to discuss sales plans, not any particular kind of sales plans, but rather the importance of having definite sales plans, and, I might say, conservative sales plans. All that I hope to do is give you a thought and suggest that you make it an active thought by working it out in some way in your business.

In the past few months, the baking industry has been disrupted even more than it was during the war period. Bread prices have been adjusted, markets reorganized, with much more work in the industry to be done. This is true of the North as well as the South. It has taken a long time to build up the public's confidence in Bread. By confidence, I mean an appreciation of Bread as a food and an appreciation of the economy and value of baker's Bread. The public is always ready to take advantage of price cuts. It is easy to make these cuts on any commodity, but it is difficult to go back to a selling price that will afford a fair margin of profit and have public opinion with you. This is particularly true of Bread. The price of silk or any kind of clothing material may increase one or two hundred per cent. without eliciting newspaper editorials. The prices of food products generally go up and down without the press taking a great deal of notice. When it comes to an increase in the price of Bread, you have a hue and cry all over the place. The Bread consumers of the country today do not know what all the Bread price agitation means. The bakers' controversies are a mystery to them. As a matter of fact, they are not greatly interested in what the bakers are doing so long as prices are on the downward trend. The baker himself is the one who is losing.

I do not have to tell you that indiscriminate lowering of prices in any business is bad. It gets the business nowhere and means losses to the individual firms who indulge in it.

In the magazine "System" each month they run a Suggestion Department under the titles: "If I Were a Butcher," "If I Were a Grocer," "If I Were a Builder," etc. I am reminded of these suggestions when I say to you that if I were a baker, I would build my business the way all successful businesses are built. I would give good value, ask a good price, and go after trade. That in the last analysis is a conservative selling plan. It is easy to give a formula of this kind and perhaps you will say not so easy to work it out, but even that point I cannot concede. If you have a good loaf of Bread, you can certainly get a good price for it and you can certainly get business. This has been done even in markets where general price cutting has been indulged in. The public is always willing to pay more for an article that has quality.

Now the point of getting business with a good loaf of Bread at a good price is the point that interests us.

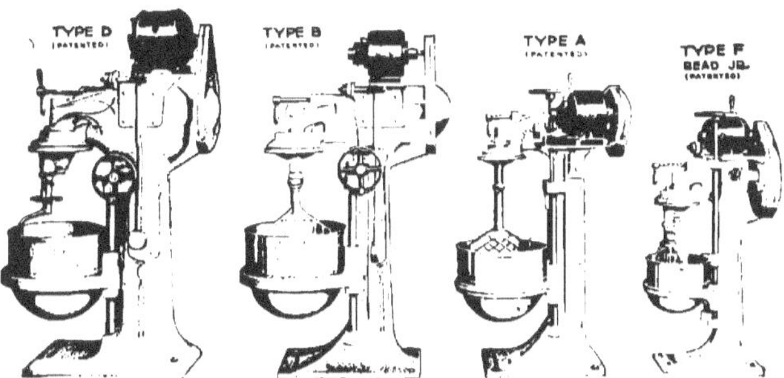

EVERYONE A READ

The Read Three-Speed Mixer is the Original. Made in Four Models, "A Size for Every Purpose." Simply Select the Type that Meets Your Requirements.

All Read Machines Carry This Mark

Which Assures You of the Original.

Write For Catalogue.

The Read Machinery Company
YORK, PA.

Also Manufacturers of

Dough Mixers, Sifting Outfits, Automatic Proofers
and Complete Equipments.

You may ask "How" and "Where" can the business be secured. The answer to "How" is "Digging"; the answer to "Where" is probably closer at hand than you imagine. It is quite possible that a good percentage of increase in your business could be secured within a radius of a few blocks of your bakery. There are few territories that have been worked up to a point where they are yielding one hundred per cent. returns on any commodity. This is particularly true of Bread. I do not know how I can better illustrate my point than by telling you a little story. It was told by J. P. Newell, Sales Manager of the Toledo Scale Co., in an article entitled "Working the Invisible Market," in a recent number of *Printers' Ink.* He tells of an applicant for a position who refused a certain territory because it was too large. The new man had been selling cash registers, and, on being pinned down to facts, he stated that it had taken him three weeks to cover the town of Beloit, Kansas. The following ensued:

"How big is Beloit?"

"Twenty-eight hundred."

"It didn't pay you to stay there that long, did it?"

"Sure. I wouldn't have stayed if it hadn't been profitable." And he went on to tell how he had sold some $2,200.00 worth of cash registers by working every possible prospect in the town. He defined a possible prospect as "anybody who could use a cash register in his business if it came to him as a Christmas present." Most of the sales he had been making for this concern were to the little fellows who had been overlooked in the days of luxurious prosperity, especially those off the beaten paths.

"The little merchant is generally pretty well pleased when I go in and try to sell him a $700.00 cash register," the explanation continued, "for nobody has ever before recognized his business as important enough to have any use for one. It is easier to sell him because of that."

"How about the credit risk?" I persisted. "Doesn't your company turn down a lot of these little fellows?"

"No, because if there is any doubt about it, I take full cash in advance with the order." And he explained further that many of these small business men, some of whom did not do business with banks even, had several hundreds of thousands of dollars put away in cash or Liberty Bonds.

This salesman was working a market that was practically invisible to his competitors, and which would even have been beyond the vision of the average credit department.

This little story brought home to me a condition that I have observed myself in working with bakers to increase their business. I will admit that I have never put the facts down in cold type, but I have had a hazy idea in the back of my head all the time that many bakers who are trying to corral the trade of a big city with meagre success could get as much business as they could handle within a small area surrounding their shop. Many bakers themselves have a vague idea

as to just where their market lies. The result is they spend a good deal of money on advertising to the general public and get a small percentage of return. Just as the man in the story finding a possible prospect as anybody who could use a cash register in his business, so I would define the possible prospect for Bread as anybody who can eat solid food. That being so, everybody in your town is a prospect, of course. A great many of you reach your market through the grocer. Some of you who do a retail business can apply the same idea that I am speaking of to the particular area of territory surrounding your retail shop. Those of you who reach your consumers through the grocer want to work this market as economically as possible and as thoroughly as it is possible to work it. The first question is: "Are the people in the neighborhood of your bakery eating as much Bread as they should eat?" "Are the grocers you now supply selling as much Bread as they can sell?" Getting more business is not necessarily a matter of increasing your distribution or increasing the number of stores you supply. It is first of all a matter of working those stores up to a point where their sale of your Bread is one hundred per cent. good. Just as the small town of Beloit could be made to yield an amazing return on cash register sales, so can the grocers in your neighborhood be made to yield an amazing return on Bread sales. To get an insight into the "invisible market" which is right at your elbow and which you are not supplying, there is nothing like getting out and spending two or three days on your Bread routes. You have the big sales angle. You will see opportunities in the stores that the route man will not see. You will be surprised yourself at the improvement you can make in the sales in stores and on routes that your route man believed had been worked to the limit. No store has been worked to the limit on Bread sales until every person entering the store buys Bread daily and recognizes the merit of your brand. No route has been worked to the limit until every grocer on the route is selling as much Bread as the families who patronize his store can eat.

Just a word about route supervision—I understand that the customary plan in connection with supervising a bakery route is for the route foreman to go with the salesman and see how efficiently this salesman is handling his trade. This means that two men are on the route for a period of eight or ten hours. I don't know how many of you gentlemen are handling the supervising of your routes in this way, but it occurs to me that it might be well to consider carefully a change in this generally accepted plan of supervising. Why not let a supervisor take a route and handle it himself? We must take it for granted in advance that he knows the route, then let the salesman go out and spend some time with the trade he serves, allowing him to go in and get into conversation with some of the store managers or store clerks, and work up an interest in the possibilities of selling Bread. Many of these salesmen are sufficiently well trained to take a group

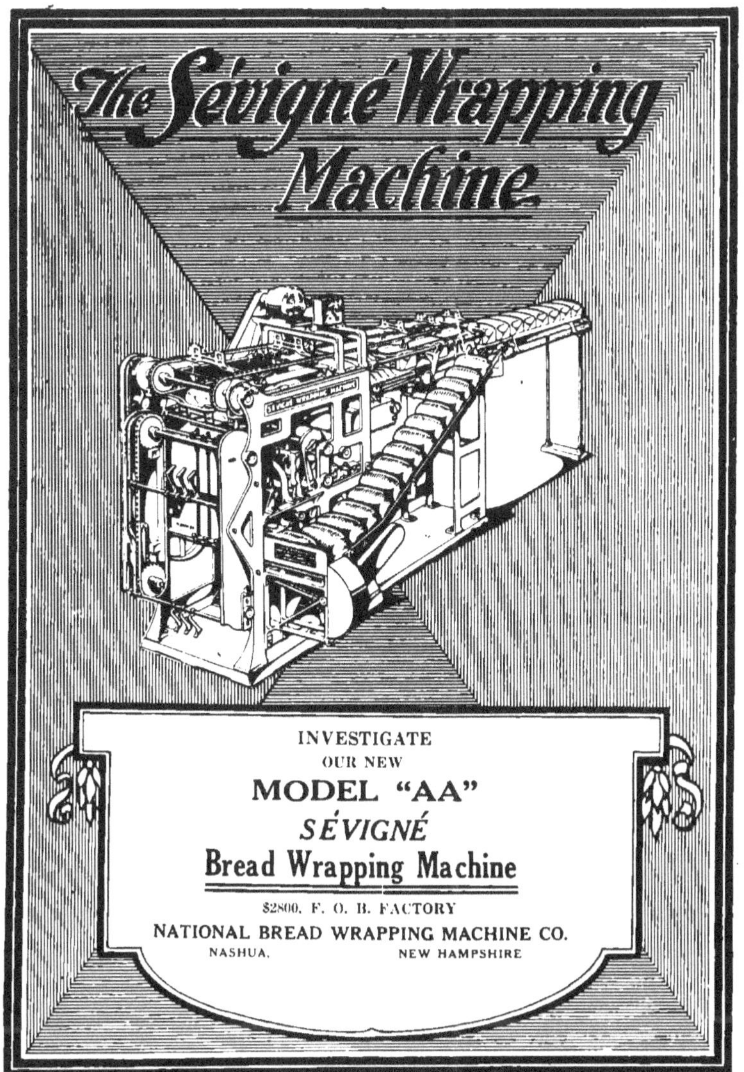
The Sévigné Wrapping Machine

INVESTIGATE
OUR NEW
MODEL "AA"
SÉVIGNÉ
Bread Wrapping Machine

$2800. F. O. B. FACTORY

NATIONAL BREAD WRAPPING MACHINE CO.
NASHUA, NEW HAMPSHIRE

of ten to fifteen stores and put on an interesting demonstration with a loaf of Bread and a jar of jam. If the salesman is supplied with some advertising material to put in these stores, his work is made so much easier because he leaves with each prospective customer a reminder of his Bread.

Building business in the South is uphill work because of the preference for hot Breads, but the job is not an impossible one, as you will all agree, when you look back and see what you have accomplished in the past few years. There is not the slightest question about your success in replacing hot Bread with light Bread on tables in the South, if you have faith in your ability to do it and keep working. Light Bread is better than hot Bread. Belief in that fact alone is going to enable you to place light Bread permanently on the tables in the South. You have got to believe in your product and the faith in your ability to put it over. Your salesmen have to be taken into the secret and sold on the idea of what you are trying to accomplish. There was a day when flying machines were regarded as absurdities. The day will come when flying machines will be cheaper than the cheapest automobile and man will go from East coast to West coast of this country between the rising and setting of the sun.

Professors of Yale are preparing to teach history with moving pictures. At one time, the moving picture was housed in vacant lots or little halls and people wondered how long it would last. The following story illustrates our point:

THE VISIONARY: A TRUE INCIDENT

BY DON LAUDER

Within the walls of a room in a Boston building, now long since torn down, an earnest group of men were assembled in the late seventies. They typified the New England spirit of that day—cautious, conservative, almost reactionary.

They represented, for the most part, important financial interests. In fact, the meeting had been called for the purpose of interesting capital in the manufacture and sale of a recent invention.

The contrivance had just been explained to the little group by its deaf inventor, and its commercial possibilities had come up for discussion.

Some were dubious as to its practicability. Others predicted a very limited market. Suddenly one man, an impetuous youth of fifty, with the fire of vision in his eyes, smote the mahogany table and exclaimed:

"Gentlemen, I can see the day when there will be one hundred thousand of these instruments in use in this country."

His words caused consternation. The deaf inventor cupped his ear, while one of the less excited repeated the remark.

"For God's sake, man," some one whispered, looking around to make sure that the door was closed, "don't let that remark get outside these four walls. People will think us crazy."

Today there are something like 12,000,000 of these instruments in use, and the controlling company in the field figures 20,000,000 as a not unlikely market.

The deaf inventor was Alexander Graham Bell. The invention was the telephone.

Light Bread consumption in the South which will equal, if not surpass the light Bread consumption in the North, is still a vision, but the faith that made the flying machine, the moving picture and the telephone necessities to the American public, will make light Bread a necessity in the South. Faith plus hard work is the recipe. Is the invisible market on your street, in your neighborhood, in your corner of the town, yielding all it can yield?

—‡—‡—‡—

Different Flours, Different Treatment

IT MAY safely be asserted that while some flour is spoiled in the process of manufacture, a far greater amount is spoiled in the baking, because the baker does not understand the peculiarities of the particular flour being used. Any one who has had even a limited experience knows that there is a marked difference in the fermentation of various doughs. Some will work much faster than others and if not taken at the proper time will not make a good bread. While these fast-working flours will, with care, produce a good loaf, any abuse will result in flat, coarse-grained, dark-colored bread. To illustrate this it is only necessary to take a strong and a weak flour and work them under the same conditions. When due care is exercised in the care of both flours the results will be the same, good bread. But treat the flours with the same ferments and give them the same amount of work, neglecting, however, some little detail. For instance, have the temperature of the liquor used in making the dough a few degrees too high, or allow the dough to stand in the pans a little too long before being placed in the oven. The usual result will be that the bread from the strong flour will be as good as when baked under perfect conditions, while that from the weak flour will be poor, coarse and dark. Dough made from strong flour will, during the fermentation process, rise up and "drop" and rise again a second and even a third time, but dough from a weak flour will not rise again if allowed to drop once. It is evident, therefore, that weak flours require very careful handling.

—‡—‡—‡—

The average man is apt to flinch when he looks back at the past.

Many a woman prays to get into heaven and fights to get into society.

Ever notice how willing people are to assist you when you don't need help?

Take care of your pennies and your heirs may dodge taxes on your dollars.

Lightning seldom strikes twice in the same place. Good luck is like lightning in that respect.

Don't buy poor material and expect good goods.

Don't buy milk and expect cream.

SUPERIOR
Double Chamber Gas Oven

THIS Oven can be operated practically as cheap as a coal or coke Oven, and is more simple to operate. All you have to do is to turn on the gas—no dirt, ashes, or coal pile. With this Oven you have a positive guarantee against fuel shortage.

In the top of the Oven there is a flue running completely around the Oven. This flue gives just enough draft to properly circulate the heat at all times.

Each baking chamber is equipped with two tile hearths and side shields, also a heavy tile bed shelf below the first baking shelf, which insures an even baking temperature on both shelves. Over the burners in the base of the Oven are heavy tile baffle

plates which, when once hot, give off a solid baking heat. It requires about forty-five minutes to get the Oven to a baking heat from the cold Oven, but you can bake for an hour, to an hour and a half, after the gas is turned off.

The charging doors in front are equipped with heavy polished re-inforced glass, which makes it unnecessary to open the door to ascertain the condition of the product in the Oven. This is a very important feature, as the baker can see his goods in the Oven from any part of the bakery without going to the Oven and opening the door. **Write or inquire for further information.**

Made in five sizes to meet your requirements.

SUPERIOR OVEN CO.

LEITER BLDG.

Western Office
SOUTHERN CALIF. SUPPLY CO.
Los Angeles, Calif.

CHICAGO, ILL.

Eastern Office
137 HUDSON ST.
New York

Ferments and Fermentation

By David Ellis, D. Sc., Ph. D., F. R. S. E., in the British Baker

BAKERS who have some practical knowledge of fermentation and living organisms, will be in a position to take up with us the consideration of the fermentation which is of extreme importance to the baker, namely, that which takes place when the yeast organism multiplies.

The name yeast is applied to those round or oval micro-organisms which multiply by *budding* and which produce alcohol and carbonic acid when placed in a sugary solution. These round or oval bodies are very small, normally about 4·5 microns in width and up to about 9 microns in length. A micron is about a thousand times smaller than the diameter of an average pin's head. It is defined exactly as one-thousandth of a millimetre. Hence, if we were to place yeast cells end on across the top of an ordinary pin's head, we should have to place a hundred end to end in order to get a line across the surface of the head of the pin.

If you wanted to make a lump of yeast cells the size of a marble, you would need at least 1,200 million yeast cells to enable you to do it.

We have stated that reproduction is by the process of *budding*. This means that the cell multiplies by forming a kind of "pimple" on its surface, which grows and grows until the "pimple" is as big as the cell which produced it. We speak gloatingly or otherwise of a birth-rate of 25 per 1,000 among human beings. If we were to multiply as do the yeasts when they are in their prime, in a year the earth would be stiff with human beings covering the whole surface, not even excepting the North Pole, and very soon there would not be room to get born in.

It is necessary for the baker to know something of the conditions which determine the growth and multiplication of these little yeast cells, for if there is no multiplication there will be no gas; and if there is no gas the dough will not rise, and those changes will not take place which transform the indigestible dough into the digestible bread.

All organisms require food, water and oxygen, also there must be a complete absence of substances that are inimical to the life of the organism in question. The yeast is no exception to other organisms. Long experience has taught bakers how to feed this prolific little micro-organism, although it is only within comparatively recent times—sixty years or so—that it has been known that the baker has been entertaining, not angels, but a micro-organism, unawares.

The food of yeast is made up of sugar, of certain nitrogenous matters, and of certain mineral matters. The sugar is perhaps the most important element in the food supply, for it is from the sugar that the gas (carbon dioxide) is produced. The name sugar in the laboratory covers a multitude of substances all belonging to the same family, and the sugar of the "man in the street" is only one of them, although by far the most important of its class.

It may be objected that the fermentation of yeast proceeds blithely even if no sugar be added. But, does it? The flour that the yeast attacks for provender contains starch, which, as everyone knows, is the main constituent of flour. In the flour and in the yeast there are ferments which change the starch into sugar. Hence the addition of sugar is not necessary, provided that flour be present. If, therefore, sugar be supplied to the yeast, it is by way of being a supplementary process and not because without its presence yeast fermentation would not take place.

The same phenomena are observed in the yeast cells as in our own bodies. Various food materials are taken into the system, but they cannot be digested until they are changed by the ferments contained in the digestive juices of our bodies. It is the same with the yeasts. The digestive juices of the organism change the raw material starch into the digestible sugar. It is therefore not a question whether sugar is initially present, but whether substances are present which the yeast can change into sugar.

As already stated, such substances are supplied plentifully by the flour itself. Where, then, is the use of adding from ½ pound to 2 pounds of sugar per sack in making bread? This is where the practical man comes into his own, for the scientist can only tell him what laws govern the process in question; it is for the baker to work them out in practice. The yeast must be supplied with substances which can be transformed by the organism into sugar. If too little sugar be present, the yeast cells are underfed, they reproduce in a very tardy fashion, and the dough becomes under-fermented. On the other hand, the baker must be careful that he does not supply too much sugar. Generous treatment is not appreciated by the yeast cells. Beyond a certain point sugar restrains fermentation, and beyond another point a little further ahead, it actually stops fermentation altogether.

And yet without it there can be no fermentation, for its presence is an absolute necessity to the multiplication of the yeast cells. The baker must then, obviously, bear in mind the various sources from which his sugar is derived, and ascertain which combination gives the best results.

There is about 2 to 3 per cent. of natural sugar in flour. This is in the form of two sugars called maltose and cane sugar, the latter being the sugar as understood by the ordinary person, the sugar with which we sweeten our tea. There is also in flour a very large percentage of starch. The yeast changes the starch into sugar. Not only so, but when the sugar is formed

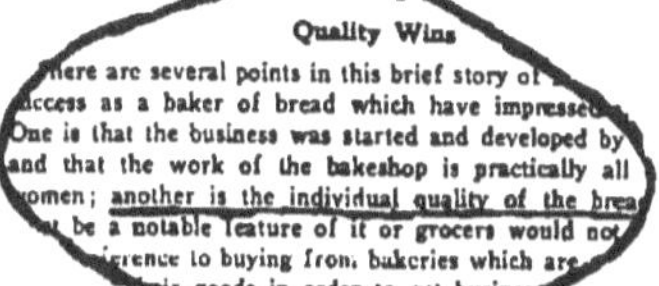

The Surest

and Quickest

Road to Success!

A LOAF OF SUPERIOR QUALITY

Another story of success—success due to *quality!* Because of a loaf of superior quality, the keenest competition and numerous other big handicaps were overcome.

Bread consumers want above all, a loaf of good quality, made of good material, a loaf that pleases the palate and satisfies the appetite. Such a loaf cannot be a "dead" one—it must stand up well with a live, fresh look that catches the eye. That's the loaf that brings the repeat orders, the mainstay of any business.

A DUTCHESS Automatic Dough Divider will save enormously in labor and material and will give you a loaf of *superior quality.* The biggest selling breads are made with DUTCHESS Dividers. No amount of advertising would sell a loaf repeatedly unless it possessed superior quality.

For a live, fresh looking loaf, use a DUTCHESS Divider.

"Our Sales Tell the Tale"

**DUTCHESS
TOOL
COMPANY
BEACON, N. Y.**

the yeast has still to transform it into the appropriate sugar—that is, into the sugar which it can assimilate.

It must be understood that maltose and cane sugar, although sugars, are not capable of digestion until they have been changed into a simpler form of sugar called glucose. This transformation is effected by ferments which the yeast possesses in addition to those which it possesses for changing sugar into alcohol and carbonic acid gas.

Again, suppose milk is added. There is sugar in this substance which can be changed into glucose by the yeast cells. In the same way there is sugar in malt in the form of maltose, which also can be transformed into glucose and digested. The addition of malt is a necessary feature in the preparation of Parisian barm, so the maker of bread by the use of this barm has a sugar content in the form of maltose. Needless to say, the addition of glucose is frequent in making bread. Theoretically it would appear that, inasmuch as the yeast changes all the different kinds of sugar presented to it into glucose, then this substance should in all cases be added. As a matter of fact, this substance is often given to the extent of about 1 pound per sack.

In dealing, however, with organic life, it is almost impossible to predict what will take place when certain substances are added to promote or retard fermentation. It is one of those cases in which an ounce of fact is worth a ton of theory. That which has been found as a result of experiment must be held to outweigh any theoretical considerations. We all know wherein lies the proof of the pudding. In order, however, to be able to make experiments along intelligent lines the baker must be in possession of the salient facts which science has discovered, and it is these facts which must guide him in initiating experiments. These facts are:

1. The yeast will stop growing if presented with too little or too much sugar.

2. All sugars must turn to glucose before they can be assimilated by yeast cells.

3. Sugars exist in different forms, and are found in different forms in malt, flour, glucose, milk, etc.

4. There are many substances (e. g., starch) which change into sugar when acted upon by ferments.

5. The yeast does not use all its sugar for purposes of food; the bulk of the sugar obtained by the transformation of starch is used to yield to the yeast cells a supply of energy which enables them to "carry on," sometimes at a prodigious rate.

These general facts supply enough material to justify the hope that experiments based on them—in other words, research work—would yield a few answers to the questions which inevitably arise when the facts are stated. This kind of research work is not to be lightly undertaken as a kind of casual experiment, but should rather be an organized effort directed by the various associations that are interested in the art of baking—or, rather, in the science which underlies this art.

The whole question of "stimulants" centers round this supply of materials which accelerate the rate of fermentation, and at present we do not appear to be very far advanced.

Turning now to the nitrogenous nutriment of the yeast, here again we find that special attention must be given to the peculiar needs of the yeast cells. Albumen, which is the staple source of a vast number of different species of animals and plants, is quite unsuitable; but if the albumen can be changed into peptone by a ferment then we have the best possible food for yeast, and the most favorable media for the artificial cultivation of this organism are to be found among those containing peptone as the nitrogenous source of food.

Fortunately a suitable nitrogenous medium is found in flour, in malt and in other natural and artificial bodies; also in all well nourished yeast cells there is a ferment which can transform these nitrogenous substances into forms suitable for consumption. We want, however, to go further than this. What about the other sources of nitrogen? Can we stimulate the yeast cells to do their work in a shorter time, or so adjust our conditions that no other contending fermentation has a chance of succeeding? Can this be done by the addition of "drugs" or by the addition of nitrogen in a form other than the organic one in which this substance is found in flour?

All this is still in the womb of time. We have, however, found out some interesting facts, not, one is sorry to record, through the researches of institutions set up by bakers, but by the zealous endeavors of brewers, who, for interested reasons, have pushed forward the scientific study of yeast quite without consideration of the fact whether the benefit was going to be immediate or more remote. We have to look in the journals supported by brewers to obtain our facts.

One important fact was unearthed when it was found that yeast cells can assimilate the nitrogen which they require from ammonium salts, but not from nitrates. Then it was ascertained that the addition of ammonium chloride to bread dough saved 30 per cent. of the yeast ordinarily used. Many other interesting facts have come to light in respect to the nitrogenous food of yeasts, and would need an article to themselves to do full justice to their significance. We will mention here only two facts which will indicate the trend of modern work. The first is that researches have been made with success to ascertain whether the yeasts cannot get the nitrogen which they need from the nitrogen of the atmosphere. The second

BUDWEISER Barley Malt—100 per cent pure—is made only from the finest barley and scientifically malted by the most modern methods. It has the advantage of Anheuser-Busch's years of malting experience in developing a diastase of just the right proportion and strength for bakers' purposes.

The result is an extract syrup of barley malt—nothing more nor less—uniformly produced at all times.

The new distributing system makes it possible to secure fresh supplies just as they are needed, without the use of the old contract system.

ANHEUSER-BUSCH SALES CORPORATION

ST. LOUIS. U. S. A.

is the investigation into the effects of drugs like adrenalin on the growth and fermentation of yeast cells.

The next feature in the life of this wonderful little organism is its behavior in respect to oxygen. Without oxygen we all die, animal and plant alike. Here, again, the investigations of the scientist have achieved a result of the highest importance to the baker. We have to distinguish between the respiration and the fermentation of yeast. By respiration we mean the taking in of oxygen and the using of it to break down food. This break down is attended by a liberation of energy, just as energy is liberated when a match is applied to gunpowder. The oxygen, like the match, sets things going, which results in energy-liberating processes.

By fermentation we mean here the particular fermentation which results in the production of alcohol and carbonic acid gas. This also is an energy-liberating process. Now, if the yeast gets plenty of oxygen it may stop producing alcohol and carbonic acid gas altogether. This would never do for the baker. Much research work has been instituted to ascertain the relationship of these two contending processes; and particularly their relationship at different temperatures.

It will be obvious that the attitude of the baker towards aeration must be different from that of the yeast manufacturer, who wants to make a quantity of yeast and does not trouble about the product. The yeast manufacturer will strive to bring about conditions which will bring the cells as much as possible into contact with the air. If the baker follows his example too far the dough will soon show the marks of his treatment.

The next feature in the nutrition of yeast is the consideration of the mineral foods of the yeast plant. We know what the absence of appropriate minerals from the food of human beings brings about—a falling off in vitality, and ultimately, if not attended to in time, death. It is the same with all plants, including the yeast micro-organism. The best combination at present known is the following:

0.1 gramme monobasic potassium phosphate.
0.1 gramme magnesium sulphate.
0.1 gramme tribasic calcium phosphate.
100 c. c. distilled water.
15 grammes candied sugar.

In making artificial media for the growth of yeasts, instead of water from the tap, it is customary to add this mixture. All yeasts must have phosphorus, potassium and magnesium. It is not, of course, proposed that this solution should be added to flour in commercial bread-making, but it is suggested that the baker should periodically ascertain whether the ingredients which he uses are deficient or not in one or more of the essential substances which are necessary for the growth of the yeast cells. The up-to-date baker should

deal with his yeast as does the medical man with his patient. The baker and the doctor alike have to deal with a living organism, which is liable to fall sick. In the training of the medical man the physiology of the human body is thoroughly taught, and when prescribing for a patient he is really applying to a specific case the general rules which regulate the physiology of the human body. In the same way the baker should know intimately the general rules which govern the physiology of the yeast cells.

We have dealt now with the food, the drink and the respiration of the yeast cells. In the bakery the conditions necessary for the proper adjustment of the ingredients have become more or less stereotyped, and the process of making bread has become more or less mechanical. So long as matters are progressing in the right direction the ordinary baker does not worry his head. Why, then, should matters occasionally go completely wrong? Upholders of the Parisian barm method of making bread must be well acquainted with the tendency for things to go wrong, apparently through sheer "cussedness." Other organisms are present in the barm besides yeast, and these must be kept down at all costs. This can be accomplished only by the adjustment of temperature, for each organism has its own optimum of temperature, and obviously if this be kept at a point which is the optimum for yeast the chances are that the other fermentations which give rise to acidity will not gain headway. To the practicing baker this matter of temperature is one of vital importance, for the adjustment of the temperature is practically the only safe means at his disposal for securing the control of his fermentation and preventing it from getting out of hand.

The only other method of control is by the addition of substances which increase or decrease the rapidity of fermentation. We are not sufficiently advanced in our research work yet to state explicitly that such and such substances should be used in specific cases, and it would not serve any useful purpose to discuss the steps that have been taken in this line of research.

—‡—‡—‡—

Allen Borton's bakery, Hillsdale, Mich., has recently been remodelled, redecorated, and new machinery installed, at a cost of about $4,000.

The Parkview Baking Company recently opened its fine, new, modern bakery at 12th and Washington streets, Manistee, Mich.

A Growing Demand

The growing demand for "Bakers' home made bread" has only been made possible by a high order of sanitary and scientific production.

An important factor in sanitary and scientific production of pure and wholesome bread is the sweet, safe, distinctive, sanitary cleanliness which always follows the use of

Knowledge of this fact has enabled thousands of bakers the country over to depend upon this cleaner to accomplish results which are greatly assisting to hasten the day when a majority of families will eat "Bakers'" bread exclusively.

This efficient and economical cleaner is so pure and purifying, providing as it does a sweet, wholesome, faultless, sanitary cleanliness, that your baking processes and display rooms are always protected from insanitation, and your product displayed under the most attractive conditions.

Wyandotte Sanitary Cleaner and Cleanser is quick and easy in its action and is entirely harmless to the hands.

Order from your supply house.

The J. B. Ford Co. SOLE MANUFACTURERS Wyandotte, Mich.

Apple Specialties in the Bakeshop

APPLE pie is undoubtedly the most demanded bake stuff in the pie line, and is made all the year round, while most of the others are manufactured only at certain times or seasons. There are various ways of making this pie filling. They may be made of canned, dried, or fresh apples. As the season is now approaching when good and fresh apples can be procured at a reasonable price, we give a few methods for the preparation of the fresh fruit.

In the first place only apples of the sour variety should be used for pie filling, as a sweet apple is useless and does not jellify, and will never get soft. Pare and core the apples, cut them up fine, sweeten with sugar and add a dash of cinnamon, and it is ready for use. This is certainly the quickest way of producing a pie filling, and if made right, the pie not baked too fast or too slow, it will give a very good result, as no flavor is lost by stewing or boiling the apples. Another method is to stew about half of the apples with a few slices of lemon (which are removed after stewing), very lightly, then mix them all together, sweeten with sugar and add a dash of cinnamon, this will also make an excellent pie filling. Still another method is to stew all the apples with some lemon, very light, just enough to be a trifle soft; drain off the surplus water, then sweeten with enough water to suit the taste, and add a pinch of cinnamon. Lemon is a great improvement in an apple pie filling, if added proportionately, say 1 lemon to 6 quarts of apples. It keeps the apples nice and white and increases the flavor.

Stewed apples mashed fine may be used advantageously in conjunction with peaches, pineapples and the like, especially when the latter fruit is scarce and high in price. When added to other fruit it should not be overdone, so as not to spoil the flavor of the original. Canned apples, before using should also be stewed and finished in the same manner.

Dried apples or apricots should be soaked over night in water and then stewed and proceeded with in the above manner.

APPLE TARTS

Line the tart molds with some pie crust; then fill them up with stewed and sweetened apples well flavored. This tart may be finished different ways. Some bakers may prefer strips across the top, or a star cut out, or some other shape, while others may prefer a meringue. If meringue is used for a finish the tarts have to be baked first and cooled off again. Some very attractive design can be piped on top, dusted over with powdered sugar and put back in the oven again to color the meringue. The strips, stars or other shaped center pieces are made of good pie crust rolled thin and cut out, brushed over with egg wash and placed on top, baked in moderate heat.

APPLE TURNOVERS

Take a piece of good puff paste, roll it about one-sixth of an inch in thickness, cut it into square pieces about four by four, or of any size to suit the trade; brush the edges over with egg wash, then have some finely chopped apples ready, sweetened and well flavored; place a spoonful in the center of each square, then lay one corner on top of the opposite one, thus forming a triangle; press the edges down well to prevent bursting open during the process of baking. Lay them upon baking tins and brush over with egg wash and bake in moderate heat. When baked sprinkle them over with powdered sugar and put them back again in flash-heat, just long enough to melt the sugar on top. This will give them a fine gloss and they are ready for sale. The size and price for this pastry differ greatly.

APPLE CAKE

This cake is mostly made and baked upon large square baking tins and cut to the size of five-cent pieces. It is sold as much in lunch rooms as in bakeries; in the former it is served in smaller pieces with coffee, tea or milk. It is also baked to a great extent in commonly called cheesecake pans. The pans are lined with coffee-cake dough, the apples are pared, cored and quartered, then laid close together in rotation upon the lined tins, sprinkled over with sugar and a few currants and slightly dusted with cinnamon and baked in a good heat. Before removing from the oven they should be examined to see that they have a good baked bottom, even more than a pie, as a coffee-cake dough absorbs a great deal of moisture from the apples, through its rising qualities during the baking. Should the apples not be soft enough when the cake is nearly baked then they should be steamed, that is, a greased paper laid over the pan to keep the steam on them. Apples of the sour variety will mostly always be soft enough when the cake is baked. Sweet apples should never be used for such goods. As some apples contain less juice than others, then the cakes should be sprinkled with water before baking, not too much sugar should be put on them before they are put in the oven, as sugar draws moisture and the cake will be soggy. To give the cake the necessary sweetness the rest of the sugar should be sprinkled on them after the baking. When the cake is finished, that is sugared, they must be baked at once, otherwise the juice will soak through, the dough will not bake a good bottom and will stick to the pan.

COVERED APPLE CAKE

This apple cake is baked in the same pans as the former. The pans are lined with sweet dough or coffee-cake dough; the apples pared, cored and finely chopped, sweetened and flavored and filled in about one inch in thickness; next roll out a thin sheet of good pie crust or scrap puff paste and cover the top with this, brush it over with egg wash, mark the top with a fork and bake in hot oven. When baked, glace the top with a thin water icing.

We will give you two or more recipes for linings which come very handy when no coffee-cake dough is on hand, and can be made in very little time and are preferable for the small cakes and tartlettes, especially the sweet dough, which is composed of the following ingredients: 2 pounds of pastry flour, 1 pound of powdered sugar, 1 pound of shortening and 6 eggs, all mixed together. This dough can be used for various articles and may be altered to suit the trade; it can be kept on hand a long time in a cool place and is always ready for use.

The second is a mixture, also adapted to line cheese-cake pans: 8 ounces of sugar worked up lightly with 8 ounces of shortening, then broken up thoroughly with 8 pounds of flour, to which are added 2 ounces of cream tartar, 1 ounce of soda, dissolved in 1 quart of milk, mixed in and worked until it gets smooth and glossy; dust over well and it is ready to line the pans. Peach cake, apricot cake, huckleberry cake and the like are made on the same lines, and the same observation holds good.

The apple peeling may be used for jelly and any economical baker should take advantage of it, as the peel contains the most jellification. The formula

would be as follows: Put the peeling in a copper kettle, add enough water to cover them; then put on a brisk fire and boil for half an hour, then drain, and to every quart of juice add from 1¼ to 1½ pounds of granulated sugar. Put this all in a copper kettle and set on hot fire and cook to a jelly, first stirring until all the sugar is dissolved. When the juice has boiled for some time and it begins to thicken, put some on a tin or saucer, which should be kept in cold water or on ice, and you can readily tell whether it has reached the proper degree.

—‡—‡—‡—

Real Puff Paste

THE coming months are the most difficult times in the year (even to those usually good at making it) to make good puff paste. We give a few points which will assist to that end, first prefacing them with the remark that those succeeding in making good puff paste in warm weather may expect like or better results in cold weather. To insure good puff paste the following points must be observed.

Use a good, tough, smooth, full flavored butter.

Wash and work out the salt, and work and knead it up smooth. Several pounds may be thus prepared and kept ahead, if kept in a cool place.

Use a good, medium strong, good colored flour.

Have the dough and butter both of equal stiffness, or they will not roll even. This and even rolling are potent factors in the production of good puff paste.

Use cold water to mix the dough, and if the butter is saltless, add salt to the water as your judgment may direct.

For each two pounds of butter you may use a quarter of an ounce of cream of tartar mixed with double its weight of flour; and if you wish your tartlets or patties to run small towards the top add a whisked white of egg to the water you mix with for each pound of flour, or the juice of a medium-size lemon for each two pounds of flour. If lemon juice is used discard the cream of tartar.

Roll the dough out to about half an inch in thickness and three times the length of its width; roll out the butter in size to three-fourths, cover that, not coming to the edge of the dough by half an inch. Lay the butter on the dough, leaving the half inch margin of dough round the sides, and on the top sprinkle the cream of tartar and flour evenly on the butter; turn the clear piece of dough over onto the butter, then the butter and dough part over onto that. This gives two layers of butter and three of dough. Press the edges together with the rolling pin, then with the pin make a few light impressions on the dough one way, then the other, just to force the whole out a little; then lightly lay on the pin, move it from you, then draw it towards you; repeat this until it is rolled out large enough to fold again; then fold in three; repeat the rolling; then fold it in four laps, roll and repeat this; then roll it out again half an inch in thickness, and with a sharp knife cut off a piece of it and examine the edge. If

you can only just discriminate between the layers of dough and butter it is ready for cutting up, which do in the usual manner. If the butter shows more than the dough, it needs another folding, which give, according to your judgment, one lap or two laps. In cold weather it will stand more folding and rolling than in warm weather.

The only difference in the method for cold and hot weather is that in hot weather it needs to be made in some cool place—no matter where, so it is cold. The only suggestions we can make is to find the coldest place possible, and use every means possible to make and keep it cool, even if it has to be kept for paste-making only. Use ice water to mix the dough. Keep the butter on ice until used. After the first rolling and each successive rolling put it in the refrigerator until cold, and so on until finished. In using it cut off only as much as you need at a time, let the balance remain in the refrigerator. When cut up, bake as quickly as possible. In cutting up use a sharp cutter, and turn each piece—if for patties or tartlets or open pastry—upside down. Do these things and you have done all you can do in this matter.

We should have stated that marble, slate or glass is the best for rolling pastry on. Only in very cold weather can good puff paste be made on a board. You must be guided as to the proportion of butter to use to each pound of flour by the price you are to receive for your goods. Of course, the greater the amount of butter, other things being equal, the better the paste. Good butterine is much better than poor butter.

—‡—‡—‡—

In the care of a horse simply use a little "horse sense" and your animal will give you long and faithful service, and that means economy anyway you look at it.

—‡—‡—‡—

August Conrad has opened the Luzerne Home Bakery at 52 Main street, Luzerne, Pa., and will specialize in fancy pastry and home-made bread, having had many years' experience in this line. The shop has been equipped with modern machinery.

Walter W. Price, formerly employed at the bakery at Hershey, Pa., has bought out the Calvin Umbenhen bakery business at Myerstown, Pa., and will shortly open same for business, making extensive improvements and installing new machinery.

The Purity Bakery formerly located at 103 E. Main street, Wilkes-Barre, Pa., has moved its plant to 153 E. Main street, that city.

P. D. and G. E. Swanson, of Warren, Pa., recently purchased the bakery business of L. L. Anderson, of Youngsville, Pa., at a cost of about $100,000.

Chas. Vaetsch has purchased a store on South Main street, Brattleboro, Vt., where he will open a bakery, after remodelling same.

J. Radek, of Centralia, Wash., has bought the Puyallup Home Bakery, of Henry and Olaf Olsen, Puyallup, Wash., and has taken possession.

A second retail branch of the New York Bakery was recently opened in the Liberty Market Building, Seattle, Wash., with Sam Mosler in charge. The bakery's main plant and retail store is at 661 Weller street, Seattle.

Recipe Department

In this department we will publish new and valuable recipes and want our readers to forward to us any recipe from which they have had good results, or that is not generally known. We wish to make this department as interesting as possible and ask our readers to help us to this end. Address.

RECIPE DEPARTMENT   THE NATIONAL BAKER

ALMOND CAKES

Six pounds flour, 2¼ ounces baking powder, 3¼ pounds butter, 3¼ pounds sugar, 1 quart eggs, 12 ounces chopped almonds, 2 ounces ground almonds, few drops essence almonds, 1½ pints milk, egg color. Beat up sugar and butter and eggs in the usual manner, add the essence, chopped and ground almonds, and mix lightly. Weigh at 13 ounces each and cover with chopped almonds. Almond paste instead of ground almonds is an improvement.

A splendid cocoanut cake can be made from this mixture by adding one pound of desiccated cocoanut with the milk of a fresh one, in which the desiccated nut has been soaked. Cherry cake should be made from a different recipe, as the cherries are likely to disappear. Bake at 400 degrees F.

CHERRY CAKES

Seven pounds flour, 2 ounces baking powder, 1 pound cherries (cut in quarters), 3 pounds butter, 3½ pounds sugar, 1 quart eggs, 8 ounces citron peel (cut small), essence of cherry, 1 quart new milk. Beat up as usual. Place 4 or 5 halves of cherries on top, and bake at 400 degrees F. Weigh at 14 ounces.

SPONGE GOODS

Sponge goods form an essential part of a middle-class trade, and the following recipes will give satisfaction if carefully followed.

One quart eggs, 2½ pounds sugar, 2½ pounds soft flour. Beat up eggs and sugar in a sponge machine until it will hardly drop from the finger, when it should be turned into a round-bottomed bowl and the flour well but lightly mixed in. Sponge cakes should be very lightly flavored, and nothing beats a very little sugar on which fresh lemon peel has been rubbed. Bake at 410 degrees F.

SPONGE BISCUITS

One and a half pounds powdered sugar, 15 eggs, 1 pound 12 ounces of flour, 1-3 of an ounce of soda, 2-3 of an ounce of cream of tartar, a good flavoring of lemon. Sift all together in a bowl, make a bay, add the eggs and flavor, and mix thoroughly. Lay out with bag and tube upon previously greased and dusted baking sheets and bake in medium heat. When baked and while yet warm, cut them off the sheets, being careful so as not to bruise the bottoms. Ice the flat or bottom side with different color water icing.

SPONGE SANDWICHES

These sandwiches are very popular, but they need to be much lighter, so as to present a greater bulk than sponge cakes. Volatile is often used in the cheap kinds, but it has a tendency to dry them. A little ordinary powder tends to give both lightness and moistness.

Five pounds eggs, 4½ pounds sugar, 4½ pounds patent flour, 1 ounce baking powder. Beat as usual. Lightly mix, and bake at 420 degrees F. if thin sandwiches; if thick, bake at 400 degrees F. They can be dusted with sugar or brushed with apricot pulp and then cocoanut dusted on. A little apricot jam brushed on the top will keep the sugar from falling off.

SAVOY FINGERS

Two pounds eggs, 1½ pounds pulverized sugar, 1¼ pounds soft flour. Separate whites from yolks. Beat up whites and sugar in a sponge machine, when thoroughly stiff stir in yolks lightly, then mix in flour. Fill bag and lay out on paper, dusting with pulverized sugar. If properly knocked up you will be able to lay all out before baking off. This is the advantage of knocking up the whites and sugar first, the fingers stand up bolder and are not inclined to run about. Bake in a hot oven about 460 to 480 degrees F.

SPONGE MOULDS

One pound of eggs, 14 ounces of sugar, 14 ounces soft flour. Beat as for sponges. In dressing the moulds it is advisable to thoroughly rub out with a soft cloth, then rub 1 ounce of flour into 8 ounces of firm lard, creaming well together; go over the mould well with this and then dust with fine sugar (not icing), give a good tap to remove the superfluous sugar, then dust with flour, knocking out again. Place a wide band of paper around your moulds, and place in a tin, being careful that the mould touches the bottom of the tin. Place just inside a cool oven (350 degrees F.) where you can just reach to try it. On no account move it until it is done. Cover with paper if inclined to color. Allow it to stand in the mould for a quarter of an hour to set, when it should be turned out on a wire.

SMALL GOODS

These are to be found in every shop, and the following recipes are typical of the general class of this kind of goods.

DROP BUNS

LEMON, ALMOND, COCOANUT, ETC.

Five pounds flour, 4 ounces baking powder, 8 eggs, 1½ pounds lard, 1½ pounds sugar, 1 quart milk, essence, egg color. Rub lard into flour, then make bay, place sugar and eggs in centre, adding milk gradually, giving a good mix at the same time. Lay out on tins and then egg wash, putting currants, almonds or cocoanut on top. Bake at 460 degrees F.

ROCK CAKES

Ten pounds flour, 7 ounces baking powder, 2½ pounds lard or compound, 3 pounds of sugar, 6 eggs, 3 pounds of currants, ¼ pound chopped peel, essence, egg color, 3 pints of milk. Mix on board as previous mixture, only this should be a stiff instead of a soft one. Lay out with a fork on sheets, and bake at 430 degrees F.

CAKES FOR HOOPS

Six pounds of flour, 4 ounces of baking powder, 2½ pounds of lard or compound, 4 pounds of sugar, 20 eggs, essence, egg color, about 1 quart of milk. Cream up, mix lightly, and allow to stand for quarter of an hour, when you should lightly mix again. Lay out in small hoops or any sort of pans. Bake at 450 degrees F. for small cakes, and 430 degrees F. for large size.

ORDINARY FERMENTED BUNS

Ferment 1 quart of milk, 1 quart of water, at 95 degrees F., 5 ounces yeast, ¾ pound of sugar, 1 pound of flour. When dropped, add 8 pounds flour (strong patent), 1¼ pounds lard, 1 pound of sugar, 1½ pounds of currants, ½ pound of peel, ½ ounce of salt. Give the dough an hour and a half proof, and then mould up, prove in steam. Egg wash and bake at 460 degrees F.

SHORT PASTE

Four pounds of flour, 2 pounds of lard, 8 ounces of sugar, 1 pint of water, ¼ ounce of salt. The above paste is an excellent one for custards, jam tarts, etc., taking a golden-brown color when baked.

SWEET PASTE FOR STRIPS, ETC.

Four pounds of flour, 2 pounds of butter, 1¼ pounds of sugar, 9 eggs. Mix without handling too much. This paste will make almond strips, etc.

FILLING FOR STRIPS

Put on stove 12 ounces of chopped almonds, 4 ounces desiccated cocoanut, 8 whites of eggs, essence of almonds. Bring this up to 140 degrees F., when it should be turned on to the strips (which have previously been in the over for ten minutes). Sprinkle with chopped almonds.

GENOESE CAKE

This cake is well adapted for cutting up and will keep moist for a considerable time if kept enclosed in a tin with a lid. Three pounds of flour, 1 quart of eggs, 2 pounds of butter, 2 pounds of sugar, 1 ounce of baking powder, essence of vanilla. Cream up well and lightly mix. This mixture will fill an ordinary sized tin. Ice with various colored fondants, and decorate to fancy.

SWISS ALMOND TARTS

Five pounds of sugar, 2 pounds of butter, 5 pounds

Cream 1 pound of butter, ½ pound of pulverized sugar, 4 whites of eggs, then add 8 ounces of ground almonds, 12 ounces of flour. Have a number of small pans slightly greased and floured, place the mixture in a bag containing a large star pipe. Pipe a round ring round the inside of the tin, and in the centre put a little raspberry jam. Bake in a slack oven, just hot enough to tinge the tops a golden brown, slightly dust with icing sugar when done. These tarts are favorites wherever introduced, as they are delicious to the palate and agreeable to the sight.

LIGHTNING CAKE

One pound of powdered sugar, 1 pound of butter, 12 yolks of eggs, 12 whites of eggs, 1 pound of pastry flour, the grated rind of 1 lemon. Cream up sugar and butter, gradually adding the yolks; then beat up the whites, adding same together with flour and lemon and mix thoroughly. Put the mixture into papered square moulds and bake in medium heat. When cold ice top with a punch icing.

LEMON SNAPS

of flour, 15 eggs, 1 ounce of ammonia, lemon flavor. Mix sugar and butter, add gradually the eggs, flavor and the ammonia, finely powdered; roll out and cut out with small cutter, lay on greased pans, and bake at good heat.

A GOOD CHEAP LAYER CAKE

Twelve ounces of powdered sugar, 5 eggs, 1 pound 2 ounces of flour, ½ pint of milk, ½ ounce of soda, 1 ounce of cream of tartar, flavor either lemon or vanilla. Mix sugar and eggs together, adding soda flavor and milk and give it a few more turns. Lastly, add the flour. Spread this mixture upon greased layer cake pans and bake in good heat.

OATMEAL COOKIES

Five pounds brown sugar, 2¼ pounds lard or compound, 1 quart buttermilk, 2 ounces soda, 3 pounds rolled oats, 6 pounds flour, ¾ pounds chopped nut meat, lemon to flavor. Yield 22 dozen.

Cut with a plain round sugar cookie cutter, and bake in a moderate oven.

The above recipe has been used with great success by several of our leading subscribers. It is very highly recommended.

MOLASSES COOKIES

Four pounds of sugar, 2 pounds of butter or lard, 7 ounces of soda, 4 ounces of ginger, 4 quarts of molasses, 2½ quarts of sweet milk. Salt and flour to make a dough that can be handled, not too soft.

Cream sugar and butter (or lard) after sifting in soda and adding ginger. Add molasses, mix up; then add milk and mix again; then add flour and salt. Be careful not to get too stiff a dough. Cut out with a crinkled edge cutter, three and one-half inch size. Cookies should be thick. Use molasses and water for wash, give a dark brown color. Be careful not to let them burn.

This recipe is a very good one by an English baker. It will make thirty dozen.

SUGAR CAKES.

This mixture is on the same lines as the above drop cake, that is, in cheapness of the mixture, and should prove even a better seller than the former, as a greater variety can be obtained by means of different cutters and finish: 6 pounds of brown sugar, 3 pounds and 12 ounces of lard, 18 eggs, 12 pounds of cake flour, 3 ounces of soda, 6 ounces of cream of tartar, 1 ounce of ammonia, 2 ounces of salt, egg color to suit, flavor with mace. Mix sugar, lard and eggs, add 3 pints of milk, in which soda and ammonia must be dissolved; then mix in the other ingredients. Put the dough on flour-dusted table and work good and dry, dust well with flour, roll out a piece about one-fourth of an inch thick and cut with any suitable shaped cutter.

For instance, the so-called "Sugar Bolivar," take a round-scalloped cutter, lay on pans and wash over with milk; next the queen cake, take small pointed round cutter, wash with egg wash and drop a few chopped almonds or peanuts mixed with granulated sugar in the centre; heart, leaf, rings, etc., will also make a good addition to the variety. These should be placed upon granulated sugar before being laid on pans. The rock cake is obtained by mixing some currants in a piece of this dough and a little more flour added, or the scraps used instead. These are rolled to the same thickness, washed over with egg-wash, marked with a fork, that is, the fork run over the surface cross-wise, and cut out with plain round cutter. For seed cakes, mix in some caraway seeds, cut out with small, pointed round cutter and finish in the same manner as Sugar Bolivars; then bake in good oven a nice yellow. This mixture we can recommend to any baker, and it will prove a good seller, with a good profit to the manufacturer, and at the same time will please his customers. We will call attention to one point where a beginner might find an obstacle, that is, in the use of soda and cream of tartar in this mixture. The workman will find it soft and puffy (like all mixtures where soda and cream of tartar are used for a raising powder), but if thoroughly worked, the sides thrown over, the top dusted and pounded down, he will get it as slick as a New Year's cake mixture and as easy to work.

—‡—‡—‡—

Frank Bauer, of Hoxie, Ark., has purchased the Hoxie Bakery from Eugene Dent, same place, and will be open for business in a short time.

Articles of incorporation have been filed for the Bright Biscuit Co., Denver, Colo., with capital of $100,000 by Walter F. Schwed, Jacob V. Schaetzel, Elsie Rohr, Burton A. Swead and Richard E. Bishop.

C. S. Ray and T. A. Belcher have purchased the F. A. G. Hammill Bakery at 703 N. Main street, Pueblo, Colo., and have re-decorated and painted the entire interior, and plan on operating a thoroughly modern and up-to-date bakery in every respect. The name will be changed to the Bonafide Bakery.

Messrs. Brode & Lipp have opened a new quality bakery at 130 W. Railroad street, Dubois, Pa. The shop has been completely renovated and placed in a first class sanitary condition. Mr. Brode is a baker of wide experience, while Mr. Lipp is also well versed in the baking business.

ESTABLISHED 1864
THOS. MILLS & BRO., Inc.
MANUFACTURERS OF
BAKERS', CONFECTIONERS' AND ICE CREAM
MACHINERY AND TOOLS
1301-1311 NORTH EIGHTH STREET :·: :·: PHILADELPHIA, PA.
ALL SIZES OF TUBS AND CANS IN STOCK
EGG WHIPS
LARGE ASSORTMENT OF INDIVIDUAL
ICE CREAM MOULDS
COMBINED ICE CREAM FREEZER
AND BREAKER
PEELS AND SWAB POLES
ALL SIZES OF TIN, STEEL
AND RUSSIA IRON PANS
ALL STYLES
OF BRUSHES
ALL SIZES OF
PIE PLATES
PATENT BEATING MACHINE
ICE CREAM REFRIGERATORS, HARD
WOOD OR MARBLE FRONTS
WE ISSUE THREE DISTINCT CATALOGS—CONFECTIONERS'
BAKERS' AND ICE CREAM

Information Department

The object of this department is to help our readers, as far as possible, to solve the various difficulties that come up from day to day. We will also answer questions about all kinds of machinery and give every possible assistance in securing detailed information. No names or addresses of manufacturers will be given in these columns. When wanted they will be sent by mail. Address,

INFORMATION DEPARTMENT   **THE NATIONAL BAKER**

SANDWICH BUNS

J. E., Conn.: One gallon of water, 14 pounds of flour, 3½ ounces of salt, 12 ounces of sugar, 12 ounces of lard, 3 ounces of yeast.

Temperature 84 when mixed. Let stand 3½ hours, punch; let stand 1¼ hours, punch; let stand ½ hour, bench; 5¼ hours in all.

After dividing the buns, ball them on the bench the same as if making split rolls; after the buns have had about ten minutes proof on the bench, take a pie crust roller and flatten them to about the size required, then place on a dry sheet pan and give good proof for the oven. Do not have the oven too flashy—use a temperature of about 475.

Note—In case of using 3 gallons, or more water to the mix 2½ ounces to the gallon, is the right amount of yeast.

In making zweiback rolls use 18 ounces of sugar and 18 ounces of lard to the above mix and work the same as given above.

The above formula will make about 15 dozen buns, that is, two-ounce buns, when scaled.

WHOLE WHEAT BREAD

W. A. C., Illinois: The portion of the whole wheat loaf which you forwarded was very much discolored, owing to mould formation, which made it rather difficult for us to examine the same. We would suggest that you use the following formula, which we believe will make a whole wheat bread very closely resembling the bread which you forwarded.

FORMULA

Hard whole wheat flour, 25 pounds; water, 15 to 15½ pounds; salt, 7 ounces; yeast, 7 ounces; malt extract, ½ pound; sugar, ½ pound; shortening, ½ pound.

METHOD

Dissolve the yeast and malt extract in about 2 quarts of water and allow it to stand. Put the balance of water, salt and sugar into the mixer and stir. Add the flour, begin mixing and then add the yeast. After these ingredients have been nearly incorporated, add the shortening and continue mixing until the dough is smooth. The dough should have a temperature of 78 to 80 degrees when mixed.

FERMENTATION

First rising. 2¼ hours; 2nd rising, 1 hour; 3rd rising, ½ hour. Allow the dough to rest 15 minutes and then divide it.

This dough will not be as elastic as a white dough when first mixed, but will gradually become more so as fermentation is carried on.

Do not give the bread too much proof in the pans, as this will produce bread having coarse texture and poor keeping quality. Be sure to use whole wheat flour or meal milled from hard wheat. The whole wheat meal milled from very soft wheat will not make good bread when used alone, but must be used in combination with a hard, white flour.

SALT RISING BREAD

R. N. H., New York: Acknowledging your favor of the 22nd, we give you herewith a good formula for Salt Rising Bread. There is no extra charge for same, as this is part of our service.

Four ounces bolted cornmeal, ¼ ounce salt, ¼ ounce soda, 1 quart fresh milk and water. Cook the milk, then pour the cooking milk in the meal, salt and soda; stir well with spatula and let stand ten to twelve hours or longer. Then place above batter in a four-gallon stone jar (jar first heated in water), add 1 gallon hot water, then have ready the flour (spring wheat) and ¼ ounce soda; mix with spatula into a soft sponge. Now let this second batter come up well, but don't let it drop, as you would a yeast sponge; place in a large wooden bowl and mix with warm flour. At the same time add 1 pound of sugar and 4 ounces of salt; also 3 gallons of hot water with 4 ounces lard. Use strong spatula and make a medium soft dough; when raised, add more flour with the hands into a not too solid dough; put up in tins at once. Let rise and bake in a good oven.

This dough must be kept very warm from the beginning to the end, if good results are expected. Temperature 90-100 degrees F. in cold shops. The batter should be kept in the proving box.

We also mail you under separate cover a former issue containing a good formula from a practical baker. Between the two you should have no trouble in making this character of bread. It will require some practical experience to get good results, but a little experimenting will, we are sure, place you on the right track.

BREAD TROUBLE

E. W. E., Penna.: In reference to the loaf of bread and sample of flour which you recently left at this office, our technical editor advises that the flour besides being too new is also very rich in gluten. Would suggest using but one-half of this flour with one-half of an older flour. New flour is weak in its action with yeast.

FORMULA

One gallon water, 4 ounces salt, 2 ounces sugar, 2 ounces powdered milk, no lard. Temperature 80 degrees. Not a soft dough, but rather firm.

Let raise two-thirds of its own height, turn over, but do not punch.

Let raise two-thirds of its own height, turn over, let raise one-half of its own height.

Should now be ready for bench. Try it by taking a pinch with the fingers and lift up; if it snaps short at a raise of 6 inches it is ready. If it raises a foot turn over again for another two-thirds raise.

New flour will never make as large a loaf as old flour. Neither will it absorb so much water. If not ready at 2½ hours to 3 hours in trough, add more yeast next time until it does be ready. New flour plays out its strength soon and that is the trouble with your loaf.

CAKE FILLING

J. A., Jr., Texas: Marshmallow filling is made the following way: Three pounds of granulated or confectioner's sugar, from 2 to 4 ounces of dissolved gum arabic, a scant pint water, all placed in a copper kettle over a brisk fire and stirred until the sugar is all dissolved. Then boil to 240 degrees on the thermometer, or to the ball degree. By the time the proper degree is reached have 16 whites of eggs beaten up stiff and slowly pour the boiling sugar in under, constantly stirring with the egg beater, then flavor with vanilla. If a strawberry or raspberry flavor is desired, the mixture should be colored pink or red according to fruit. For different kinds of marshmallow filling some finely chopped walnuts or roasted filberts or almonds ground fine can be added. All sorts of fruit jams, jelly or marmalade are appropriate cake fillings. Custard cream, as for cream puffs, with different flavors or an addition of nuts, as described, for marshmallow is another excellent filling. Whipped cream sweetened with 4 ounces of powdered sugar to 1 quart of cream, flavored with vanilla, maraschino, rum or kirsch is a most desirable filling for light cakes, like sponge cakes.

W. B., Michigan: We don't know of any reliable substitute for cream puffs, for any similar cake has to be filled either with boiled custard or with whipped cream. Custard as well as whipped cream gets sour very soon in summer time, and it is for this reason that people don't like to buy such filled cakes in hot weather.

Ice cream and fancy cakes which go with them are most wanted, therefore we would advise making small meringues and selling them filled with ice cream; or else make a round small cake with jelly or jam inside. Both the meringues and cakes can be made the day before they are needed. You may also fill the cakes with custard or with whipped cream and dip them in thin cream fondant icing.

METHOD FOR MAKING LIGHT AND SMOOTH SPONGE CAKE

M. M. B., Ohio: Place 7 ounces of sugar in a large bowl, add gradually 12 yolks of eggs, 7 ounces of pastry flour, and stir vigorously into a light smooth paste. Beat the whites of the eggs as stiff as you can, and draw carefully under the sugar, yolks and flour moisture; fill into canvas dressing bag with lady finger tube and lay out dots of the size of large walnuts on baking paper and bake in good oven. They should be very smooth. When cold, double them with jelly or fruit jam, or else cut out the inside, fill with custard, whipped cream, or with ice cream. When filled with ice cream the shells should be placed in the refrigerator. You may also ice the shells first with thin cream fondant so that they are ready for immediate use. A very nice cake is produced when rolling the shells in shredded cocoanut right after they are iced, and filled with a white marshmallow filling.

PUFF PASTE

P. A., Vermont: Your formula for puff paste, as stated, is nearly right, and if made properly it should raise in the oven, providing you use good butter and the right sort of flour. You would not need so much cream tartar, as it toughens your puff paste and makes the rolling harder. Try 2 pounds of flour with 2 pounds of good waxy butter and very little cream tartar. Seeing that your stock dough is of nearly the same consistency as your butter. Wash and work your butter good and smooth, to be of an easy rolling nature, then envelope in dough. Give it six turns, only two at one time, and let stand between turns, have each turn of three layers, same as you would fold a letter. When the paste is rolled down ready to be folded, brush off all flour that may adhere to same.

PIE TROUBLES

H. A. W., West Va.: To have the right proportions of pie seasoning always ready, we would advise you to keep them on hand already mixed. Many times the lemon rinds are thrown away which could be grated off and used for this. Grate off the outer yellow rind of enough lemons to make 1 cupful; add 4 tablespoonfuls of cinnamon, 3 tablespoonfuls of allspice, 2 nutmegs, grated; 4 cupfuls of granulated or light brown sugar; mix all well and put away in a jar, when it will be always ready for use for seasoning.

When canned fruits are used very often the juice runs out or soaks through the bottom. To avoid this pour off the juice; add to each pint of juice half a pound of sugar, little salt, and boil; then stir in one and a half ounces of dissolved corn starch; stir until it thickens; then add the fruit.

FROSTING FOR LEMON PIES

J. R. S., Boston, Mass.: "I have gained much valuable information from THE NATIONAL BAKER since I have been a subscriber and find it to be the best paper I have ever taken. Your pie articles have helped me greatly. Will you give me a good formula for the best frosting for frosted lemon pies, and oblige."

The mixture used for frosting lemon pies is nothing more nor less than a meringue mixture, composed of 8 egg whites to every pound of sugar. Beat up the egg whites to a stiff froth, beating in some of the sugar gradually. When beaten stiff, that means as stiff as it can possibly be beaten, add the remainder of the sugar, mixing lightly but thoroughly. Then the mixture is ready to be applied.

—:—:—:—

Power and Lighting Economies in the Bake Shop

Concluded from May issue.

on the meter, but these troubles can only be remedied by an experienced electrician and cannot be taken up here. The motor should be given a periodical inspection by someone qualified for this work, preferably by a representative of the light and power company. The power plant is anxious to keep their lines free from faults and leaks, and will quickly remedy any trouble that may arise, more for their own benefit than for yours, so you may be sure that you will get a "square deal" from them in this respect if in no other.

Learn to read your meter and keep a record of the readings together with the current consumed. Readings should be taken at least once per week, and when the operating conditions are entered parallel to them, a basis of comparison is had by which faults in the equipment and operation may be quickly detected.

LIGHTING ECONOMY

Any condition which prolongs or increases the amount of daylight admitted to the shop of course correspondingly reduces the amount of lighting current necessary. Clean windows, white or light colored interior walls, or Luxfer prisms in the windows all contribute to the amount of natural daylight available and therefore are instrumental in saving current. By the same token, light colored paints increase the effectiveness of the artificial lighting and therefore produce a second saving. While large windows are generally a great item in the first cost of a building they soon pay for themselves in the reduction of the artificial lighting cost.

By keeping the electric bulbs clean, that is, cleaning them at least once per week, the amount of light is increased by a surprising amount, and for equal intensities fewer lamps are needed. Even a thin dull haze over the bulb cuts down the light from 10 to 20 per cent., while the same increase will be had by a frequent cleaning of the reflectors and other light reflecting surfaces. In bake shops and other similar places where cooking is done, the oily vapors produced condense and collect on the bulbs, forming a greasy film which attracts and holds much dirt. These bulbs are therefore much more difficult to keep clean than when the dust is dry.

—:—:—:—

Samuel Miller has purchased the bakery and equipment of M. Nesin and Charles Korrick at 84 Hartford avenue, New Britain, Conn.

Business Chances

"WANT" and "FOR SALE" advertisements inserted in THE NATIONAL BAKER for three cents a word, payable in advance. Stamps accepted in payment.

MACHINERY FOR SALE

1—2-Pocket American Dough Divider and Motor.

3—Complete Cruller Outfits.

1—American Rounder and Motor.

1—Champion Cake Mixer, New.

1—Union Divider and Motor, used three weeks.

3—Day Sifters.

1—Thomson Zerah Bailer and Motor.

1—20-in. Thomson Moulder Extension, New.

1—2½-bbl. Day Dough Mixer.

2—Peerless Dough Mixers and Motors, 1½ bbl.

1—2-bbl. Century Dough Mixer and Motor.

2—Union Bun Rounders.

1—Union Combination Bun and Bread Rounder.

2—2-bbl. Read Dough Mixers and Motors.

1—1-bbl. Read Dough Mixer and Motor.

1—Type B. Read Cake Mixer and Motor. Like New.

1—8-in. Peerless Bread Moulder and Motor. Like New.

2—Wood Proof Closets, For Window Bakery.

Cake Machines, Bread Racks, Troughs and Equipment of every description ready for immediate shipment, new or rebuilt. Rebuilt machines guaranteed same as new ones.

J. H. BAST & CO.

649 W. Pratt St.   Baltimore, Md.

FOR SALE—FOR A VERY LOW price you can secure the following slightly used equipment:

Two Yankee Reel Ovens, $100 each.

DOUGH MIXERS

1 Dutchess, 3 bbl.	J. H. Day, 3 bbl.
1 Champion, 4 bbl.	2 Rockwell, 3 bbl.
2 Read, 1½ bbl.	1 Read, 5 bbl.
1 Peerless, 1½ bbl.	
1 Champion Sifting Machine, 3 bbl.	
1 Read Sifting Machine, 5 bbl.	

CAKE MACHINES

Read	1 Champion
1 Hobart with D. C. motor attached	

Dutchess 6-Pocket Divider

Dutchess Roll Dividers

Bread and Pan Racks

Proofing Closets	Troughs
Work Tables	Bread Pans
1 Day Egg Clipper	Shipping Boxes

MACHINERY FOR SALE

Champion Dough Brake, A1 condition, motor drive

2 Doughnut Fryers with trays

I. KALFUS COMPANY

119-127 Ridge Street

New York City

BAKERIES FOR SALE

FOR SALE—GOOD BAKERY IN town of 10,000 population, together with wagons, horses and all tools. Only bakery in town or in the towns around it. Address Baldowski Bros., 72 West Main Street, Miners Mills, Penna.

FOR SALE—BAKERY IN GOOD, live town of 1,500; two railroads, one running east and west and the other running north and south. Nearest bakery in county 14 miles. Town contains brick plant employing 70 men daily. Everything in first-class condition and sanitary. Priced at a bargain. Half cash and balance in five years. For further particulars write City Bakery, I. T. Mains, proprietor, St. Elmo, Ill.

FOR SALE — BAKERY, DOING good business, equipped with No. 11½ Hubbard Oven, dough mixer, moulder, bun divider, steam boiler, tank, etc. Good opportunity. Write Maloy Baking Co., corner Second and Oak Sts., London, Ohio.

FOR SALE—BAKERY IN CITY OF 80,000. Full Meek gas equipment. New brick oven. Peerless 1½ bbl. mixer, doughnut machine, dough roller, one truck. A wholesale and retail trade. Cash. Address Sanitary Bakery, Wichita, Kans.

FOR SALE — WHOLESALE BAKery in town of 16,000 population. Equipped with bread and cake mixer, bread moulder and wrapping machine. Also sell property. Wm. H. Fox, 312 E. Broad Street, Millville, N. J.

FOR SALE—MODERN BAKERY— Marshall-Middleby Oven, gas-oven, Read bread mixer, Read cake mixer, Union cookie machine, fried cake machine, bread wrapper. All in first-class condition, and now doing good business. Selling out on account of ill health. Address Dan Deegan, Geneva, N. Y.

BAKERIES FOR SALE

FOR SALE — GOOD RETAIL bakery, best location in good Ohio town of 5,000. Equipment as good as new. Price right, best reasons for selling. Address D-12, care THE NATIONAL BAKER, 411 Walnut St., Philadelphia, Pa.

BAKERY FOR SALE ON ACcount of ill health of owner. Only wholesale bakery in town of 15,000 inhabitants. Getting 7c per loaf, running 9 to 10 bbls. per day. Well equipped plant. Price $6,500 cash. Address E. E. care THE NATIONAL BAKER, 411 Walnut St., Philadelphia, Pa.

OVENS FOR SALE

FOR SALE—GOOD MASTER REEL Oven. You set the price. Walt Ozburn, Du Quoin, Ill.

SITUATION WANTED

EXPERIENCED MALT SALESman open for engagement; am practical baker; will consider any line with a good house, on salary or commission, with advance drawing account. Am well known in the Southern States, but will travel anywhere. Address P. O. Box 912, Clearwater, Florida.

MISCELLANEOUS

TURNER'S RAPID RECIPE BOOK oner simplifies cost accounting so that it is a matter of only a few minutes to get the cost of a batch of any size, and of any class of goods. The baker is saved all the trouble in counting up the cost; it is already done for him. Tables are given of the cost of each ounce of flour at a price per barrel from $4.00 upward, of other materials from $0.01 to $0.60 by the pound, and the cost of each ounce. One is needed in every bake-shop, and the cost is but $2.00 postpaid. For sale by THE NATIONAL BAKER, 411 Walnut Street, Philadelphia, Pa.

A Classified List of Goods Needed by Bakers

Automobile Trucks—
Republic Truck Sales Corp., Alma, Mich.

Almond Paste—
Henry Heide, Inc., New York.

Bakery Advertising—
L. B. Nordham Co., N. Y.
Schulze Advert. Service, Chicago.
W. E. Long Co., Chicago.

Bakers' Institute—
Siebel Institute, Chicago.

Bakers' Machinery—
Champion Machine Co., Joliet, Ill.
J. H. Day Co., Cincinnati, O.
Dutchess Tool Co., Beacon, N. Y.
Jaburg-Miller Co., New York.
Pearless Bread Mch. Co., Sidney, O.
Read Machinery Co., York, Pa.
Reeves Pulley Co., Columbus, Ind.
Thomson Mch. Co., Bellevue, N. J.
Thomas Mills & Bro., Philadelphia.
Union Machinery Co., Joliet, Ill.

Bakers' Pans—
Jaburg Bros., New York.
Jaburg-Miller Co., New York.
Edward Katzinger Co., Chicago.
The Aug. Maag Co., Baltimore.
Thomas Mills & Bro., Philadelphia.

Bakers' Tools—
Jaburg Bros., New York.
Jaburg-Miller Co., New York.
Edward Katzinger Co., Chicago.
The Aug. Maag Co., Baltimore.
Thomas Mills & Bro., Philadelphia.
Union Steel Products Co., Albion.

Books for Bakers—
Malzbender's Recipe Book.
Turner's Rapid Recipe Reckoner.

Bread Labels—
Mirror Printing Co., Kalamazoo.

Bread Wrapping and Sealing Machines—
National Bread Wrapping Machine Co., Nashua, N. H.
Lambooy Label & Wrapper Co., Kalamazoo, Mich.
Union Machinery Co., Joliet, Ill.

Cash Registers—
National Cash Register Company.

Chocolate—
Walter Baker & Co., Ltd., Dorchester.

Cooking Oil
Corn Products Ref. Co., New York.

Dough Mixers and Kneaders—
Champion Machinery Co., Joliet, Ill.
J. H. Day Co., Cincinnati, O.
Read Machinery Co., York, Pa.

Eggs-Desiccated—Egg Products—
Joe Lowe Co., N. Y.

Flour—
Big Diamond Mills Co., Minn.
Commander Mills, Minneapolis.
Empire Milling Co., Minneapolis.
W. J. Jennison & Co., Minneapolis.
Russell-Miller Milling Co., Minn.
Washburn-Crosby Co., Minneapolis.

Food Colors—
National Aniline & Chem. Co., N. Y.

Fruit Growers—
California Associated Raisin Co.
California Prune & Apricot Growers.

Ice Cream Tools and Supplies—
Atlas Mfg. Co., New Haven.
Chr. Hansen's Lab., Little Falls, N. Y.
The Aug. Maag Co., Baltimore.
Thomas Mills & Bro., Philadelphia.

Malt, Extract and Dry—
American Diamalt Co.
Anheuser-Busch, Inc., St. Louis.
P. Ballantine & Sons, Newark.
Freihofer Baking Co., Philadelphia.
Malt Diastase Co., N. Y.

Milk, Powdered and Condensed—
Consolidated Prod. Co., Lincoln, Neb.
L. H. Nestor & Co., Philadelphia.

Ovens—
Bennett Oven Co., Battle Creek.
Duhrkop Oven Co., New York.
Hubbard Oven Co., Chicago.
Meak Oven Mfg. Co., Westport, Conn.
Middleby Oven Co., New York.
Middleby-Marshall Co., Chicago.
Standard Oven Co., Pittsburgh.
Superior Oven Co., Chicago, Ill.

Oven Lights and Doors—
Dutchess Tool Co., Beacon, N. Y.
Chas. Robson & Co., Philadelphia.

Papers (Parchment and Waxed)—
Lambooy Label & Wrapper Co., Kalamazoo, Mich.
Menasha Ptg. & Carton Co., Menasha, Wis.
Waterproof Paper & Board Co., Cincinnati.

Pie Machinery—
Edwin E. Bartlett, Nashua, N. H.
J. H. Day Co., Cincinnati, O.
Union Machinery Co., Joliet, Ill.

Potato Flour—
Falk American Potato Flour Co., Pittsburgh, Pa.

Pyrometers—
Hubbard Oven Co., Chicago.
Philadelphia Thermometer Co.
Chas. Robson & Co., Philadelphia.

Shipping Boxes (Wood and Paper)—
A. Backus, Jr., & Son, Detroit.
Rob't Gaylord, Inc., St. Louis.

Shortening—
Corn Products Refining Co., N. Y.
Procter & Gamble Co., Cincinnati.

Stoves for Bakers and Confectioners—
Edward Katzinger Co., Chicago.
Thomas Mills & Bro., Philadelphia.

Sugar and Sugar Syrups—
American Sugar Ref. Co., N. Y.
Corn Products Ref. Co., New York.
Franklin Sugar Ref. Co., Philadelphia.

Supplies—
Jaburg Bros., New York.
Joe Lowe Co., N. Y.
Stein-Hall Mfg. Co., Chicago and N. Y.
Ward Baking Co., New York.

Thermometers—
Phila. Thermometer Co., Phila.

Washing and Cleaning Material—
J. B. Ford Co.

Yeast—
The Fleischmann Co., New York.

INDEX TO ADVERTISEMENTS

	Page
American Diamalt Co.	13
Anheuser-Busch Sales Corp.	47
American Sugar Refining Co.	15
Baker & Co., Ltd., Walter	53
Ballantine & Sons, P.	14
Bennett Oven Co.	5
Big Diamond Mills Co.	4
Business Chances	61
California Associated Raisin Co.	11
Carter, Rice & Co. Corporation	41
Commander Mills	51
Corn Products Ref. Co.	9
Day Co., The J. H.	7
Duhrkop Oven Co.	8
Dutchess Tool Co.	14, 45
Empire Milling Co.	16
Fleischmann Co., The	13
Ford Co., J. B.	49
Freihofer Baking Co.	51
Heide, Inc., Henry	59
Hubbard Portable Oven Co.	Cover
Jennison Co., W. J.	16
Katzinger Co., Edward	Cover
Lambooy Label & Wrapper Co.	4
W. E. Long Co.	37
Maag Co., The Aug.	Cover
Malt Diastase Co.	16
Malzbender, M.	53
Middleby-Marshall Oven Co.	5
Middleby Oven Co., N. Y.	15
Mills & Bro., Inc., Thomas	57
National Bread Wrapping Mach. Co.	41
Philadelphia Thermometer Co.	4
Procter & Gamble Co.	7
Read Machinery Co.	39
Reeves Pulley Co.	7
Republic Truck Sales Corp.	3
Robson & Co., Charles	15
Russell-Miller Milling Co.	10
Siebel Institute	17
Standard Oven Co.	5
Sun-Maid Raisins	11
Superior Oven Co.	48
Tanglefoot	55
Thomson Machine Co.	6
Turner, A. R.	55
Union Steel Products Co.	
Union Machinery Co.	4
Ward Baking Co.	33
Washburn-Crosby Co.	Cover
Water-proof Paper & Board Co.	13

KLEEN-KRUST
RIVETLESS
REG. U.S. PAT. OFF.
"STEEL-SHOD"
BREAD PANS
(Patented Jan. 21, 1913; Jan. 16, 1917.)

The Appearance of the Loaf is of Prime Importance--

—it goes a long way in creating a demand for your bread. If you would turn out loaves of exceptional uniformity—clean, spotless loaves—you will bake in Kleen-Krust Rivetless "Steel-Shod" Bread Pans.

Entirely Different from Any Other Pan on the Market

Their construction, the most rigid and sanitary ever devised, entirely eliminates strapping, therefore neither dirt nor grease can collect.

The outer face of the end pans is protected by a sheet of steel which acts as a piece of armor-plate. This steers the peel underneath the pans, eliminating all danger of battering the end pan.

Kleen-Krust Rivetless "Steel-Shod" Bread Pans are manufactured under letters patent granted by the U. S. Government. We are sole manufacturers.

The advantages of Kleen-Krust Rivetless "Steel-Shod" Bread Pans go a long way toward creating a demand for your bread by improving the appearance of the loaf. In order that you may find out these advantages for yourself, we will forward a sample set of open Pans for immediate practical use in your oven room.

With Covers for Pullman or Sandwich Loaves

Specially Adapted for Traveling Ovens

We have issued a New Catalog illustrating and describing our Kleen-Krust Rivetless "Steel Shod" Bread Pans and Kleen-Krust Rivetless Pullman or Sandwich Bread Pans. Catalog mailed on request.

THE AUGUST MAAG CO.
509-11 W. Lombard St.
BALTIMORE, MD.

The Rye Flour You Want
— When You Want It:

You surely want

> the Rye Flour of exactly the right color, with good, rich, ripe, rye flavor, that comes only from carefully selected, skillfully milled Mississippi Valley grown grain.

And you also want

> to buy your Rye Flour from the Company that can and will deliver both quality and amount exactly as you want when you want it.

Therefore buy

GOLD MEDAL RYE FLOUR

WASHBURN CROSBY CO.
The World's Largest Millers

MINNEAPOLIS   BUFFALO   NEW YORK
U. S. A.

CREAM OF RYE
PURE WHITE RYE

HOFMULLER
PURE DARK RYE

O O O RYE
PURE MEDIUM RYE

BLENDED
WHEAT and RYE

RYE MEAL

IRON DUKE for RYE MIX
WHEAT FIRST CLEAR